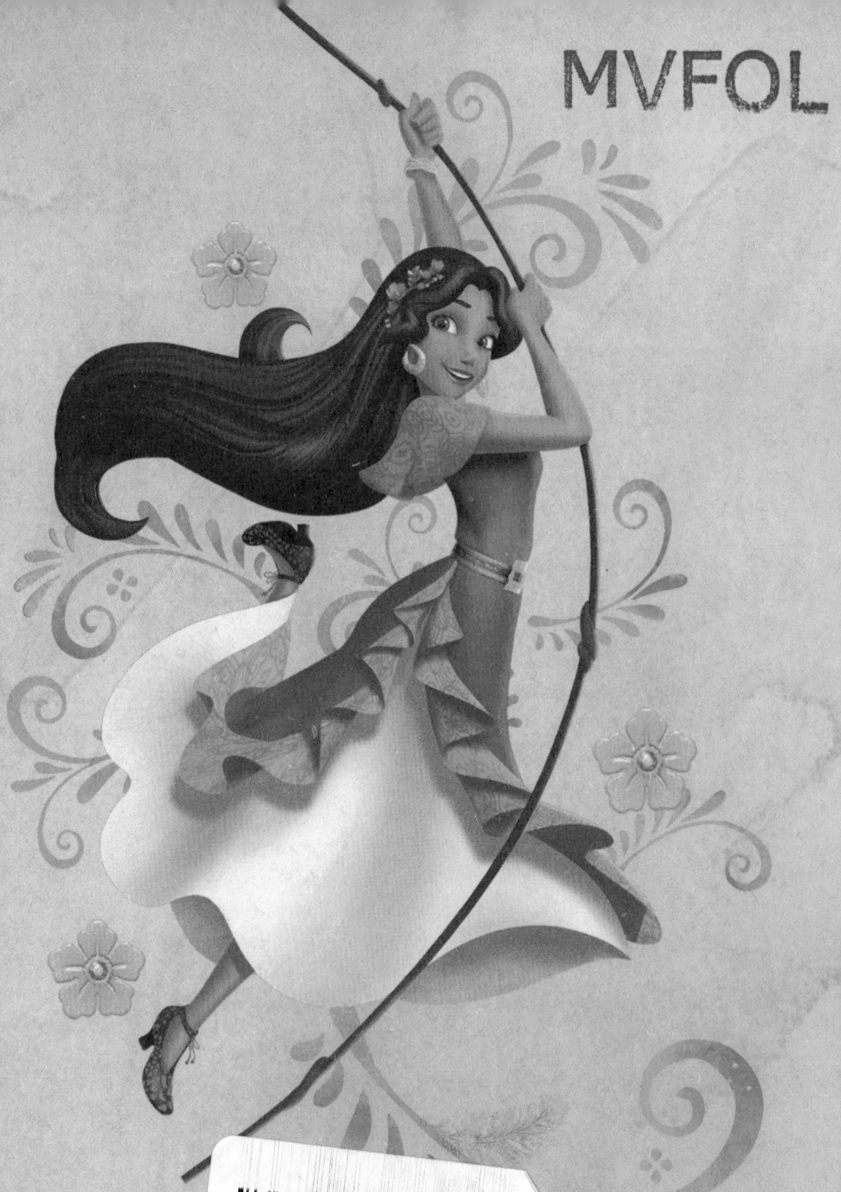

Also from Joe Books

Disney Frozen Cinestory Comic
Disney Cinderella Cinestory Comic
Disney 101 Dalmatians Cinestory Comic
Disney Princess Comics Treasury
Disney • Pixar Comics Treasury
Disney Darkwing Duck: The Definitively Dangerous Edition
Disney Frozen: The Story of the Movie in Comics
Disney Big Hero 6 Cinestory Comic
Disney • Pixar Inside Out Cinestory Comic
Disney • Pixar Inside Out Fun Book
Disney Gravity Falls Cinestory Comic Volume One
Disney Gravity Falls Cinestory Comic Volume Two
Disney • Pixar The Good Dinosaur Cinestory Comic
Disney • Pixar The Good Dinosaur Fun Book
Disney Zootopia Cinestory Comic
Disney Winnie the Pooh Cinestory Comic
Disney Descendants Wicked World Cinestory Comic Volume One
Disney Descendants Wicked World Cinestory Comic Volume Two
Disney Alice in Wonderland Cinestory Comic
Disney • Pixar Finding Nemo Cinestory Comic
Disney • Pixar Finding Dory Cinestory Comic
Disney Star vs the Forces of Evil Cinestory Comic
Disney • Pixar Finding Dory Graphic Novel
Disney Zootopia Comics Collection
Disney Princess Comic Strips Collection Volume One
Marvel Thor: Dueling with Giants
Marvel Guardians of the Galaxy: Castaways

Don't miss our monthly comics...

Disney Darkwing Duck
Disney • Pixar Finding Dory
Disney Frozen
Disney Pirates of the Caribbean
Disney Princess
Disney Star vs the Forces of Evil

Disney

Elena of Avalor

Ready to Rule

Cinestory Comic

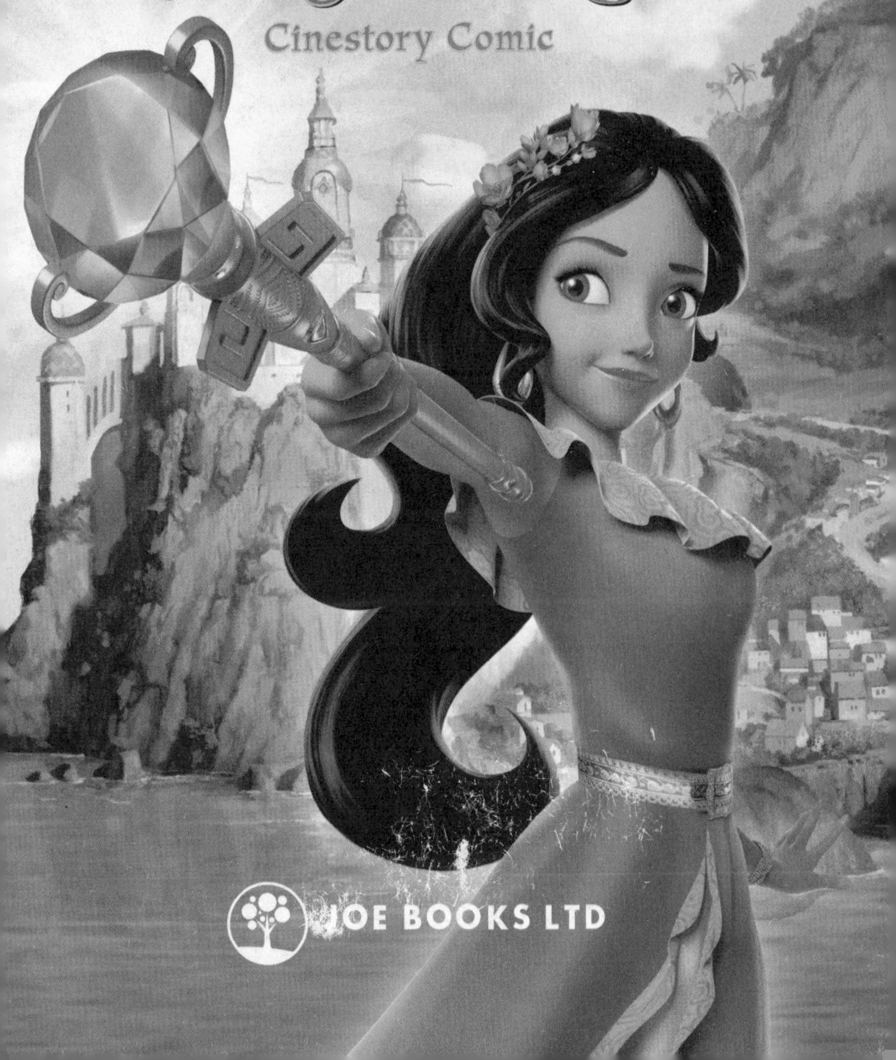

JOE BOOKS LTD

Published in the United States and Canada by Joe Books Ltd
489 College Street, Toronto, ON, M6G 1A5

www.joebooks.com

First Joe Books Ltd edition: December 2016

Print ISBN: 978-1-77275-462-9
ebook ISBN: 978-1-77275-471-1

Elena of Avalor (Main Title)
Words and Music by John Kavanaugh and Craig Gerber
© 2016 Walt Disney Music Company (ASCAP) /
Wonderland Music Company, Inc. (BMI)
Performed by Elena
Under License by Walt Disney Records
All Rights Reserved.

Ready To Rule
Words and Music by John Kavanaugh and Craig Gerber
© 2016 Walt Disney Music Company (ASCAP) /
Wonderland Music Company, Inc. (BMI)
Performed by Cast – Elena of Avalor
Under License by Walt Disney Records
All Rights Reserved.

Sister Time
Words and Music by John Kavanaugh, Becca Topol, and Craig Gerber
© 2016 Walt Disney Music Company (ASCAP) /
Wonderland Music Company, Inc. (BMI)
Performed by Cast – Elena of Avalor
Under License by Walt Disney Records
All Rights Reserved.

Blow My Top
Words and Music by John Kavanaugh, Craig Gerber, and Tom Rogers
© 2016 Walt Disney Music Company (ASCAP) /
Wonderland Music Company, Inc. (BMI)
Performed by Cast – Elena of Avalor
Under License by Walt Disney Records
All Rights Reserved.

Adaptation, design, lettering, layout, and editing by First Image.

Library and Archives Canada Cataloguing in Publication
information is available upon request.

Printed and bound in Canada
1 3 5 7 9 10 8 6 4 2

Created by
Craig Gerber

Episode 1 "First Day of Rule"

Written by
Craig Gerber

Directed by
Elliot M. Bour

Executive Producer
Craig Gerber

Episode 2 "Model Sister"

Written by
Becca Topol

Directed by
Elliot M. Bour

Executive Producer
Craig Gerber

Episode 3 "All Heated Up"

Written by
Tom Rogers

Directed by
Elliot M. Bour

Executive Producer
Craig Gerber

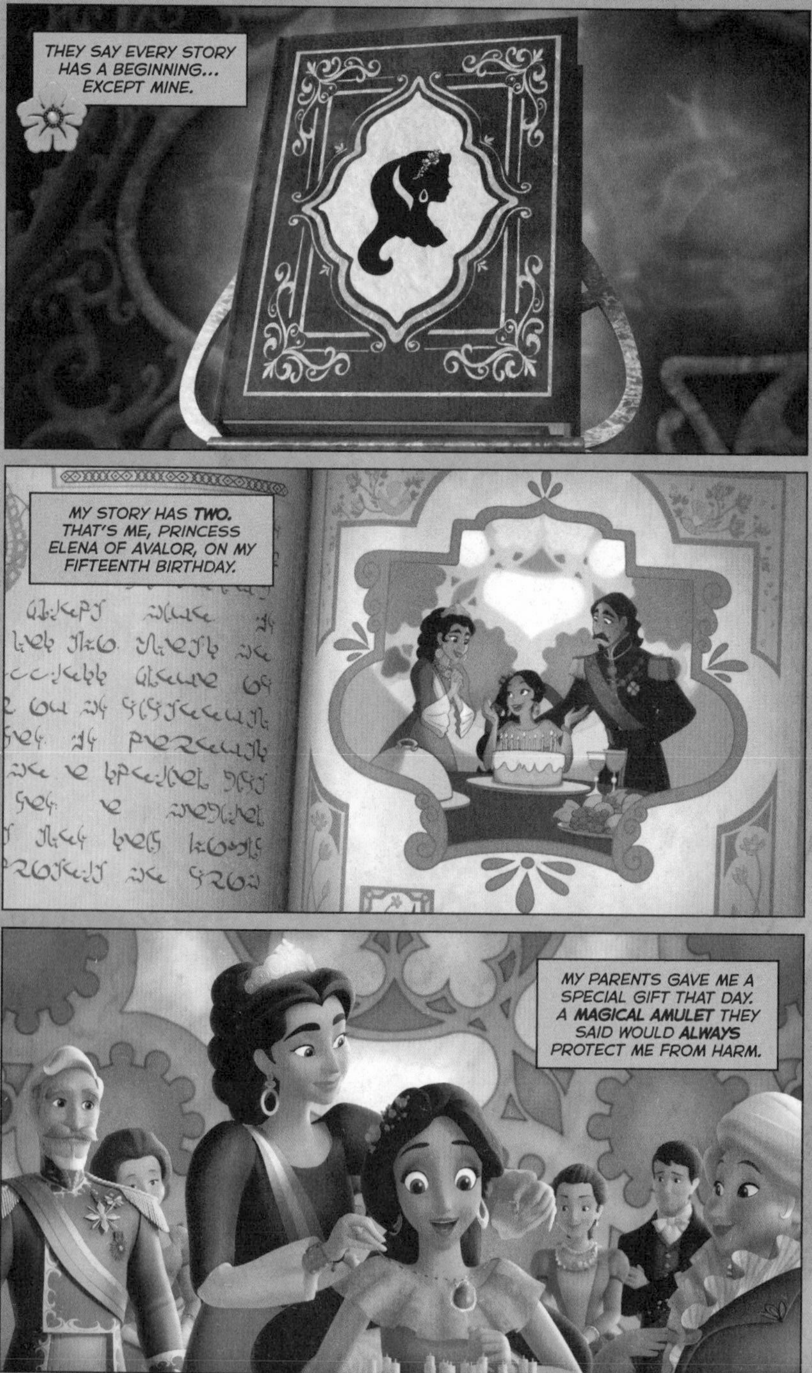
THEY SAY EVERY STORY HAS A BEGINNING... EXCEPT MINE.
MY STORY HAS **TWO.** THAT'S ME, PRINCESS ELENA OF AVALOR, ON MY FIFTEENTH BIRTHDAY.
MY PARENTS GAVE ME A SPECIAL GIFT THAT DAY. A **MAGICAL AMULET** THEY SAID WOULD **ALWAYS** PROTECT ME FROM HARM.

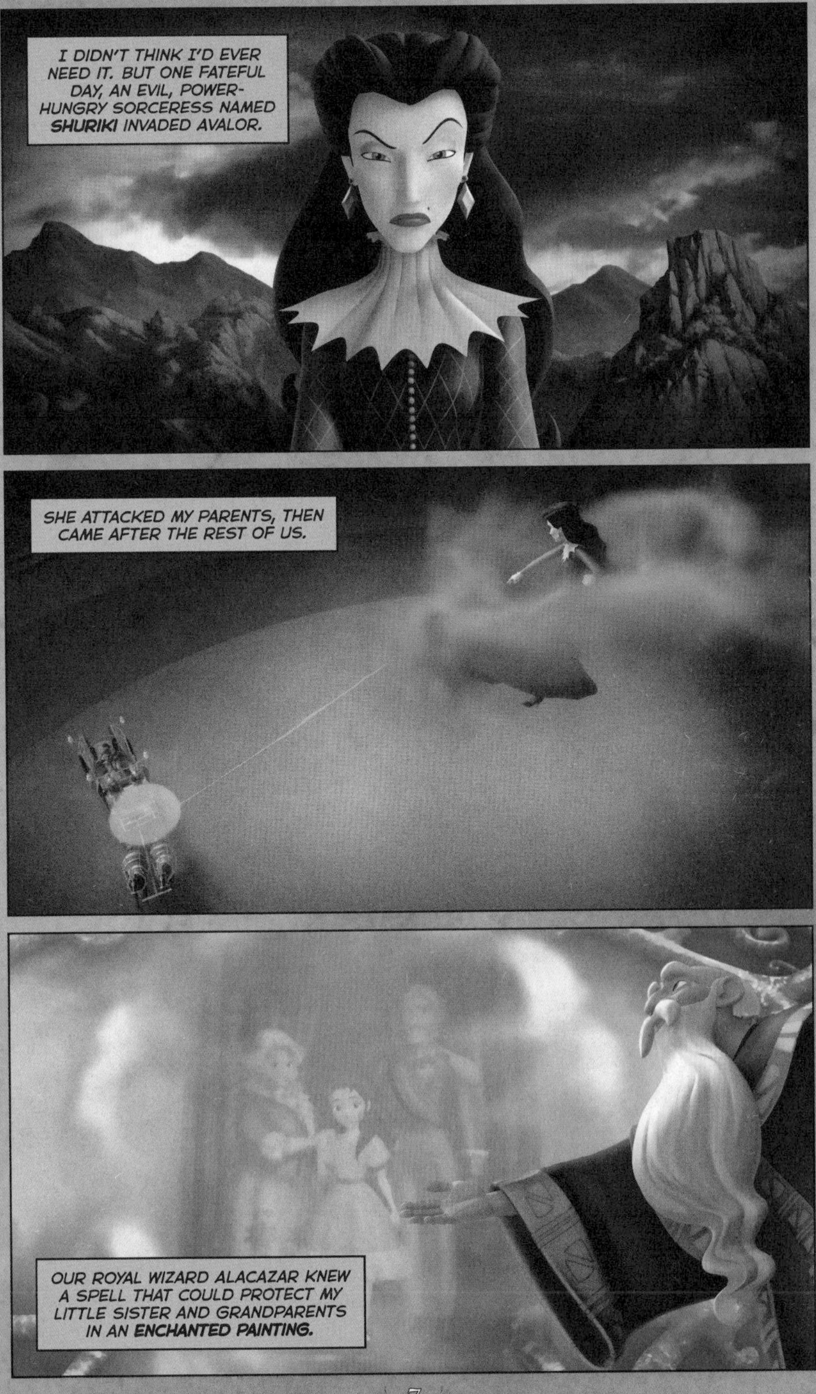
I DIDN'T THINK I'D EVER NEED IT. BUT ONE FATEFUL DAY, AN EVIL, POWER-HUNGRY SORCERESS NAMED SHURIKI INVADED AVALOR.
SHE ATTACKED MY PARENTS, THEN CAME AFTER THE REST OF US.
OUR ROYAL WIZARD ALACAZAR KNEW A SPELL THAT COULD PROTECT MY LITTLE SISTER AND GRANDPARENTS IN AN ENCHANTED PAINTING.

BUT HE NEEDED TIME TO CAST IT. SO I DECIDED TO FACE SHURIKI **ON MY OWN.**

SHURIKI TRIED TO STRIKE ME DOWN...

...BUT THE AMULET **SAVED MY LIFE** BY PULLING ME INSIDE IT.

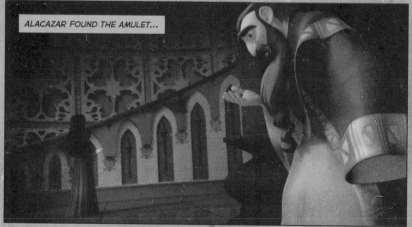

ALACAZAR FOUND THE AMULET...

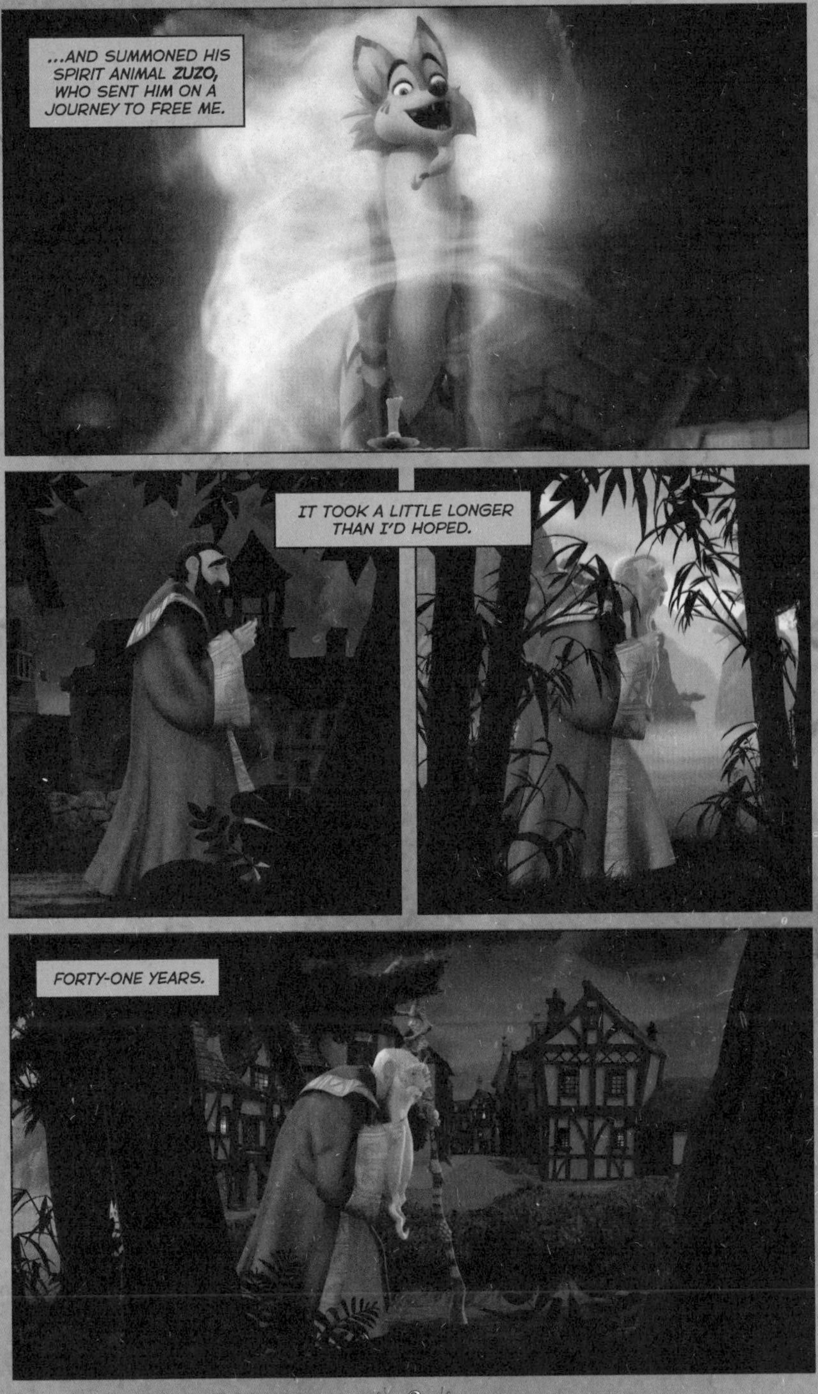
...AND SUMMONED HIS SPIRIT ANIMAL ZUZO, WHO SENT HIM ON A JOURNEY TO FREE ME.
IT TOOK A LITTLE LONGER THAN I'D HOPED.
FORTY-ONE YEARS.

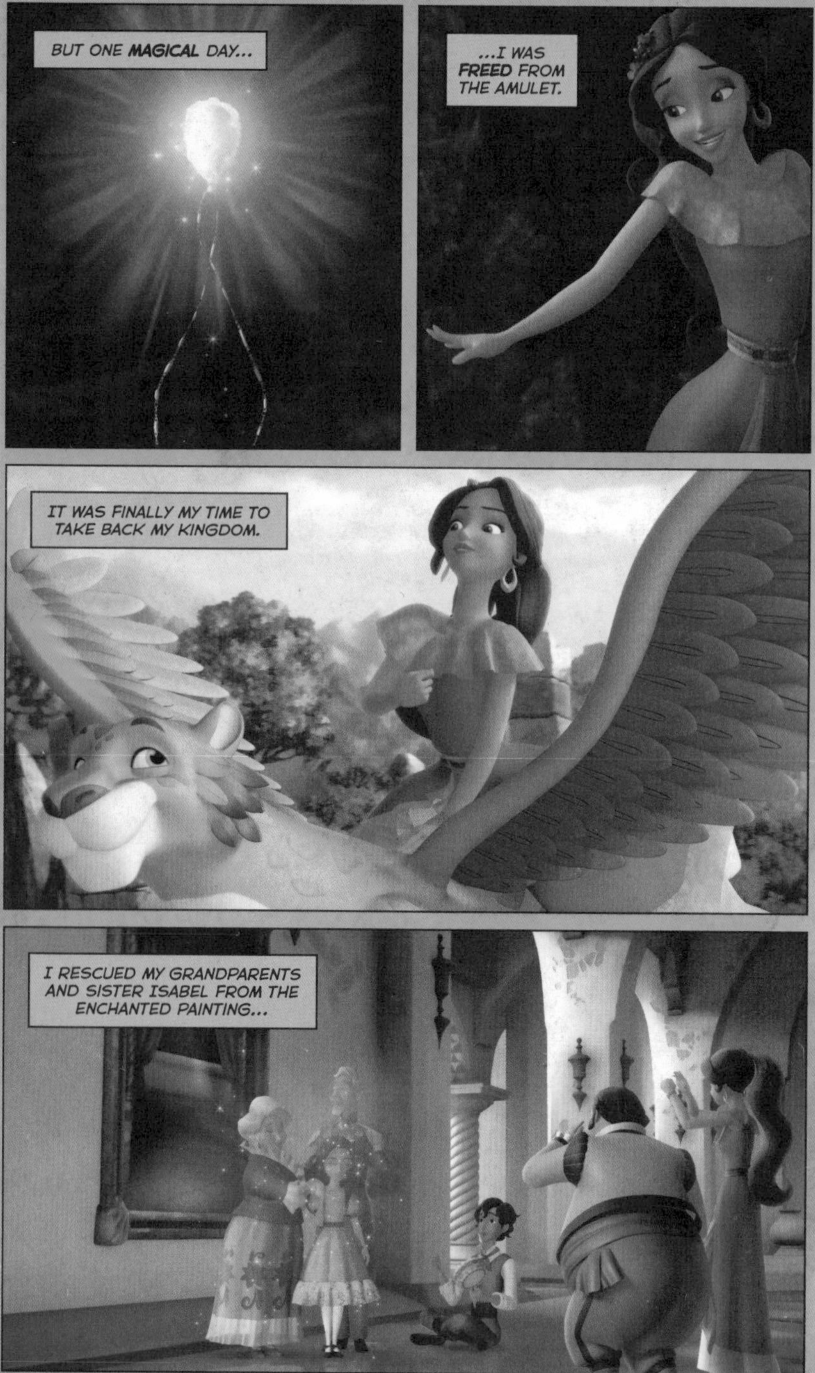
BUT ONE MAGICAL DAY...
...I WAS FREED FROM THE AMULET.
IT WAS FINALLY MY TIME TO TAKE BACK MY KINGDOM.
I RESCUED MY GRANDPARENTS AND SISTER ISABEL FROM THE ENCHANTED PAINTING...

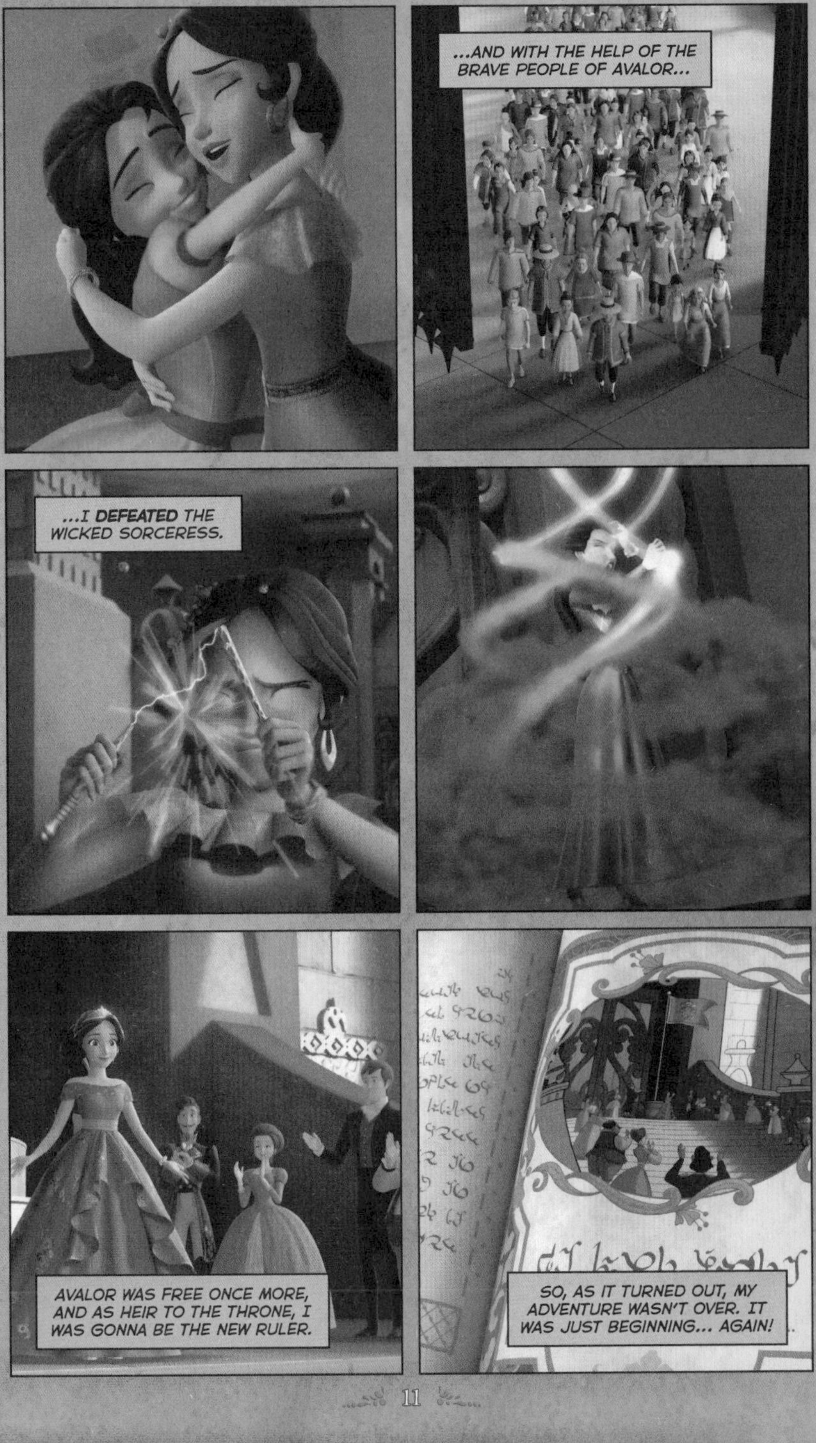
...AND WITH THE HELP OF THE BRAVE PEOPLE OF AVALOR...
...I DEFEATED THE WICKED SORCERESS.
AVALOR WAS FREE ONCE MORE, AND AS HEIR TO THE THRONE, I WAS GONNA BE THE NEW RULER.
SO, AS IT TURNED OUT, MY ADVENTURE WASN'T OVER. IT WAS JUST BEGINNING... AGAIN!

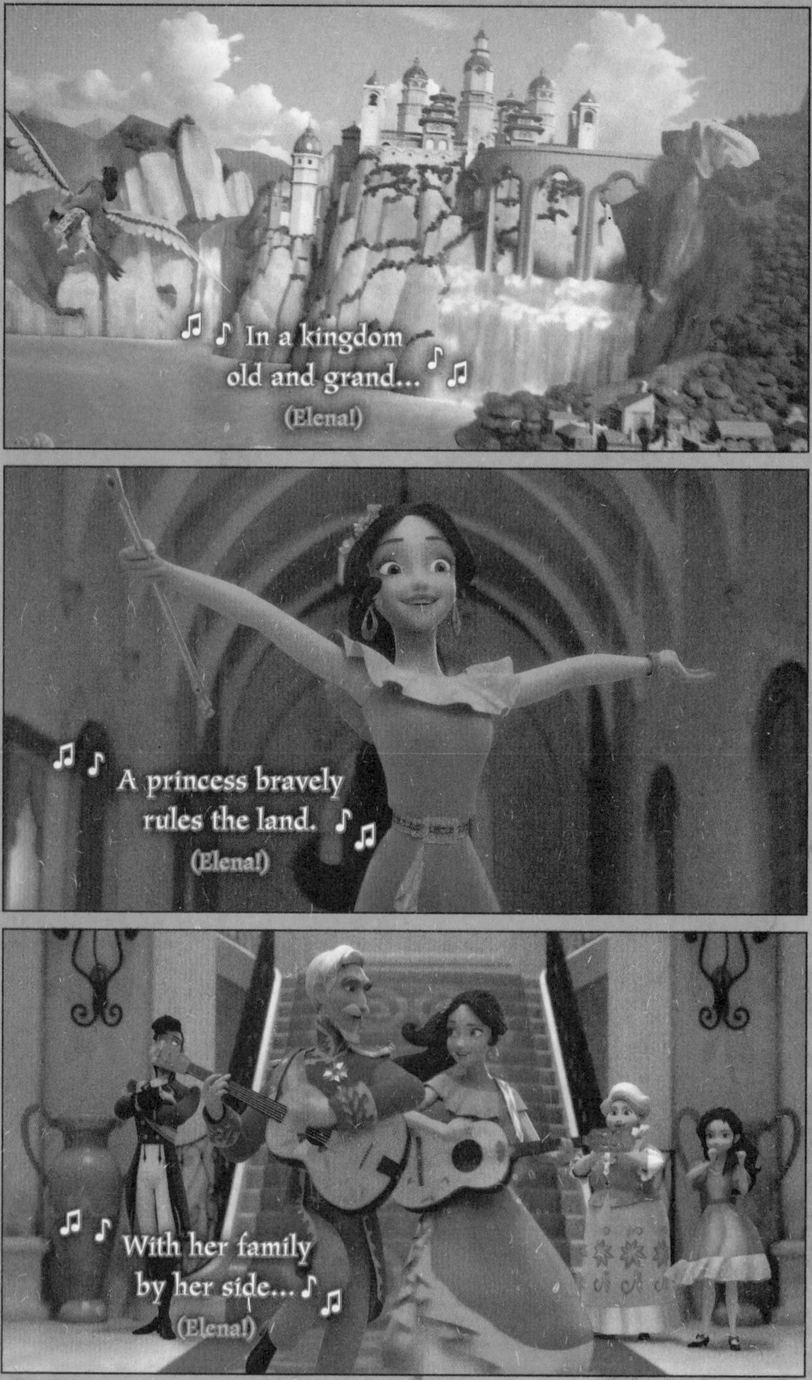
♫ ♪ In a kingdom old and grand... ♪ ♫
(Elena!)
♫ ♪ A princess bravely rules the land. ♪ ♫
(Elena!)
♫ ♪ With her family by her side... ♪ ♫
(Elena!)

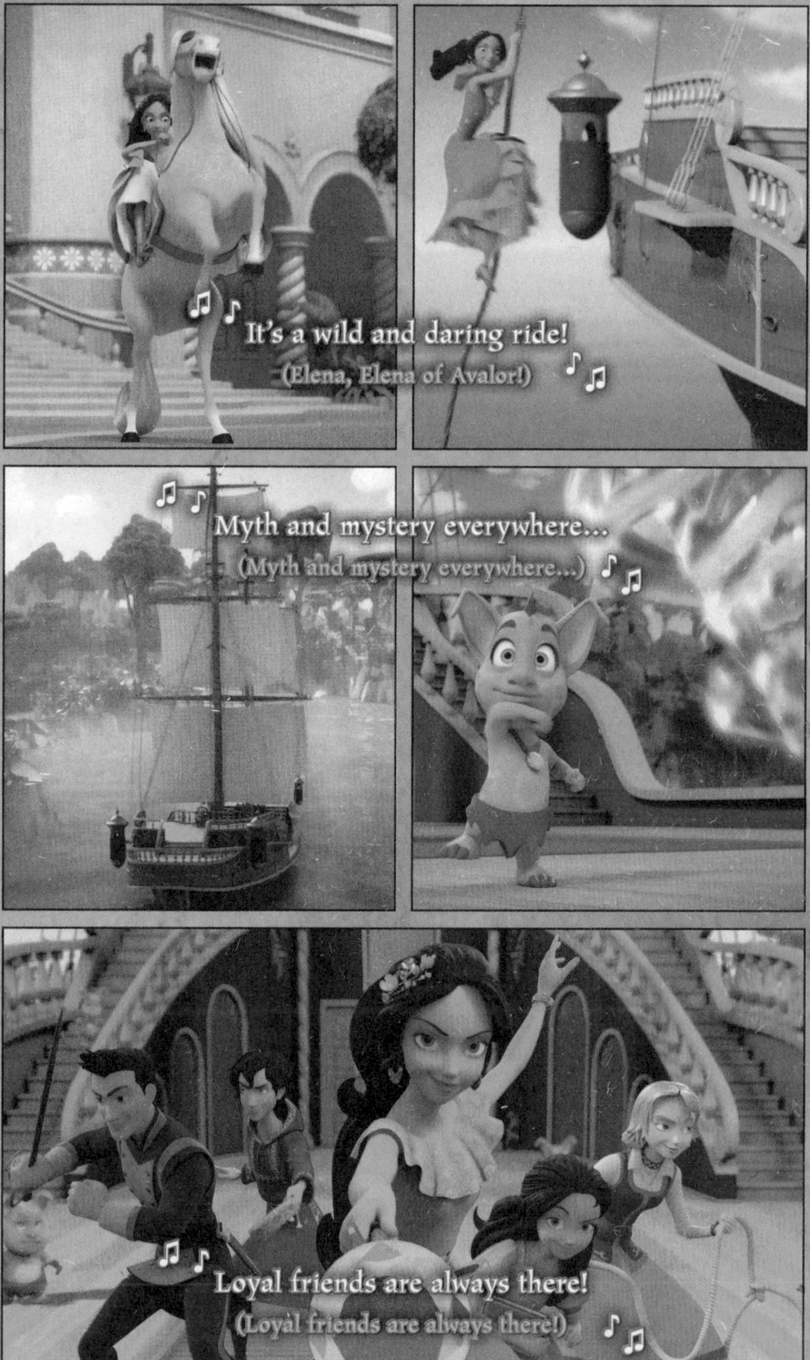
It's a wild and daring ride!
(Elena, Elena of Avalor!)
Myth and mystery everywhere...
(Myth and mystery everywhere...)
Loyal friends are always there!
(Loyal friends are always there!)

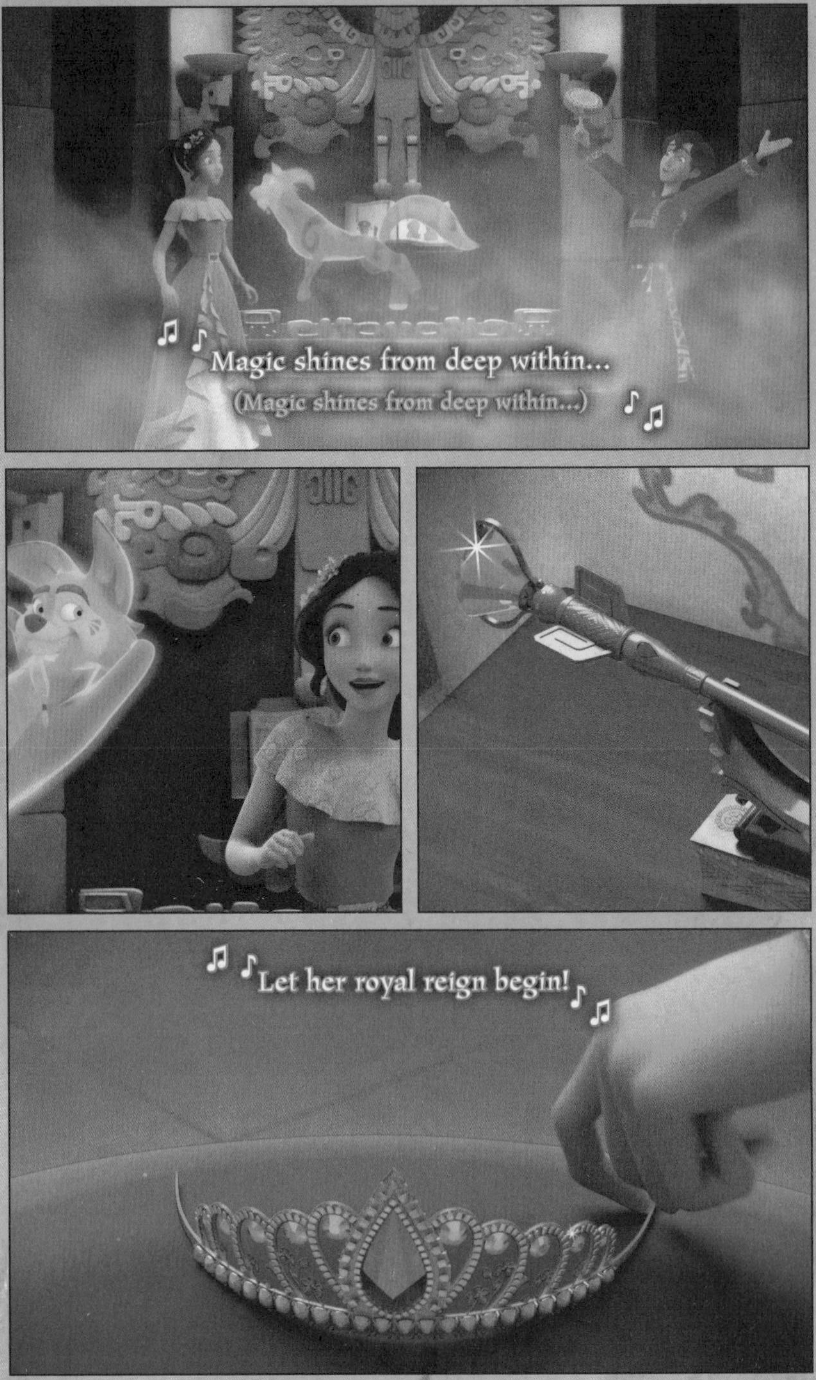
Magic shines from deep within...
(Magic shines from deep within...)
Let her royal reign begin!

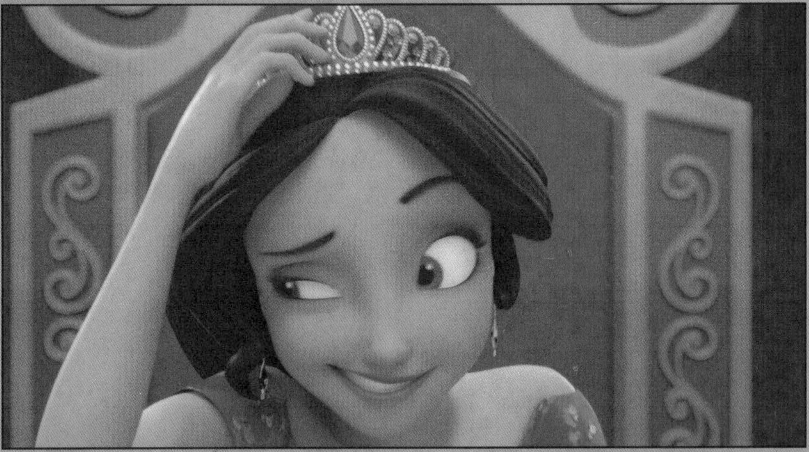

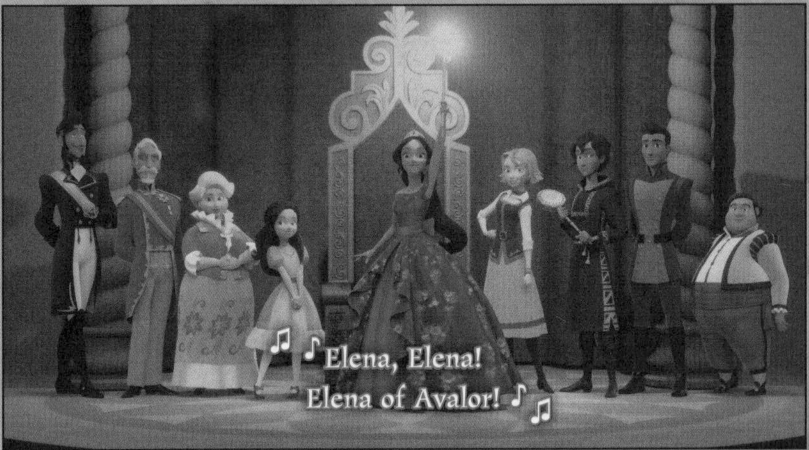
♫ ♪ Elena, Elena!
Elena of Avalor! ♪ ♫

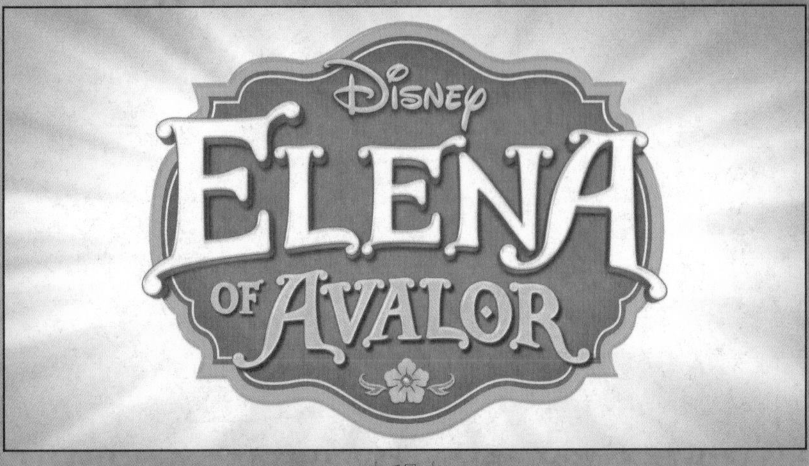
Disney
Elena
of Avalor

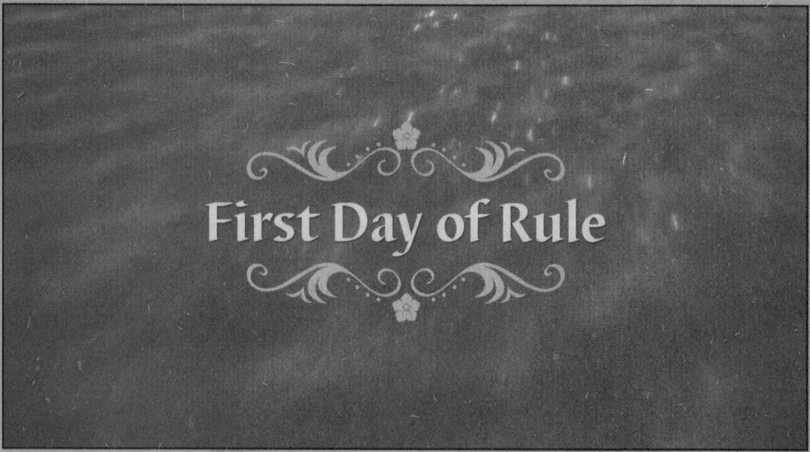
First Day of Rule

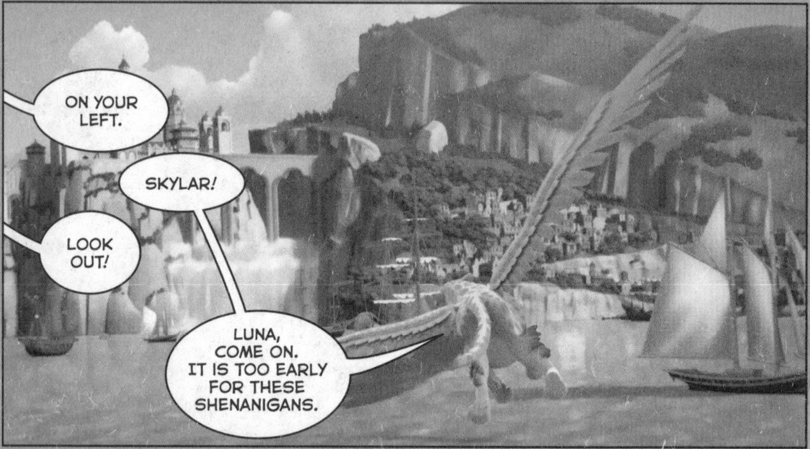
ON YOUR LEFT.
SKYLAR!
LOOK OUT!
LUNA, COME ON. IT IS TOO EARLY FOR THESE SHENANIGANS.

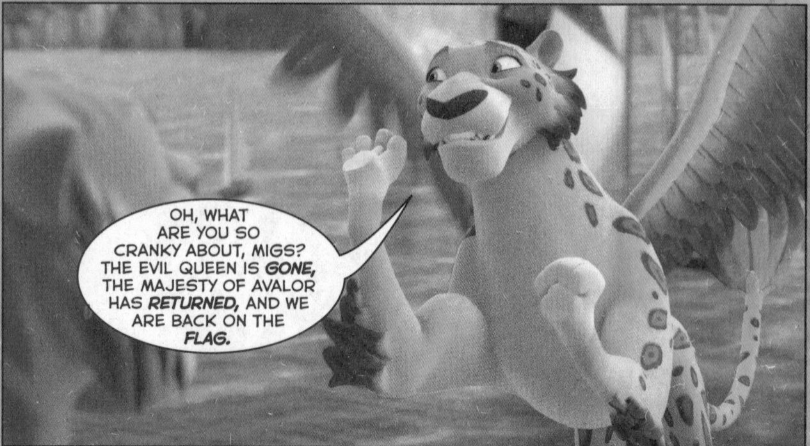
OH, WHAT ARE YOU SO CRANKY ABOUT, MIGS? THE EVIL QUEEN IS *GONE,* THE MAJESTY OF AVALOR HAS *RETURNED,* AND WE ARE BACK ON THE *FLAG.*

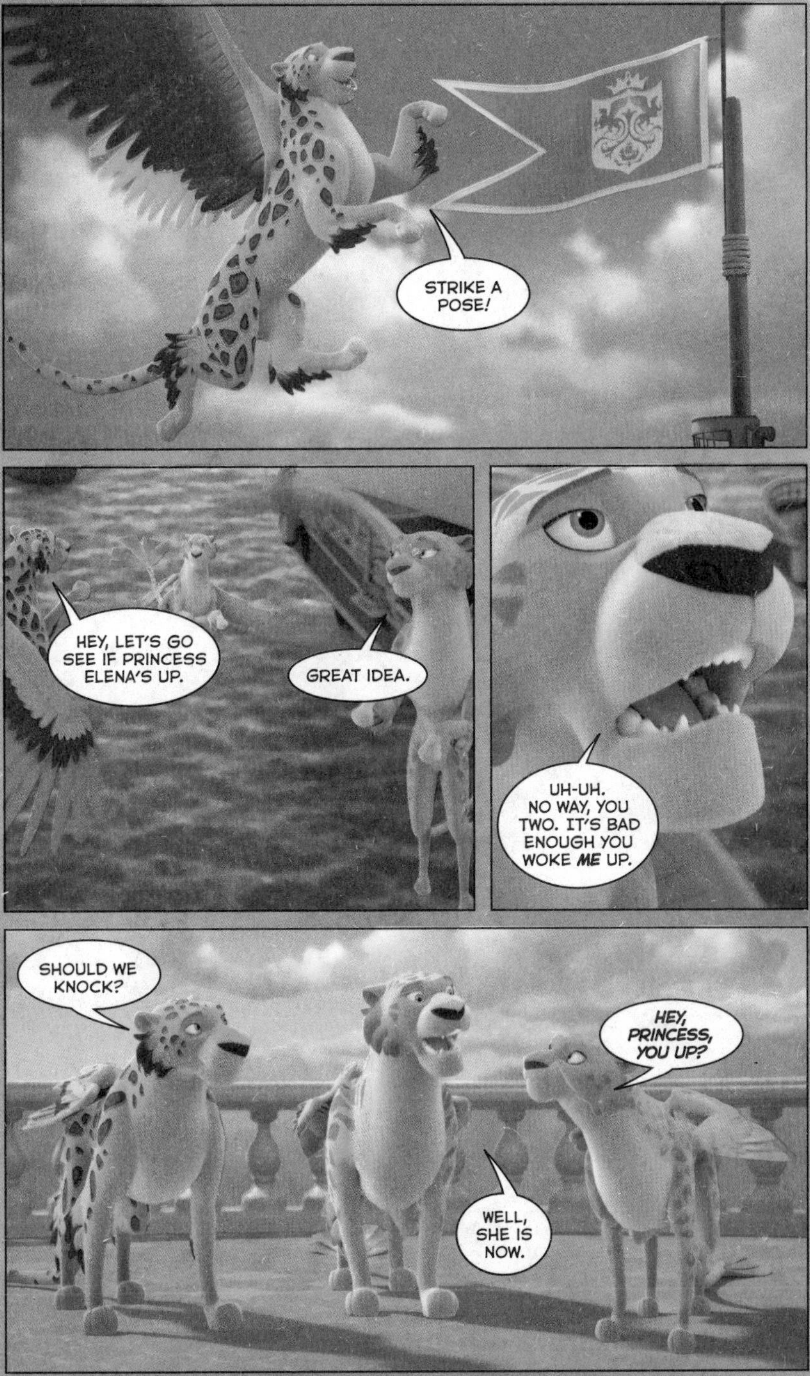
STRIKE A POSE!
HEY, LET'S GO SEE IF PRINCESS ELENA'S UP.
GREAT IDEA.
UH-UH. NO WAY, YOU TWO. IT'S BAD ENOUGH YOU WOKE ME UP.
SHOULD WE KNOCK?
HEY, PRINCESS, YOU UP?
WELL, SHE IS NOW.

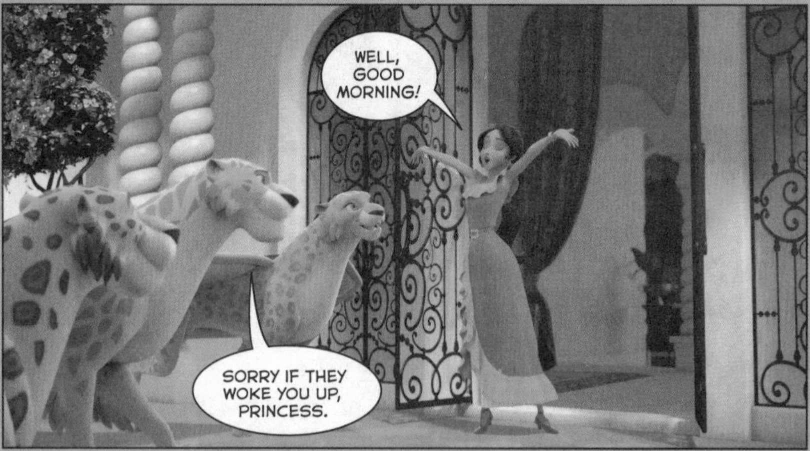
WELL, GOOD MORNING!
SORRY IF THEY WOKE YOU UP, PRINCESS.

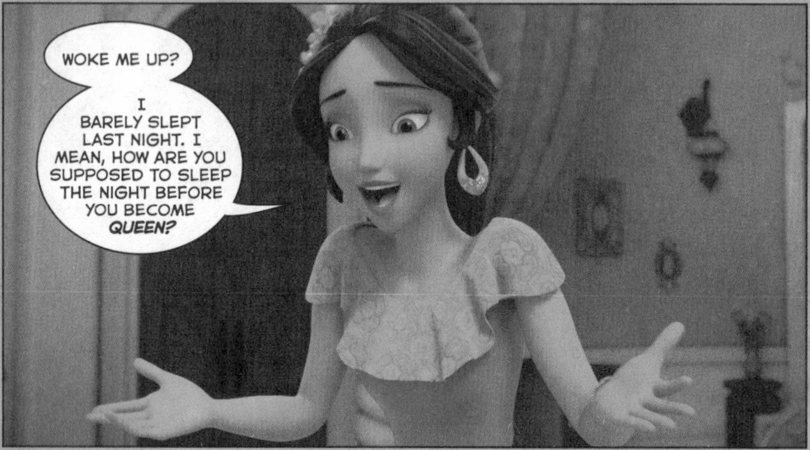
WOKE ME UP?
I BARELY SLEPT LAST NIGHT. I MEAN, HOW ARE YOU SUPPOSED TO SLEEP THE NIGHT BEFORE YOU BECOME QUEEN?

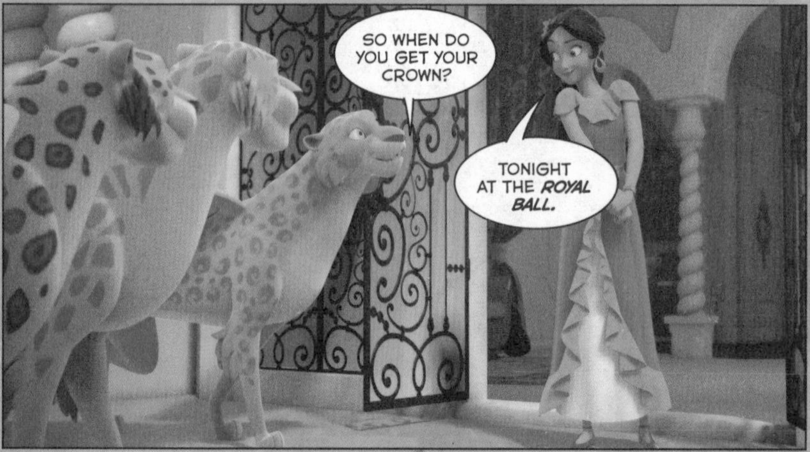
SO WHEN DO YOU GET YOUR CROWN?
TONIGHT AT THE ROYAL BALL.

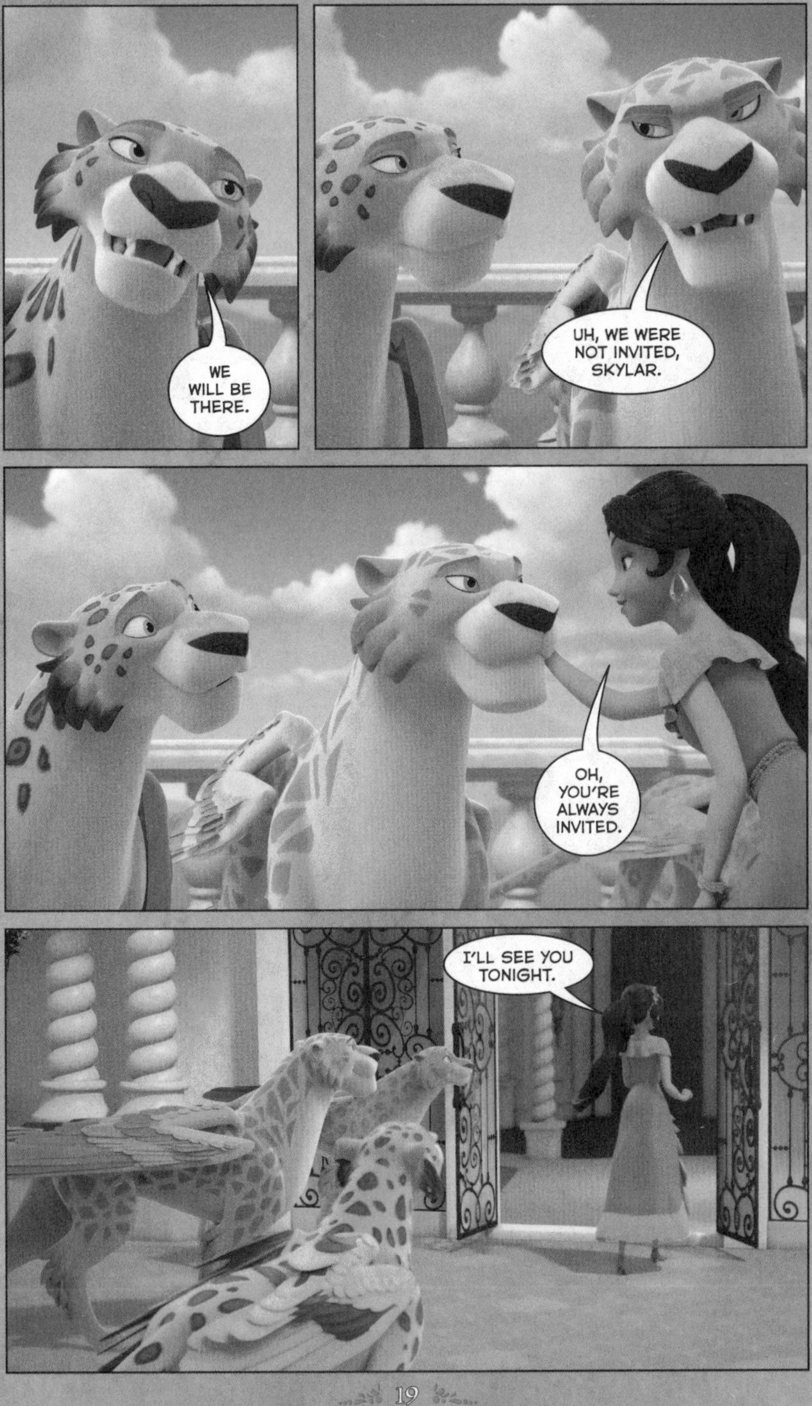
WE WILL BE THERE.
UH, WE WERE NOT INVITED, SKYLAR.
OH, YOU'RE ALWAYS INVITED.
I'LL SEE YOU TONIGHT.

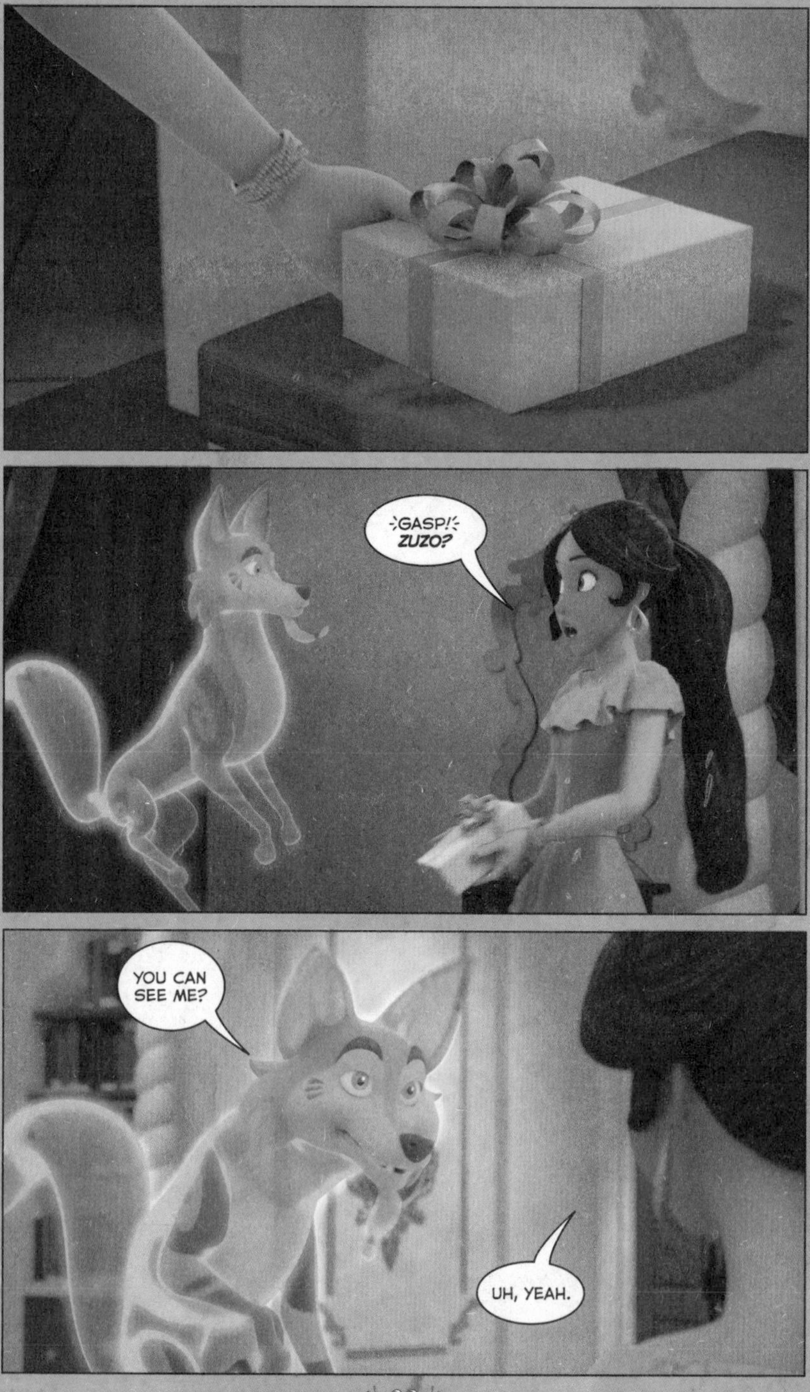
GASP! ZUZO?
YOU CAN SEE ME?
UH, YEAH.

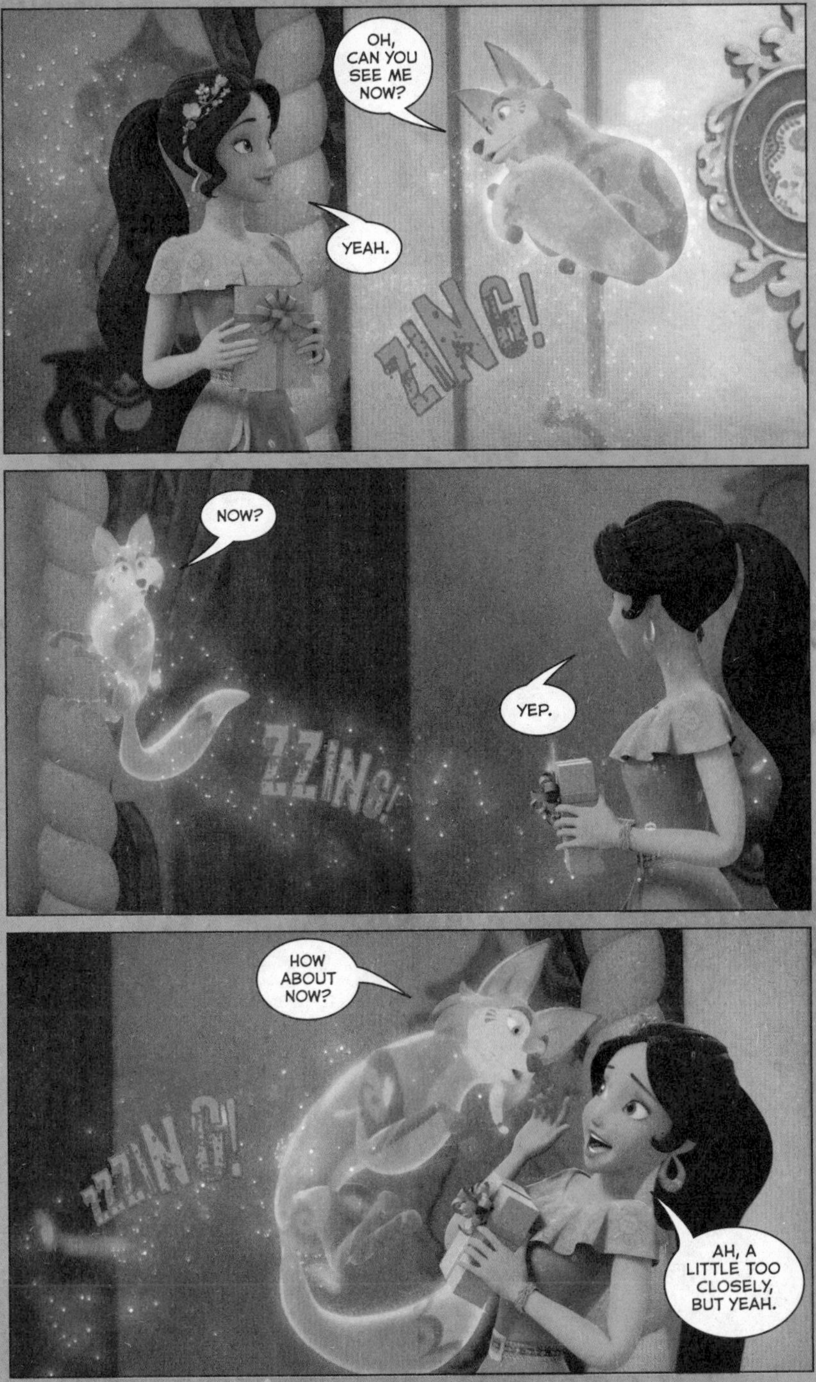
OH, CAN YOU SEE ME NOW?
YEAH.
ZING!
NOW?
YEP.
ZZING!
HOW ABOUT NOW?
ZZZING!
AH, A LITTLE TOO CLOSELY, BUT YEAH.

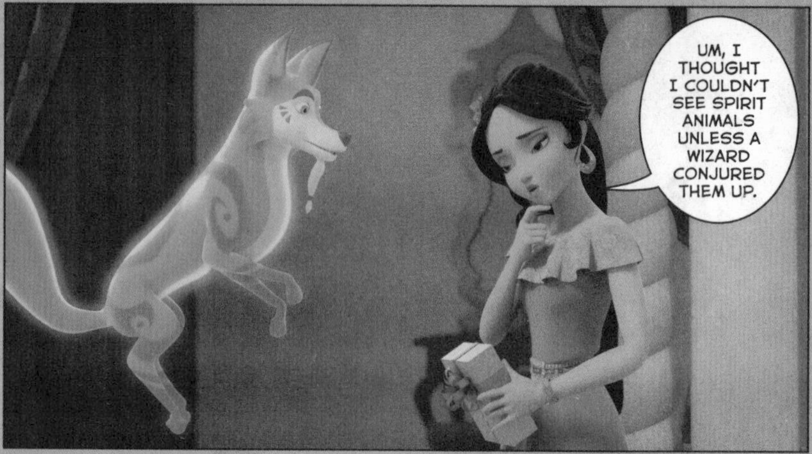
UM, I THOUGHT I COULDN'T SEE SPIRIT ANIMALS UNLESS A WIZARD CONJURED THEM UP.

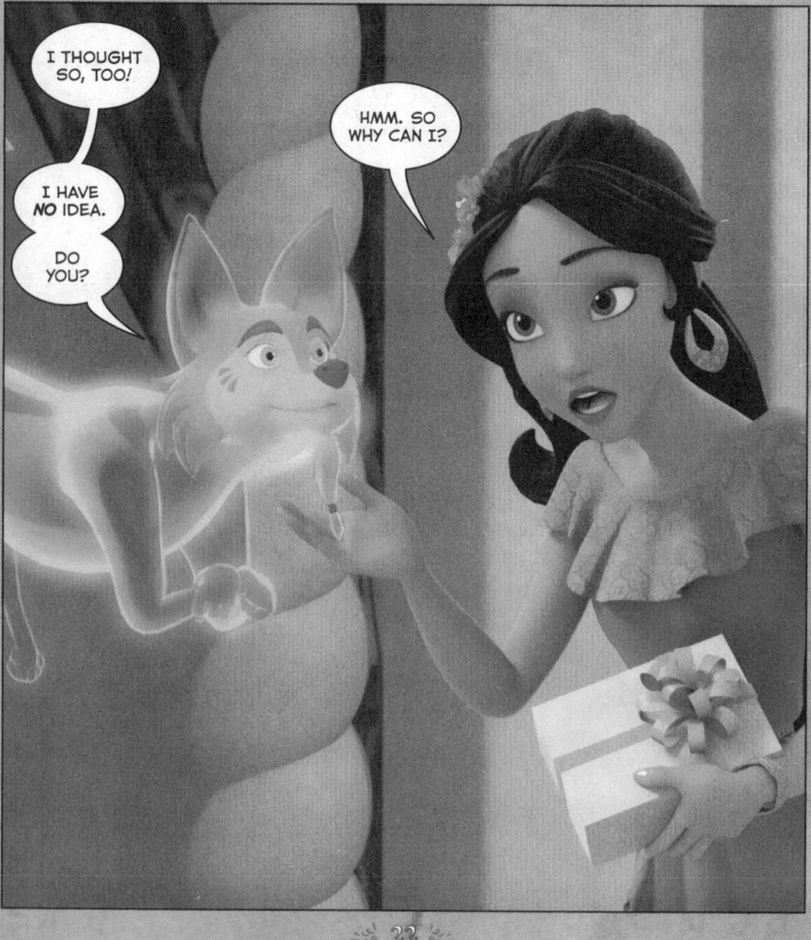
I THOUGHT SO, TOO!
I HAVE *NO* IDEA.
DO YOU?
HMM. SO WHY CAN I?

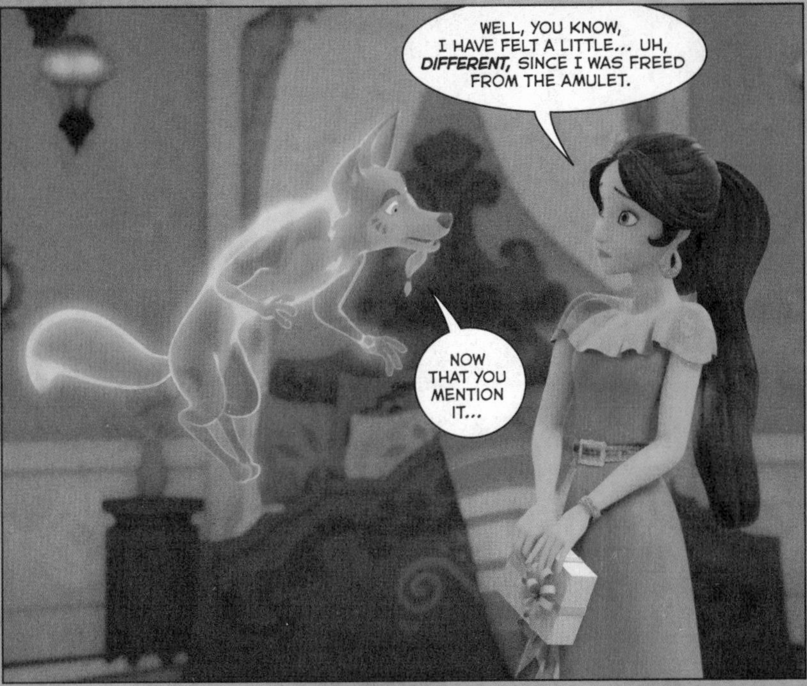
WELL, YOU KNOW, I HAVE FELT A LITTLE... UH, ***DIFFERENT,*** SINCE I WAS FREED FROM THE AMULET.
NOW THAT YOU MENTION IT...

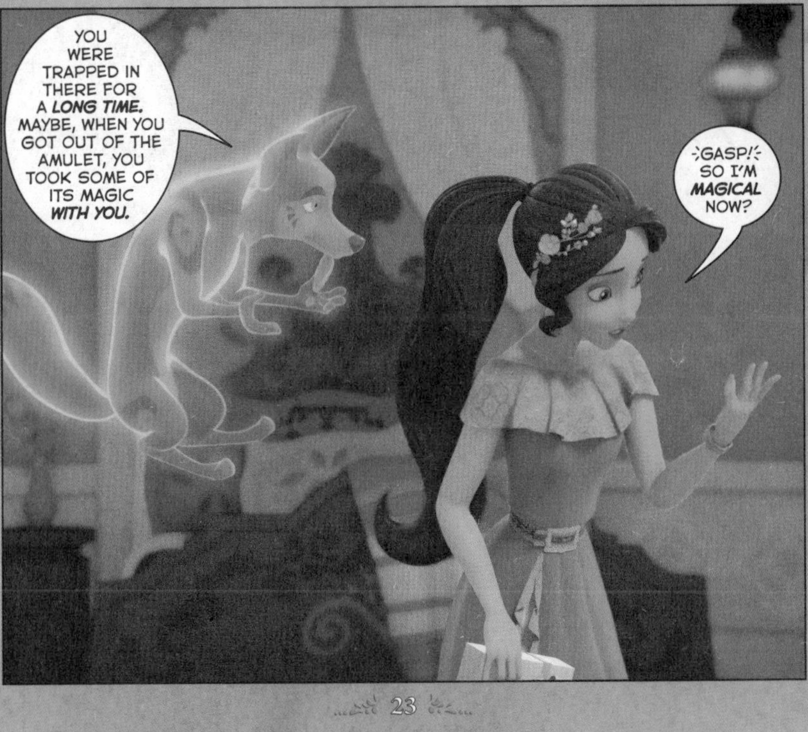
YOU WERE TRAPPED IN THERE FOR A ***LONG TIME.*** MAYBE, WHEN YOU GOT OUT OF THE AMULET, YOU TOOK SOME OF ITS MAGIC ***WITH YOU.***
GASP! SO I'M ***MAGICAL*** NOW?

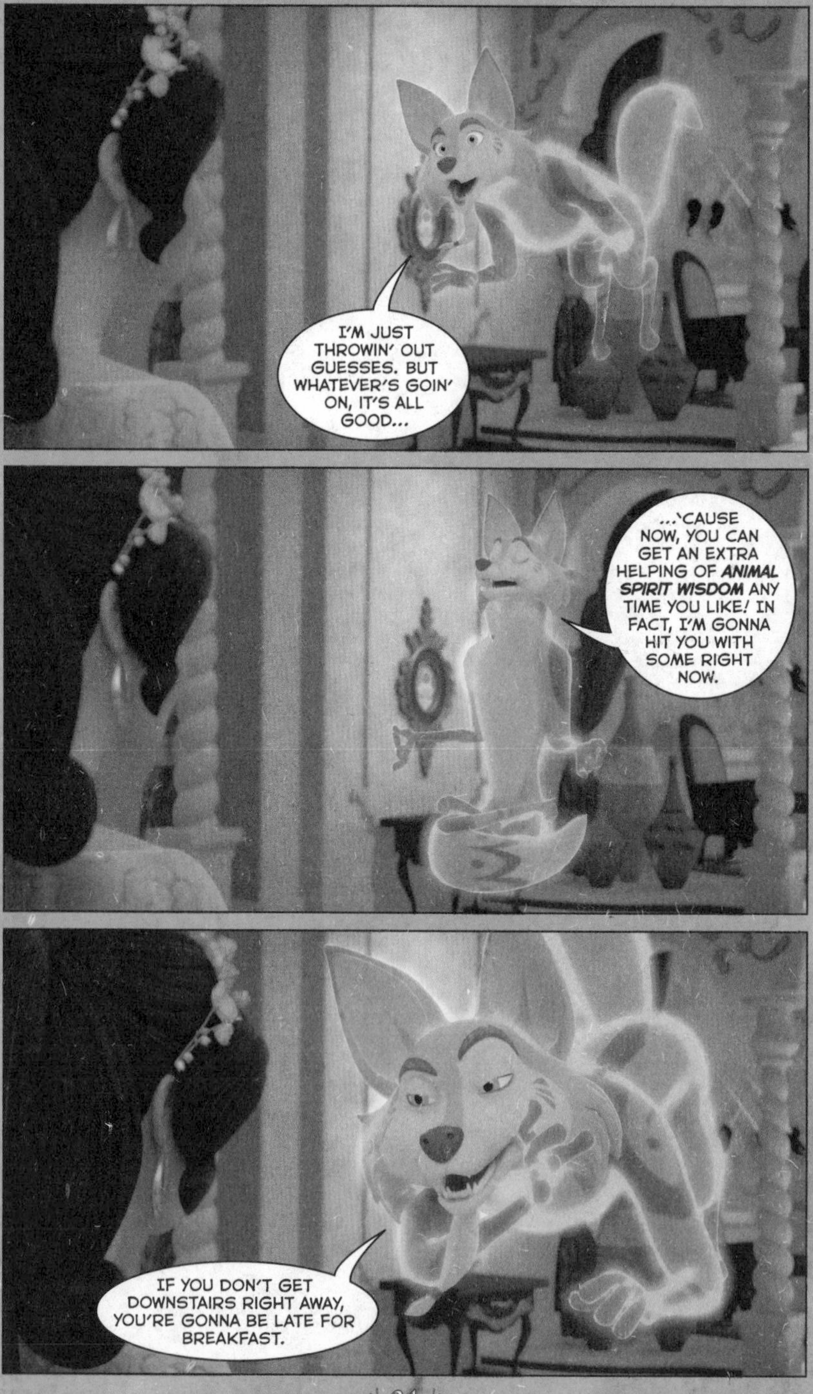
I'M JUST THROWIN' OUT GUESSES. BUT WHATEVER'S GOIN' ON, IT'S ALL GOOD...
...'CAUSE NOW, YOU CAN GET AN EXTRA HELPING OF ***ANIMAL SPIRIT WISDOM*** ANY TIME YOU LIKE! IN FACT, I'M GONNA HIT YOU WITH SOME RIGHT NOW.
IF YOU DON'T GET DOWNSTAIRS RIGHT AWAY, YOU'RE GONNA BE LATE FOR BREAKFAST.

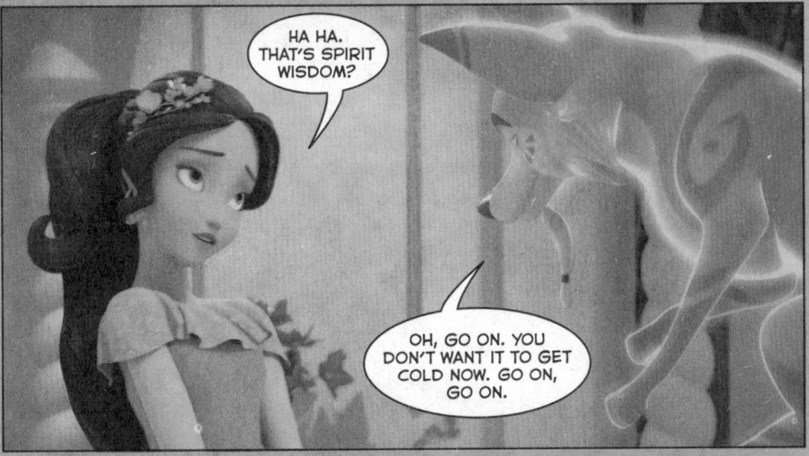
HA HA. THAT'S SPIRIT WISDOM?
OH, GO ON. YOU DON'T WANT IT TO GET COLD NOW. GO ON, GO ON.

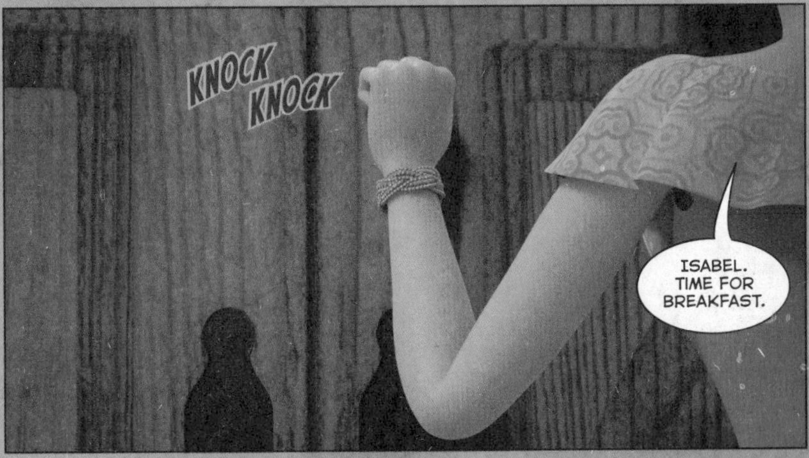
KNOCK KNOCK
ISABEL. TIME FOR BREAKFAST.

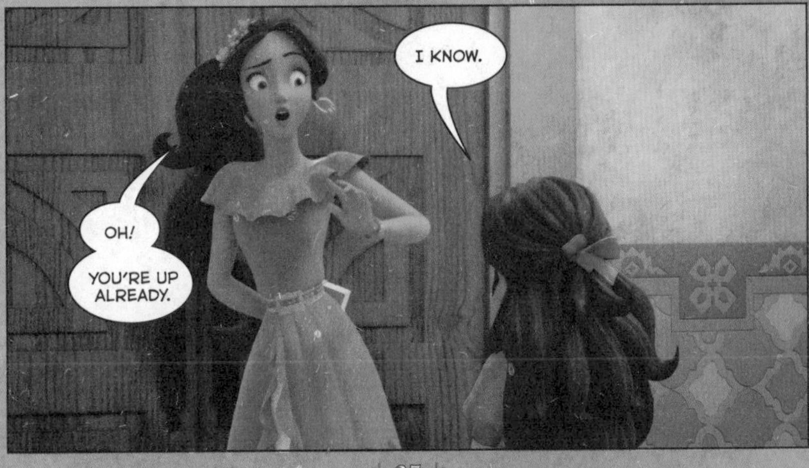
OH!
YOU'RE UP ALREADY.
I KNOW.

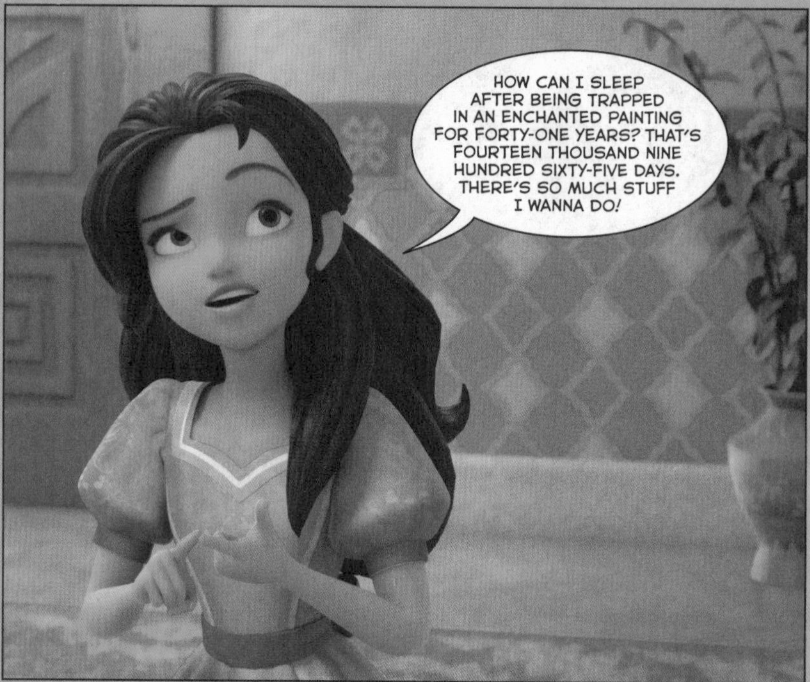
HOW CAN I SLEEP AFTER BEING TRAPPED IN AN ENCHANTED PAINTING FOR FORTY-ONE YEARS? THAT'S FOURTEEN THOUSAND NINE HUNDRED SIXTY-FIVE DAYS. THERE'S SO MUCH STUFF I WANNA DO!

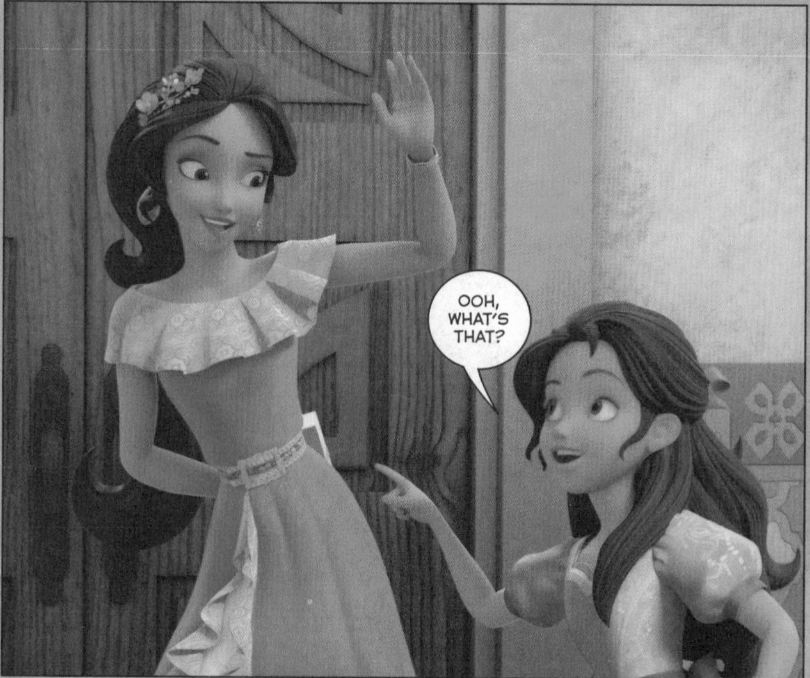
OOH, WHAT'S THAT?

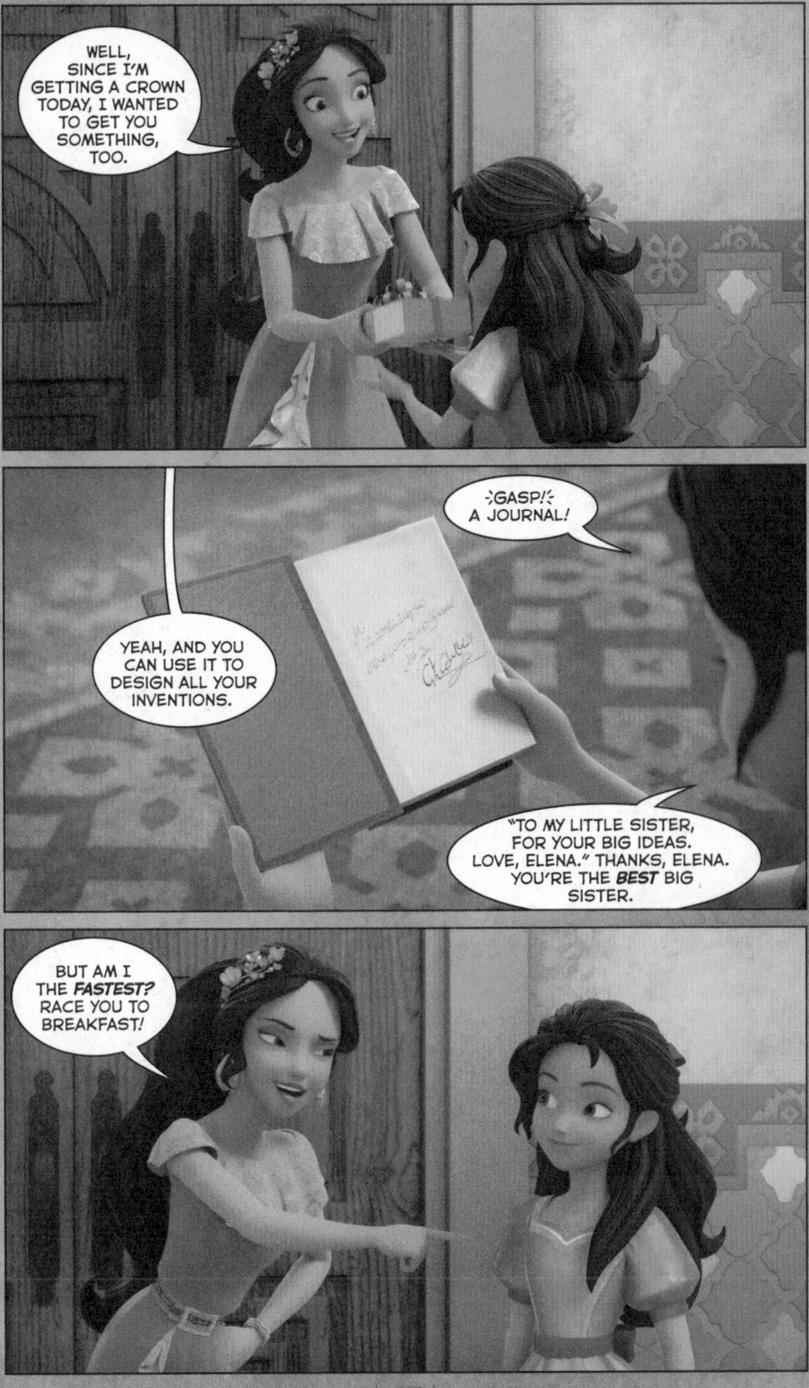
WELL, SINCE I'M GETTING A CROWN TODAY, I WANTED TO GET YOU SOMETHING, TOO.
GASP! A JOURNAL!
YEAH, AND YOU CAN USE IT TO DESIGN ALL YOUR INVENTIONS.
"TO MY LITTLE SISTER, FOR YOUR BIG IDEAS. LOVE, ELENA." THANKS, ELENA. YOU'RE THE ***BEST*** BIG SISTER.
BUT AM I THE ***FASTEST?*** RACE YOU TO BREAKFAST!

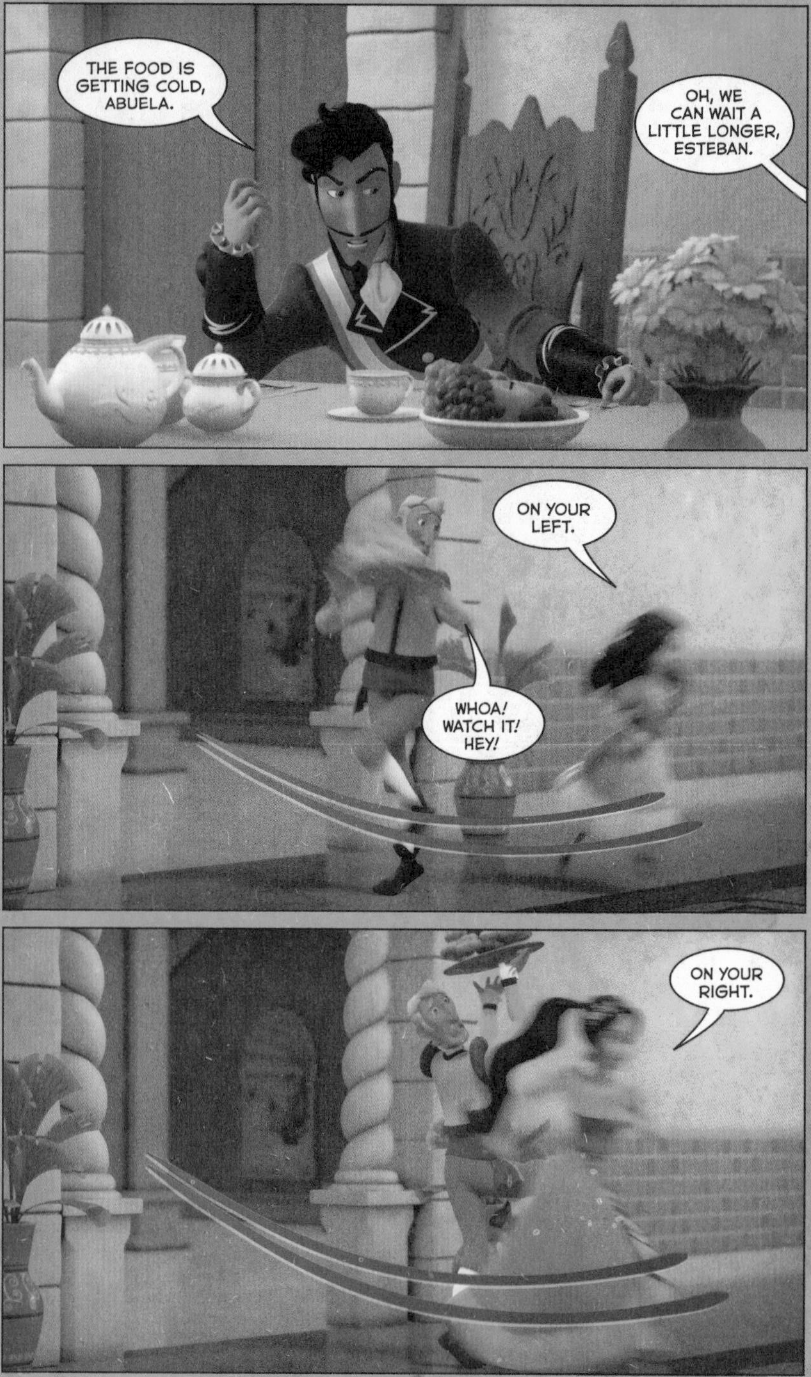
THE FOOD IS GETTING COLD, ABUELA.
OH, WE CAN WAIT A LITTLE LONGER, ESTEBAN.
ON YOUR LEFT.
WHOA! WATCH IT! HEY!
ON YOUR RIGHT.

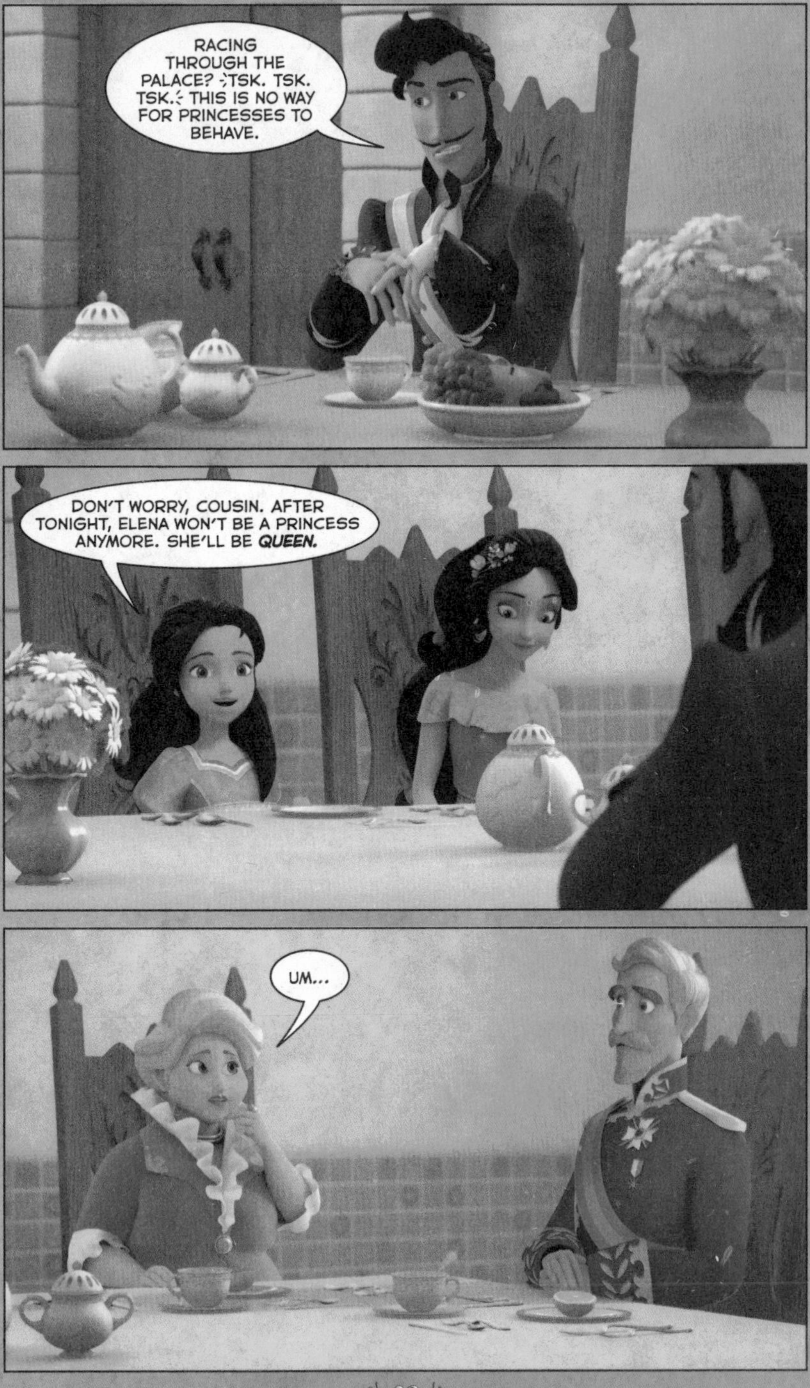
RACING THROUGH THE PALACE? TSK. TSK. TSK. THIS IS NO WAY FOR PRINCESSES TO BEHAVE.
DON'T WORRY, COUSIN. AFTER TONIGHT, ELENA WON'T BE A PRINCESS ANYMORE. SHE'LL BE ***QUEEN.***
UM...

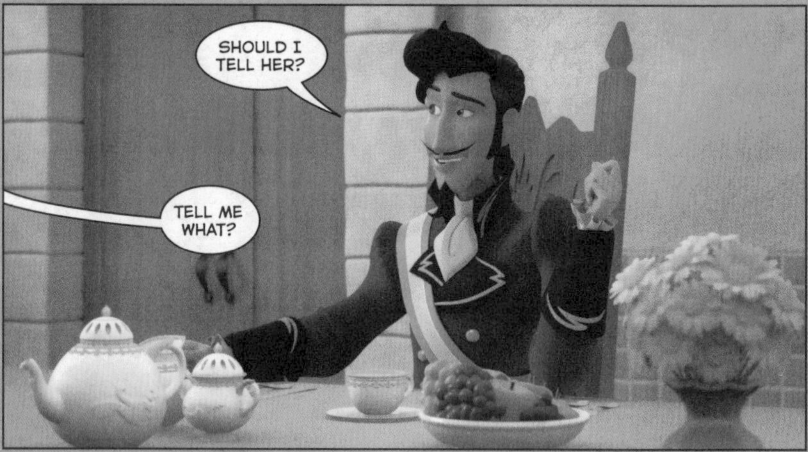
SHOULD I
TELL HER?
TELL ME
WHAT?

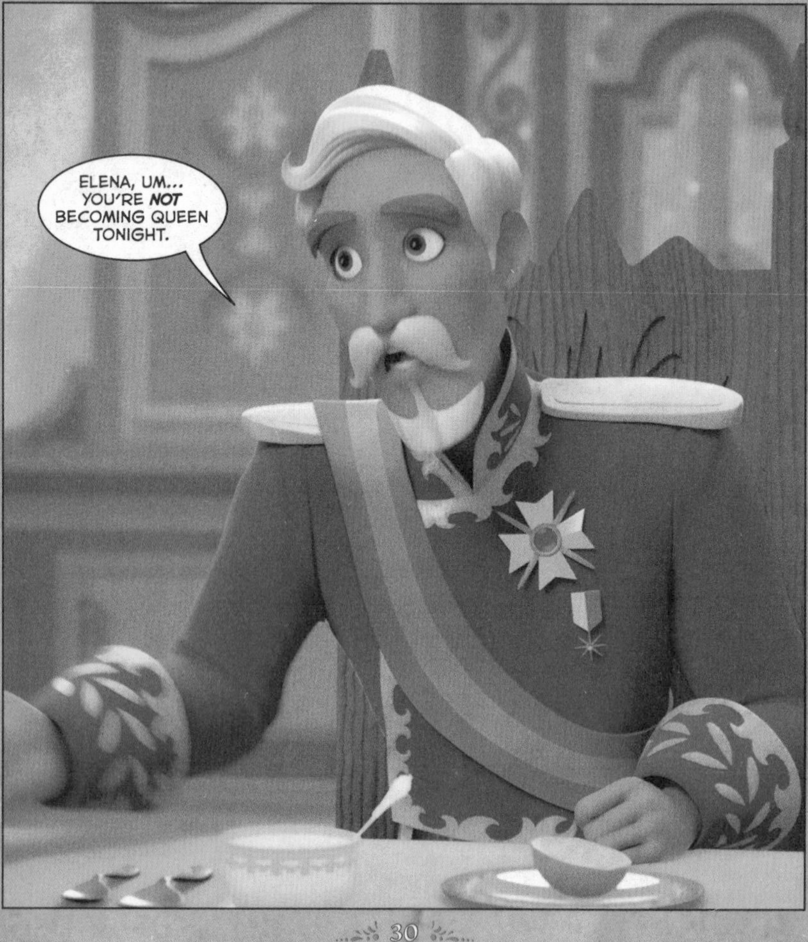
ELENA, UM...
YOU'RE **NOT**
BECOMING QUEEN
TONIGHT.

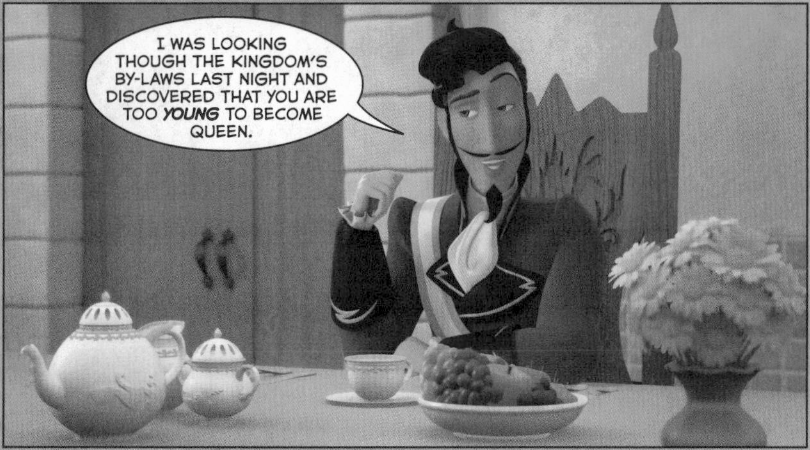
I WAS LOOKING THOUGH THE KINGDOM'S BY-LAWS LAST NIGHT AND DISCOVERED THAT YOU ARE TOO *YOUNG* TO BECOME QUEEN.

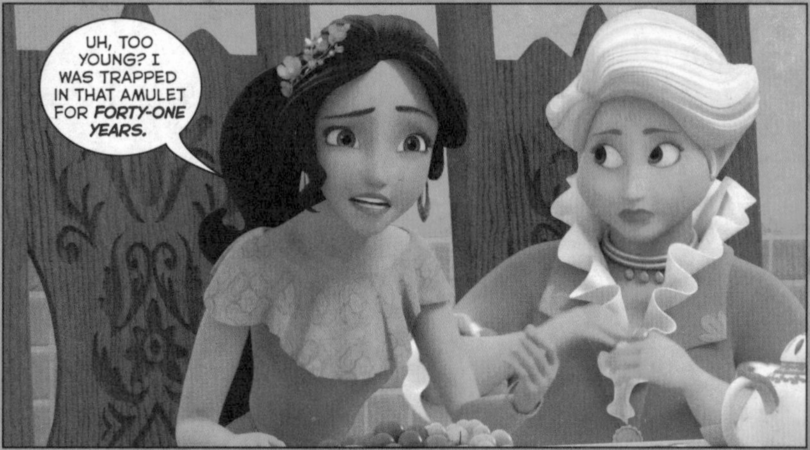
UH, TOO YOUNG? I WAS TRAPPED IN THAT AMULET FOR *FORTY-ONE YEARS.*

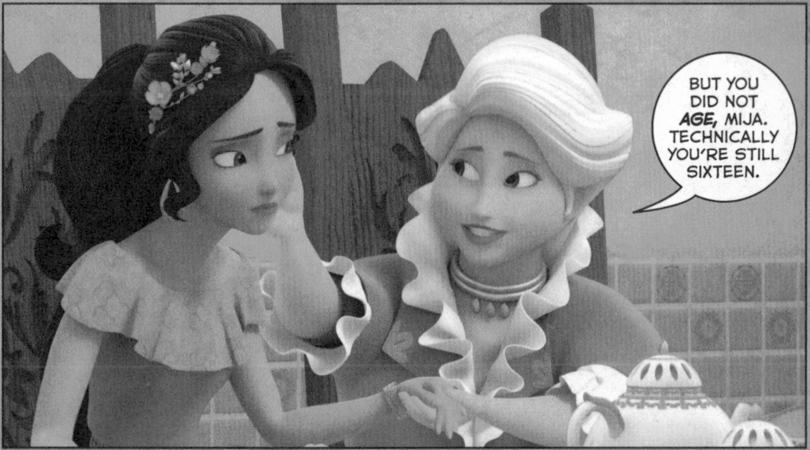
BUT YOU DID NOT *AGE,* MIJA. TECHNICALLY YOU'RE STILL SIXTEEN.

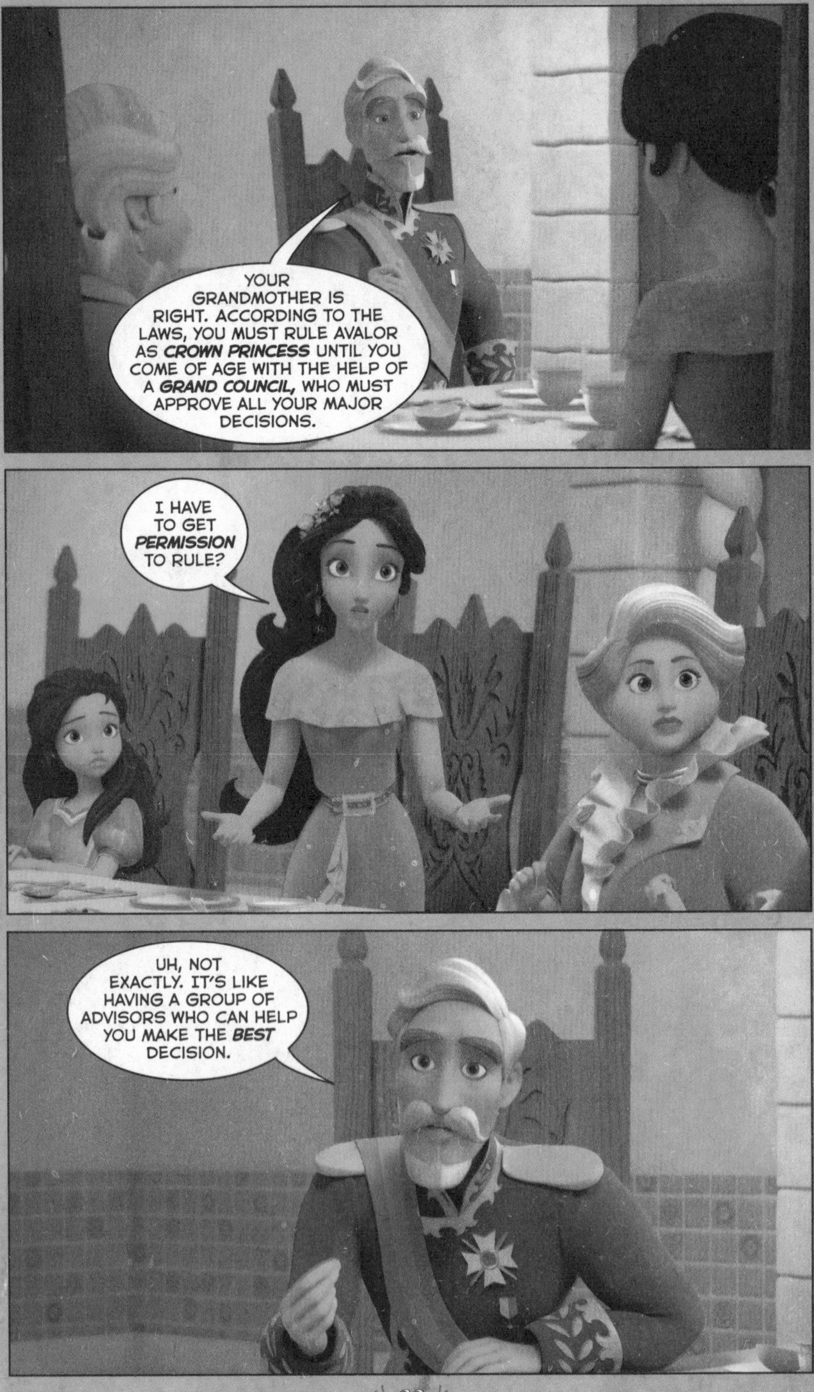
YOUR GRANDMOTHER IS RIGHT. ACCORDING TO THE LAWS, YOU MUST RULE AVALOR AS *CROWN PRINCESS* UNTIL YOU COME OF AGE WITH THE HELP OF A *GRAND COUNCIL,* WHO MUST APPROVE ALL YOUR MAJOR DECISIONS.
I HAVE TO GET *PERMISSION* TO RULE?
UH, NOT EXACTLY. IT'S LIKE HAVING A GROUP OF ADVISORS WHO CAN HELP YOU MAKE THE *BEST* DECISION.

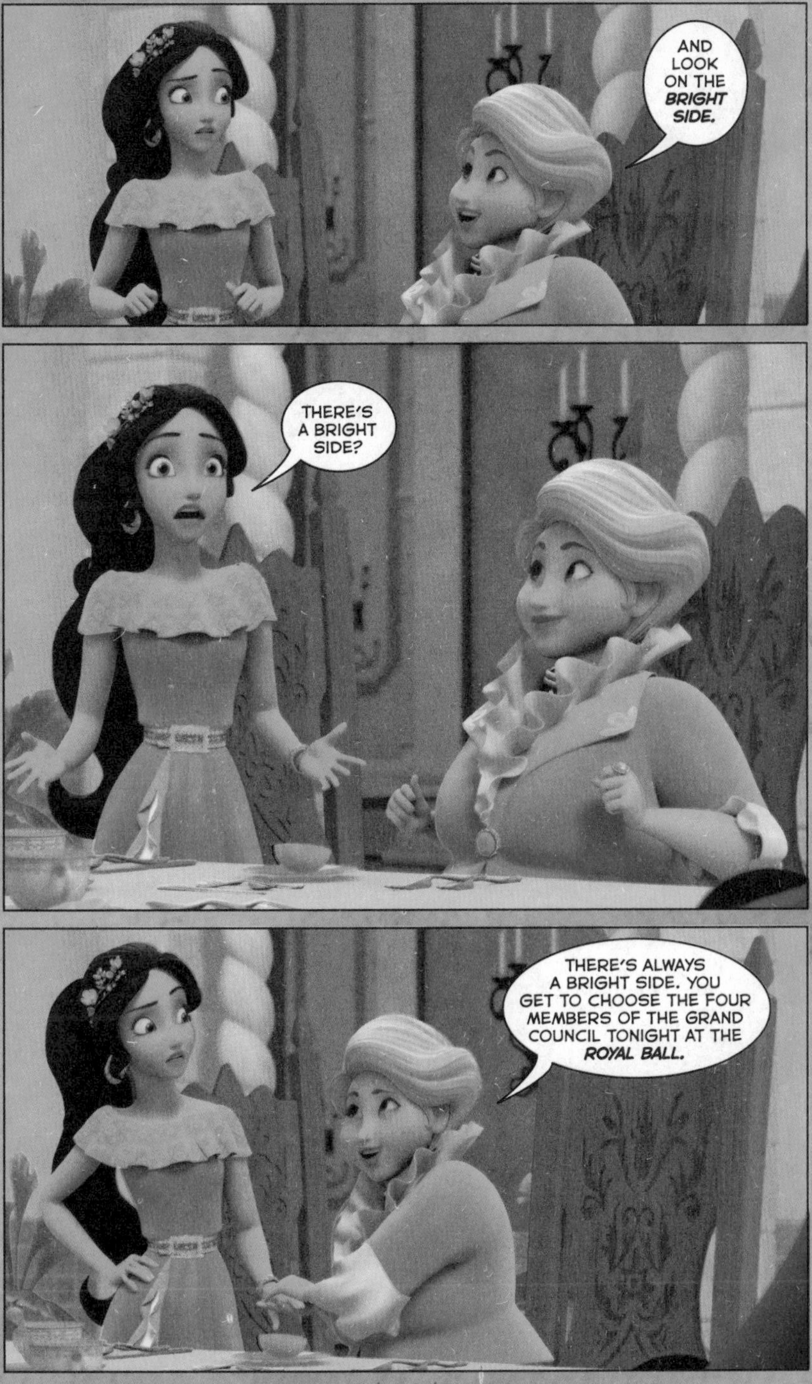
AND LOOK ON THE BRIGHT SIDE.
THERE'S A BRIGHT SIDE?
THERE'S ALWAYS A BRIGHT SIDE. YOU GET TO CHOOSE THE FOUR MEMBERS OF THE GRAND COUNCIL TONIGHT AT THE ROYAL BALL.

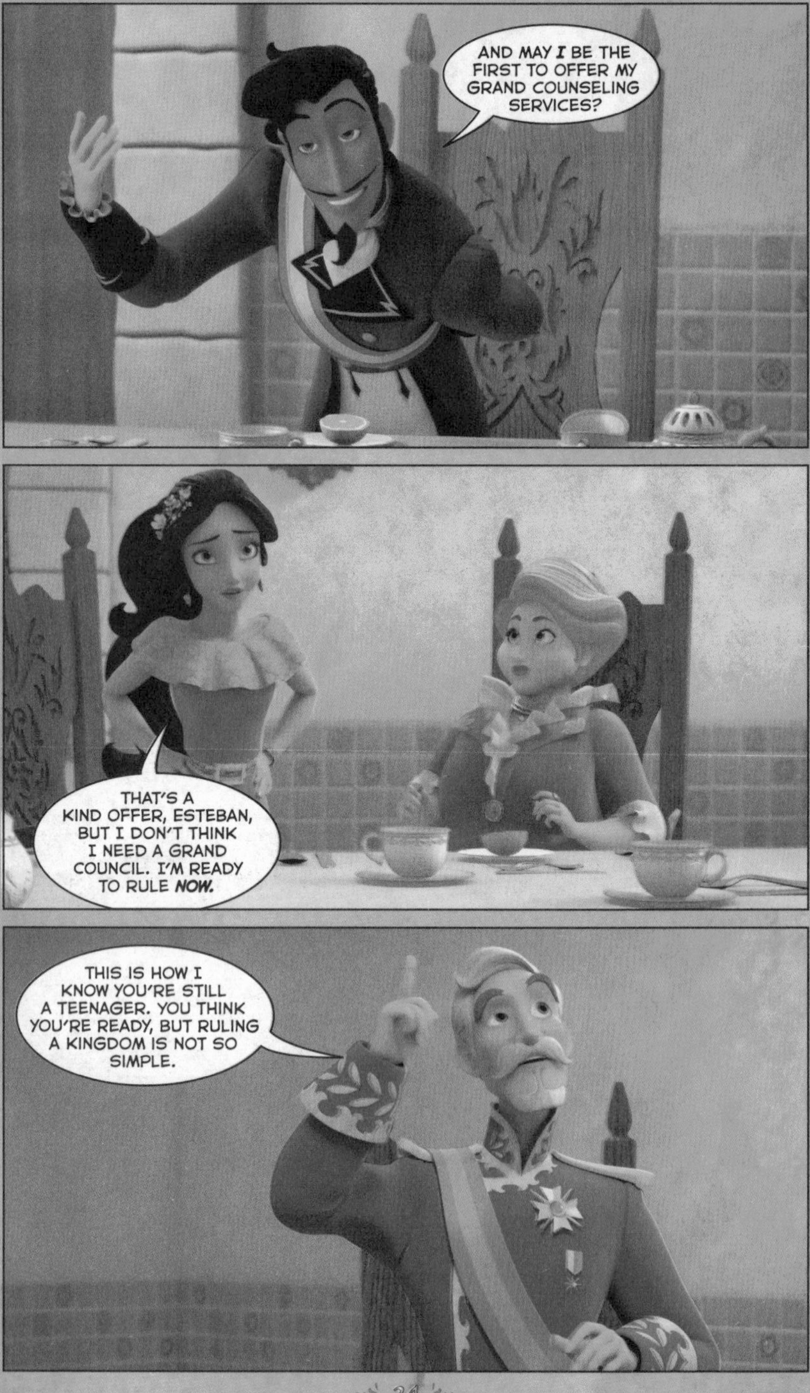
AND MAY *I* BE THE FIRST TO OFFER MY GRAND COUNSELING SERVICES?
THAT'S A KIND OFFER, ESTEBAN, BUT I DON'T THINK I NEED A GRAND COUNCIL. I'M READY TO RULE *NOW.*
THIS IS HOW I KNOW YOU'RE STILL A TEENAGER. YOU THINK YOU'RE READY, BUT RULING A KINGDOM IS NOT SO SIMPLE.

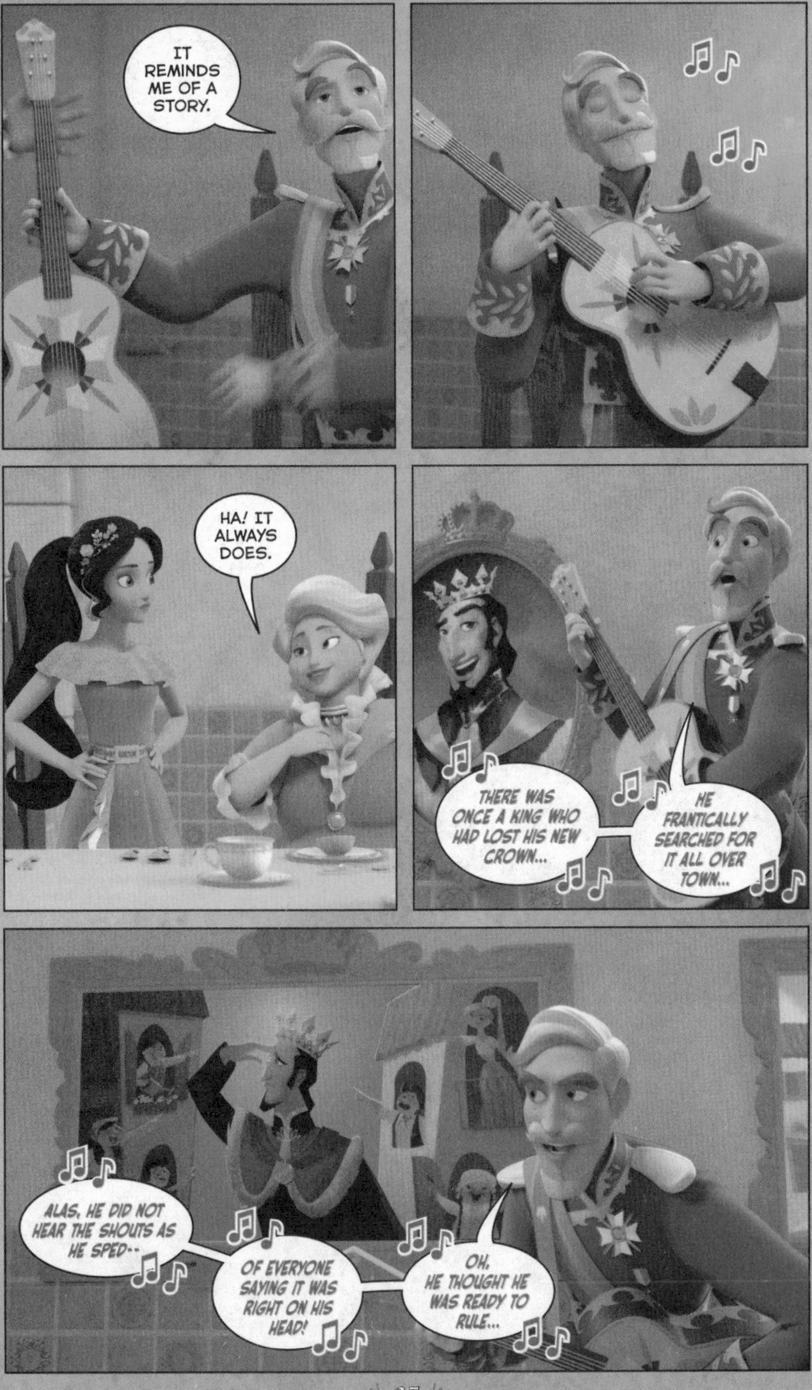
IT REMINDS ME OF A STORY.
HA! IT ALWAYS DOES.
THERE WAS ONCE A KING WHO HAD LOST HIS NEW CROWN...
HE FRANTICALLY SEARCHED FOR IT ALL OVER TOWN...
OH, HE THOUGHT HE WAS READY TO RULE...
ALAS, HE DID NOT HEAR THE SHOUTS AS HE SPED--
OF EVERYONE SAYING IT WAS RIGHT ON HIS HEAD!

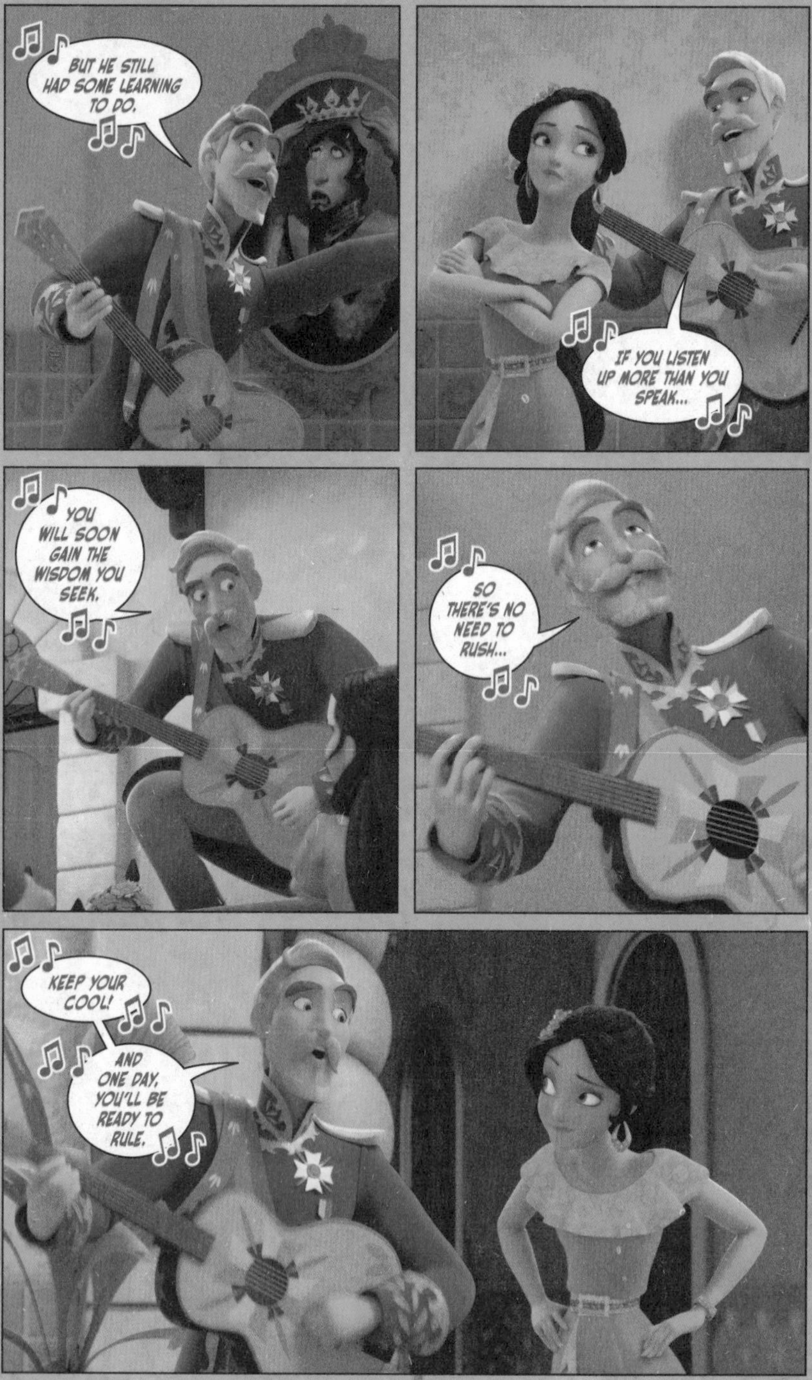
BUT HE STILL HAD SOME LEARNING TO DO.
IF YOU LISTEN UP MORE THAN YOU SPEAK...
YOU WILL SOON GAIN THE WISDOM YOU SEEK.
SO THERE'S NO NEED TO RUSH...
KEEP YOUR COOL!
AND ONE DAY, YOU'LL BE READY TO RULE.

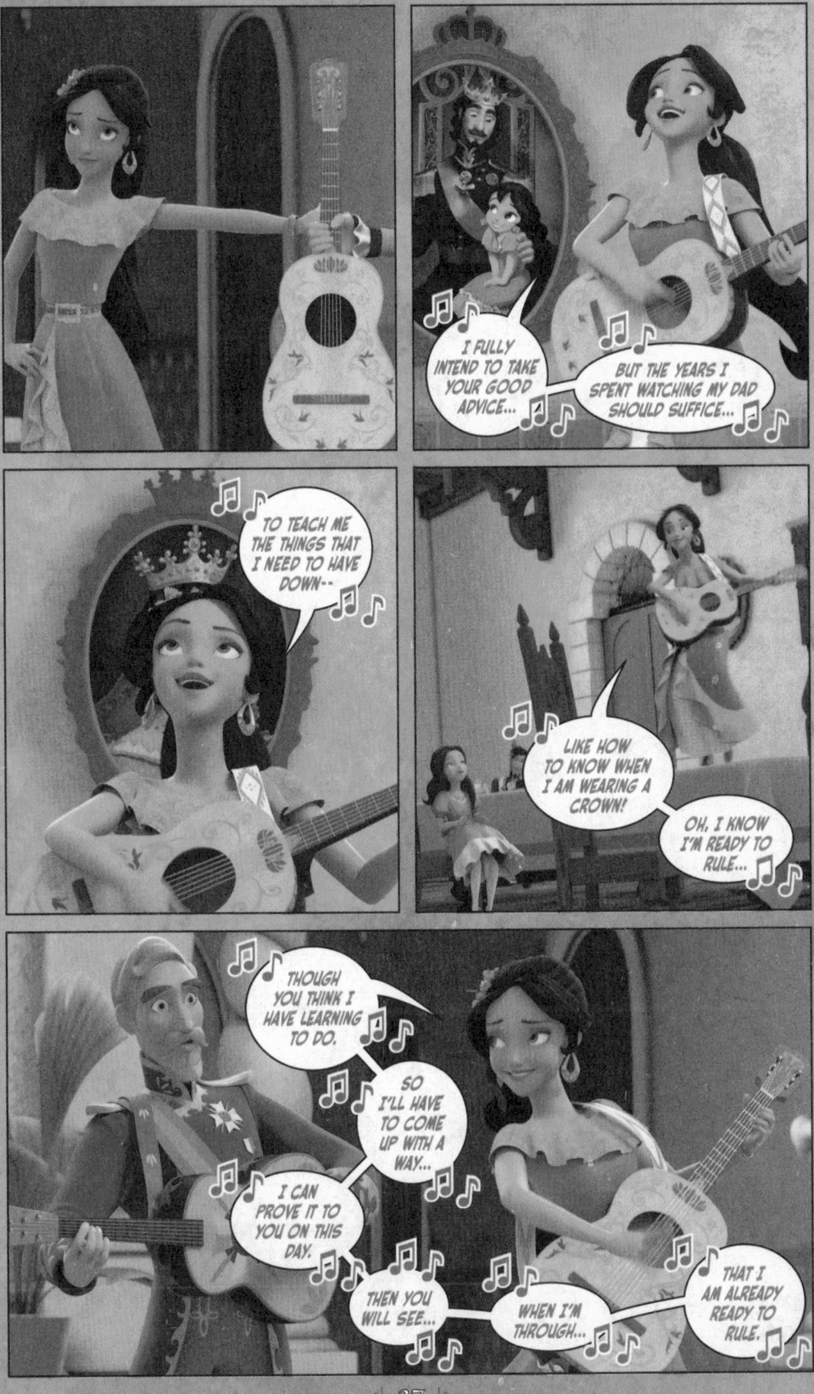
I FULLY INTEND TO TAKE YOUR GOOD ADVICE...
BUT THE YEARS I SPENT WATCHING MY DAD SHOULD SUFFICE...
TO TEACH ME THE THINGS THAT I NEED TO HAVE DOWN--
LIKE HOW TO KNOW WHEN I AM WEARING A CROWN!
OH, I KNOW I'M READY TO RULE...
THOUGH YOU THINK I HAVE LEARNING TO DO.
SO I'LL HAVE TO COME UP WITH A WAY...
I CAN PROVE IT TO YOU ON THIS DAY.
THEN YOU WILL SEE...
WHEN I'M THROUGH...
THAT I AM ALREADY READY TO RULE.

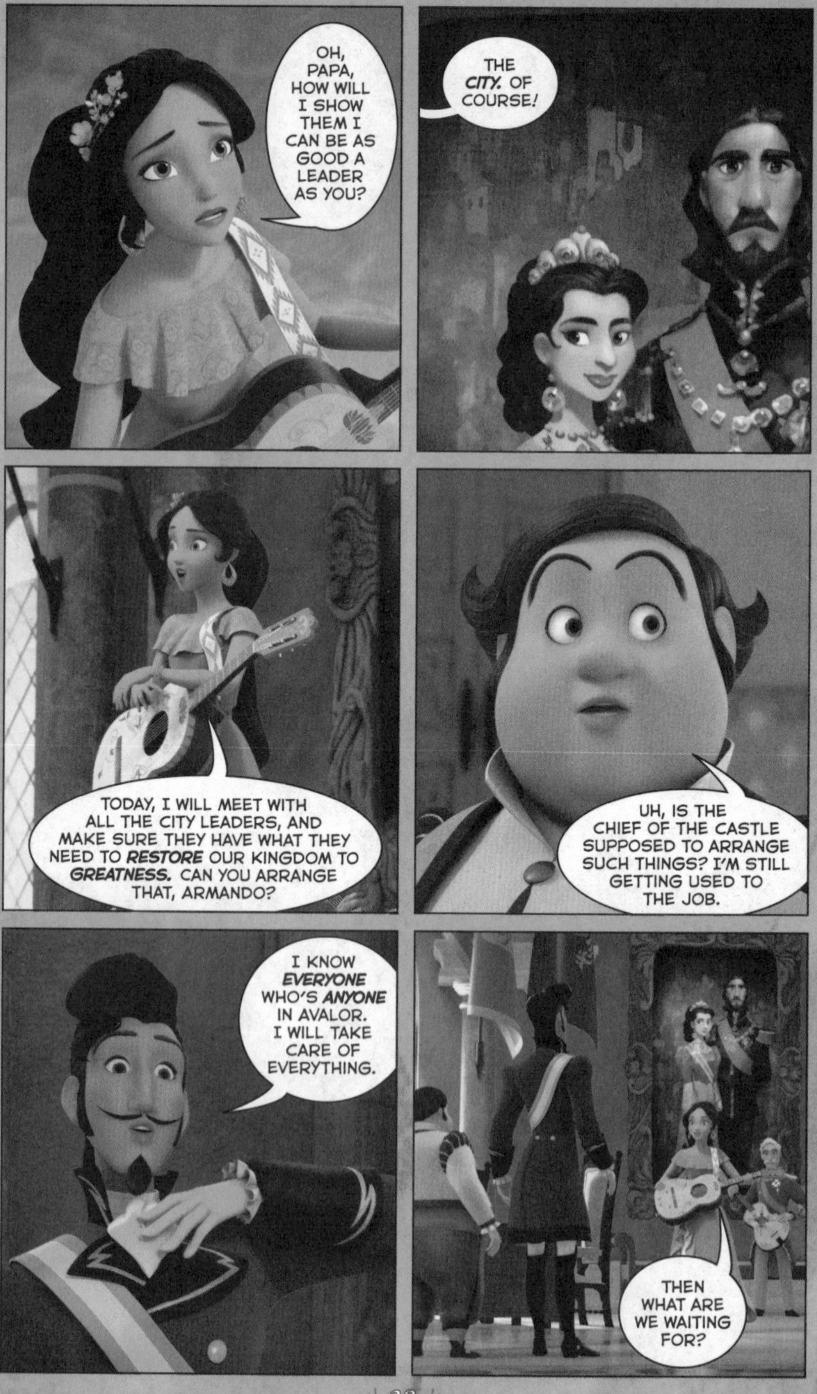
OH, PAPA, HOW WILL I SHOW THEM I CAN BE AS GOOD A LEADER AS YOU?
THE *CITY*, OF COURSE!
TODAY, I WILL MEET WITH ALL THE CITY LEADERS, AND MAKE SURE THEY HAVE WHAT THEY NEED TO ***RESTORE*** OUR KINGDOM TO ***GREATNESS.*** CAN YOU ARRANGE THAT, ARMANDO?
UH, IS THE CHIEF OF THE CASTLE SUPPOSED TO ARRANGE SUCH THINGS? I'M STILL GETTING USED TO THE JOB.
I KNOW ***EVERYONE*** WHO'S ***ANYONE*** IN AVALOR. I WILL TAKE CARE OF EVERYTHING.
THEN WHAT ARE WE WAITING FOR?

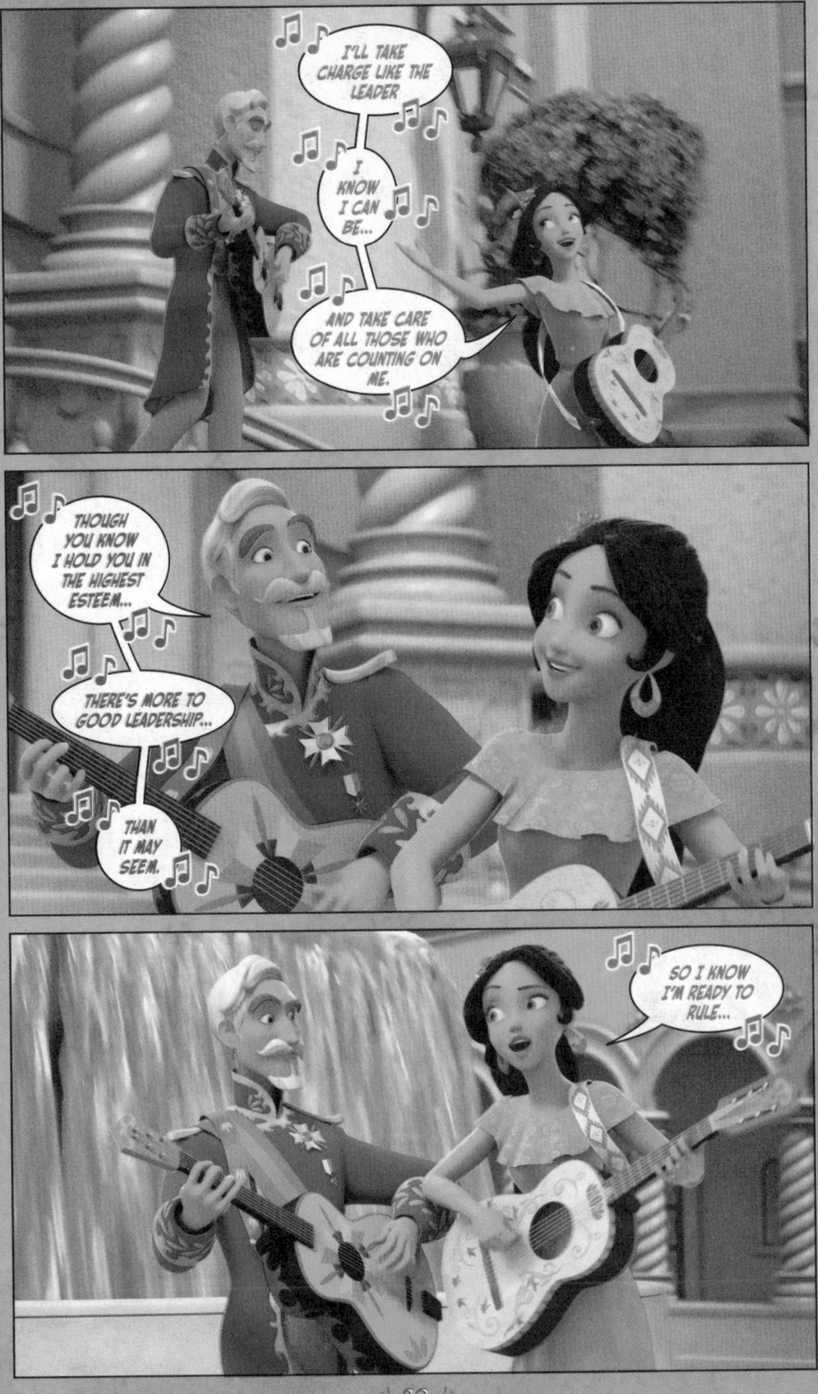
I'LL TAKE CHARGE LIKE THE LEADER
I KNOW I CAN BE...
AND TAKE CARE OF ALL THOSE WHO ARE COUNTING ON ME.
THOUGH YOU KNOW I HOLD YOU IN THE HIGHEST ESTEEM...
THERE'S MORE TO GOOD LEADERSHIP...
THAN IT MAY SEEM.
SO I KNOW I'M READY TO RULE...

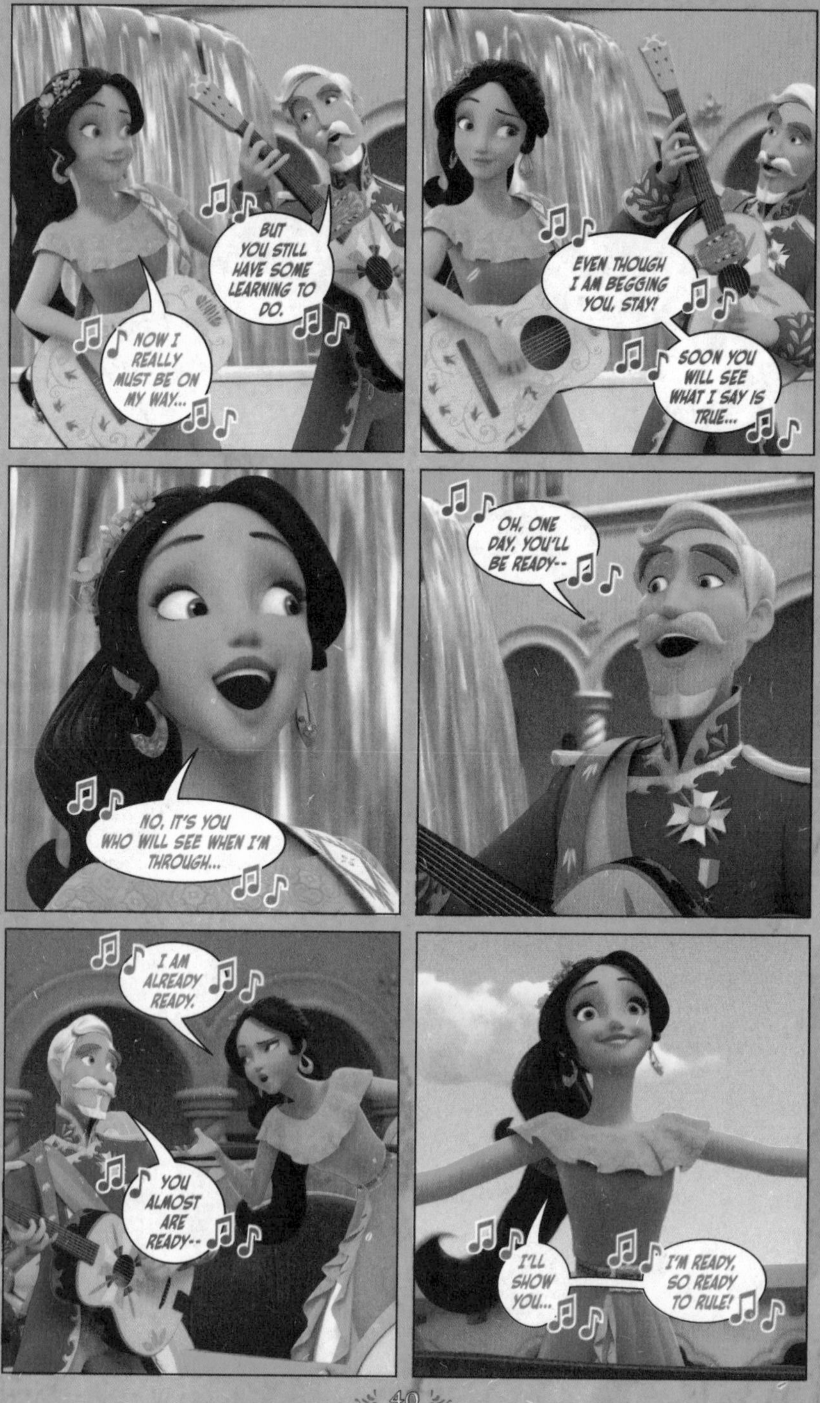

BUT YOU STILL HAVE SOME LEARNING TO DO.
NOW I REALLY MUST BE ON MY WAY...
EVEN THOUGH I AM BEGGING YOU, STAY!
SOON YOU WILL SEE WHAT I SAY IS TRUE...
NO, IT'S YOU WHO WILL SEE WHEN I'M THROUGH...
OH, ONE DAY, YOU'LL BE READY--
I AM ALREADY READY.
YOU ALMOST ARE READY--
I'LL SHOW YOU...
I'M READY, SO READY TO RULE!

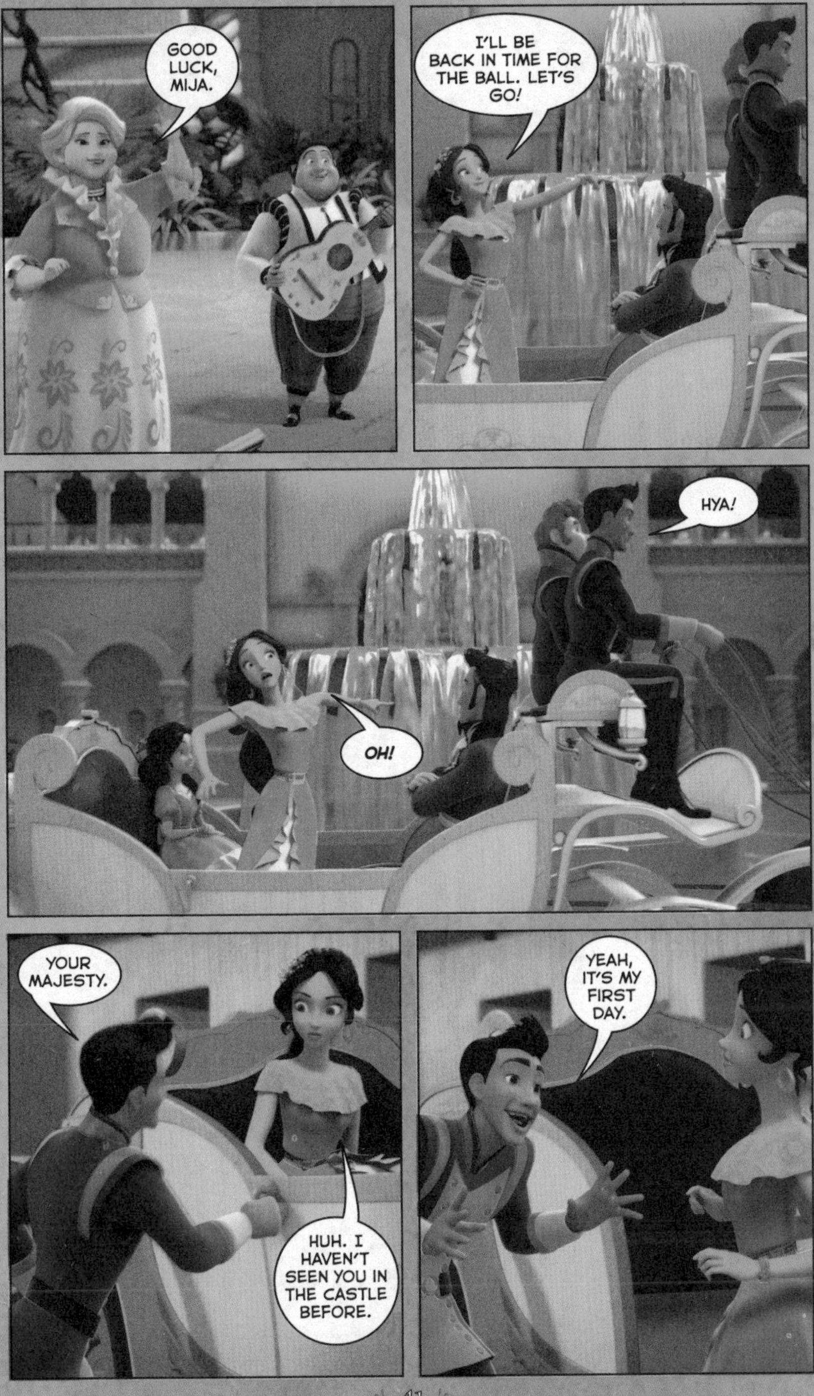
GOOD LUCK, MIJA.
I'LL BE BACK IN TIME FOR THE BALL. LET'S GO!
HYA!
OH!
YOUR MAJESTY.
HUH. I HAVEN'T SEEN YOU IN THE CASTLE BEFORE.
YEAH, IT'S MY FIRST DAY.

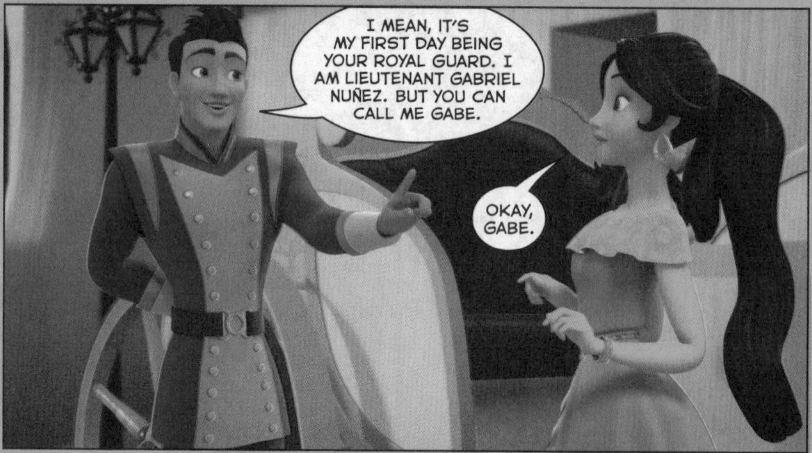
I MEAN, IT'S MY FIRST DAY BEING YOUR ROYAL GUARD. I AM LIEUTENANT GABRIEL NUÑEZ. BUT YOU CAN CALL ME GABE.
OKAY, GABE.

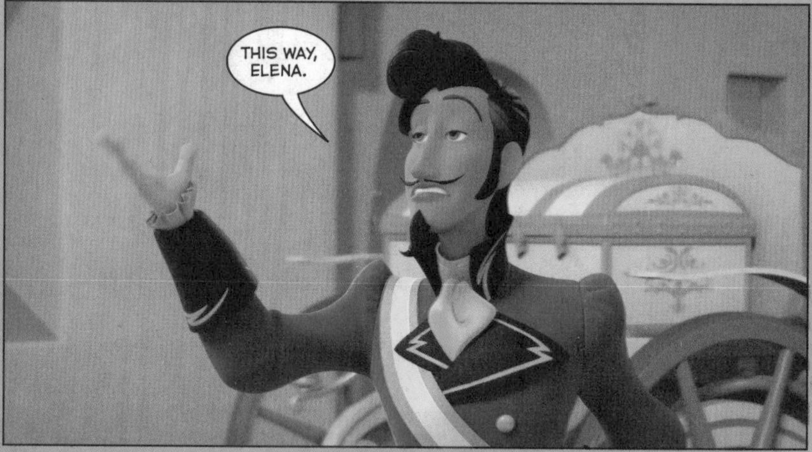
THIS WAY, ELENA.

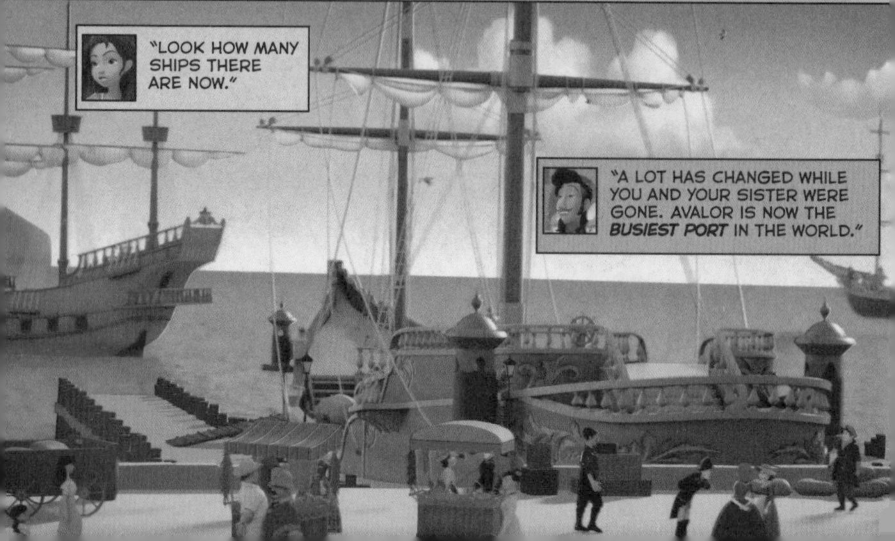
"LOOK HOW MANY SHIPS THERE ARE NOW."
"A LOT HAS CHANGED WHILE YOU AND YOUR SISTER WERE GONE. AVALOR IS NOW THE BUSIEST PORT IN THE WORLD."

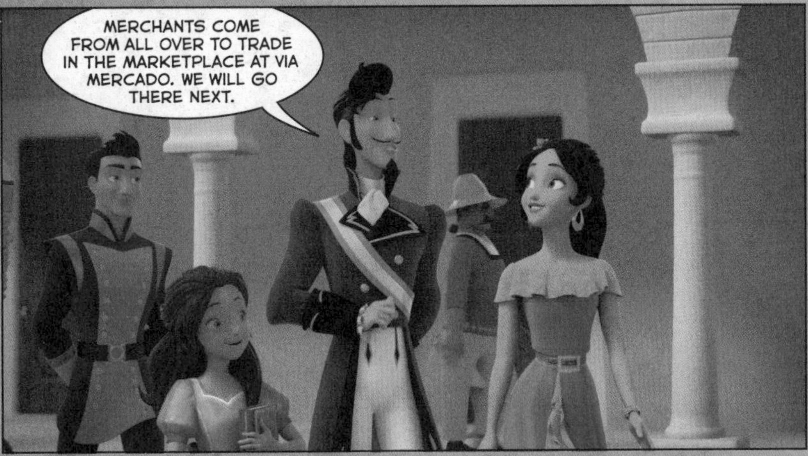
MERCHANTS COME FROM ALL OVER TO TRADE IN THE MARKETPLACE AT VIA MERCADO. WE WILL GO THERE NEXT.

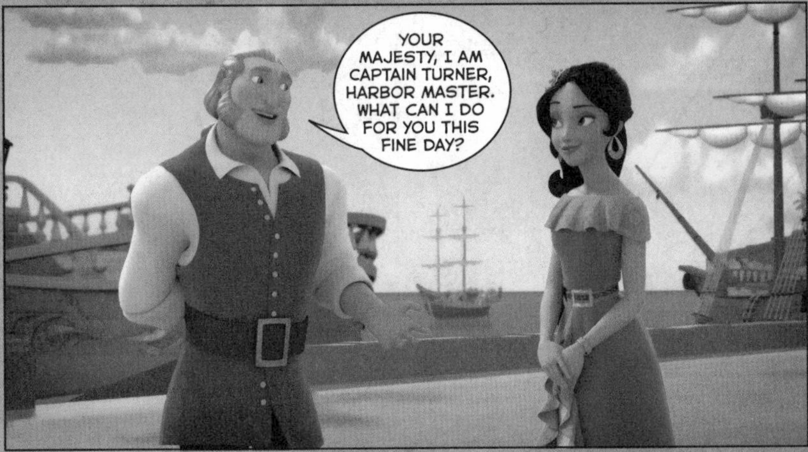
YOUR MAJESTY, I AM CAPTAIN TURNER, HARBOR MASTER. WHAT CAN I DO FOR YOU THIS FINE DAY?

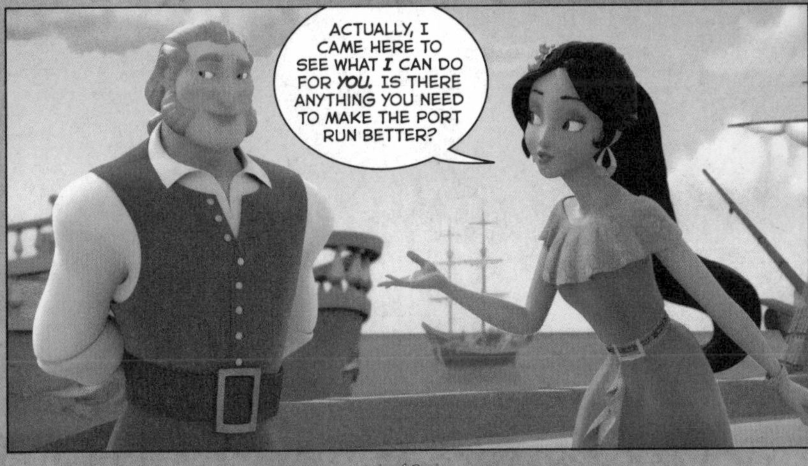
ACTUALLY, I CAME HERE TO SEE WHAT *I* CAN DO FOR ***YOU.*** IS THERE ANYTHING YOU NEED TO MAKE THE PORT RUN BETTER?

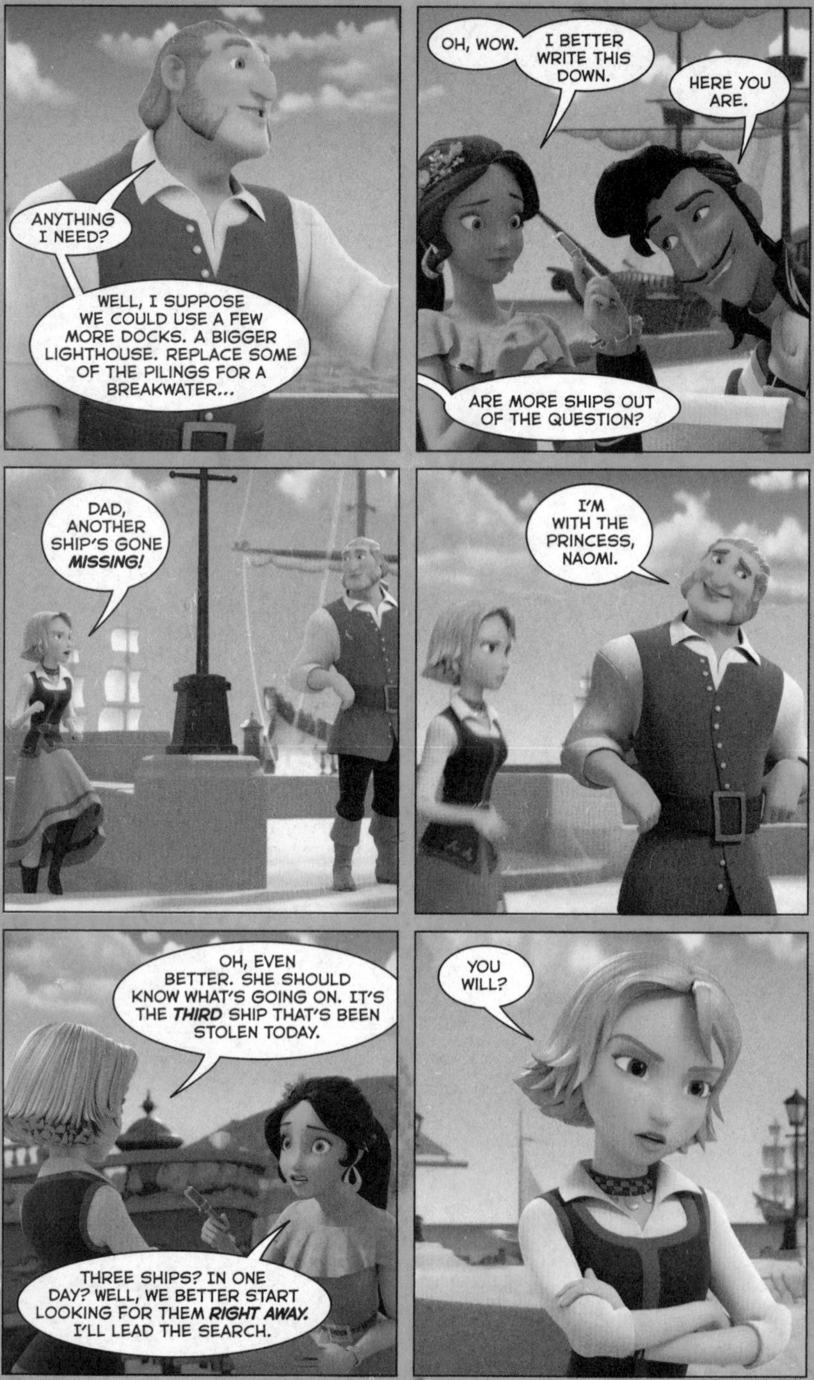
ANYTHING I NEED?
WELL, I SUPPOSE WE COULD USE A FEW MORE DOCKS. A BIGGER LIGHTHOUSE. REPLACE SOME OF THE PILINGS FOR A BREAKWATER...
OH, WOW.
I BETTER WRITE THIS DOWN.
HERE YOU ARE.
ARE MORE SHIPS OUT OF THE QUESTION?
DAD, ANOTHER SHIP'S GONE *MISSING!*
I'M WITH THE PRINCESS, NAOMI.
OH, EVEN BETTER. SHE SHOULD KNOW WHAT'S GOING ON. IT'S THE *THIRD* SHIP THAT'S BEEN STOLEN TODAY.
THREE SHIPS? IN ONE DAY? WELL, WE BETTER START LOOKING FOR THEM *RIGHT AWAY.* I'LL LEAD THE SEARCH.
YOU WILL?

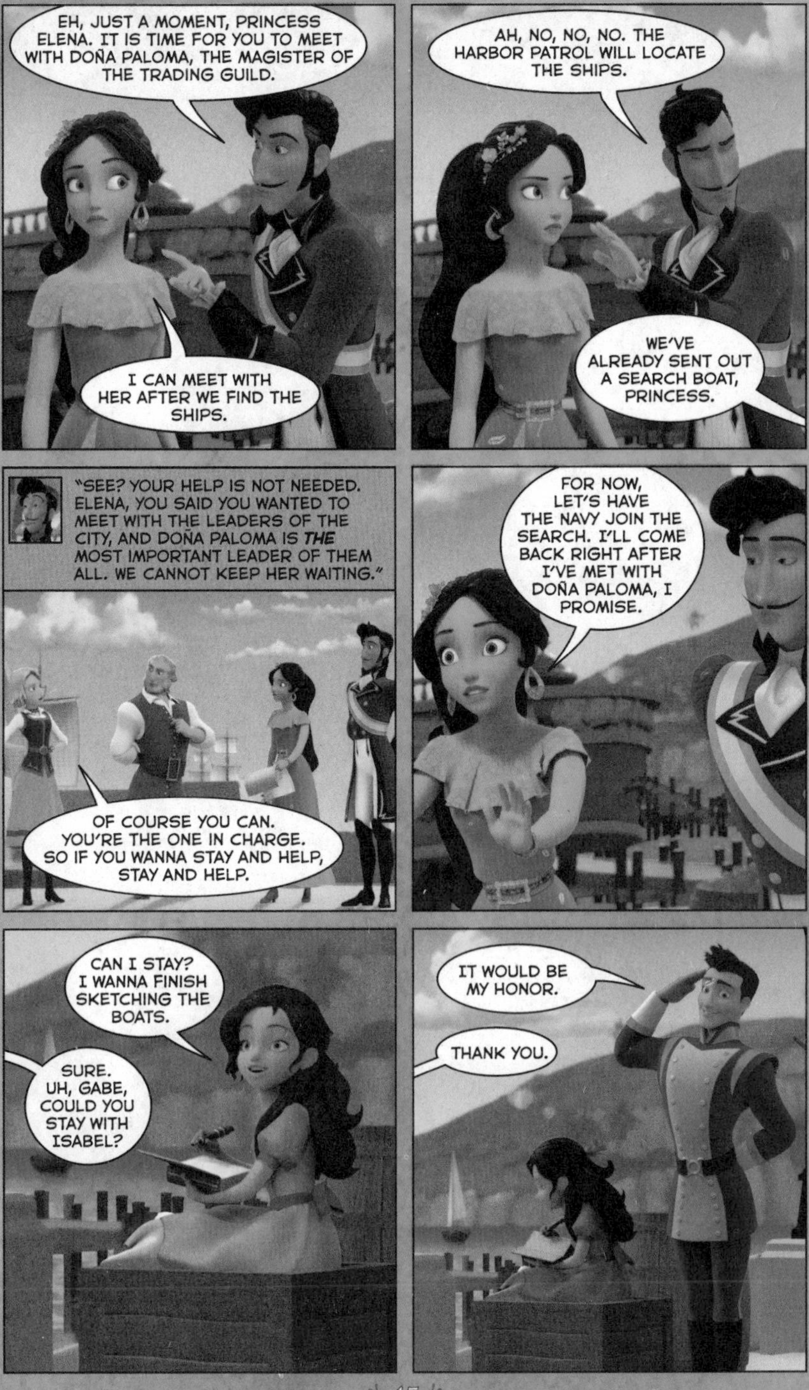
EH, JUST A MOMENT, PRINCESS ELENA. IT IS TIME FOR YOU TO MEET WITH DOÑA PALOMA, THE MAGISTER OF THE TRADING GUILD.
I CAN MEET WITH HER AFTER WE FIND THE SHIPS.
AH, NO, NO, NO. THE HARBOR PATROL WILL LOCATE THE SHIPS.
WE'VE ALREADY SENT OUT A SEARCH BOAT, PRINCESS.
"SEE? YOUR HELP IS NOT NEEDED. ELENA, YOU SAID YOU WANTED TO MEET WITH THE LEADERS OF THE CITY, AND DOÑA PALOMA IS *THE* MOST IMPORTANT LEADER OF THEM ALL. WE CANNOT KEEP HER WAITING."
OF COURSE YOU CAN. YOU'RE THE ONE IN CHARGE. SO IF YOU WANNA STAY AND HELP, STAY AND HELP.
FOR NOW, LET'S HAVE THE NAVY JOIN THE SEARCH. I'LL COME BACK RIGHT AFTER I'VE MET WITH DOÑA PALOMA, I PROMISE.
CAN I STAY? I WANNA FINISH SKETCHING THE BOATS.
SURE. UH, GABE, COULD YOU STAY WITH ISABEL?
IT WOULD BE MY HONOR.
THANK YOU.

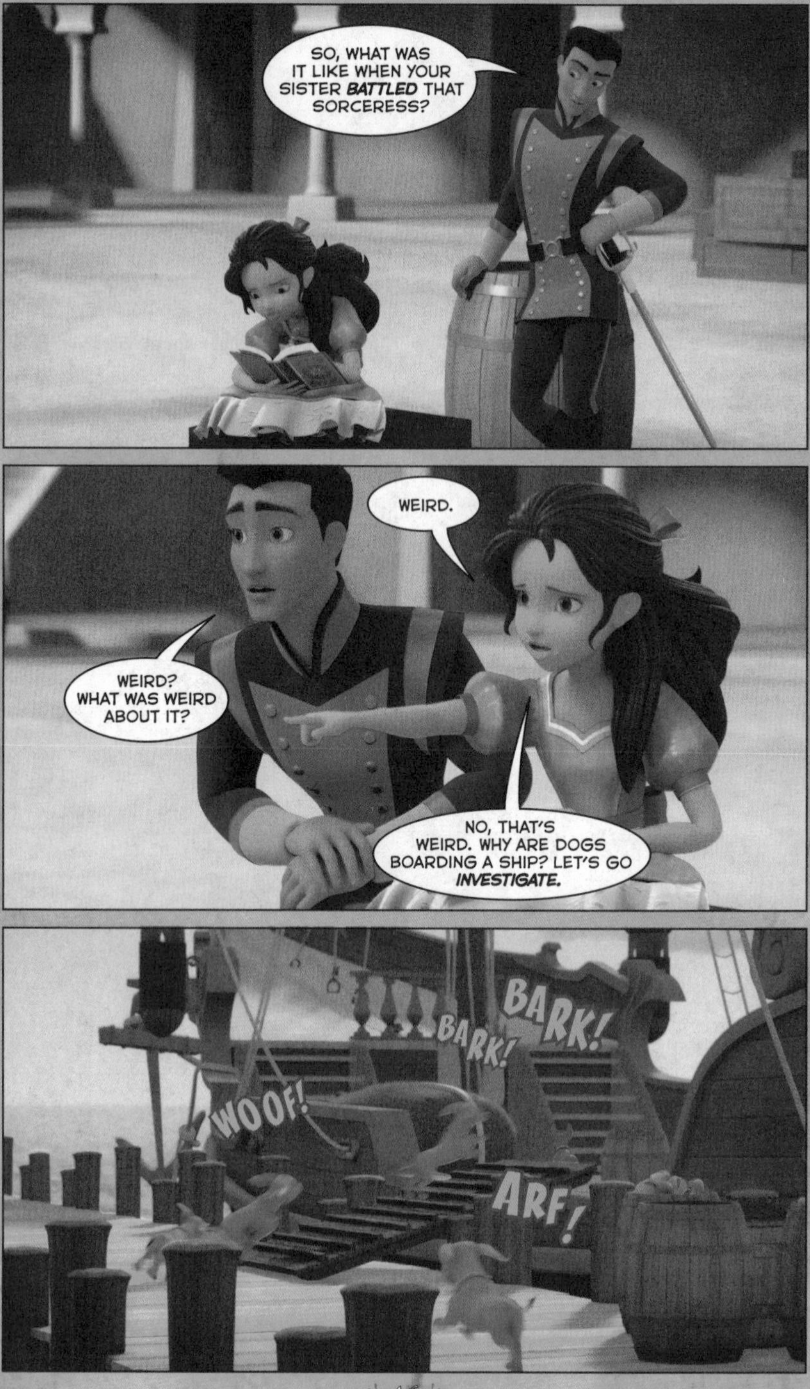
SO, WHAT WAS IT LIKE WHEN YOUR SISTER BATTLED THAT SORCERESS?
WEIRD.
WEIRD? WHAT WAS WEIRD ABOUT IT?
NO, THAT'S WEIRD. WHY ARE DOGS BOARDING A SHIP? LET'S GO INVESTIGATE.
BARK!
BARK!
WOOF!
ARF!

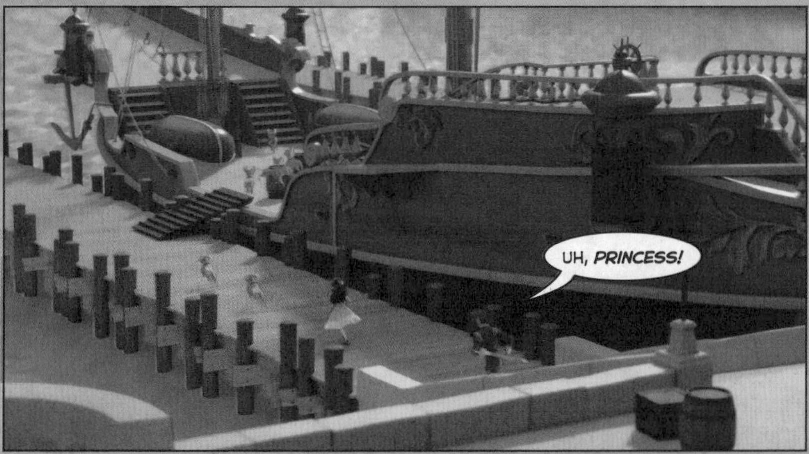
UH, PRINCESS!

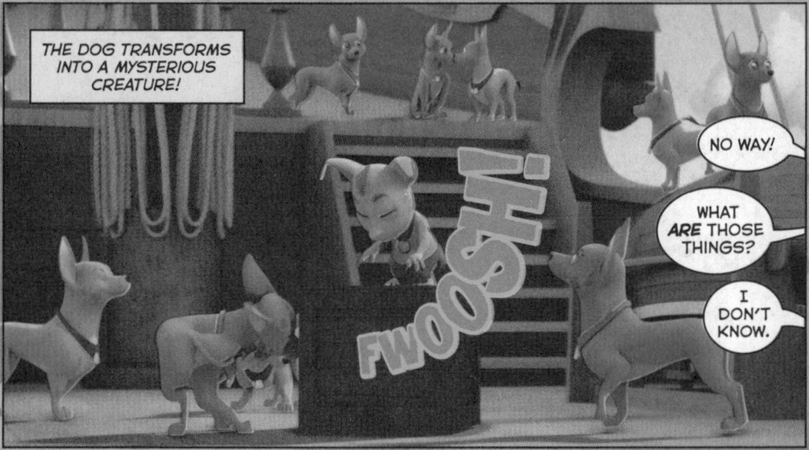
THE DOG TRANSFORMS INTO A MYSTERIOUS CREATURE!
FWOOSH!
NO WAY!
WHAT ARE THOSE THINGS?
I DON'T KNOW.

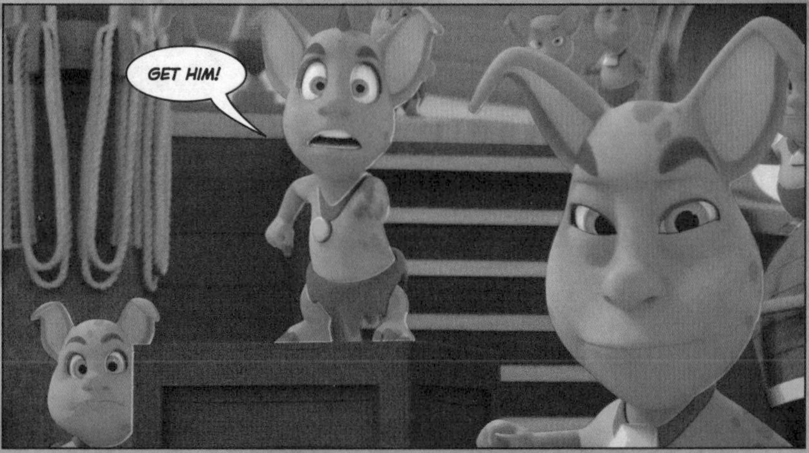
GET HIM!

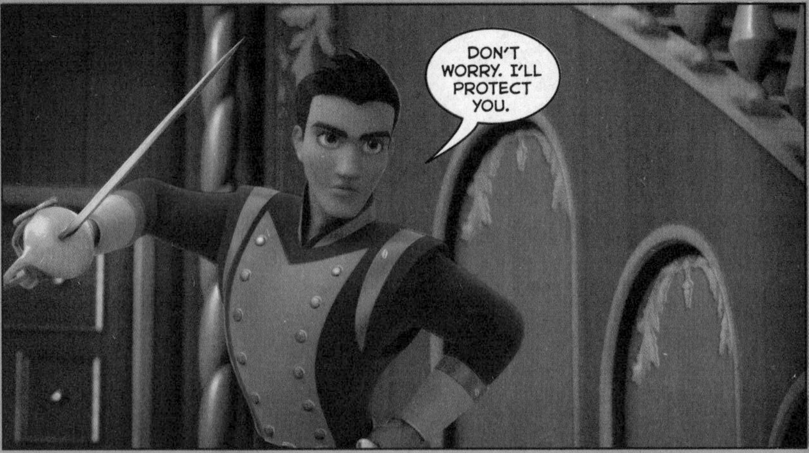
DON'T WORRY. I'LL PROTECT YOU.

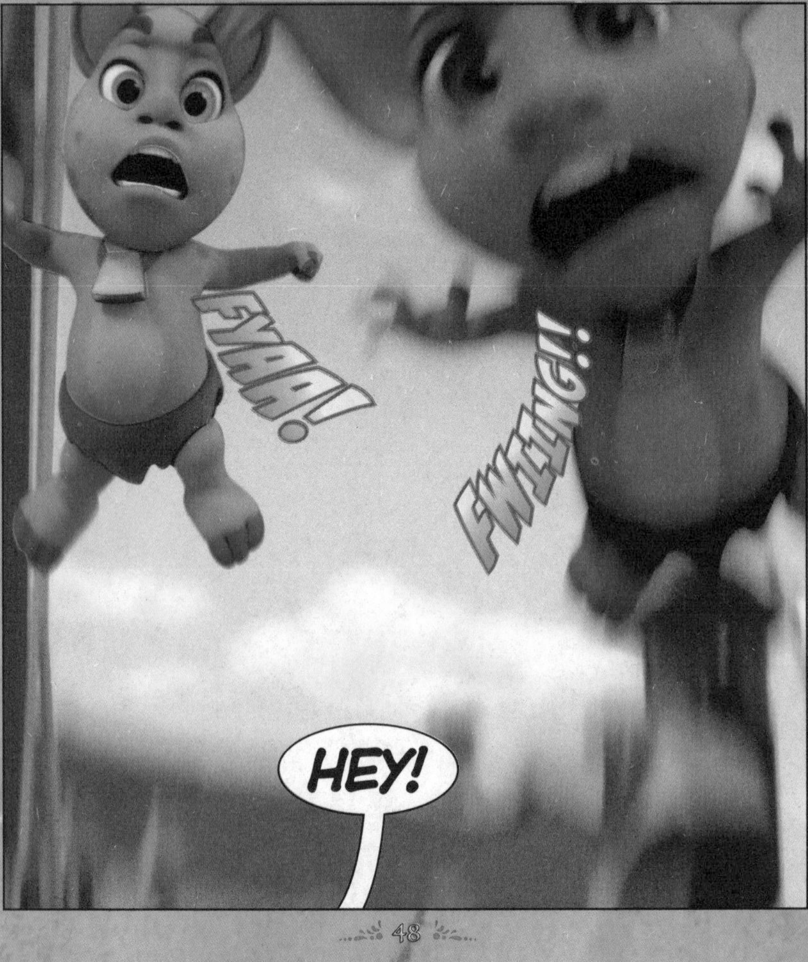
FYAA!
FWEENG!!
HEY!

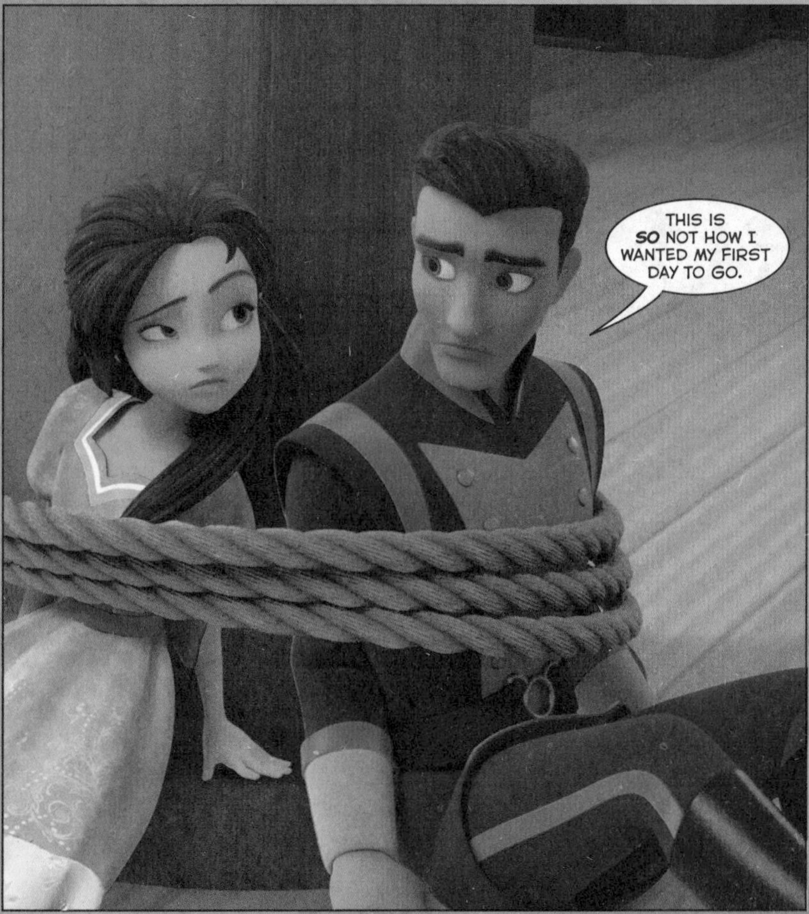
THIS IS
SO NOT HOW I
WANTED MY FIRST
DAY TO GO.

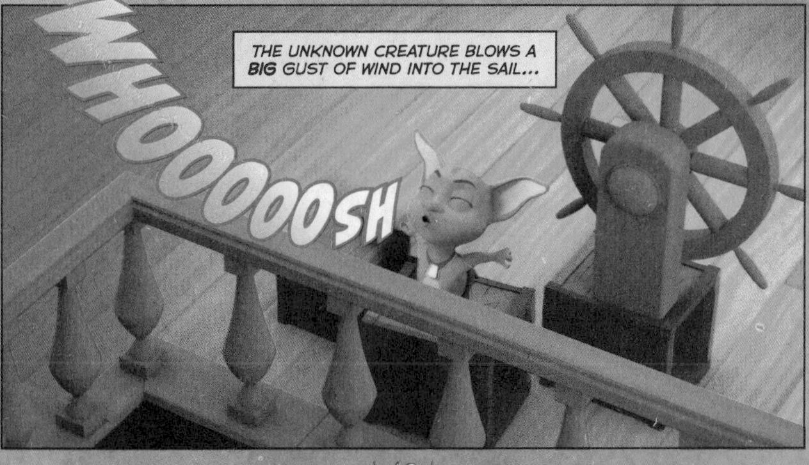
THE UNKNOWN CREATURE BLOWS A BIG GUST OF WIND INTO THE SAIL...
WHOOOOOOSH

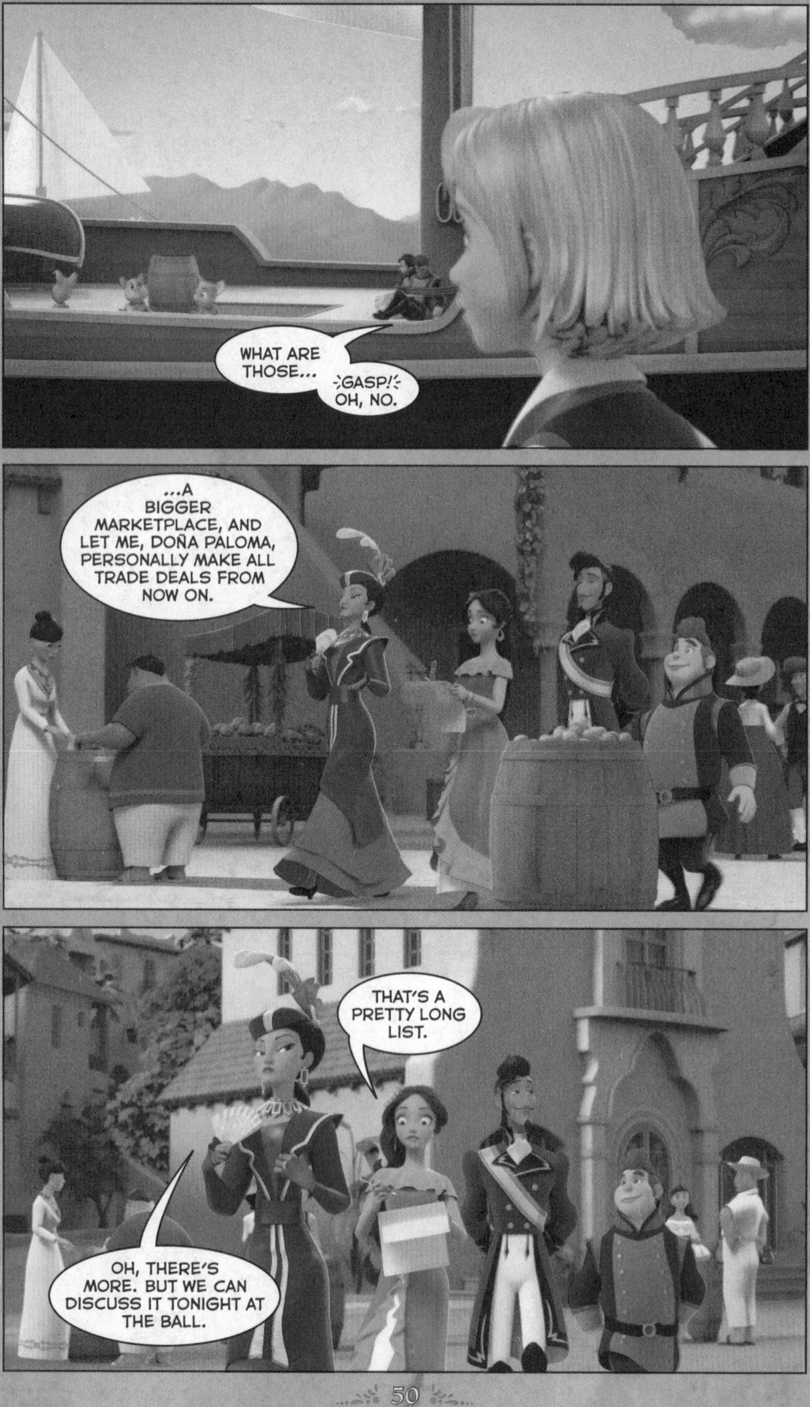
WHAT ARE THOSE...
GASP! OH, NO.
...A BIGGER MARKETPLACE, AND LET ME, DOÑA PALOMA, PERSONALLY MAKE ALL TRADE DEALS FROM NOW ON.
THAT'S A PRETTY LONG LIST.
OH, THERE'S MORE. BUT WE CAN DISCUSS IT TONIGHT AT THE BALL.

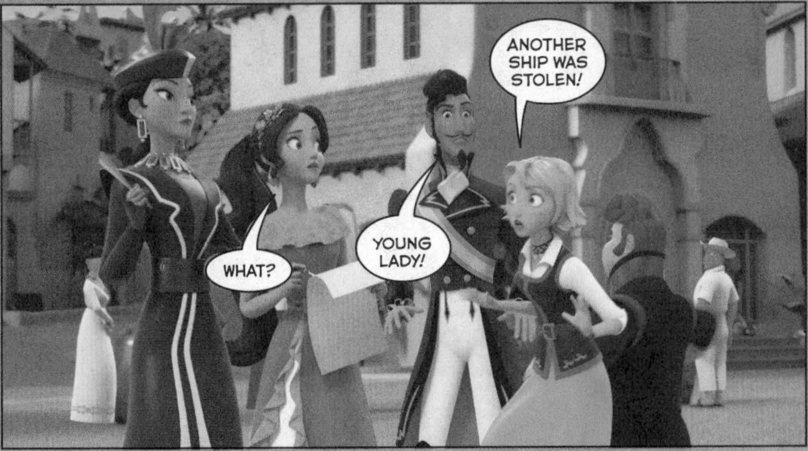
ANOTHER SHIP WAS STOLEN!
WHAT?
YOUNG LADY!

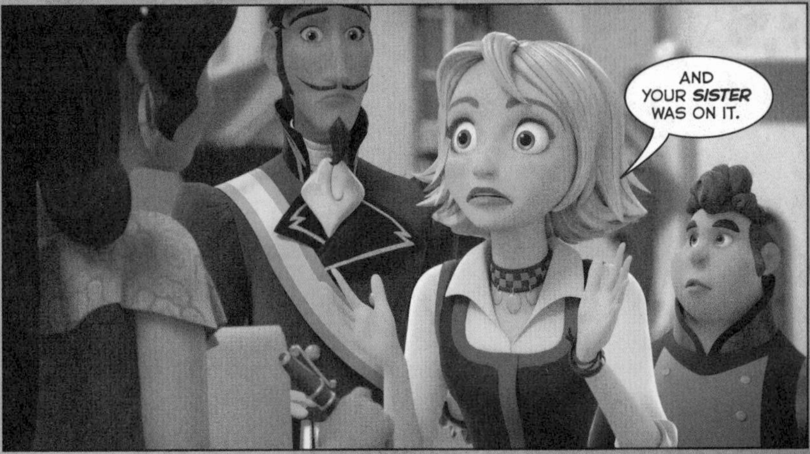
AND YOUR **SISTER** WAS ON IT.

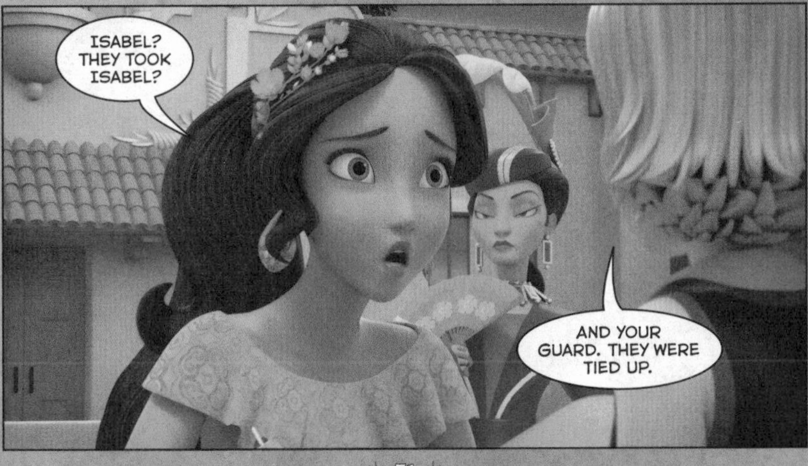
ISABEL? THEY TOOK ISABEL?
AND YOUR GUARD. THEY WERE TIED UP.

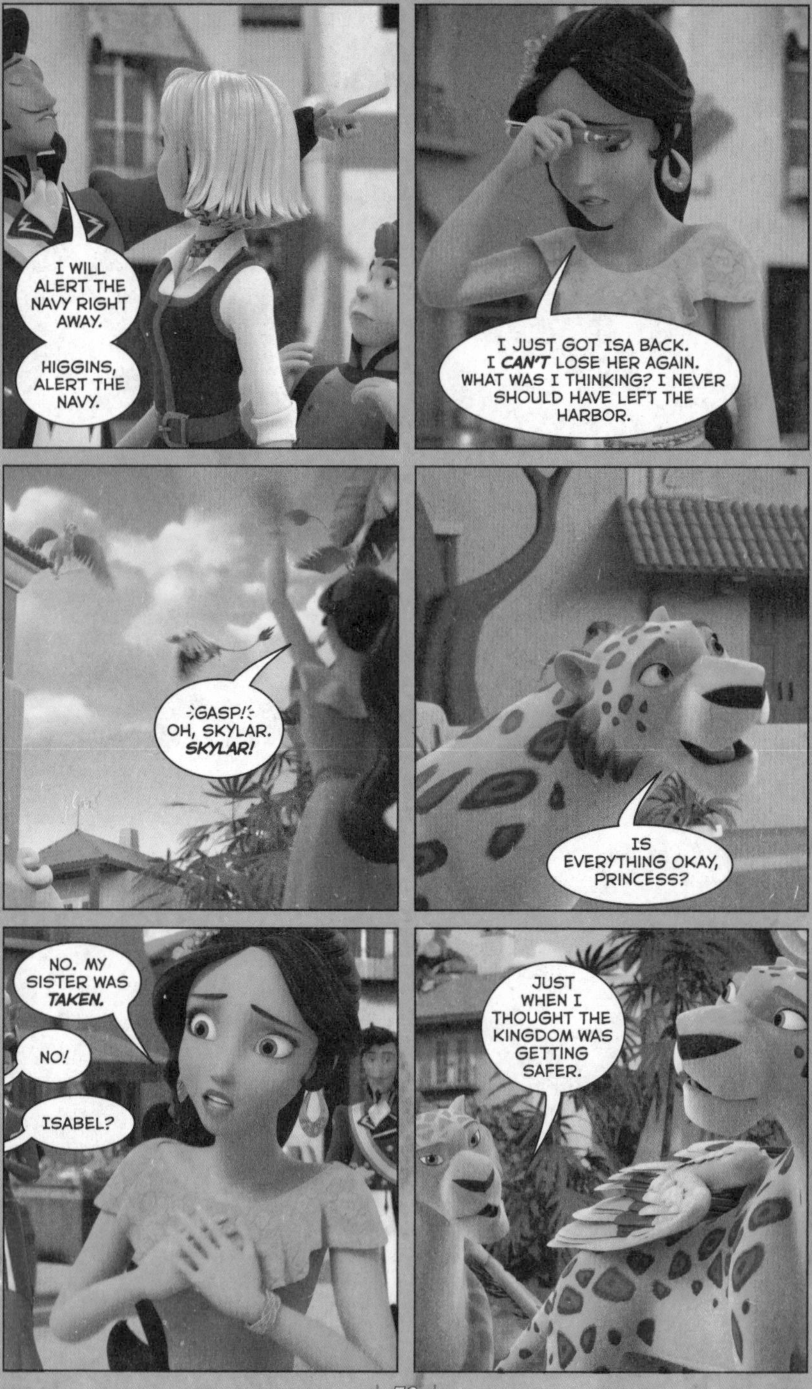
I WILL ALERT THE NAVY RIGHT AWAY.
HIGGINS, ALERT THE NAVY.
I JUST GOT ISA BACK. I *CAN'T* LOSE HER AGAIN. WHAT WAS I THINKING? I NEVER SHOULD HAVE LEFT THE HARBOR.
GASP! OH, SKYLAR. ***SKYLAR!***
IS EVERYTHING OKAY, PRINCESS?
NO. MY SISTER WAS ***TAKEN.***
NO!
ISABEL?
JUST WHEN I THOUGHT THE KINGDOM WAS GETTING SAFER.

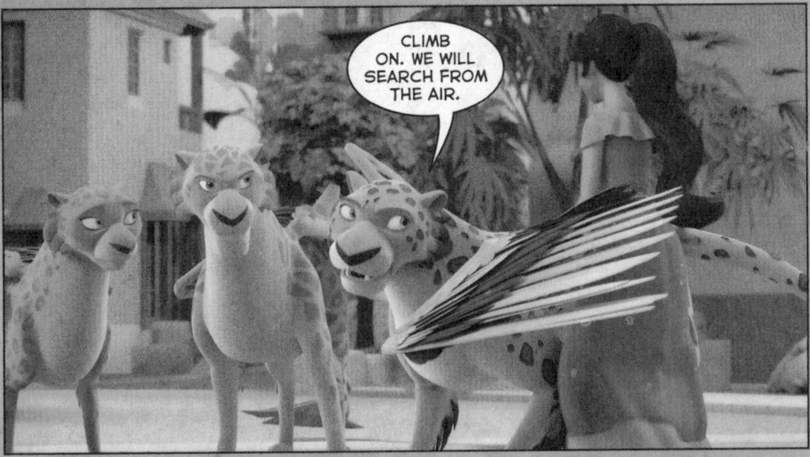
CLIMB ON. WE WILL SEARCH FROM THE AIR.

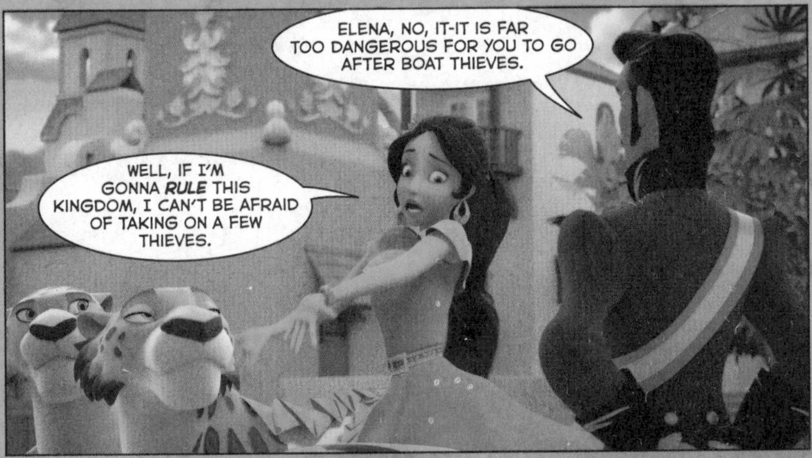
ELENA, NO, IT-IT IS FAR TOO DANGEROUS FOR YOU TO GO AFTER BOAT THIEVES.
WELL, IF I'M GONNA ***RULE*** THIS KINGDOM, I CAN'T BE AFRAID OF TAKING ON A FEW THIEVES.

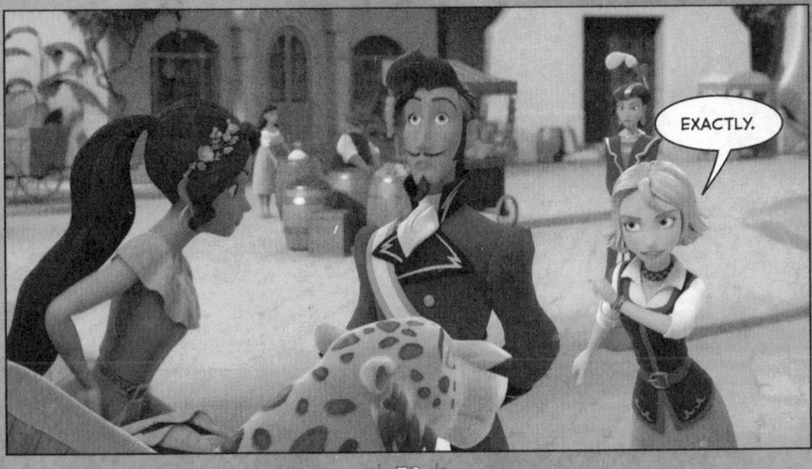
EXACTLY.

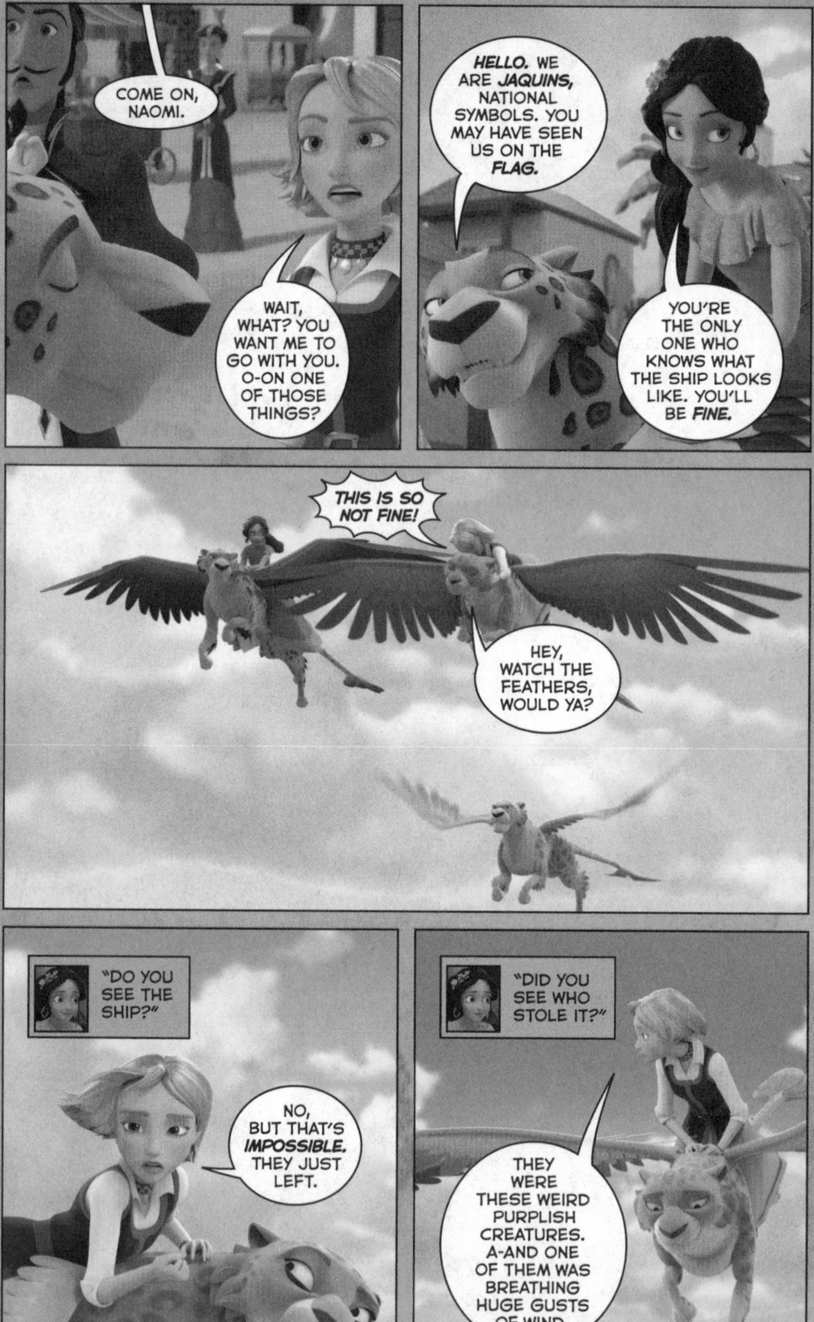
COME ON, NAOMI.
WAIT, WHAT? YOU WANT ME TO GO WITH YOU. O-ON ONE OF THOSE THINGS?
HELLO. WE ARE JAQUINS, NATIONAL SYMBOLS. YOU MAY HAVE SEEN US ON THE FLAG.
YOU'RE THE ONLY ONE WHO KNOWS WHAT THE SHIP LOOKS LIKE. YOU'LL BE FINE.
THIS IS SO NOT FINE!
HEY, WATCH THE FEATHERS, WOULD YA?
"DO YOU SEE THE SHIP?"
NO, BUT THAT'S IMPOSSIBLE. THEY JUST LEFT.
"DID YOU SEE WHO STOLE IT?"
THEY WERE THESE WEIRD PURPLISH CREATURES. A-AND ONE OF THEM WAS BREATHING HUGE GUSTS OF WIND.

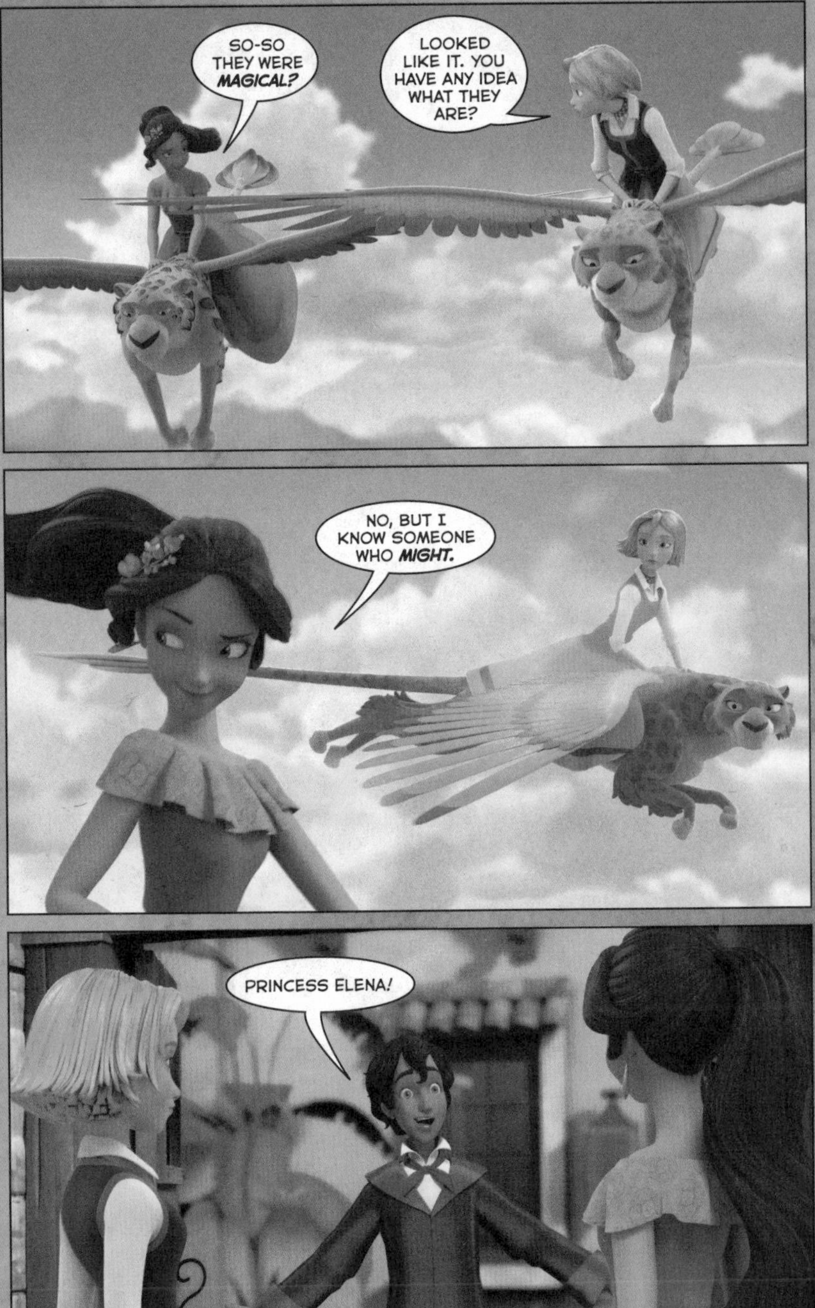
SO-SO THEY WERE *MAGICAL?*
LOOKED LIKE IT. YOU HAVE ANY IDEA WHAT THEY ARE?
NO, BUT I KNOW SOMEONE WHO *MIGHT.*
PRINCESS ELENA!

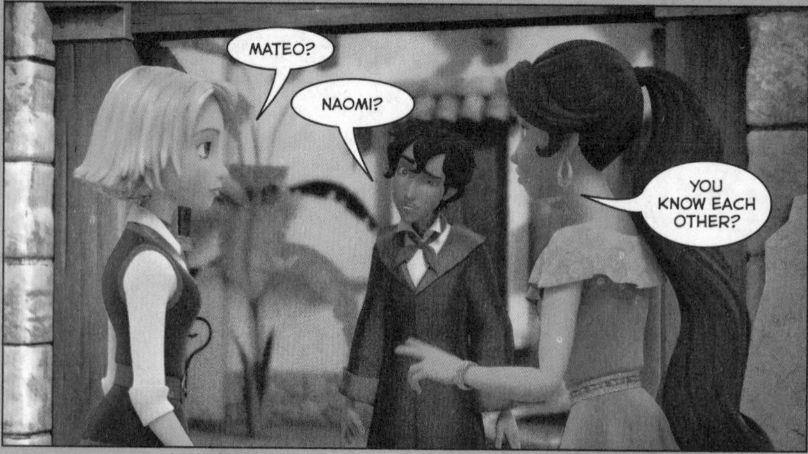
MATEO?
NAOMI?
YOU KNOW EACH OTHER?

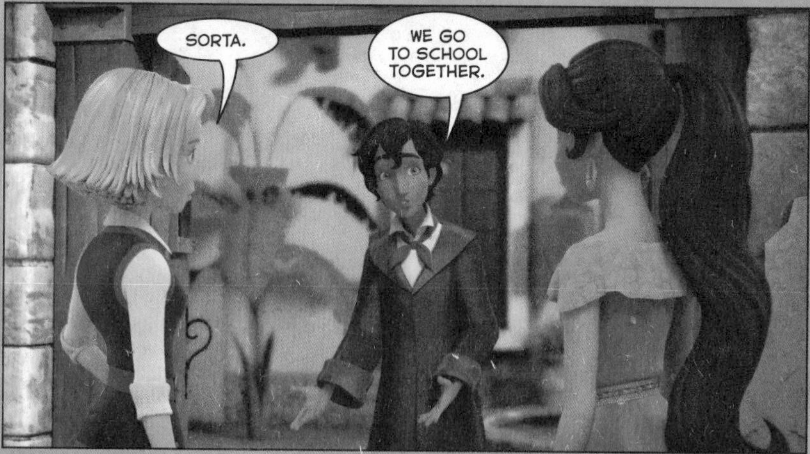
SORTA.
WE GO TO SCHOOL TOGETHER.

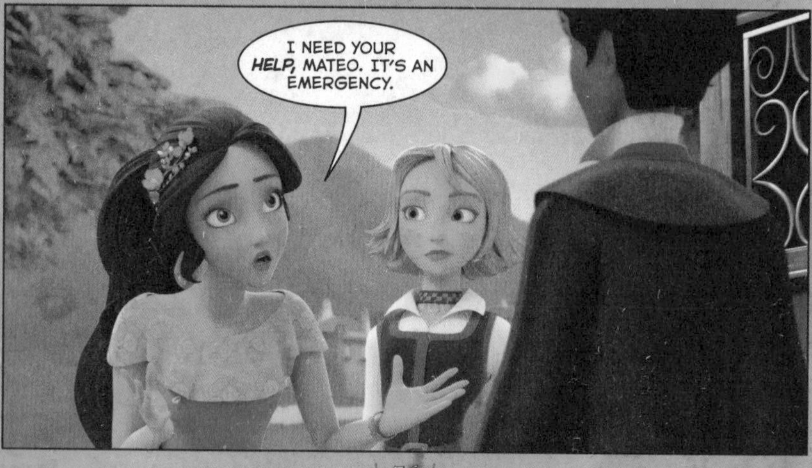
I NEED YOUR *HELP,* MATEO. IT'S AN EMERGENCY.

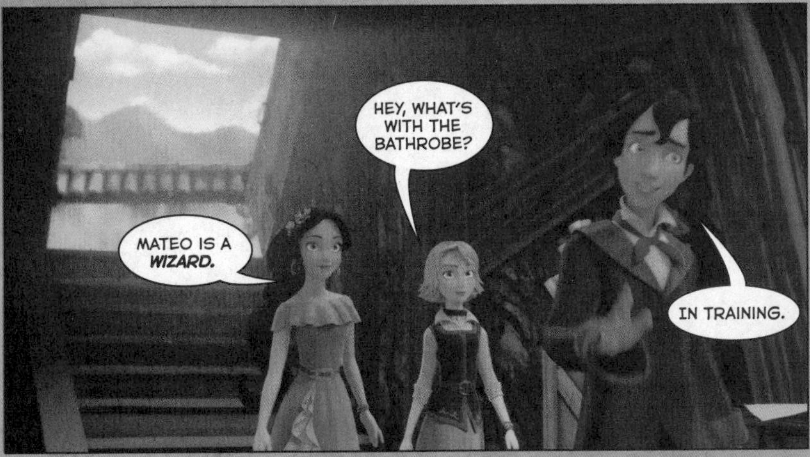
MATEO IS A *WIZARD.*
HEY, WHAT'S WITH THE BATHROBE?
IN TRAINING.

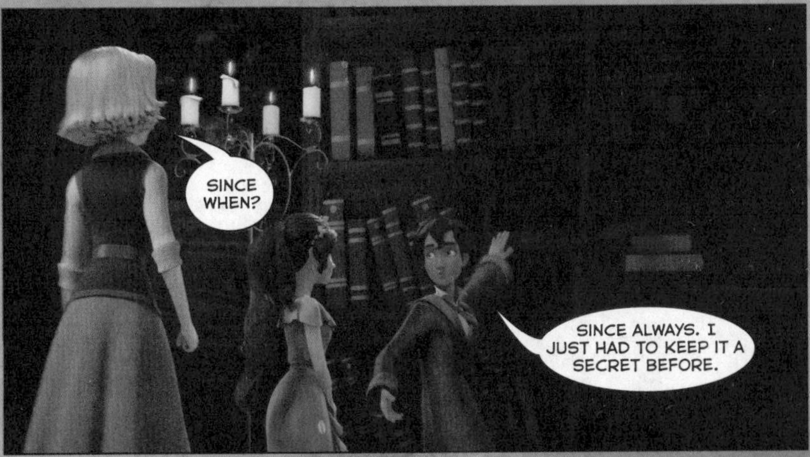
SINCE WHEN?
SINCE ALWAYS. I JUST HAD TO KEEP IT A SECRET BEFORE.

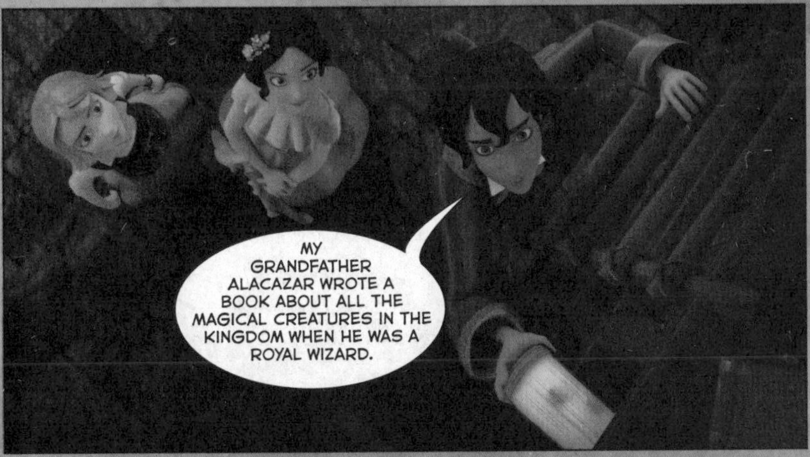
MY GRANDFATHER ALACAZAR WROTE A BOOK ABOUT ALL THE MAGICAL CREATURES IN THE KINGDOM WHEN HE WAS A ROYAL WIZARD.

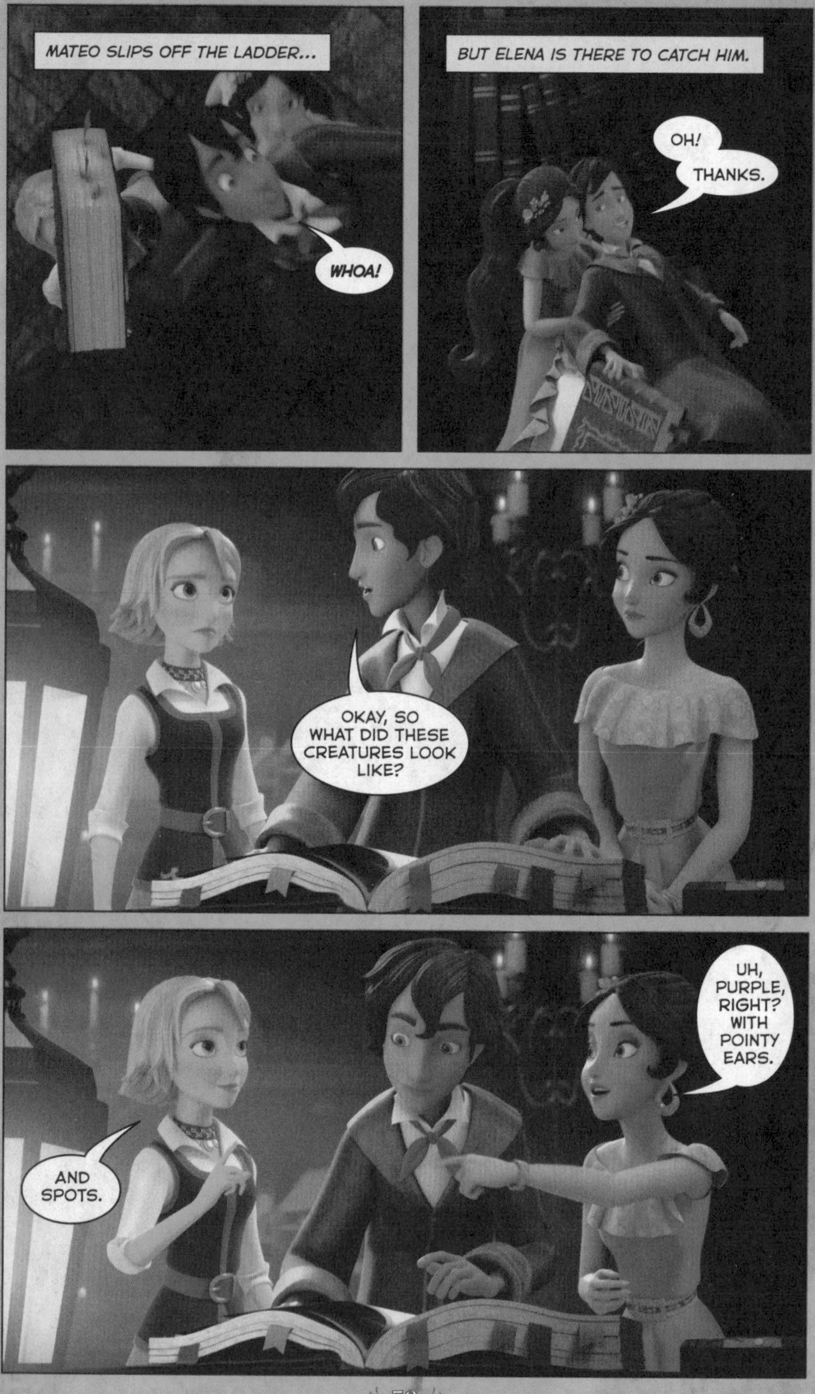
MATEO SLIPS OFF THE LADDER...
WHOA!
BUT ELENA IS THERE TO CATCH HIM.
OH!
THANKS.
OKAY, SO WHAT DID THESE CREATURES LOOK LIKE?
UH, PURPLE, RIGHT? WITH POINTY EARS.
AND SPOTS.

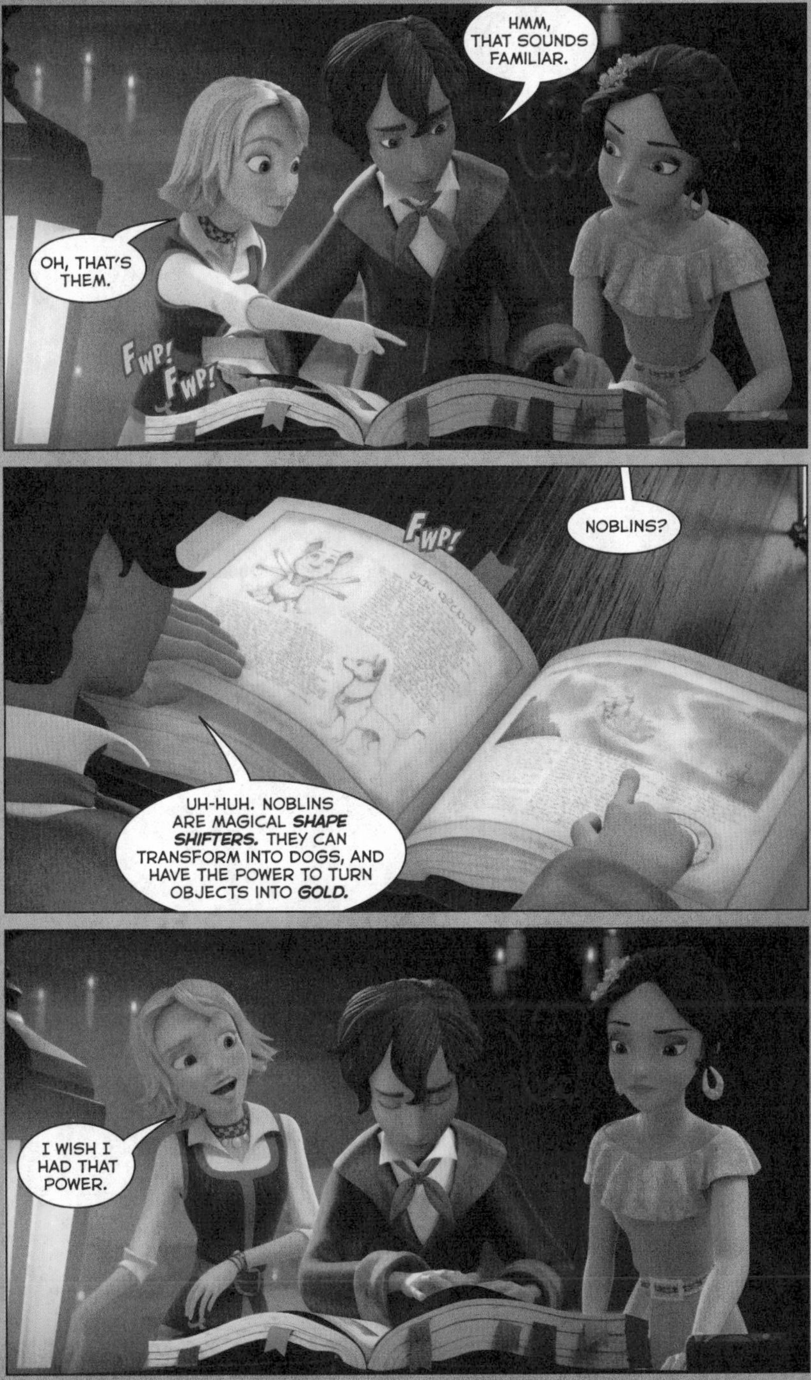
HMM, THAT SOUNDS FAMILIAR.
OH, THAT'S THEM.
FWP! FWP!
NOBLINS?
FWP!
UH-HUH. NOBLINS ARE MAGICAL **SHAPE SHIFTERS.** THEY CAN TRANSFORM INTO DOGS, AND HAVE THE POWER TO TURN OBJECTS INTO **GOLD.**
I WISH I HAD THAT POWER.

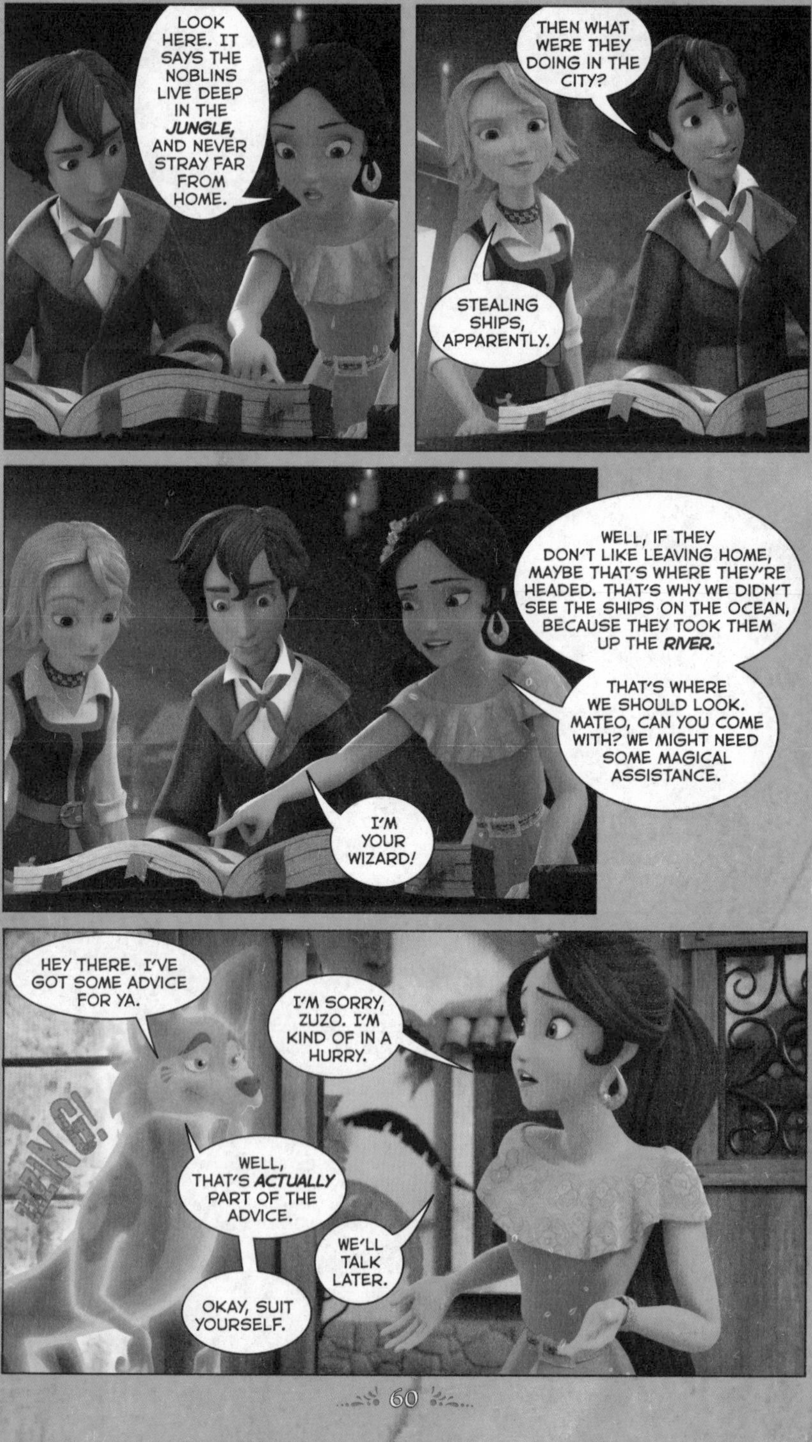
LOOK HERE. IT SAYS THE NOBLINS LIVE DEEP IN THE *JUNGLE,* AND NEVER STRAY FAR FROM HOME.
THEN WHAT WERE THEY DOING IN THE CITY?
STEALING SHIPS, APPARENTLY.
WELL, IF THEY DON'T LIKE LEAVING HOME, MAYBE THAT'S WHERE THEY'RE HEADED. THAT'S WHY WE DIDN'T SEE THE SHIPS ON THE OCEAN, BECAUSE THEY TOOK THEM UP THE *RIVER.*
THAT'S WHERE WE SHOULD LOOK. MATEO, CAN YOU COME WITH? WE MIGHT NEED SOME MAGICAL ASSISTANCE.
I'M YOUR WIZARD!
HEY THERE. I'VE GOT SOME ADVICE FOR YA.
I'M SORRY, ZUZO. I'M KIND OF IN A HURRY.
WELL, THAT'S *ACTUALLY* PART OF THE ADVICE.
WE'LL TALK LATER.
OKAY, SUIT YOURSELF.

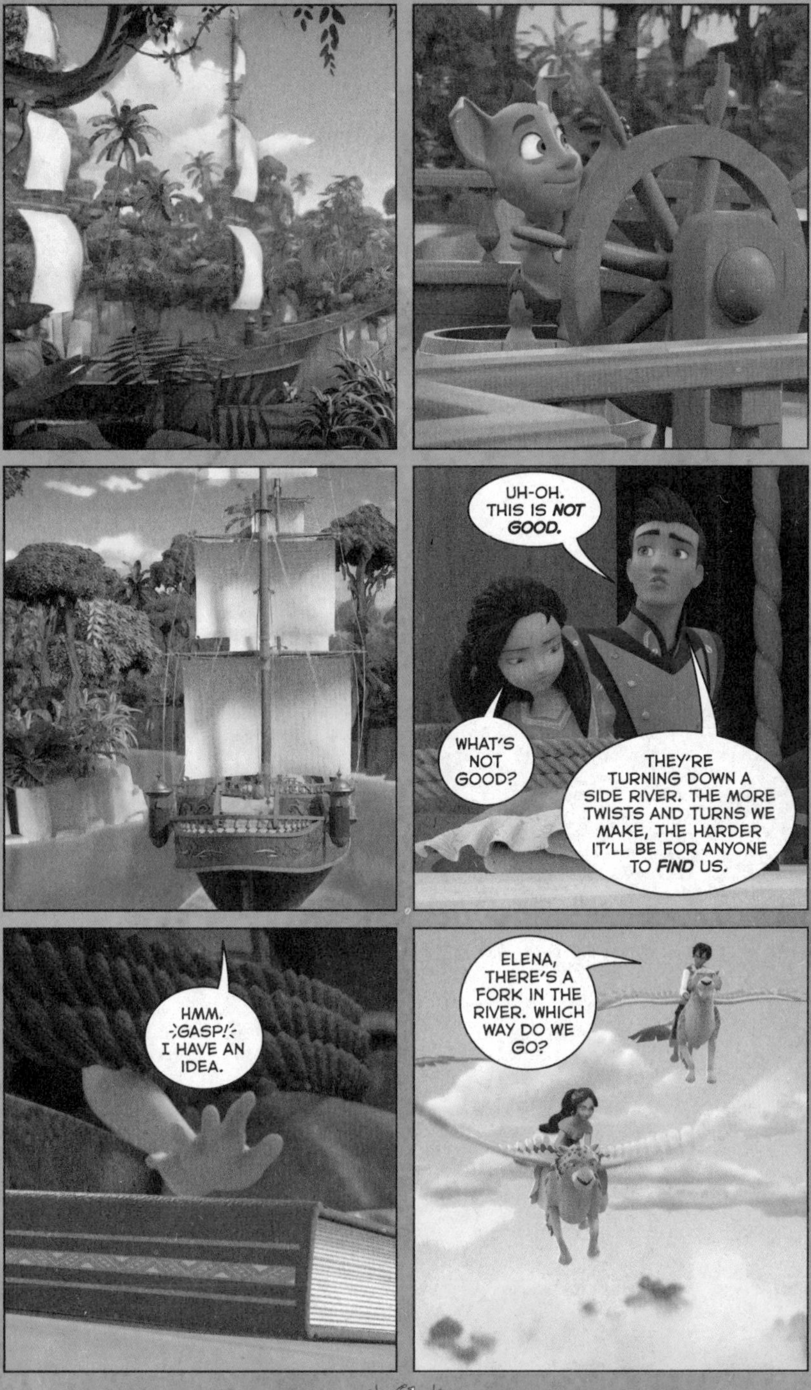
UH-OH. THIS IS NOT GOOD.
WHAT'S NOT GOOD?
THEY'RE TURNING DOWN A SIDE RIVER. THE MORE TWISTS AND TURNS WE MAKE, THE HARDER IT'LL BE FOR ANYONE TO FIND US.
HMM. -GASP!- I HAVE AN IDEA.
ELENA, THERE'S A FORK IN THE RIVER. WHICH WAY DO WE GO?

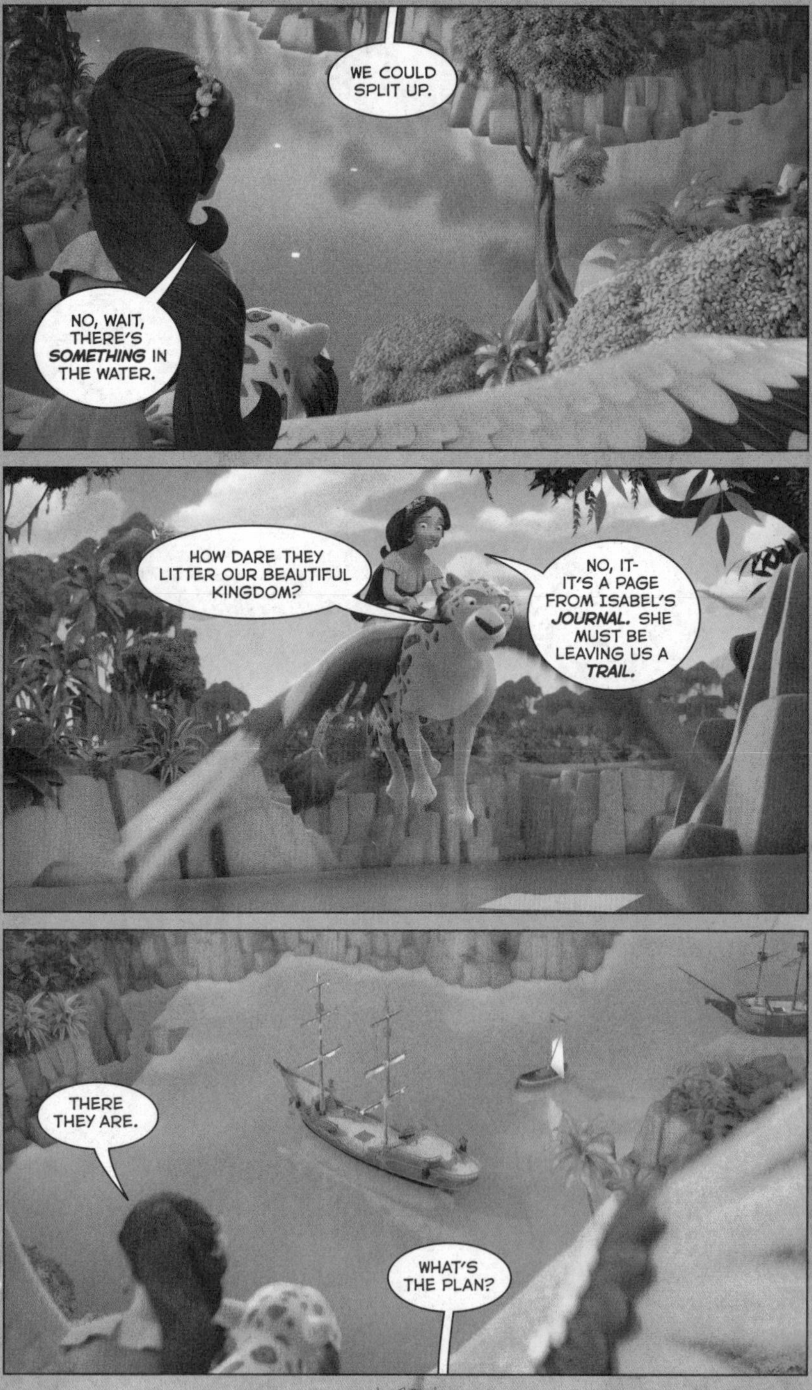
WE COULD SPLIT UP.
NO, WAIT, THERE'S *SOMETHING* IN THE WATER.
HOW DARE THEY LITTER OUR BEAUTIFUL KINGDOM?
NO, IT- IT'S A PAGE FROM ISABEL'S *JOURNAL.* SHE MUST BE LEAVING US A *TRAIL.*
THERE THEY ARE.
WHAT'S THE PLAN?

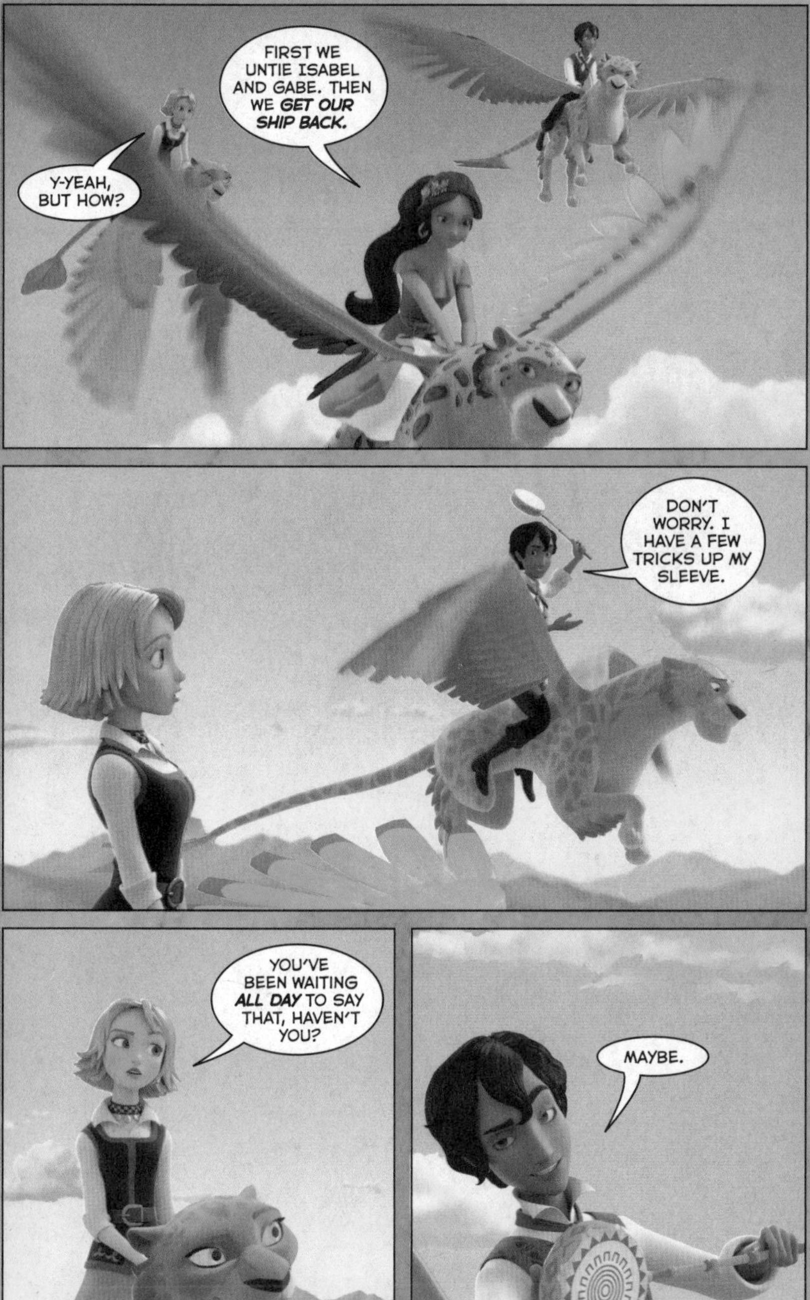
FIRST WE UNTIE ISABEL AND GABE. THEN WE **GET OUR SHIP BACK.**
Y-YEAH, BUT HOW?
DON'T WORRY. I HAVE A FEW TRICKS UP MY SLEEVE.
YOU'VE BEEN WAITING **ALL DAY** TO SAY THAT, HAVEN'T YOU?
MAYBE.

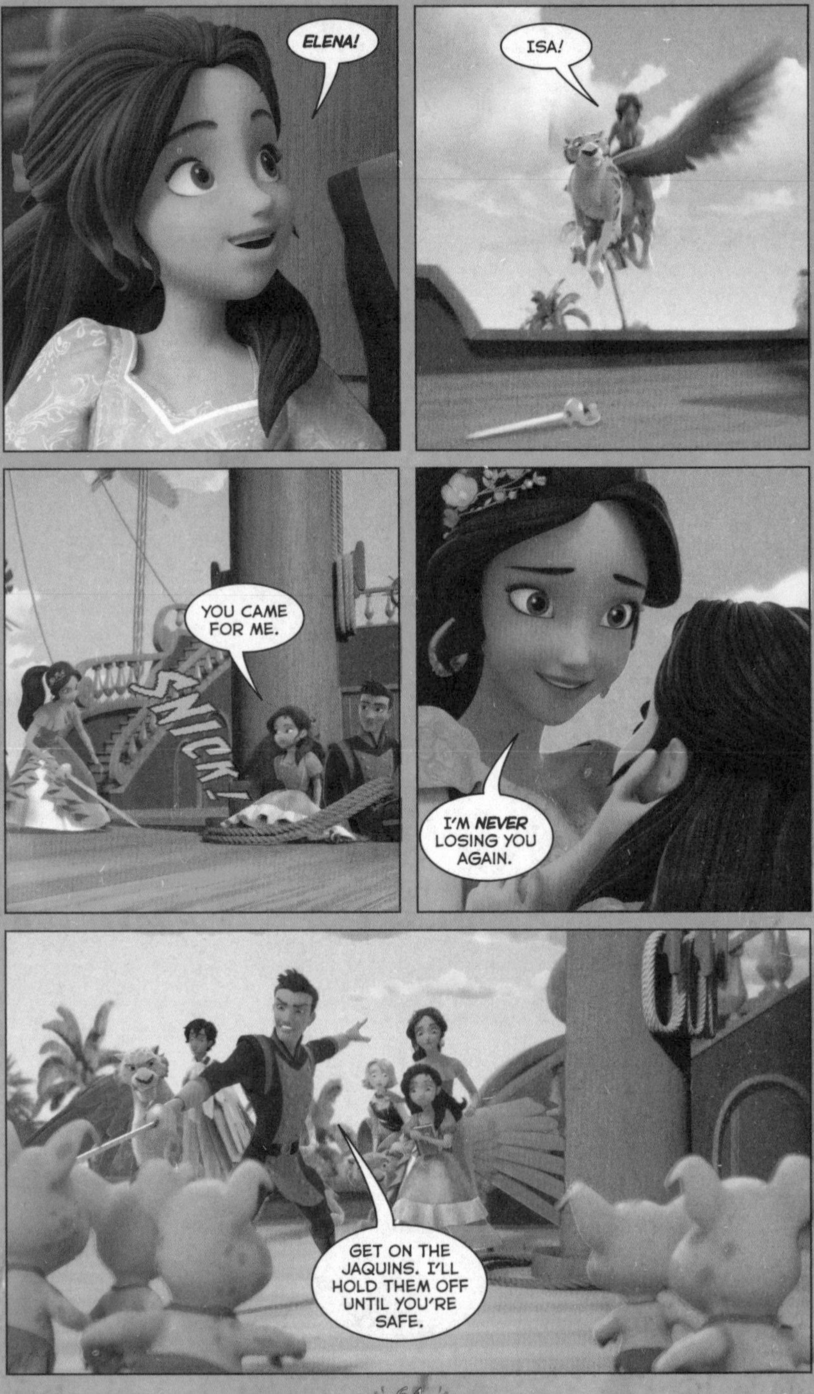
ELENA!
ISA!
YOU CAME FOR ME.
SNICK!
I'M ***NEVER*** LOSING YOU AGAIN.
GET ON THE JAQUINS. I'LL HOLD THEM OFF UNTIL YOU'RE SAFE.

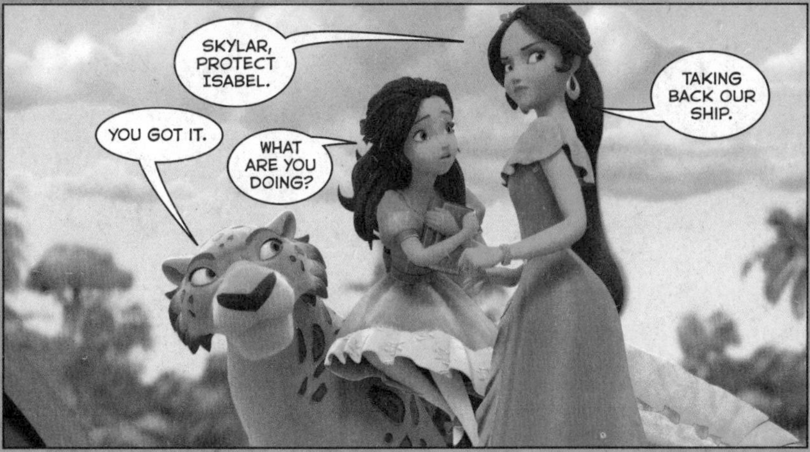
SKYLAR, PROTECT ISABEL.
YOU GOT IT.
WHAT ARE YOU DOING?
TAKING BACK OUR SHIP.

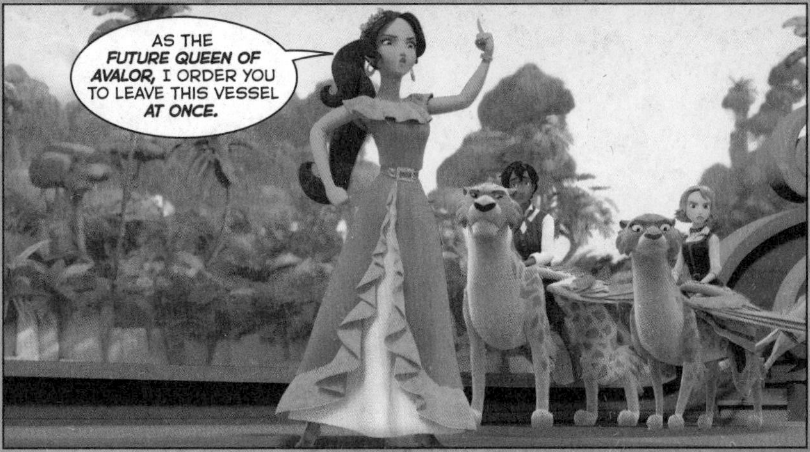
AS THE ***FUTURE QUEEN OF AVALOR,*** I ORDER YOU TO LEAVE THIS VESSEL ***AT ONCE.***

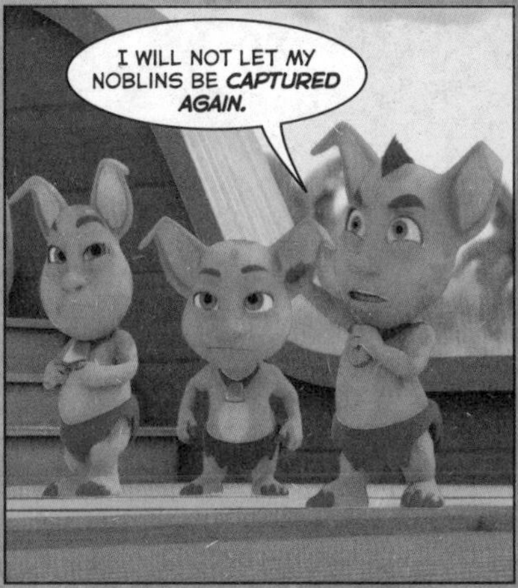
I WILL NOT LET MY NOBLINS BE ***CAPTURED AGAIN.***

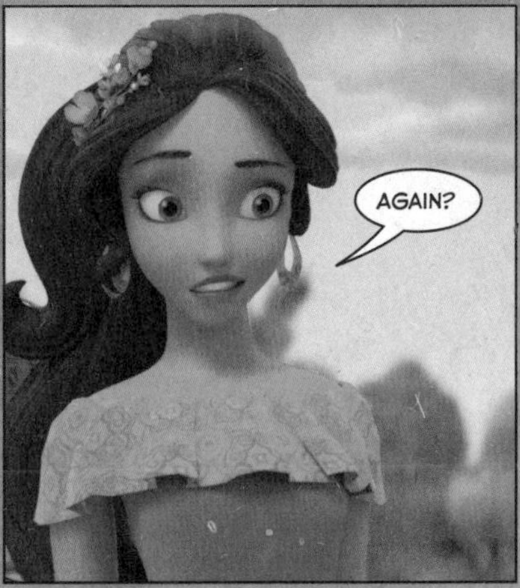
AGAIN?

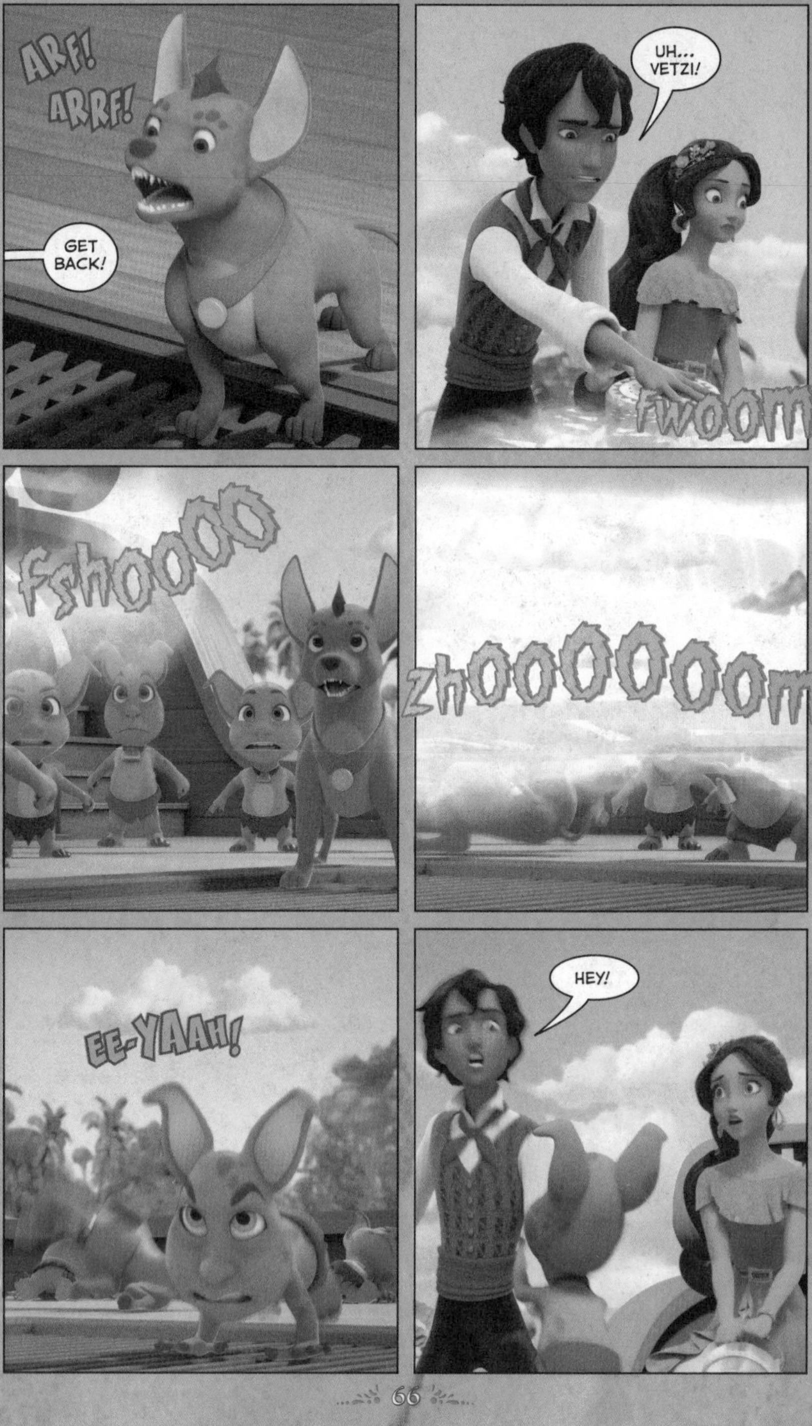
ARF! ARRF!
GET BACK!
UH... VETZI!
FWOOM
FSHOOOO
ZHOOOOOOM
EE-YAAH!
HEY!

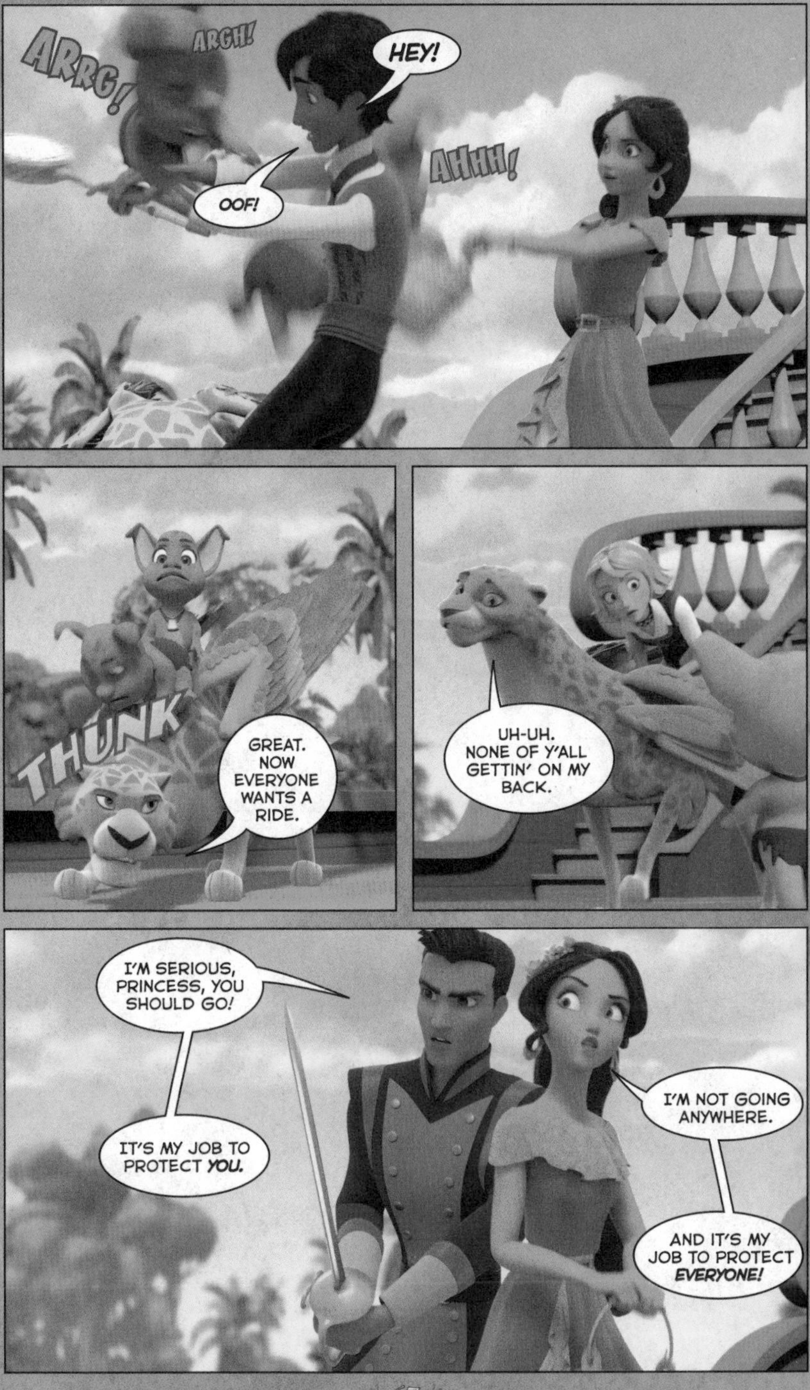
ARRG!
ARGH!
HEY!
OOF!
AHHH!
THUNK
GREAT. NOW EVERYONE WANTS A RIDE.
UH-UH. NONE OF Y'ALL GETTIN' ON MY BACK.
I'M SERIOUS, PRINCESS, YOU SHOULD GO!
IT'S MY JOB TO PROTECT *YOU.*
I'M NOT GOING ANYWHERE.
AND IT'S MY JOB TO PROTECT *EVERYONE!*

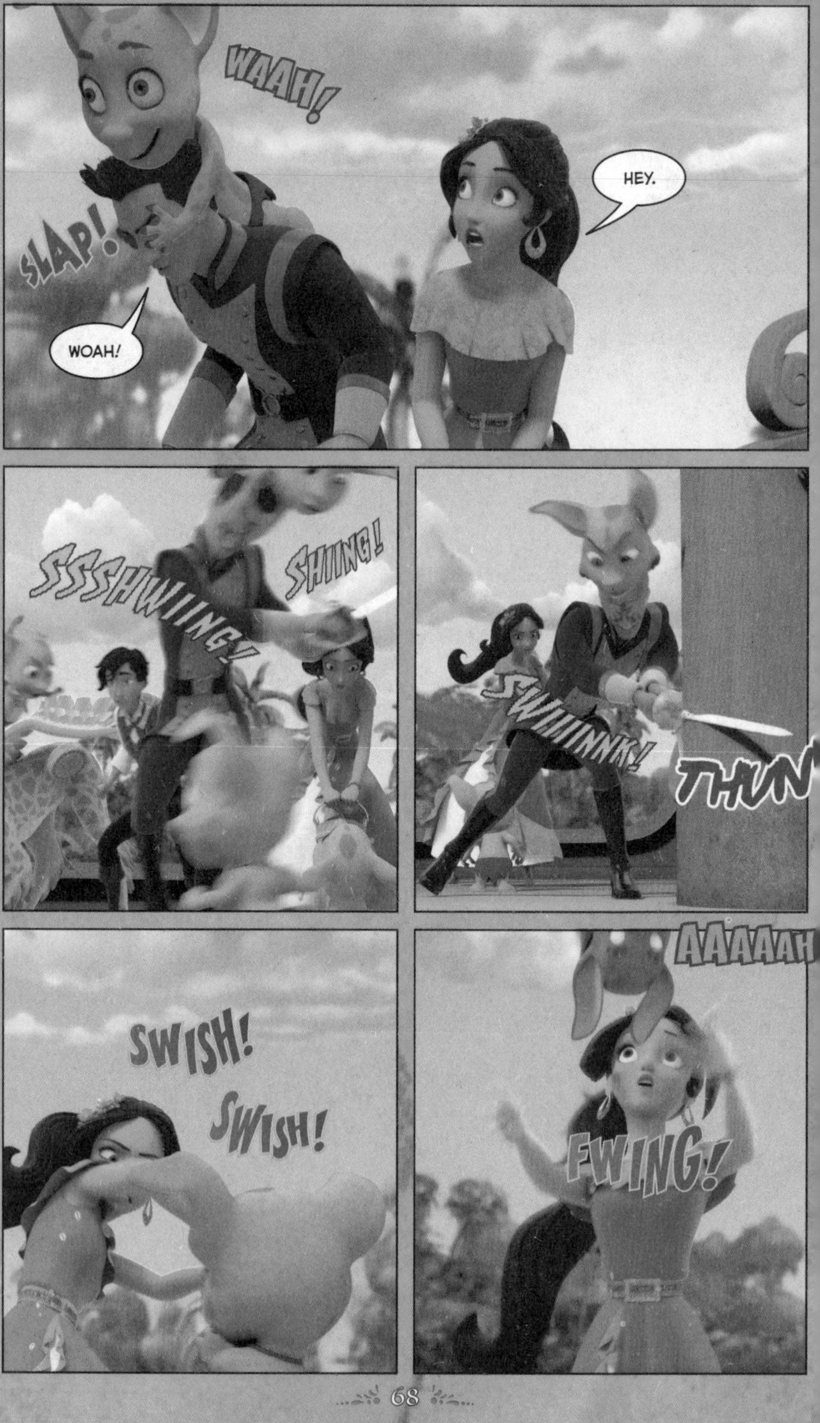
WAAH!
SLAP!
WOAH!
HEY.
SSSHWIIING!
SHIING!
SWIIIINNK!
THUN
SWISH!
SWISH!
AAAAAH
FWING!

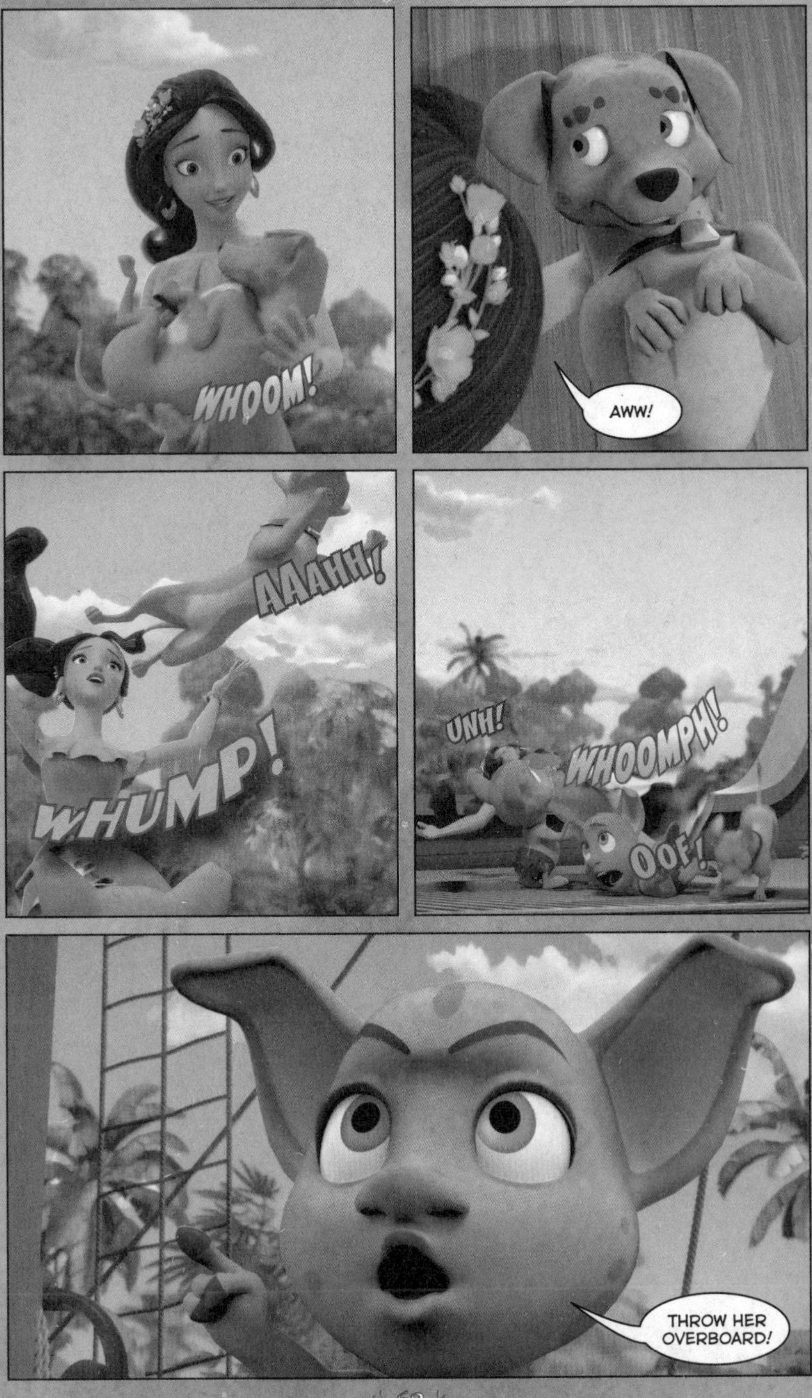
WHOOM!
AWW!
AAAHH!
WHUMP!
UNH!
WHOOMPH!
OOF!
THROW HER OVERBOARD!

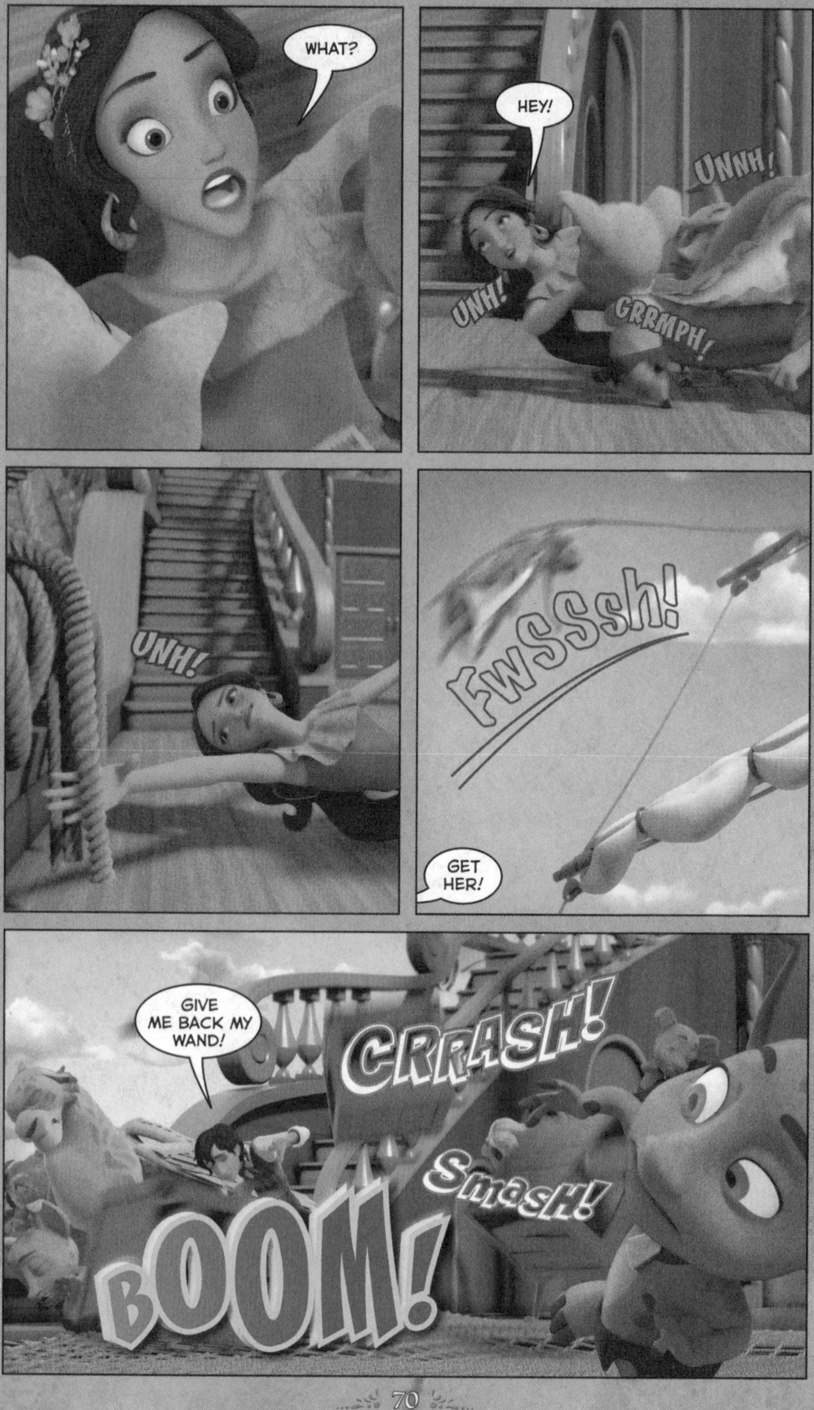
WHAT?
HEY!
UNNH!
UNH!
GRRMPH!
UNH!
FwSSsh!
GET HER!
GIVE ME BACK MY WAND!
CRRASH!
Smash!
BOOM!

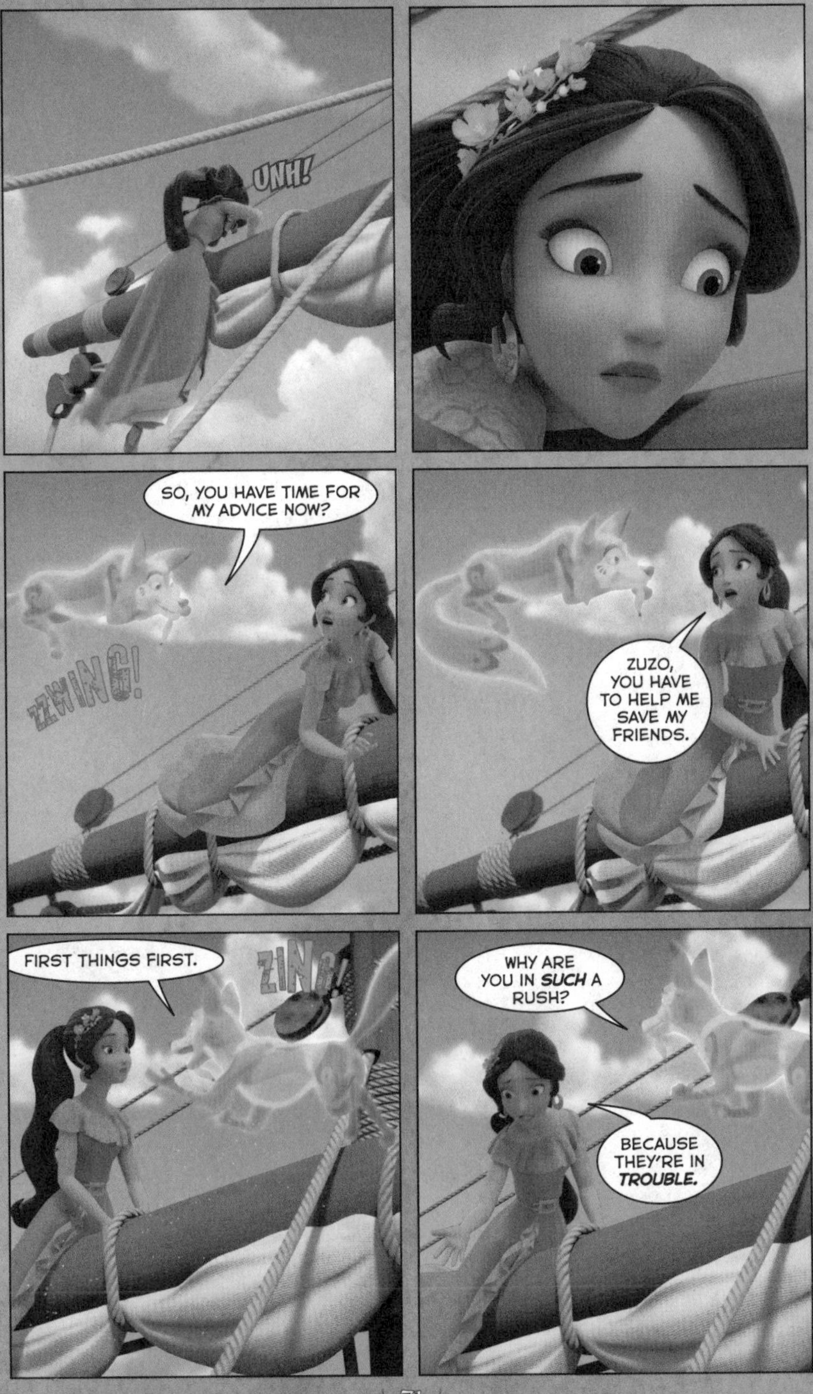
UNH!
SO, YOU HAVE TIME FOR MY ADVICE NOW?
ZWING!
ZUZO, YOU HAVE TO HELP ME SAVE MY FRIENDS.
FIRST THINGS FIRST.
WHY ARE YOU IN *SUCH* A RUSH?
BECAUSE THEY'RE IN ***TROUBLE.***

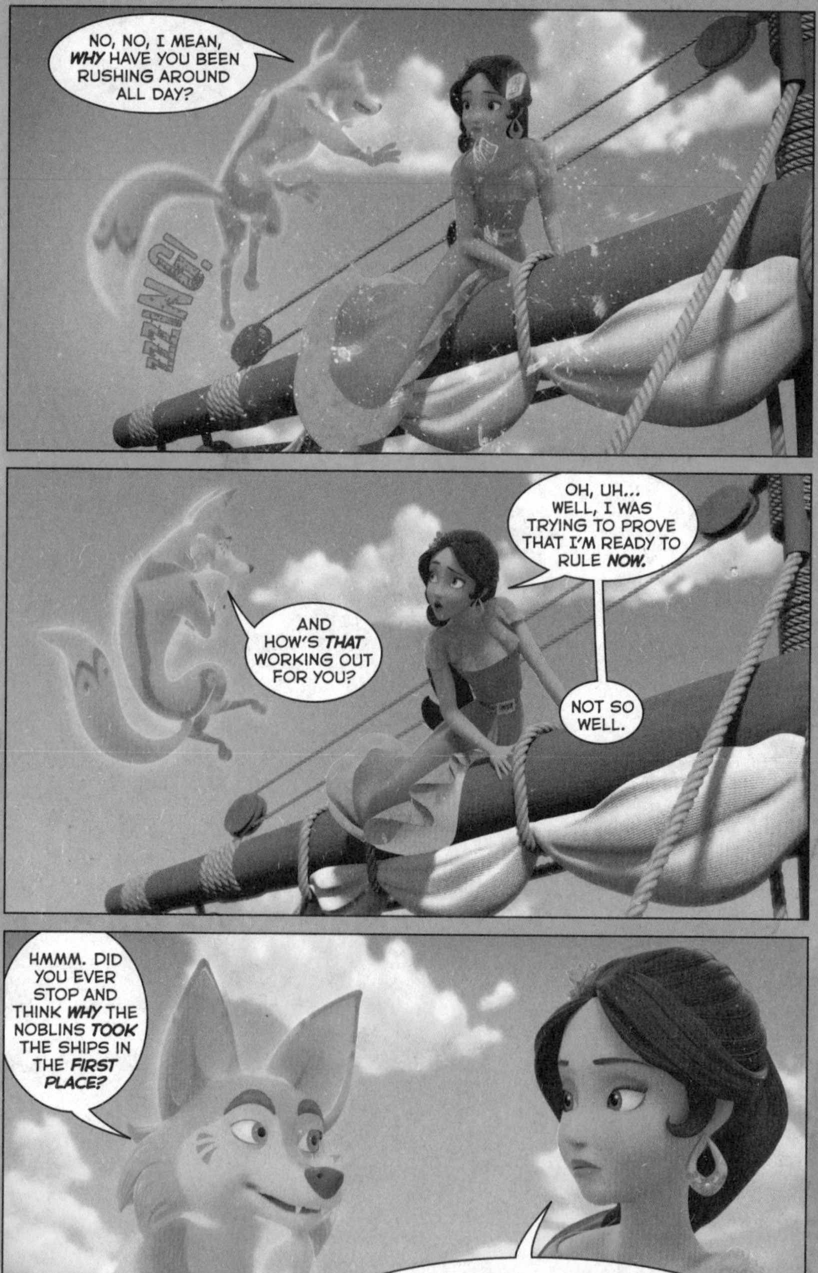
NO, NO, I MEAN, *WHY* HAVE YOU BEEN RUSHING AROUND ALL DAY?
ZZING!
OH, UH... WELL, I WAS TRYING TO PROVE THAT I'M READY TO RULE ***NOW.***
AND HOW'S ***THAT*** WORKING OUT FOR YOU?
NOT SO WELL.
HMMM. DID YOU EVER STOP AND THINK ***WHY*** THE NOBLINS ***TOOK*** THE SHIPS IN THE ***FIRST PLACE?***
NO, BUT YOU'RE RIGHT. I SHOULD'VE. UGH, I WAS SO BUSY TRYING TO ***PROVE*** I COULD BE A GREAT QUEEN, I FORGOT TO ***ACT*** LIKE ONE. MY GRANDFATHER WAS RIGHT. I'M NOT READY TO RULE.

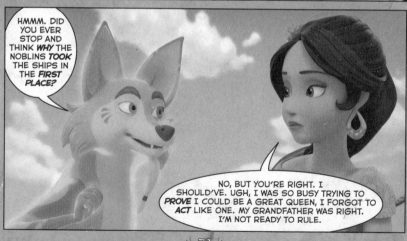

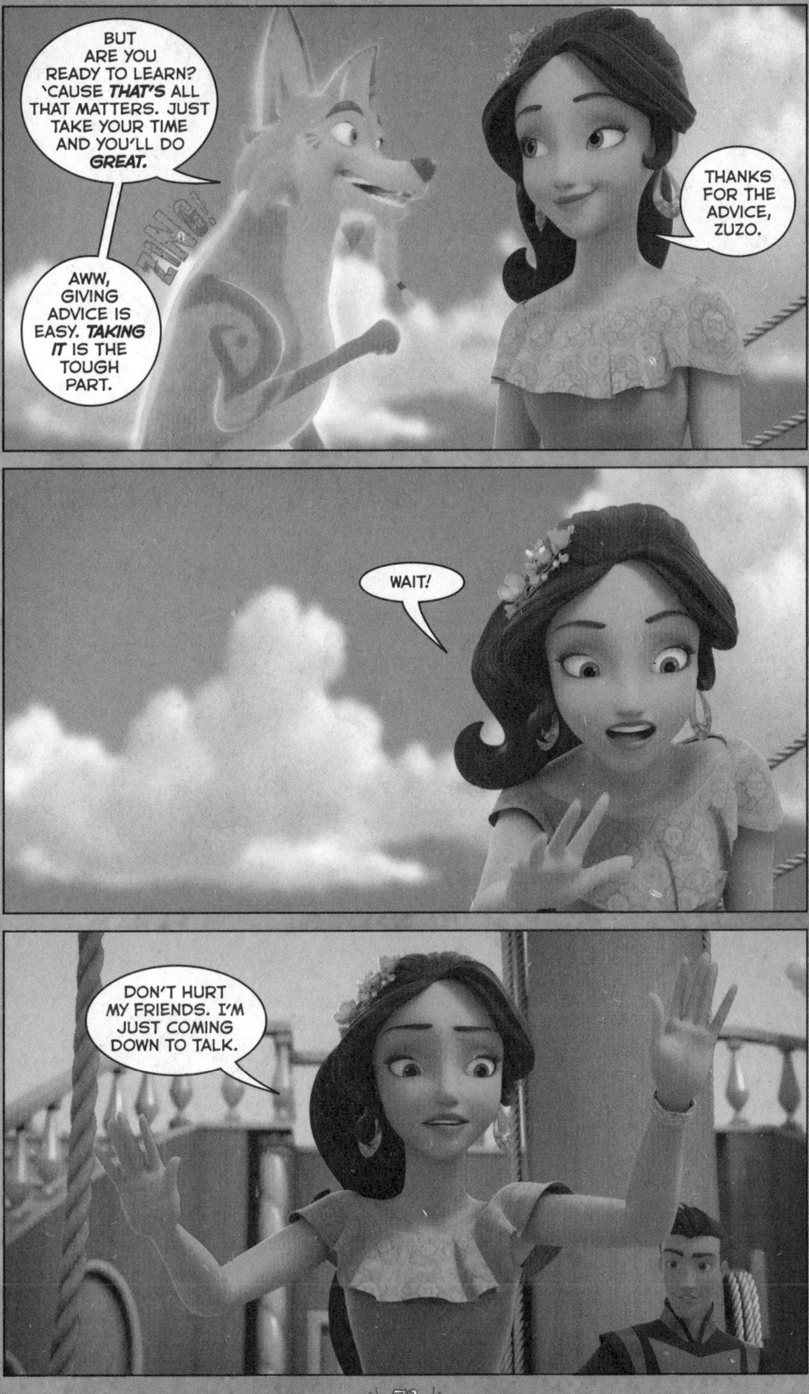
BUT ARE YOU READY TO LEARN? 'CAUSE **THAT'S** ALL THAT MATTERS. JUST TAKE YOUR TIME AND YOU'LL DO **GREAT.**
AWW, GIVING ADVICE IS EASY. **TAKING IT** IS THE TOUGH PART.
THANKS FOR THE ADVICE, ZUZO.
WAIT!
DON'T HURT MY FRIENDS. I'M JUST COMING DOWN TO TALK.

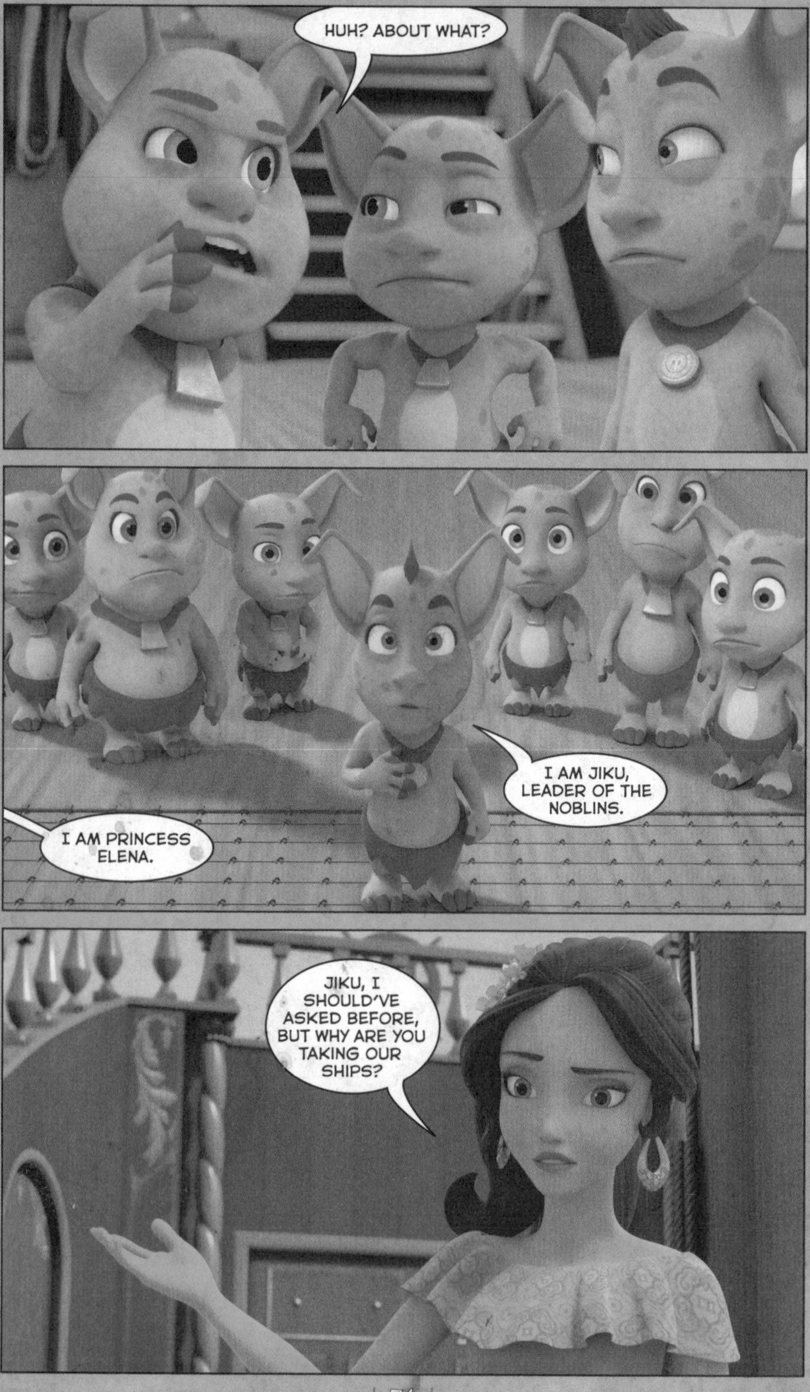
HUH? ABOUT WHAT?
I AM JIKU, LEADER OF THE NOBLINS.
I AM PRINCESS ELENA.
JIKU, I SHOULD'VE ASKED BEFORE, BUT WHY ARE YOU TAKING OUR SHIPS?

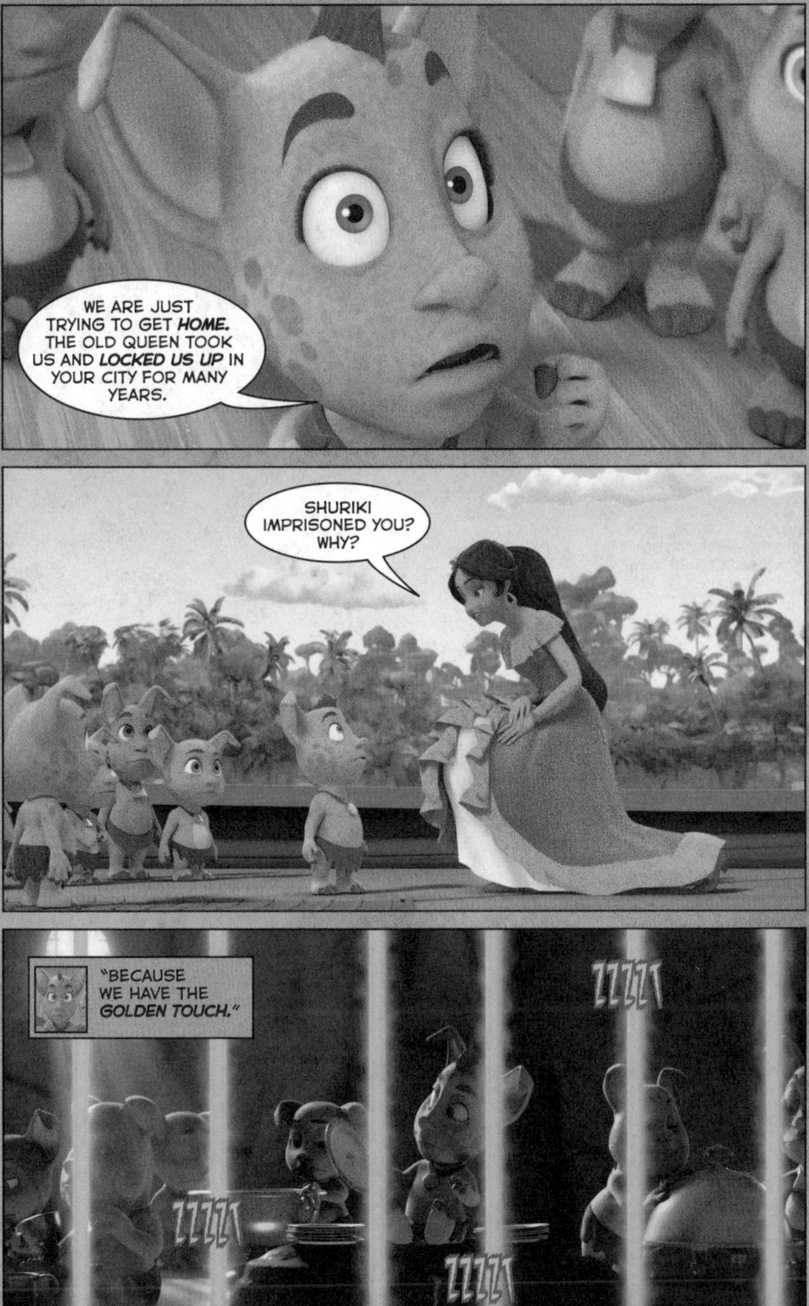
WE ARE JUST TRYING TO GET HOME. THE OLD QUEEN TOOK US AND LOCKED US UP IN YOUR CITY FOR MANY YEARS.
SHURIKI IMPRISONED YOU? WHY?
"BECAUSE WE HAVE THE GOLDEN TOUCH."
ZZZZZ
ZZZZZ
ZZZZZ

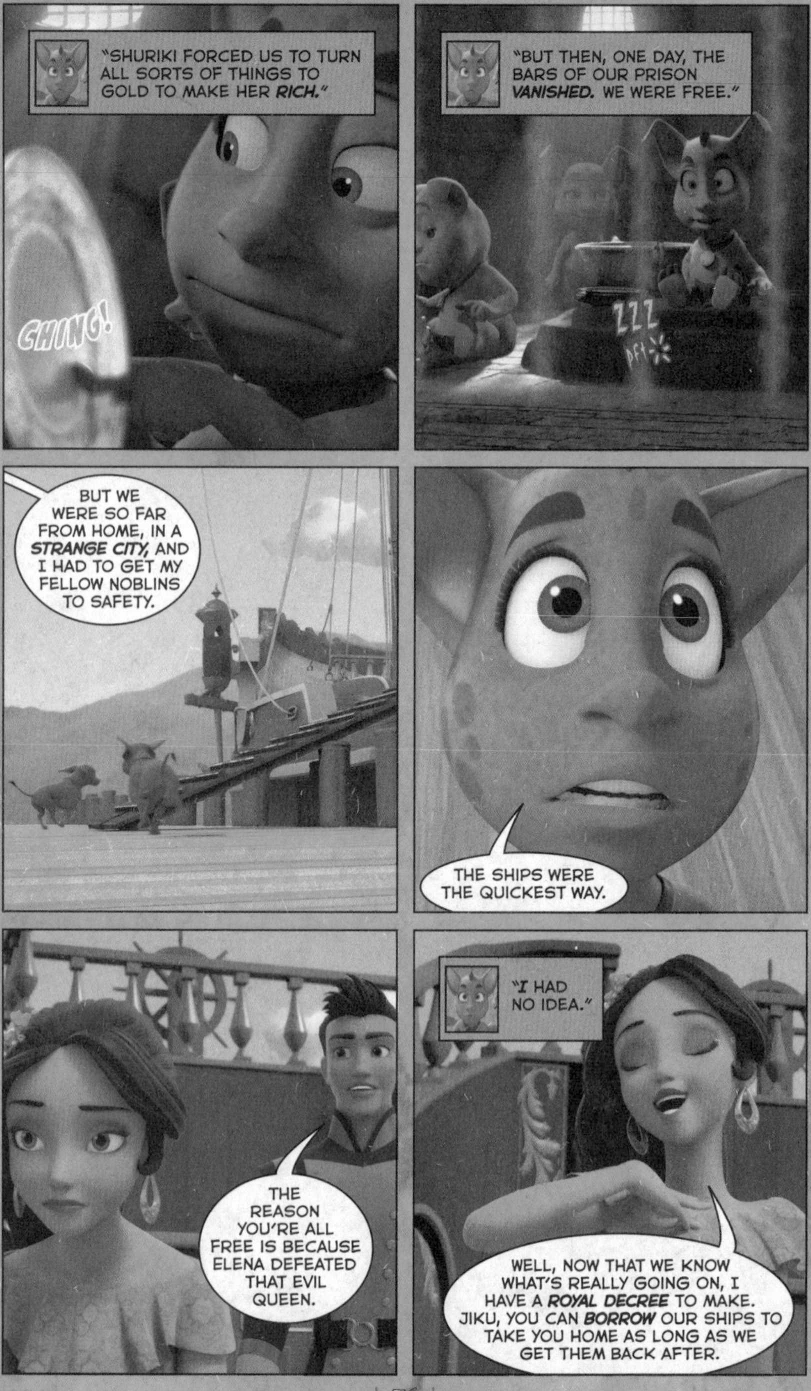
"SHURIKI FORCED US TO TURN ALL SORTS OF THINGS TO GOLD TO MAKE HER RICH."
CHING!
"BUT THEN, ONE DAY, THE BARS OF OUR PRISON VANISHED. WE WERE FREE."
ZZZ
pft
BUT WE WERE SO FAR FROM HOME, IN A STRANGE CITY, AND I HAD TO GET MY FELLOW NOBLINS TO SAFETY.
THE SHIPS WERE THE QUICKEST WAY.
THE REASON YOU'RE ALL FREE IS BECAUSE ELENA DEFEATED THAT EVIL QUEEN.
"I HAD NO IDEA."
WELL, NOW THAT WE KNOW WHAT'S REALLY GOING ON, I HAVE A ROYAL DECREE TO MAKE. JIKU, YOU CAN BORROW OUR SHIPS TO TAKE YOU HOME AS LONG AS WE GET THEM BACK AFTER.

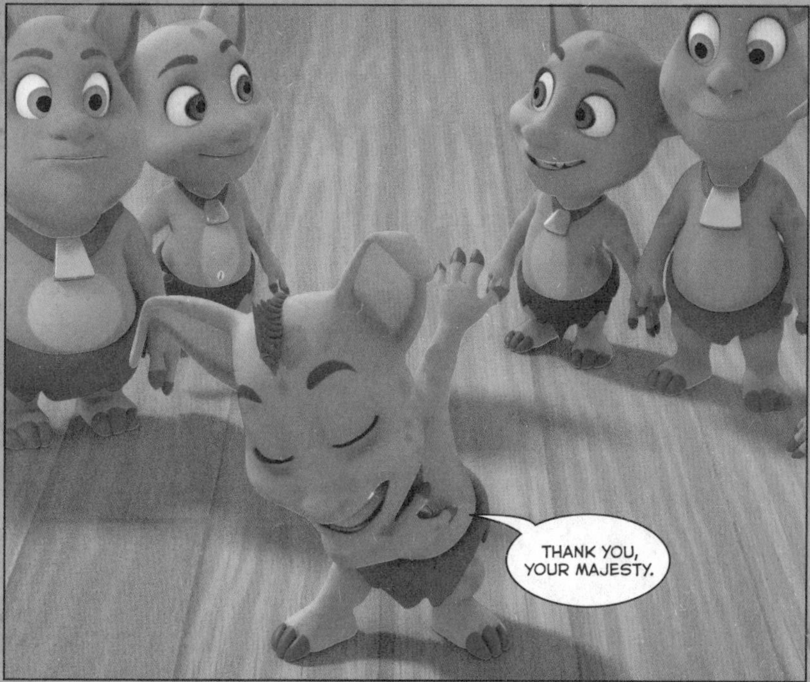
THANK YOU, YOUR MAJESTY.

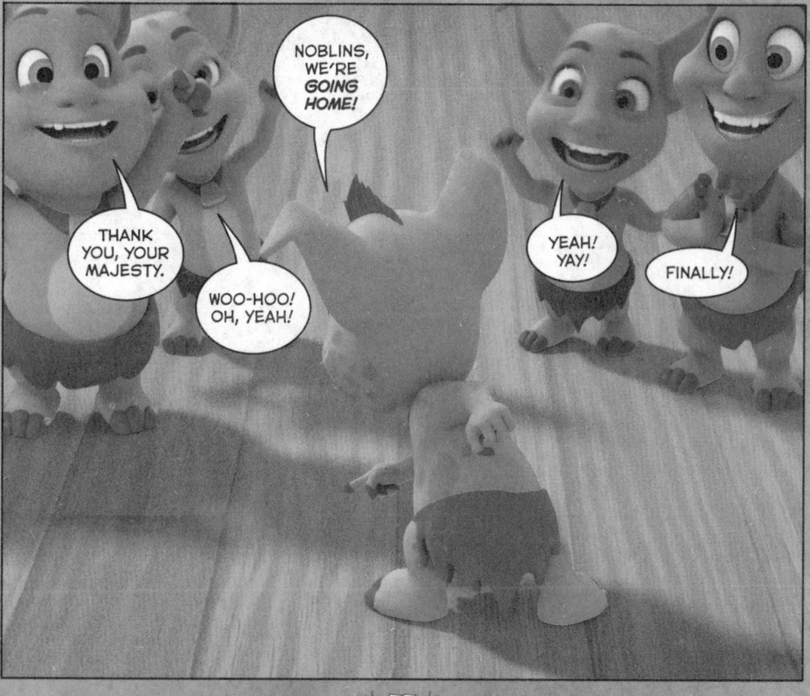
NOBLINS, WE'RE *GOING HOME!*
THANK YOU, YOUR MAJESTY.
WOO-HOO! OH, YEAH!
YEAH! YAY!
FINALLY!

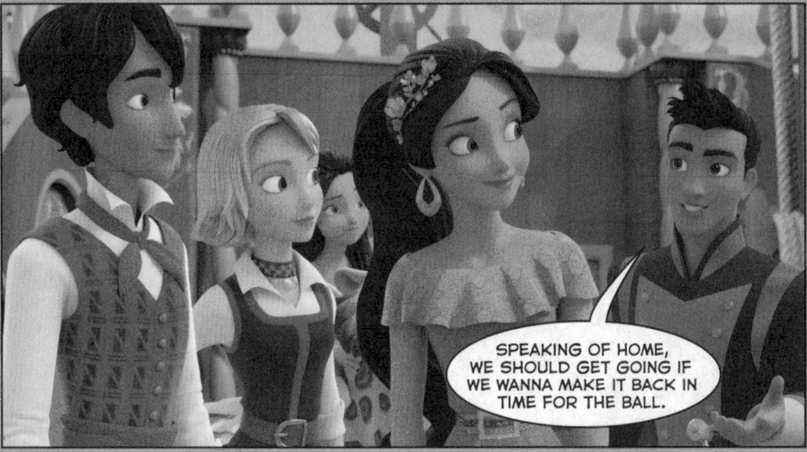
SPEAKING OF HOME, WE SHOULD GET GOING IF WE WANNA MAKE IT BACK IN TIME FOR THE BALL.

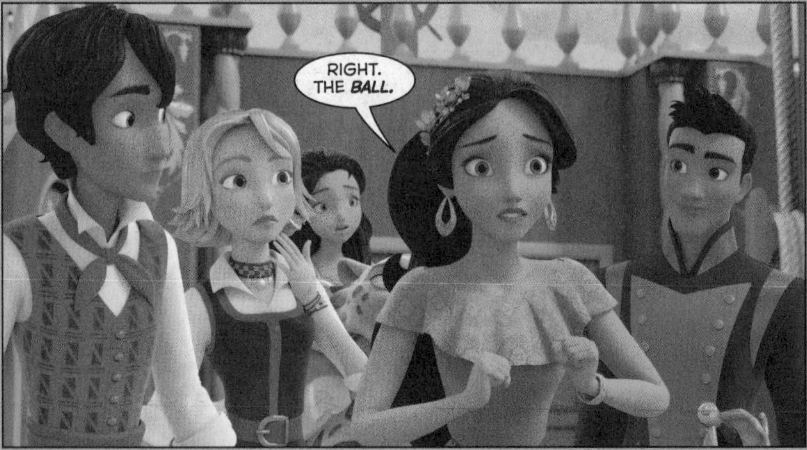
RIGHT. THE *BALL.*

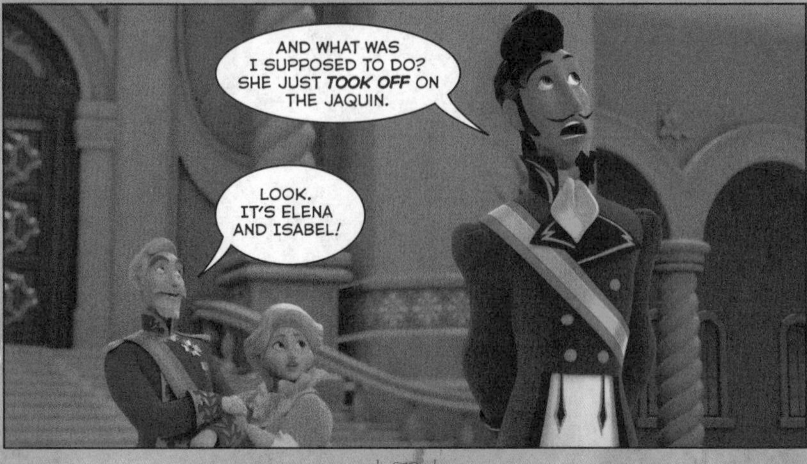
AND WHAT WAS I SUPPOSED TO DO? SHE JUST *TOOK OFF* ON THE JAQUIN.
LOOK. IT'S ELENA AND ISABEL!

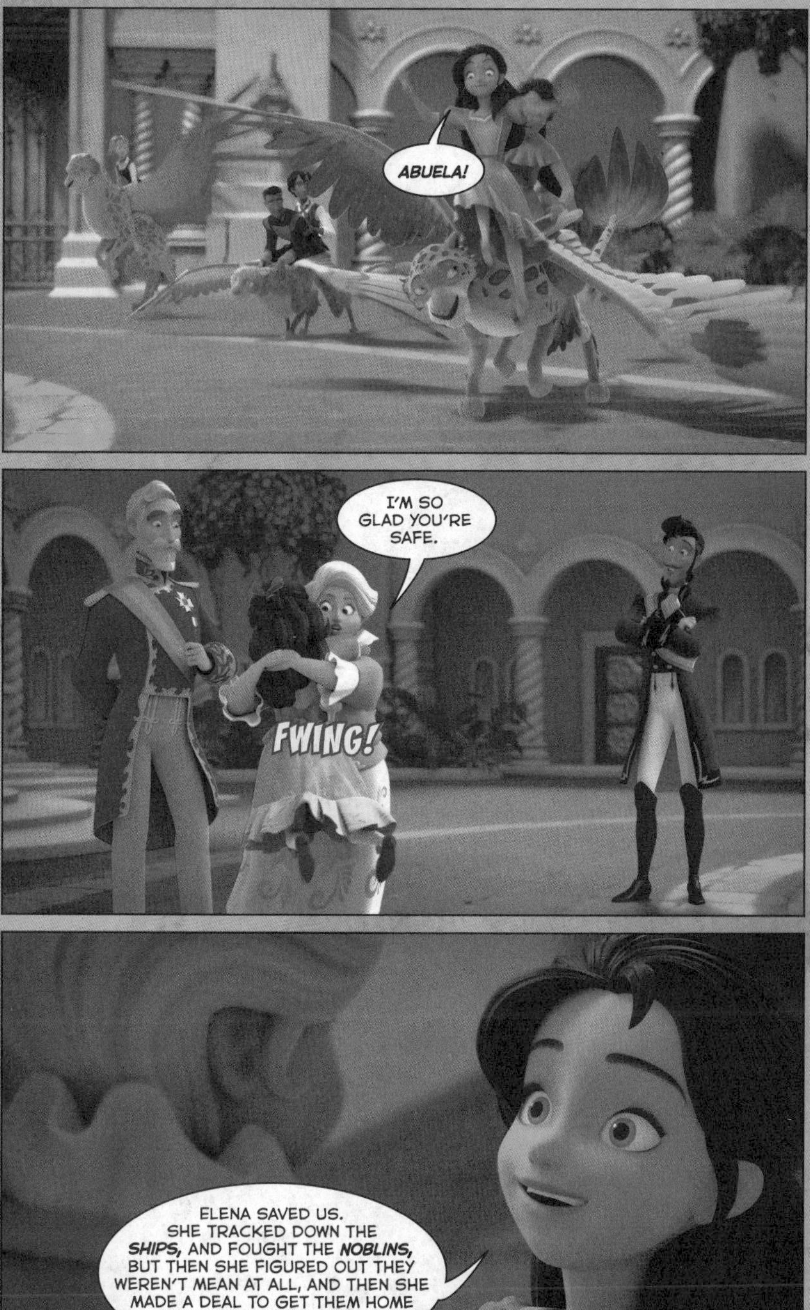
ABUELA!
I'M SO GLAD YOU'RE SAFE.
FWING!
ELENA SAVED US. SHE TRACKED DOWN THE SHIPS, AND FOUGHT THE NOBLINS, BUT THEN SHE FIGURED OUT THEY WEREN'T MEAN AT ALL, AND THEN SHE MADE A DEAL TO GET THEM HOME SAFE AND GET OUR SHIPS BACK.

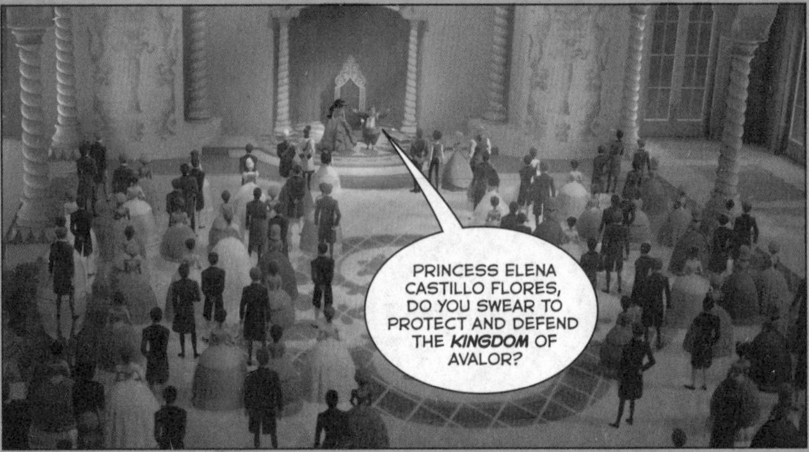
PRINCESS ELENA CASTILLO FLORES, DO YOU SWEAR TO PROTECT AND DEFEND THE KINGDOM OF AVALOR?

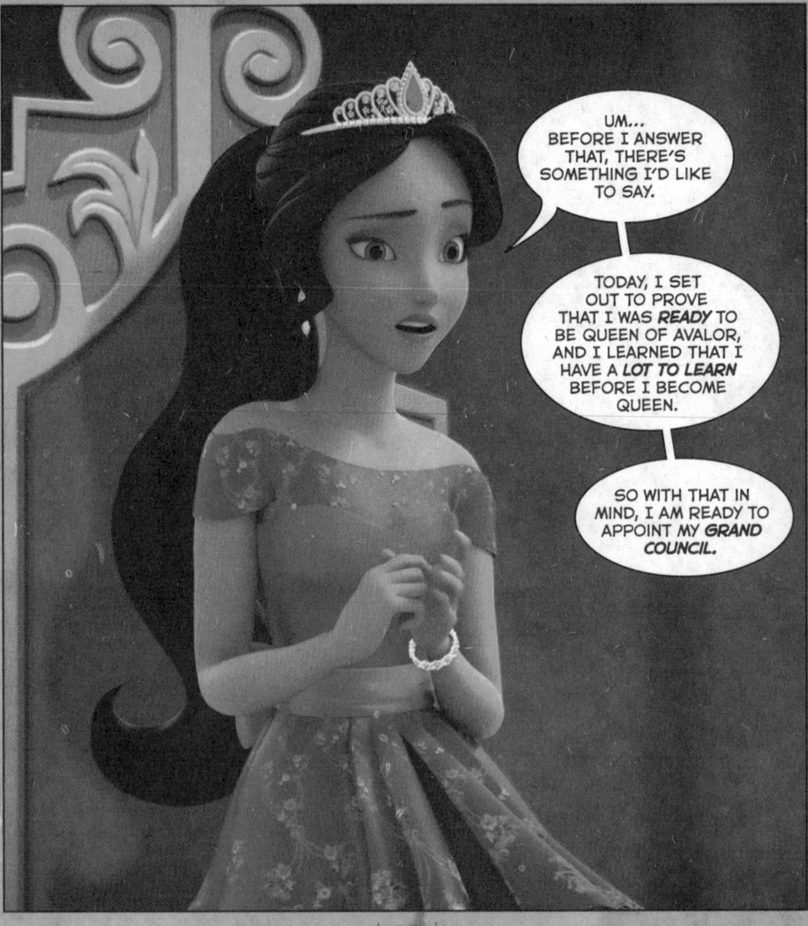
UM... BEFORE I ANSWER THAT, THERE'S SOMETHING I'D LIKE TO SAY.
TODAY, I SET OUT TO PROVE THAT I WAS READY TO BE QUEEN OF AVALOR, AND I LEARNED THAT I HAVE A LOT TO LEARN BEFORE I BECOME QUEEN.
SO WITH THAT IN MIND, I AM READY TO APPOINT MY GRAND COUNCIL.

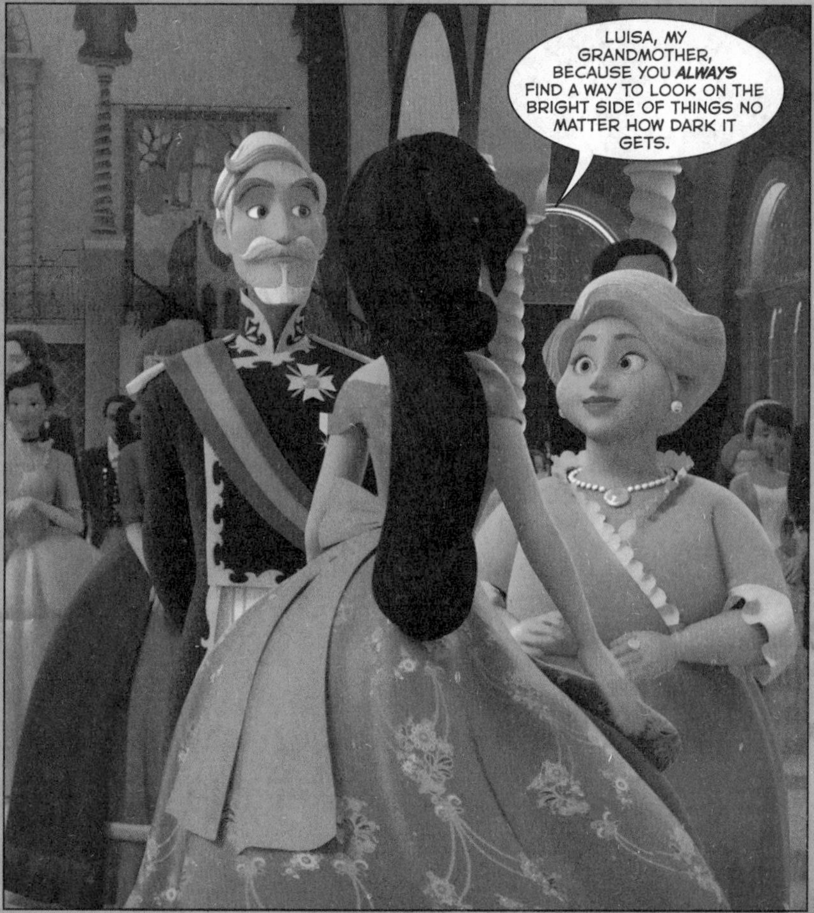
LUISA, MY GRANDMOTHER, BECAUSE YOU *ALWAYS* FIND A WAY TO LOOK ON THE BRIGHT SIDE OF THINGS NO MATTER HOW DARK IT GETS.

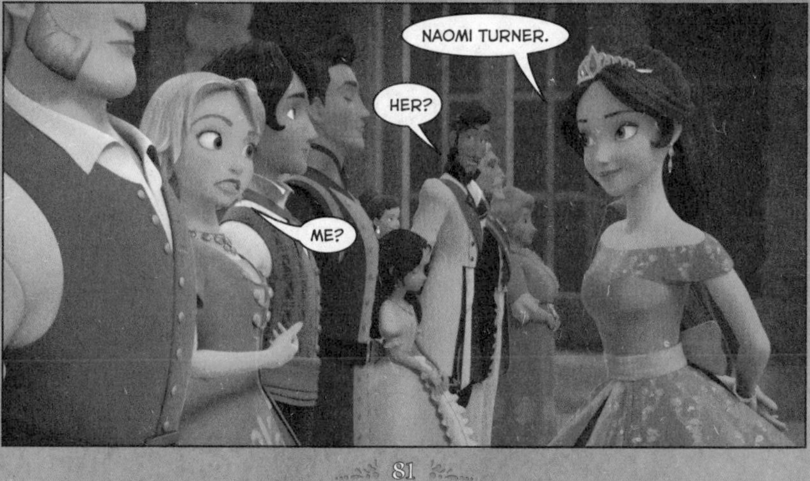
NAOMI TURNER.
HER?
ME?

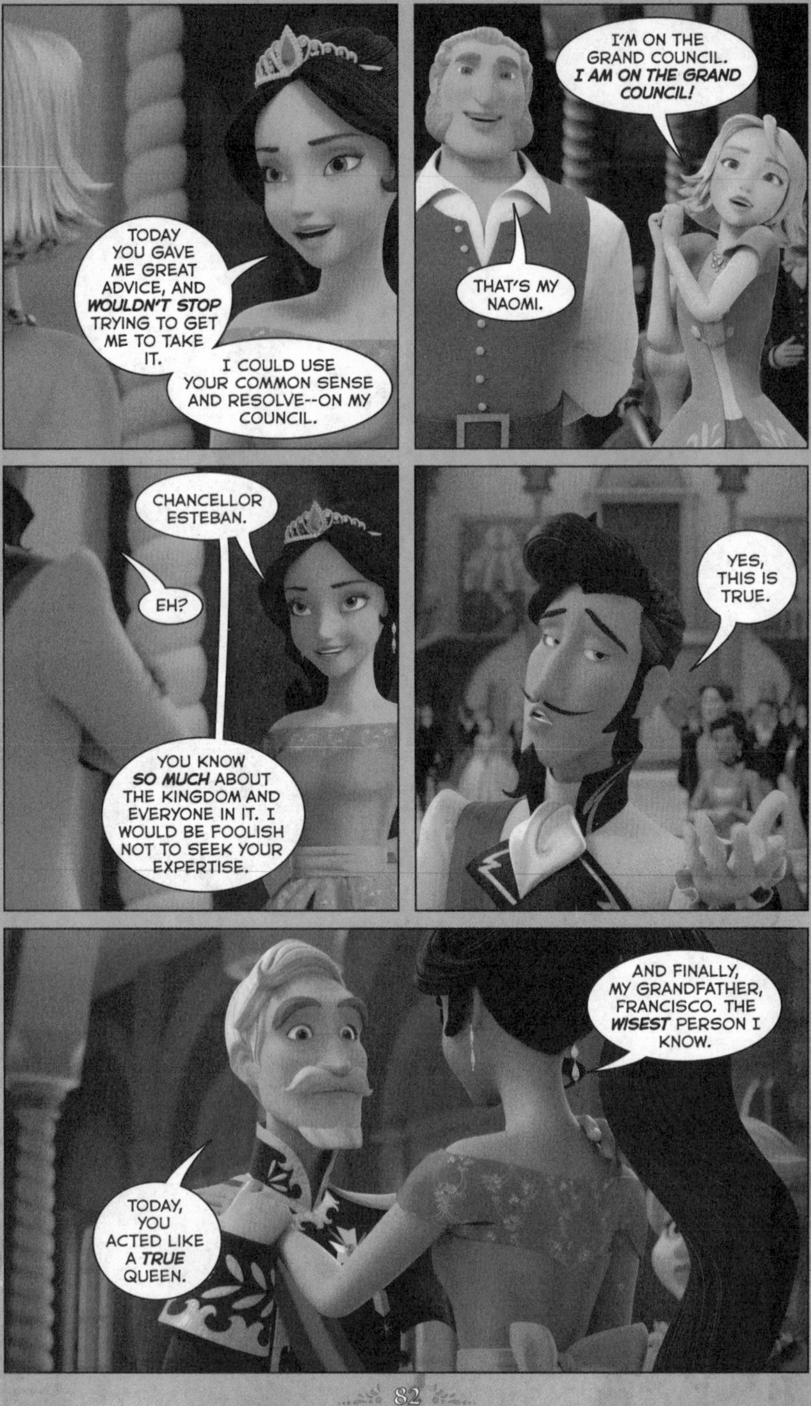
TODAY YOU GAVE ME GREAT ADVICE, AND WOULDN'T STOP TRYING TO GET ME TO TAKE IT.
I COULD USE YOUR COMMON SENSE AND RESOLVE--ON MY COUNCIL.
I'M ON THE GRAND COUNCIL. I AM ON THE GRAND COUNCIL!
THAT'S MY NAOMI.
CHANCELLOR ESTEBAN.
EH?
YOU KNOW SO MUCH ABOUT THE KINGDOM AND EVERYONE IN IT. I WOULD BE FOOLISH NOT TO SEEK YOUR EXPERTISE.
YES, THIS IS TRUE.
AND FINALLY, MY GRANDFATHER, FRANCISCO. THE WISEST PERSON I KNOW.
TODAY, YOU ACTED LIKE A TRUE QUEEN.

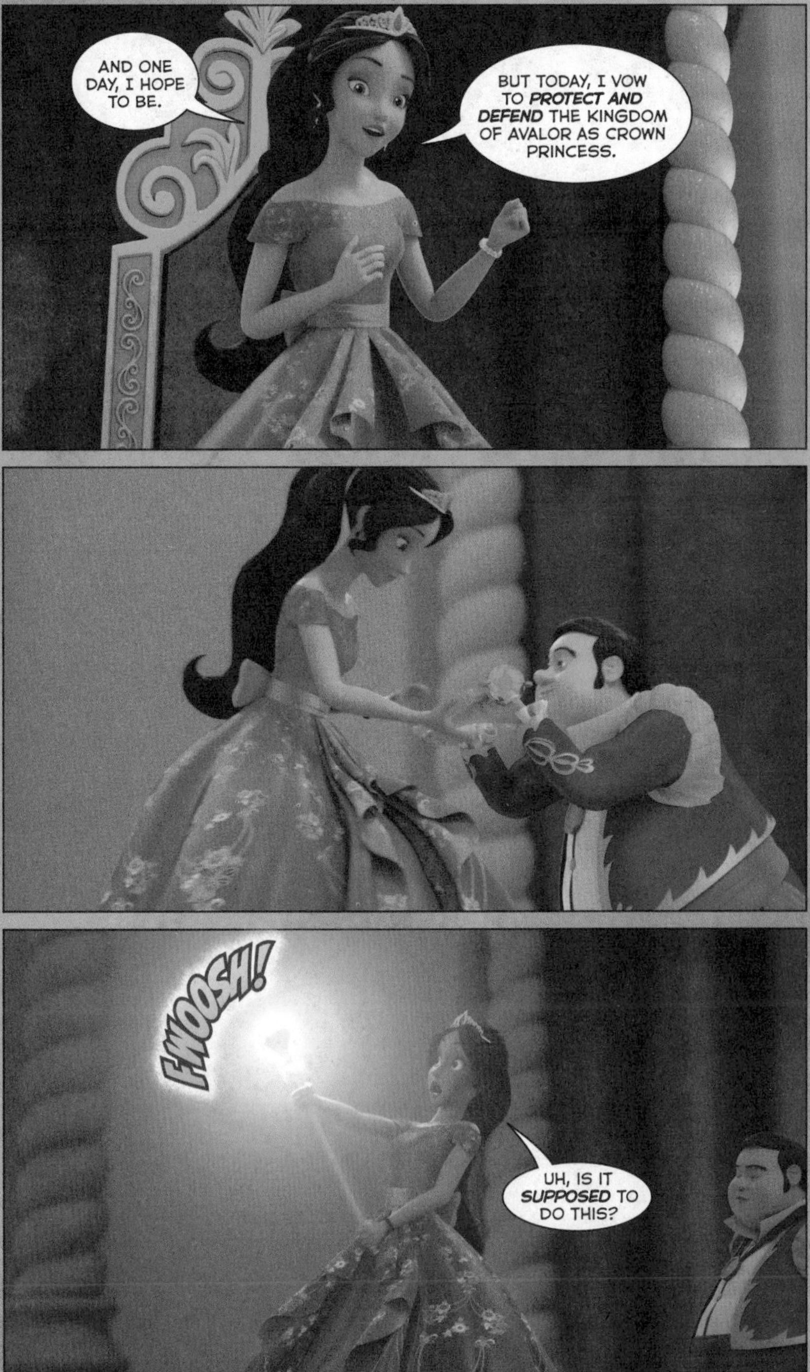
AND ONE DAY, I HOPE TO BE.
BUT TODAY, I VOW TO **PROTECT AND DEFEND** THE KINGDOM OF AVALOR AS CROWN PRINCESS.
FWOOSH!
UH, IS IT **SUPPOSED** TO DO THIS?

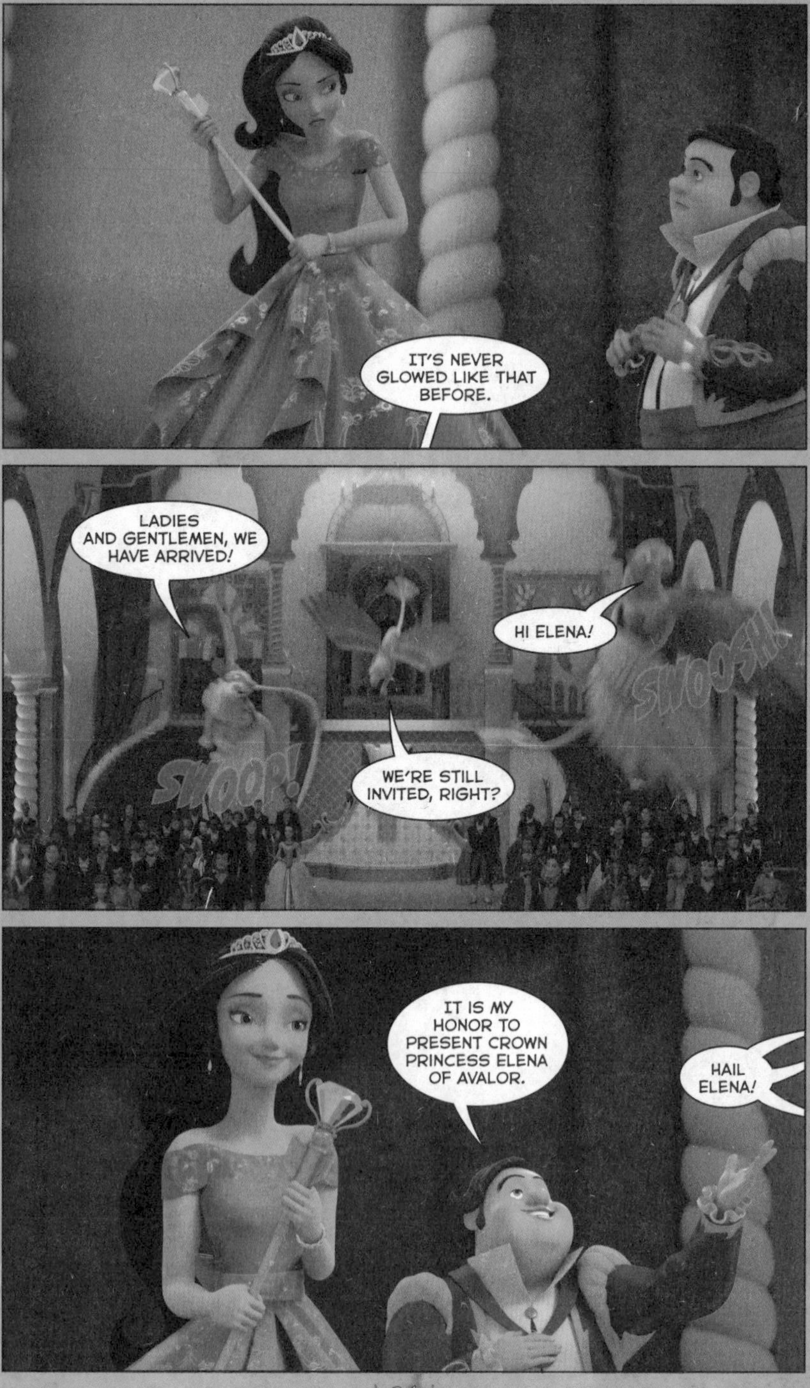
IT'S NEVER GLOWED LIKE THAT BEFORE.
LADIES AND GENTLEMEN, WE HAVE ARRIVED!
SWOOP!
WE'RE STILL INVITED, RIGHT?
HI ELENA!
SWOOSH!
IT IS MY HONOR TO PRESENT CROWN PRINCESS ELENA OF AVALOR.
HAIL ELENA!

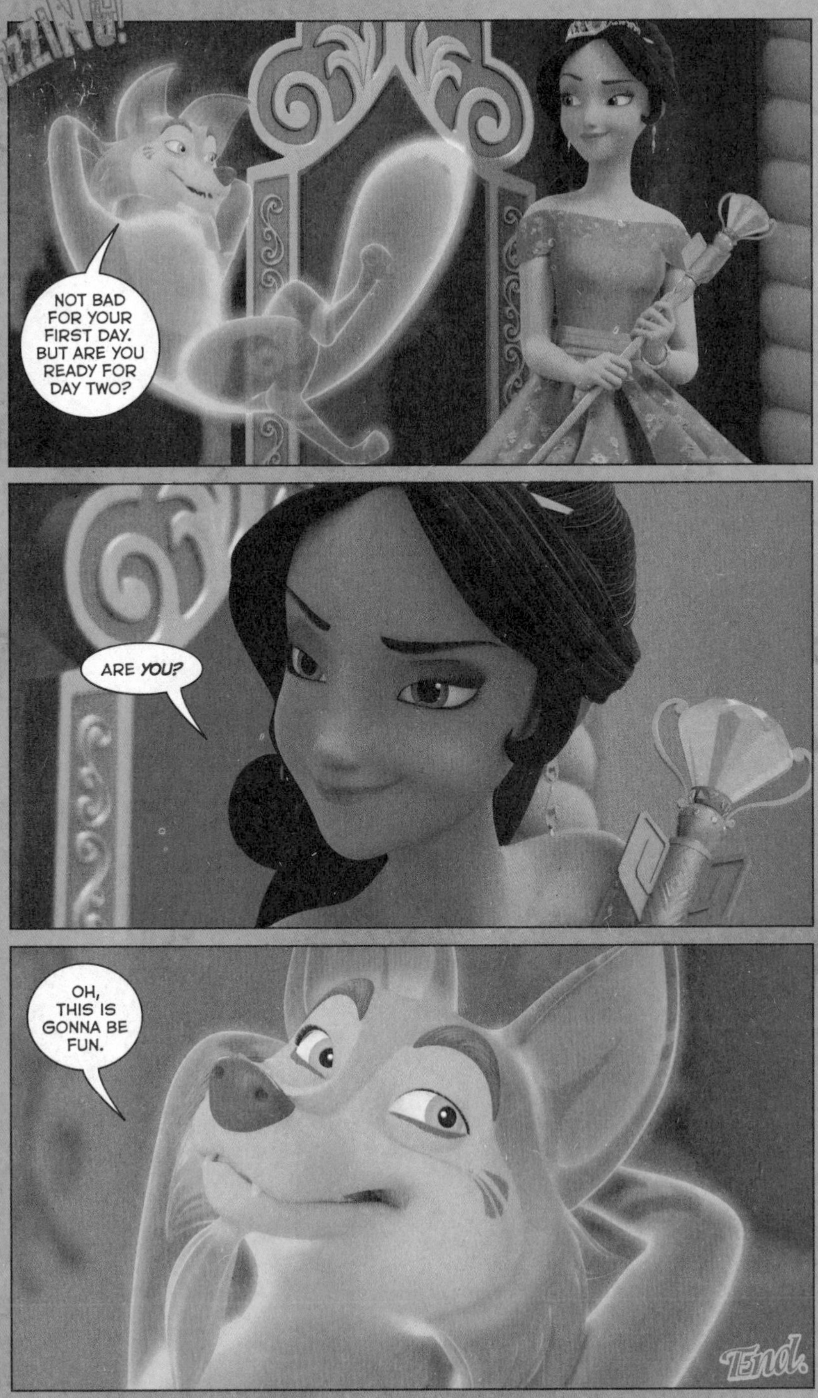
ZZING!
NOT BAD FOR YOUR FIRST DAY. BUT ARE YOU READY FOR DAY TWO?
ARE *YOU?*
OH, THIS IS GONNA BE FUN.
End.

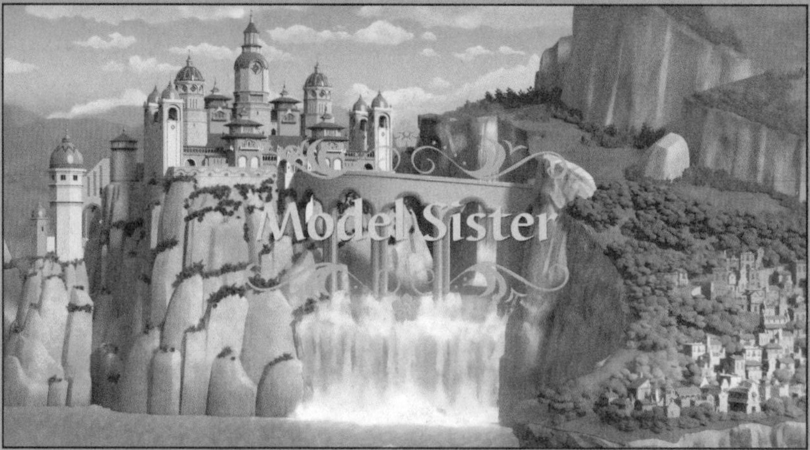
Model Sister

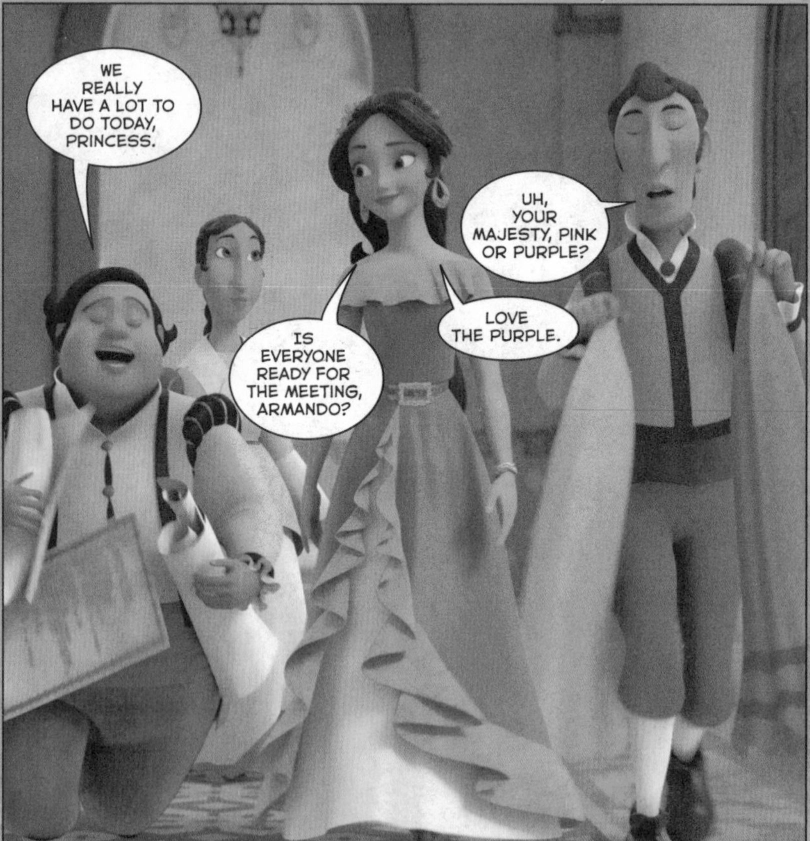
WE REALLY HAVE A LOT TO DO TODAY, PRINCESS.
IS EVERYONE READY FOR THE MEETING, ARMANDO?
UH, YOUR MAJESTY, PINK OR PURPLE?
LOVE THE PURPLE.

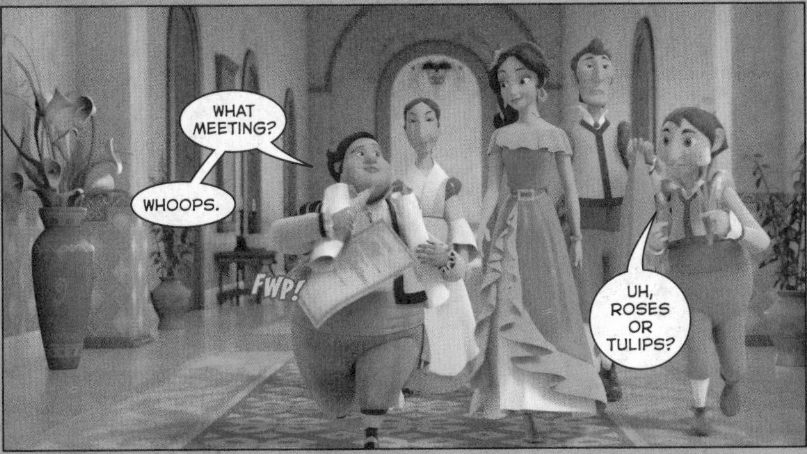

WHAT MEETING?
WHOOPS.
FWP!
UH, ROSES OR TULIPS?

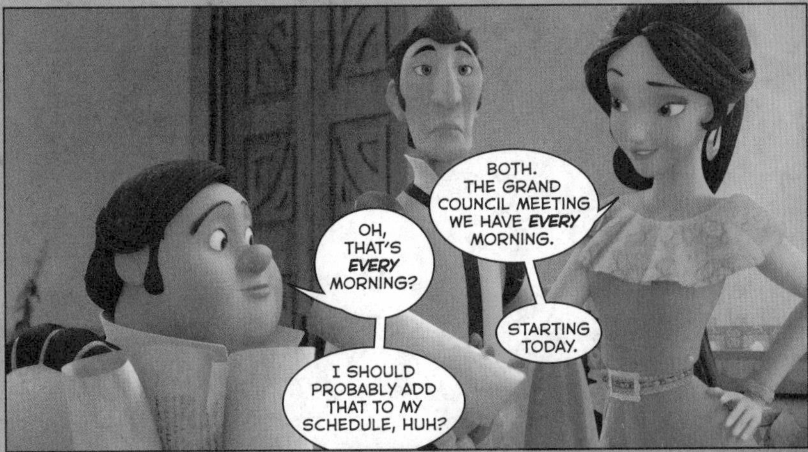

BOTH. THE GRAND COUNCIL MEETING WE HAVE *EVERY* MORNING.
OH, THAT'S *EVERY* MORNING?
STARTING TODAY.
I SHOULD PROBABLY ADD THAT TO MY SCHEDULE, HUH?

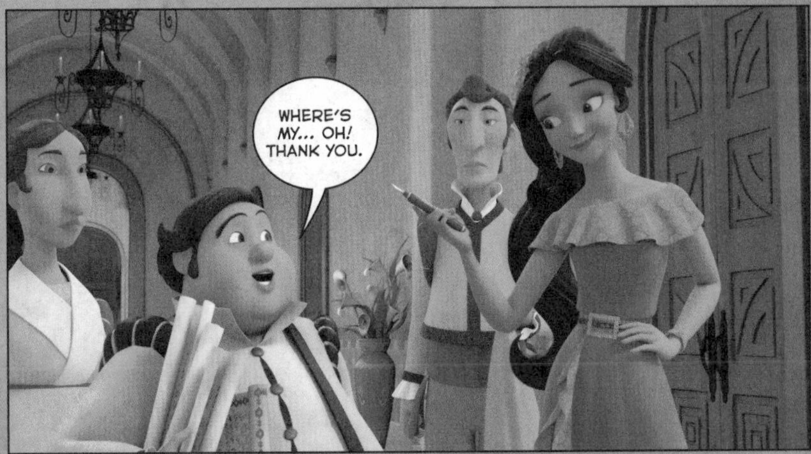

WHERE'S MY... OH! THANK YOU.

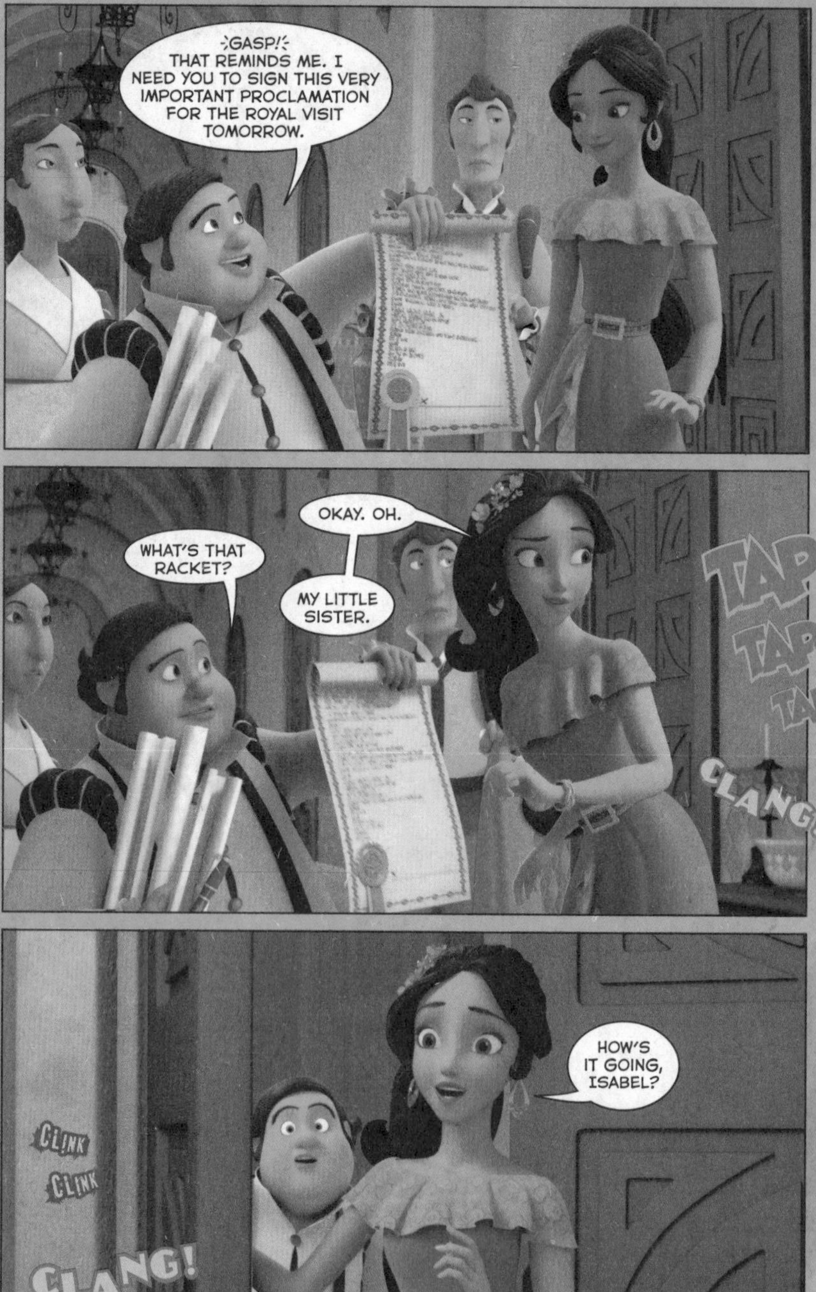

GASP!
THAT REMINDS ME. I NEED YOU TO SIGN THIS VERY IMPORTANT PROCLAMATION FOR THE ROYAL VISIT TOMORROW.
WHAT'S THAT RACKET?
OKAY. OH.
MY LITTLE SISTER.
CLANG!
CLINK
CLINK
CLANG!
HOW'S IT GOING, ISABEL?

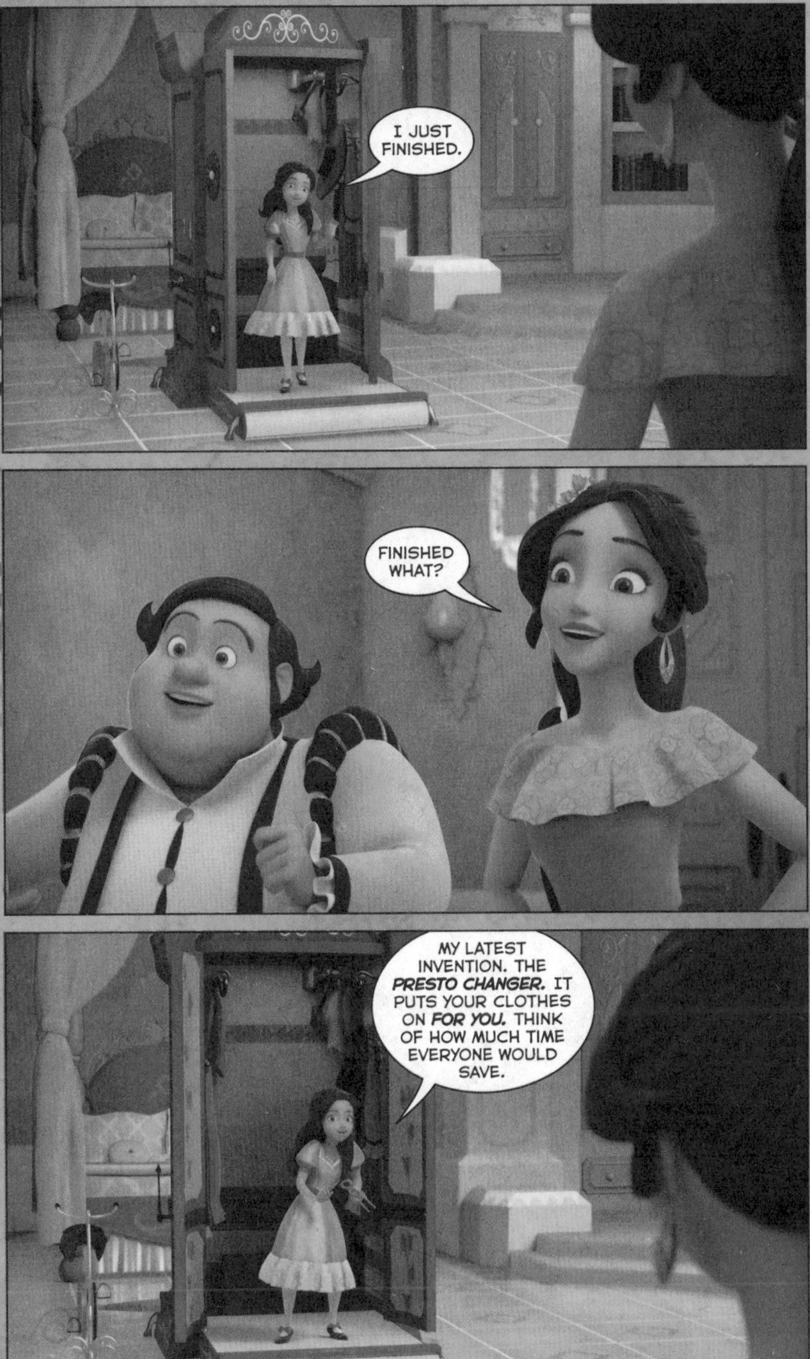
I JUST FINISHED.
FINISHED WHAT?
MY LATEST INVENTION. THE **PRESTO CHANGER.** IT PUTS YOUR CLOTHES ON **FOR YOU.** THINK OF HOW MUCH TIME EVERYONE WOULD SAVE.

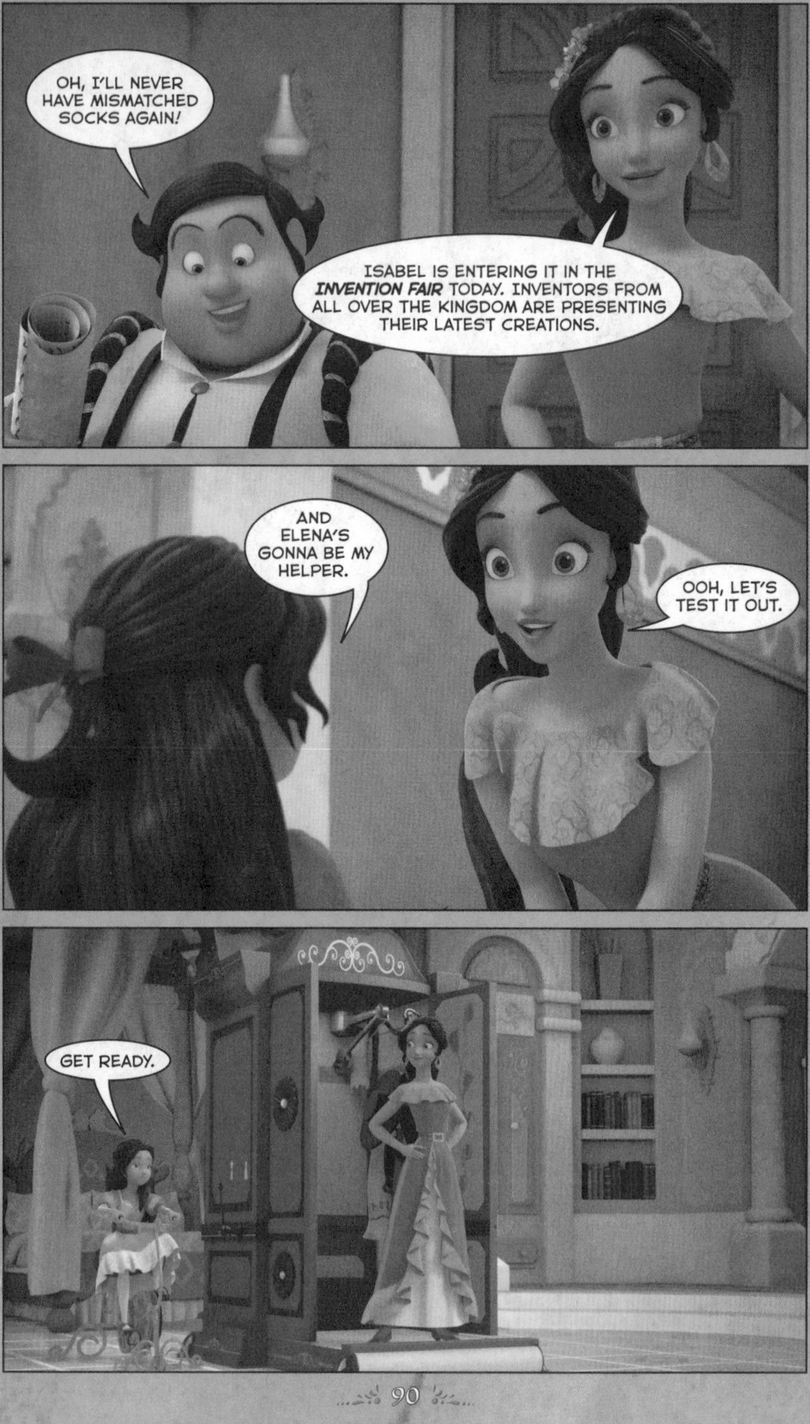
OH, I'LL NEVER HAVE MISMATCHED SOCKS AGAIN!
ISABEL IS ENTERING IT IN THE *INVENTION FAIR* TODAY. INVENTORS FROM ALL OVER THE KINGDOM ARE PRESENTING THEIR LATEST CREATIONS.
AND ELENA'S GONNA BE MY HELPER.
OOH, LET'S TEST IT OUT.
GET READY.

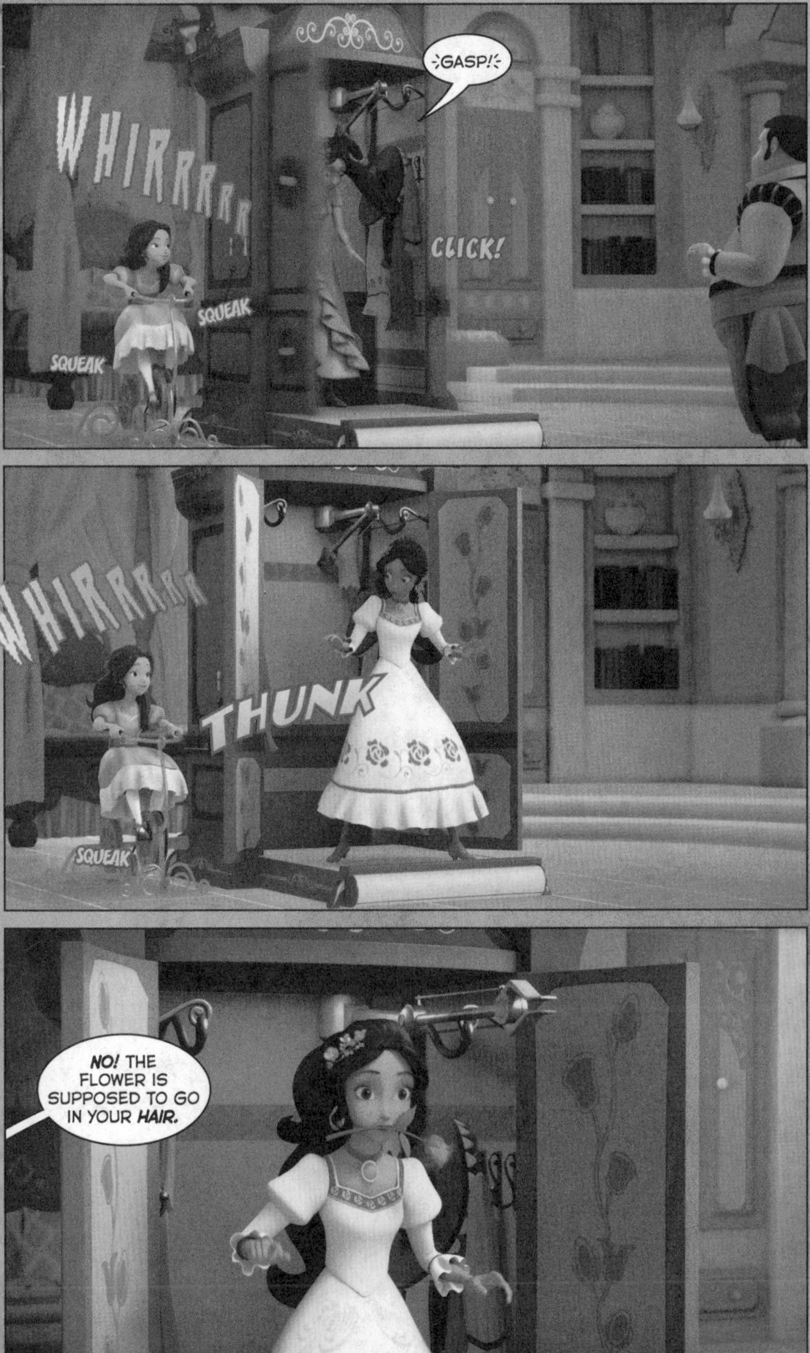

WHIRRRRRR
:GASP!:
SQUEAK
SQUEAK
CLICK!
WHIRRRRR
THUNK
SQUEAK
NO! THE FLOWER IS SUPPOSED TO GO IN YOUR HAIR.

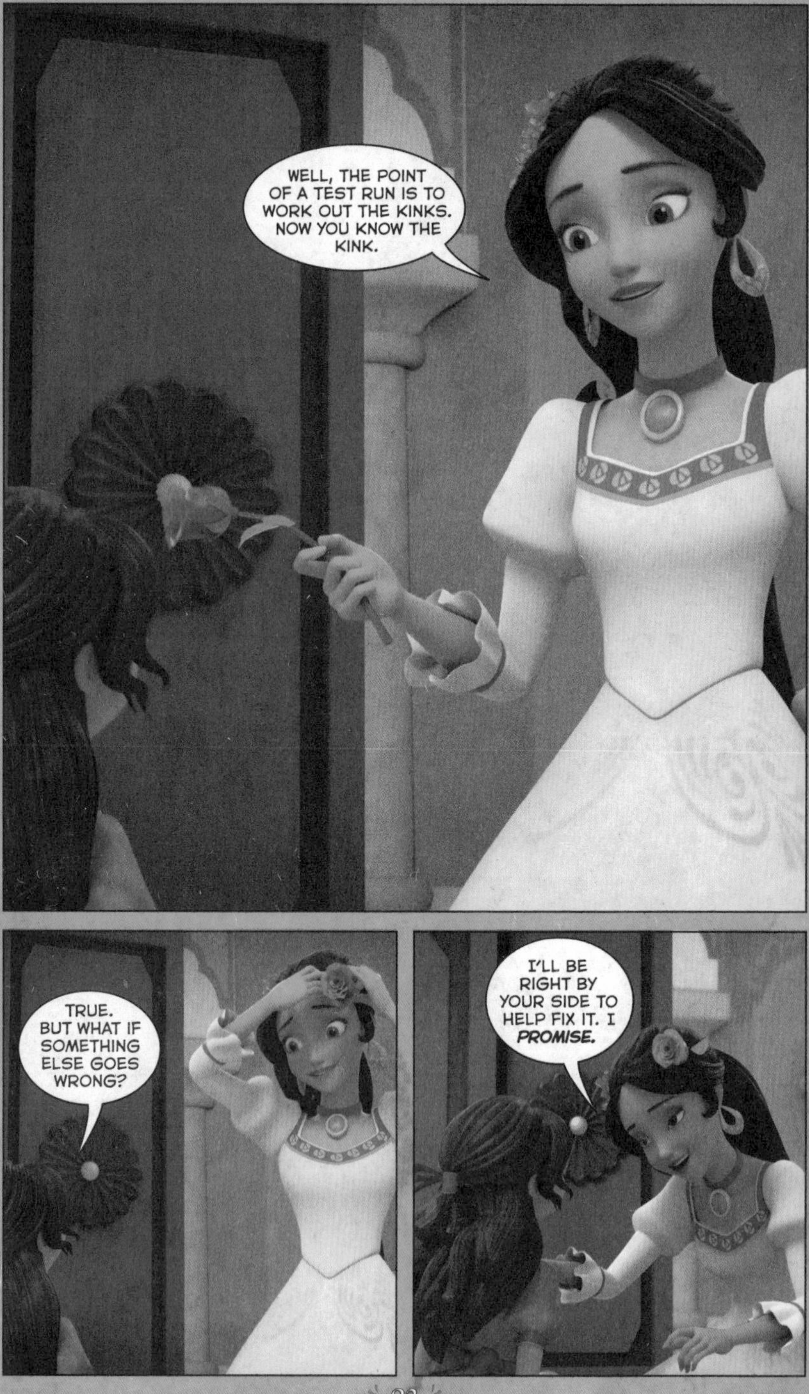
WELL, THE POINT OF A TEST RUN IS TO WORK OUT THE KINKS. NOW YOU KNOW THE KINK.
TRUE. BUT WHAT IF SOMETHING ELSE GOES WRONG?
I'LL BE RIGHT BY YOUR SIDE TO HELP FIX IT. I *PROMISE.*

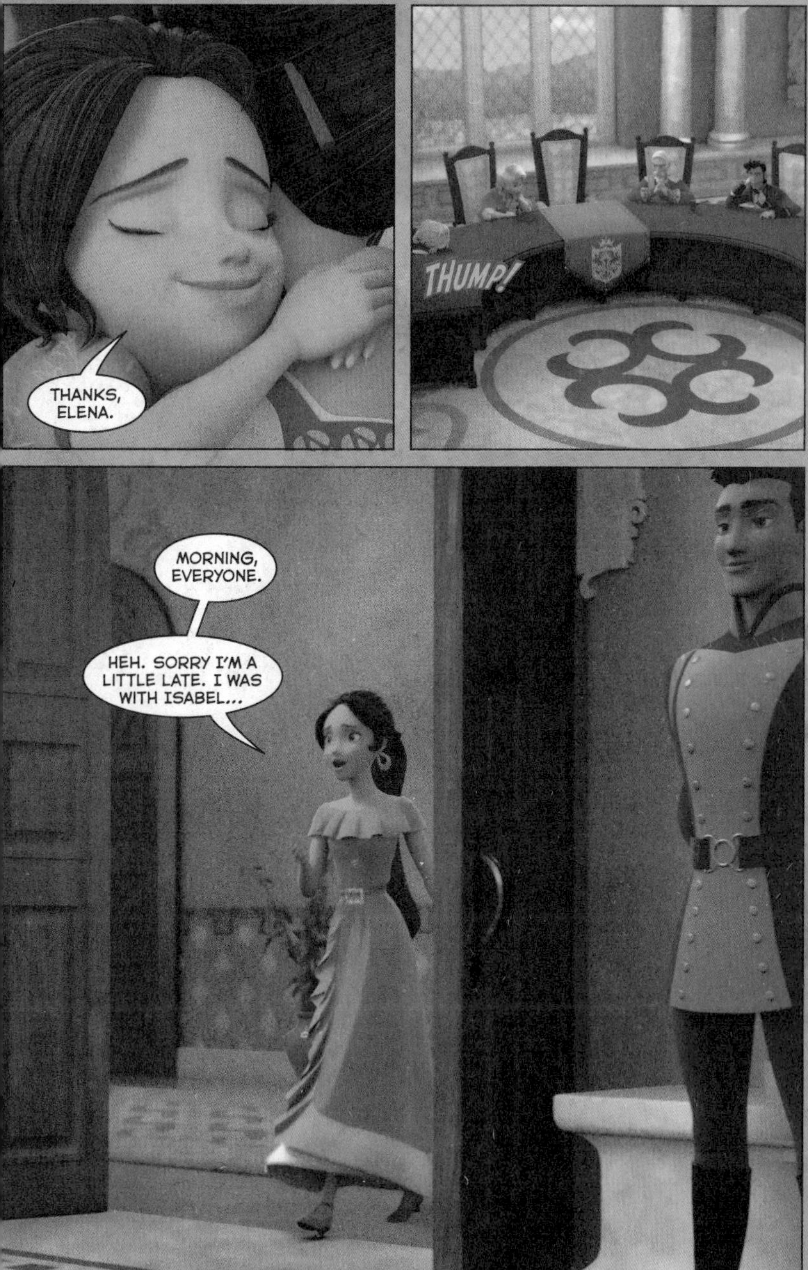
THANKS, ELENA.
THUMP!
MORNING, EVERYONE.
HEH. SORRY I'M A LITTLE LATE. I WAS WITH ISABEL...

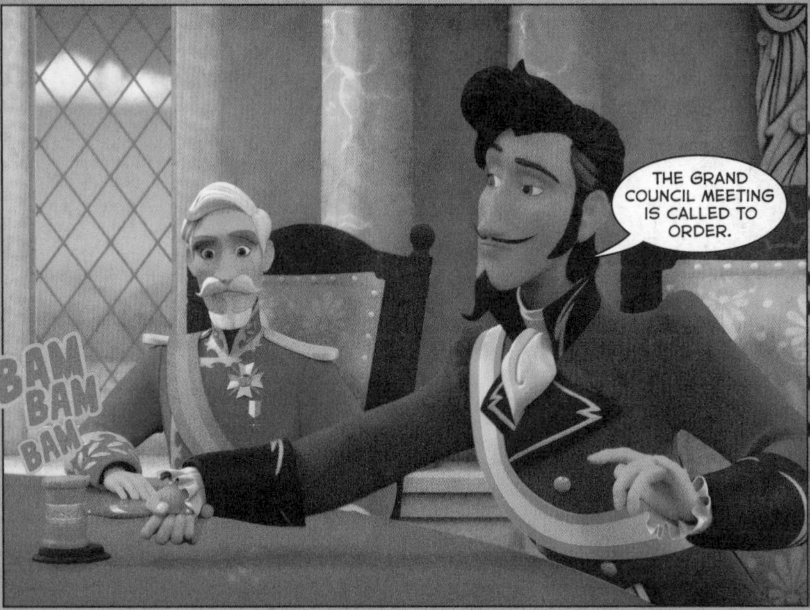
THE GRAND COUNCIL MEETING IS CALLED TO ORDER.
BAM BAM BAM

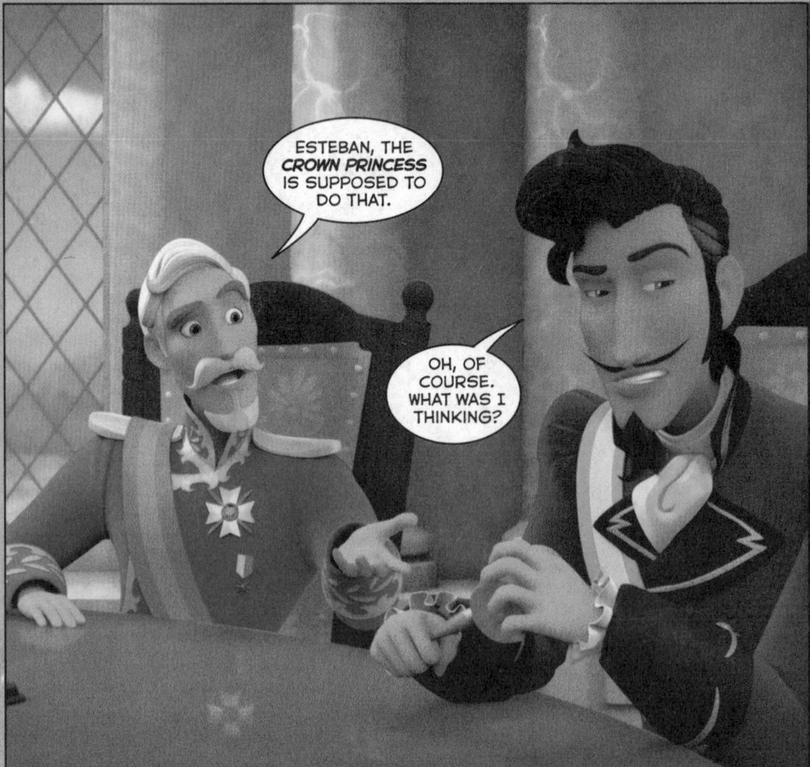
ESTEBAN, THE *CROWN PRINCESS* IS SUPPOSED TO DO THAT.
OH, OF COURSE. WHAT WAS I THINKING?

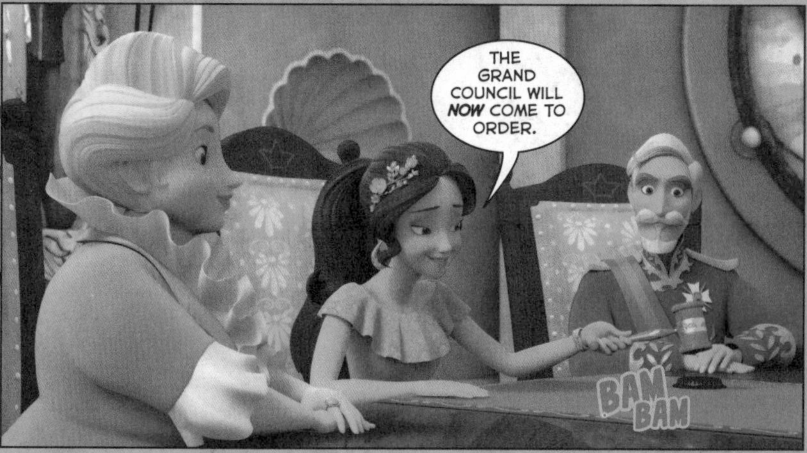
THE GRAND COUNCIL WILL *NOW* COME TO ORDER.
BAM BAM

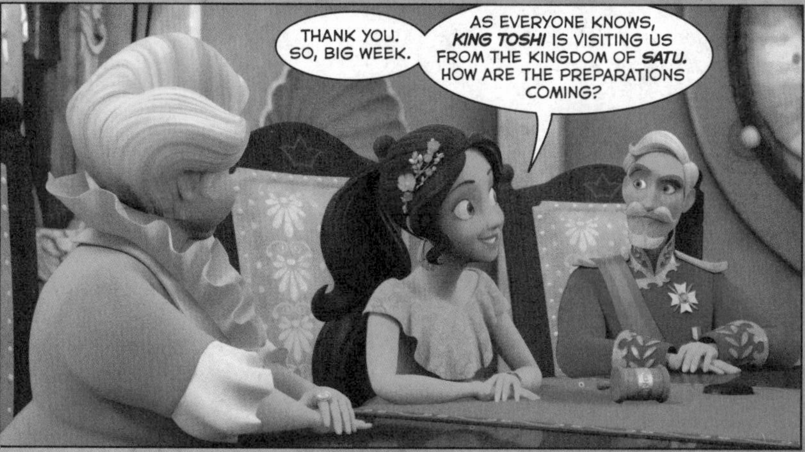
THANK YOU. SO, BIG WEEK.
AS EVERYONE KNOWS, ***KING TOSHI*** IS VISITING US FROM THE KINGDOM OF ***SATU.*** HOW ARE THE PREPARATIONS COMING?

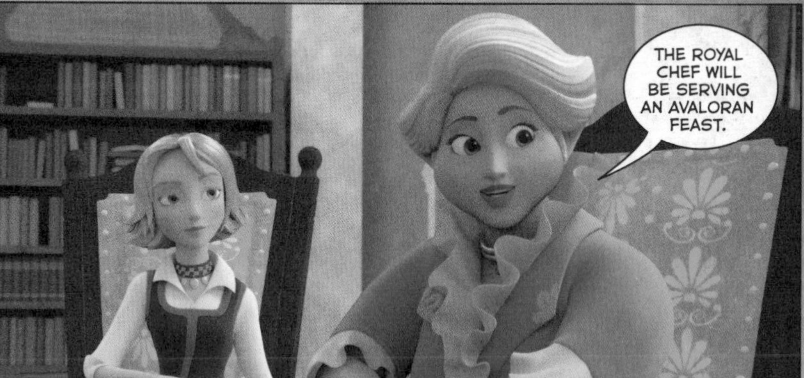
THE ROYAL CHEF WILL BE SERVING AN AVALORAN FEAST.

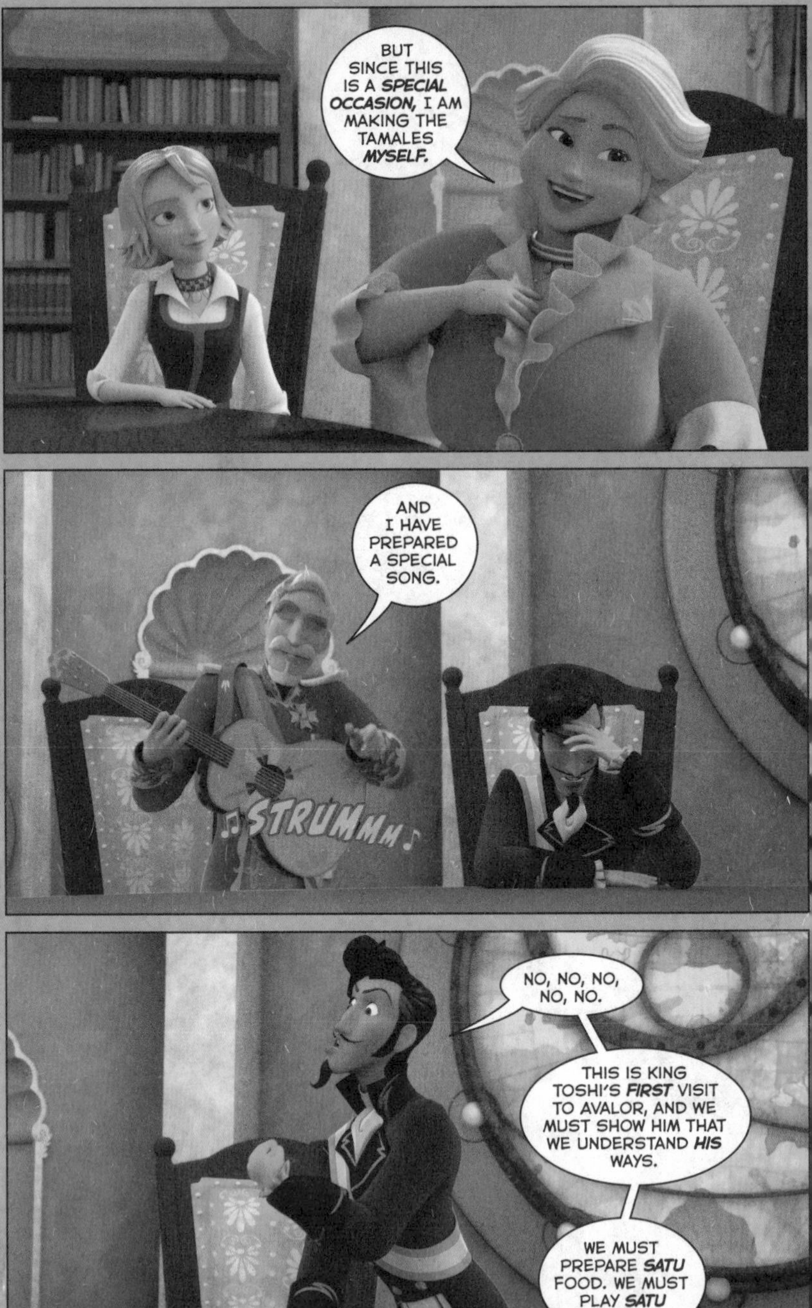
BUT SINCE THIS IS A SPECIAL OCCASION, I AM MAKING THE TAMALES MYSELF.
AND I HAVE PREPARED A SPECIAL SONG.
STRUMMM
NO, NO, NO, NO, NO.
THIS IS KING TOSHI'S FIRST VISIT TO AVALOR, AND WE MUST SHOW HIM THAT WE UNDERSTAND HIS WAYS.
WE MUST PREPARE SATU FOOD. WE MUST PLAY SATU MUSIC.

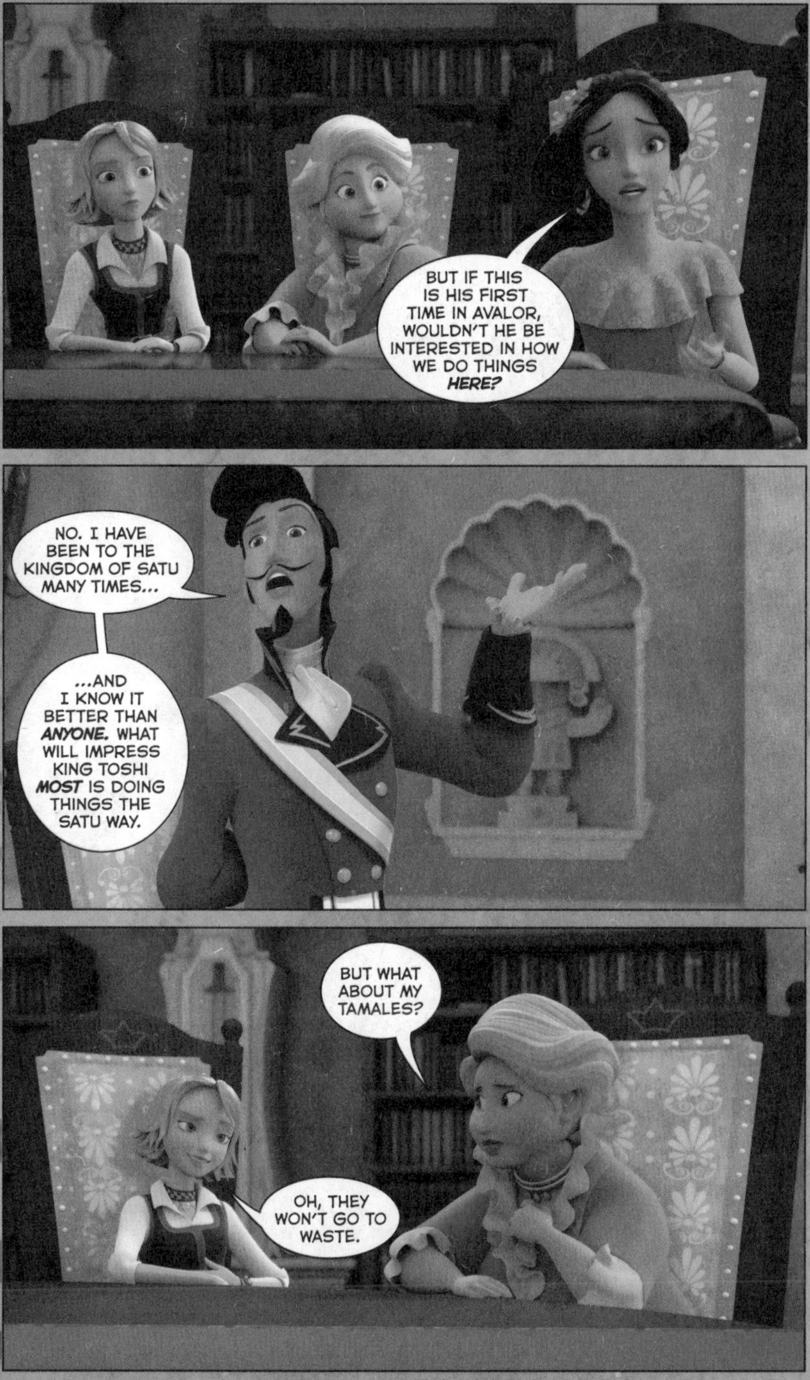
BUT IF THIS IS HIS FIRST TIME IN AVALOR, WOULDN'T HE BE INTERESTED IN HOW WE DO THINGS *HERE?*
NO. I HAVE BEEN TO THE KINGDOM OF SATU MANY TIMES...
...AND I KNOW IT BETTER THAN *ANYONE.* WHAT WILL IMPRESS KING TOSHI *MOST* IS DOING THINGS THE SATU WAY.
BUT WHAT ABOUT MY TAMALES?
OH, THEY WON'T GO TO WASTE.

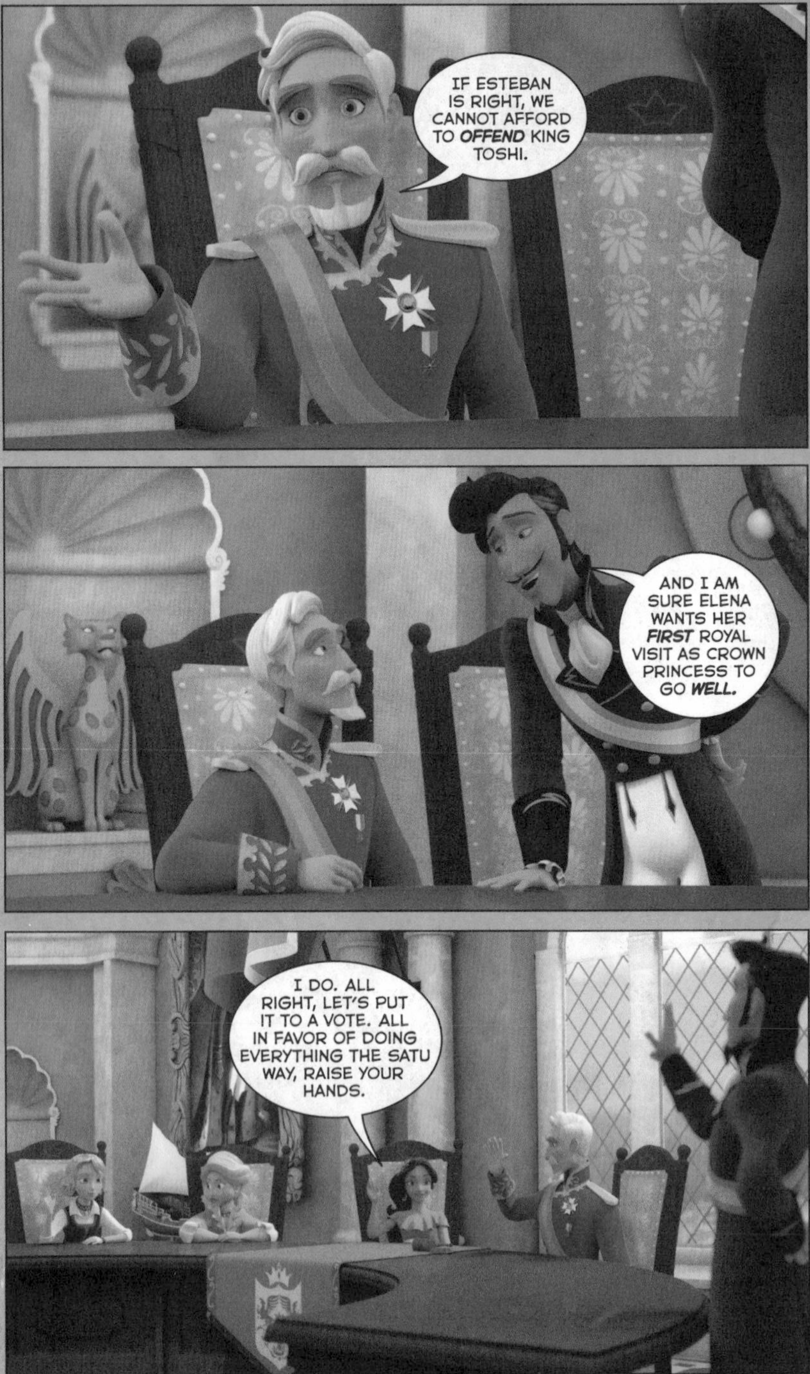
IF ESTEBAN IS RIGHT, WE CANNOT AFFORD TO *OFFEND* KING TOSHI.
AND I AM SURE ELENA WANTS HER *FIRST* ROYAL VISIT AS CROWN PRINCESS TO GO *WELL.*
I DO. ALL RIGHT, LET'S PUT IT TO A VOTE. ALL IN FAVOR OF DOING EVERYTHING THE SATU WAY, RAISE YOUR HANDS.

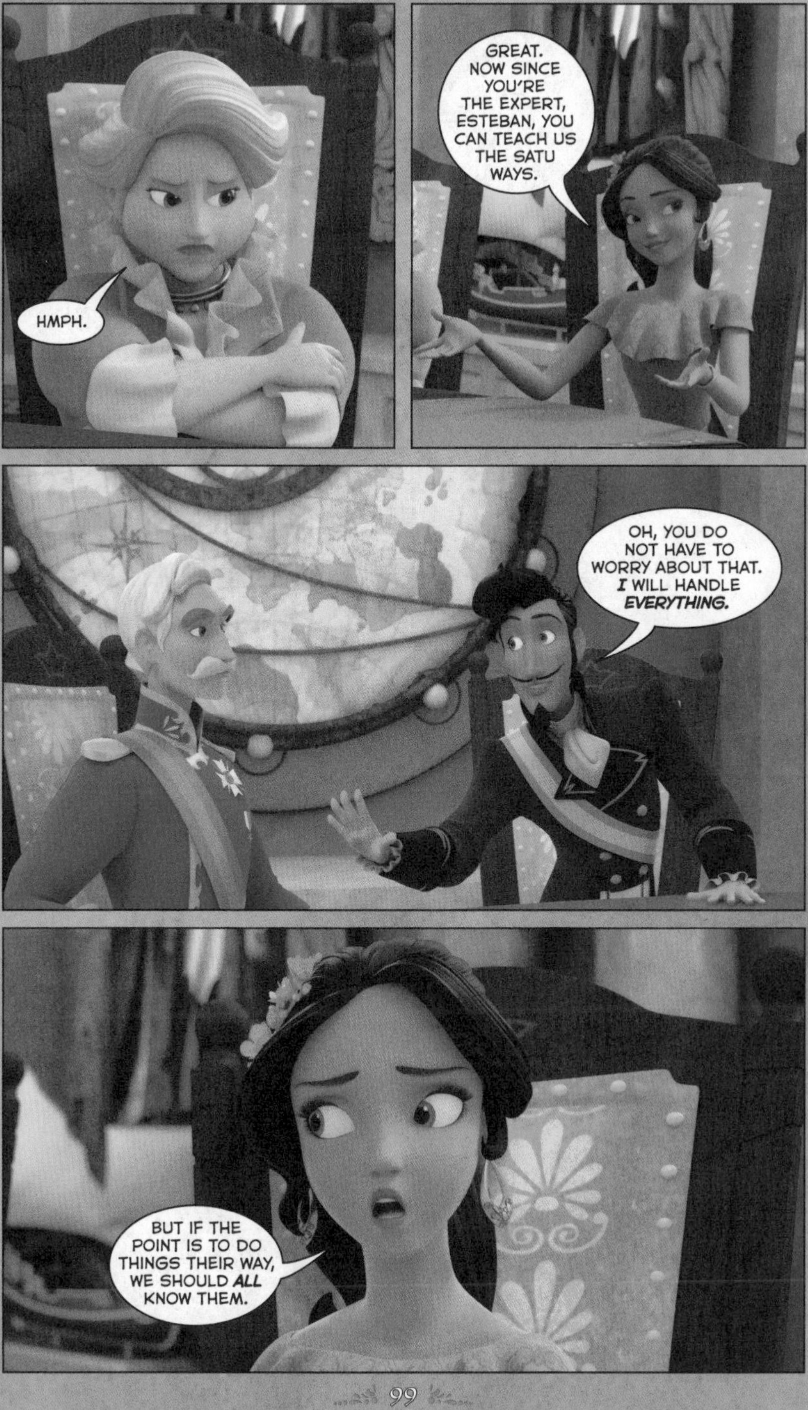
HMPH.
GREAT. NOW SINCE YOU'RE THE EXPERT, ESTEBAN, YOU CAN TEACH US THE SATU WAYS.
OH, YOU DO NOT HAVE TO WORRY ABOUT THAT. I WILL HANDLE EVERYTHING.
BUT IF THE POINT IS TO DO THINGS THEIR WAY, WE SHOULD ALL KNOW THEM.

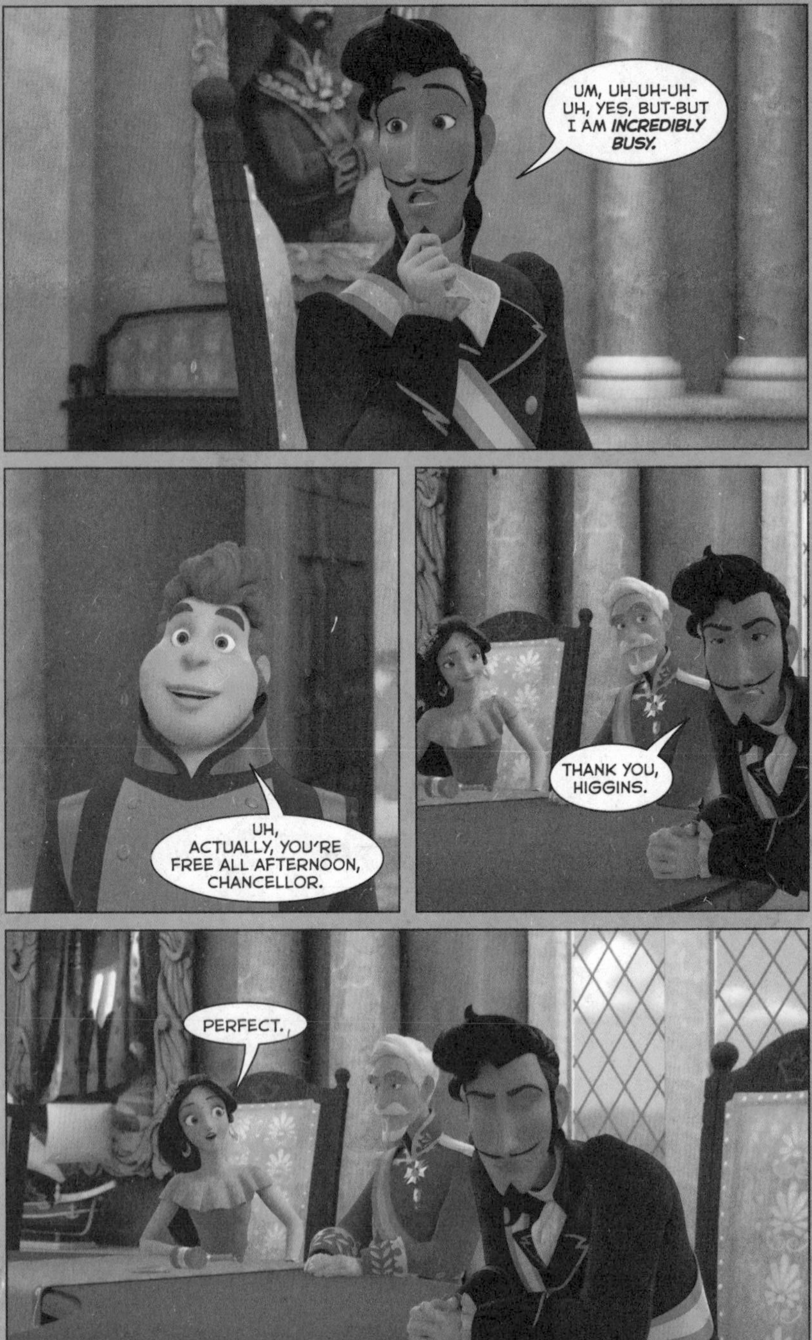
UM, UH-UH-UH-UH, YES, BUT-BUT I AM *INCREDIBLY BUSY.*
UH, ACTUALLY, YOU'RE FREE ALL AFTERNOON, CHANCELLOR.
THANK YOU, HIGGINS.
PERFECT.

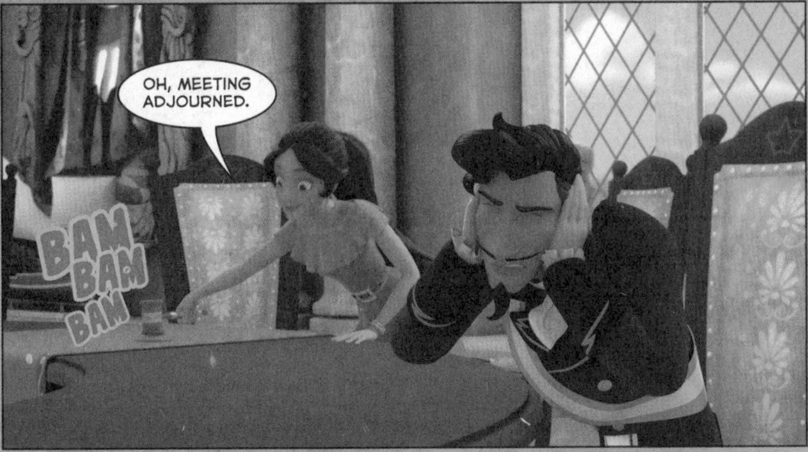
OH, MEETING ADJOURNED.
BAM BAM BAM

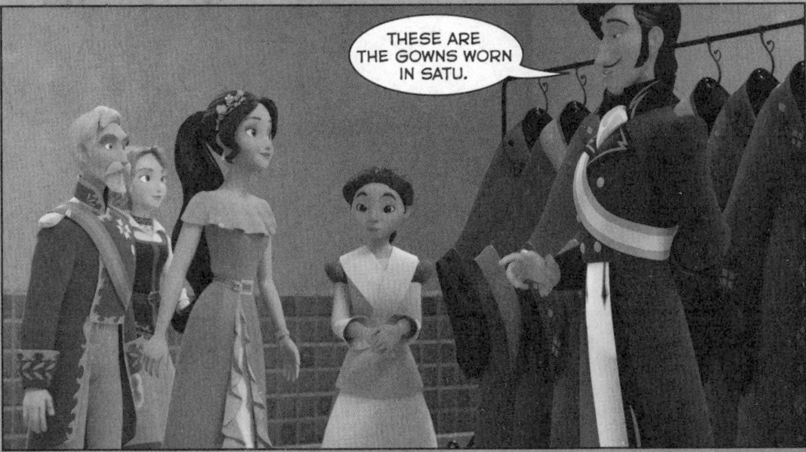
THESE ARE THE GOWNS WORN IN SATU.

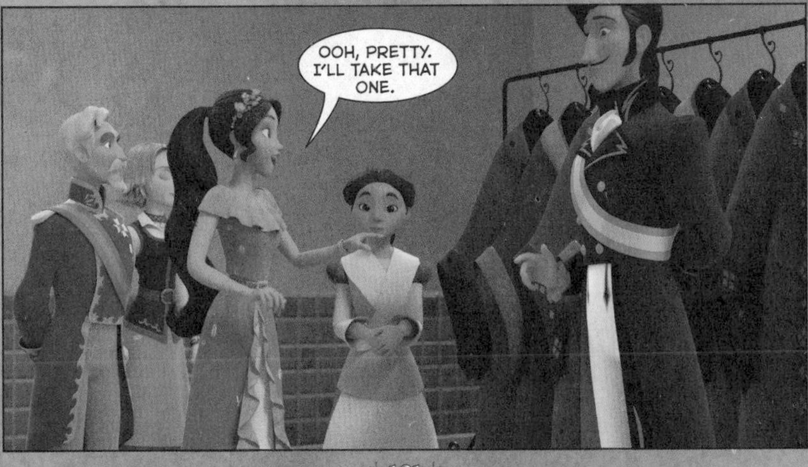
OOH, PRETTY. I'LL TAKE THAT ONE.

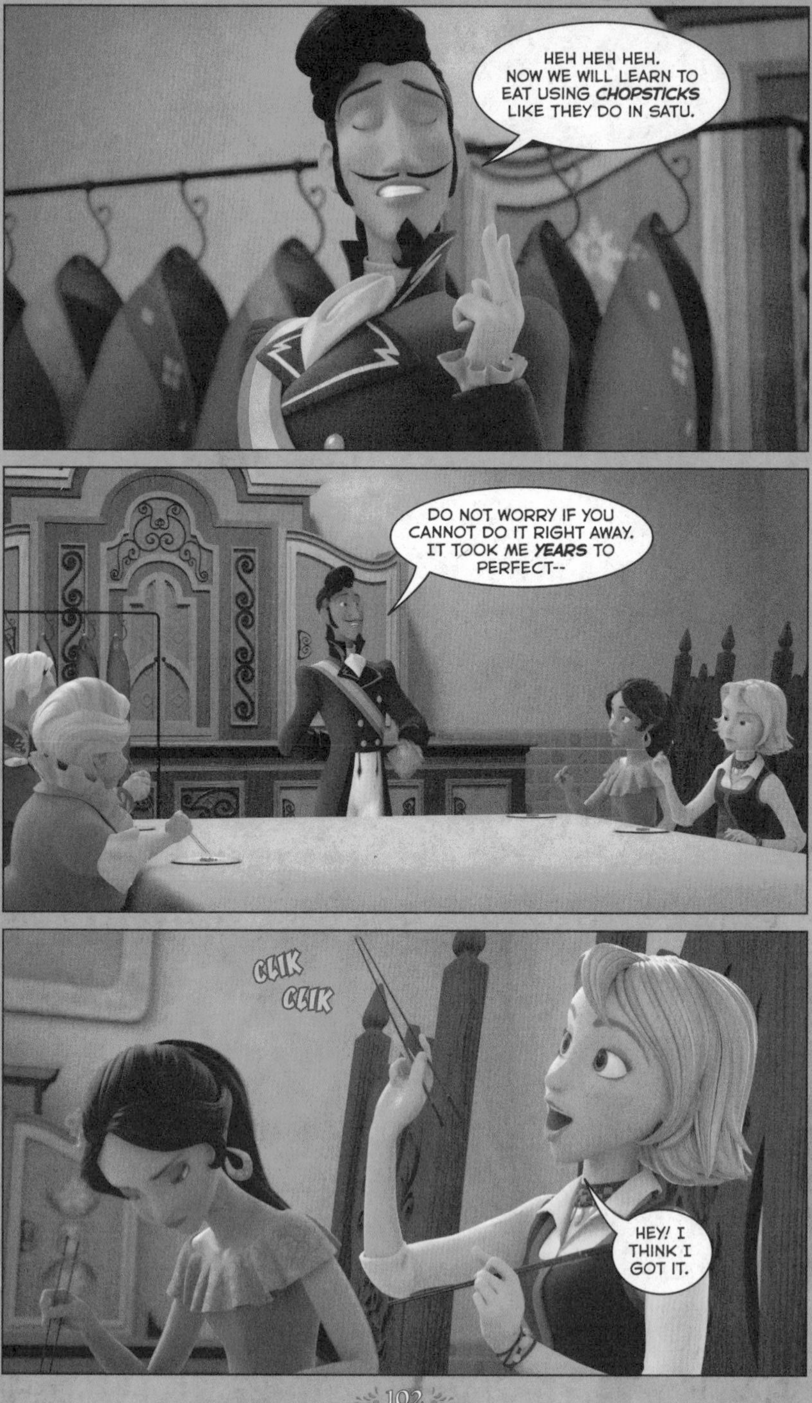
HEH HEH HEH. NOW WE WILL LEARN TO EAT USING CHOPSTICKS LIKE THEY DO IN SATU.
DO NOT WORRY IF YOU CANNOT DO IT RIGHT AWAY. IT TOOK ME YEARS TO PERFECT--
CLIK CLIK
HEY! I THINK I GOT IT.

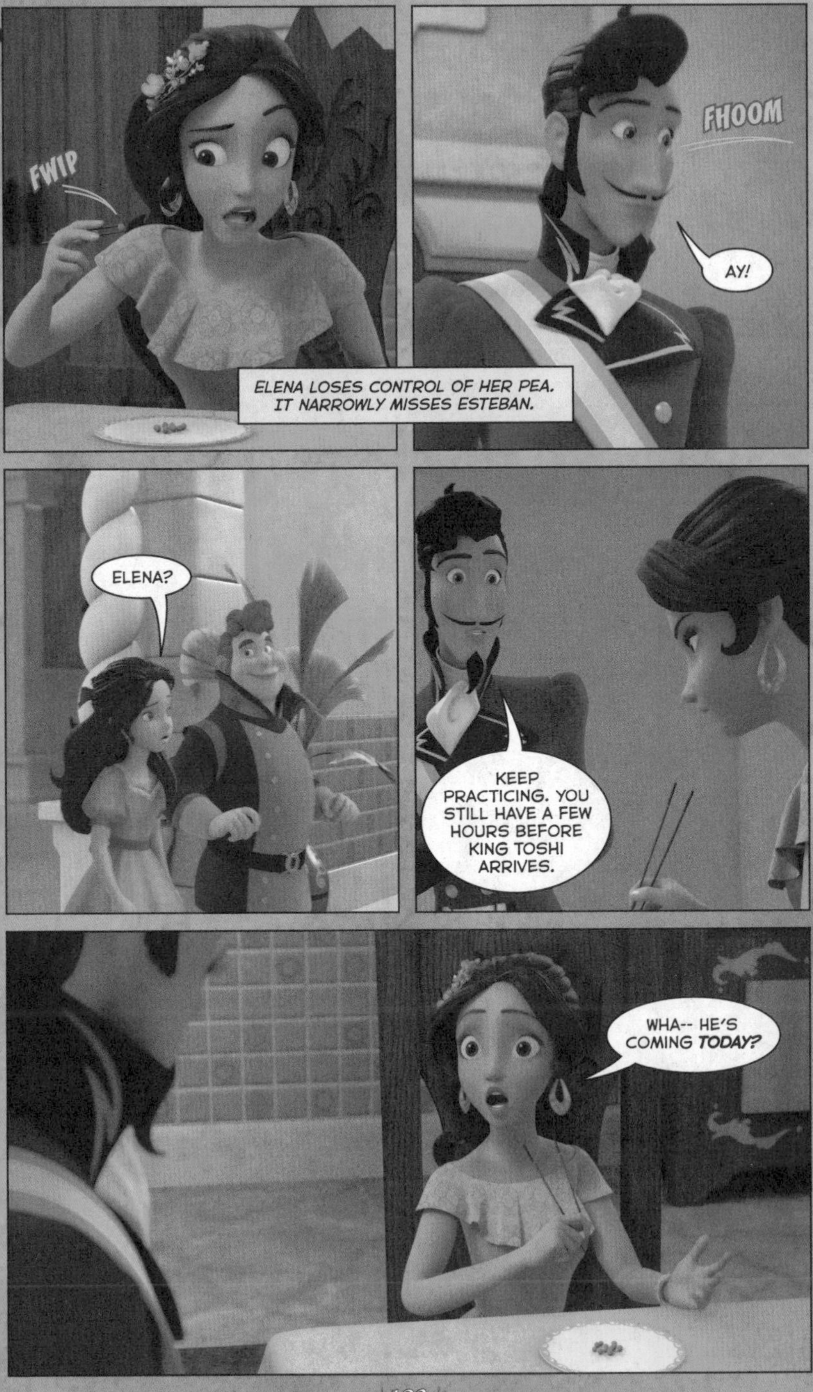
FWIP
FHOOM
AY!
ELENA LOSES CONTROL OF HER PEA. IT NARROWLY MISSES ESTEBAN.
ELENA?
KEEP PRACTICING. YOU STILL HAVE A FEW HOURS BEFORE KING TOSHI ARRIVES.
WHA-- HE'S COMING TODAY?

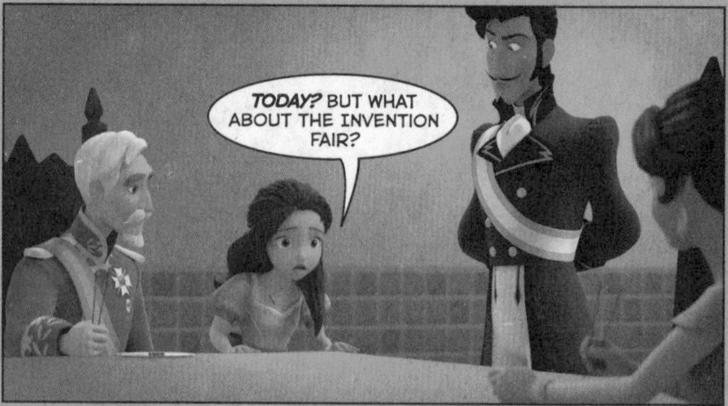
TODAY? BUT WHAT ABOUT THE INVENTION FAIR?

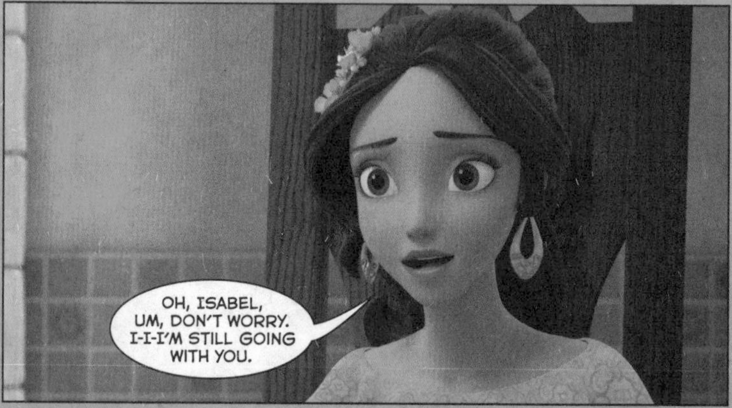
OH, ISABEL, UM, DON'T WORRY. I-I-I'M STILL GOING WITH YOU.

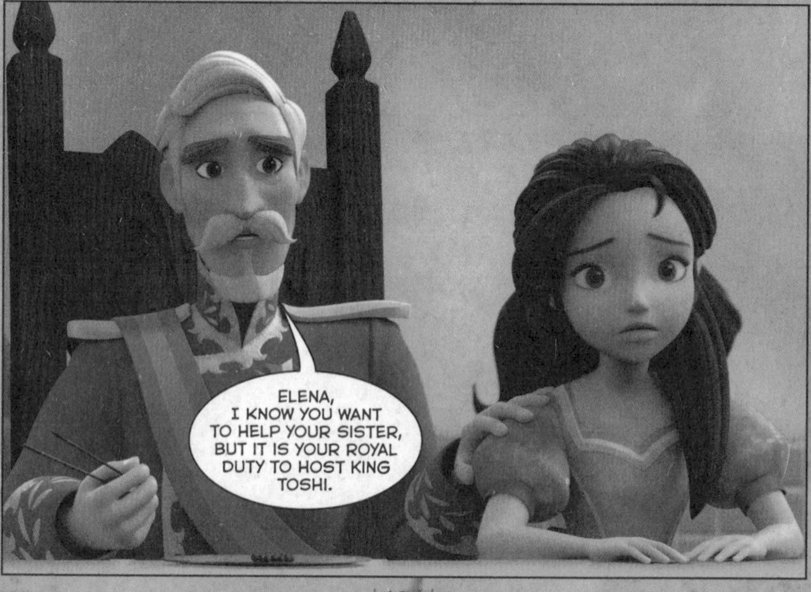
ELENA, I KNOW YOU WANT TO HELP YOUR SISTER, BUT IT IS YOUR ROYAL DUTY TO HOST KING TOSHI.

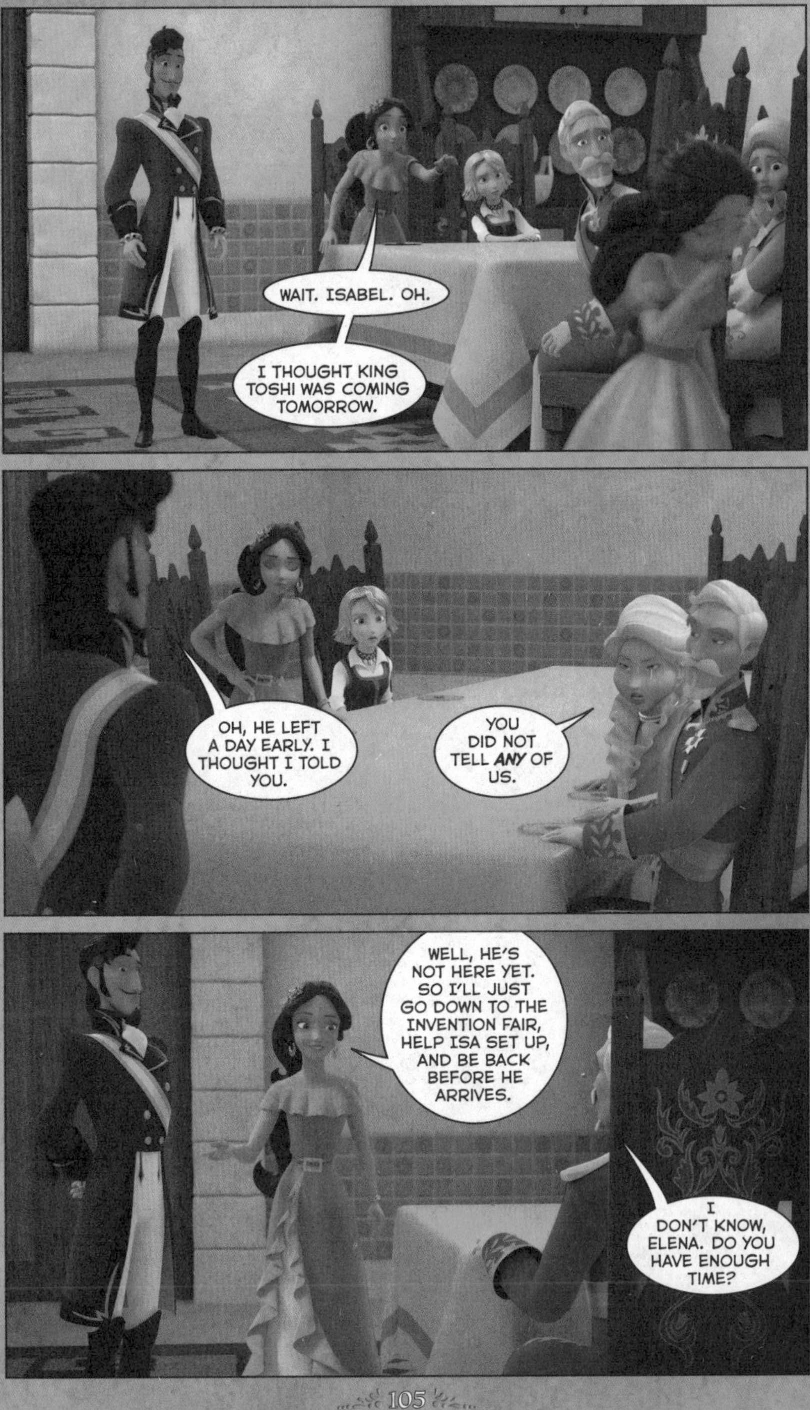
WAIT. ISABEL. OH.
I THOUGHT KING TOSHI WAS COMING TOMORROW.
OH, HE LEFT A DAY EARLY. I THOUGHT I TOLD YOU.
YOU DID NOT TELL *ANY* OF US.
WELL, HE'S NOT HERE YET. SO I'LL JUST GO DOWN TO THE INVENTION FAIR, HELP ISA SET UP, AND BE BACK BEFORE HE ARRIVES.
I DON'T KNOW, ELENA. DO YOU HAVE ENOUGH TIME?

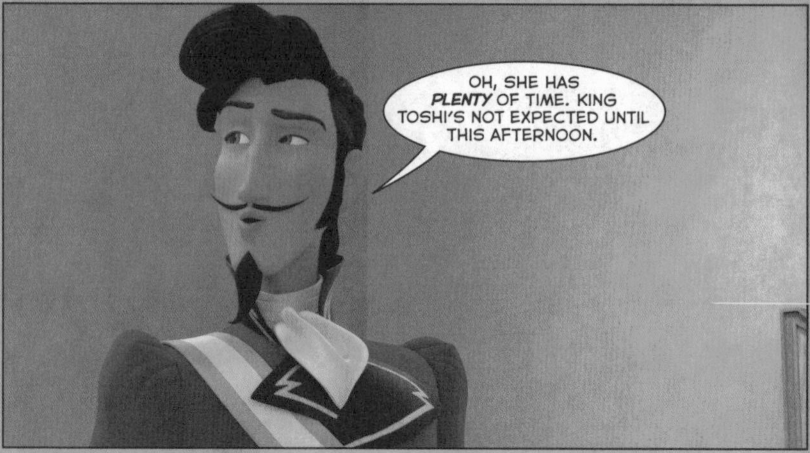
OH, SHE HAS *PLENTY* OF TIME. KING TOSHI'S NOT EXPECTED UNTIL THIS AFTERNOON.

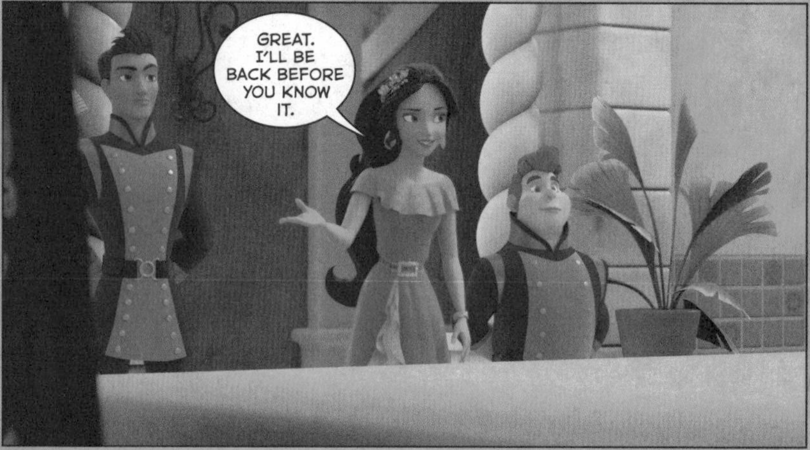
GREAT. I'LL BE BACK BEFORE YOU KNOW IT.

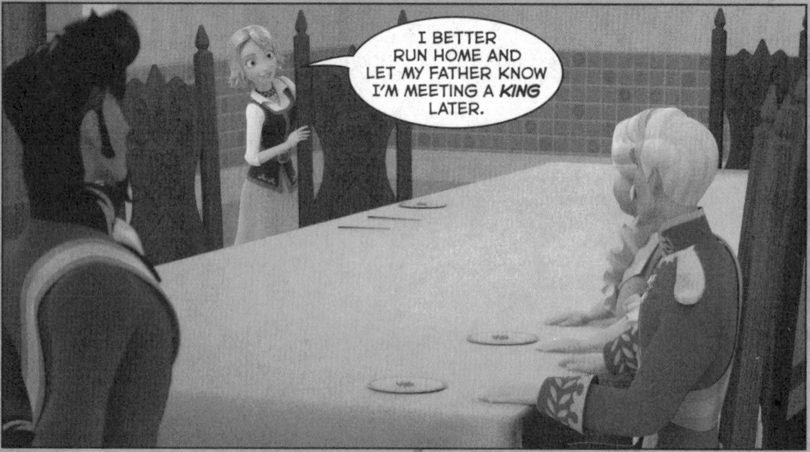
I BETTER RUN HOME AND LET MY FATHER KNOW I'M MEETING A *KING* LATER.

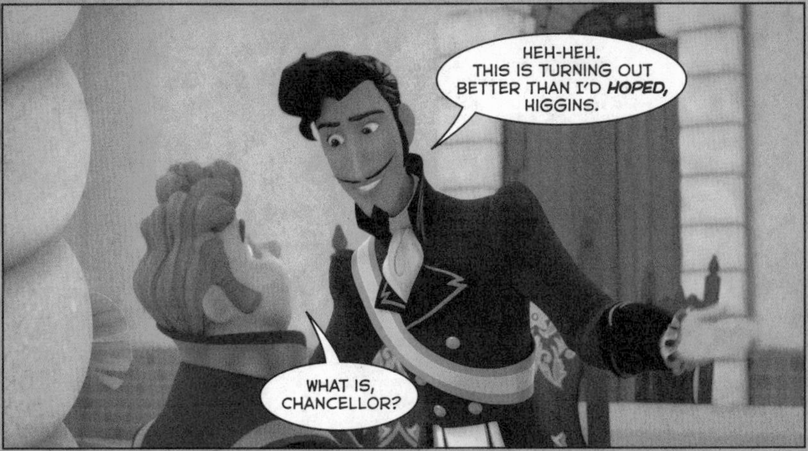
HEH-HEH.
THIS IS TURNING OUT BETTER THAN I'D *HOPED,* HIGGINS.
WHAT IS, CHANCELLOR?

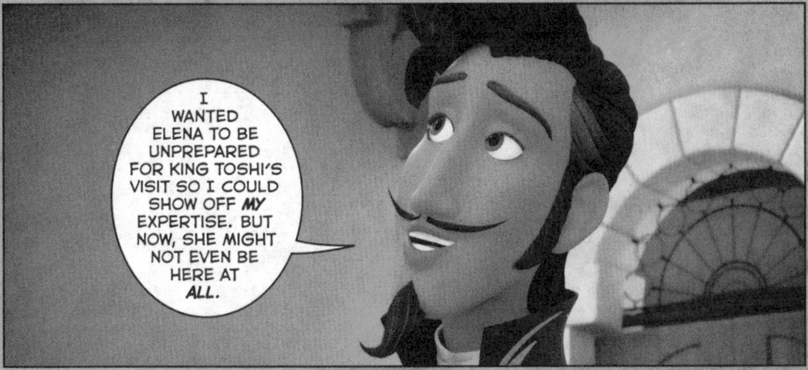
I WANTED ELENA TO BE UNPREPARED FOR KING TOSHI'S VISIT SO I COULD SHOW OFF *MY* EXPERTISE. BUT NOW, SHE MIGHT NOT EVEN BE HERE AT *ALL.*

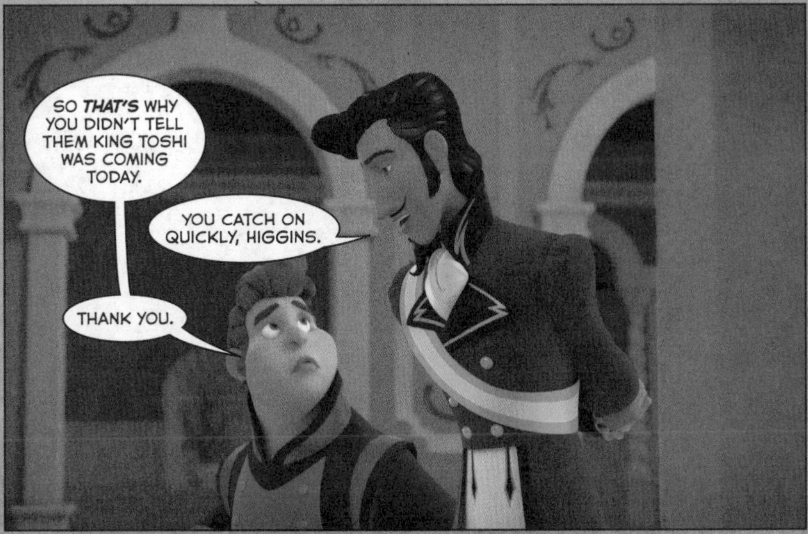
SO *THAT'S* WHY YOU DIDN'T TELL THEM KING TOSHI WAS COMING TODAY.
YOU CATCH ON QUICKLY, HIGGINS.
THANK YOU.

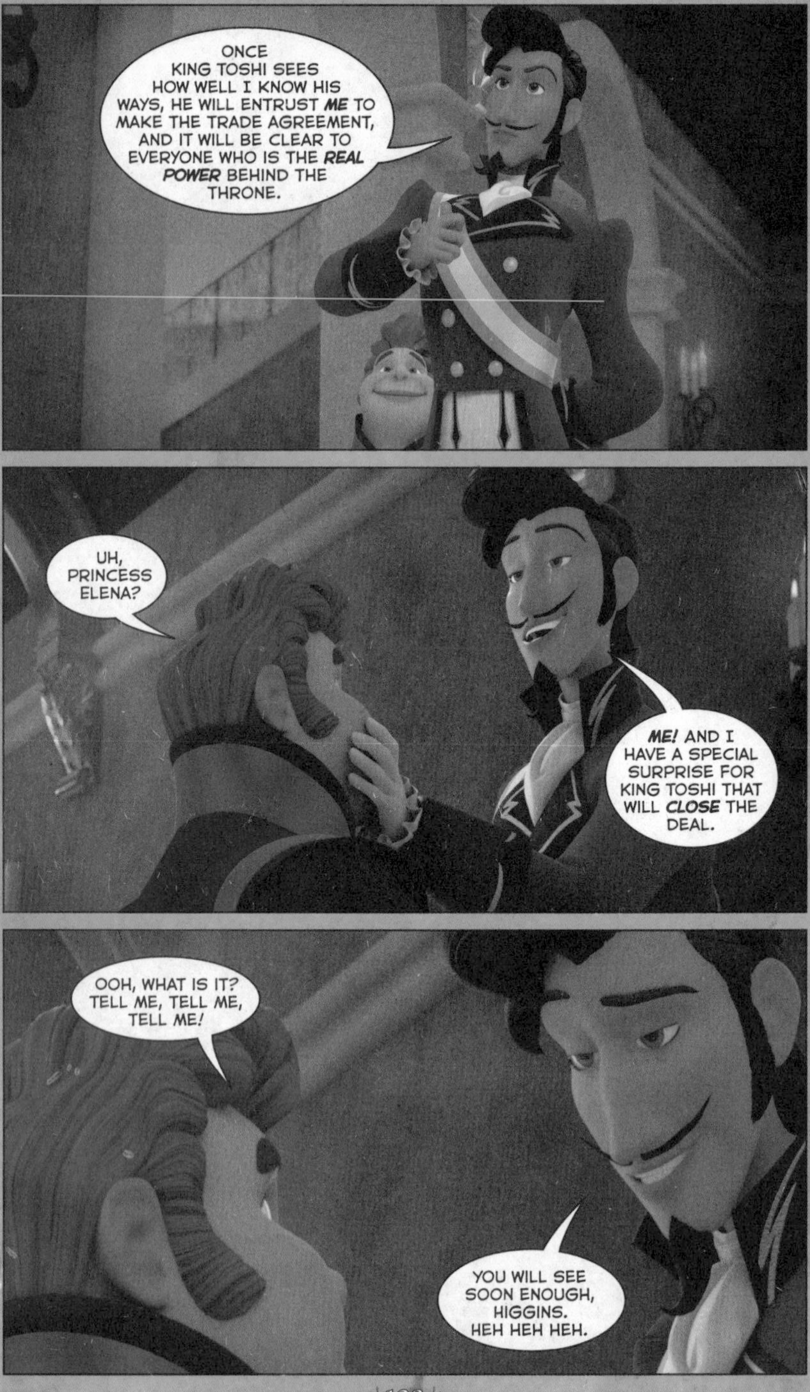
ONCE KING TOSHI SEES HOW WELL I KNOW HIS WAYS, HE WILL ENTRUST *ME* TO MAKE THE TRADE AGREEMENT, AND IT WILL BE CLEAR TO EVERYONE WHO IS THE *REAL POWER* BEHIND THE THRONE.
UH, PRINCESS ELENA?
ME! AND I HAVE A SPECIAL SURPRISE FOR KING TOSHI THAT WILL *CLOSE* THE DEAL.
OOH, WHAT IS IT? TELL ME, TELL ME, TELL ME!
YOU WILL SEE SOON ENOUGH, HIGGINS. HEH HEH HEH.

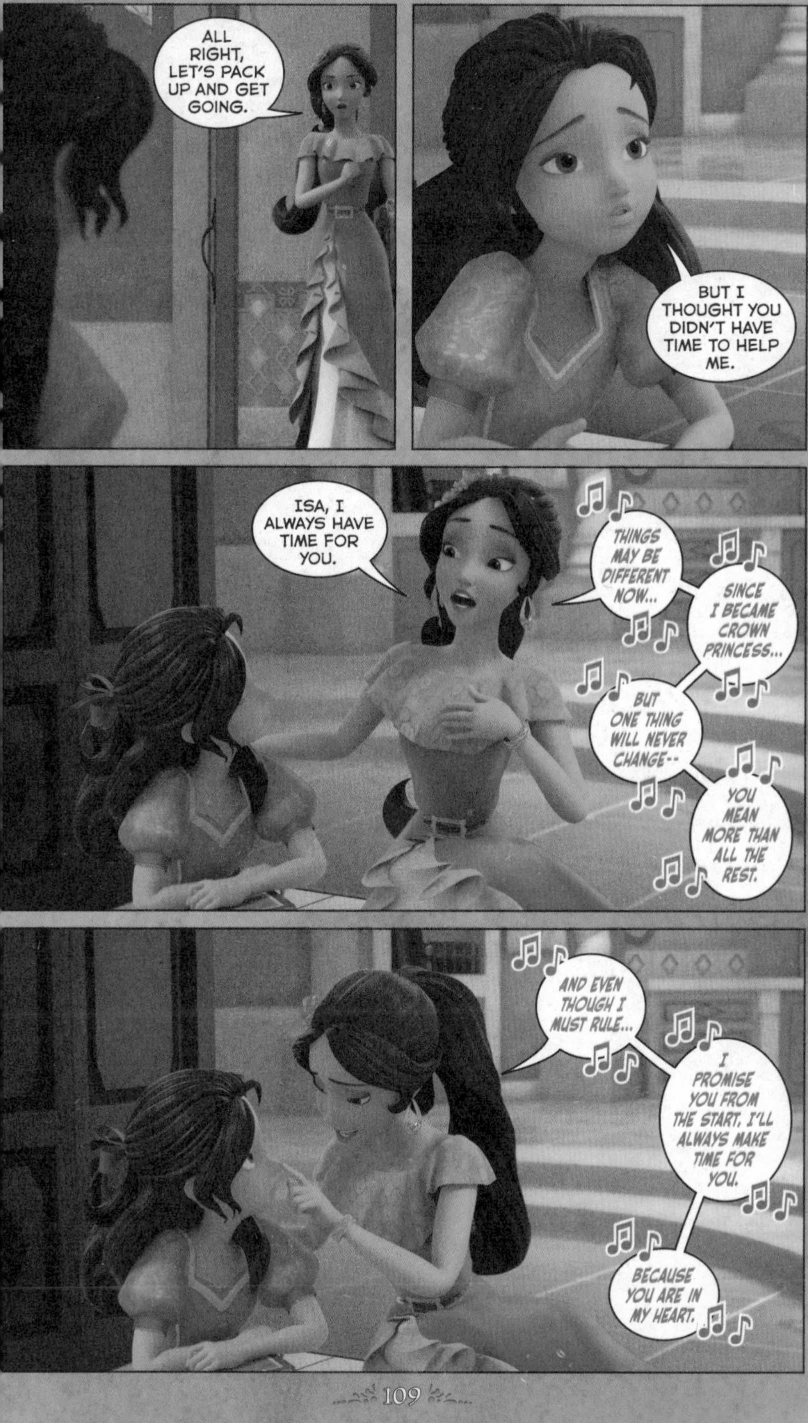
ALL RIGHT, LET'S PACK UP AND GET GOING.
BUT I THOUGHT YOU DIDN'T HAVE TIME TO HELP ME.
ISA, I ALWAYS HAVE TIME FOR YOU.
THINGS MAY BE DIFFERENT NOW...
SINCE I BECAME CROWN PRINCESS...
BUT ONE THING WILL NEVER CHANGE--
YOU MEAN MORE THAN ALL THE REST.
AND EVEN THOUGH I MUST RULE...
I PROMISE YOU FROM THE START, I'LL ALWAYS MAKE TIME FOR YOU.
BECAUSE YOU ARE IN MY HEART.

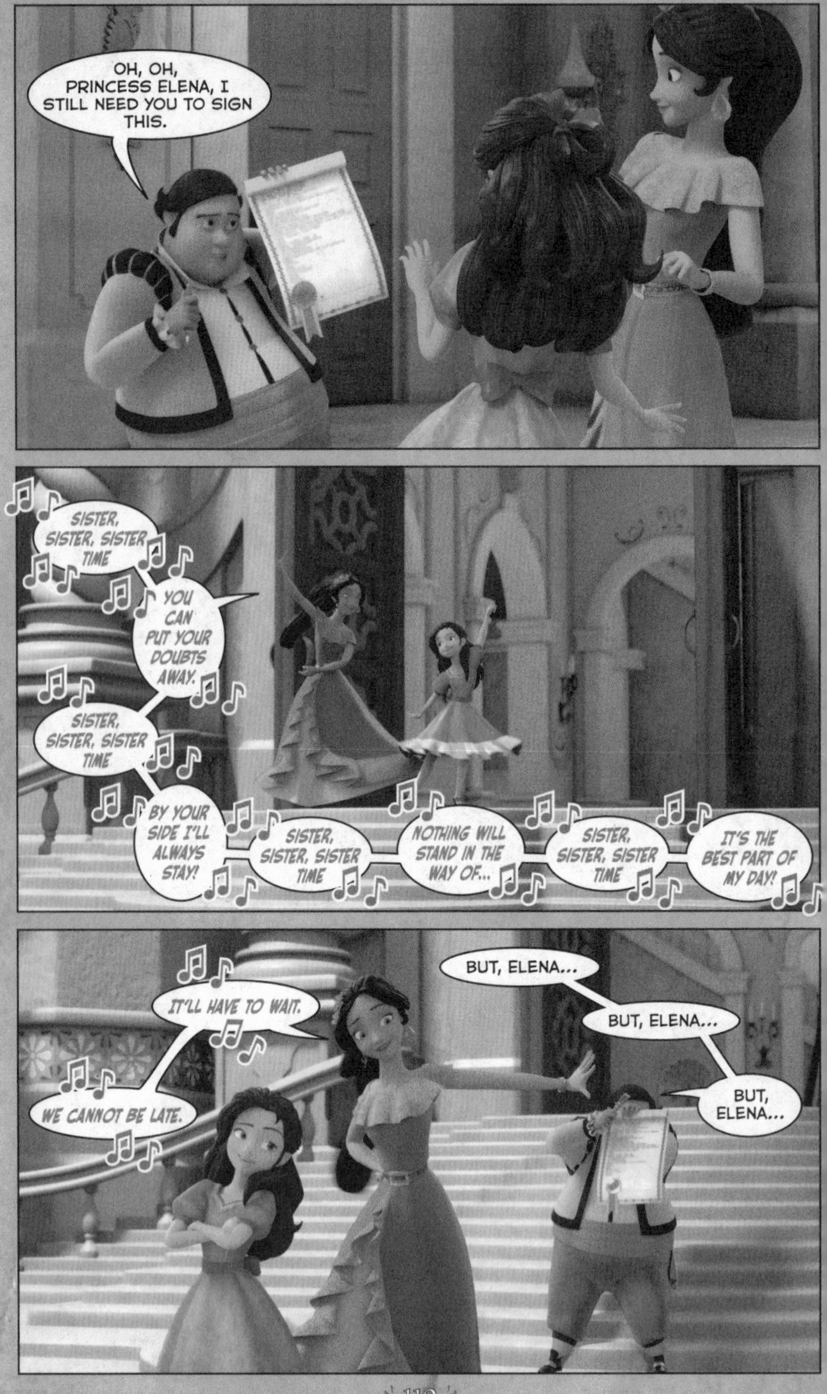
OH, OH, PRINCESS ELENA, I STILL NEED YOU TO SIGN THIS.
SISTER, SISTER, SISTER TIME
YOU CAN PUT YOUR DOUBTS AWAY.
SISTER, SISTER, SISTER TIME
BY YOUR SIDE I'LL ALWAYS STAY!
SISTER, SISTER, SISTER TIME
NOTHING WILL STAND IN THE WAY OF...
SISTER, SISTER, SISTER TIME
IT'S THE BEST PART OF MY DAY!
IT'LL HAVE TO WAIT.
WE CANNOT BE LATE.
BUT, ELENA...
BUT, ELENA...
BUT, ELENA...

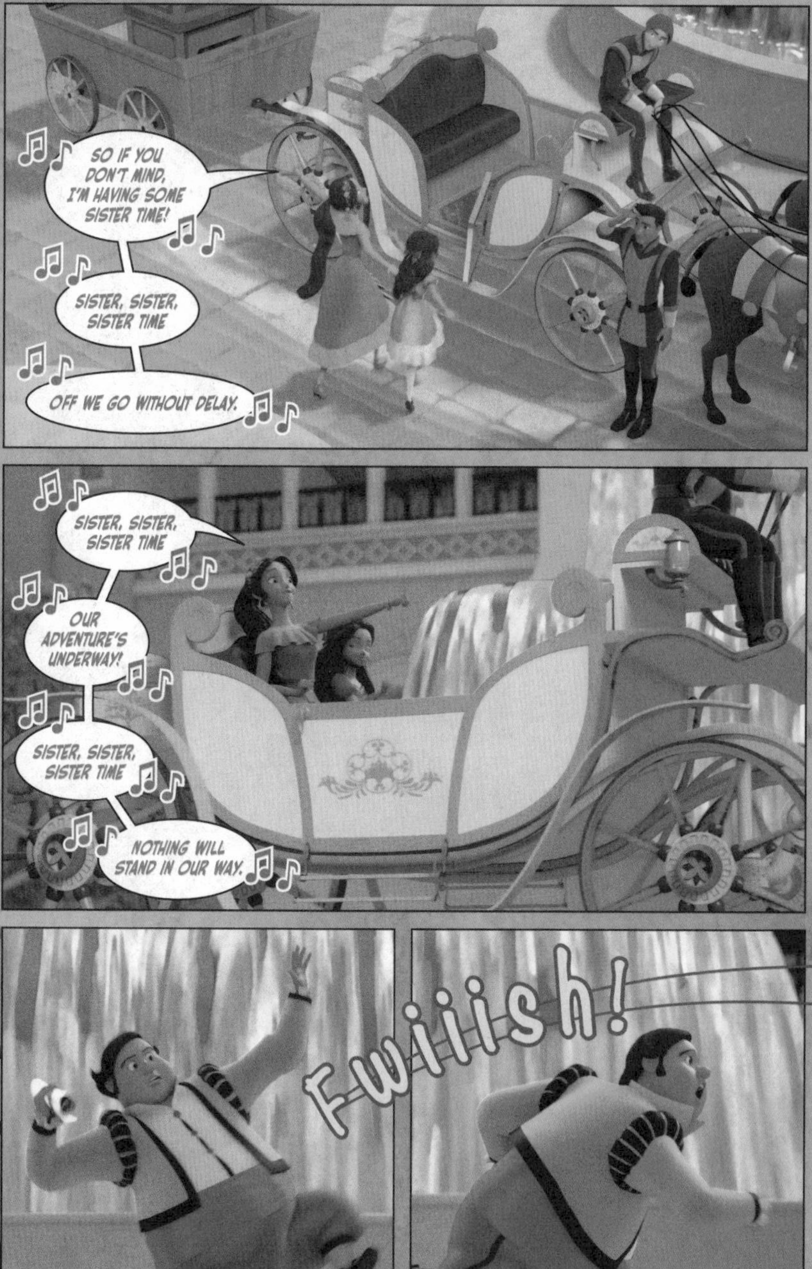
SO IF YOU DON'T MIND, I'M HAVING SOME SISTER TIME!
SISTER, SISTER, SISTER TIME
OFF WE GO WITHOUT DELAY.
SISTER, SISTER, SISTER TIME
OUR ADVENTURE'S UNDERWAY!
SISTER, SISTER, SISTER TIME
NOTHING WILL STAND IN OUR WAY.
Fwiiish!

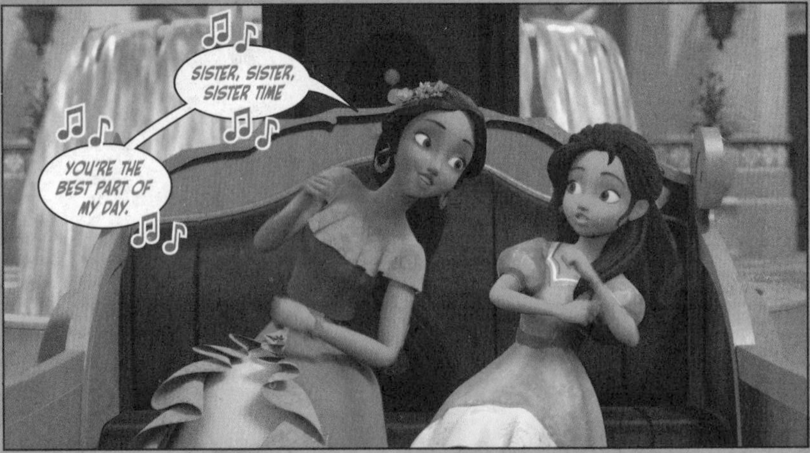
SISTER, SISTER, SISTER TIME
YOU'RE THE BEST PART OF MY DAY.

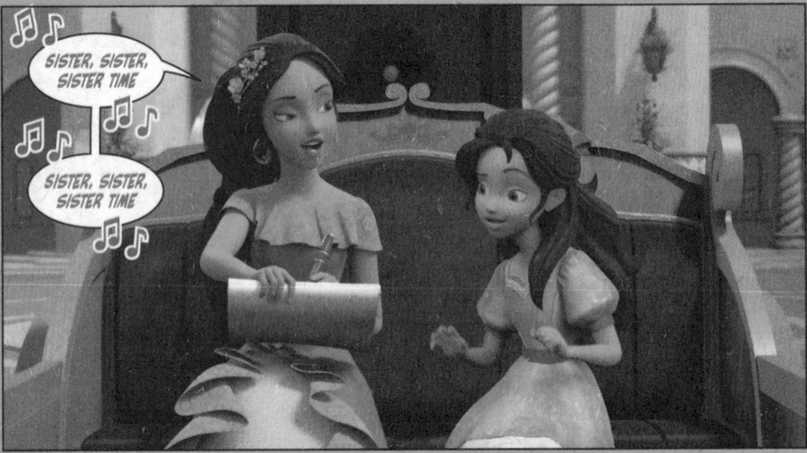
SISTER, SISTER, SISTER TIME
SISTER, SISTER, SISTER TIME

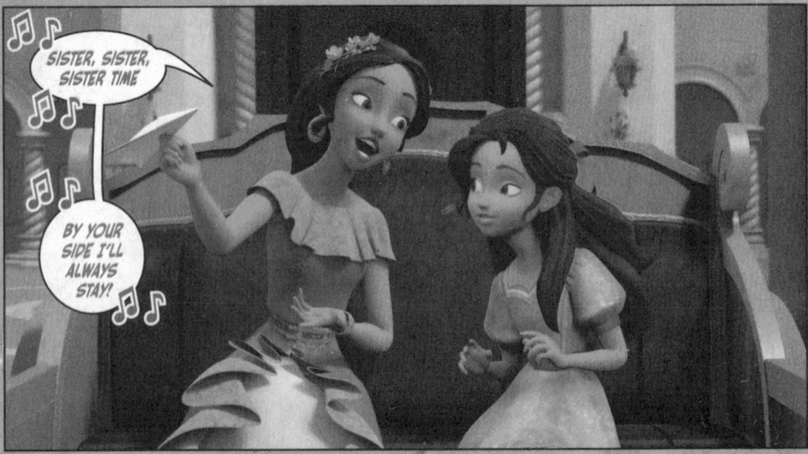
SISTER, SISTER, SISTER TIME
BY YOUR SIDE I'LL ALWAYS STAY!

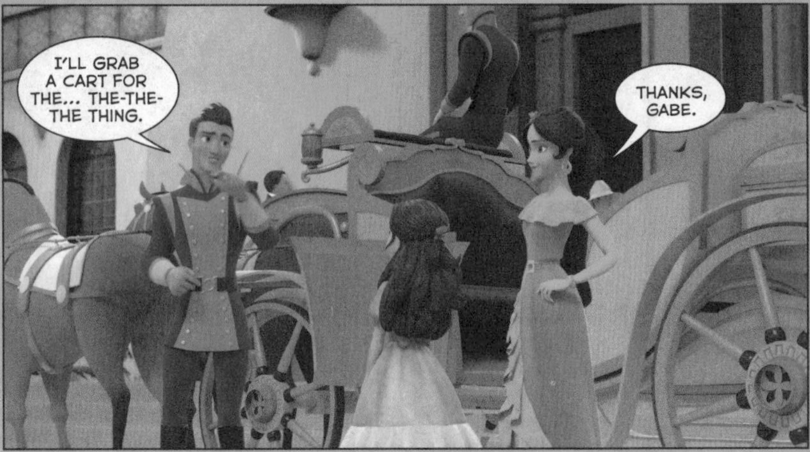
I'LL GRAB A CART FOR THE... THE-THE-THE THING.
THANKS, GABE.

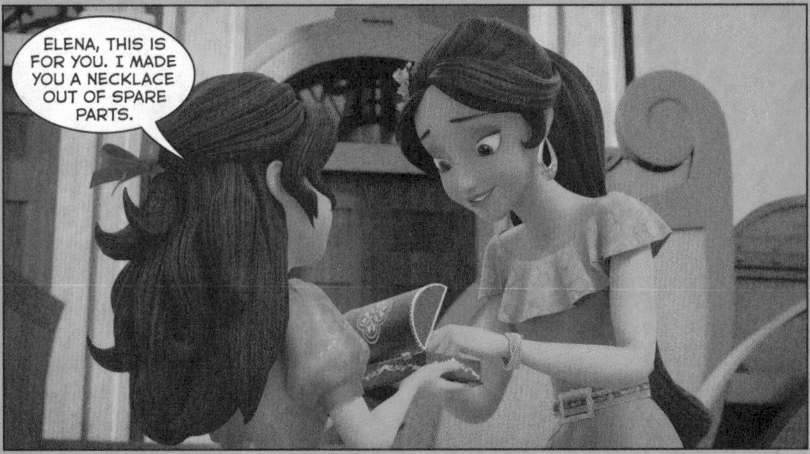
ELENA, THIS IS FOR YOU. I MADE YOU A NECKLACE OUT OF SPARE PARTS.

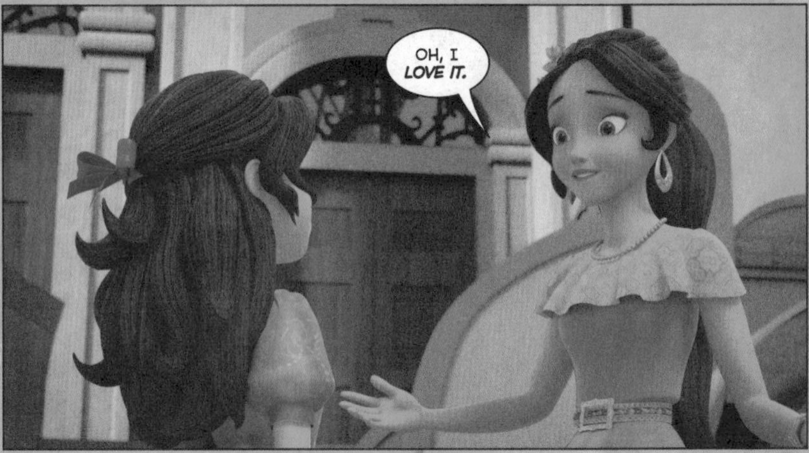
OH, I *LOVE IT.*

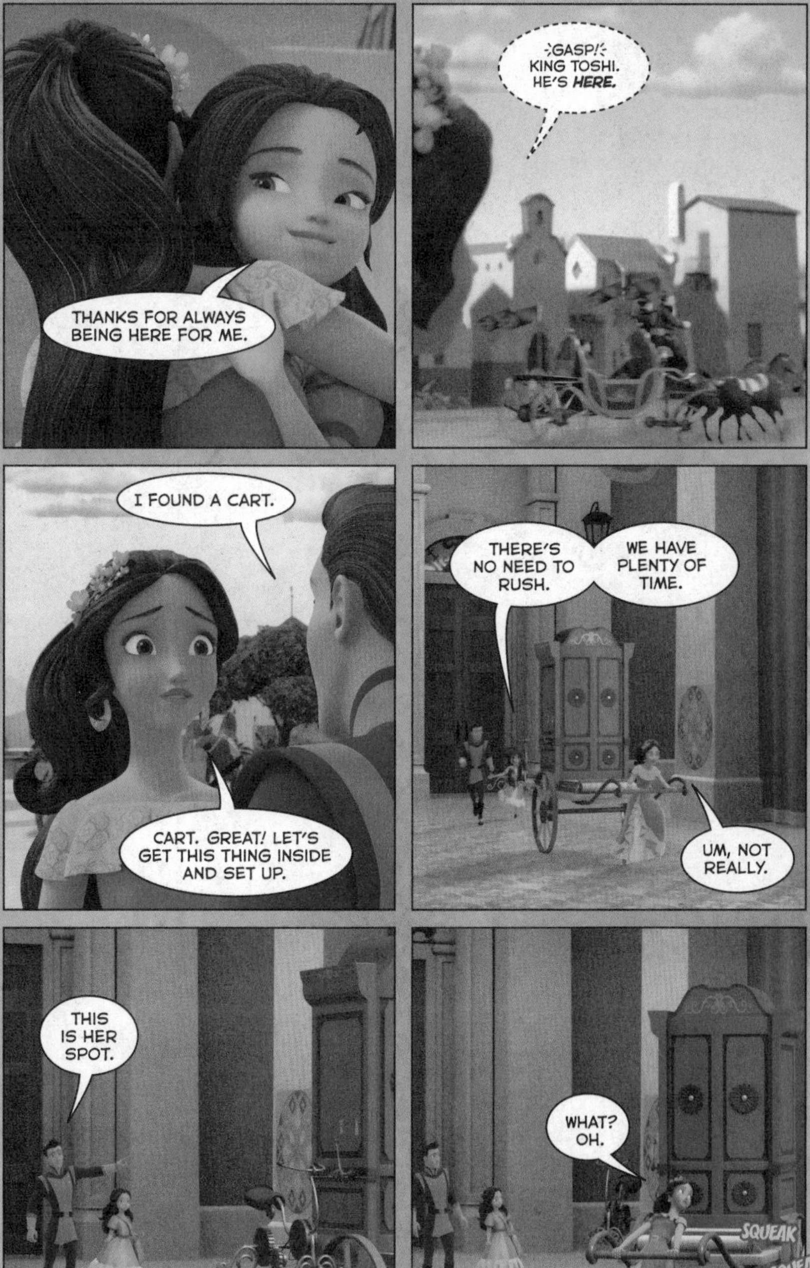
THANKS FOR ALWAYS BEING HERE FOR ME.
GASP! KING TOSHI. HE'S *HERE.*
I FOUND A CART.
CART. GREAT! LET'S GET THIS THING INSIDE AND SET UP.
THERE'S NO NEED TO RUSH.
WE HAVE PLENTY OF TIME.
UM, NOT REALLY.
THIS IS HER SPOT.
WHAT? OH.
SQUEAK
SQUEAK

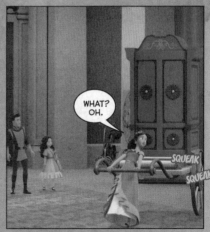

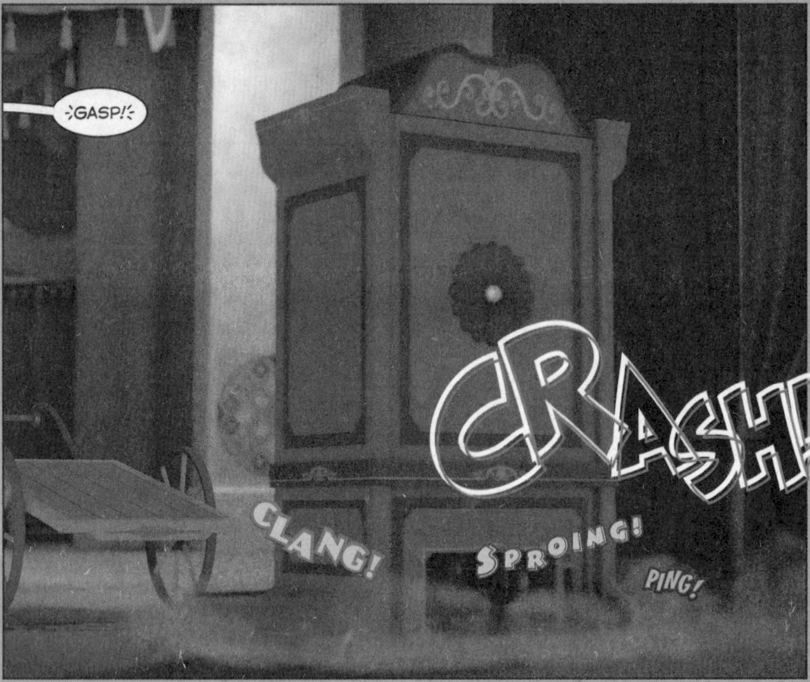

GASP!
CRASH!
CLANG!
SPROING!
PING!

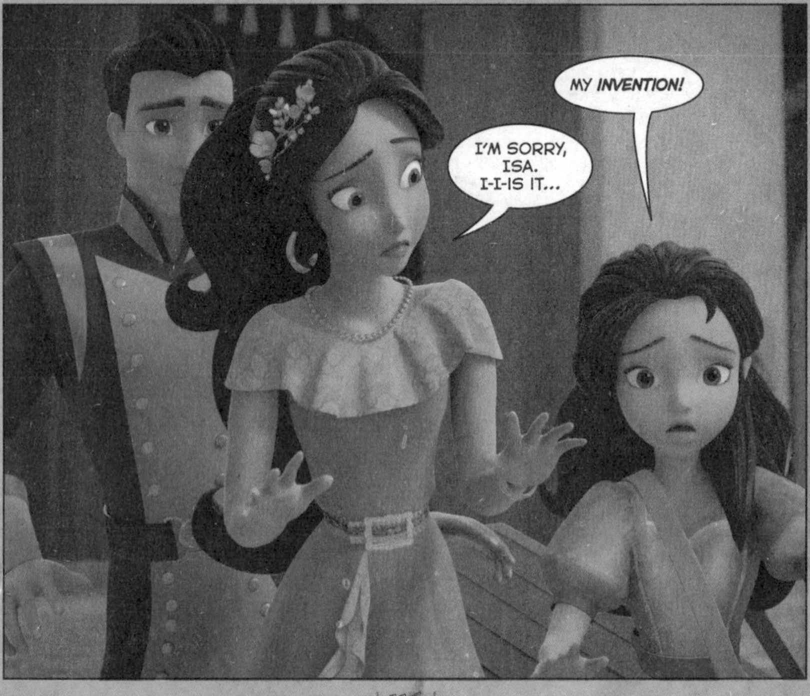

MY INVENTION!
I'M SORRY, ISA. I-I-IS IT...

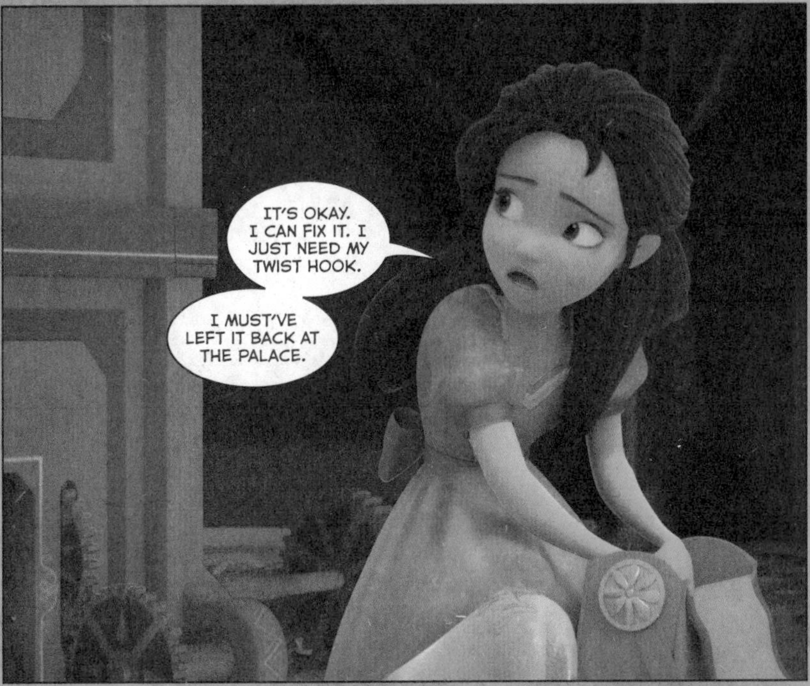
IT'S OKAY. I CAN FIX IT. I JUST NEED MY TWIST HOOK.
I MUST'VE LEFT IT BACK AT THE PALACE.

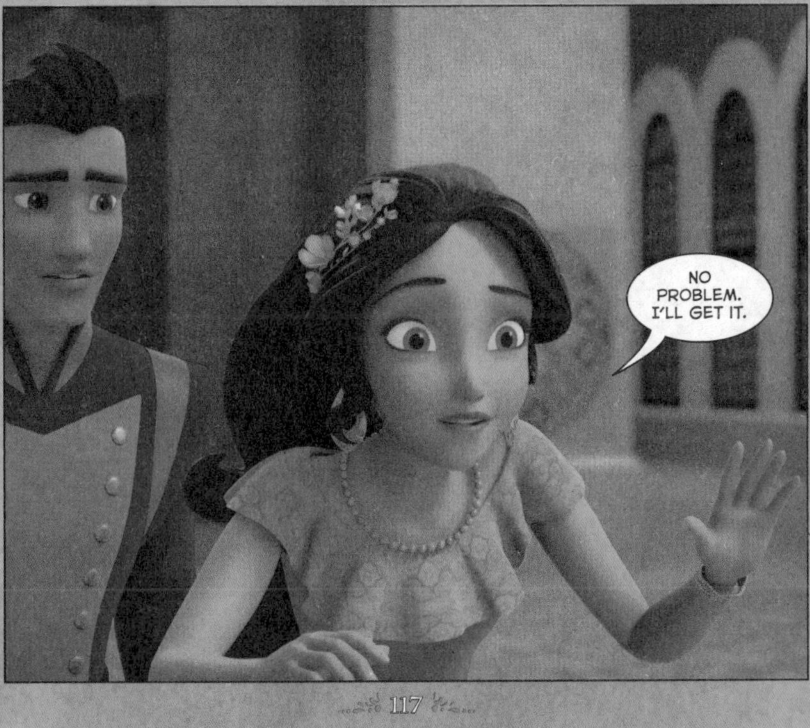
NO PROBLEM. I'LL GET IT.

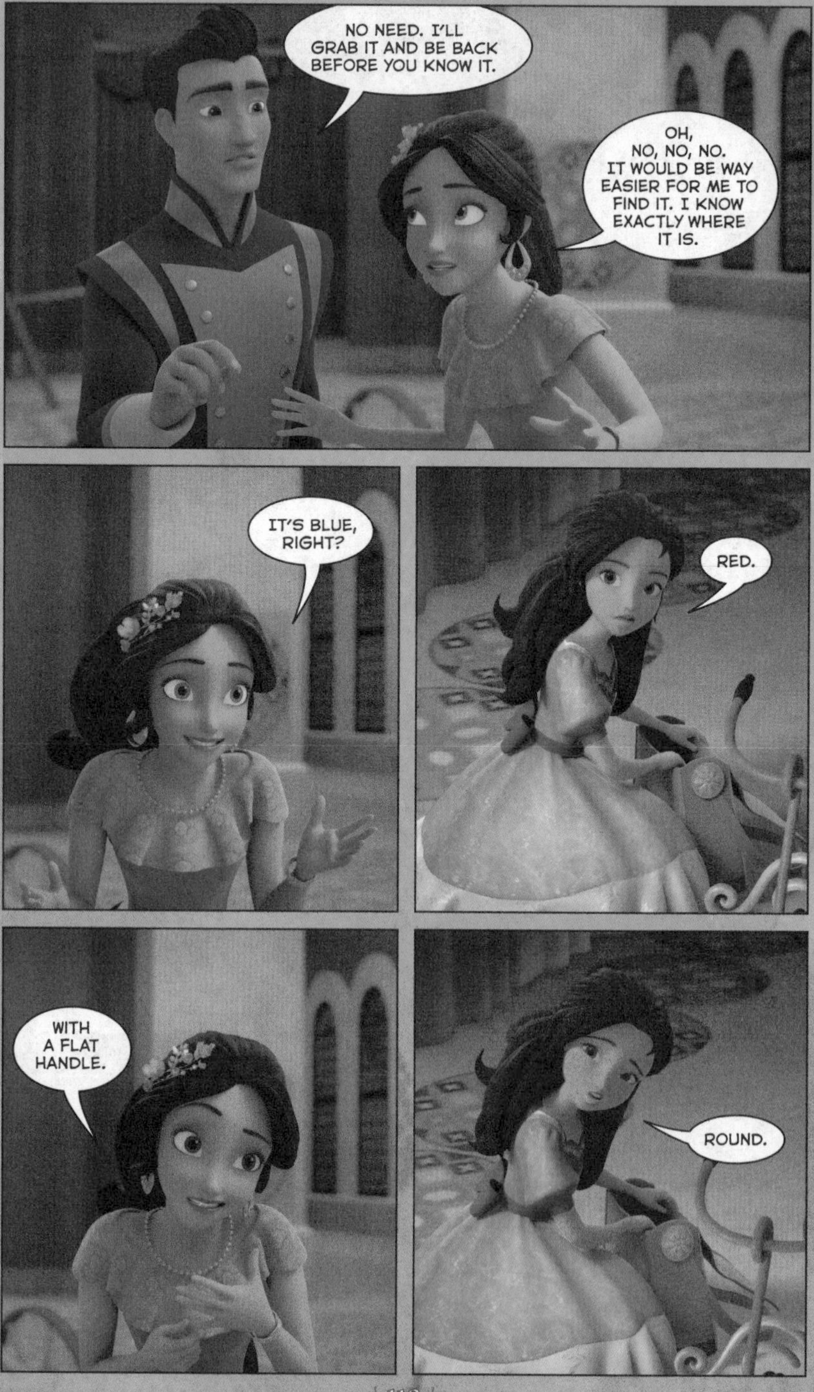
NO NEED. I'LL GRAB IT AND BE BACK BEFORE YOU KNOW IT.
OH, NO, NO, NO. IT WOULD BE WAY EASIER FOR ME TO FIND IT. I KNOW EXACTLY WHERE IT IS.
IT'S BLUE, RIGHT?
RED.
WITH A FLAT HANDLE.
ROUND.

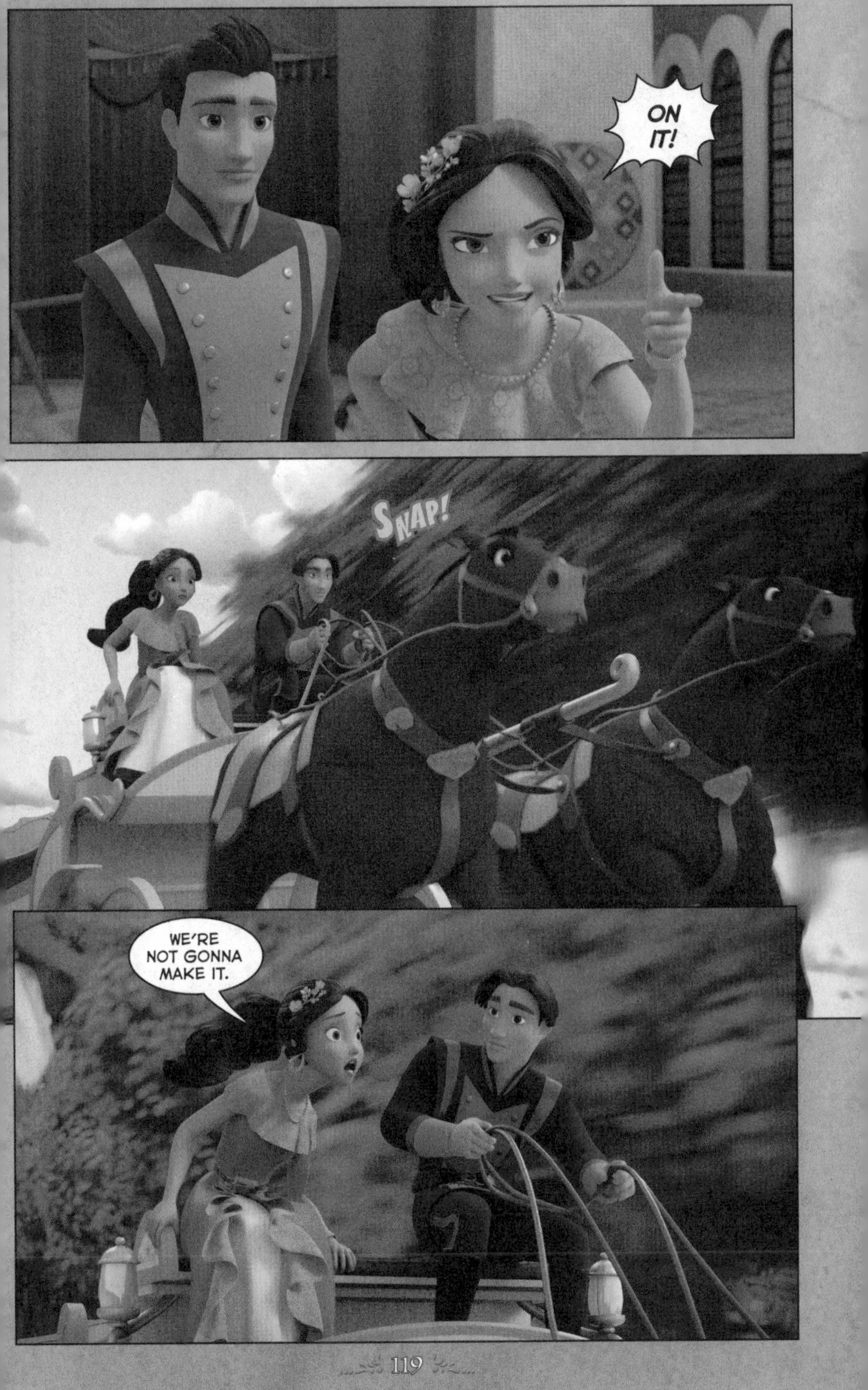
ON IT!
SNAP!
WE'RE NOT GONNA MAKE IT.

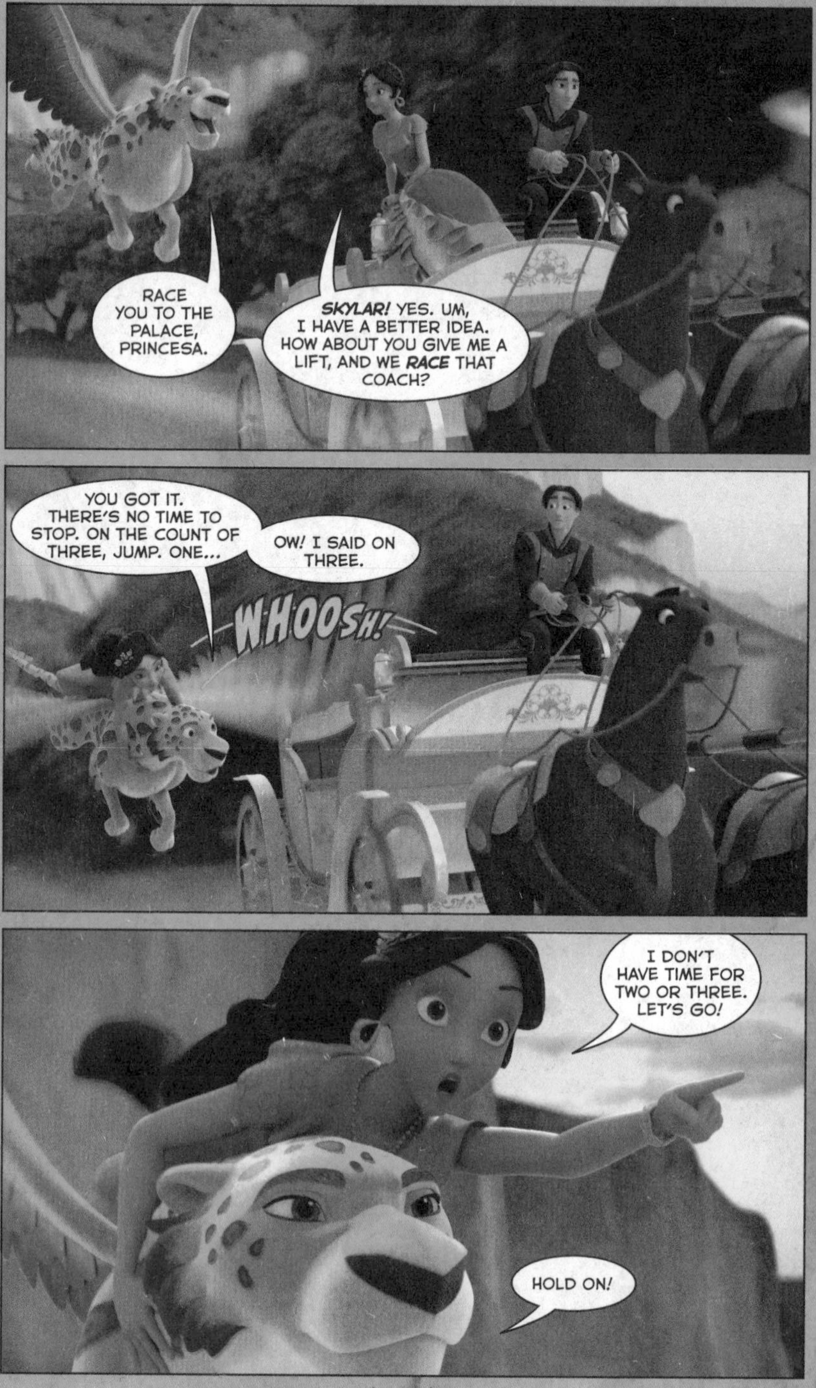
RACE YOU TO THE PALACE, PRINCESA.
SKYLAR! YES. UM, I HAVE A BETTER IDEA. HOW ABOUT YOU GIVE ME A LIFT, AND WE RACE THAT COACH?
YOU GOT IT. THERE'S NO TIME TO STOP. ON THE COUNT OF THREE, JUMP. ONE...
OW! I SAID ON THREE.
WHOOSH!
I DON'T HAVE TIME FOR TWO OR THREE. LET'S GO!
HOLD ON!

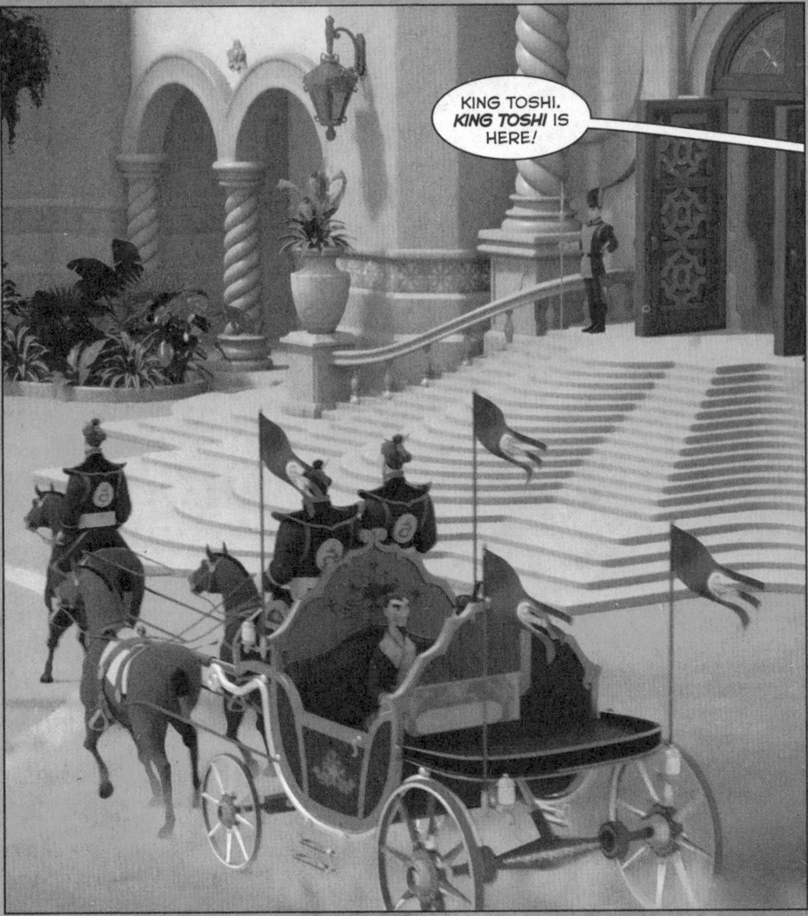
KING TOSHI. *KING TOSHI* IS HERE!

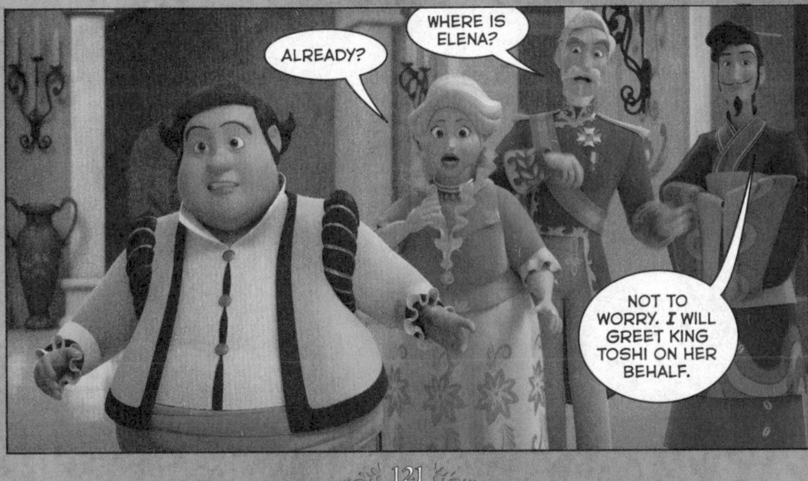
ALREADY?
WHERE IS ELENA?
NOT TO WORRY. *I* WILL GREET KING TOSHI ON HER BEHALF.

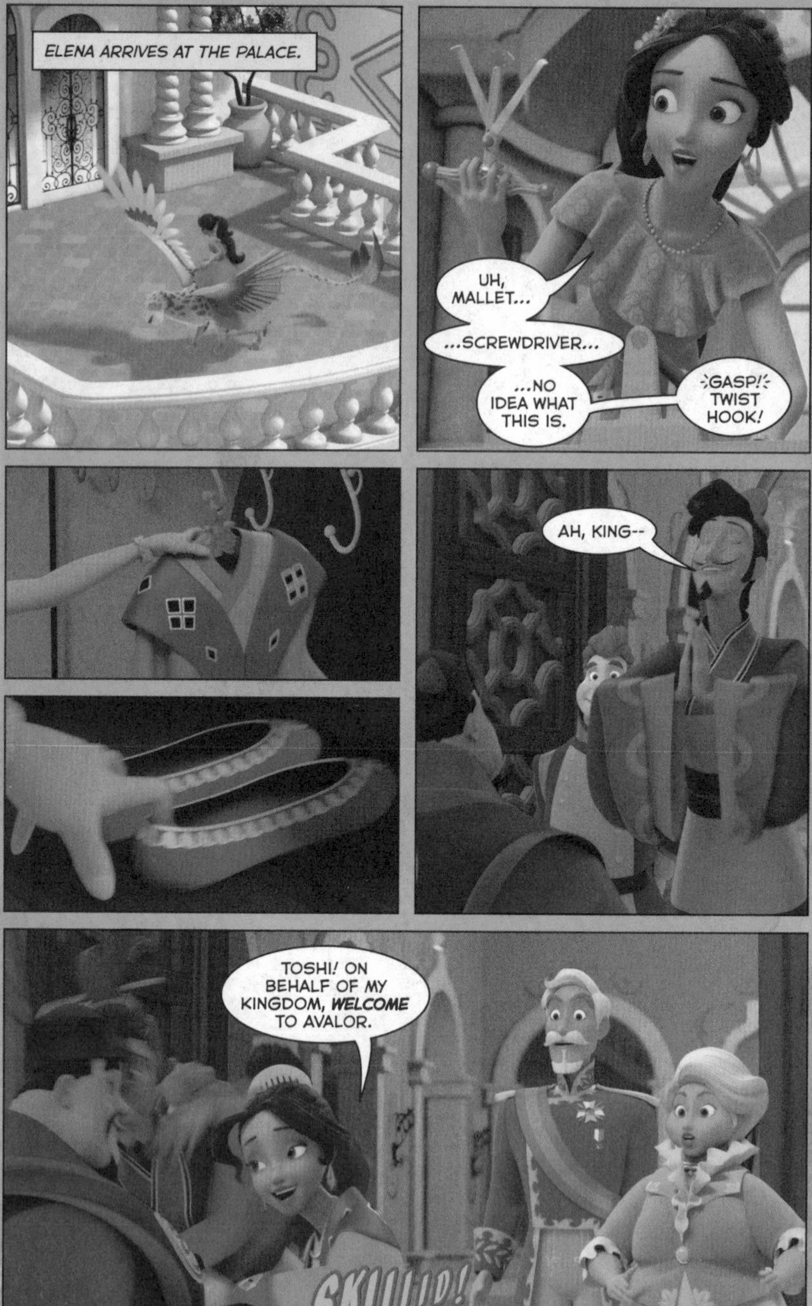
ELENA ARRIVES AT THE PALACE.
UH, MALLET...
...SCREWDRIVER...
...NO IDEA WHAT THIS IS.
GASP! TWIST HOOK!
AH, KING--
TOSHI! ON BEHALF OF MY KINGDOM, WELCOME TO AVALOR.
SKIIIID!

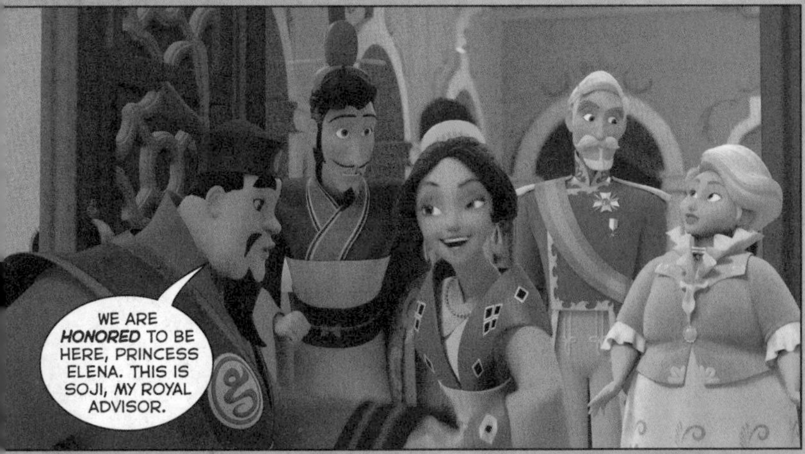
WE ARE *HONORED* TO BE HERE, PRINCESS ELENA. THIS IS SOJI, MY ROYAL ADVISOR.

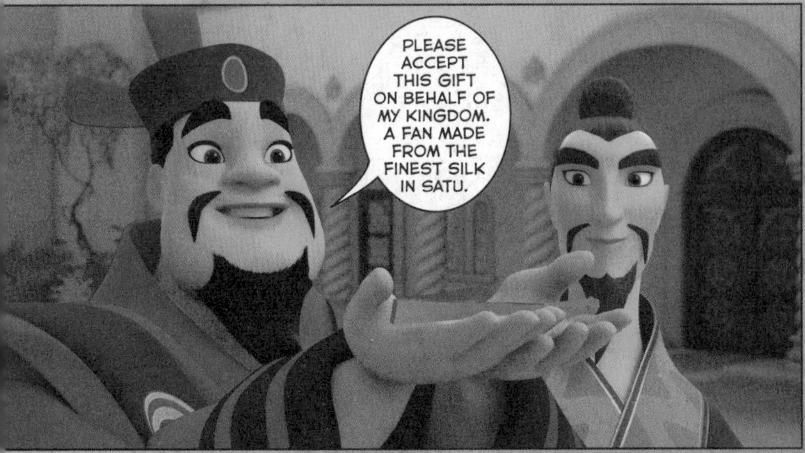
PLEASE ACCEPT THIS GIFT ON BEHALF OF MY KINGDOM. A FAN MADE FROM THE FINEST SILK IN SATU.

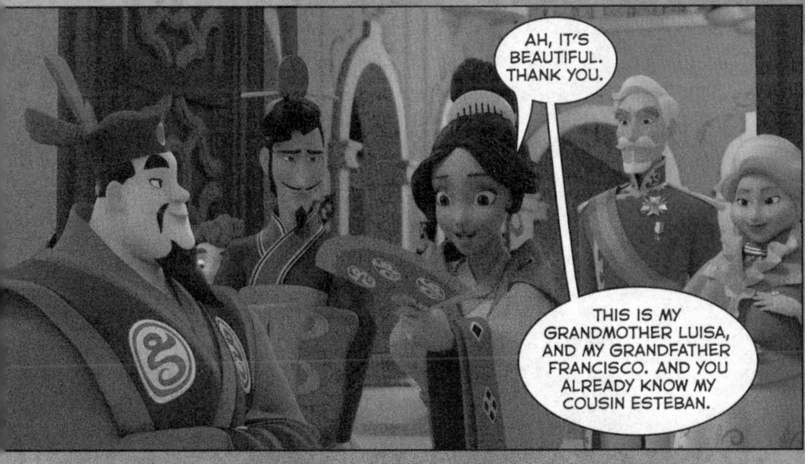
AH, IT'S BEAUTIFUL. THANK YOU.
THIS IS MY GRANDMOTHER LUISA, AND MY GRANDFATHER FRANCISCO. AND YOU ALREADY KNOW MY COUSIN ESTEBAN.

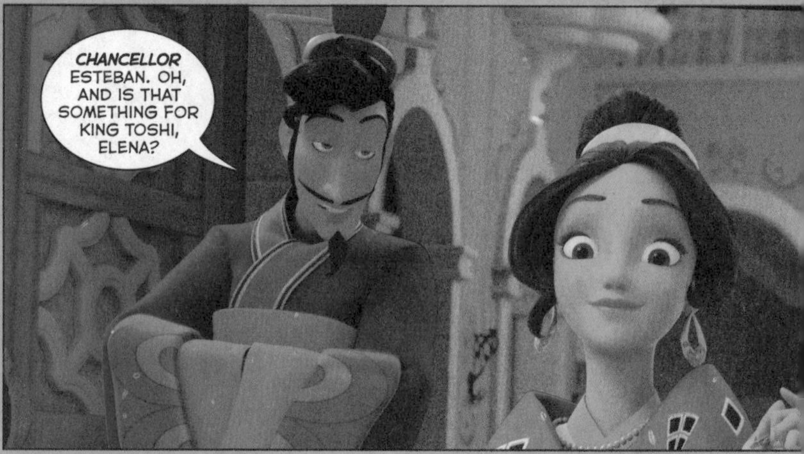
CHANCELLOR ESTEBAN. OH, AND IS THAT SOMETHING FOR KING TOSHI, ELENA?

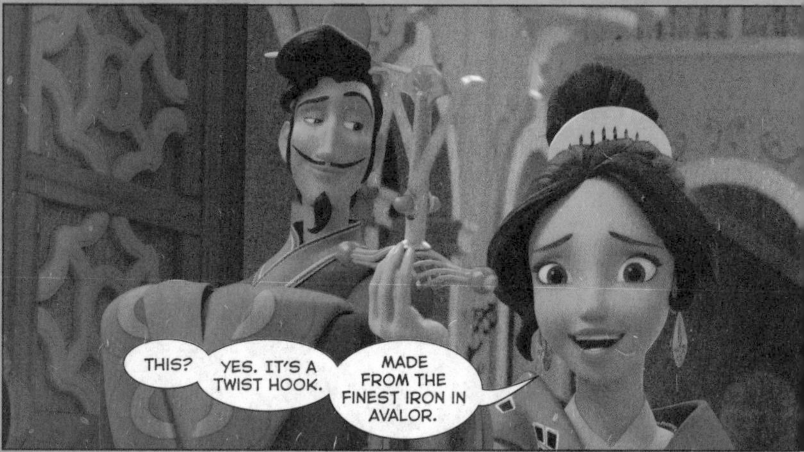
THIS?
YES. IT'S A TWIST HOOK.
MADE FROM THE FINEST IRON IN AVALOR.

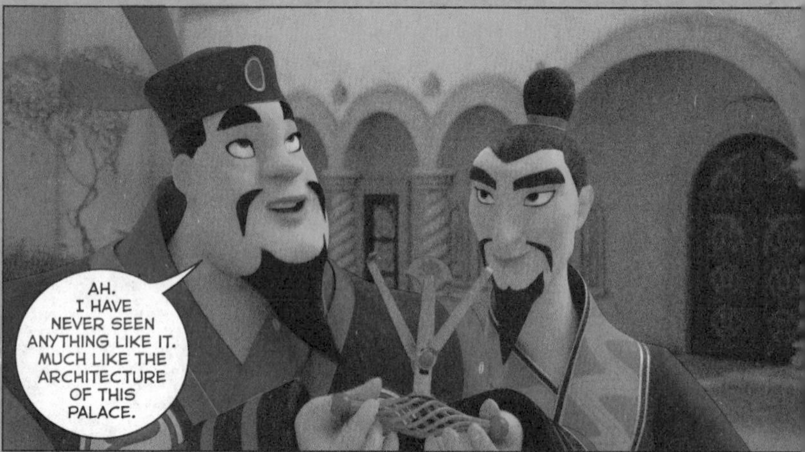
AH. I HAVE NEVER SEEN ANYTHING LIKE IT. MUCH LIKE THE ARCHITECTURE OF THIS PALACE.

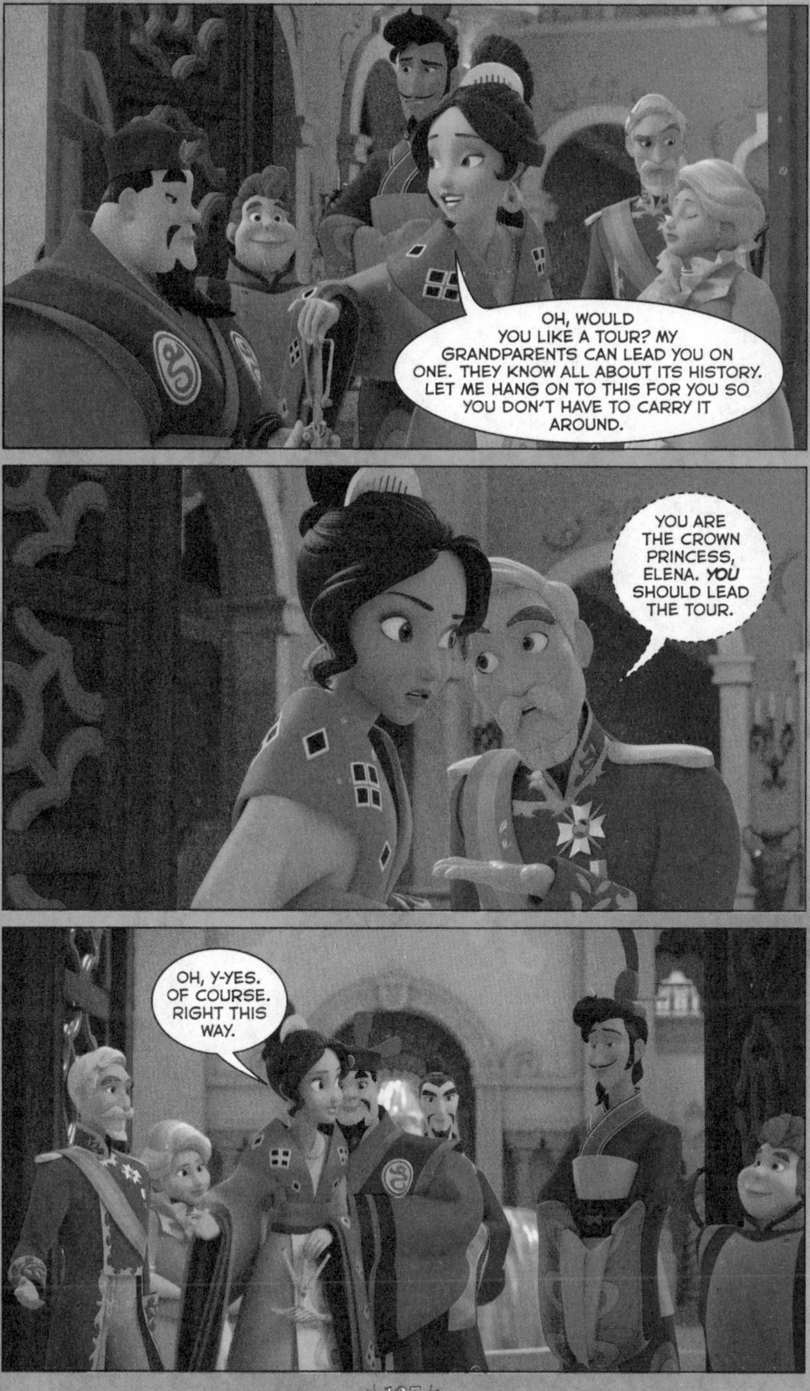
OH, WOULD YOU LIKE A TOUR? MY GRANDPARENTS CAN LEAD YOU ON ONE. THEY KNOW ALL ABOUT ITS HISTORY. LET ME HANG ON TO THIS FOR YOU SO YOU DON'T HAVE TO CARRY IT AROUND.
YOU ARE THE CROWN PRINCESS, ELENA. *YOU* SHOULD LEAD THE TOUR.
OH, Y-YES. OF COURSE. RIGHT THIS WAY.

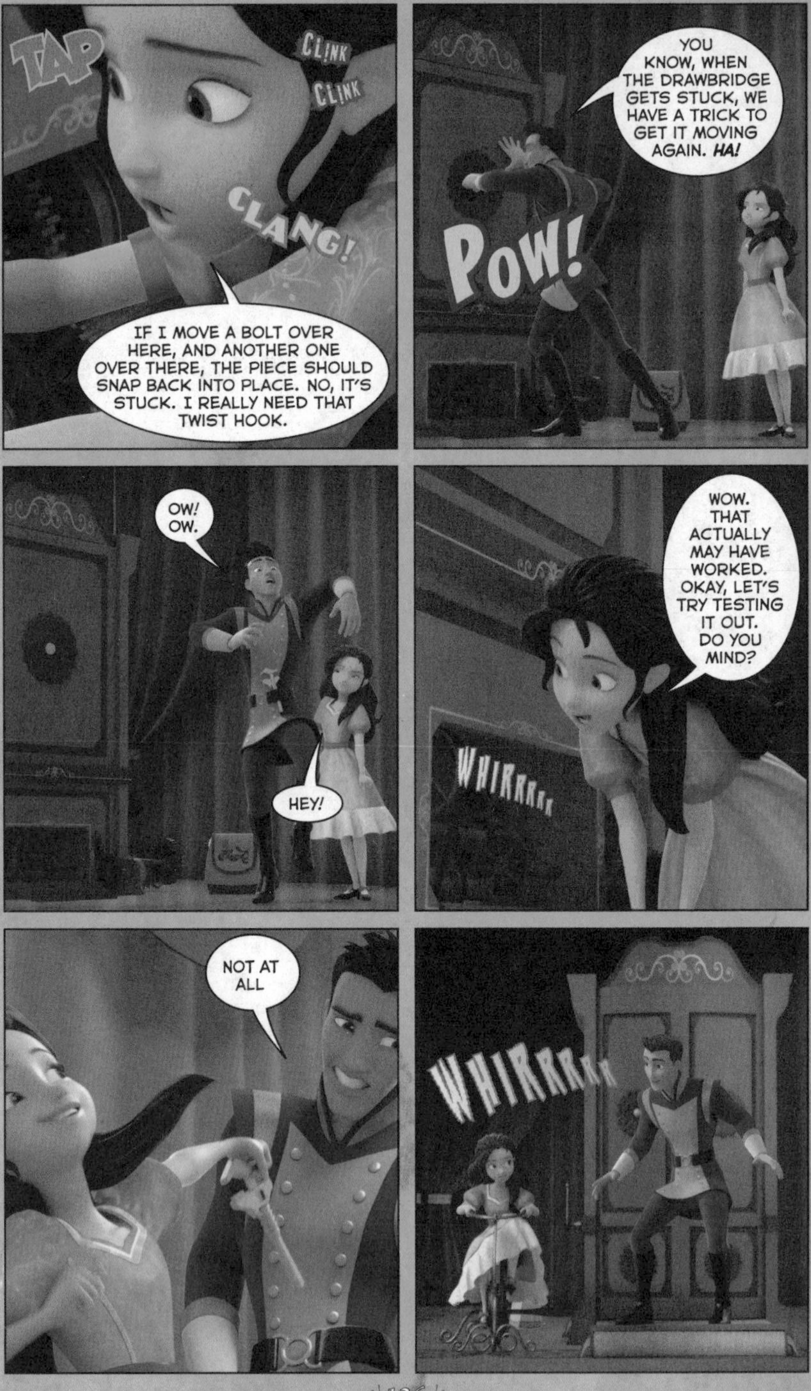
TAP
CLINK
CLINK
CLANG!
IF I MOVE A BOLT OVER HERE, AND ANOTHER ONE OVER THERE, THE PIECE SHOULD SNAP BACK INTO PLACE. NO, IT'S STUCK. I REALLY NEED THAT TWIST HOOK.
YOU KNOW, WHEN THE DRAWBRIDGE GETS STUCK, WE HAVE A TRICK TO GET IT MOVING AGAIN. HA!
POW!
OW! OW.
HEY!
WOW. THAT ACTUALLY MAY HAVE WORKED. OKAY, LET'S TRY TESTING IT OUT. DO YOU MIND?
WHIRRRRR
NOT AT ALL
WHIRRRRR

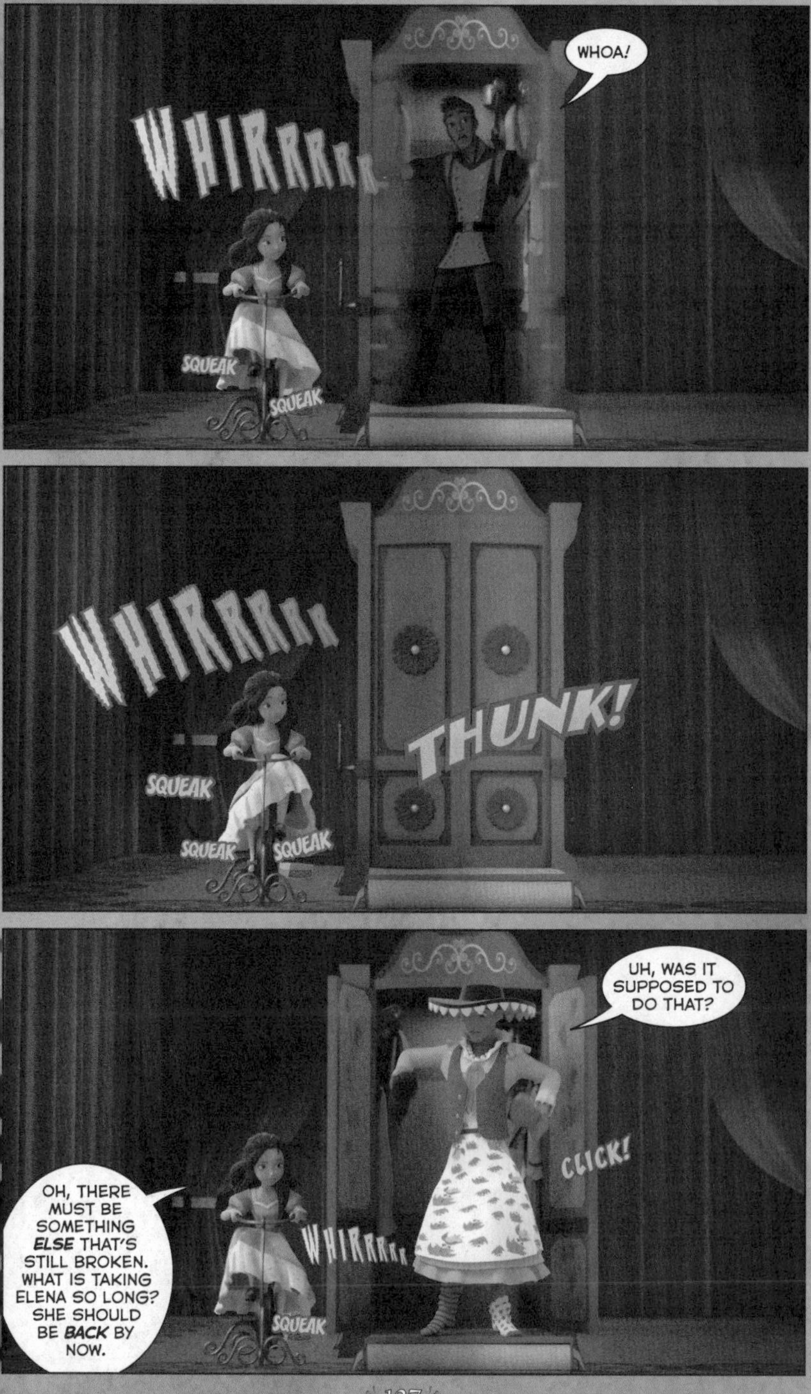
WHIRRRRR
WHOA!
SQUEAK
SQUEAK
WHIRRRRR
THUNK!
SQUEAK
SQUEAK
SQUEAK
UH, WAS IT SUPPOSED TO DO THAT?
CLICK!
OH, THERE MUST BE SOMETHING *ELSE* THAT'S STILL BROKEN. WHAT IS TAKING ELENA SO LONG? SHE SHOULD BE *BACK* BY NOW.
WHIRRRRR
SQUEAK

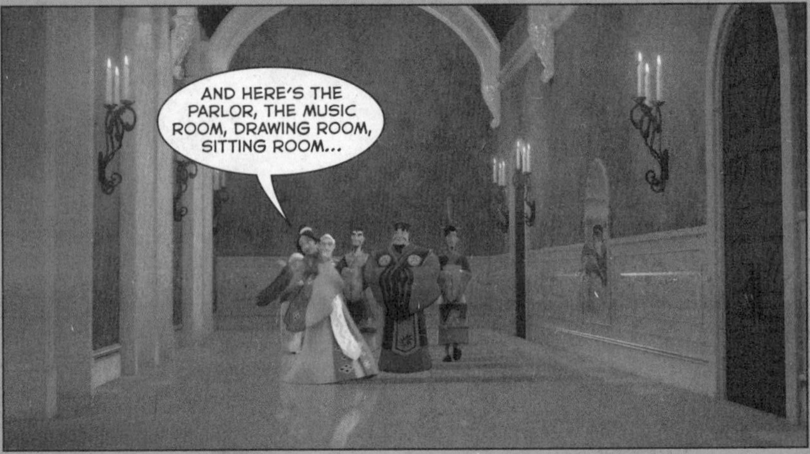
AND HERE'S THE PARLOR, THE MUSIC ROOM, DRAWING ROOM, SITTING ROOM...

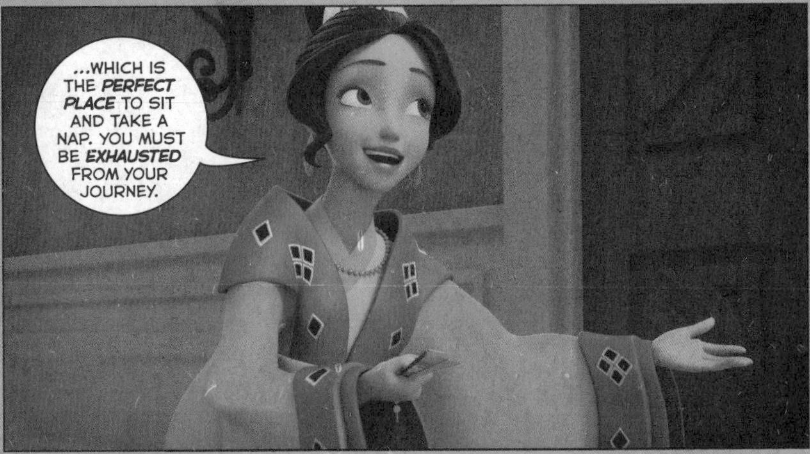
...WHICH IS THE *PERFECT PLACE* TO SIT AND TAKE A NAP. YOU MUST BE *EXHAUSTED* FROM YOUR JOURNEY.

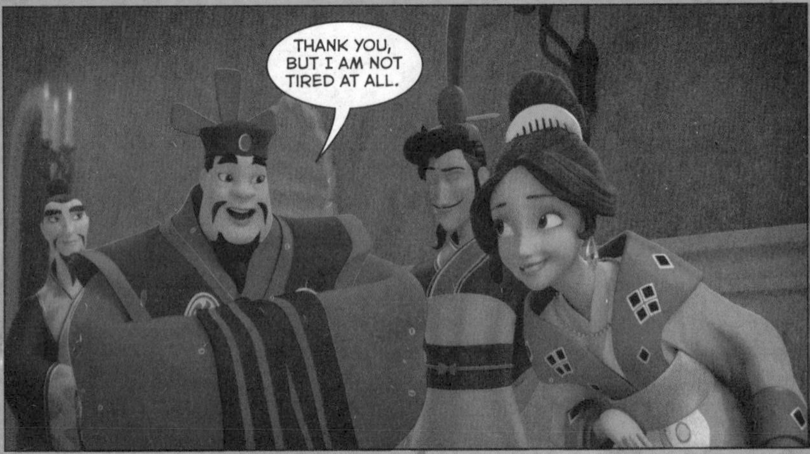
THANK YOU, BUT I AM NOT TIRED AT ALL.

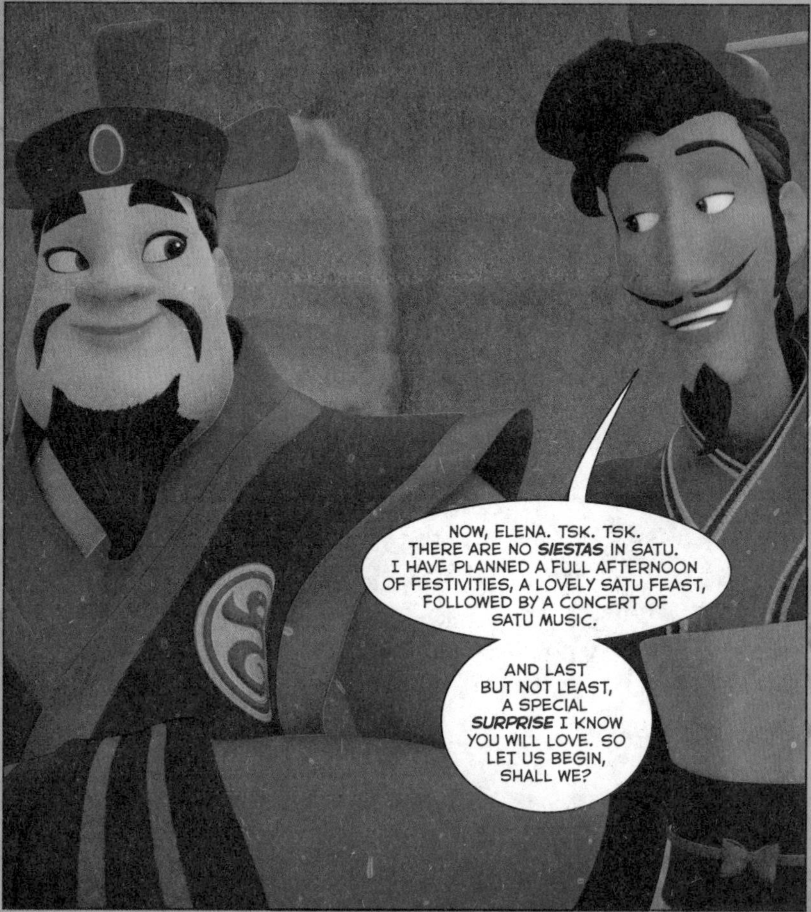
NOW, ELENA. TSK. TSK. THERE ARE NO SIESTAS IN SATU. I HAVE PLANNED A FULL AFTERNOON OF FESTIVITIES, A LOVELY SATU FEAST, FOLLOWED BY A CONCERT OF SATU MUSIC.
AND LAST BUT NOT LEAST, A SPECIAL SURPRISE I KNOW YOU WILL LOVE. SO LET US BEGIN, SHALL WE?

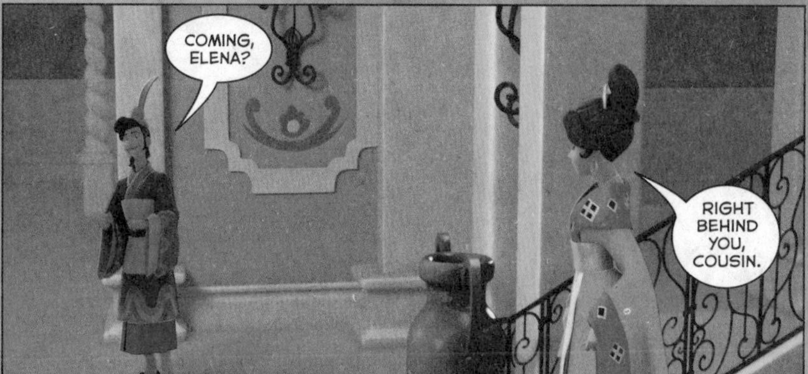
COMING, ELENA?
RIGHT BEHIND YOU, COUSIN.

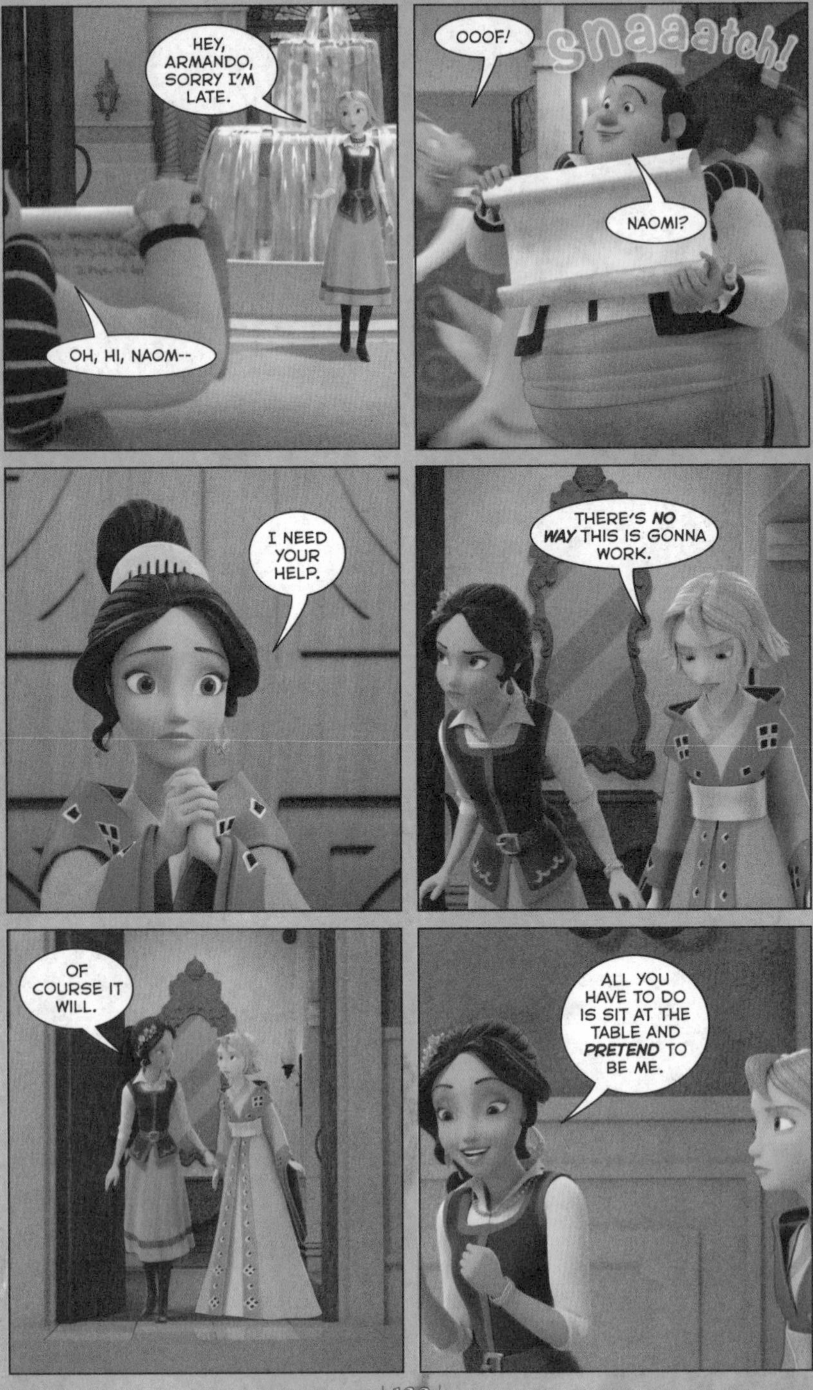
HEY, ARMANDO, SORRY I'M LATE.
OH, HI, NAOM--
OOOF!
snaaatch!
NAOMI?
I NEED YOUR HELP.
THERE'S **NO WAY** THIS IS GONNA WORK.
OF COURSE IT WILL.
ALL YOU HAVE TO DO IS SIT AT THE TABLE AND ***PRETEND*** TO BE ME.

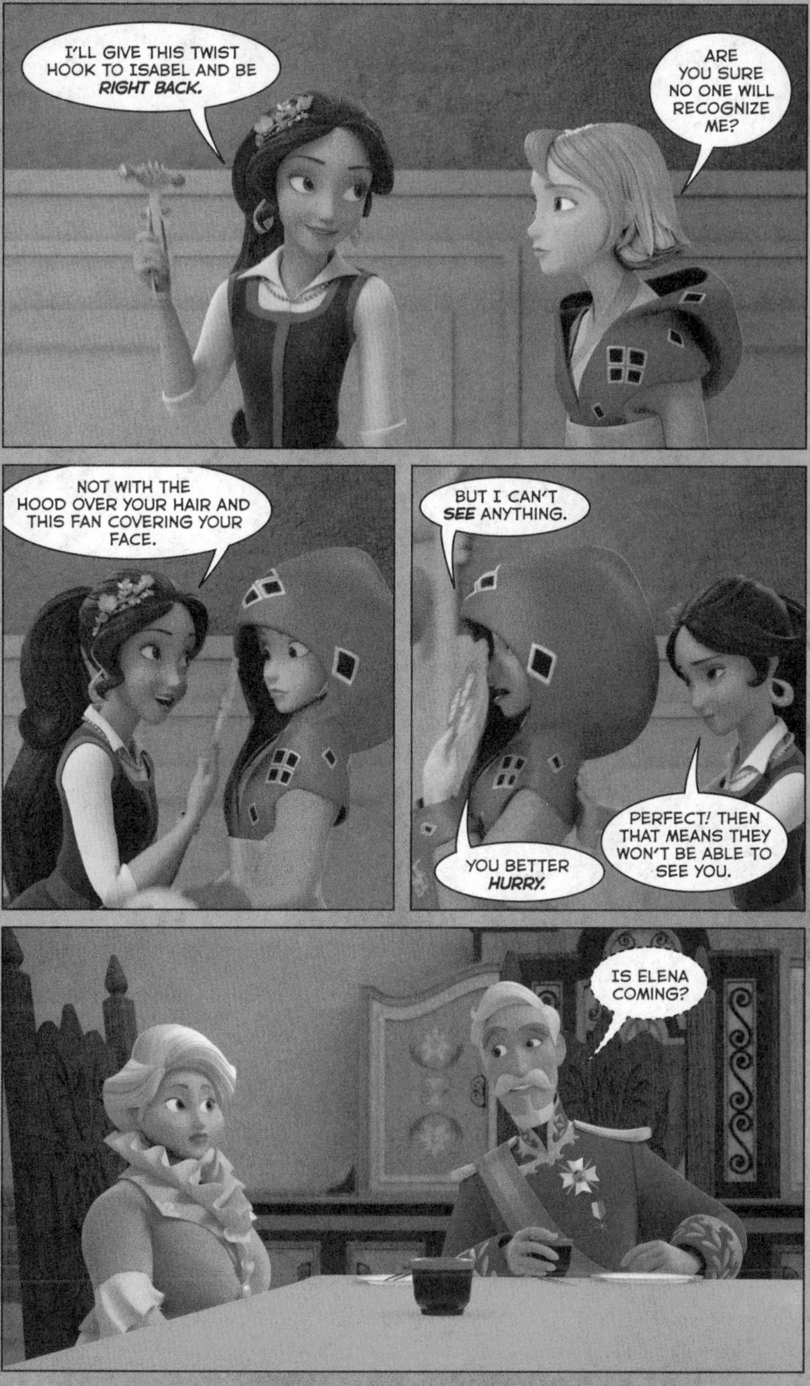
I'LL GIVE THIS TWIST HOOK TO ISABEL AND BE RIGHT BACK.
ARE YOU SURE NO ONE WILL RECOGNIZE ME?
NOT WITH THE HOOD OVER YOUR HAIR AND THIS FAN COVERING YOUR FACE.
BUT I CAN'T SEE ANYTHING.
PERFECT! THEN THAT MEANS THEY WON'T BE ABLE TO SEE YOU.
YOU BETTER HURRY.
IS ELENA COMING?

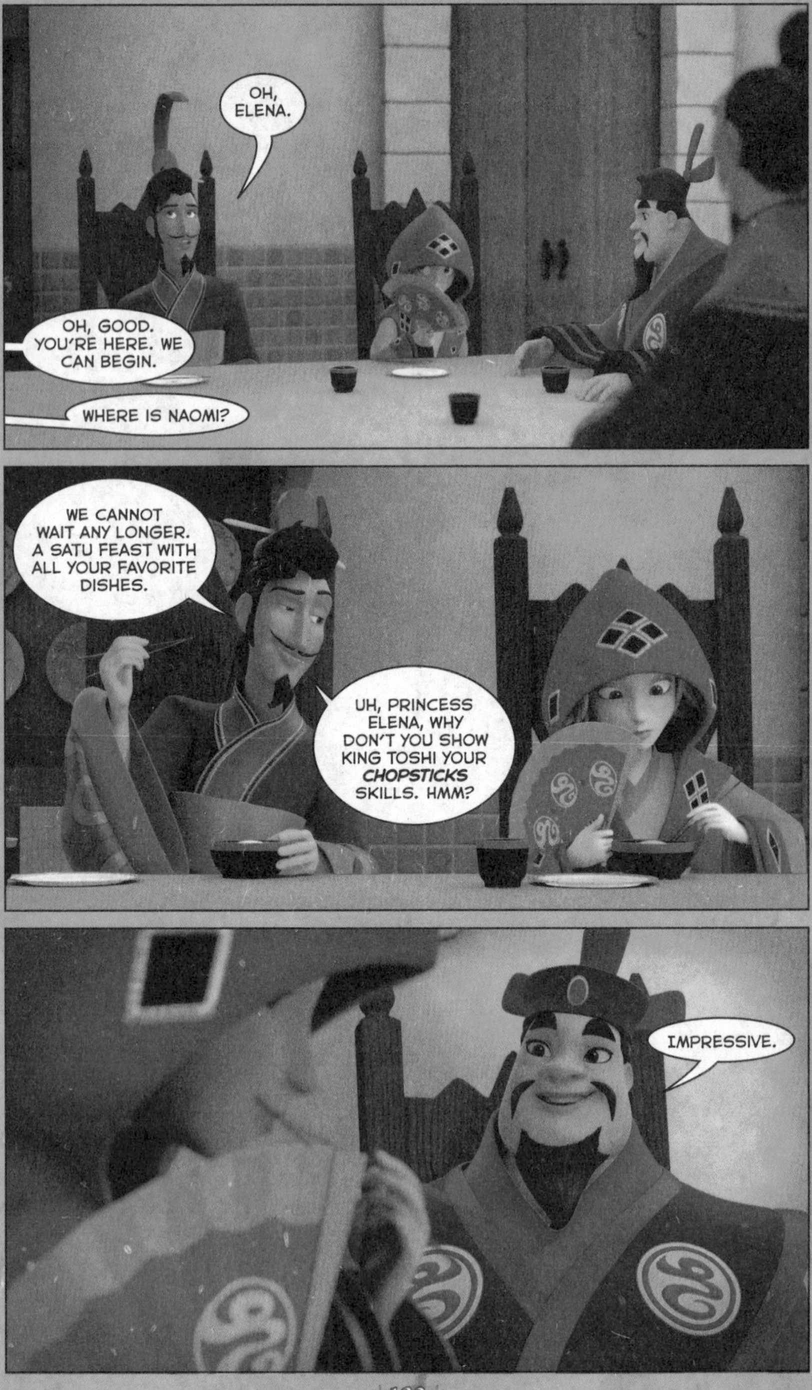
OH, ELENA.
OH, GOOD. YOU'RE HERE. WE CAN BEGIN.
WHERE IS NAOMI?
WE CANNOT WAIT ANY LONGER. A SATU FEAST WITH ALL YOUR FAVORITE DISHES.
UH, PRINCESS ELENA, WHY DON'T YOU SHOW KING TOSHI YOUR *CHOPSTICKS* SKILLS. HMM?
IMPRESSIVE.

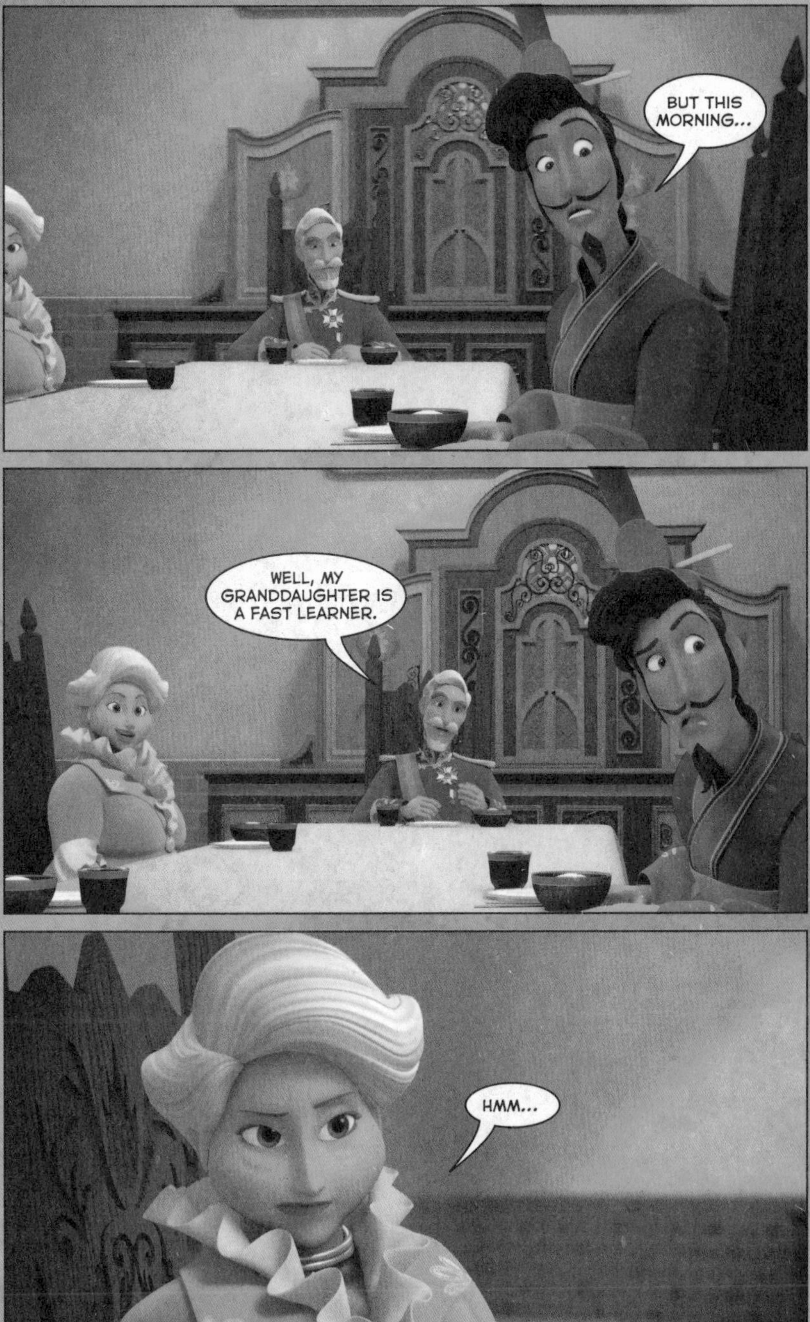
BUT THIS MORNING...
WELL, MY GRANDDAUGHTER IS A FAST LEARNER.
HMM...

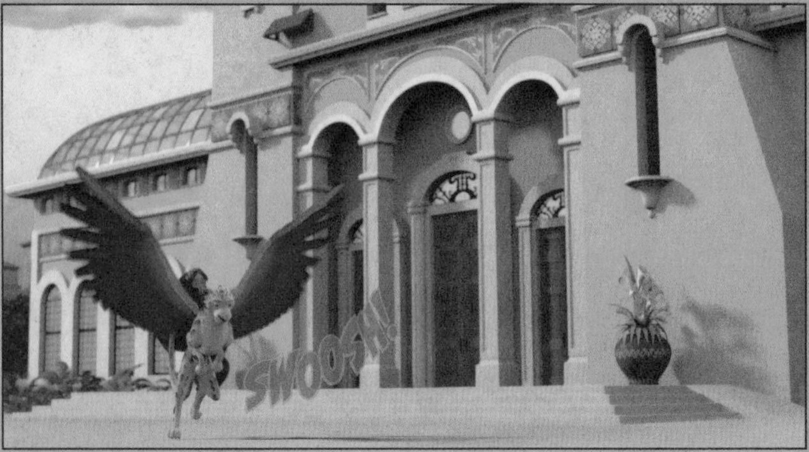
SWOOSH!

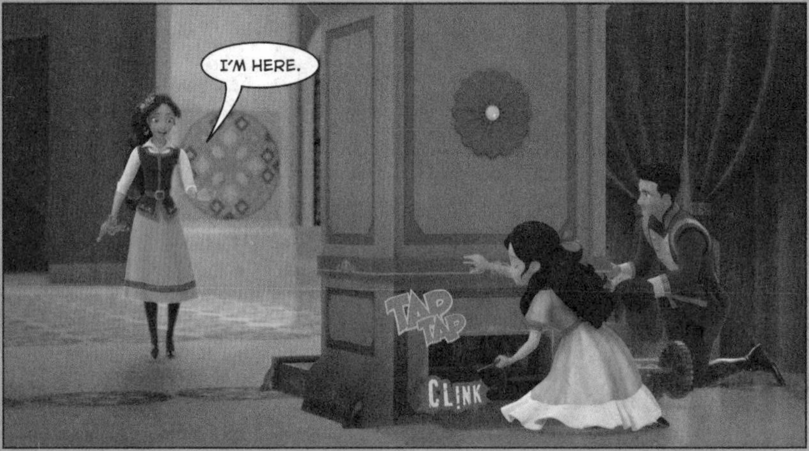
I'M HERE.
TAP TAP
CLINK

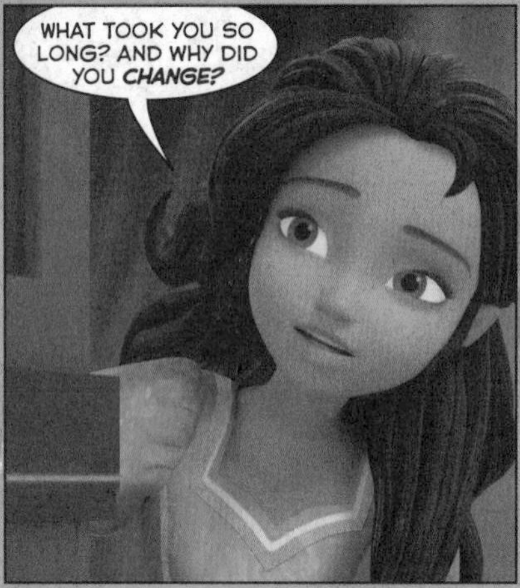
WHAT TOOK YOU SO LONG? AND WHY DID YOU *CHANGE?*

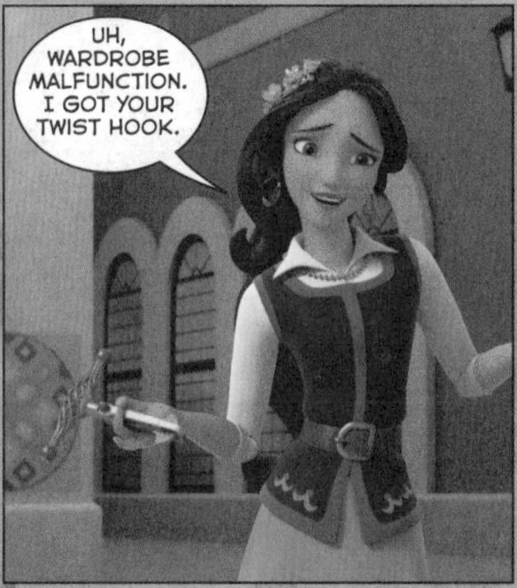
UH, WARDROBE MALFUNCTION. I GOT YOUR TWIST HOOK.

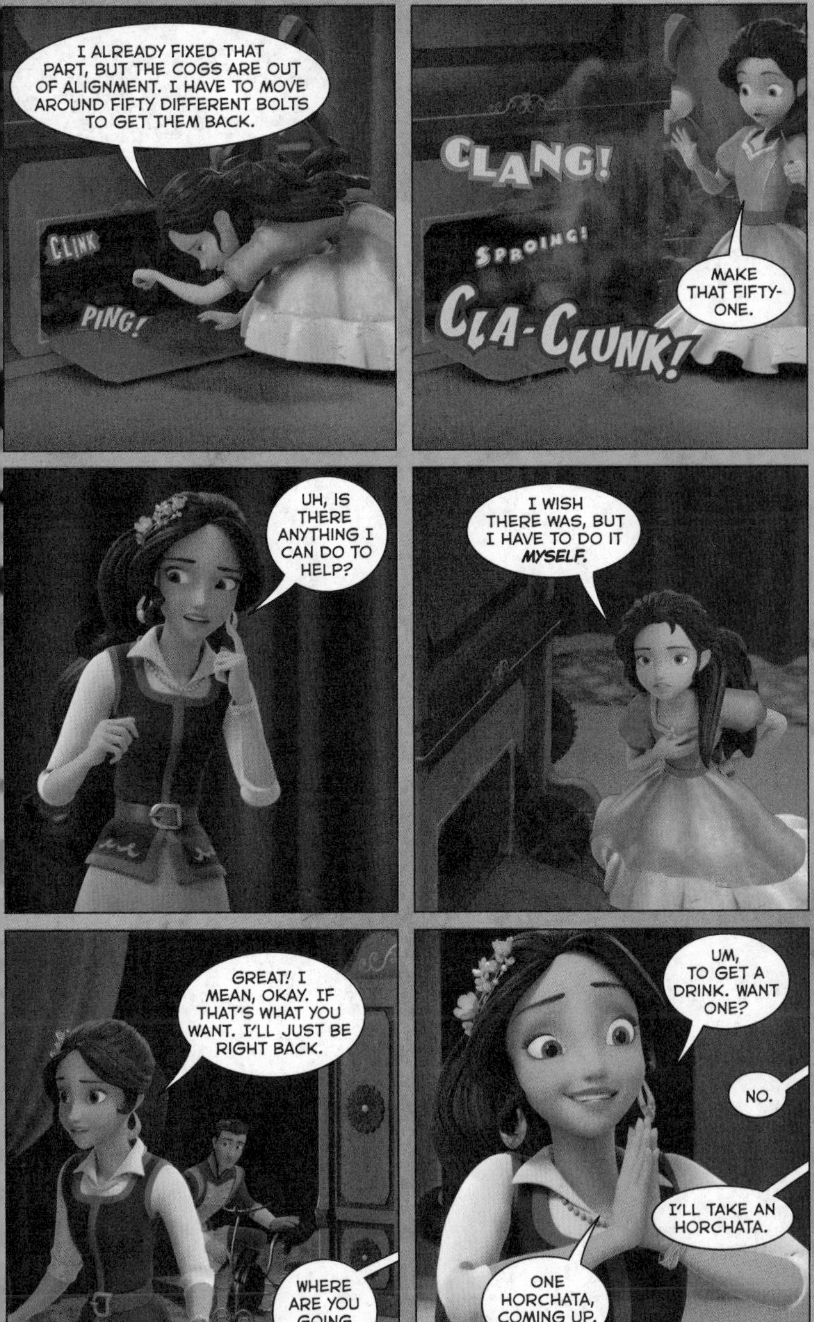
I ALREADY FIXED THAT PART, BUT THE COGS ARE OUT OF ALIGNMENT. I HAVE TO MOVE AROUND FIFTY DIFFERENT BOLTS TO GET THEM BACK.
CLINK
PING!
CLANG!
SPROING!
CLA-CLUNK!
MAKE THAT FIFTY-ONE.
UH, IS THERE ANYTHING I CAN DO TO HELP?
I WISH THERE WAS, BUT I HAVE TO DO IT *MYSELF.*
GREAT! I MEAN, OKAY. IF THAT'S WHAT YOU WANT. I'LL JUST BE RIGHT BACK.
WHERE ARE YOU GOING *NOW?*
UM, TO GET A DRINK. WANT ONE?
NO.
I'LL TAKE AN HORCHATA.
ONE HORCHATA, COMING UP.

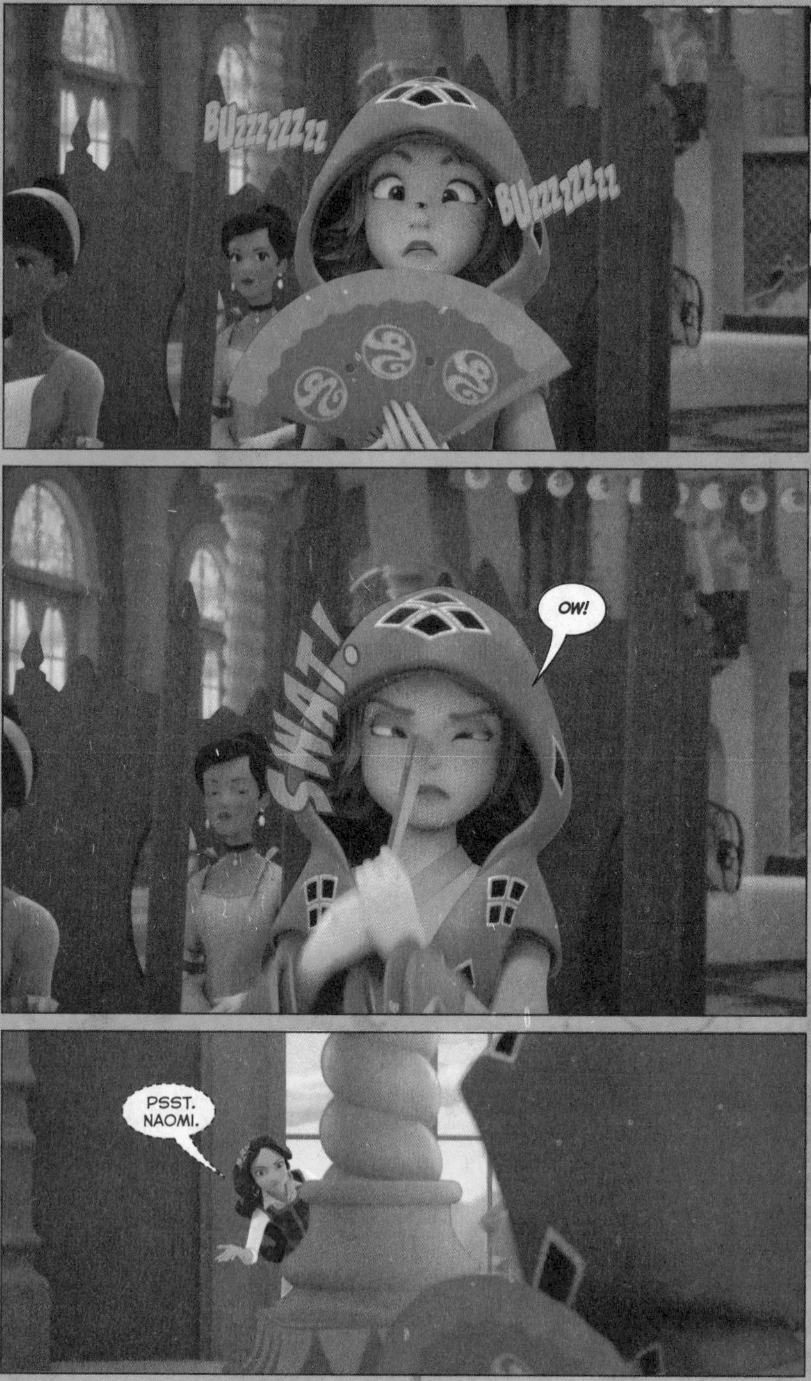
BUzzzzzzzz
BUzzzzzzzz
SWAT!
OW!
PSST. NAOMI.

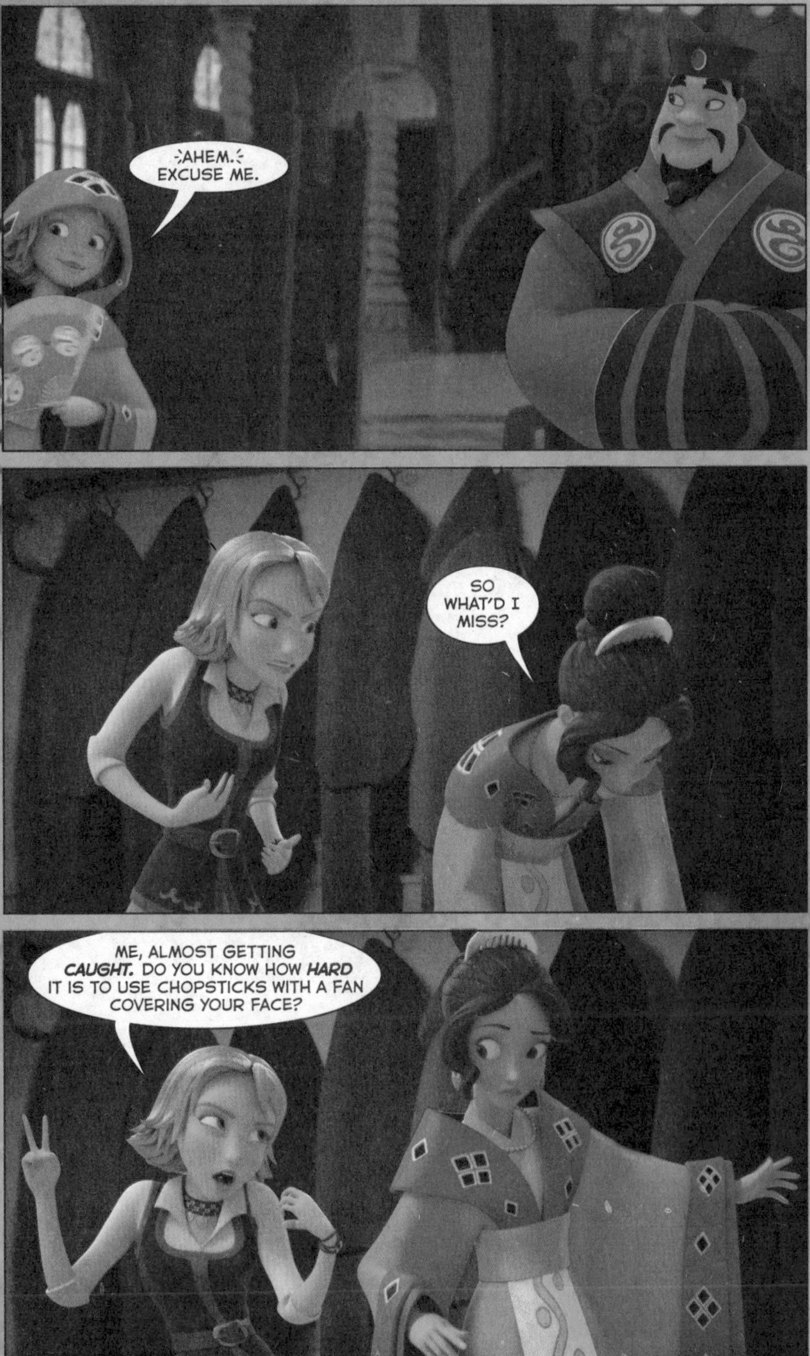

AHEM.
EXCUSE ME.
SO WHAT'D I MISS?
ME, ALMOST GETTING *CAUGHT.* DO YOU KNOW HOW *HARD* IT IS TO USE CHOPSTICKS WITH A FAN COVERING YOUR FACE?

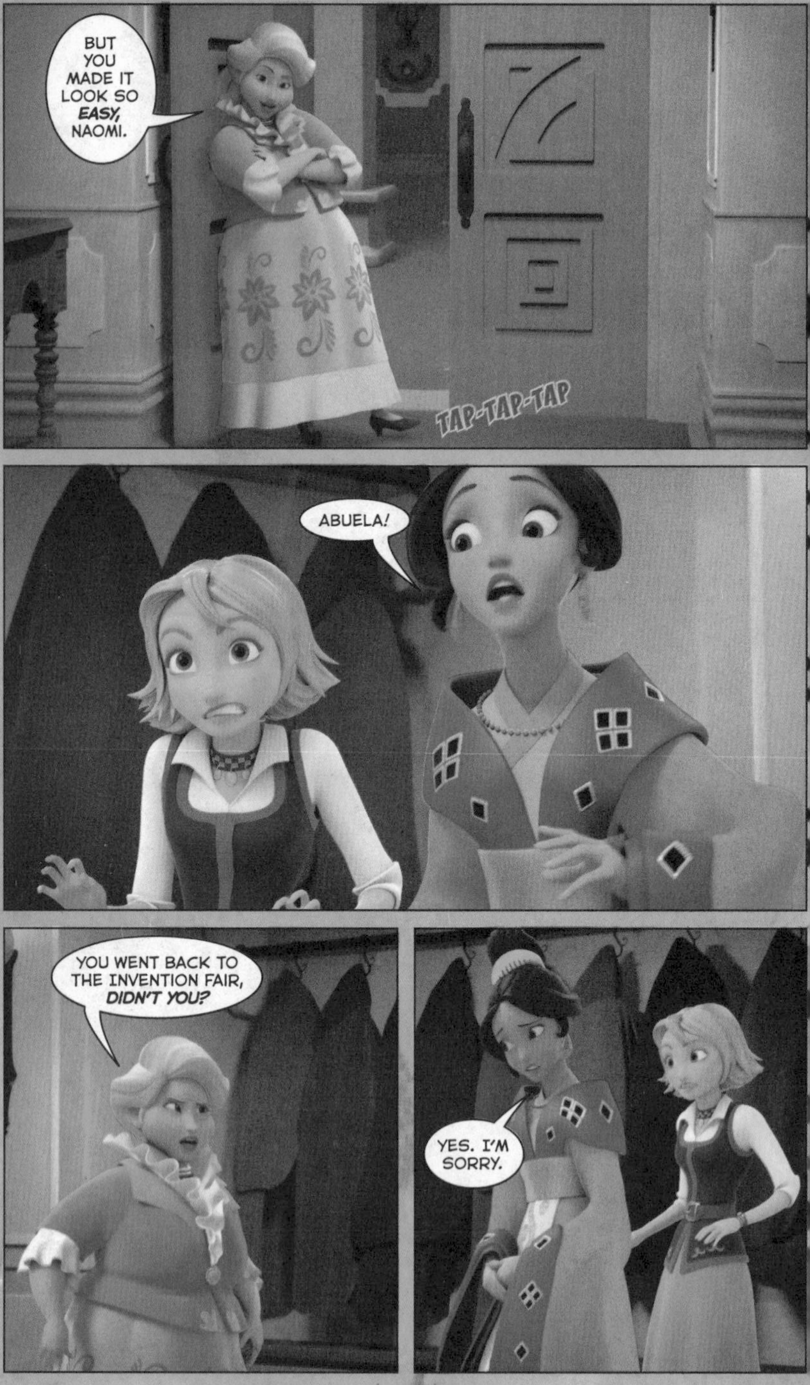
BUT YOU MADE IT LOOK SO *EASY,* NAOMI.
TAP-TAP-TAP
ABUELA!
YOU WENT BACK TO THE INVENTION FAIR, *DIDN'T YOU?*
YES. I'M SORRY.

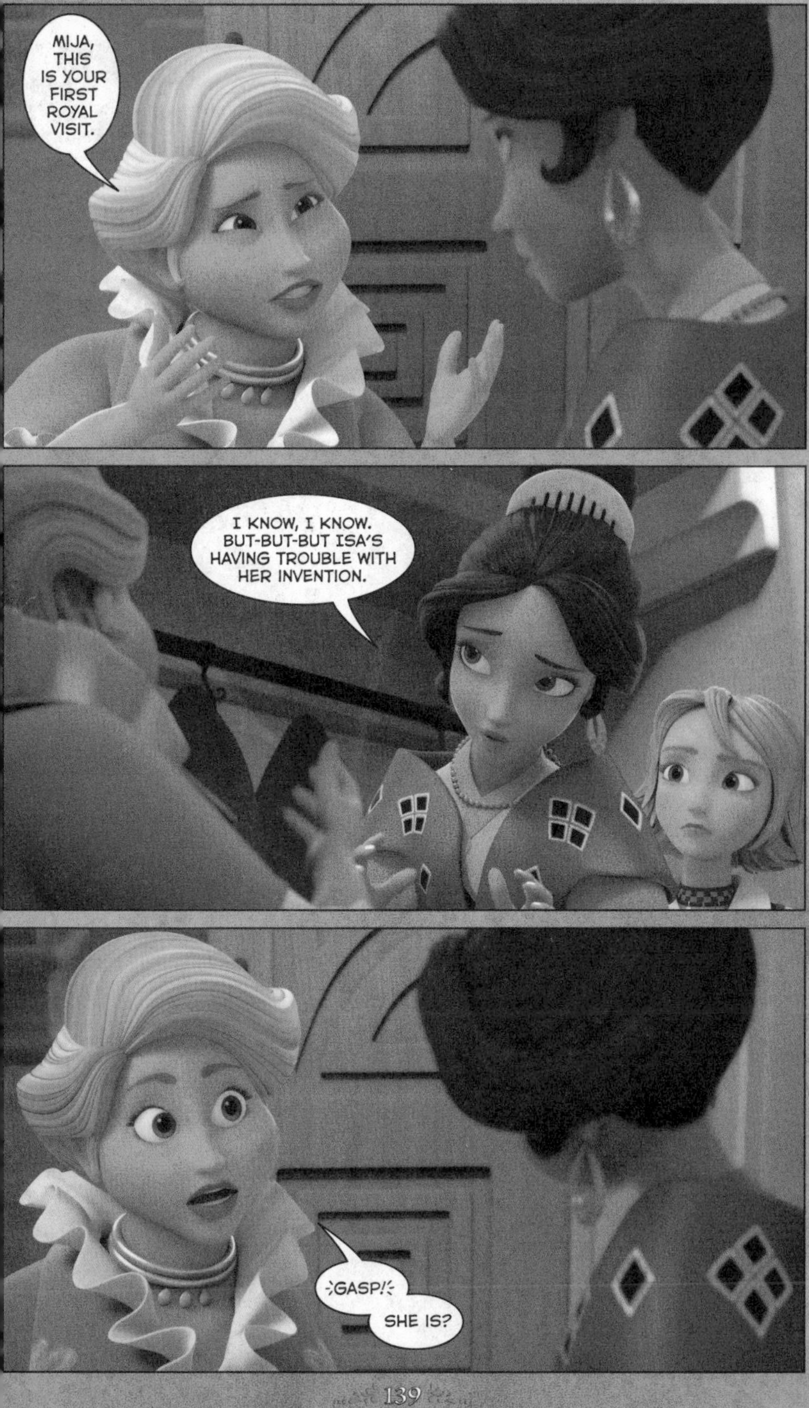
MIJA, THIS IS YOUR FIRST ROYAL VISIT.
I KNOW, I KNOW. BUT-BUT-BUT ISA'S HAVING TROUBLE WITH HER INVENTION.
GASP!
SHE IS?

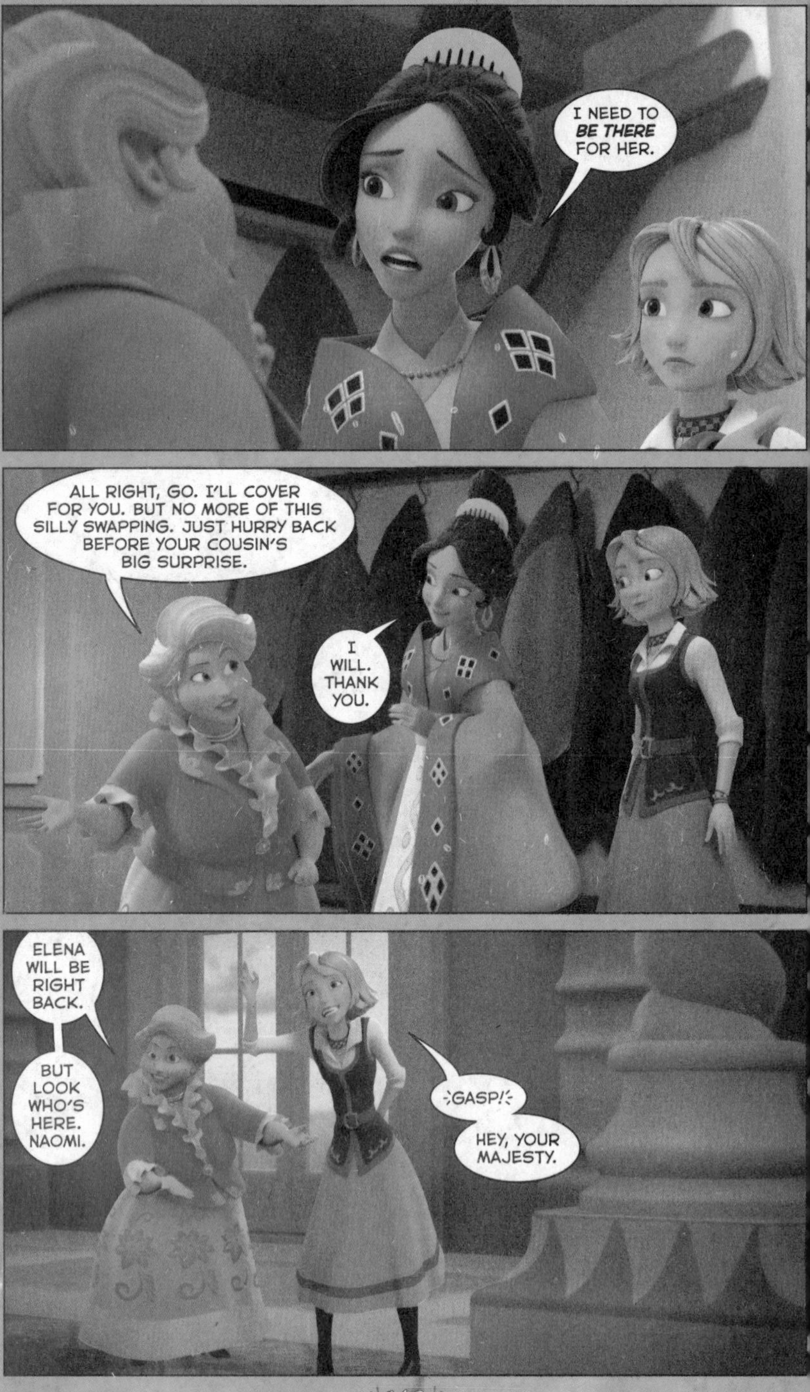
I NEED TO *BE THERE* FOR HER.
ALL RIGHT, GO. I'LL COVER FOR YOU. BUT NO MORE OF THIS SILLY SWAPPING. JUST HURRY BACK BEFORE YOUR COUSIN'S BIG SURPRISE.
I WILL. THANK YOU.
ELENA WILL BE RIGHT BACK.
BUT LOOK WHO'S HERE. NAOMI.
GASP!
HEY, YOUR MAJESTY.

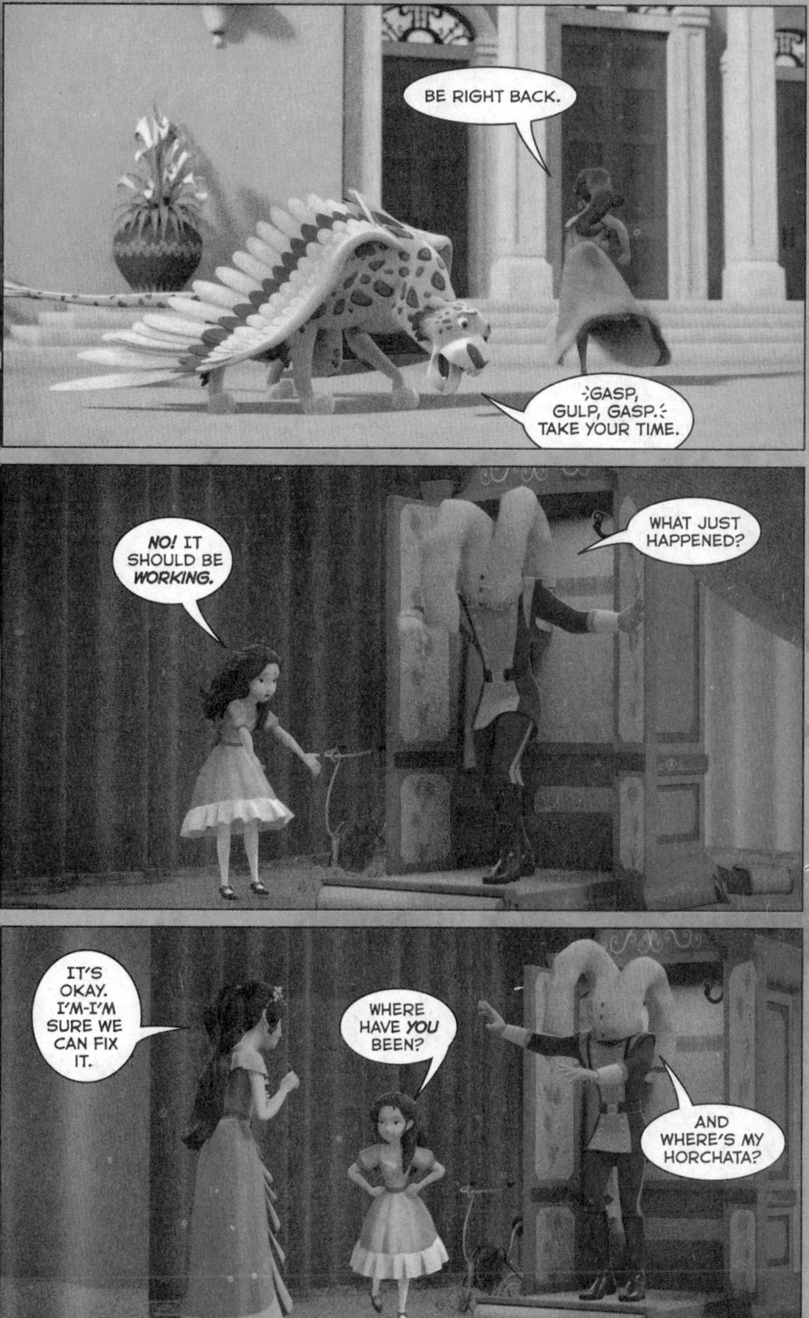
BE RIGHT BACK.
GASP, GULP, GASP. TAKE YOUR TIME.
NO! IT SHOULD BE WORKING.
WHAT JUST HAPPENED?
IT'S OKAY. I'M-I'M SURE WE CAN FIX IT.
WHERE HAVE YOU BEEN?
AND WHERE'S MY HORCHATA?

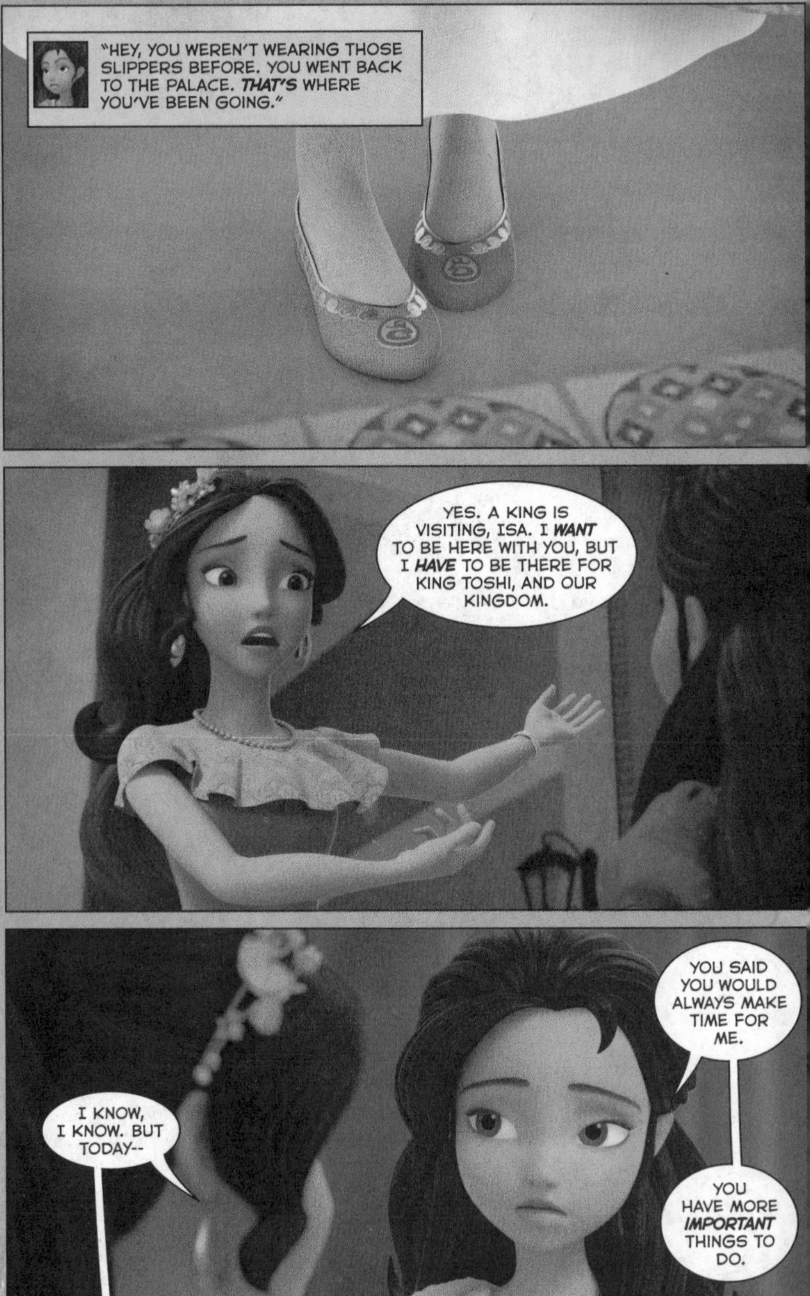
"HEY, YOU WEREN'T WEARING THOSE SLIPPERS BEFORE. YOU WENT BACK TO THE PALACE. ***THAT'S*** WHERE YOU'VE BEEN GOING."
YES. A KING IS VISITING, ISA. I ***WANT*** TO BE HERE WITH YOU, BUT I ***HAVE*** TO BE THERE FOR KING TOSHI, AND OUR KINGDOM.
YOU SAID YOU WOULD ALWAYS MAKE TIME FOR ME.
I KNOW, I KNOW. BUT TODAY--
YOU HAVE MORE ***IMPORTANT*** THINGS TO DO.
NO, I--

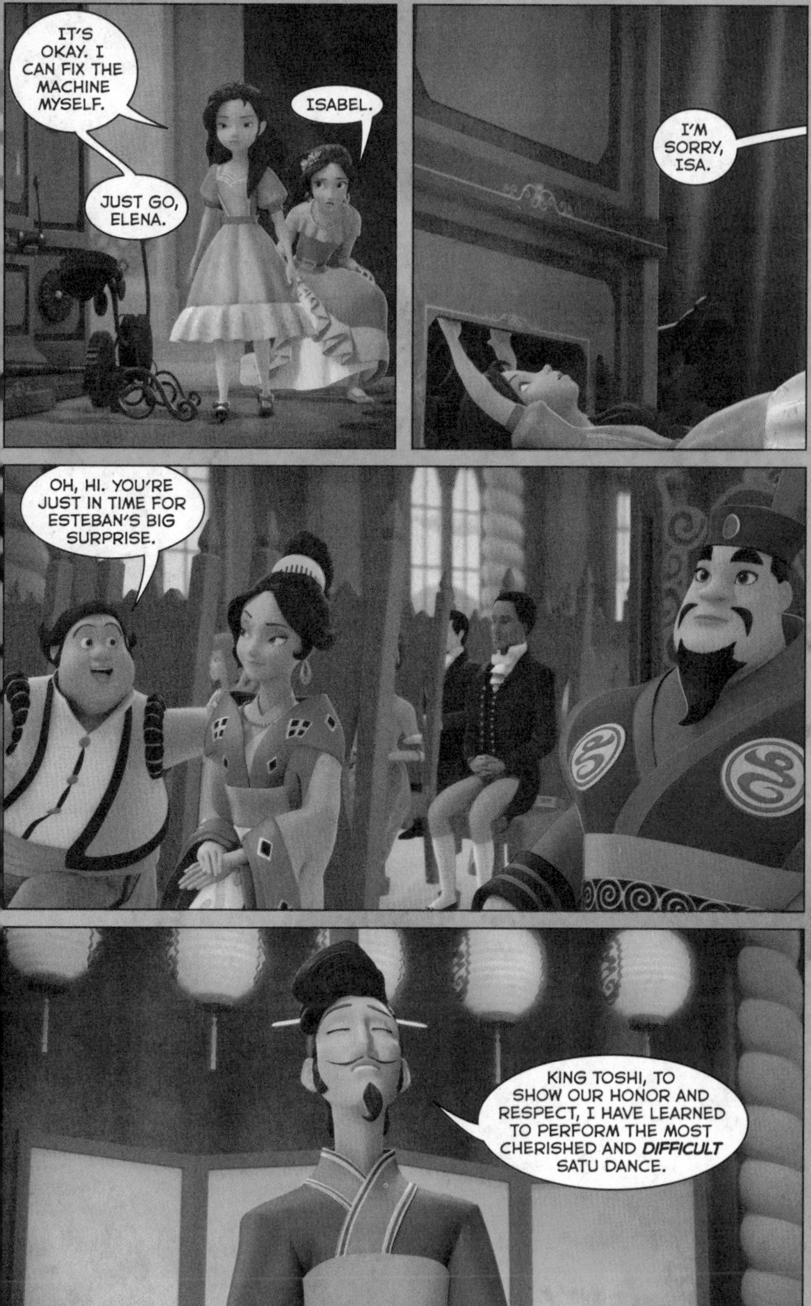
IT'S OKAY. I CAN FIX THE MACHINE MYSELF.
JUST GO, ELENA.
ISABEL.
I'M SORRY, ISA.
OH, HI. YOU'RE JUST IN TIME FOR ESTEBAN'S BIG SURPRISE.
KING TOSHI, TO SHOW OUR HONOR AND RESPECT, I HAVE LEARNED TO PERFORM THE MOST CHERISHED AND *DIFFICULT* SATU DANCE.

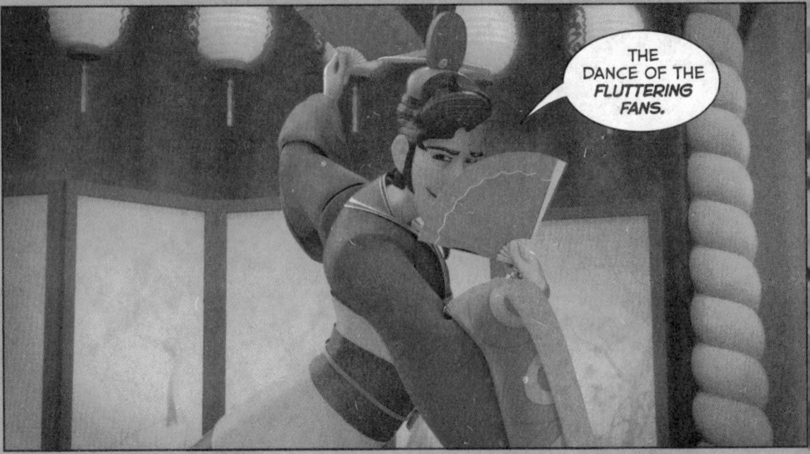
THE DANCE OF THE *FLUTTERING* FANS.

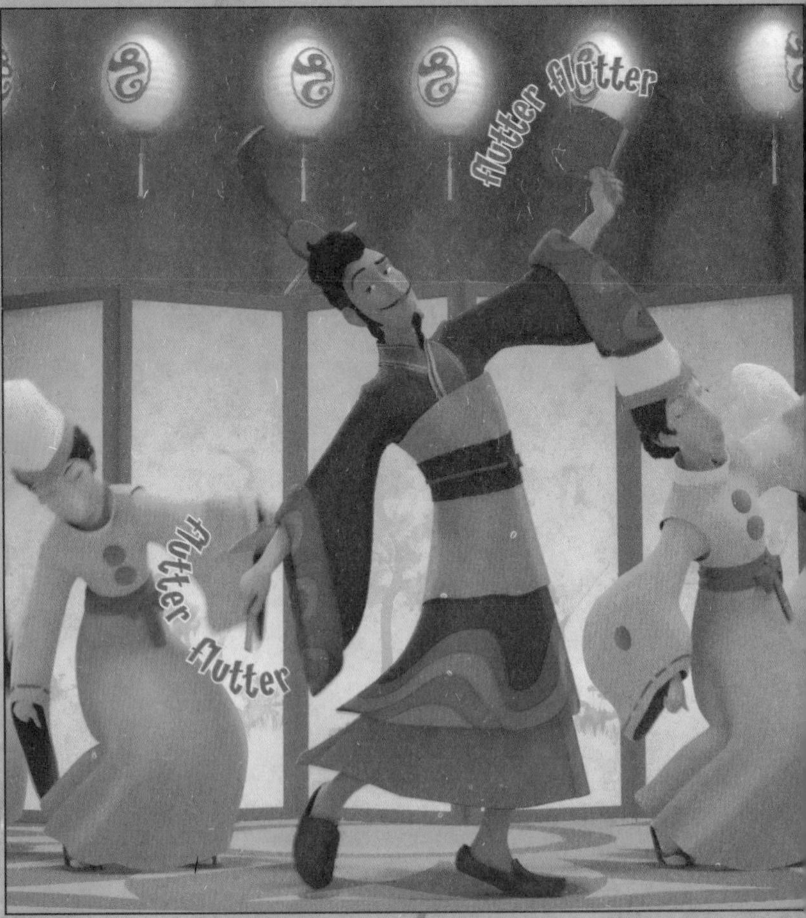
flutter flutter
flutter flutter

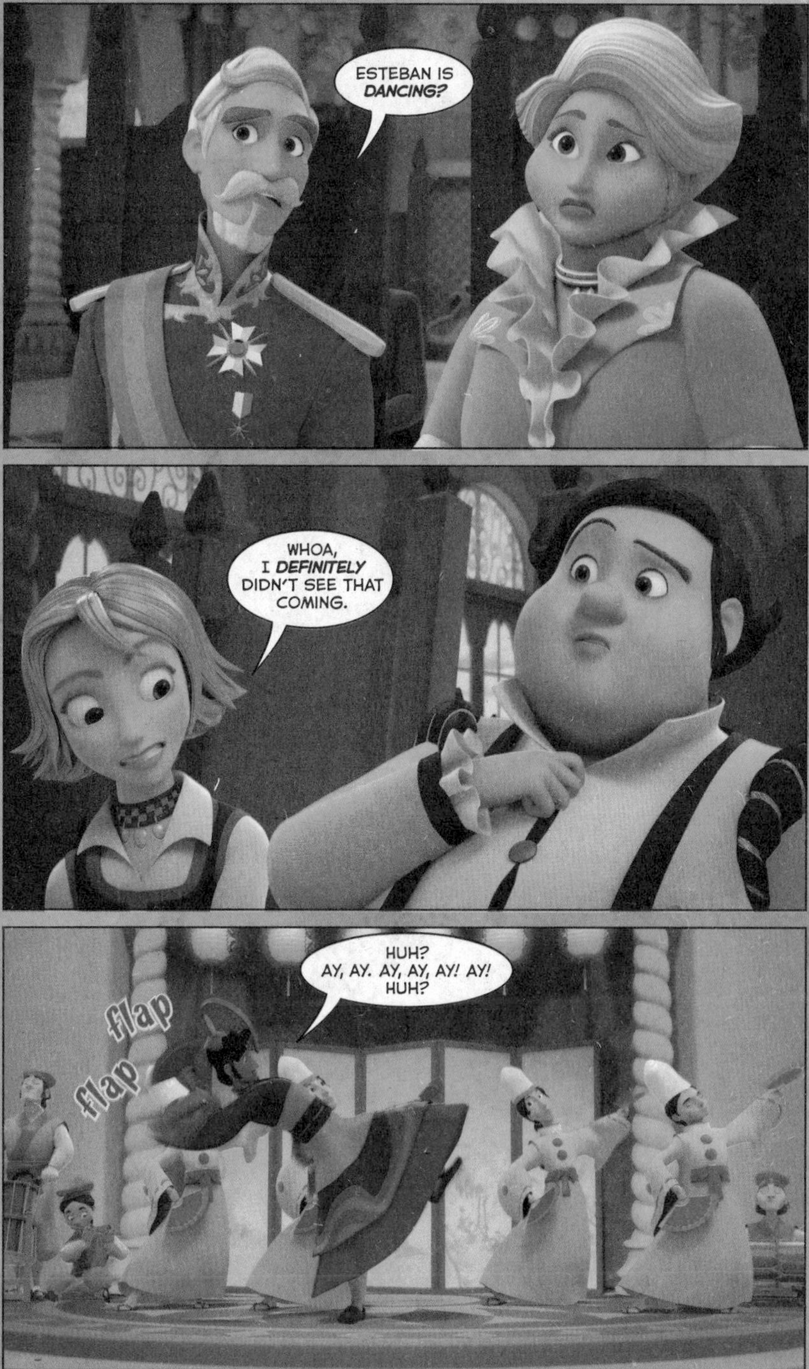
ESTEBAN IS DANCING?
WHOA, I DEFINITELY DIDN'T SEE THAT COMING.
HUH? AY, AY. AY, AY, AY! AY! HUH?
flap
flap

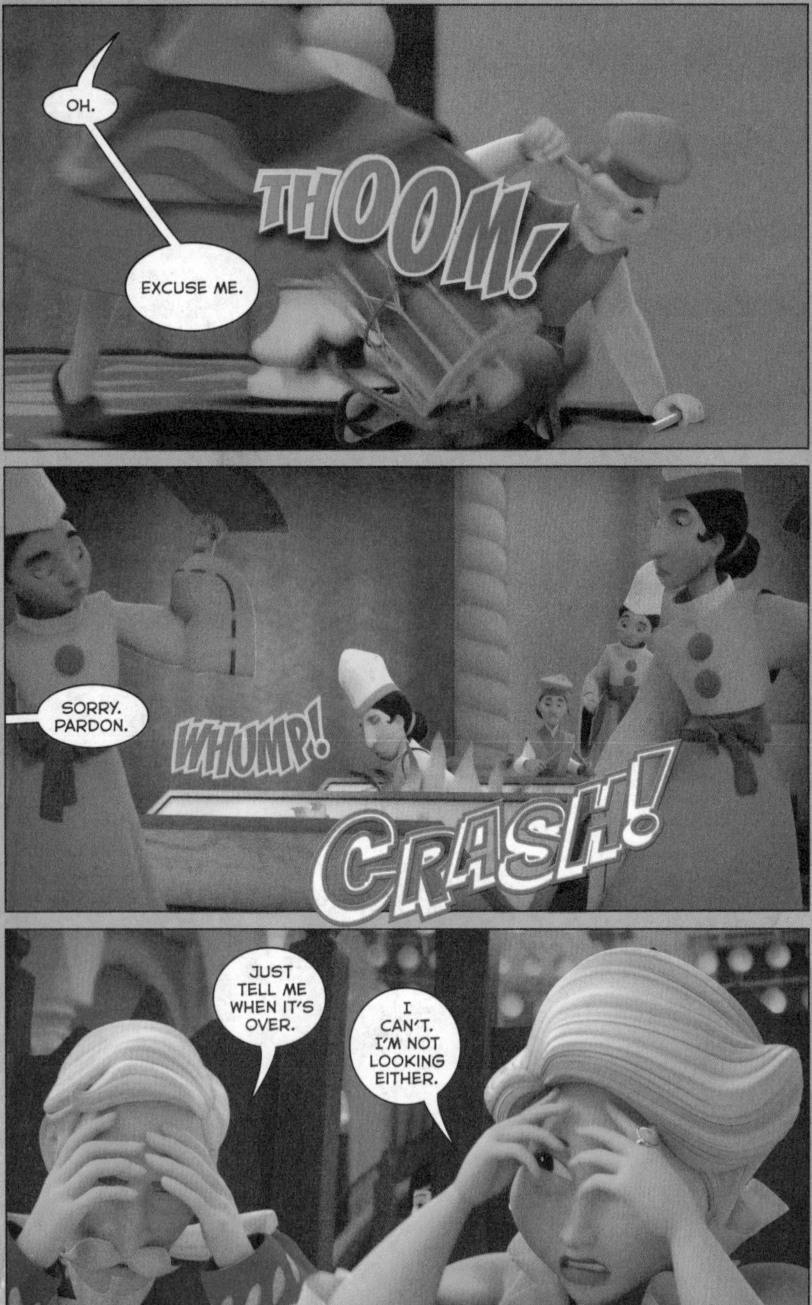
OH.
EXCUSE ME.
THOOM!
SORRY. PARDON.
WHUMP!
CRASH!
JUST TELL ME WHEN IT'S OVER.
I CAN'T. I'M NOT LOOKING EITHER.

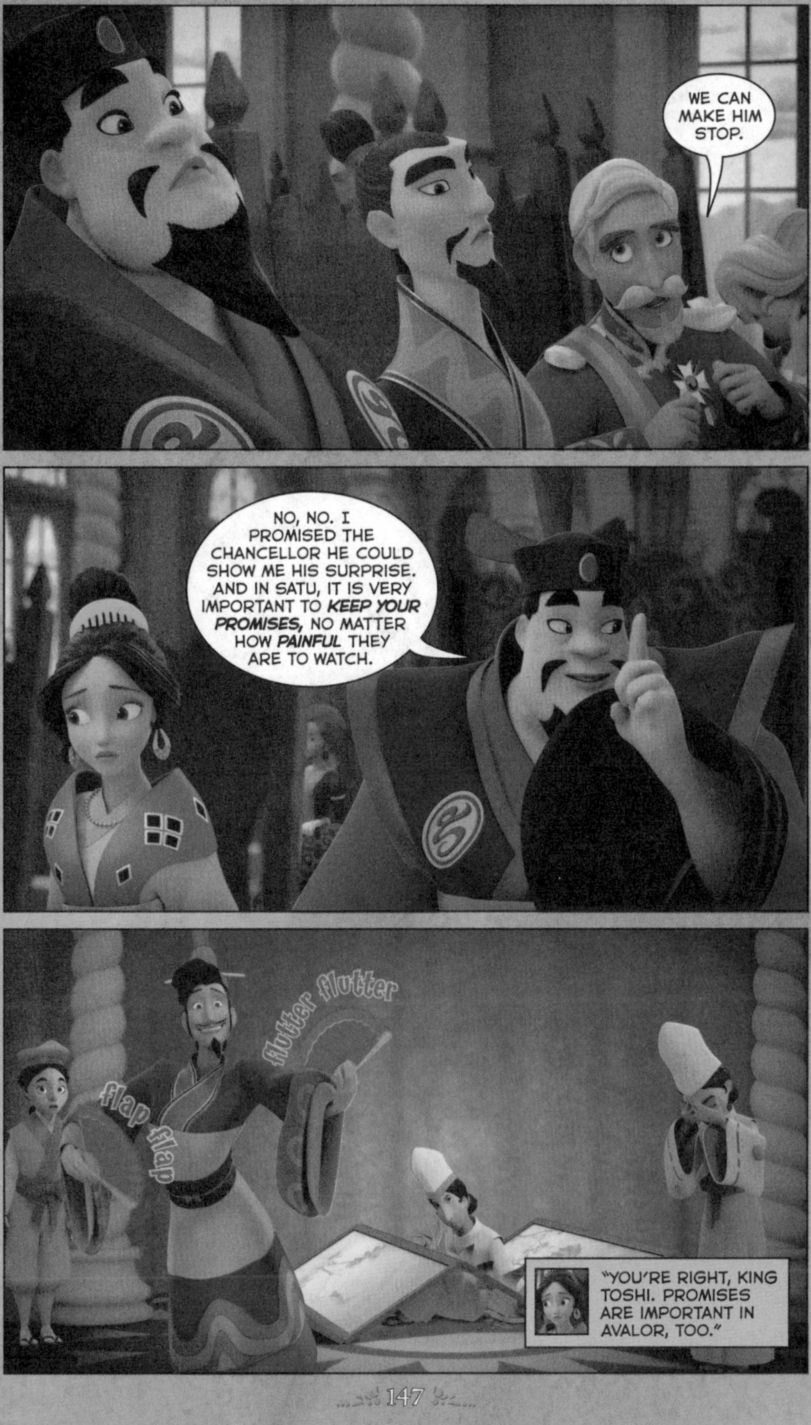
WE CAN MAKE HIM STOP.
NO, NO. I PROMISED THE CHANCELLOR HE COULD SHOW ME HIS SURPRISE. AND IN SATU, IT IS VERY IMPORTANT TO ***KEEP YOUR PROMISES,*** NO MATTER HOW ***PAINFUL*** THEY ARE TO WATCH.
flutter flutter
flap flap
"YOU'RE RIGHT, KING TOSHI. PROMISES ARE IMPORTANT IN AVALOR, TOO."

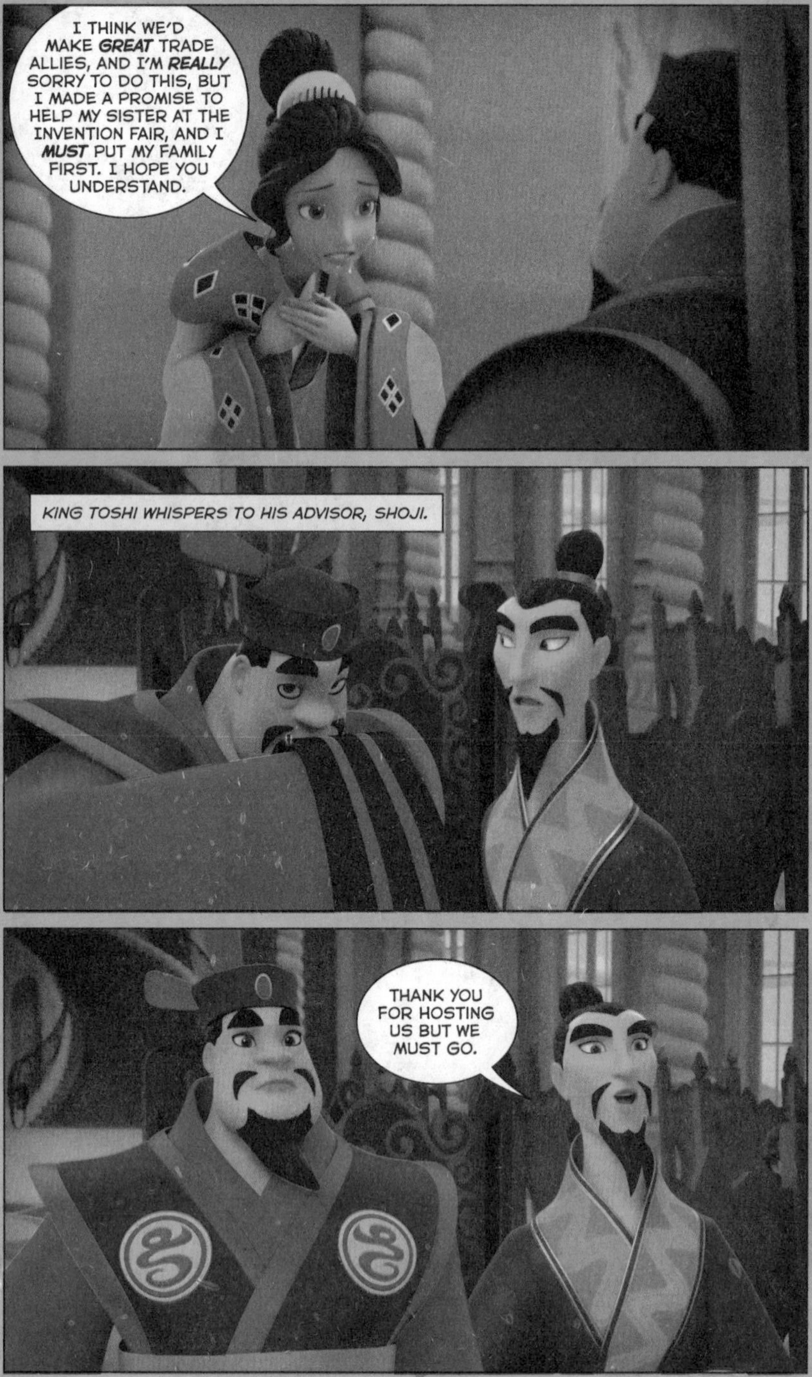
I THINK WE'D MAKE GREAT TRADE ALLIES, AND I'M REALLY SORRY TO DO THIS, BUT I MADE A PROMISE TO HELP MY SISTER AT THE INVENTION FAIR, AND I MUST PUT MY FAMILY FIRST. I HOPE YOU UNDERSTAND.
KING TOSHI WHISPERS TO HIS ADVISOR, SHOJI.
THANK YOU FOR HOSTING US BUT WE MUST GO.

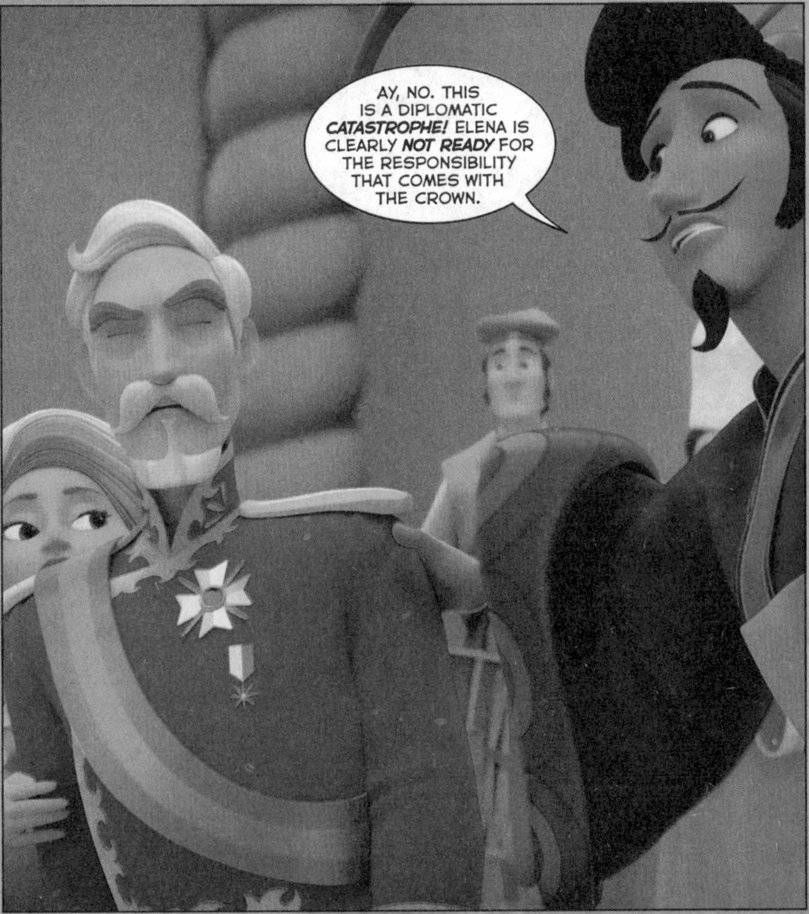
AY, NO. THIS IS A DIPLOMATIC *CATASTROPHE!* ELENA IS CLEARLY *NOT READY* FOR THE RESPONSIBILITY THAT COMES WITH THE CROWN.

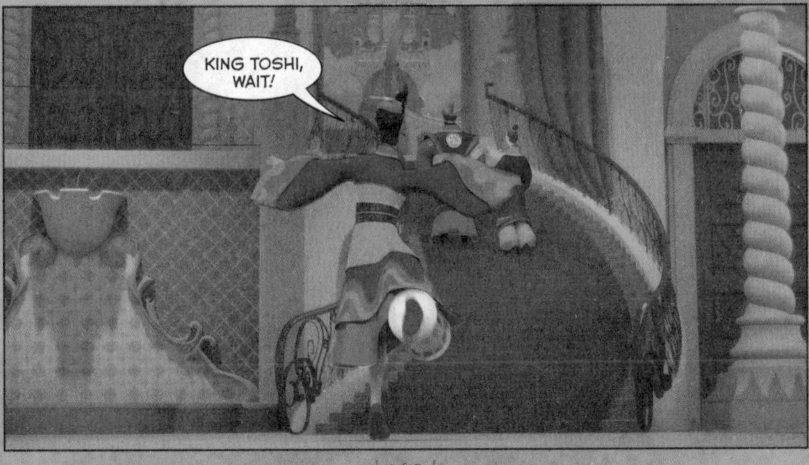
KING TOSHI, WAIT!

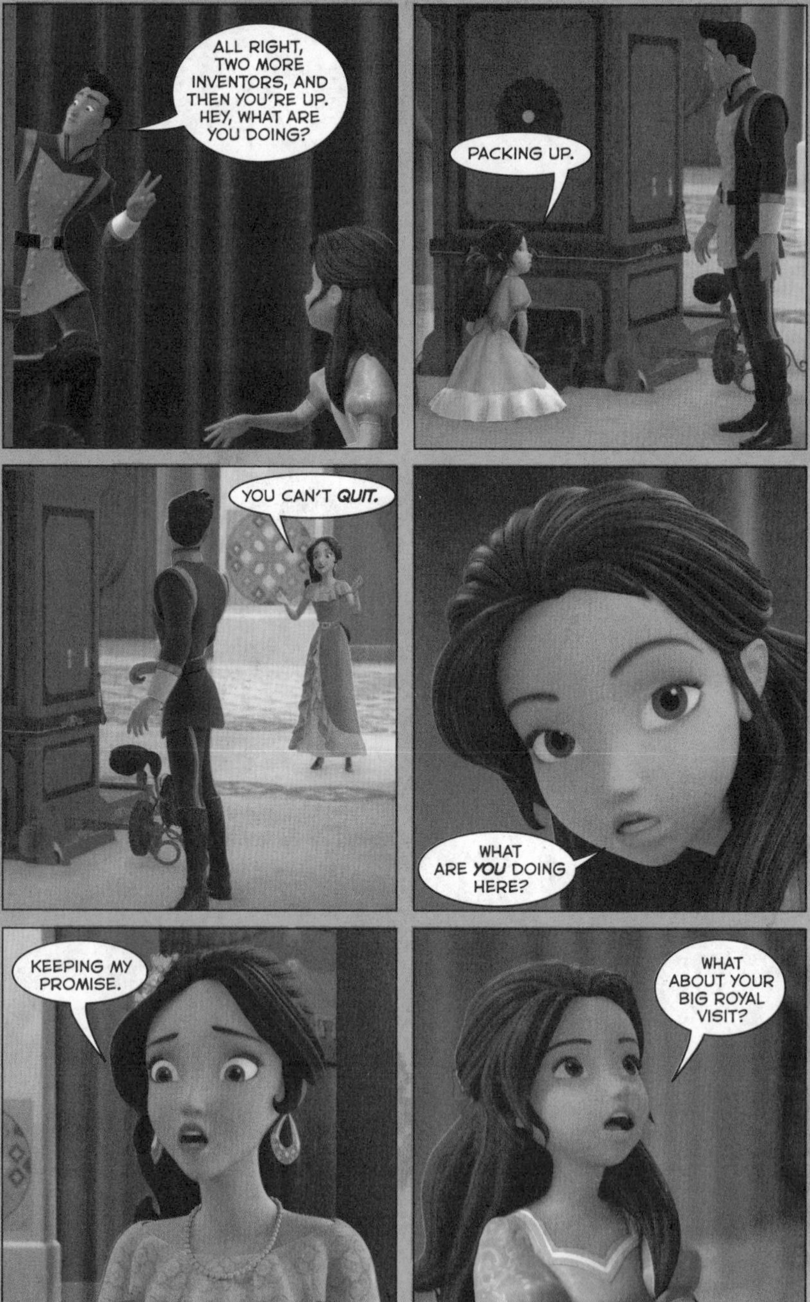
ALL RIGHT, TWO MORE INVENTORS, AND THEN YOU'RE UP. HEY, WHAT ARE YOU DOING?
PACKING UP.
YOU CAN'T QUIT.
WHAT ARE YOU DOING HERE?
KEEPING MY PROMISE.
WHAT ABOUT YOUR BIG ROYAL VISIT?

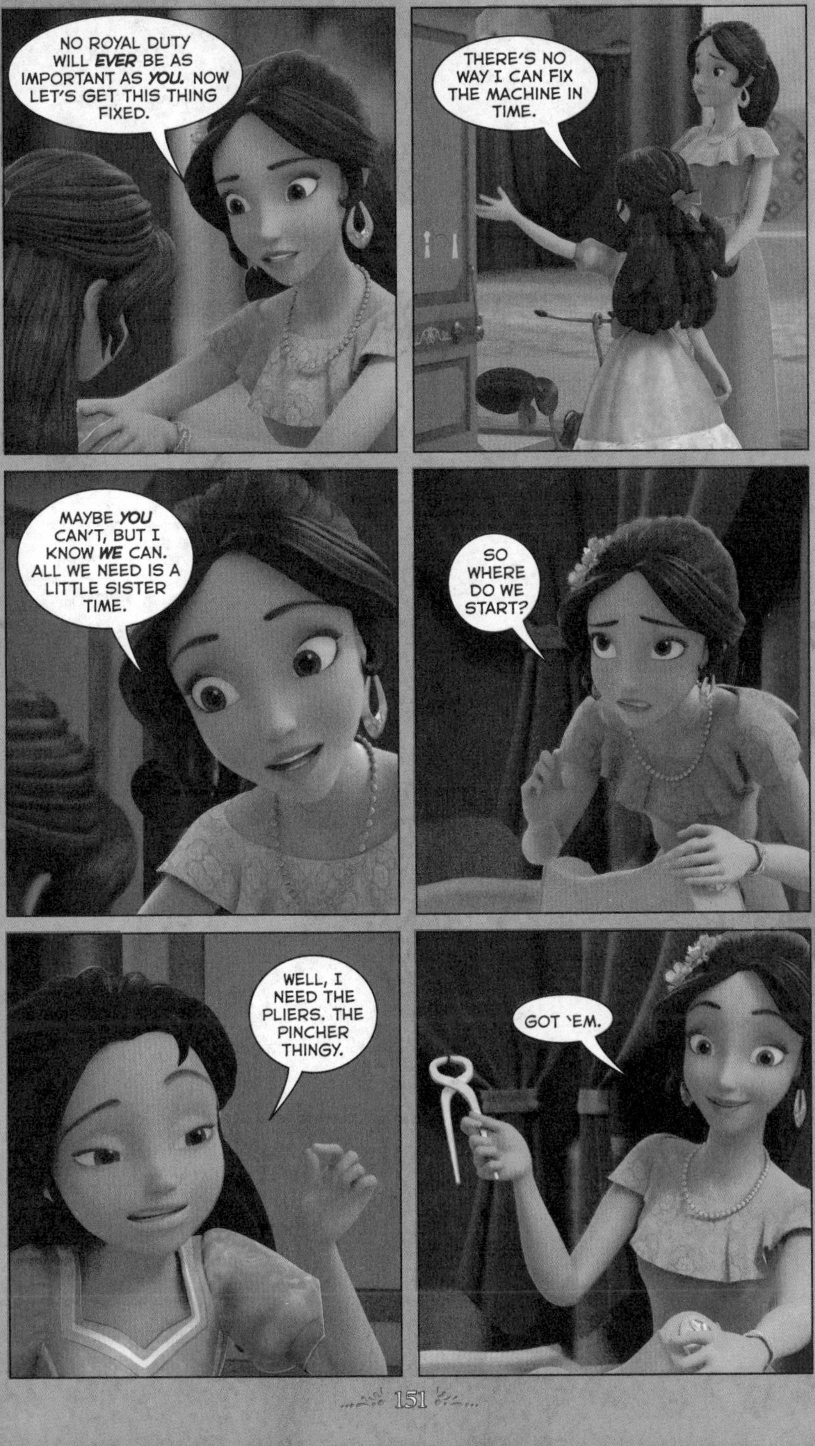
NO ROYAL DUTY WILL EVER BE AS IMPORTANT AS YOU. NOW LET'S GET THIS THING FIXED.
THERE'S NO WAY I CAN FIX THE MACHINE IN TIME.
MAYBE YOU CAN'T, BUT I KNOW WE CAN. ALL WE NEED IS A LITTLE SISTER TIME.
SO WHERE DO WE START?
WELL, I NEED THE PLIERS. THE PINCHER THINGY.
GOT 'EM.

SQUIGGLY BOLT.

SILVER FLAT DOUGHNUT THINGY.

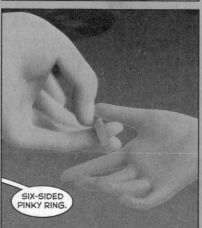

SIX-SIDED PINKY RING.

OH! THIS IS WHY THE COGS KEEP COMING LOOSE. THE CHAIN IS *BROKEN,* AND I DON'T HAVE ANOTHER ONE.

OKAY, DON'T PANIC. WE CAN FIGURE THIS OUT. WE JUST NEED TO GET *CREATIVE.* HEY, W-WHAT ABOUT MY NECKLACE? IT KINDA LOOKS LIKE A CHAIN.

⸸GASP!⸸ YOU'RE *RIGHT!* IT'S THE RIGHT LENGTH.

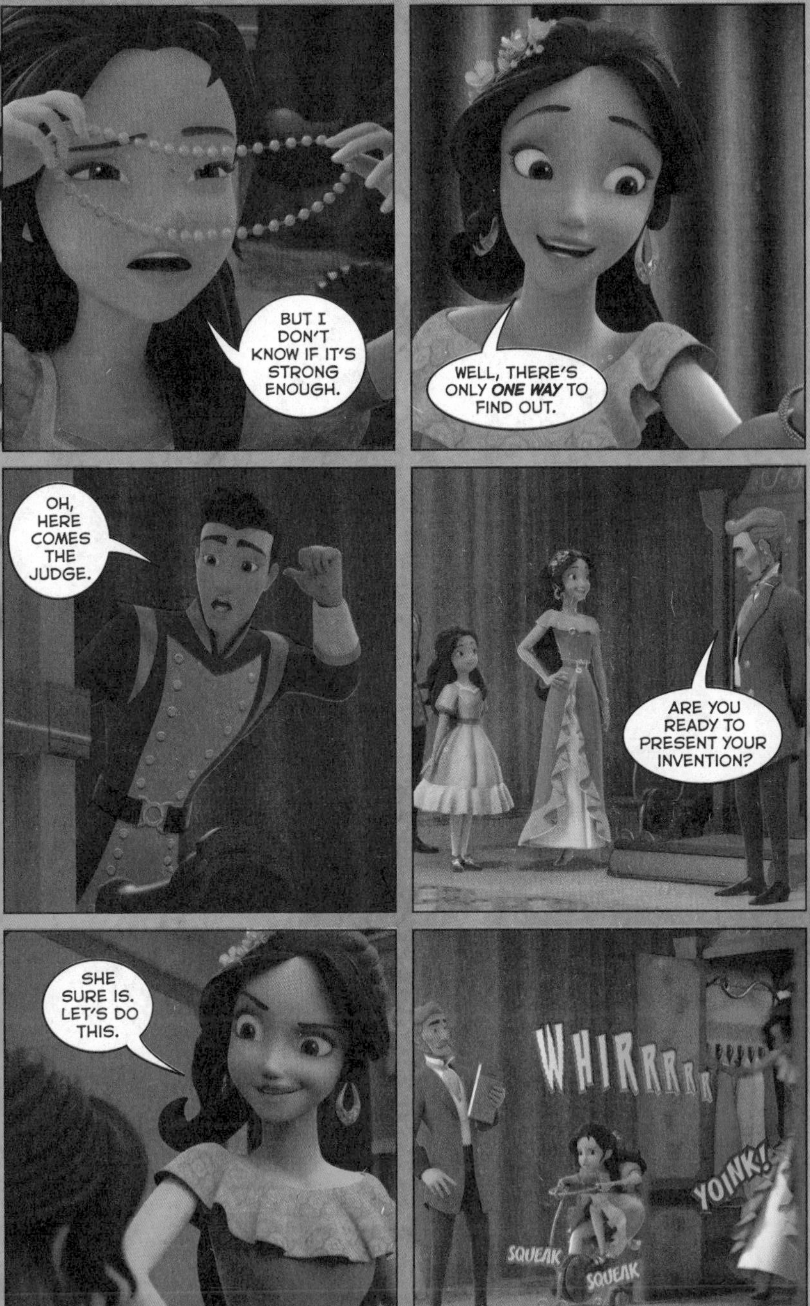
BUT I DON'T KNOW IF IT'S STRONG ENOUGH.
WELL, THERE'S ONLY *ONE WAY* TO FIND OUT.
OH, HERE COMES THE JUDGE.
ARE YOU READY TO PRESENT YOUR INVENTION?
SHE SURE IS. LET'S DO THIS.
WHIRRRRR
YOINK!
SQUEAK
SQUEAK

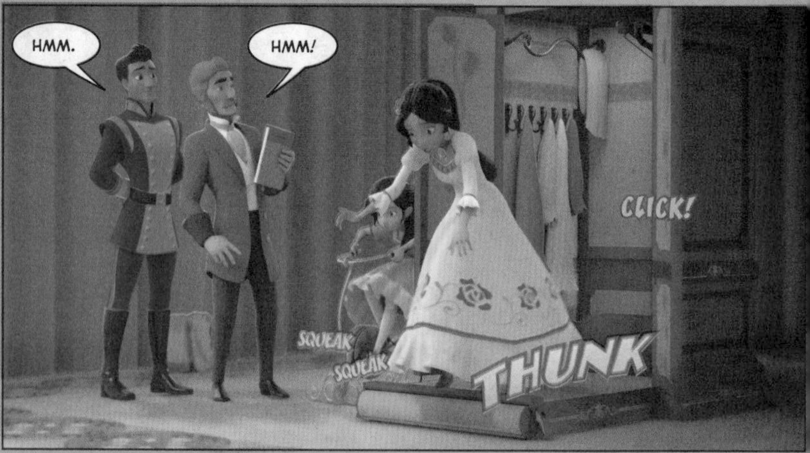
HMM.
HMM!
CLICK!
SQUEAK
SQUEAK
THUNK

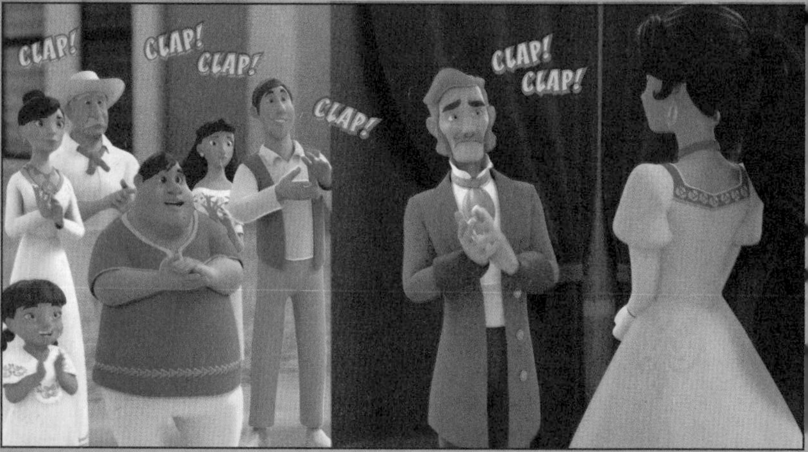
CLAP!
CLAP!
CLAP!
CLAP!
CLAP!
CLAP!

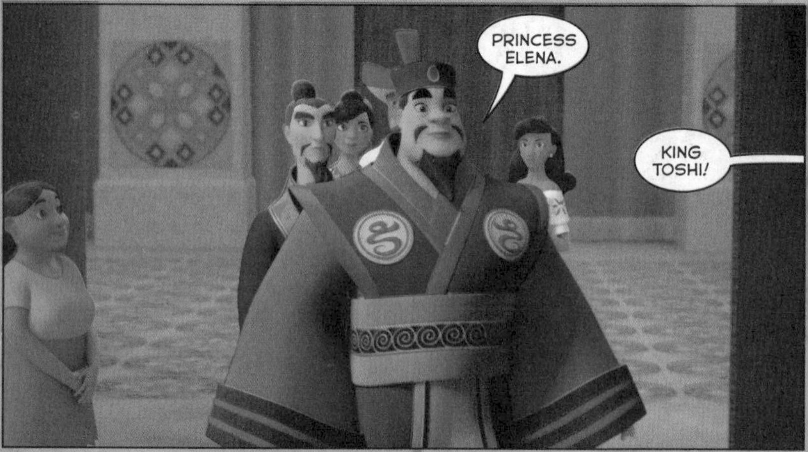
PRINCESS ELENA.
KING TOSHI!

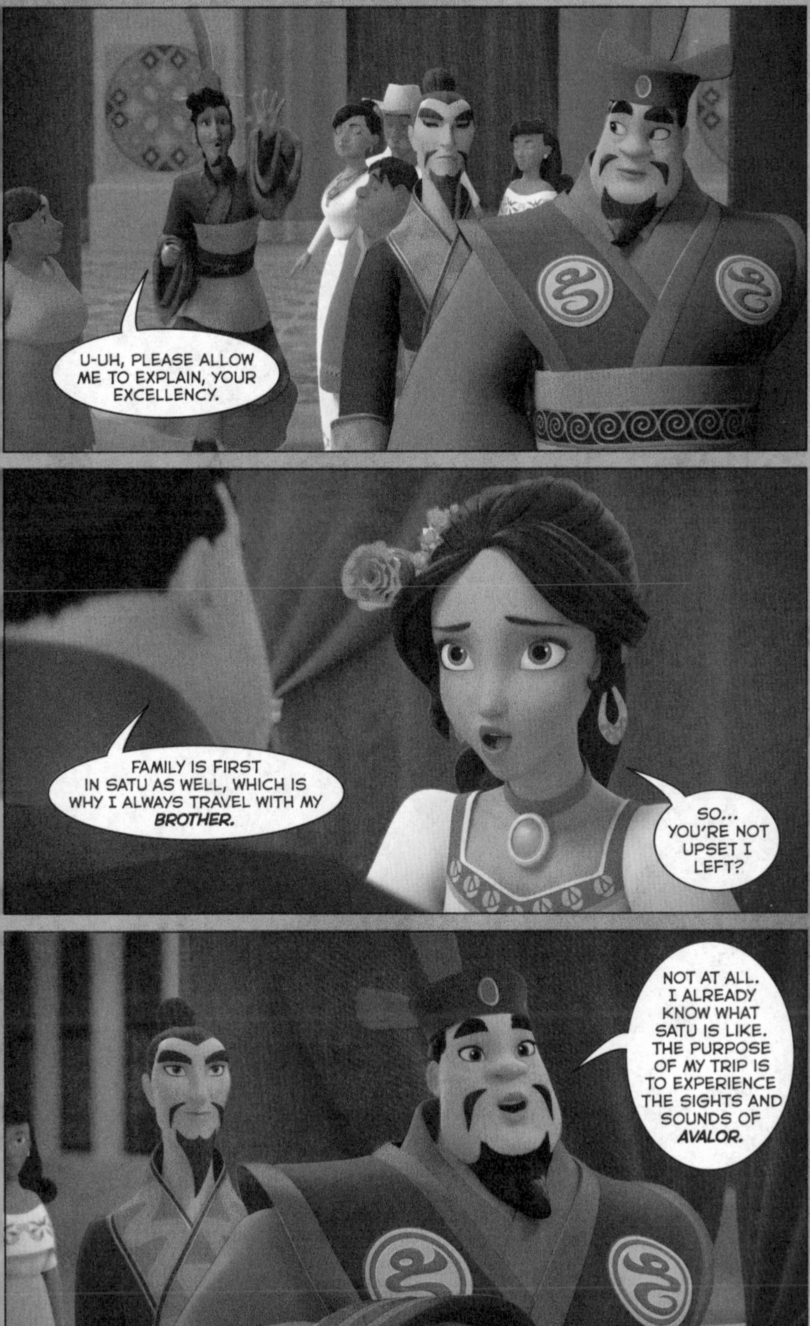
U-UH, PLEASE ALLOW ME TO EXPLAIN, YOUR EXCELLENCY.
FAMILY IS FIRST IN SATU AS WELL, WHICH IS WHY I ALWAYS TRAVEL WITH MY **BROTHER.**
SO... YOU'RE NOT UPSET I LEFT?
NOT AT ALL. I ALREADY KNOW WHAT SATU IS LIKE. THE PURPOSE OF MY TRIP IS TO EXPERIENCE THE SIGHTS AND SOUNDS OF **AVALOR.**

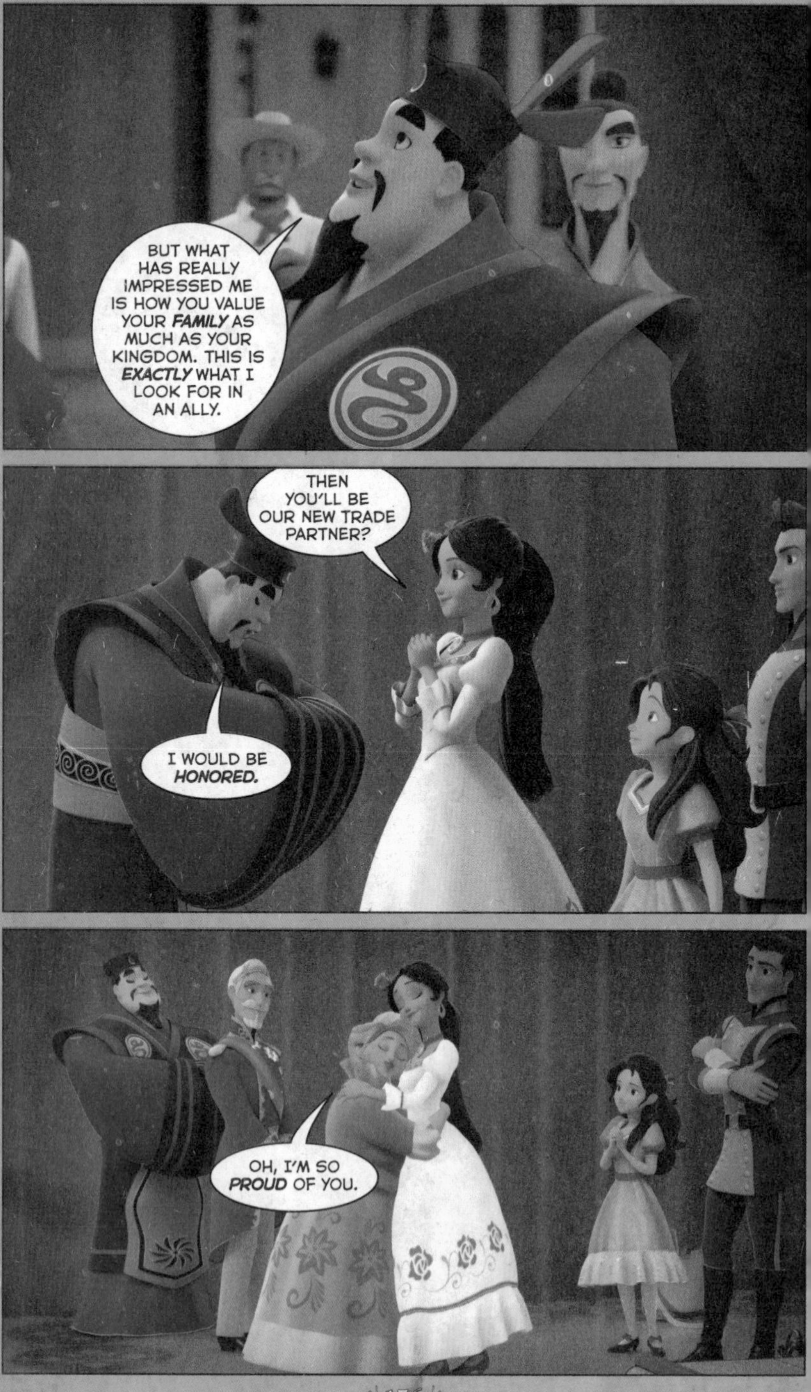
BUT WHAT HAS REALLY IMPRESSED ME IS HOW YOU VALUE YOUR FAMILY AS MUCH AS YOUR KINGDOM. THIS IS EXACTLY WHAT I LOOK FOR IN AN ALLY.
THEN YOU'LL BE OUR NEW TRADE PARTNER?
I WOULD BE HONORED.
OH, I'M SO PROUD OF YOU.

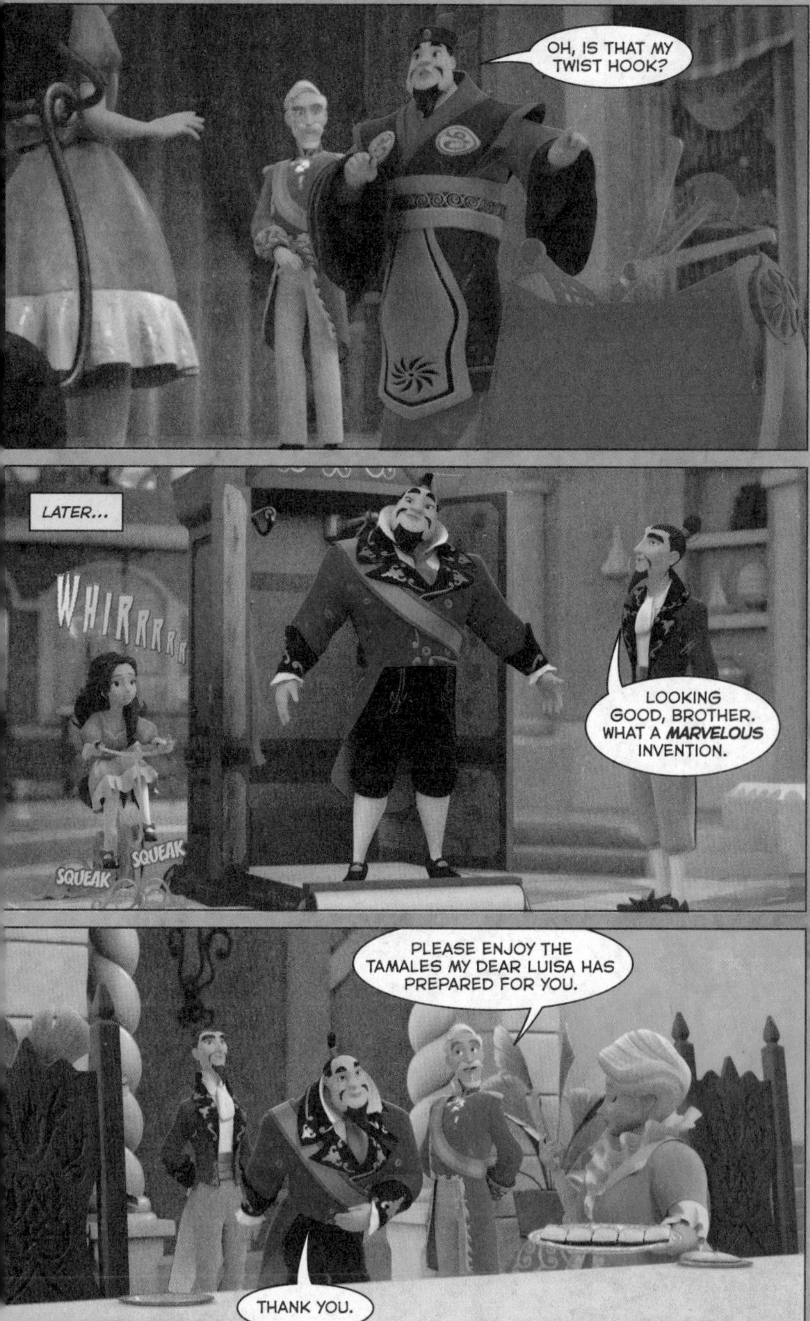

OH, IS THAT MY TWIST HOOK?
LATER...
WHIRRRRR
SQUEAK
SQUEAK
LOOKING GOOD, BROTHER. WHAT A *MARVELOUS* INVENTION.
PLEASE ENJOY THE TAMALES MY DEAR LUISA HAS PREPARED FOR YOU.
THANK YOU.

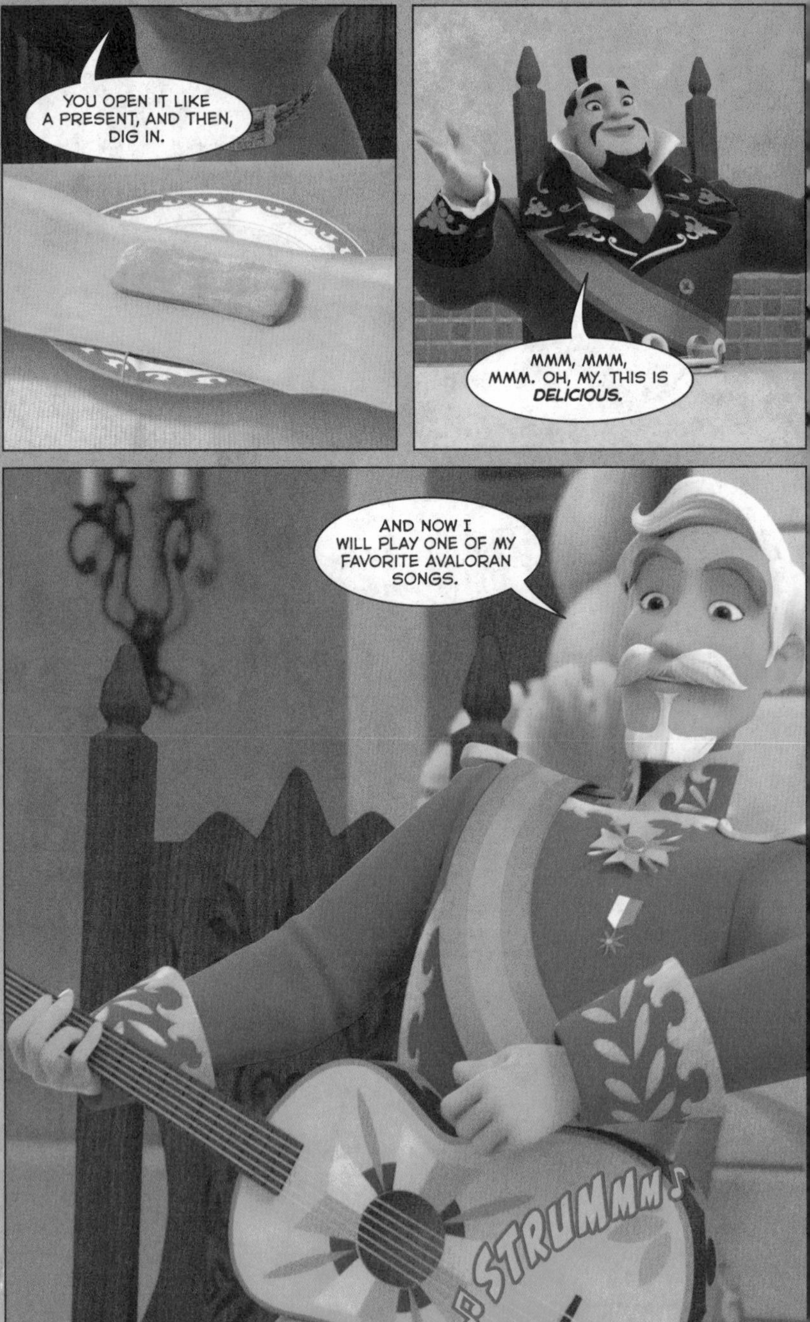
YOU OPEN IT LIKE A PRESENT, AND THEN, DIG IN.
MMM, MMM, MMM. OH, MY. THIS IS DELICIOUS.
AND NOW I WILL PLAY ONE OF MY FAVORITE AVALORAN SONGS.
STRUMMM

ESTEBAN TRIES TO EAT HIS TAMALE WITH CHOPSTICKS.

AH.

FWP! FWP! FWP!

SIGH.

CHANCELLOR ESTEBAN, WHEN IN AVALOR, PERHAPS YOU SHOULD DO IT THE *AVALORAN* WAY.

THANK YOU, ELENA. YOU WERE REALLY THERE FOR ME TODAY.

THAT'S WHAT SISTERS DO.

End.

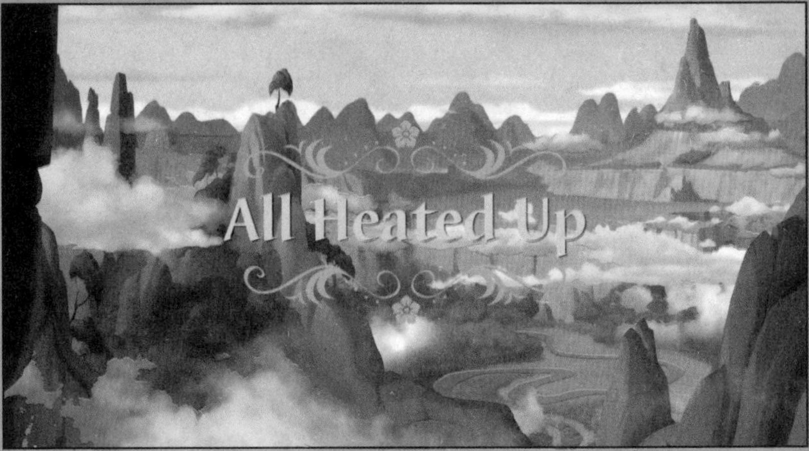
All Heated Up

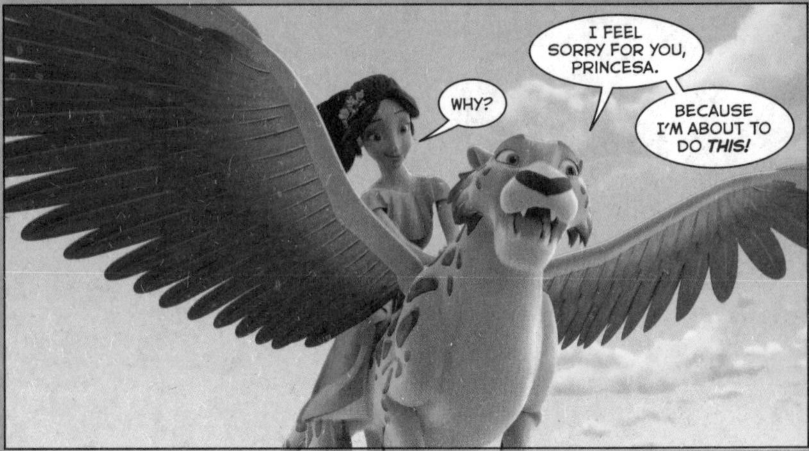
WHY?
I FEEL SORRY FOR YOU, PRINCESA.
BECAUSE I'M ABOUT TO DO *THIS!*

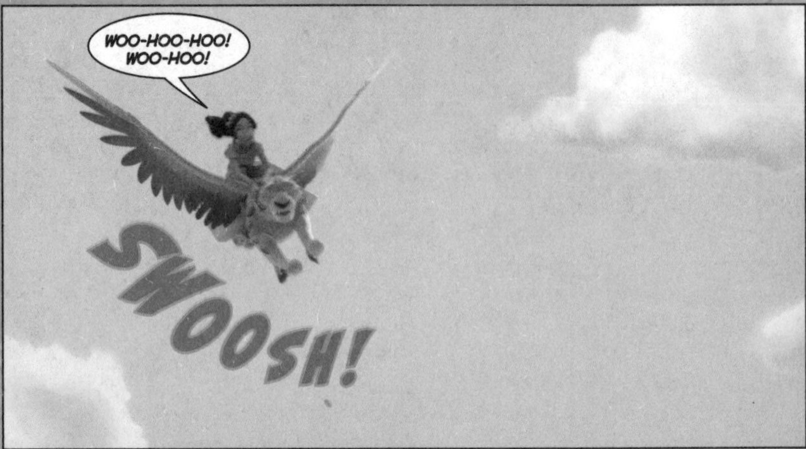
WOO-HOO-HOO! WOO-HOO!
SWOOSH!

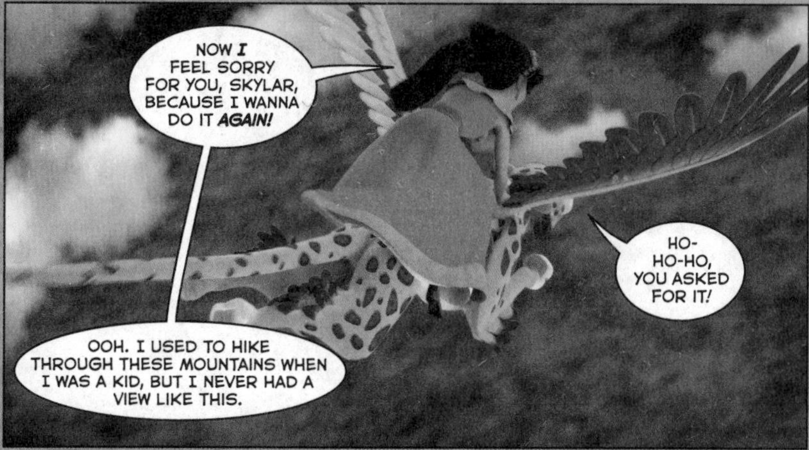
NOW I FEEL SORRY FOR YOU, SKYLAR, BECAUSE I WANNA DO IT AGAIN!
HO-HO-HO, YOU ASKED FOR IT!
OOH. I USED TO HIKE THROUGH THESE MOUNTAINS WHEN I WAS A KID, BUT I NEVER HAD A VIEW LIKE THIS.

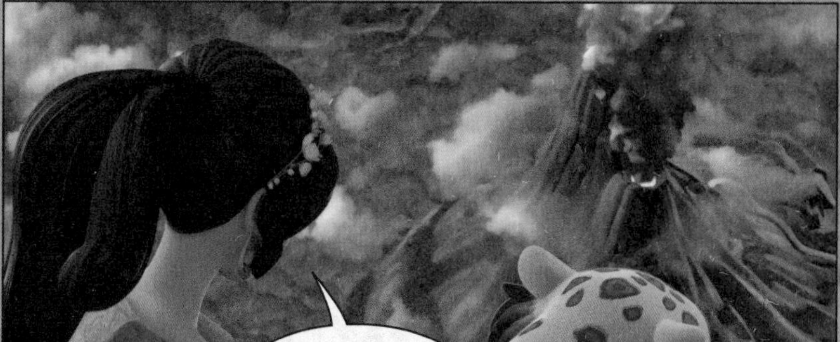
WHOA! BUT I DO NOT REMEMBER THAT MONFUEGO BEING ACTIVE.

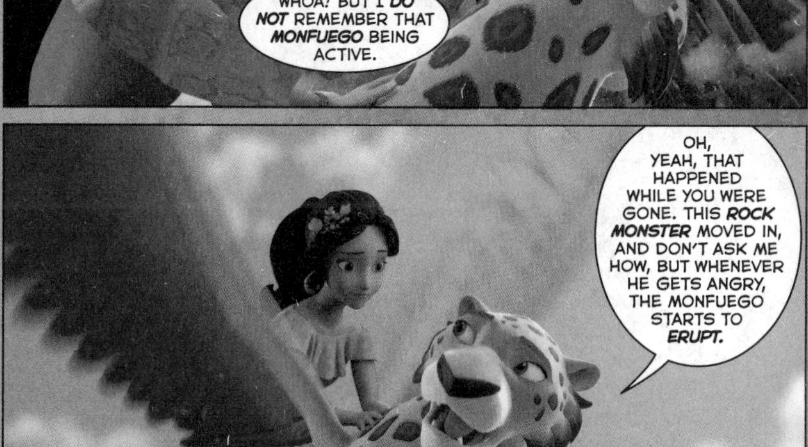
OH, YEAH, THAT HAPPENED WHILE YOU WERE GONE. THIS ROCK MONSTER MOVED IN, AND DON'T ASK ME HOW, BUT WHENEVER HE GETS ANGRY, THE MONFUEGO STARTS TO ERUPT.

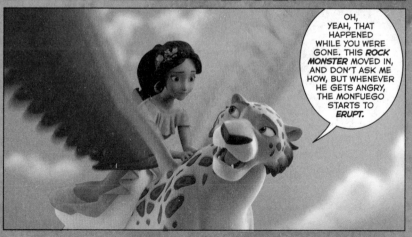

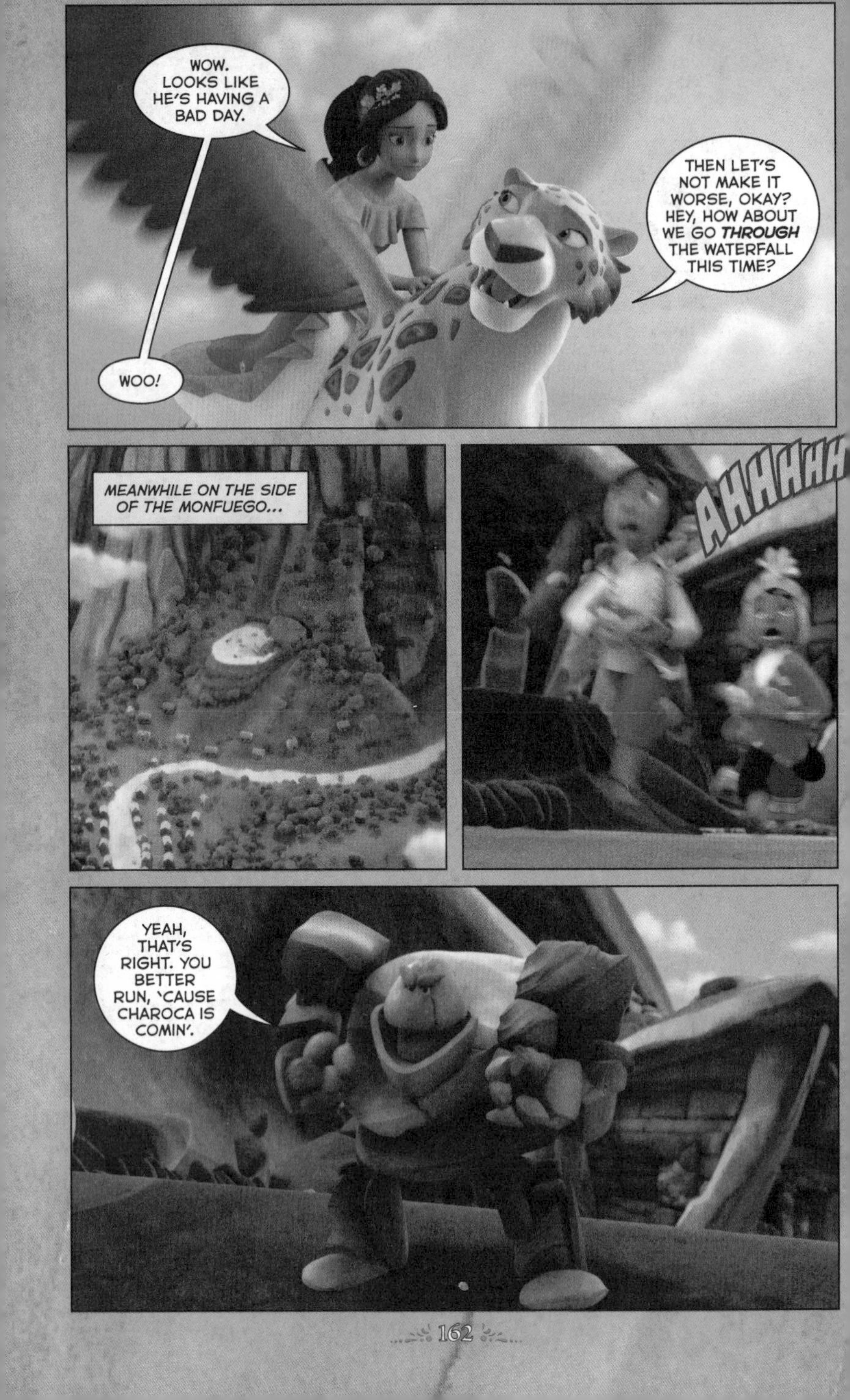
WOW. LOOKS LIKE HE'S HAVING A BAD DAY.
WOO!
THEN LET'S NOT MAKE IT WORSE, OKAY? HEY, HOW ABOUT WE GO *THROUGH* THE WATERFALL THIS TIME?
MEANWHILE ON THE SIDE OF THE MONFUEGO...
AHHHHHH
YEAH, THAT'S RIGHT. YOU BETTER RUN, 'CAUSE CHAROCA IS COMIN'.

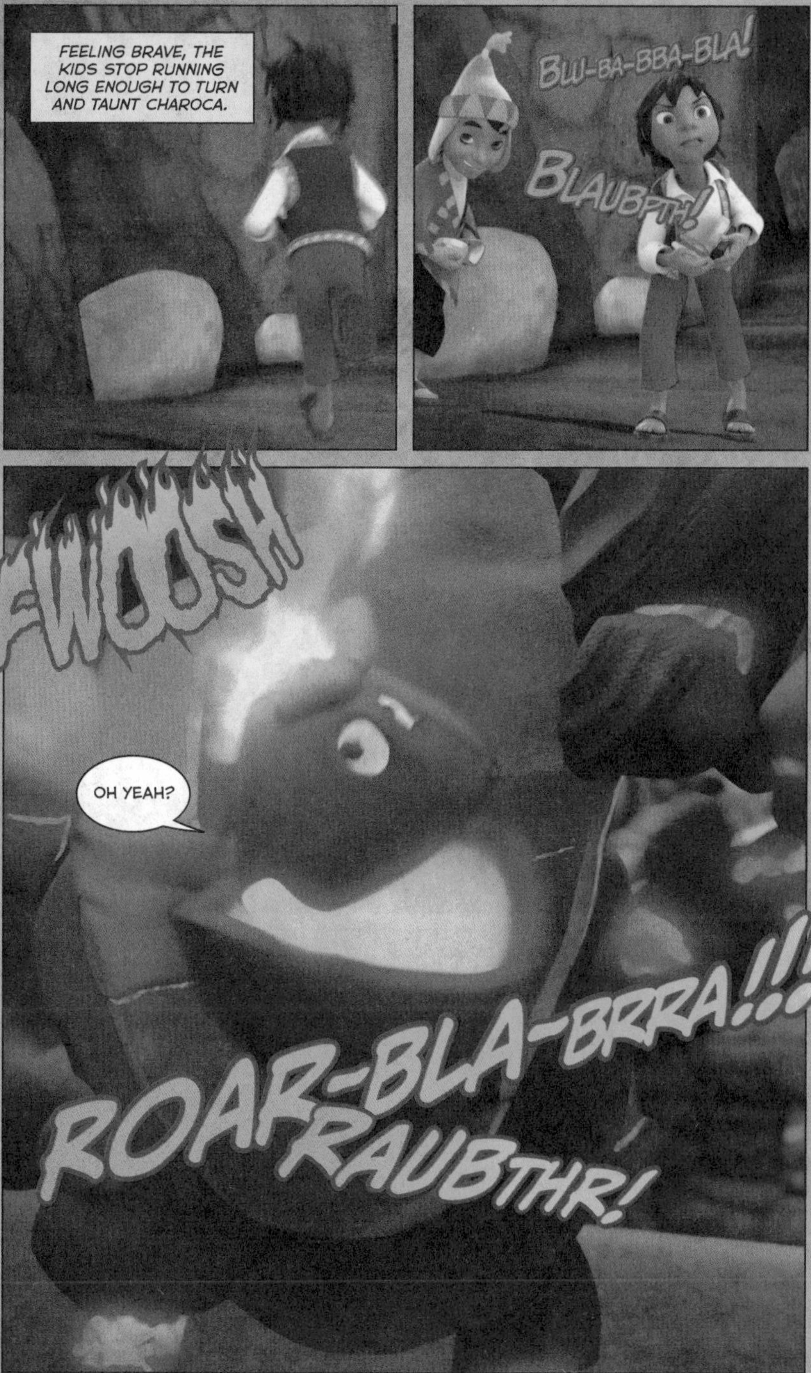

FEELING BRAVE, THE KIDS STOP RUNNING LONG ENOUGH TO TURN AND TAUNT CHAROCA.
BLU-BA-BBA-BLA!
BLAUBPTH!
FWOOSH
OH YEAH?
ROAR-BLA-BRRA!!!
RAUBTHR!

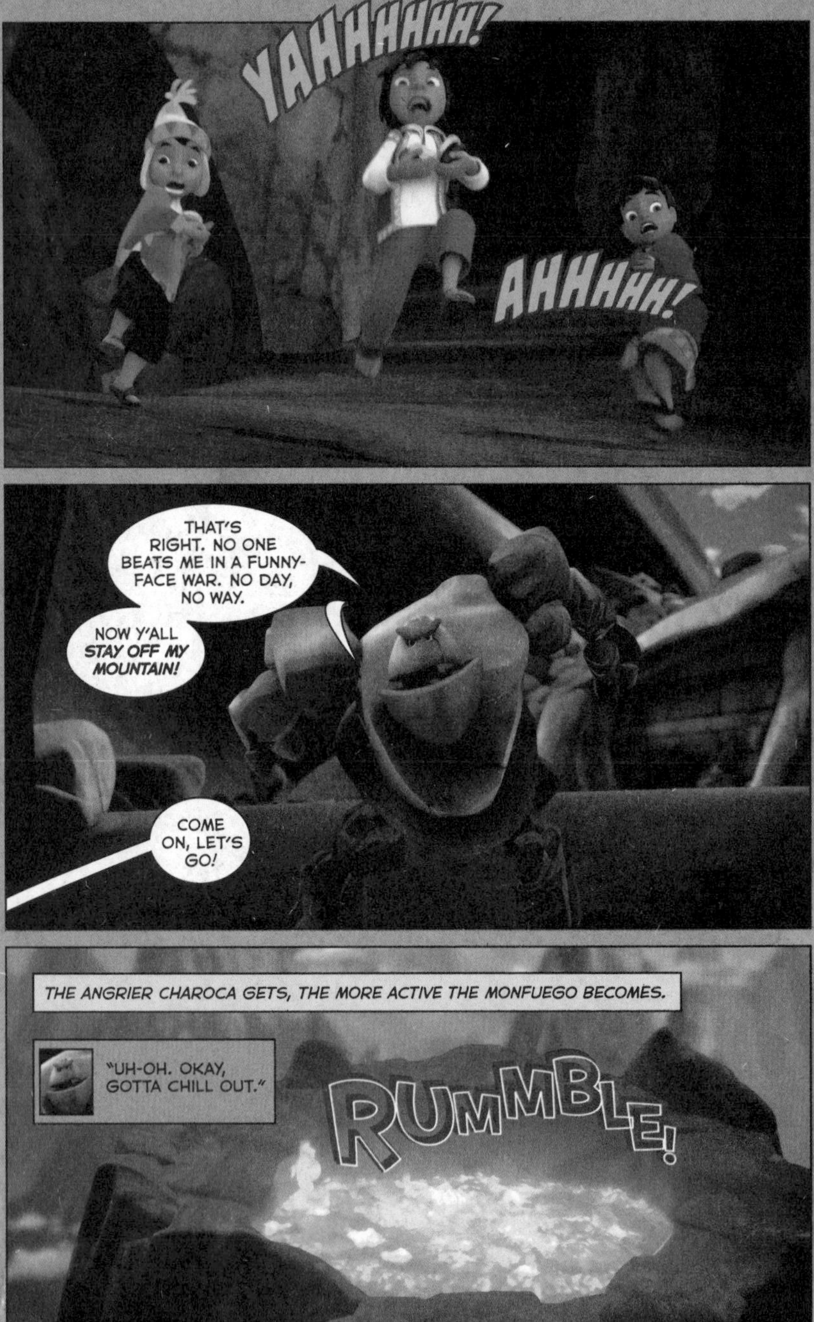
YAHHHHHH!
AHHHHH!
THAT'S RIGHT. NO ONE BEATS ME IN A FUNNY-FACE WAR. NO DAY, NO WAY.
NOW Y'ALL STAY OFF MY MOUNTAIN!
COME ON, LET'S GO!
THE ANGRIER CHAROCA GETS, THE MORE ACTIVE THE MONFUEGO BECOMES.
"UH-OH. OKAY, GOTTA CHILL OUT."
RUMMBLE!

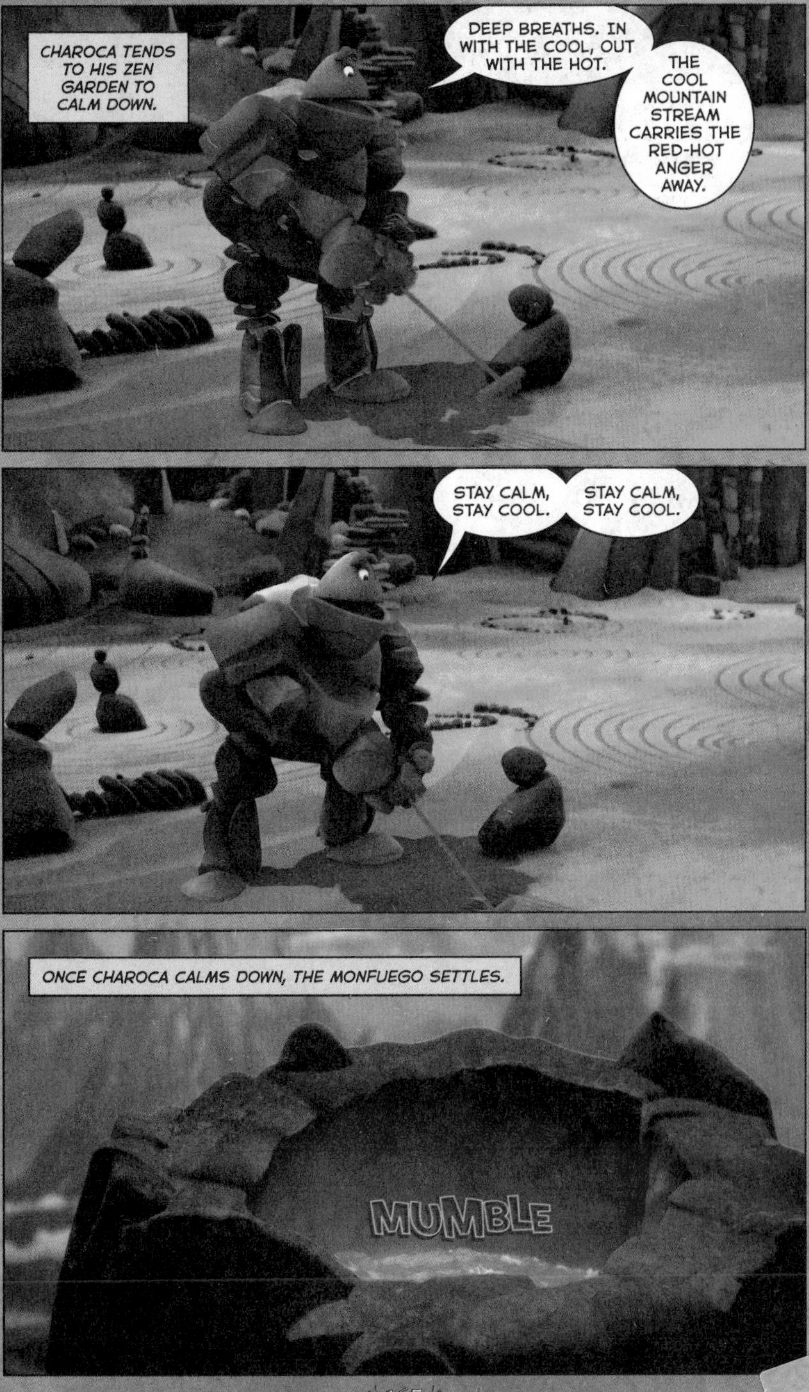
CHAROCA TENDS TO HIS ZEN GARDEN TO CALM DOWN.
DEEP BREATHS. IN WITH THE COOL, OUT WITH THE HOT.
THE COOL MOUNTAIN STREAM CARRIES THE RED-HOT ANGER AWAY.
STAY CALM, STAY COOL.
STAY CALM, STAY COOL.
ONCE CHAROCA CALMS DOWN, THE MONFUEGO SETTLES.
MUMBLE

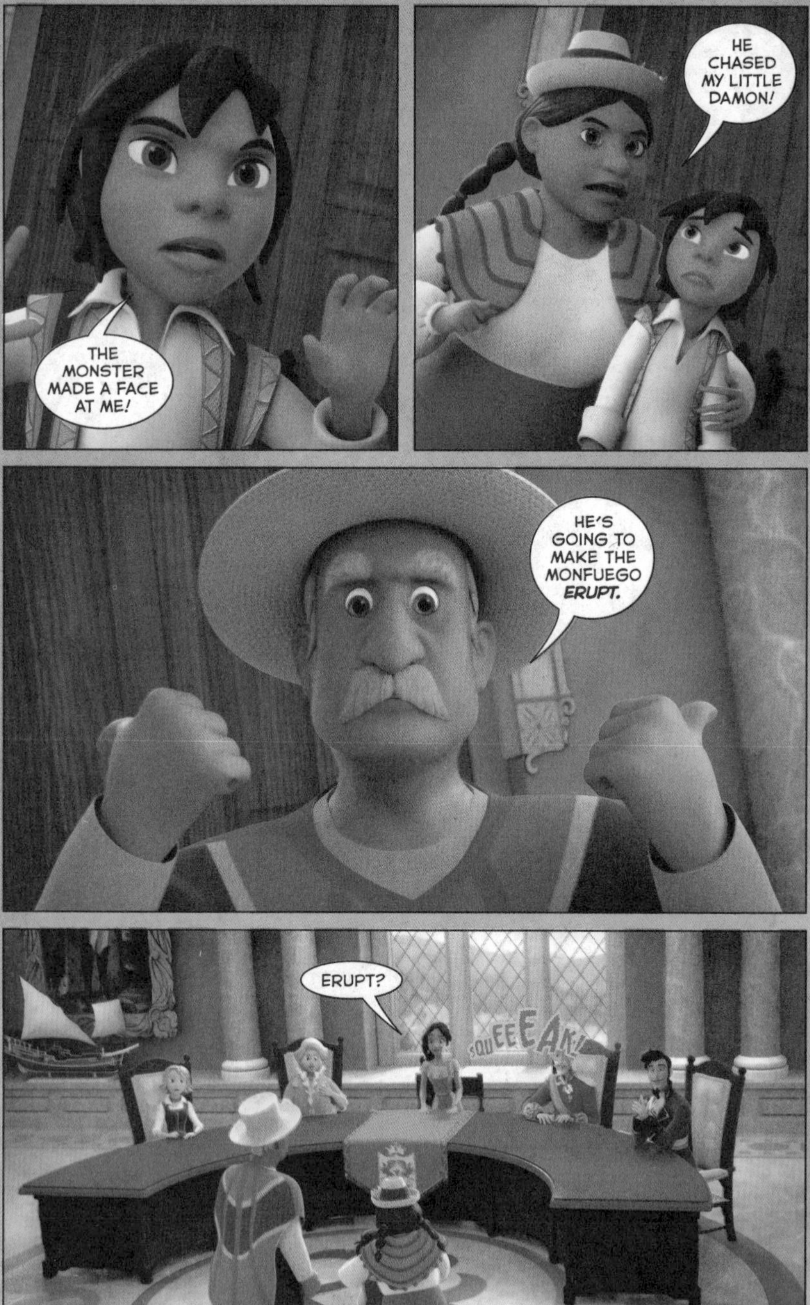
THE MONSTER MADE A FACE AT ME!
HE CHASED MY LITTLE DAMON!
HE'S GOING TO MAKE THE MONFUEGO *ERUPT.*
ERUPT?
SQUEEEAK!

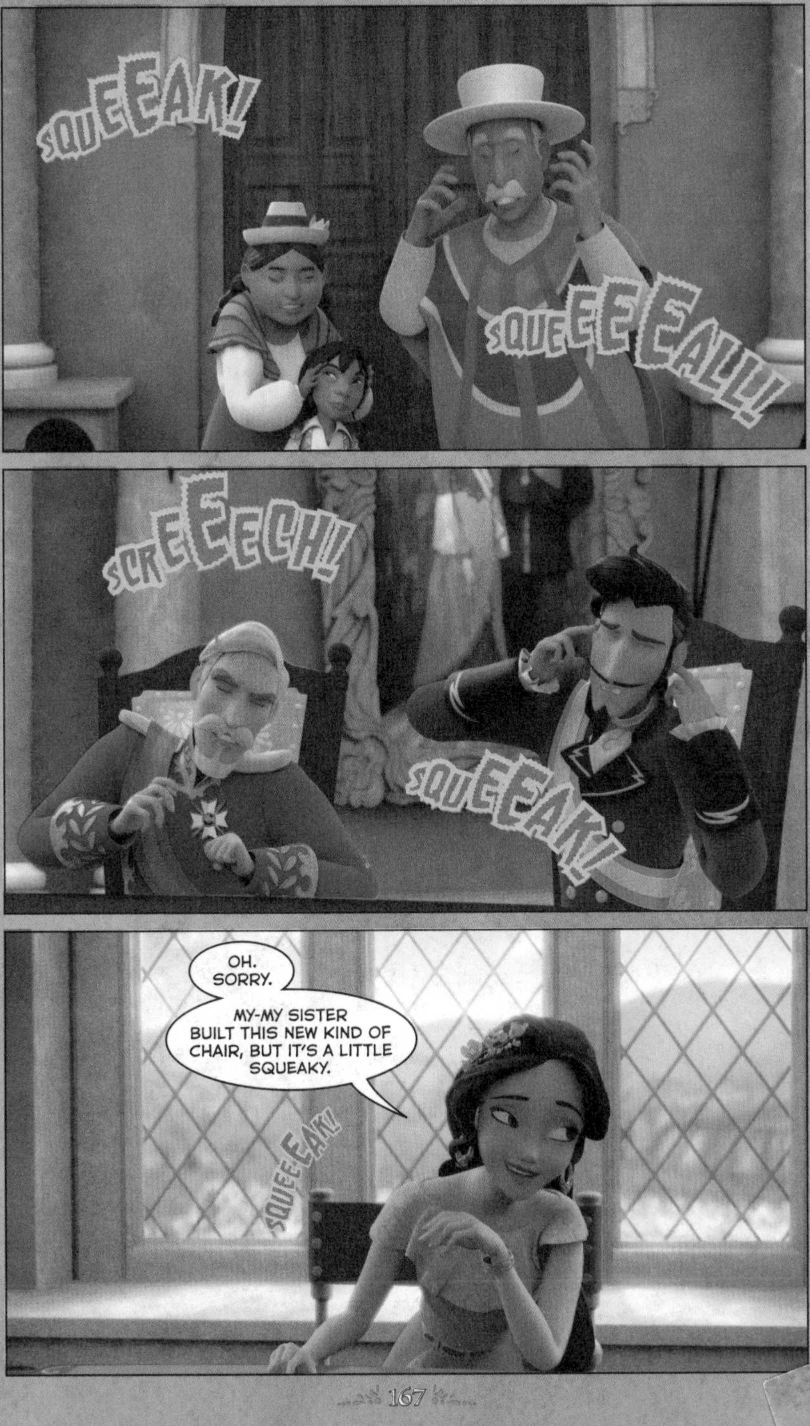
SQUEEAK!!
SQUEEEEALL!!
SCREEEECH!!
SQUEEAK!!
OH. SORRY.
MY-MY SISTER BUILT THIS NEW KIND OF CHAIR, BUT IT'S A LITTLE SQUEAKY.
SQUEEEAK!

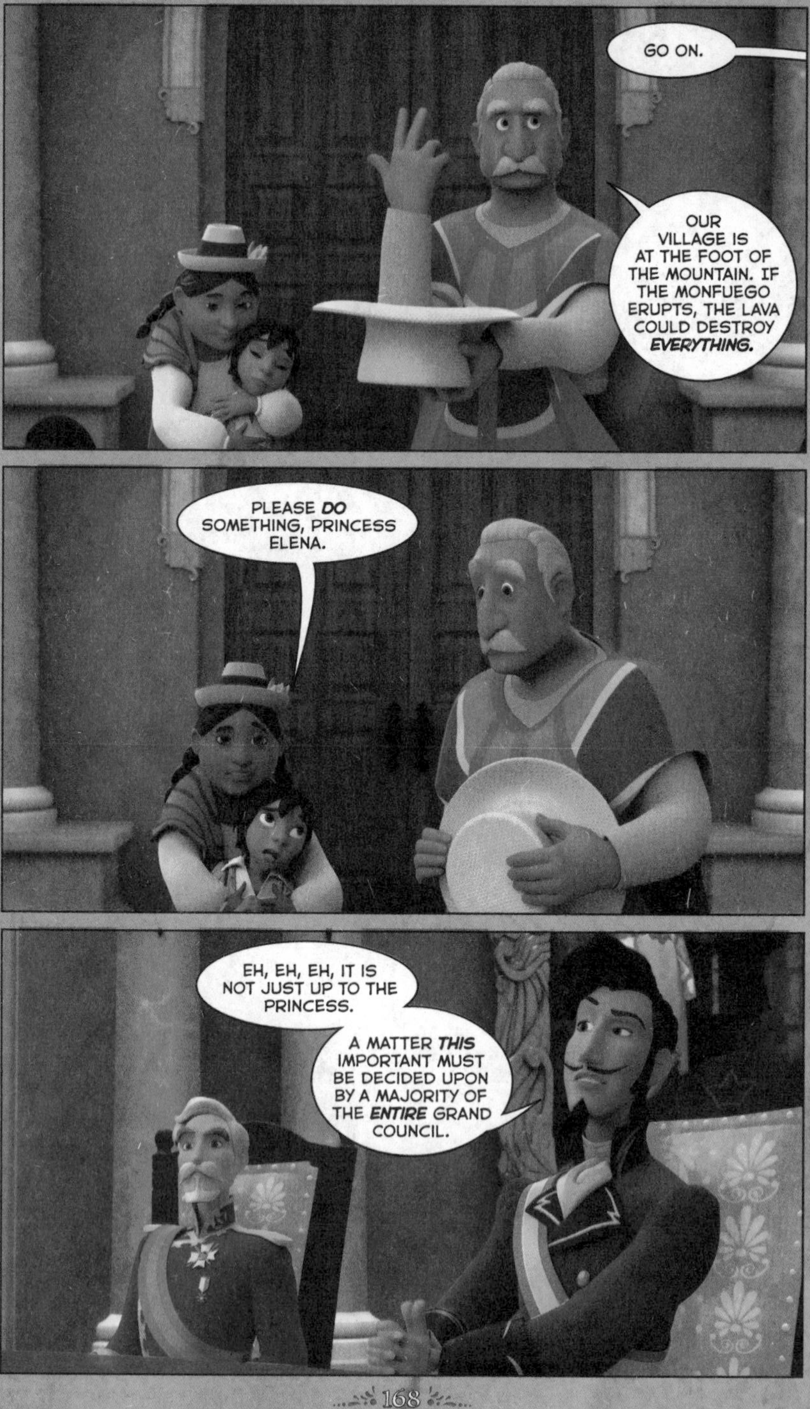
GO ON.
OUR VILLAGE IS AT THE FOOT OF THE MOUNTAIN. IF THE MONFUEGO ERUPTS, THE LAVA COULD DESTROY *EVERYTHING.*
PLEASE *DO* SOMETHING, PRINCESS ELENA.
EH, EH, EH, IT IS NOT JUST UP TO THE PRINCESS.
A MATTER *THIS* IMPORTANT MUST BE DECIDED UPON BY A MAJORITY OF THE *ENTIRE* GRAND COUNCIL.

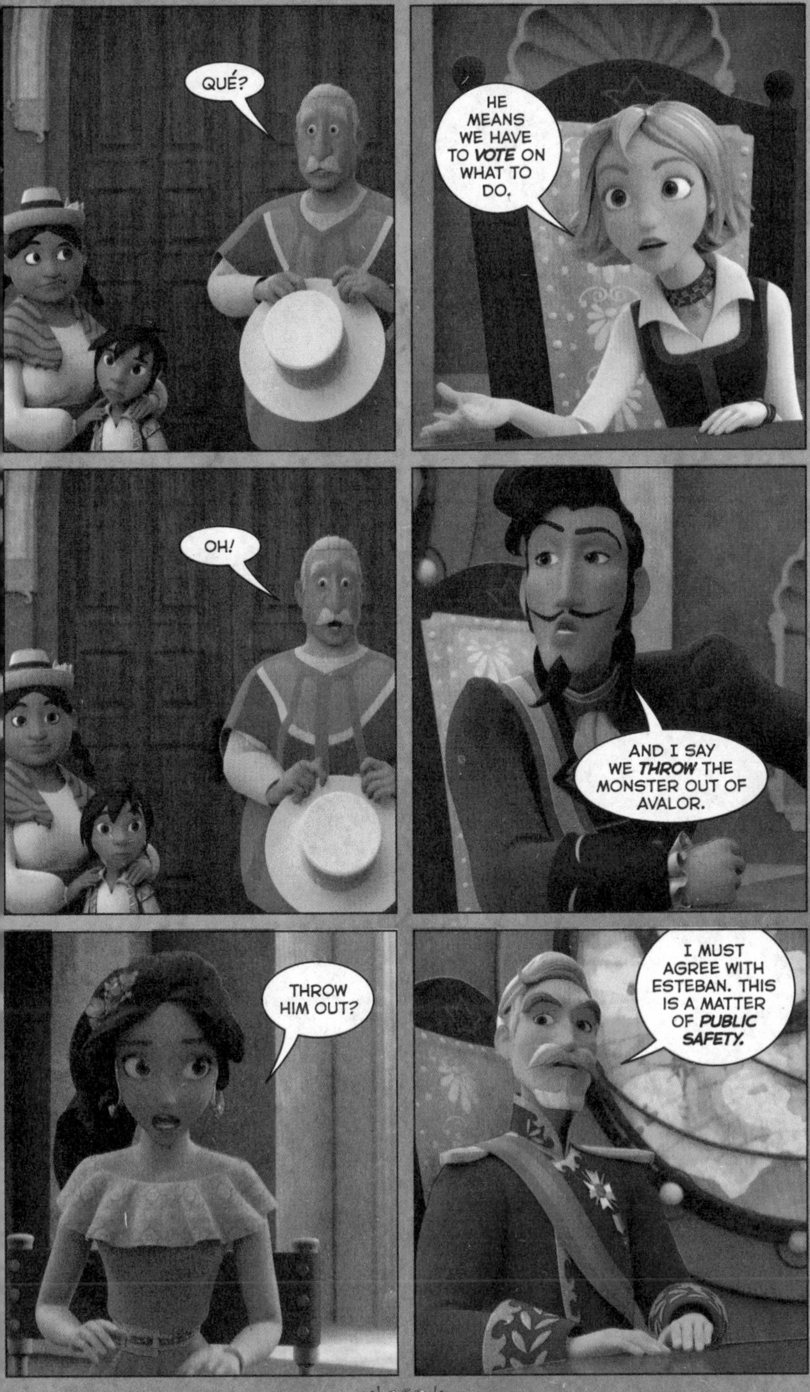
QUÉ?
HE MEANS WE HAVE TO VOTE ON WHAT TO DO.
OH!
AND I SAY WE THROW THE MONSTER OUT OF AVALOR.
THROW HIM OUT?
I MUST AGREE WITH ESTEBAN. THIS IS A MATTER OF PUBLIC SAFETY.

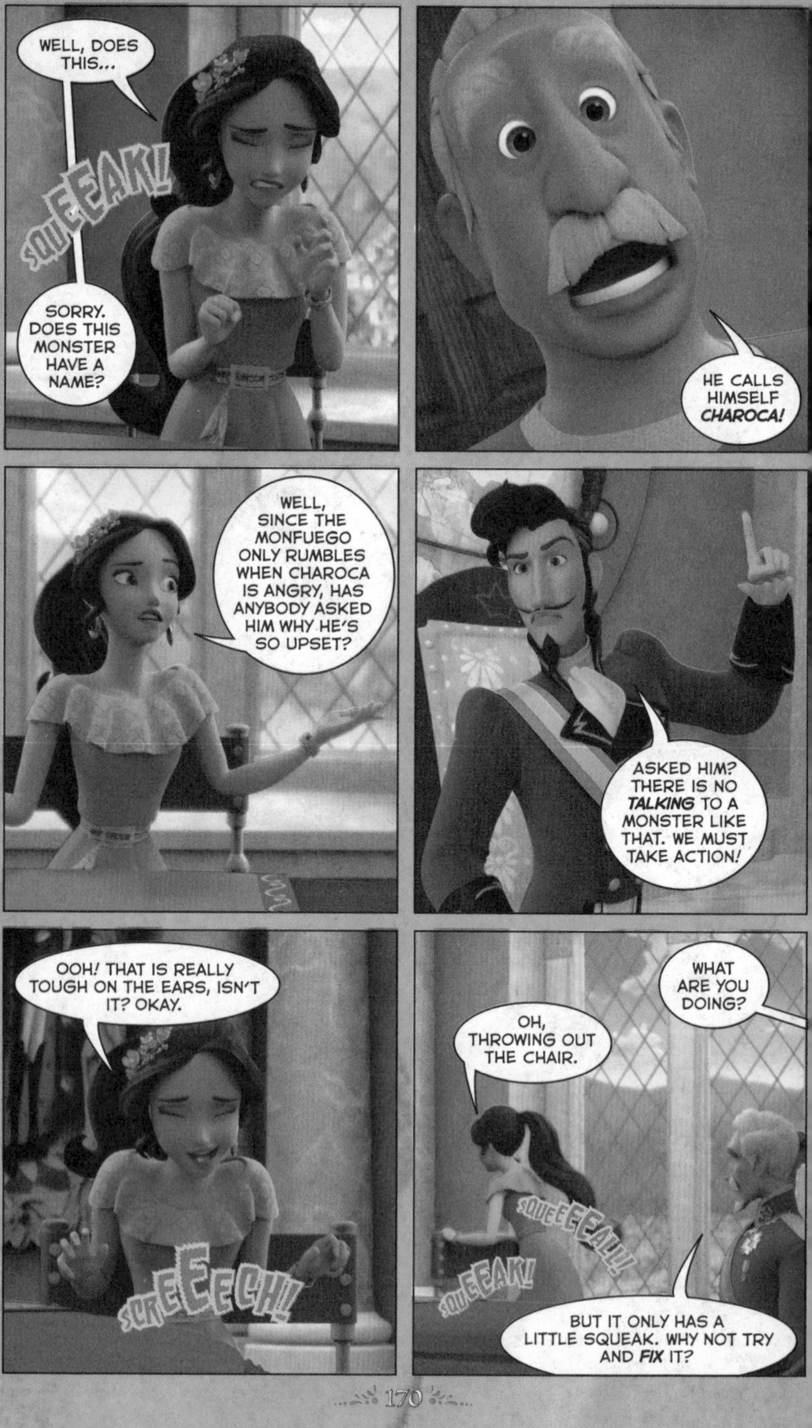

WELL, DOES THIS...
SQUEEAK!
SORRY. DOES THIS MONSTER HAVE A NAME?
HE CALLS HIMSELF *CHAROCA!*
WELL, SINCE THE MONFUEGO ONLY RUMBLES WHEN CHAROCA IS ANGRY, HAS ANYBODY ASKED HIM WHY HE'S SO UPSET?
ASKED HIM? THERE IS NO *TALKING* TO A MONSTER LIKE THAT. WE MUST TAKE ACTION!
OOH! THAT IS REALLY TOUGH ON THE EARS, ISN'T IT? OKAY.
SCREEECH!!
WHAT ARE YOU DOING?
OH, THROWING OUT THE CHAIR.
SQUEEEEAK!!
SQUEEAK!
BUT IT ONLY HAS A LITTLE SQUEAK. WHY NOT TRY AND *FIX* IT?

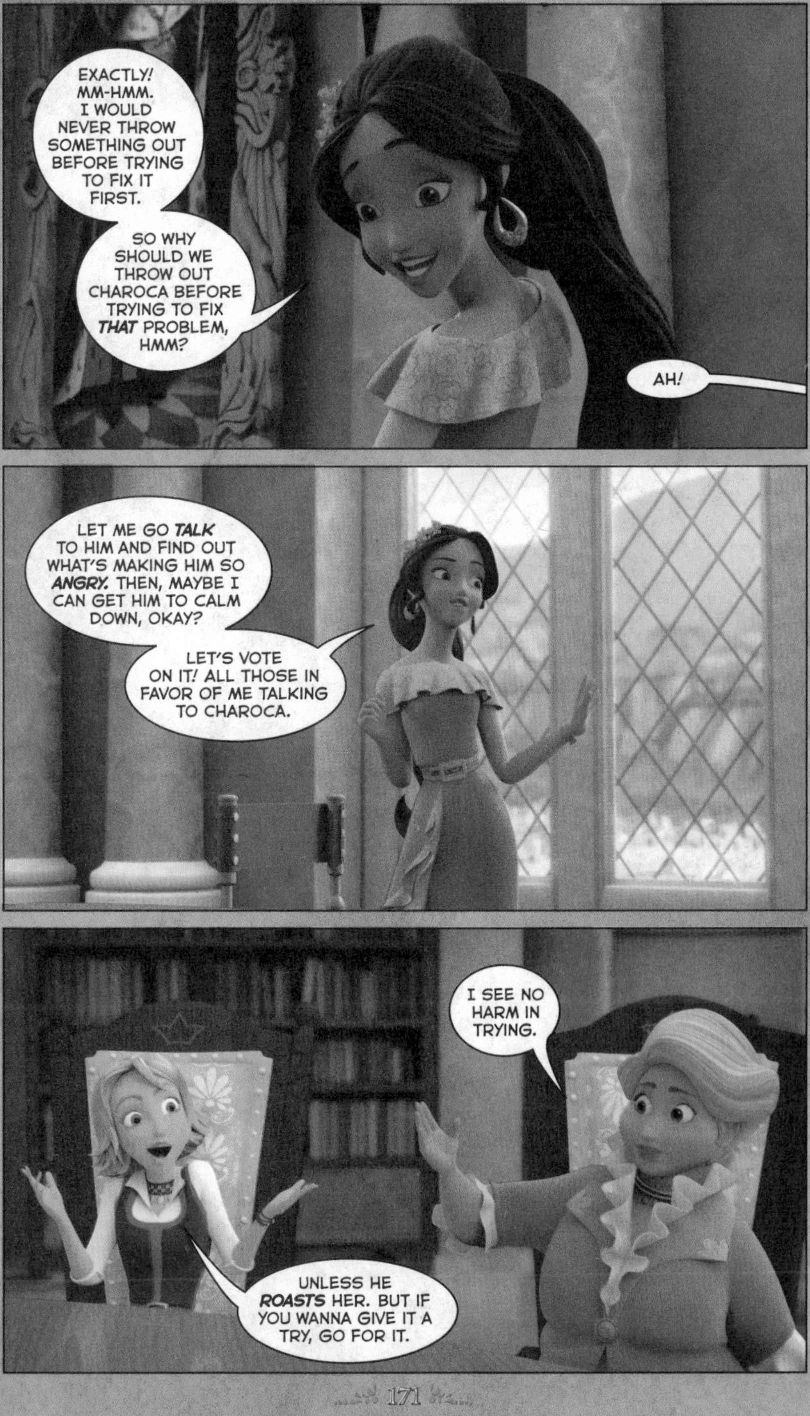
EXACTLY! MM-HMM. I WOULD NEVER THROW SOMETHING OUT BEFORE TRYING TO FIX IT FIRST.
SO WHY SHOULD WE THROW OUT CHAROCA BEFORE TRYING TO FIX *THAT* PROBLEM, HMM?
AH!
LET ME GO *TALK* TO HIM AND FIND OUT WHAT'S MAKING HIM SO *ANGRY.* THEN, MAYBE I CAN GET HIM TO CALM DOWN, OKAY?
LET'S VOTE ON IT! ALL THOSE IN FAVOR OF ME TALKING TO CHAROCA.
I SEE NO HARM IN TRYING.
UNLESS HE *ROASTS* HER. BUT IF YOU WANNA GIVE IT A TRY, GO FOR IT.

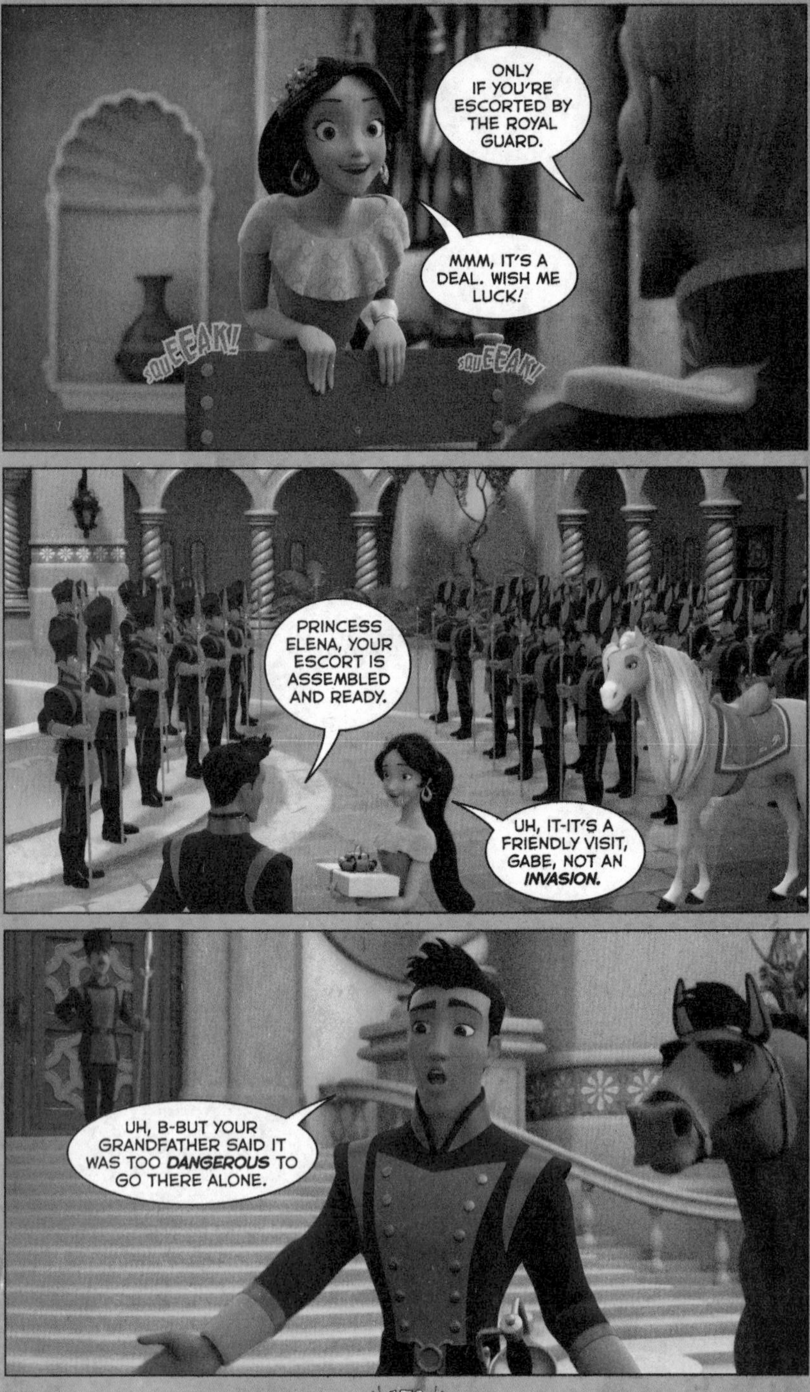
ONLY IF YOU'RE ESCORTED BY THE ROYAL GUARD.
MMM, IT'S A DEAL. WISH ME LUCK!
SQUEEAK!
SQUEEAK!
PRINCESS ELENA, YOUR ESCORT IS ASSEMBLED AND READY.
UH, IT-IT'S A FRIENDLY VISIT, GABE, NOT AN *INVASION*.
UH, B-BUT YOUR GRANDFATHER SAID IT WAS TOO *DANGEROUS* TO GO THERE ALONE.

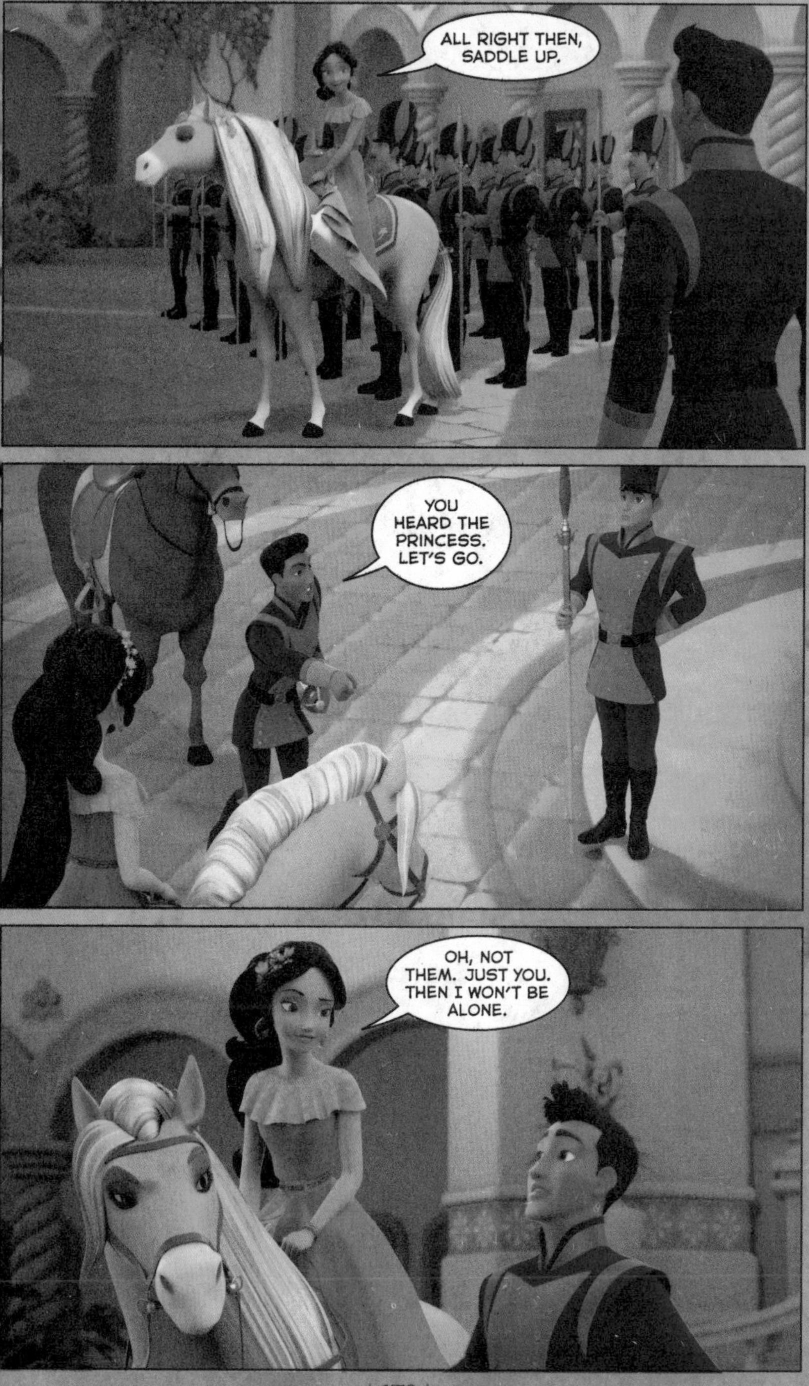
ALL RIGHT THEN, SADDLE UP.
YOU HEARD THE PRINCESS. LET'S GO.
OH, NOT THEM. JUST YOU. THEN I WON'T BE ALONE.

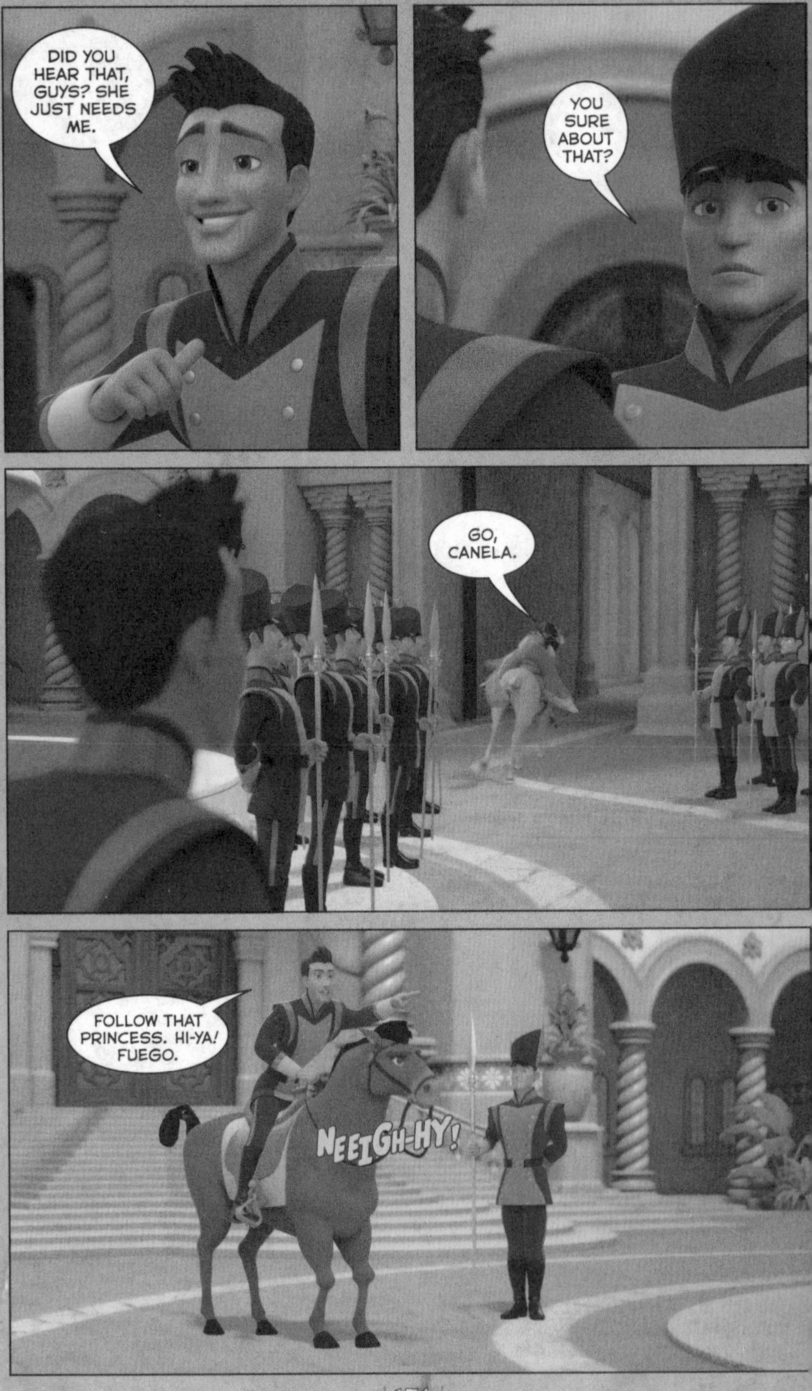
DID YOU HEAR THAT, GUYS? SHE JUST NEEDS ME.
YOU SURE ABOUT THAT?
GO, CANELA.
FOLLOW THAT PRINCESS. HI-YA! FUEGO.
NEEIGH-HY!

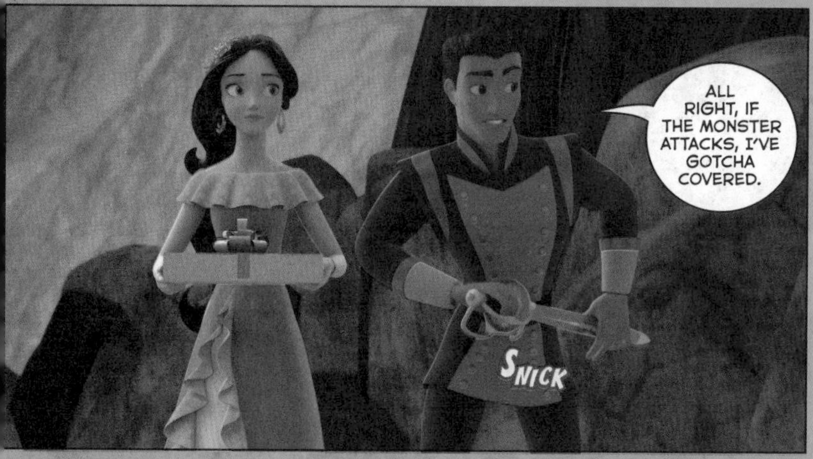
ALL RIGHT, IF THE MONSTER ATTACKS, I'VE GOTCHA COVERED.
SNICK

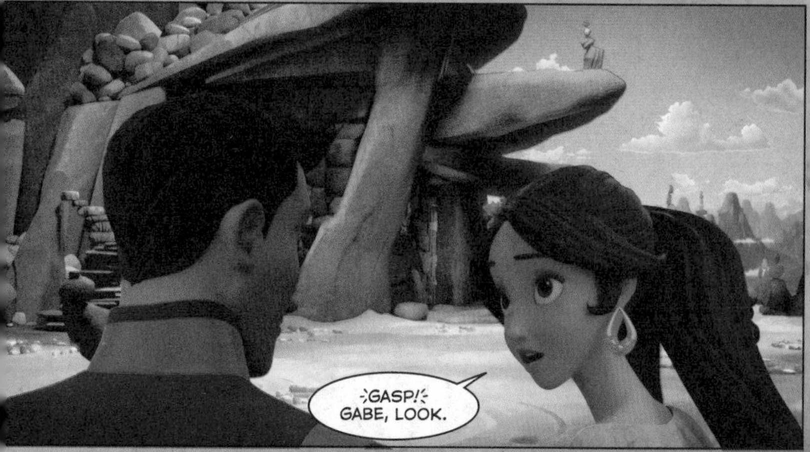
GASP! GABE, LOOK.

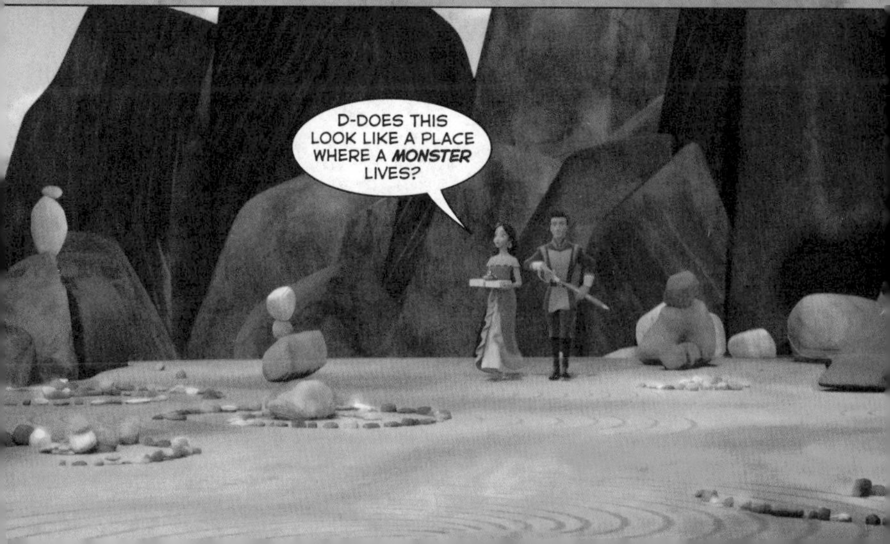
D-DOES THIS LOOK LIKE A PLACE WHERE A MONSTER LIVES?

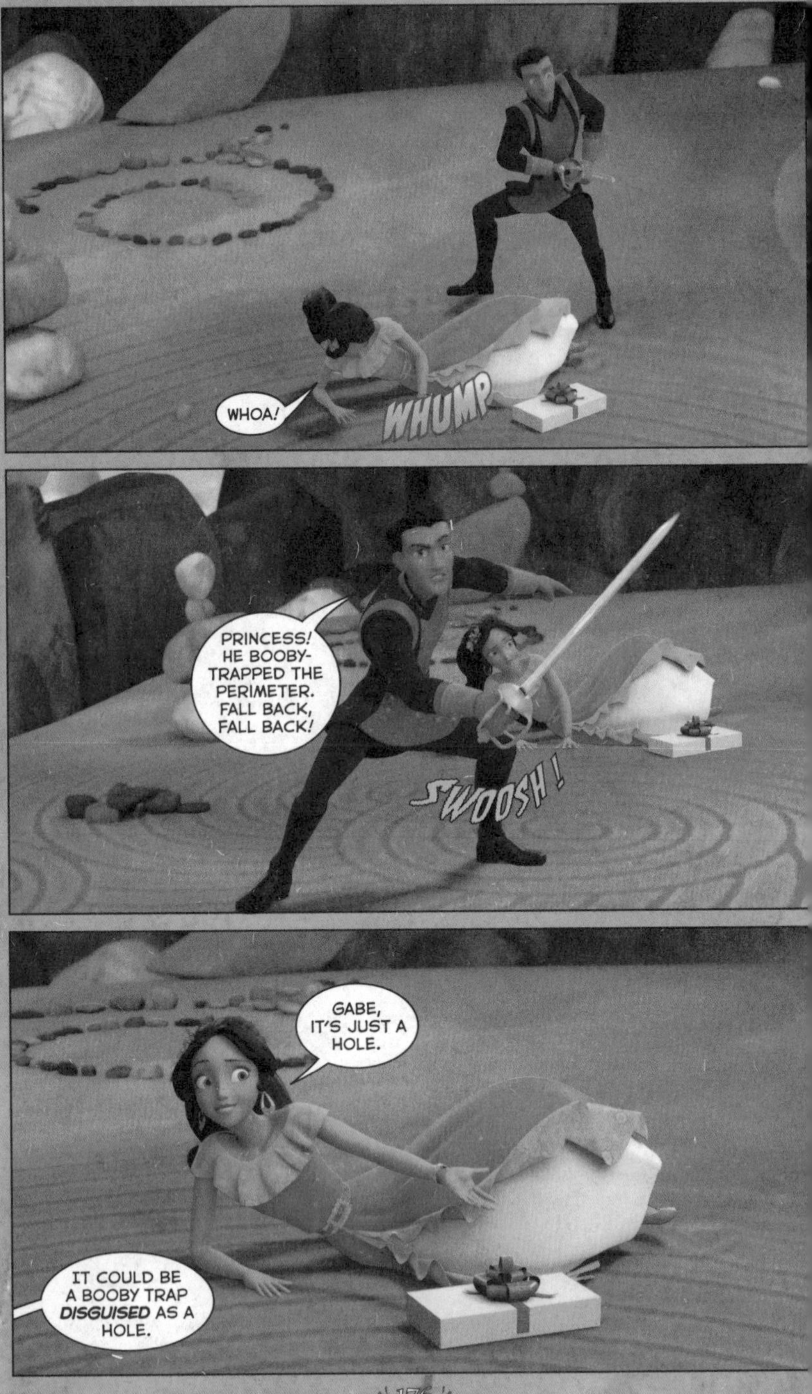
WHOA!
WHUMP
PRINCESS! HE BOOBY-TRAPPED THE PERIMETER. FALL BACK, FALL BACK!
SWOOSH!
GABE, IT'S JUST A HOLE.
IT COULD BE A BOOBY TRAP *DISGUISED* AS A HOLE.

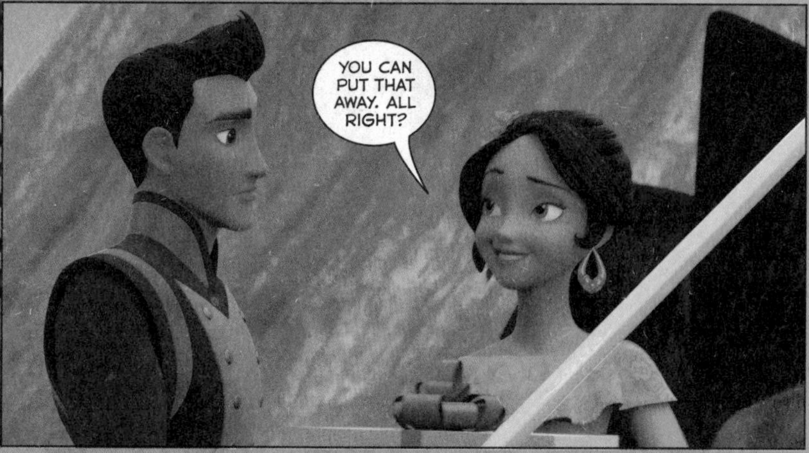
YOU CAN PUT THAT AWAY. ALL RIGHT?

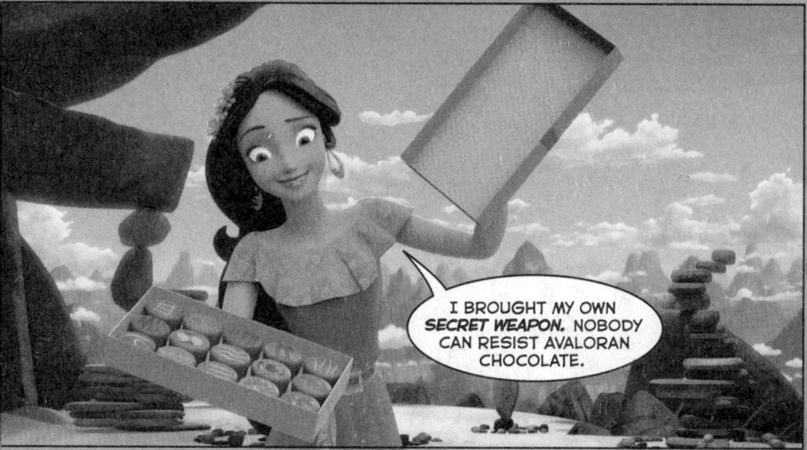
I BROUGHT MY OWN *SECRET WEAPON.* NOBODY CAN RESIST AVALORAN CHOCOLATE.

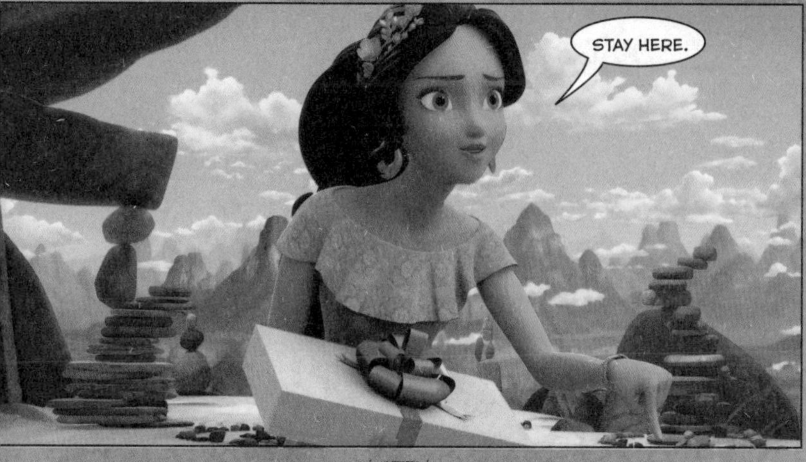
STAY HERE.

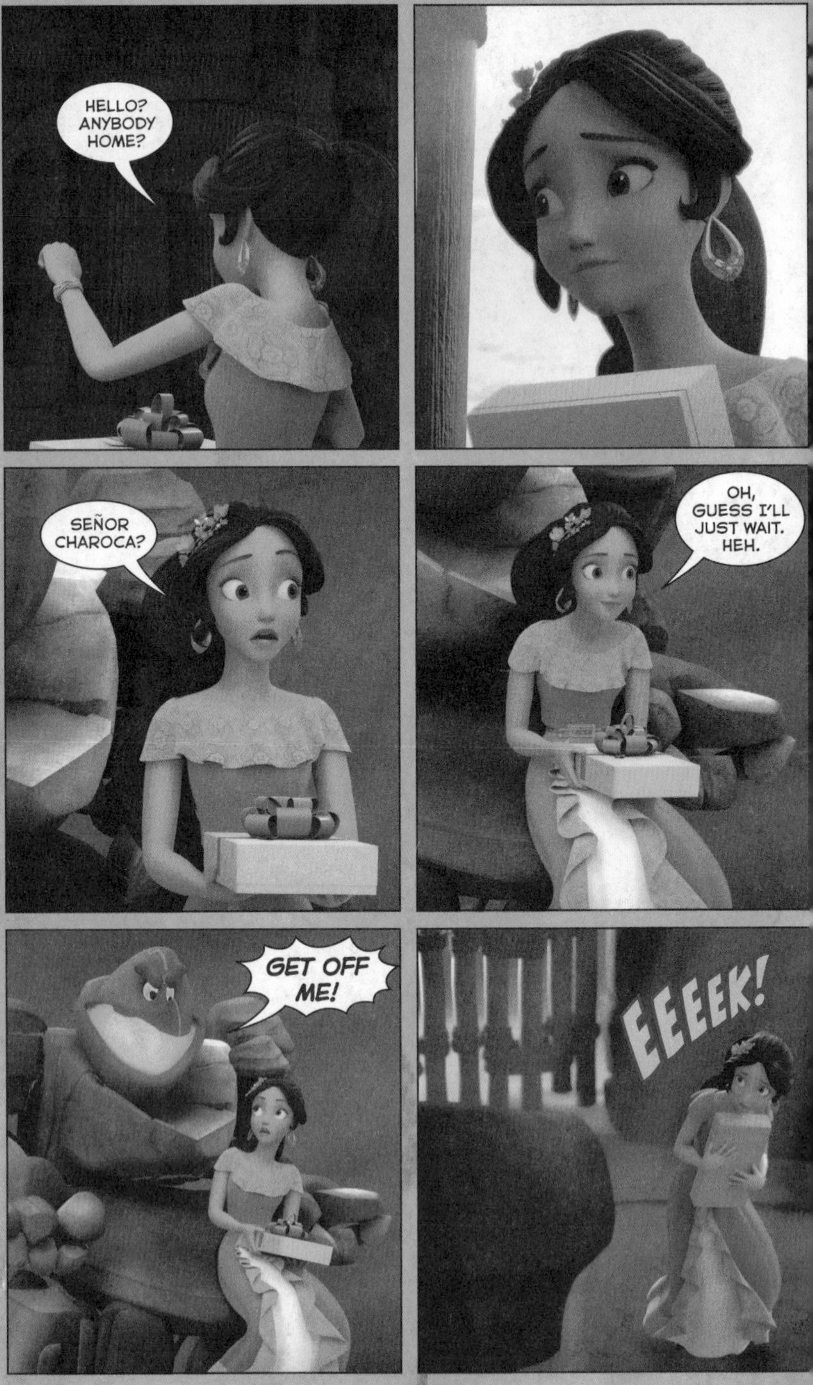
HELLO? ANYBODY HOME?
SEÑOR CHAROCA?
OH, GUESS I'LL JUST WAIT. HEH.
GET OFF ME!
EEEEK!

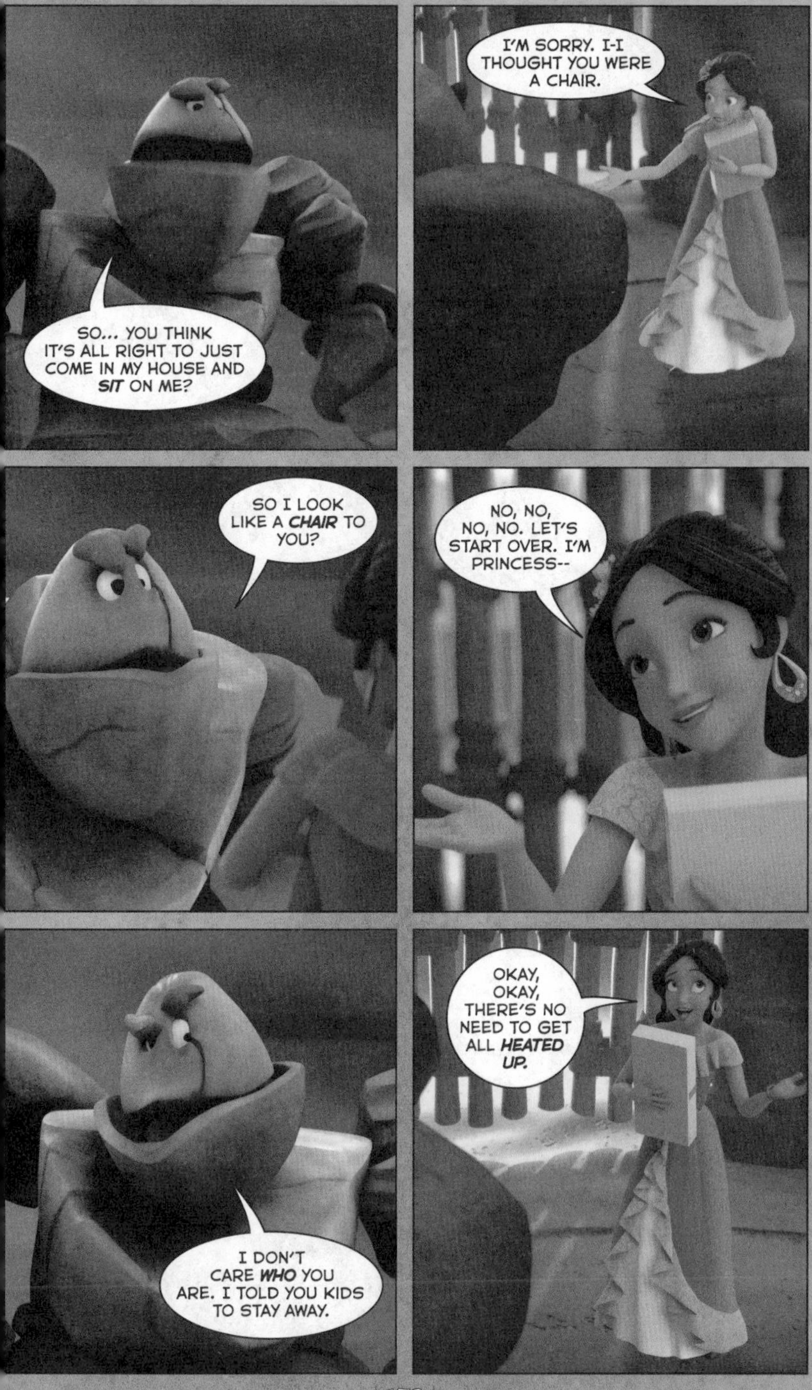
SO... YOU THINK IT'S ALL RIGHT TO JUST COME IN MY HOUSE AND *SIT* ON ME?
I'M SORRY. I-I THOUGHT YOU WERE A CHAIR.
SO I LOOK LIKE A *CHAIR* TO YOU?
NO, NO, NO, NO. LET'S START OVER. I'M PRINCESS--
I DON'T CARE *WHO* YOU ARE. I TOLD YOU KIDS TO STAY AWAY.
OKAY, OKAY, THERE'S NO NEED TO GET ALL *HEATED UP.*

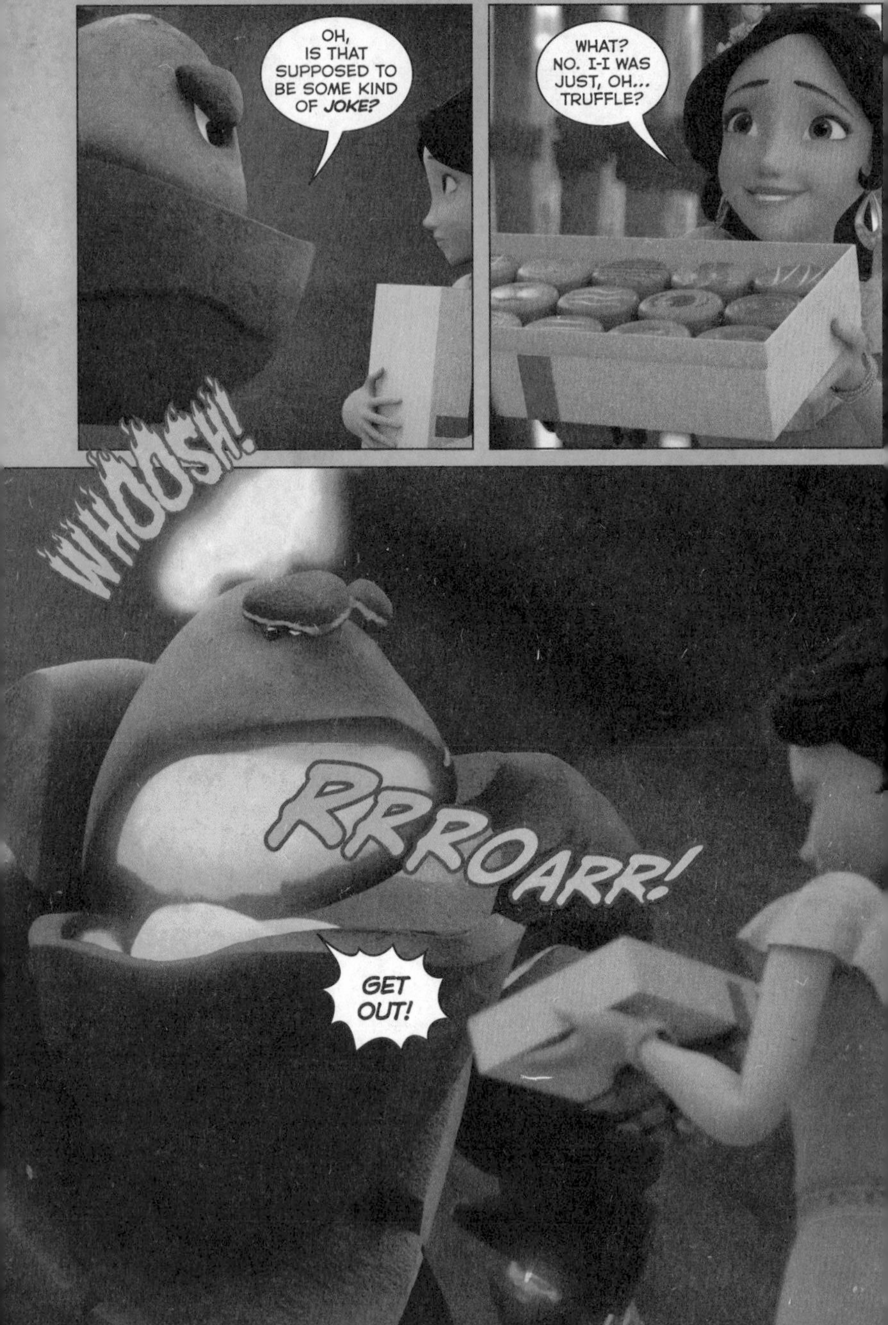
OH, IS THAT SUPPOSED TO BE SOME KIND OF JOKE?
WHAT? NO. I-I WAS JUST, OH... TRUFFLE?
WHOOSH!
RRROARR!
GET OUT!

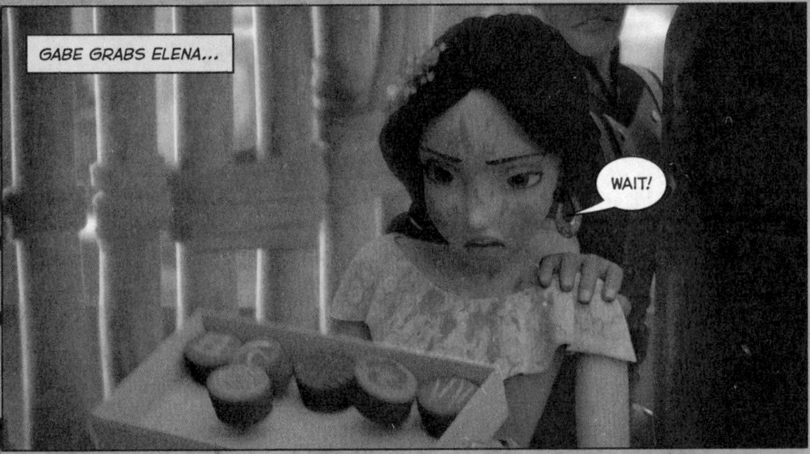
GABE GRABS ELENA...
WAIT!
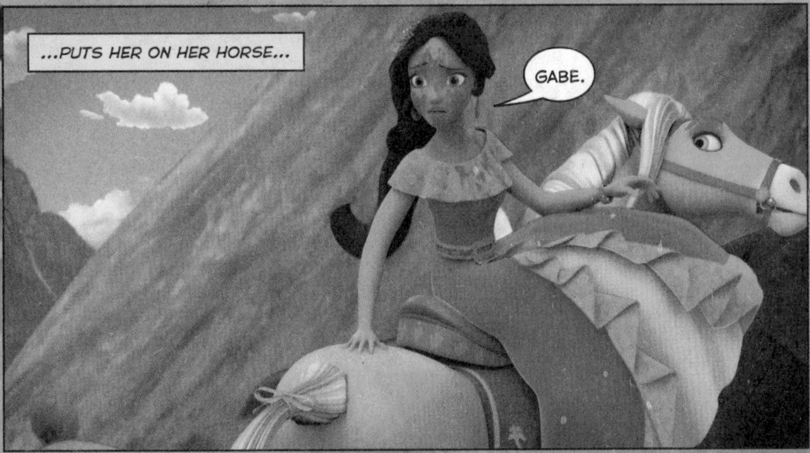
...PUTS HER ON HER HORSE...
GABE.
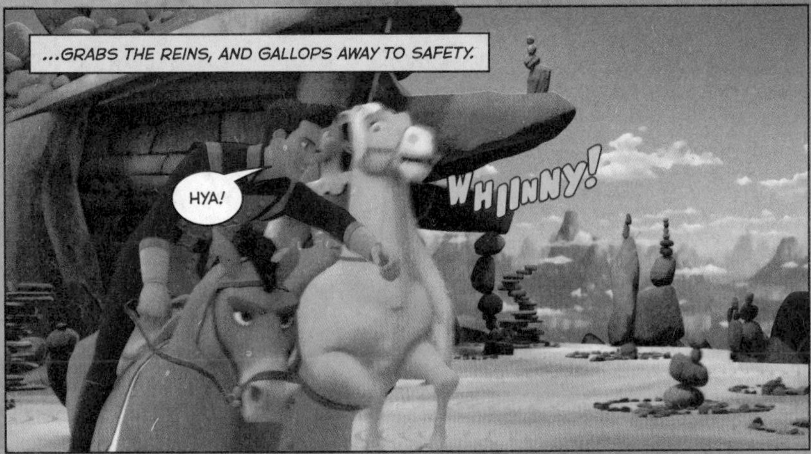
...GRABS THE REINS, AND GALLOPS AWAY TO SAFETY.
HYA!
WHIINNY!

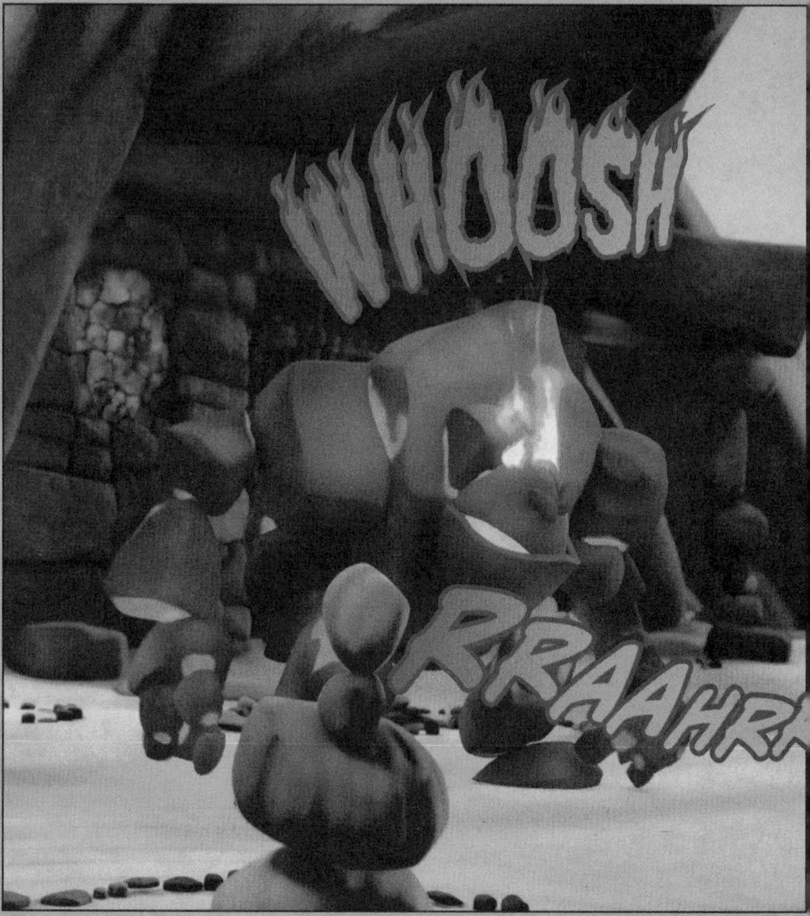
WHOOSH
RRAAHR

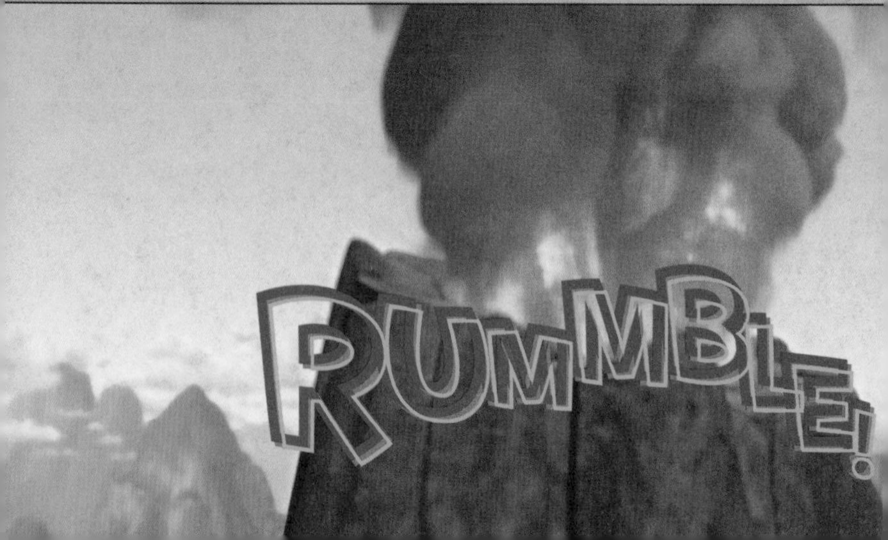
RUMMBLE!

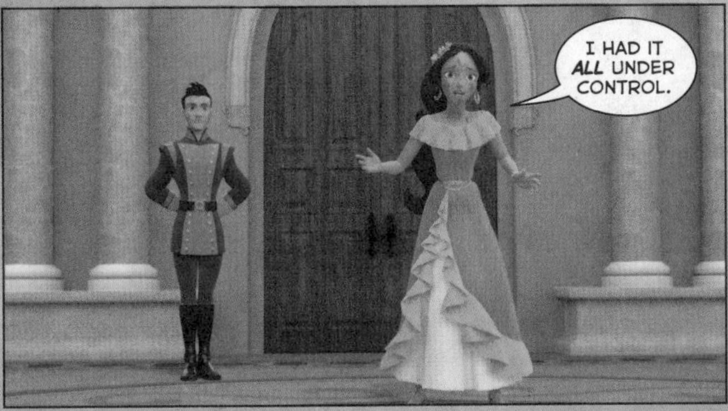
I HAD IT ALL UNDER CONTROL.

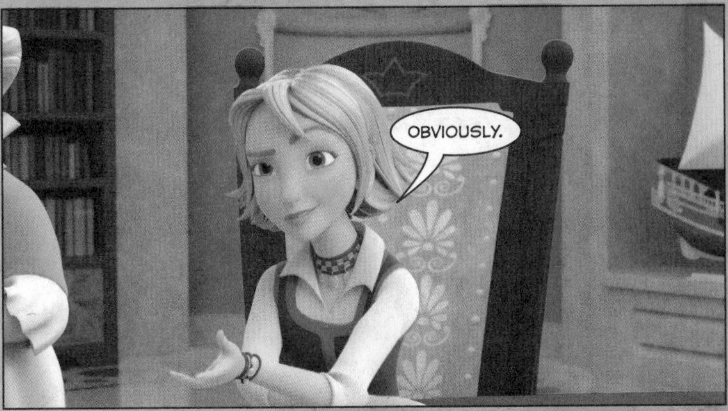
OBVIOUSLY.

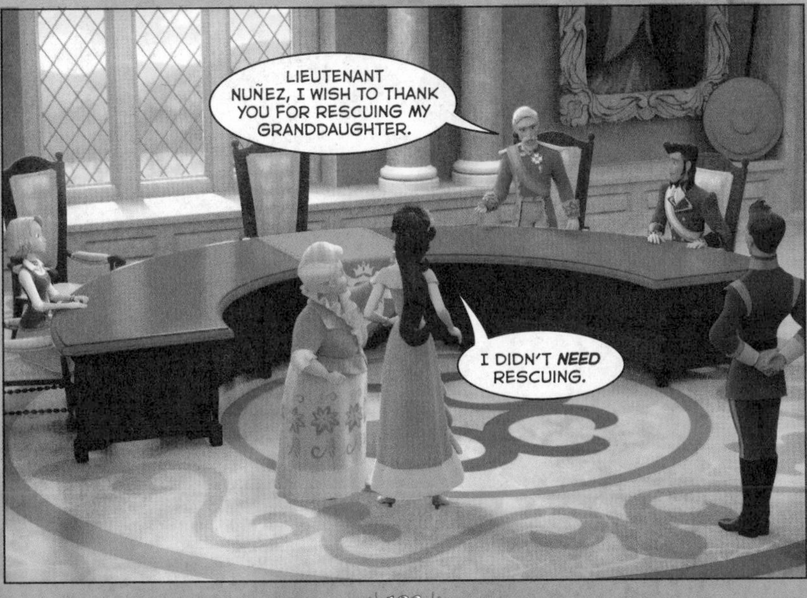
LIEUTENANT NUÑEZ, I WISH TO THANK YOU FOR RESCUING MY GRANDDAUGHTER.
I DIDN'T NEED RESCUING.

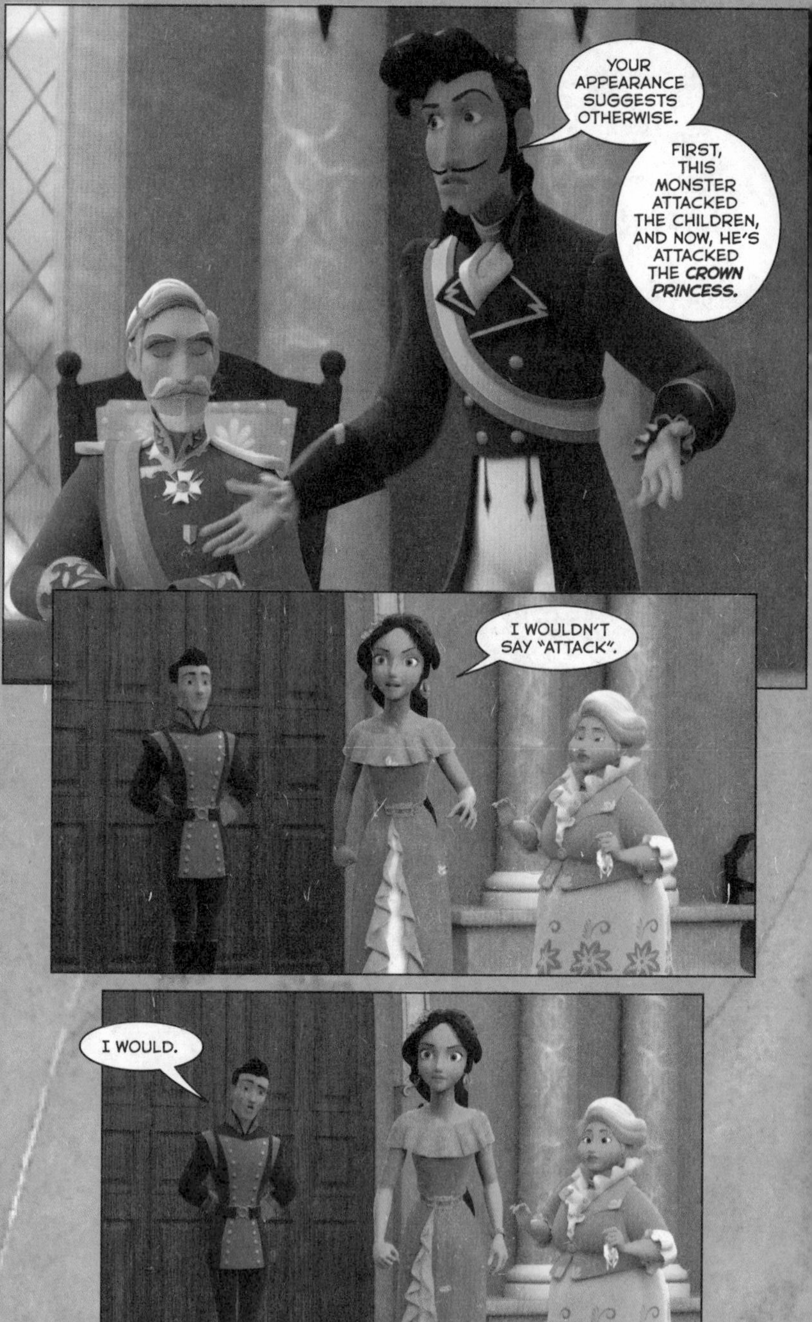
YOUR APPEARANCE SUGGESTS OTHERWISE.
FIRST, THIS MONSTER ATTACKED THE CHILDREN, AND NOW, HE'S ATTACKED THE *CROWN PRINCESS.*
I WOULDN'T SAY "ATTACK".
I WOULD.

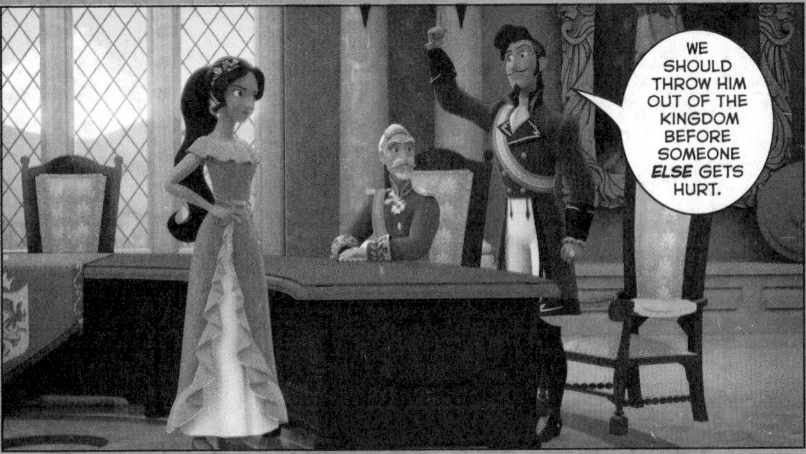
WE SHOULD THROW HIM OUT OF THE KINGDOM BEFORE SOMEONE ELSE GETS HURT.
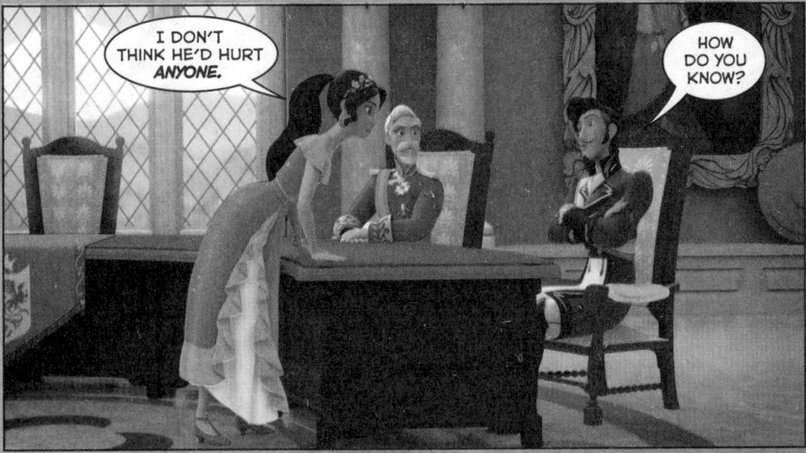
I DON'T THINK HE'D HURT ANYONE.
HOW DO YOU KNOW?
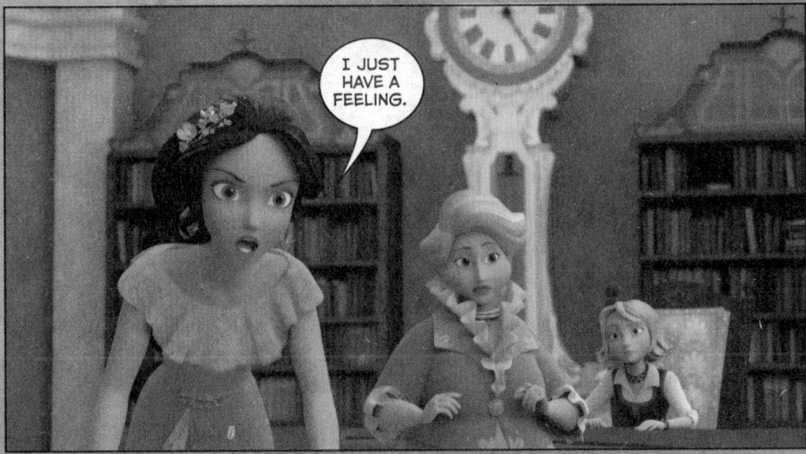
I JUST HAVE A FEELING.

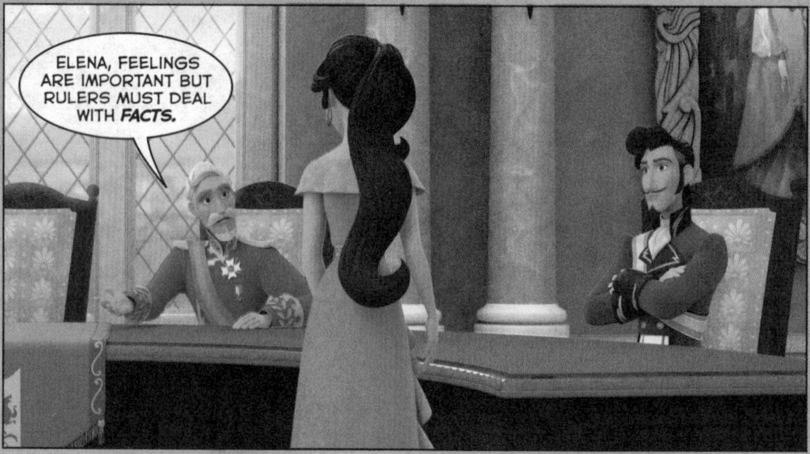
ELENA, FEELINGS ARE IMPORTANT BUT RULERS MUST DEAL WITH *FACTS.*

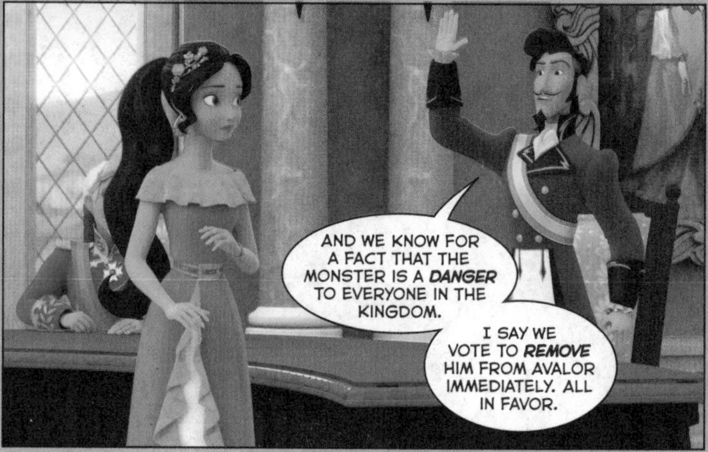
AND WE KNOW FOR A FACT THAT THE MONSTER IS A *DANGER* TO EVERYONE IN THE KINGDOM.
I SAY WE VOTE TO *REMOVE* HIM FROM AVALOR IMMEDIATELY. ALL IN FAVOR.

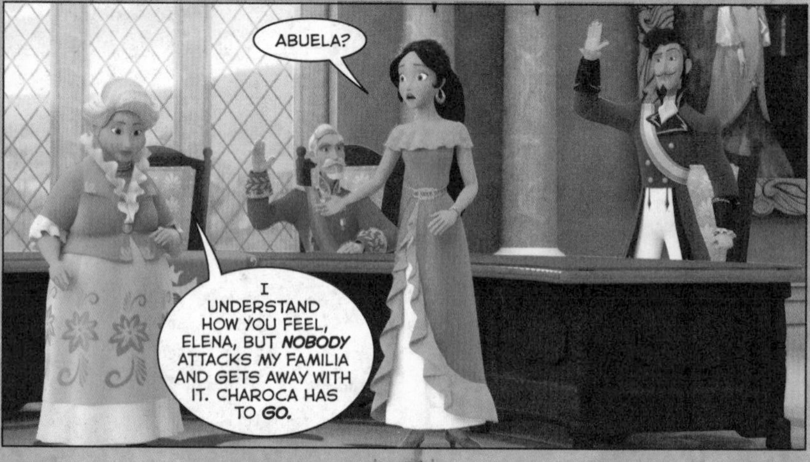
ABUELA?
I UNDERSTAND HOW YOU FEEL, ELENA, BUT *NOBODY* ATTACKS MY FAMILIA AND GETS AWAY WITH IT. CHAROCA HAS TO *GO.*

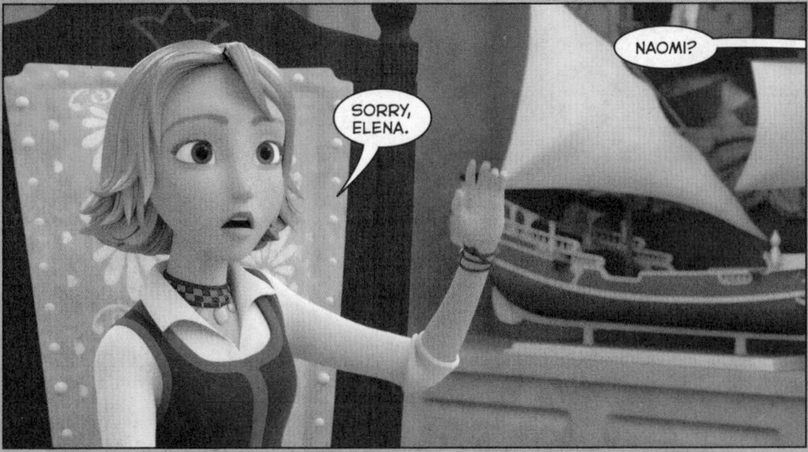
NAOMI?
SORRY, ELENA.

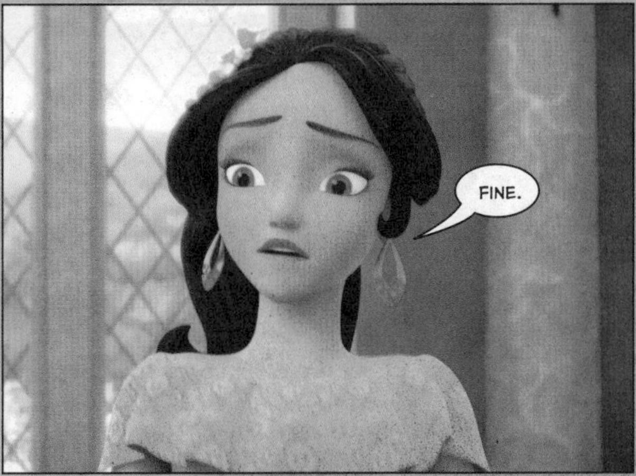
FINE.

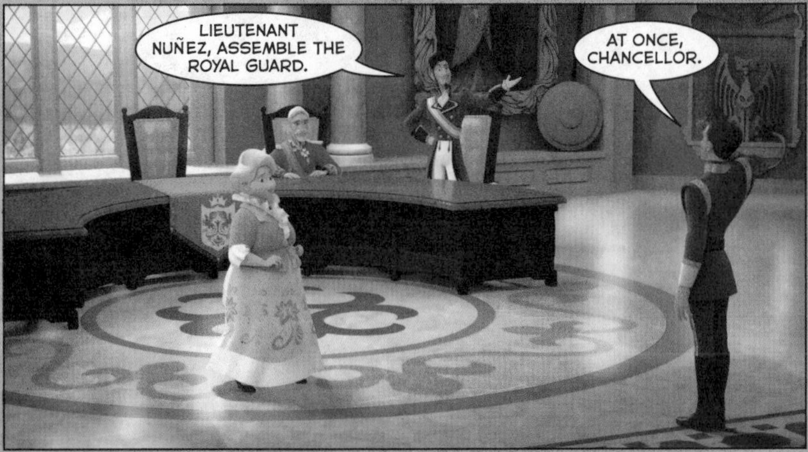
LIEUTENANT NUÑEZ, ASSEMBLE THE ROYAL GUARD.
AT ONCE, CHANCELLOR.

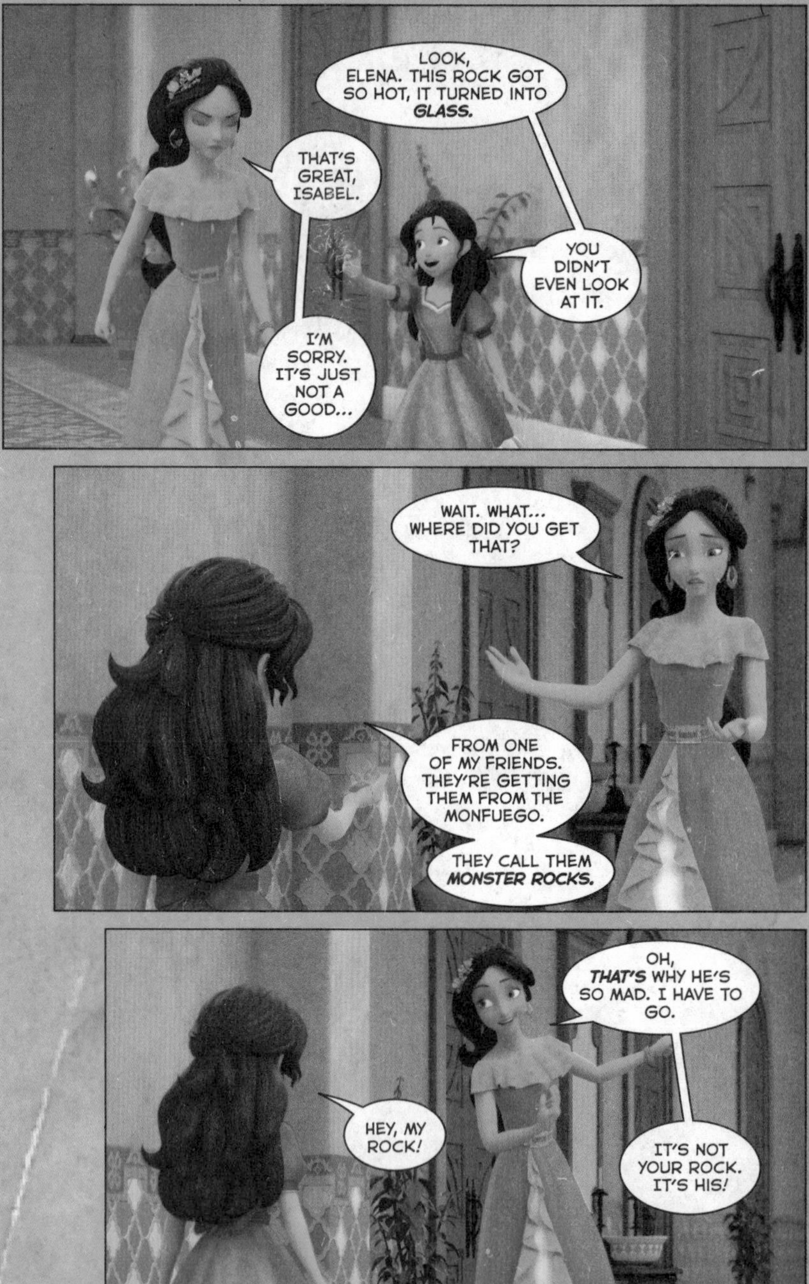
LOOK, ELENA. THIS ROCK GOT SO HOT, IT TURNED INTO ***GLASS.***
THAT'S GREAT, ISABEL.
YOU DIDN'T EVEN LOOK AT IT.
I'M SORRY. IT'S JUST NOT A GOOD...
WAIT. WHAT... WHERE DID YOU GET THAT?
FROM ONE OF MY FRIENDS. THEY'RE GETTING THEM FROM THE MONFUEGO.
THEY CALL THEM ***MONSTER ROCKS.***
OH, ***THAT'S*** WHY HE'S SO MAD. I HAVE TO GO.
HEY, MY ROCK!
IT'S NOT YOUR ROCK. IT'S HIS!

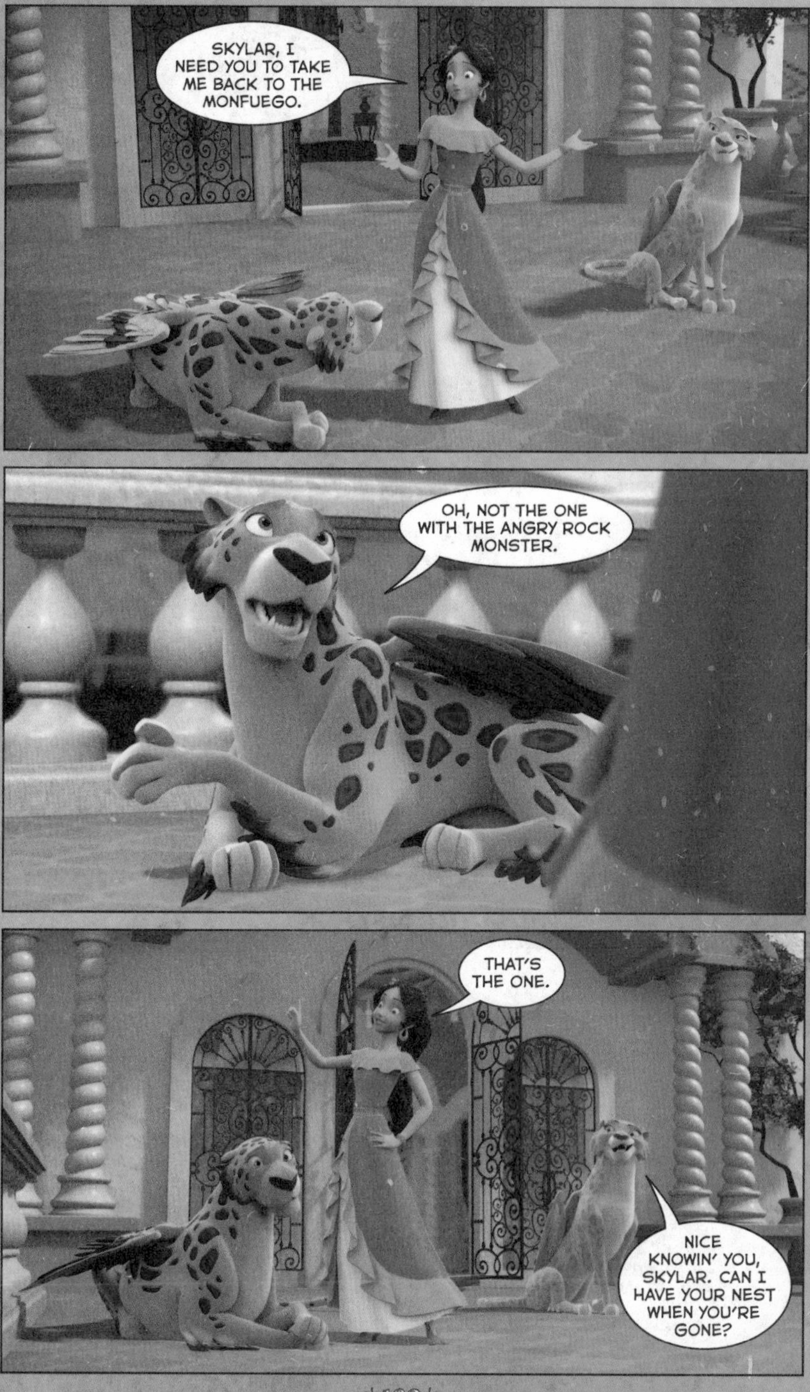
SKYLAR, I NEED YOU TO TAKE ME BACK TO THE MONFUEGO.
OH, NOT THE ONE WITH THE ANGRY ROCK MONSTER.
THAT'S THE ONE.
NICE KNOWIN' YOU, SKYLAR. CAN I HAVE YOUR NEST WHEN YOU'RE GONE?

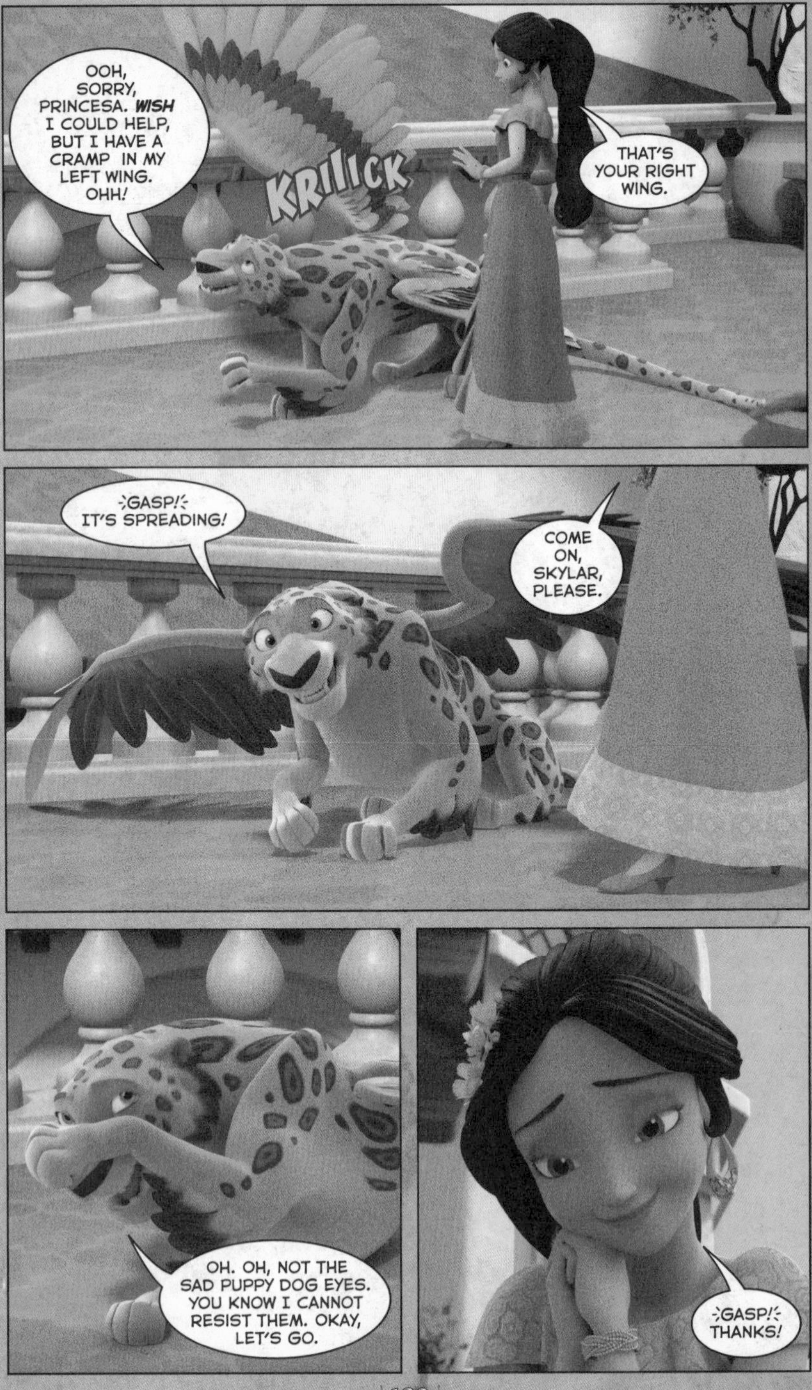
OOH, SORRY, PRINCESA. WISH I COULD HELP, BUT I HAVE A CRAMP IN MY LEFT WING. OHH!
KRIIICK
THAT'S YOUR RIGHT WING.
GASP! IT'S SPREADING!
COME ON, SKYLAR, PLEASE.
OH. OH, NOT THE SAD PUPPY DOG EYES. YOU KNOW I CANNOT RESIST THEM. OKAY, LET'S GO.
GASP! THANKS!

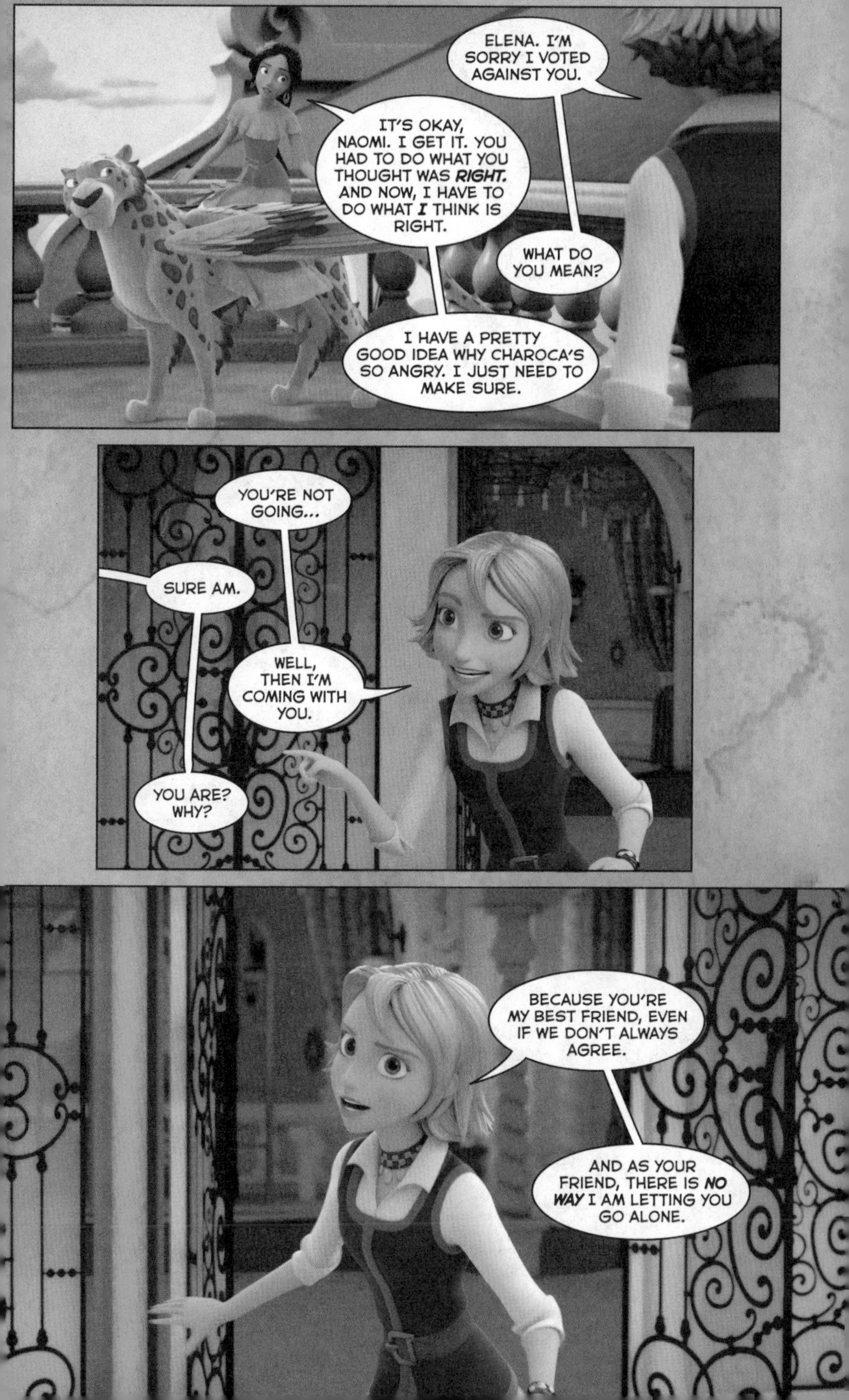
ELENA. I'M SORRY I VOTED AGAINST YOU.
IT'S OKAY, NAOMI. I GET IT. YOU HAD TO DO WHAT YOU THOUGHT WAS ***RIGHT.*** AND NOW, I HAVE TO DO WHAT ***I*** THINK IS RIGHT.
WHAT DO YOU MEAN?
I HAVE A PRETTY GOOD IDEA WHY CHAROCA'S SO ANGRY. I JUST NEED TO MAKE SURE.
YOU'RE NOT GOING...
SURE AM.
WELL, THEN I'M COMING WITH YOU.
YOU ARE? WHY?
BECAUSE YOU'RE MY BEST FRIEND, EVEN IF WE DON'T ALWAYS AGREE.
AND AS YOUR FRIEND, THERE IS ***NO WAY*** I AM LETTING YOU GO ALONE.

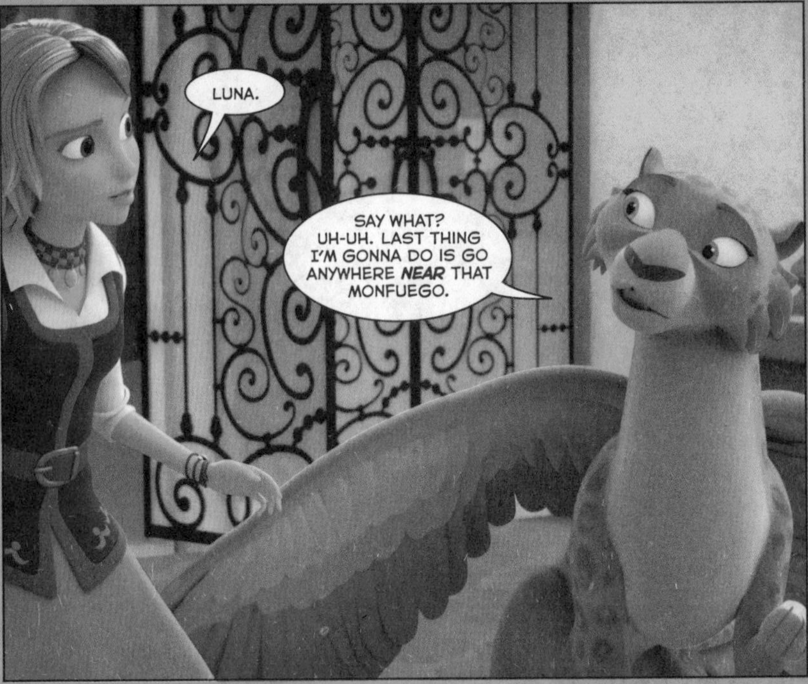
LUNA.
SAY WHAT? UH-UH. LAST THING I'M GONNA DO IS GO ANYWHERE *NEAR* THAT MONFUEGO.

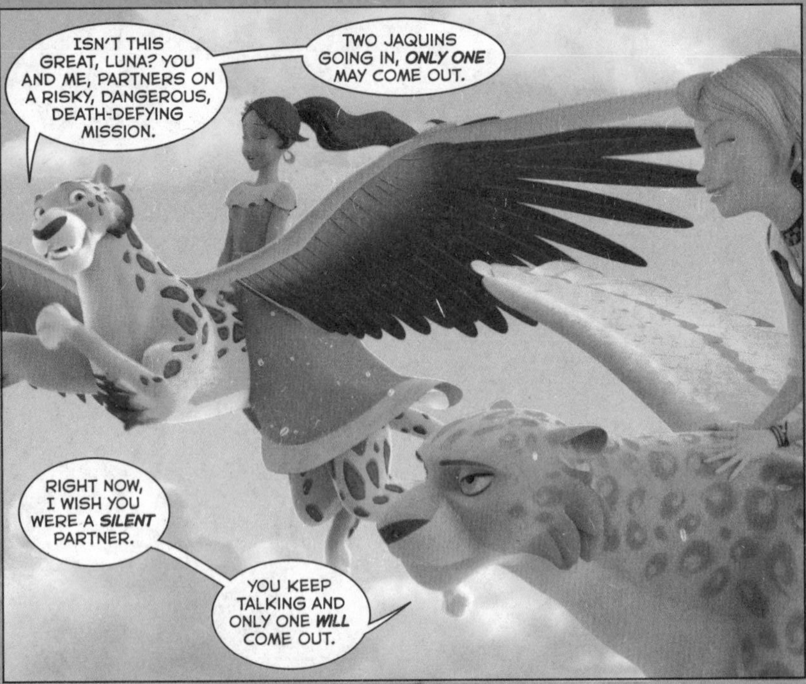
ISN'T THIS GREAT, LUNA? YOU AND ME, PARTNERS ON A RISKY, DANGEROUS, DEATH-DEFYING MISSION.
TWO JAQUINS GOING IN, *ONLY ONE* MAY COME OUT.
RIGHT NOW, I WISH YOU WERE A *SILENT* PARTNER.
YOU KEEP TALKING AND ONLY ONE *WILL* COME OUT.

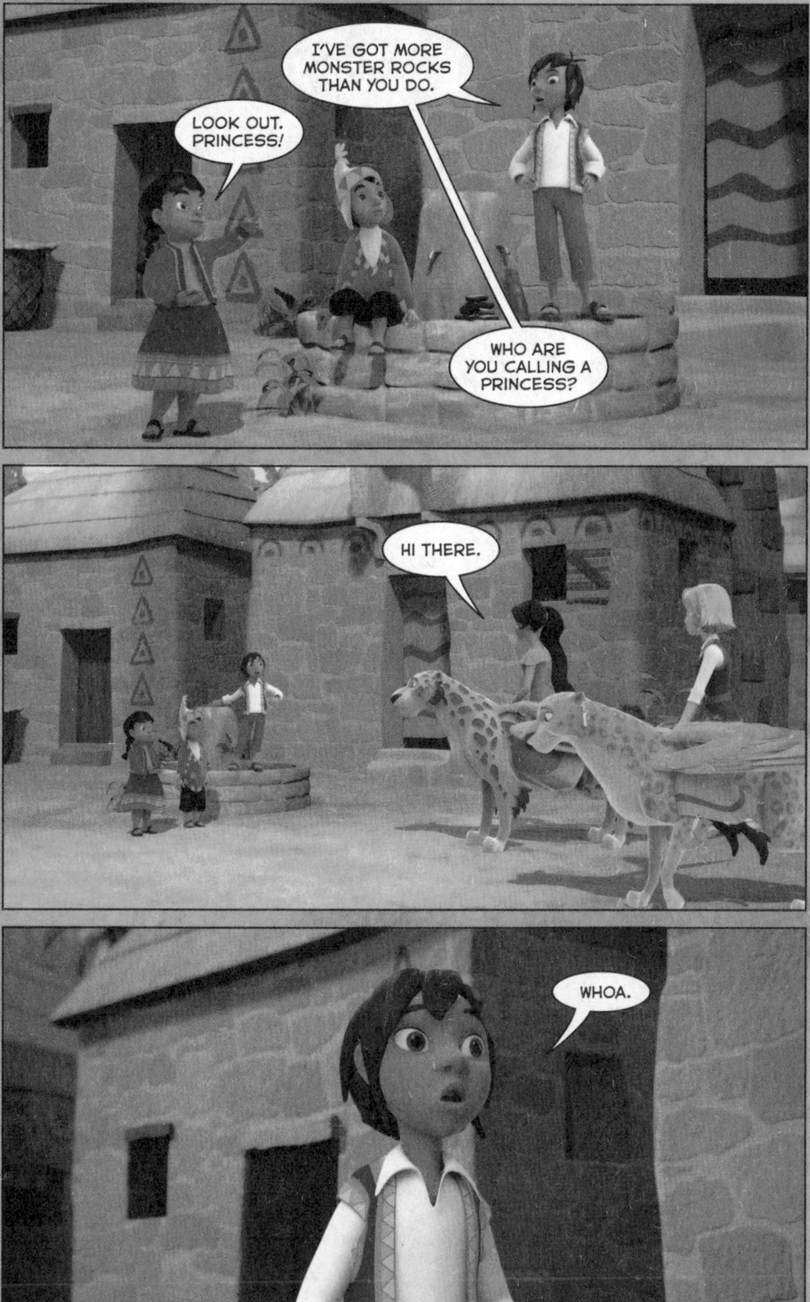
LOOK OUT. PRINCESS!
I'VE GOT MORE MONSTER ROCKS THAN YOU DO.
WHO ARE YOU CALLING A PRINCESS?
HI THERE.
WHOA.

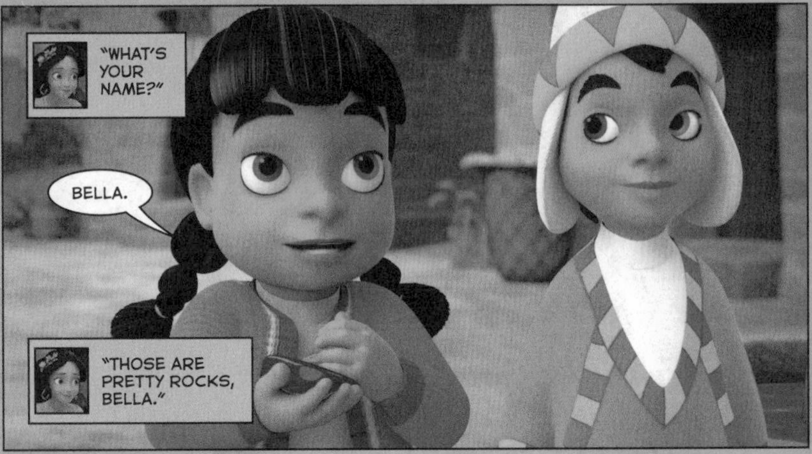
"WHAT'S YOUR NAME?"
BELLA.
"THOSE ARE PRETTY ROCKS, BELLA."

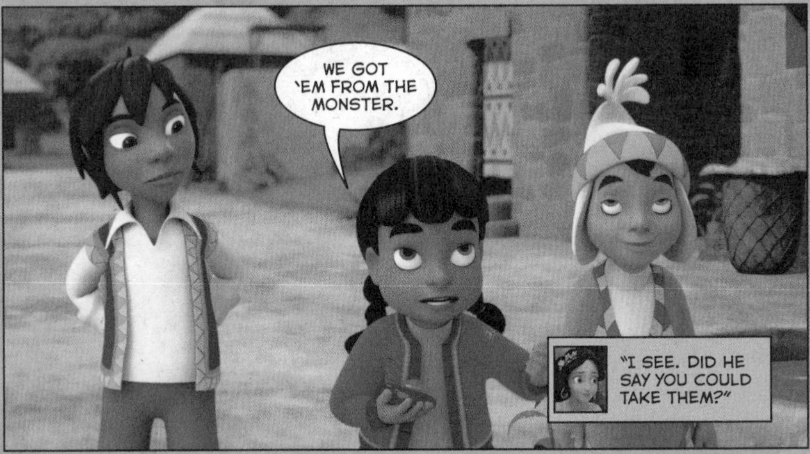
WE GOT 'EM FROM THE MONSTER.
"I SEE. DID HE SAY YOU COULD TAKE THEM?"

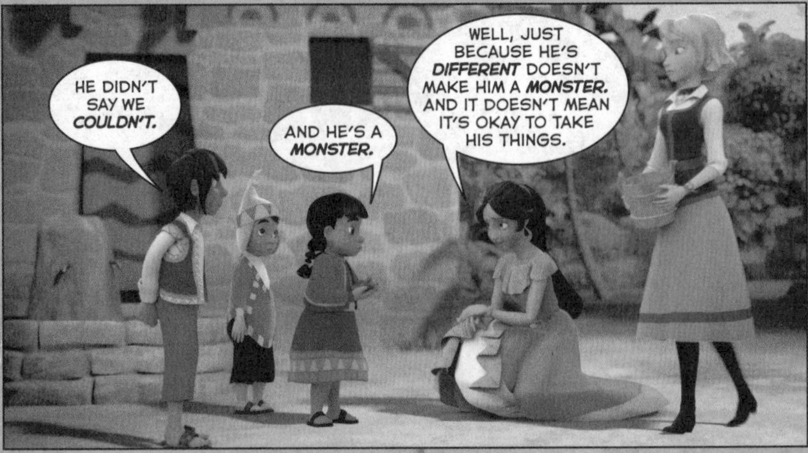
HE DIDN'T SAY WE ***COULDN'T.***
AND HE'S A ***MONSTER.***
WELL, JUST BECAUSE HE'S ***DIFFERENT*** DOESN'T MAKE HIM A ***MONSTER.*** AND IT DOESN'T MEAN IT'S OKAY TO TAKE HIS THINGS.

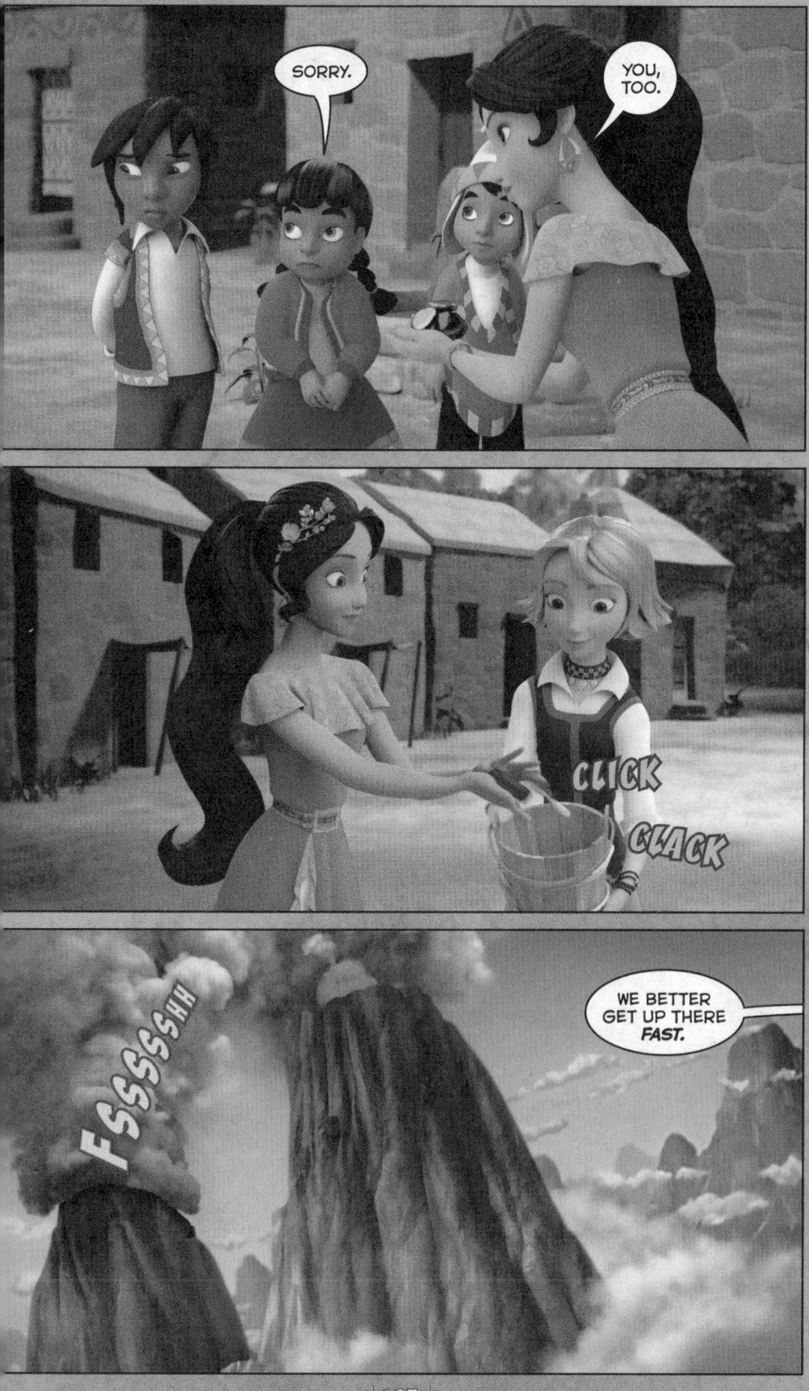
SORRY.
YOU, TOO.
CLICK
CLACK
WE BETTER GET UP THERE *FAST.*
FSSSSSHH

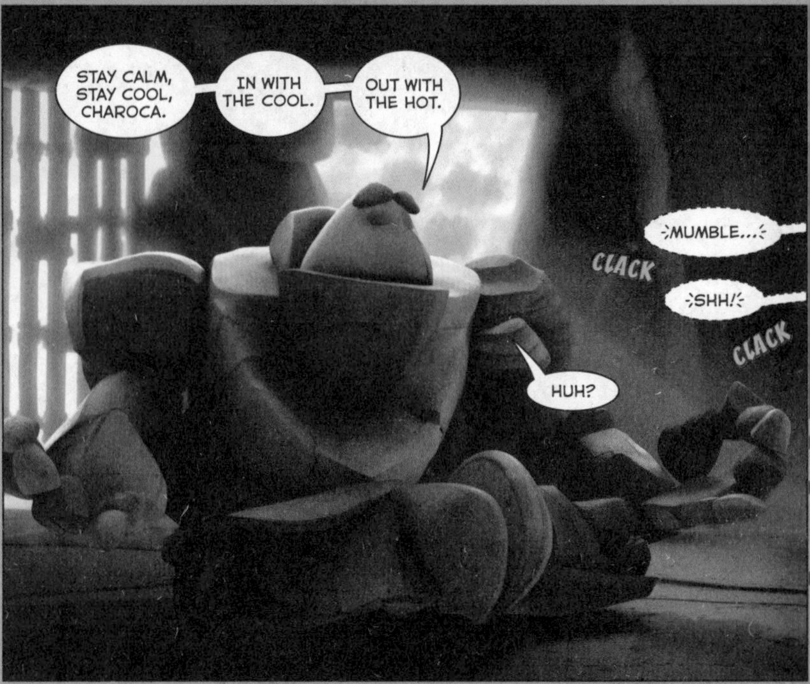
STAY CALM, STAY COOL, CHAROCA.
IN WITH THE COOL.
OUT WITH THE HOT.
MUMBLE...
CLACK
SHH!
CLACK
HUH?

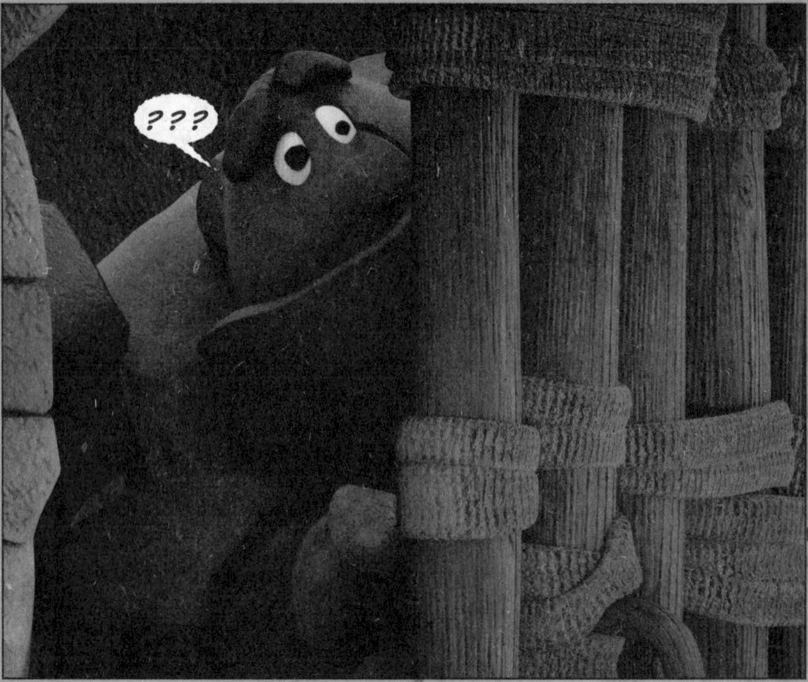
???

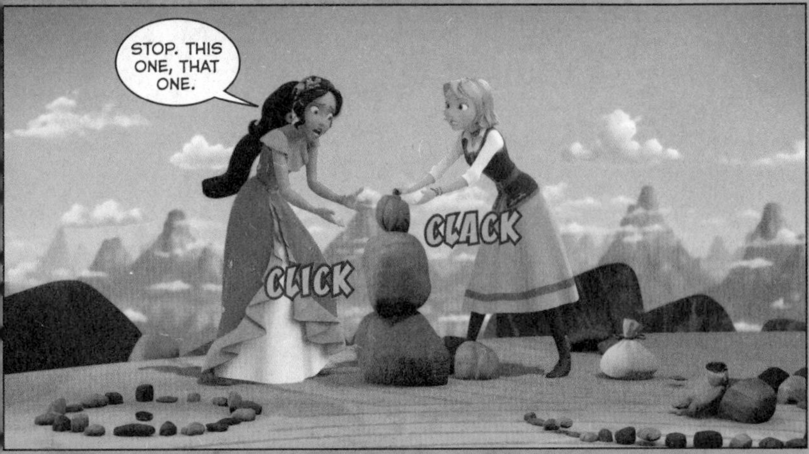
STOP. THIS ONE, THAT ONE.
CLICK
CLACK

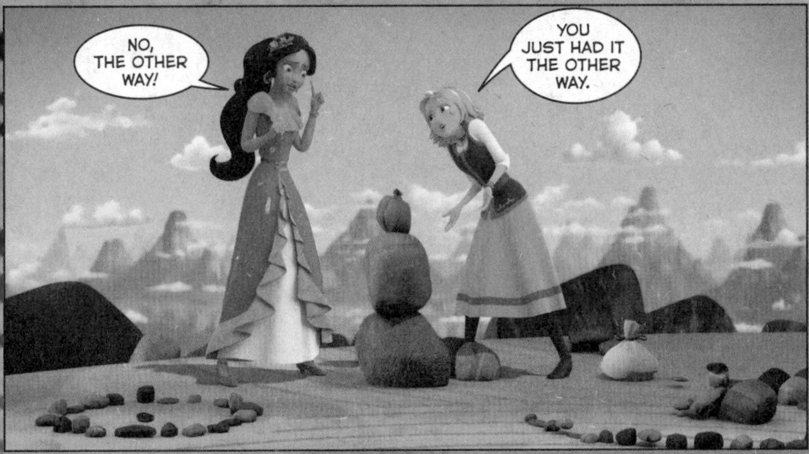
NO, THE OTHER WAY!
YOU JUST HAD IT THE OTHER WAY.

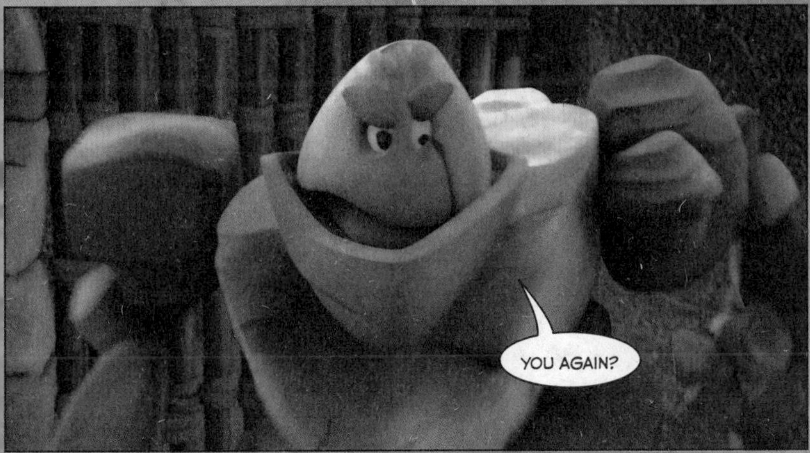
YOU AGAIN?

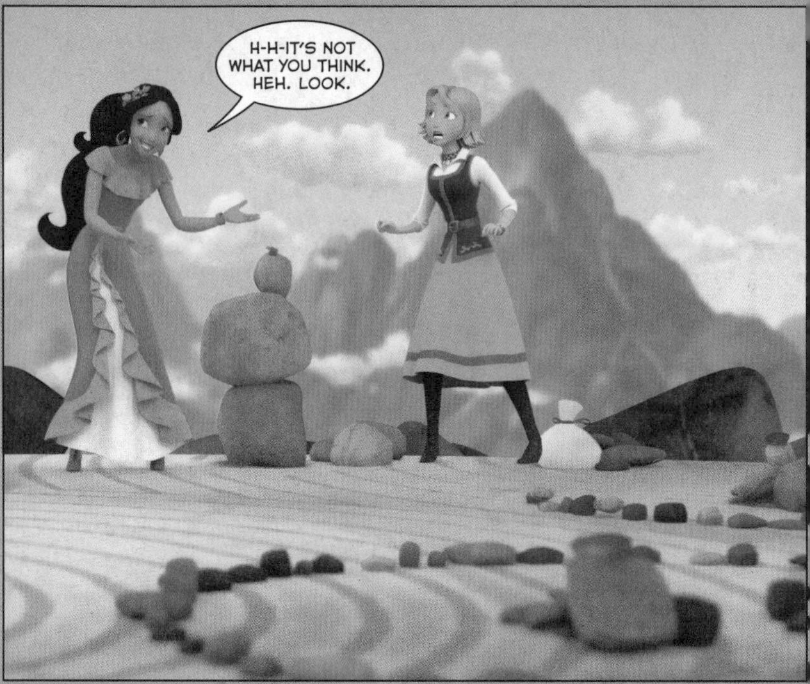
H-H-IT'S NOT WHAT YOU THINK. HEH. LOOK.

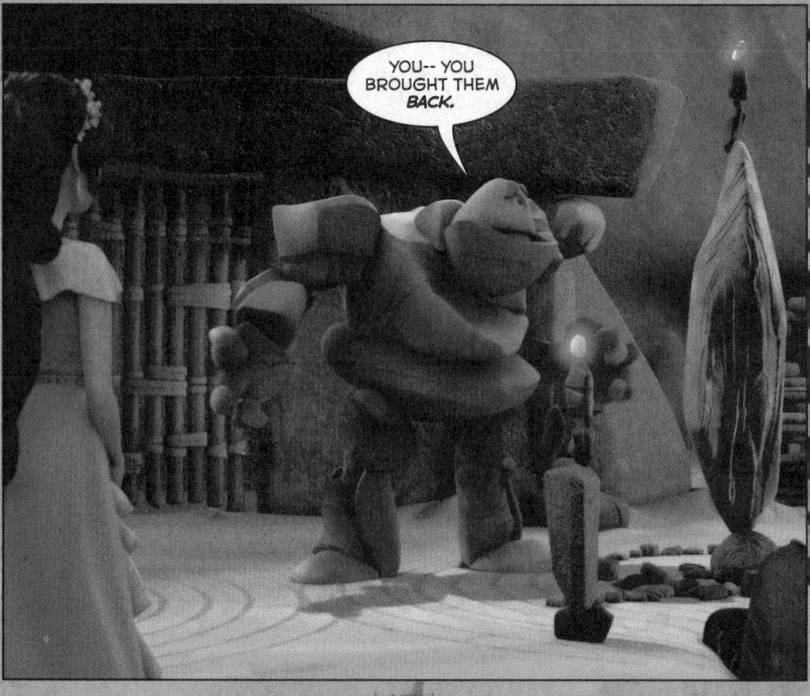
YOU-- YOU BROUGHT THEM *BACK.*

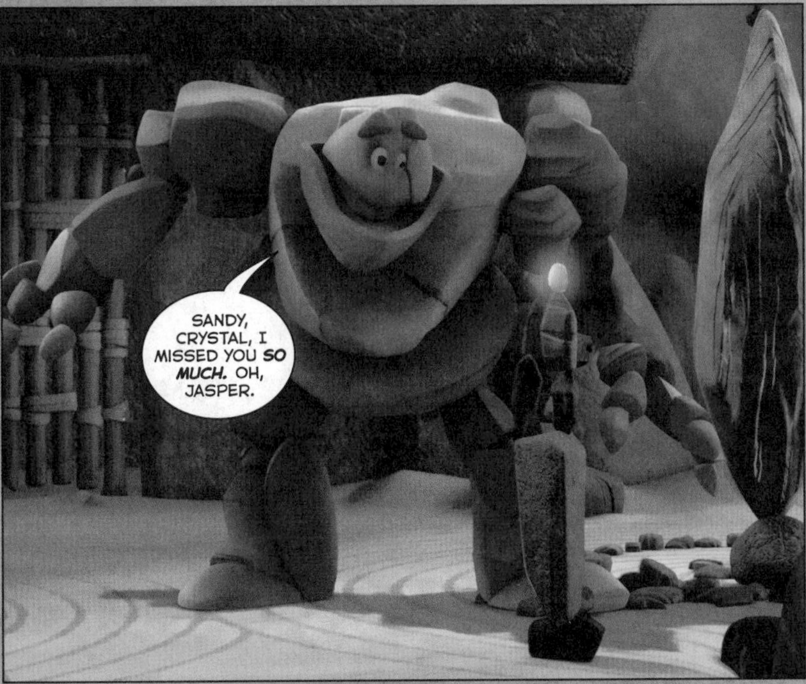
SANDY, CRYSTAL, I MISSED YOU **SO** ***MUCH.*** OH, JASPER.

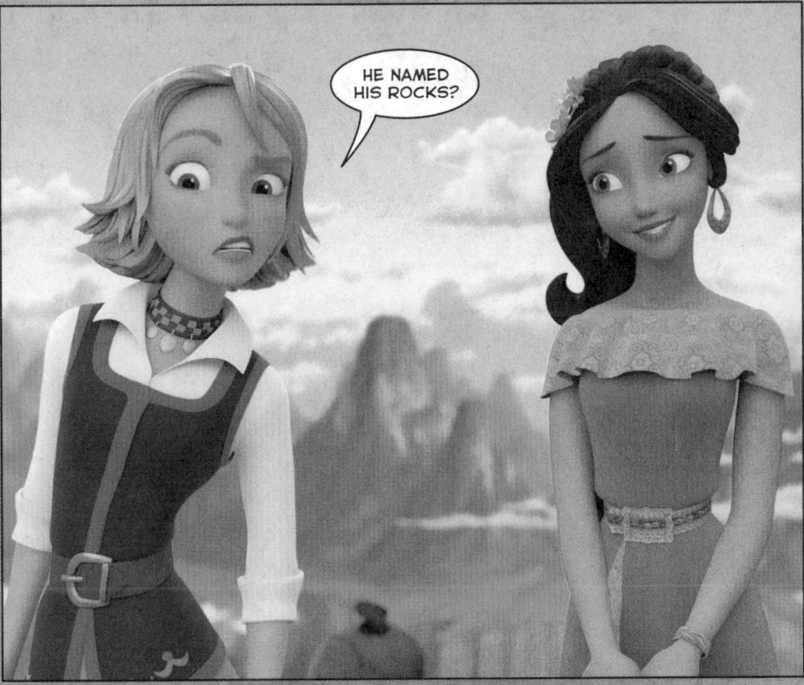
HE NAMED HIS ROCKS?

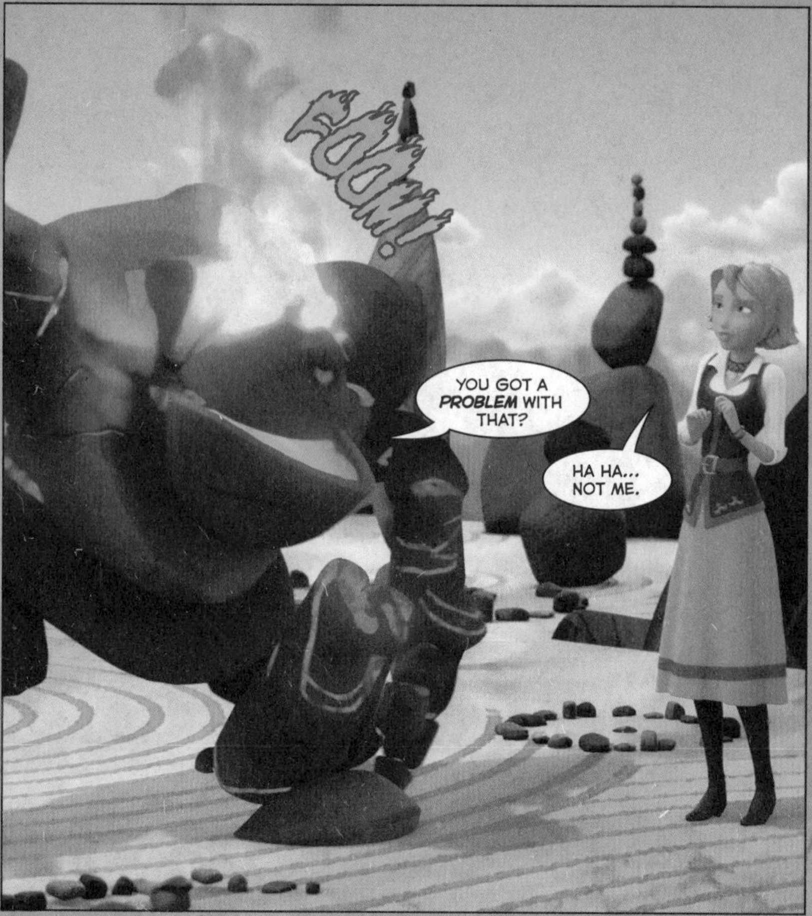
FOOM!
YOU GOT A *PROBLEM* WITH THAT?
HA HA... NOT ME.

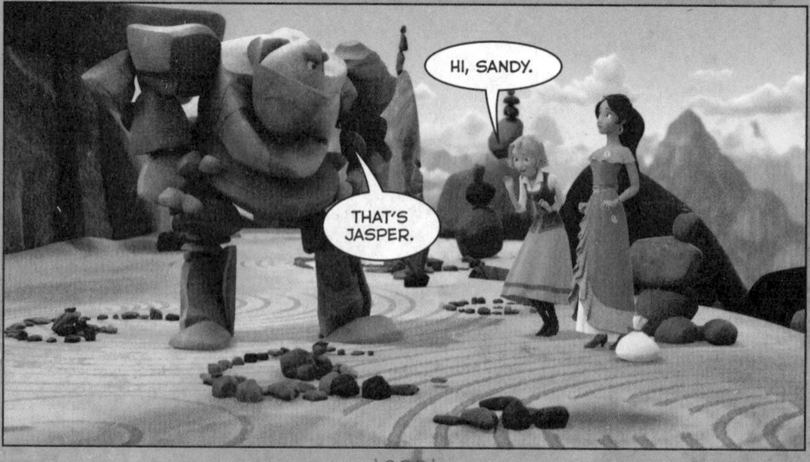
HI, SANDY.
THAT'S JASPER.

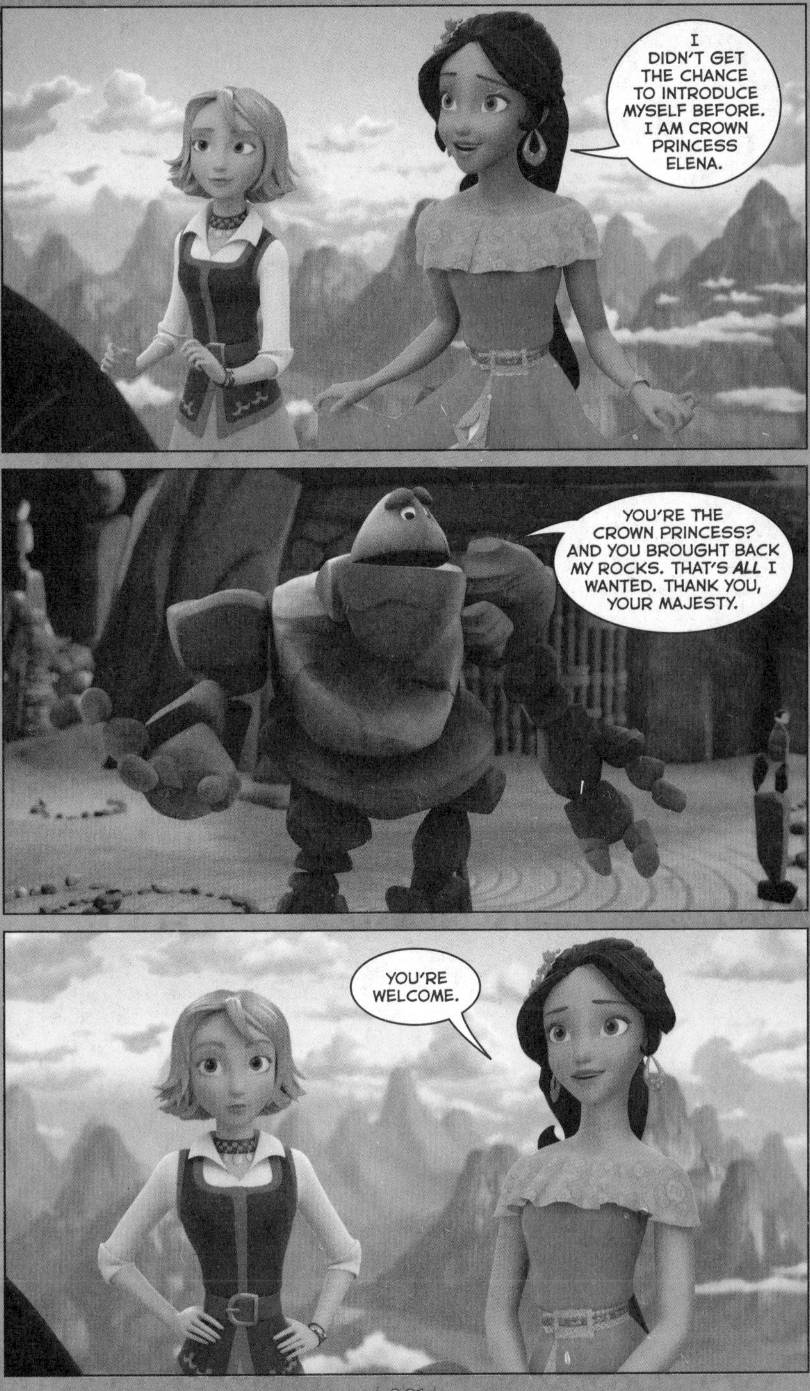
I DIDN'T GET THE CHANCE TO INTRODUCE MYSELF BEFORE. I AM CROWN PRINCESS ELENA.
YOU'RE THE CROWN PRINCESS? AND YOU BROUGHT BACK MY ROCKS. THAT'S *ALL* I WANTED. THANK YOU, YOUR MAJESTY.
YOU'RE WELCOME.

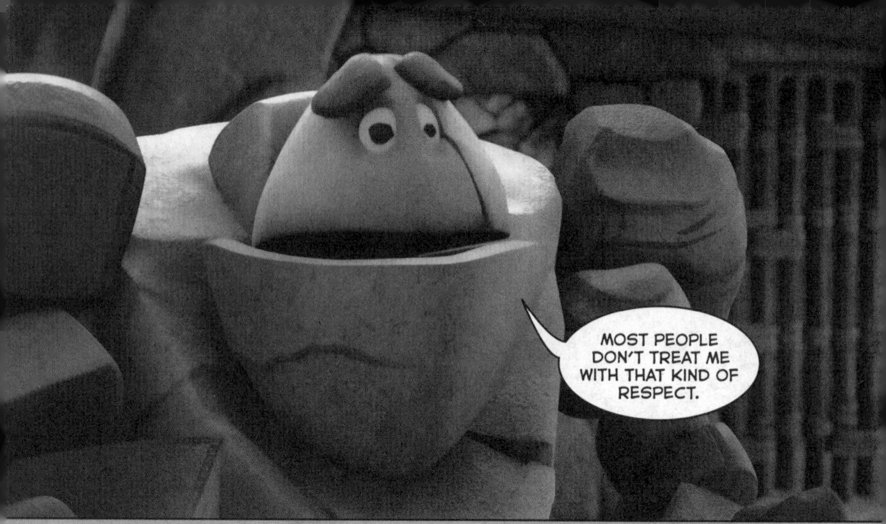
MOST PEOPLE DON'T TREAT ME WITH THAT KIND OF RESPECT.

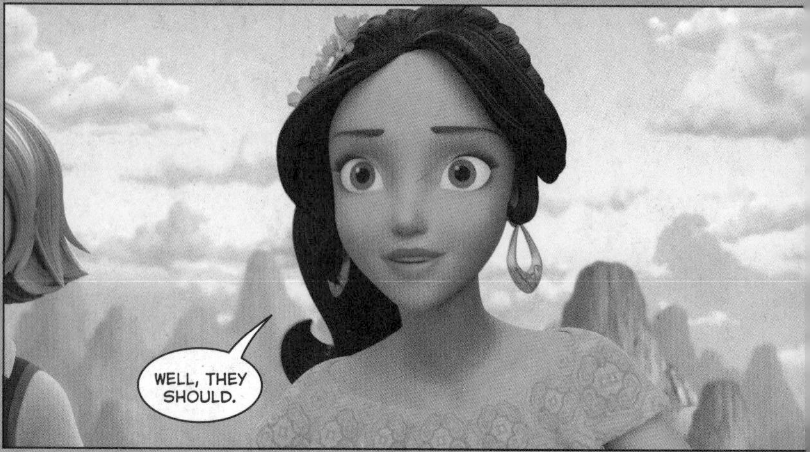
WELL, THEY SHOULD.

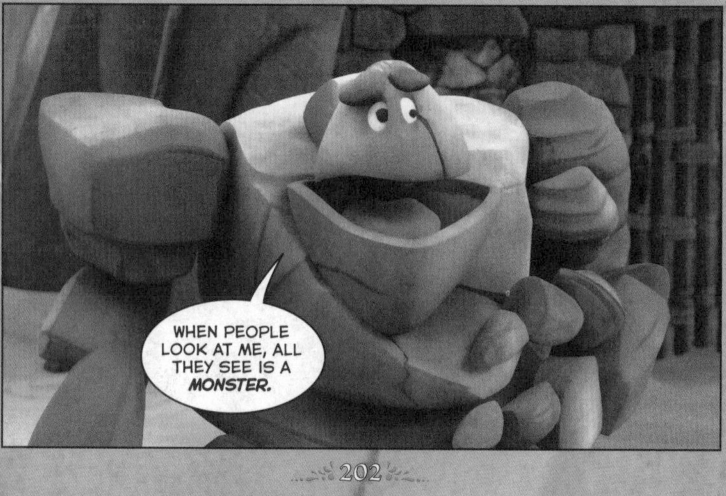
WHEN PEOPLE LOOK AT ME, ALL THEY SEE IS A *MONSTER.*

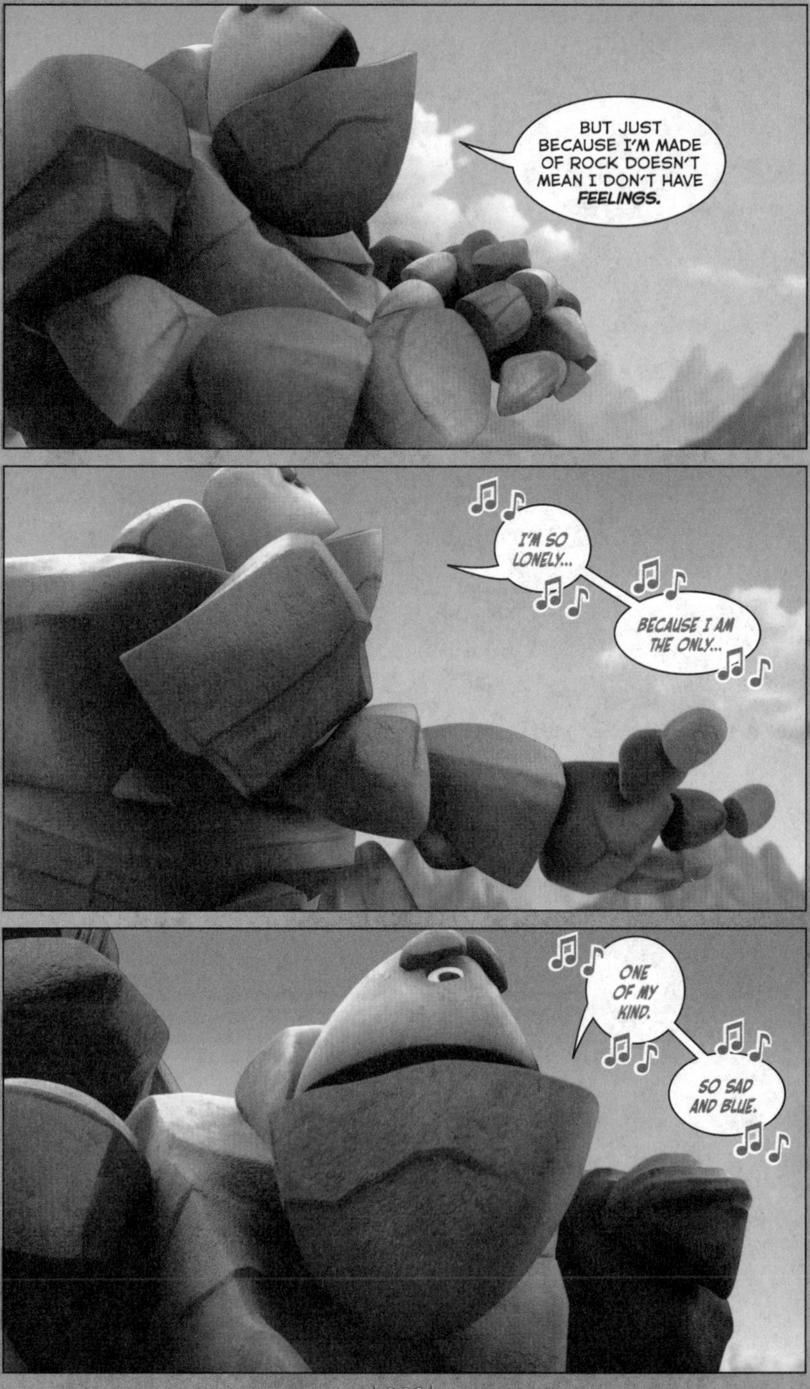
BUT JUST BECAUSE I'M MADE OF ROCK DOESN'T MEAN I DON'T HAVE **FEELINGS.**
I'M SO LONELY...
BECAUSE I AM THE ONLY...
ONE OF MY KIND.
SO SAD AND BLUE.

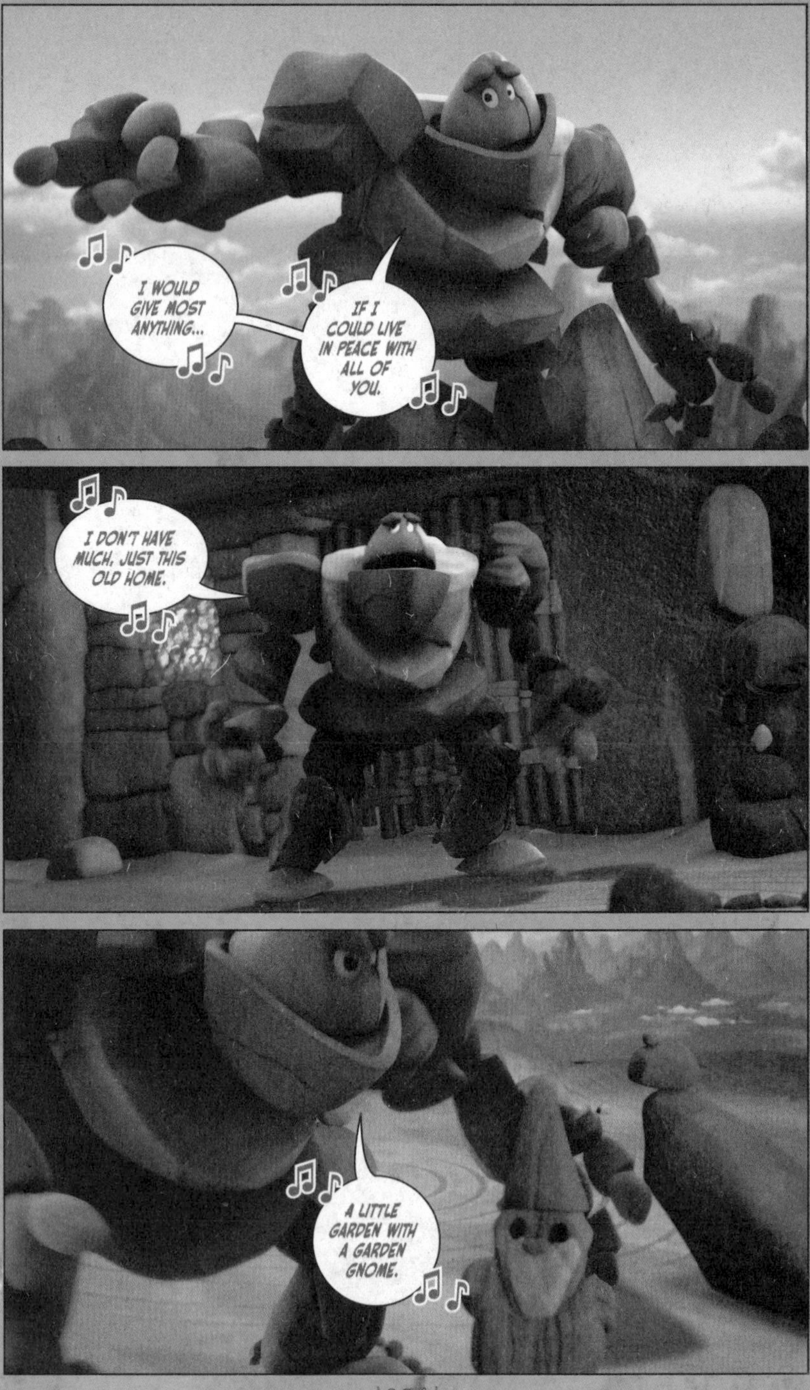
I WOULD GIVE MOST ANYTHING...
IF I COULD LIVE IN PEACE WITH ALL OF YOU.
I DON'T HAVE MUCH, JUST THIS OLD HOME.
A LITTLE GARDEN WITH A GARDEN GNOME.

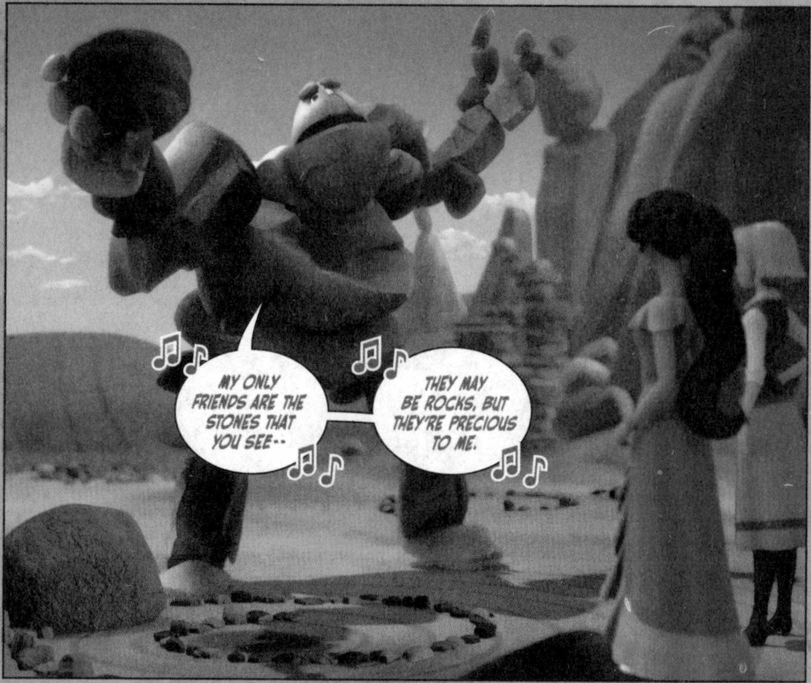
MY ONLY FRIENDS ARE THE STONES THAT YOU SEE--
THEY MAY BE ROCKS, BUT THEY'RE PRECIOUS TO ME.

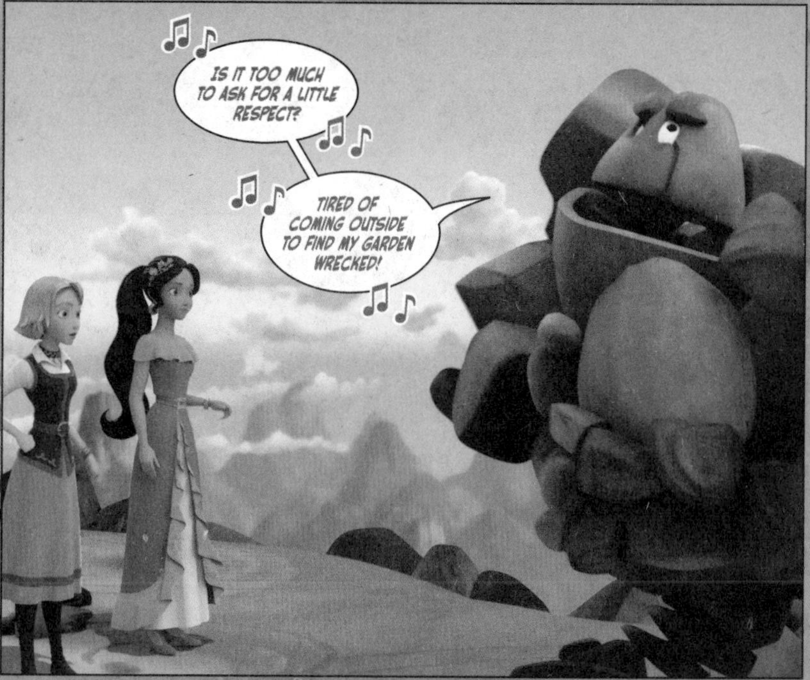
IS IT TOO MUCH TO ASK FOR A LITTLE RESPECT?
TIRED OF COMING OUTSIDE TO FIND MY GARDEN WRECKED!

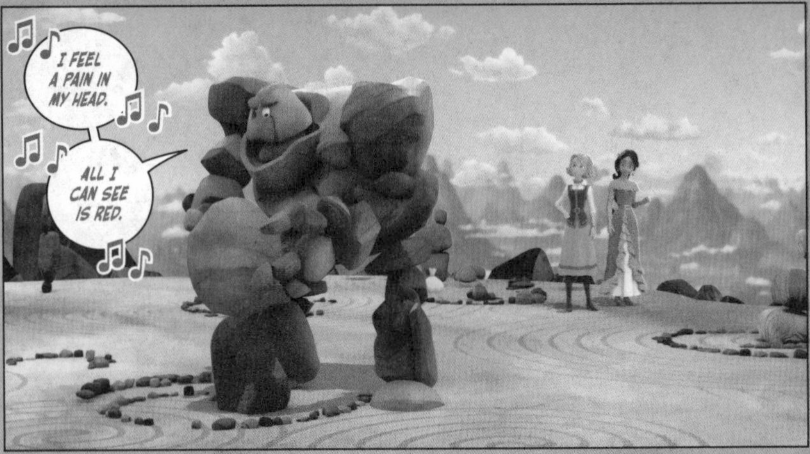
I FEEL A PAIN IN MY HEAD.
ALL I CAN SEE IS RED.

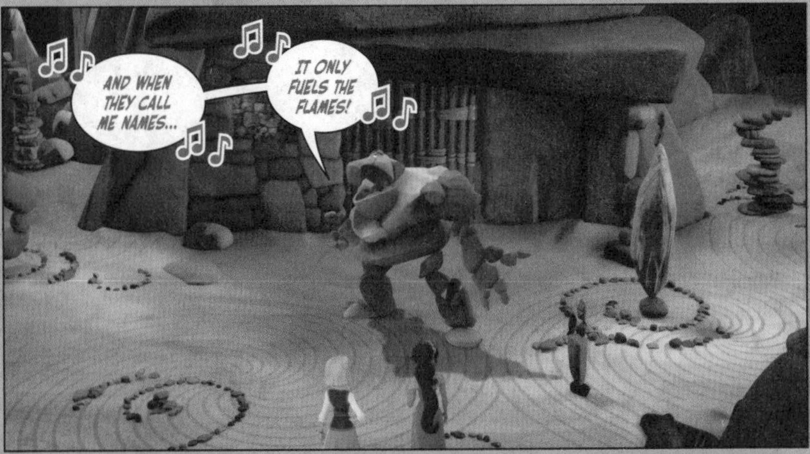
AND WHEN THEY CALL ME NAMES...
IT ONLY FUELS THE FLAMES!

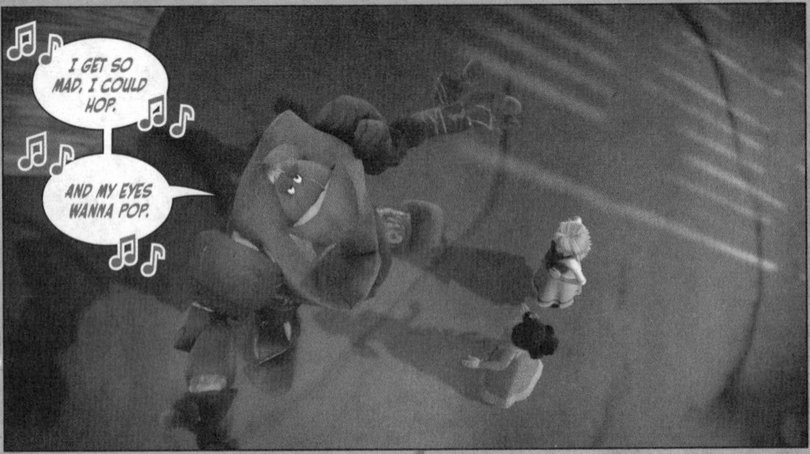
I GET SO MAD, I COULD HOP.
AND MY EYES WANNA POP.

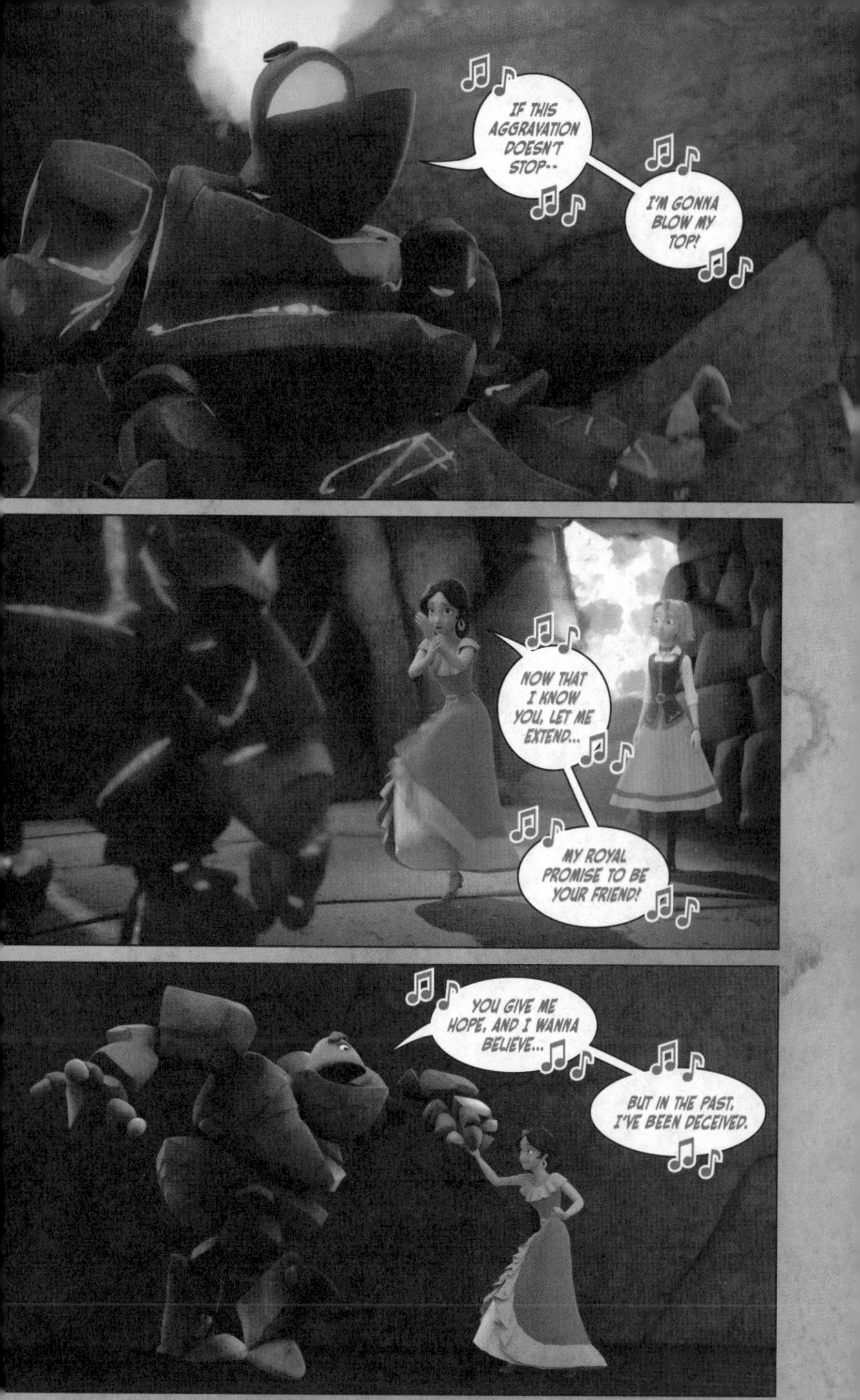
IF THIS AGGRAVATION DOESN'T STOP--
I'M GONNA BLOW MY TOP!
NOW THAT I KNOW YOU, LET ME EXTEND...
MY ROYAL PROMISE TO BE YOUR FRIEND!
YOU GIVE ME HOPE, AND I WANNA BELIEVE...
BUT IN THE PAST, I'VE BEEN DECEIVED.

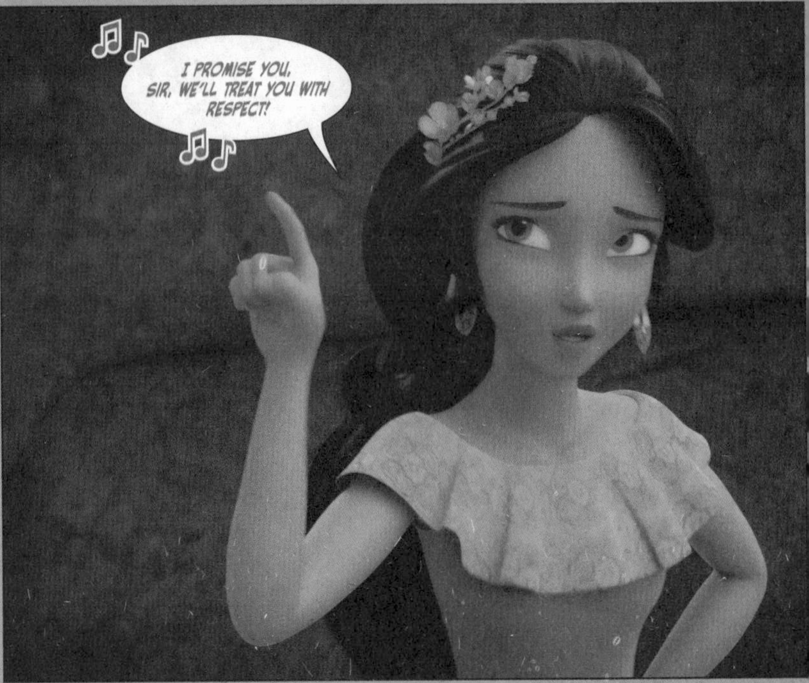
I PROMISE YOU, SIR, WE'LL TREAT YOU WITH RESPECT!

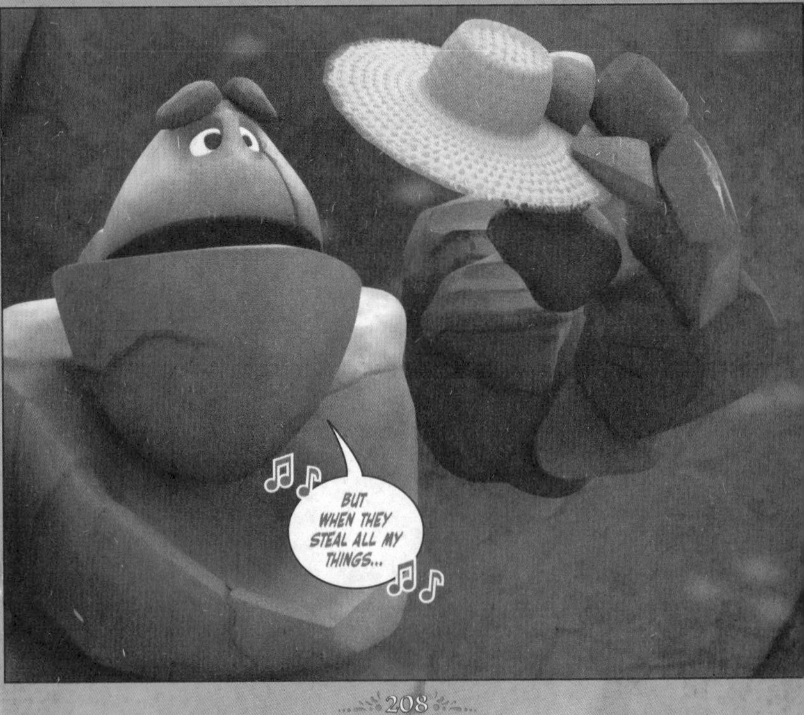
BUT WHEN THEY STEAL ALL MY THINGS...

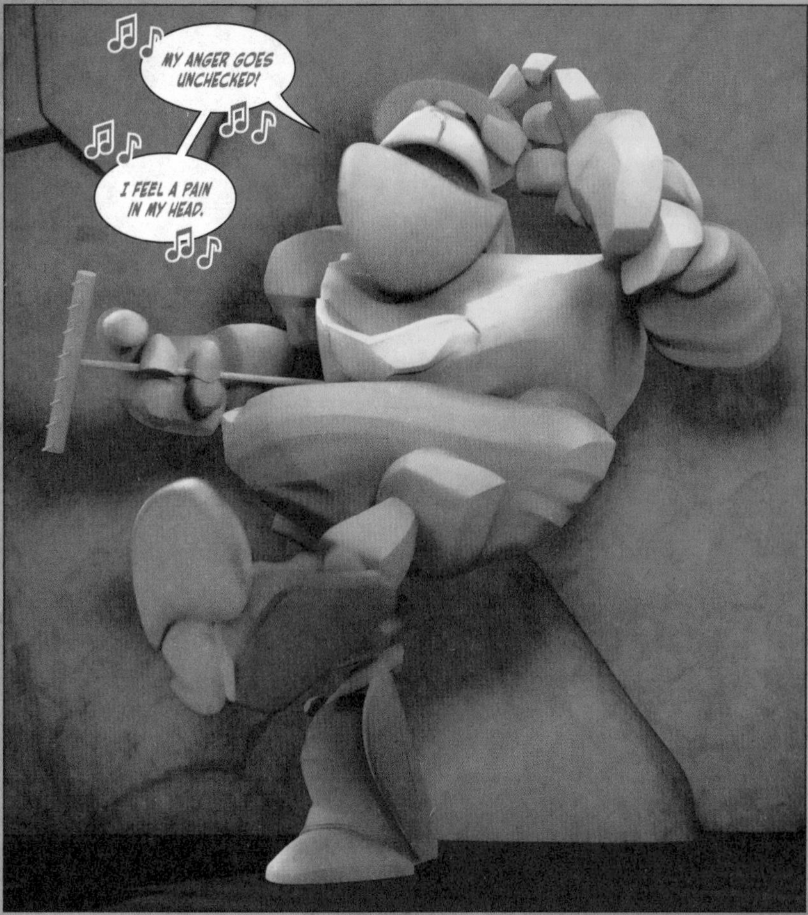
MY ANGER GOES UNCHECKED!
I FEEL A PAIN IN MY HEAD.

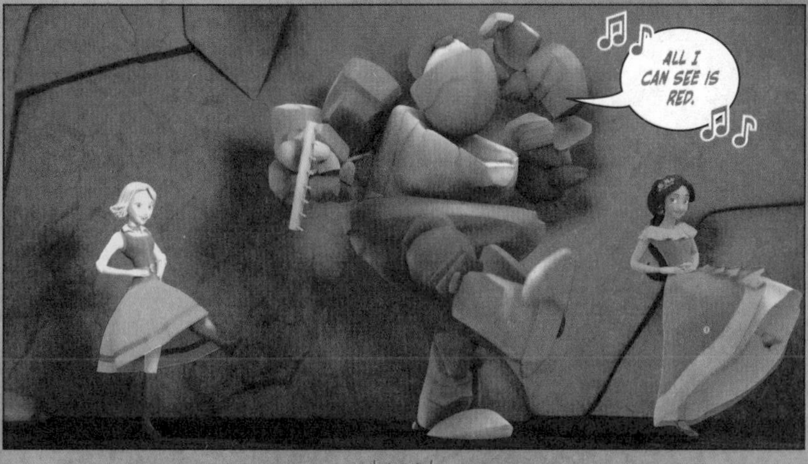
ALL I CAN SEE IS RED.

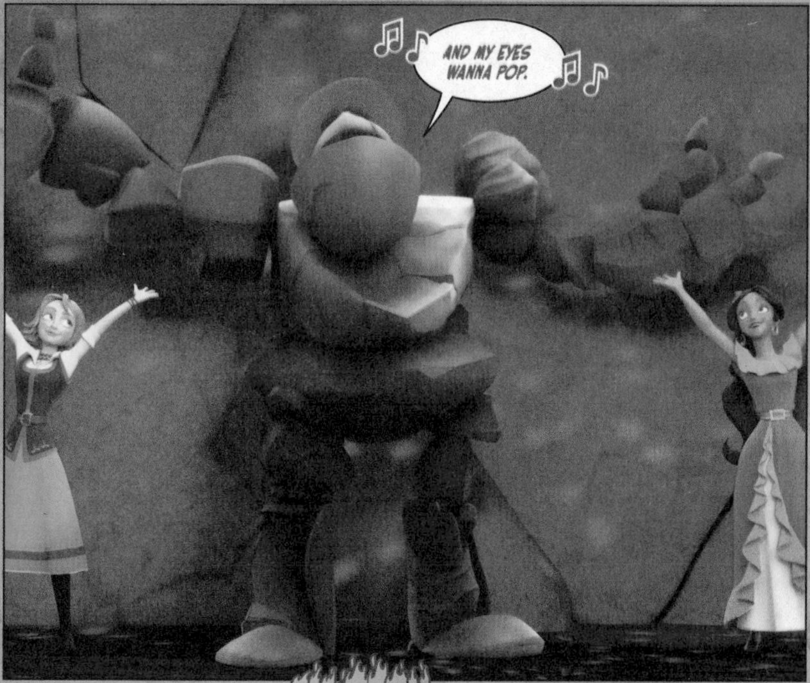
AND MY EYES WANNA POP.

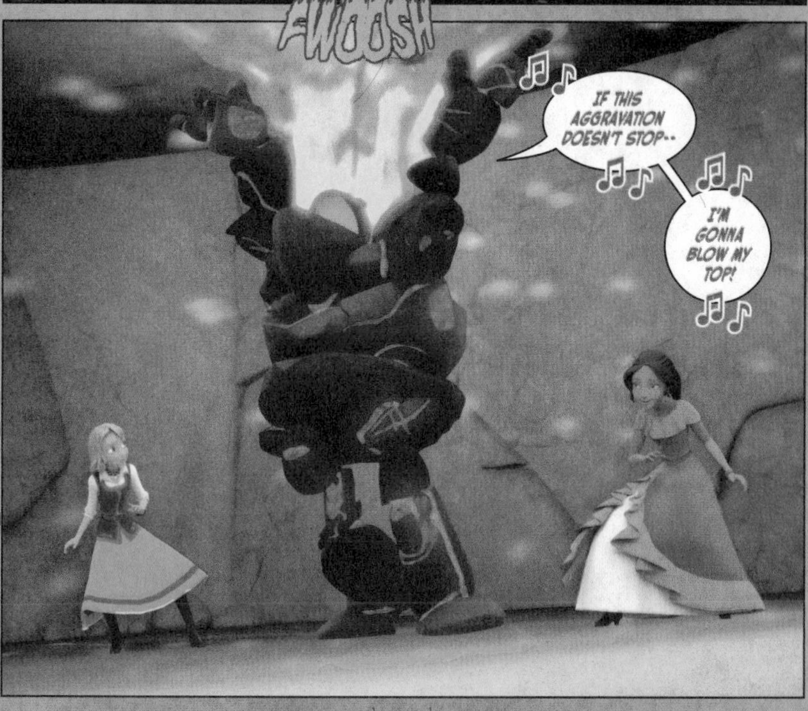
FWOOSH
IF THIS AGGRAVATION DOESN'T STOP--
I'M GONNA BLOW MY TOP!

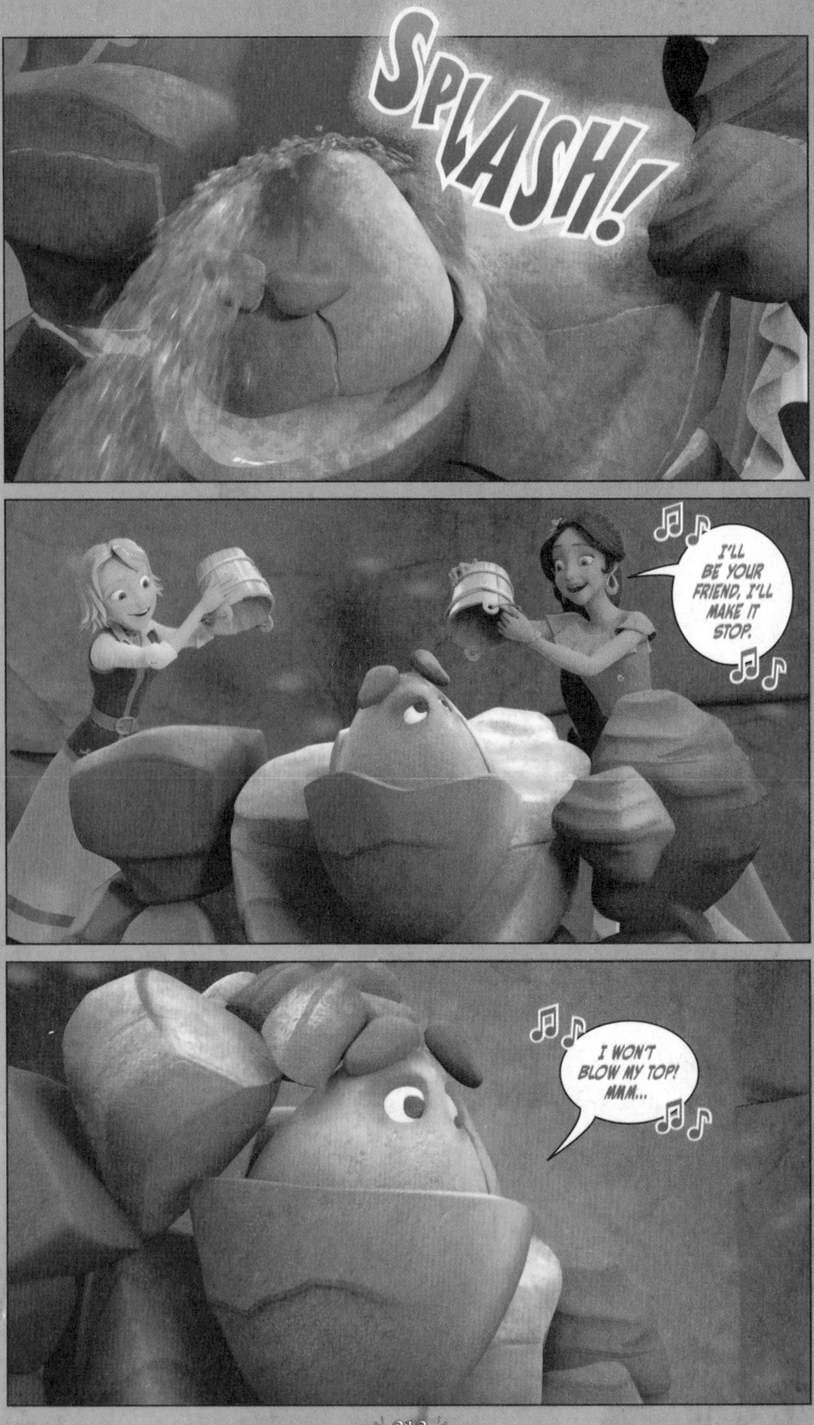
SPLASH!
I'LL BE YOUR FRIEND, I'LL MAKE IT STOP.
I WON'T BLOW MY TOP! MMM...

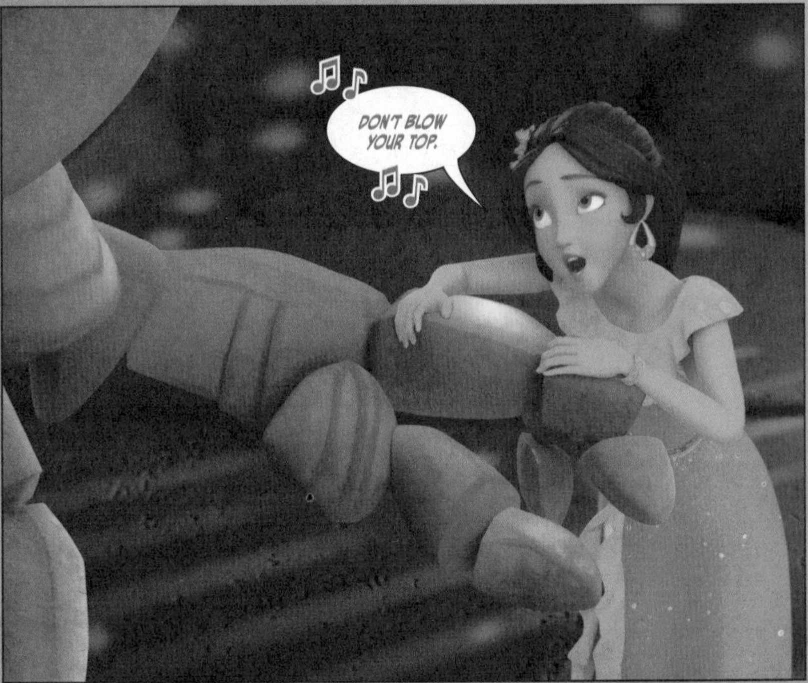
DON'T BLOW YOUR TOP.

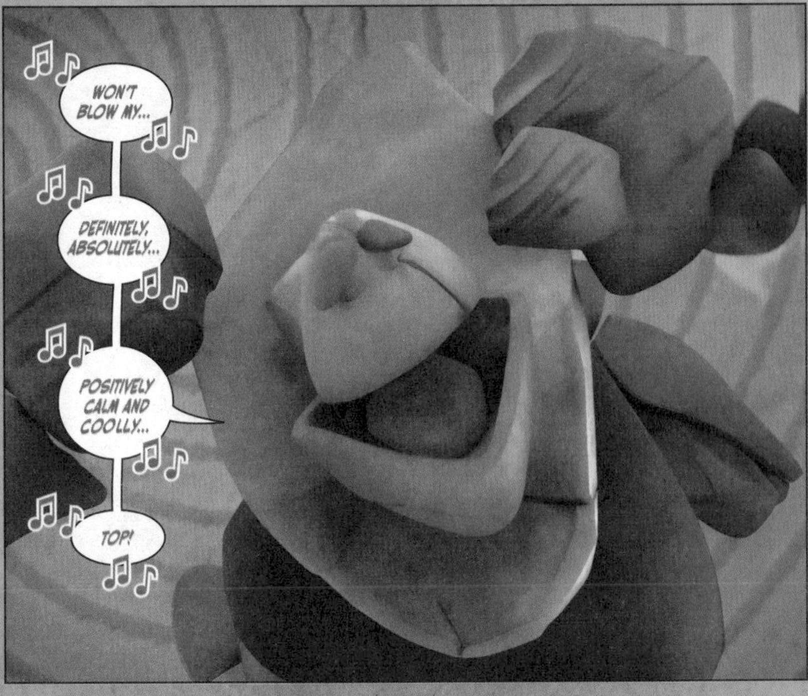
WON'T BLOW MY...
DEFINITELY, ABSOLUTELY...
POSITIVELY CALM AND COOLLY...
TOP!

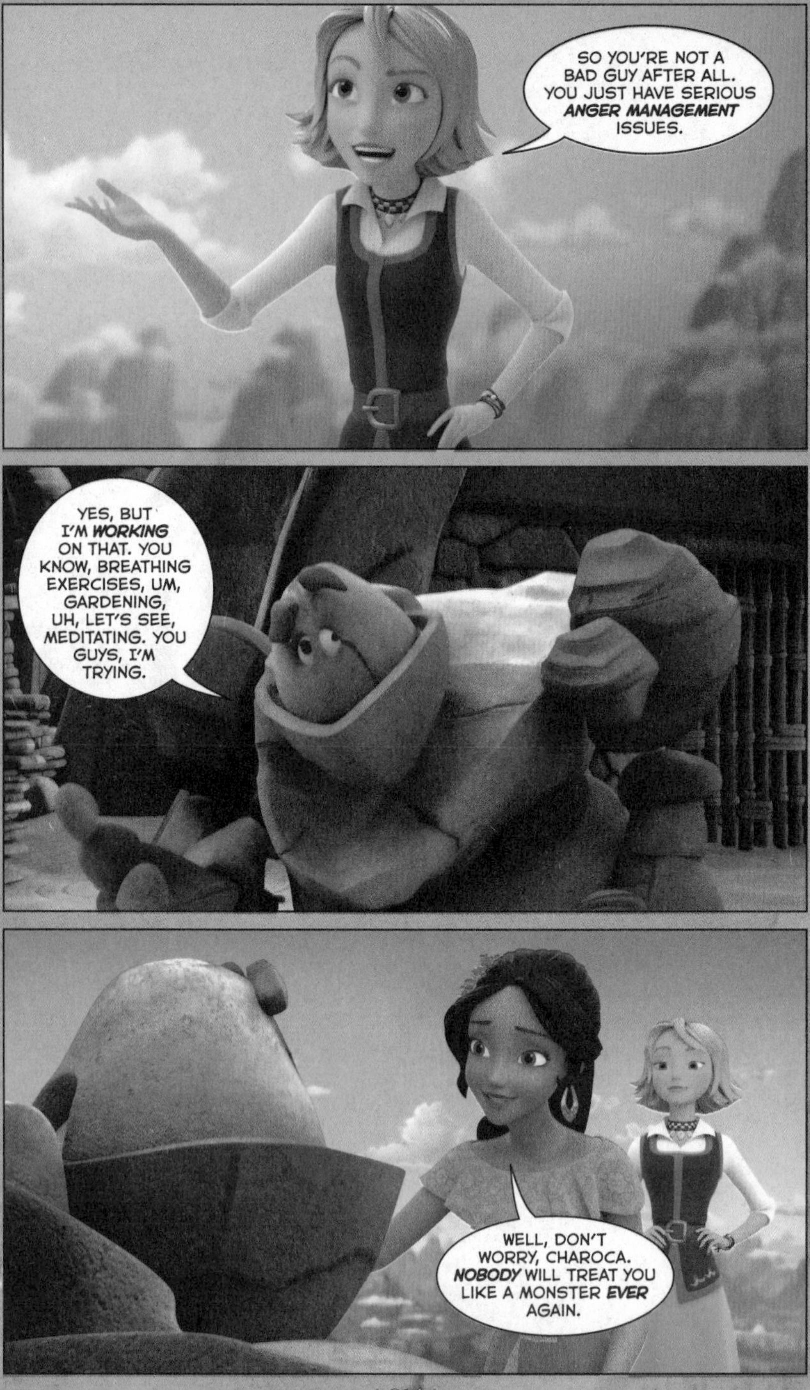
SO YOU'RE NOT A BAD GUY AFTER ALL. YOU JUST HAVE SERIOUS ***ANGER MANAGEMENT*** ISSUES.
YES, BUT I'M ***WORKING*** ON THAT. YOU KNOW, BREATHING EXERCISES, UM, GARDENING, UH, LET'S SEE, MEDITATING. YOU GUYS, I'M TRYING.
WELL, DON'T WORRY, CHAROCA. ***NOBODY*** WILL TREAT YOU LIKE A MONSTER ***EVER*** AGAIN.

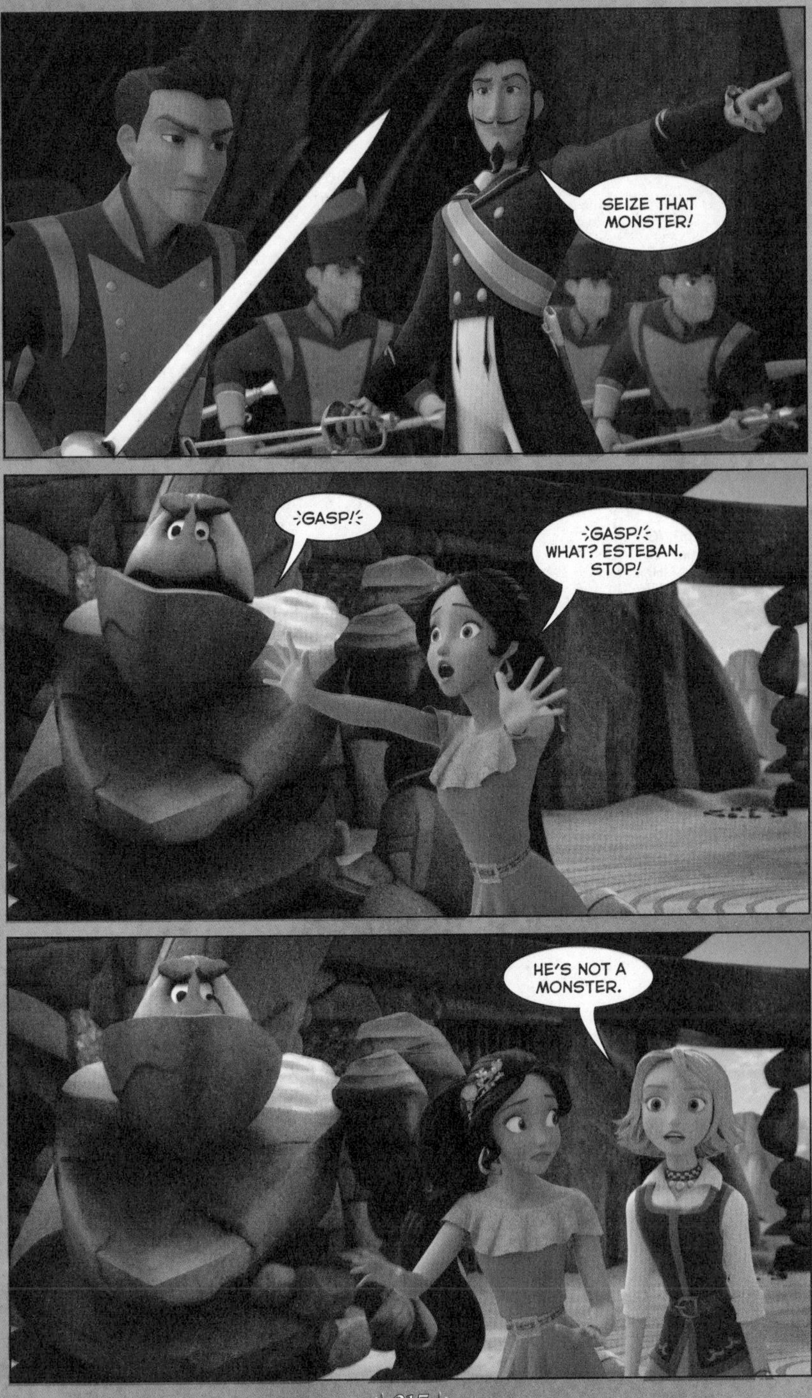
SEIZE THAT MONSTER!
GASP!
GASP! WHAT? ESTEBAN. STOP!
HE'S NOT A MONSTER.

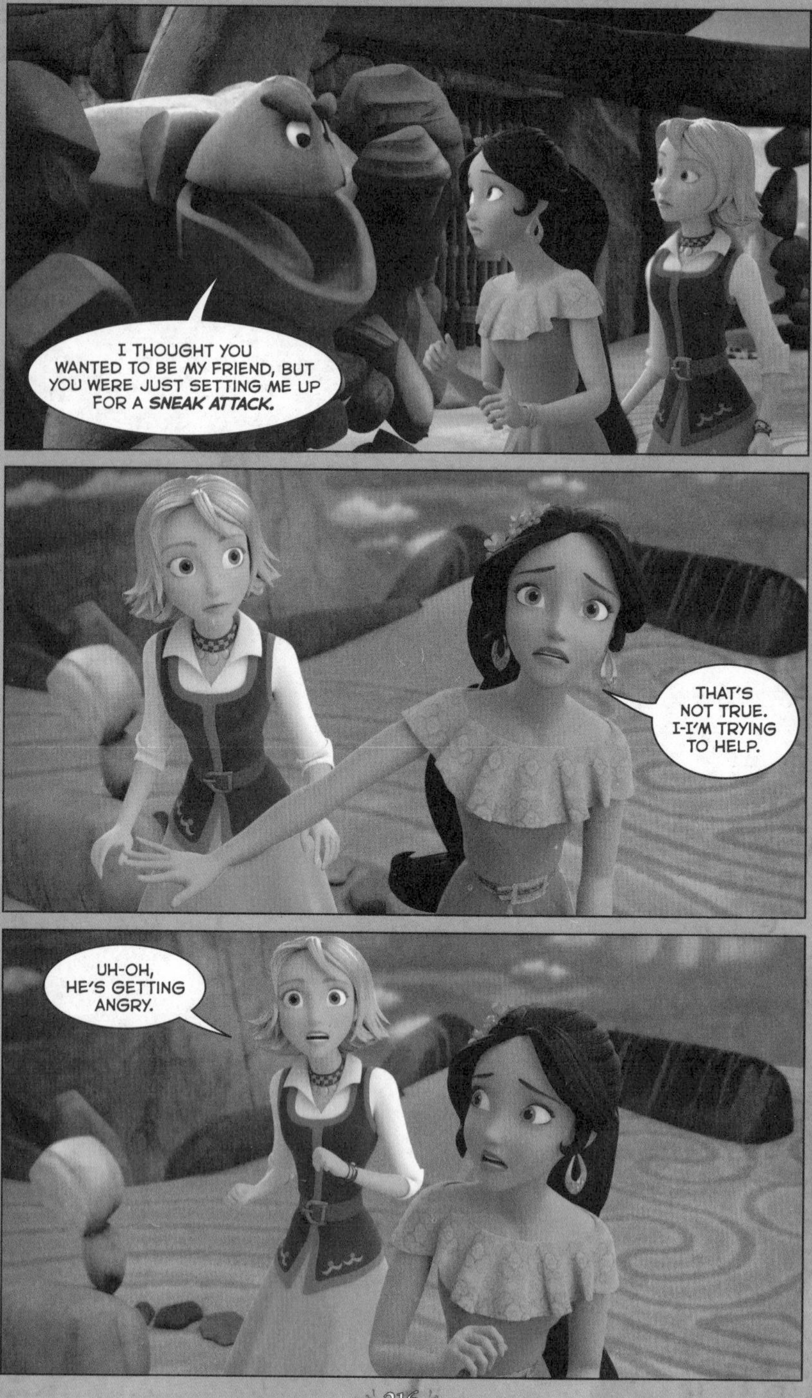
I THOUGHT YOU WANTED TO BE MY FRIEND, BUT YOU WERE JUST SETTING ME UP FOR A **SNEAK ATTACK.**
THAT'S NOT TRUE. I-I'M TRYING TO HELP.
UH-OH, HE'S GETTING ANGRY.

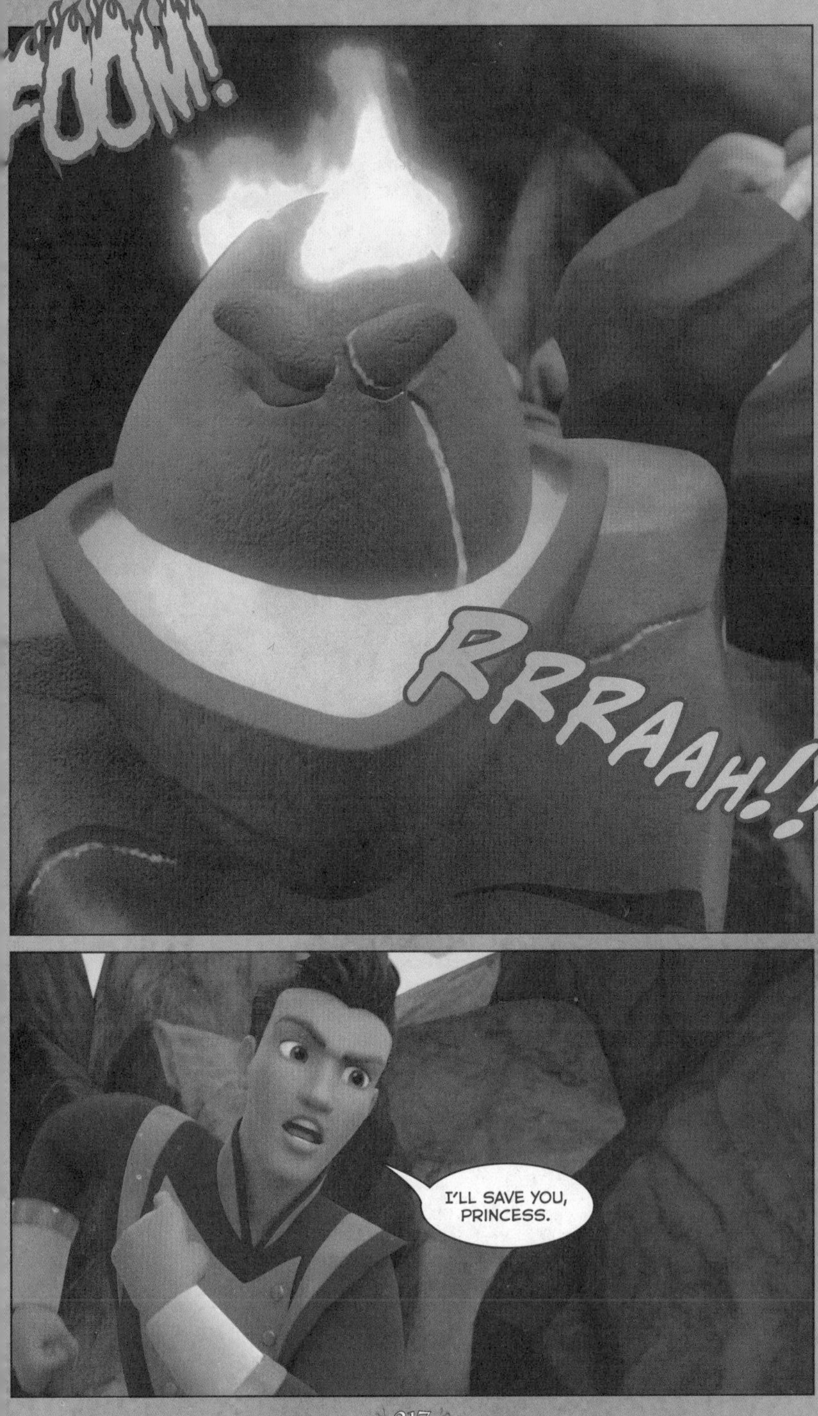
FOOM!
RRRAAH!!
I'LL SAVE YOU, PRINCESS.

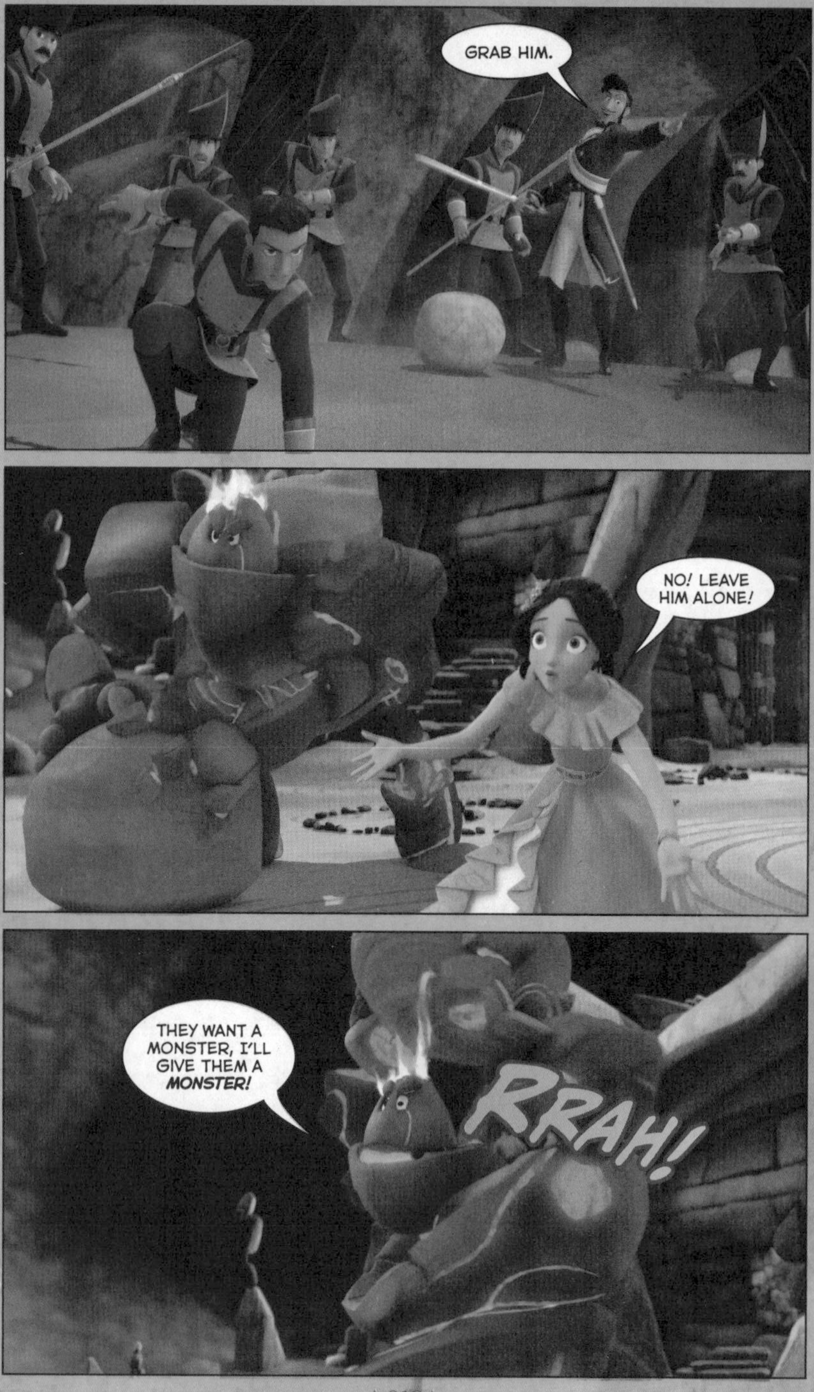
GRAB HIM.
NO! LEAVE HIM ALONE!
THEY WANT A MONSTER, I'LL GIVE THEM A *MONSTER!*
RRAH!

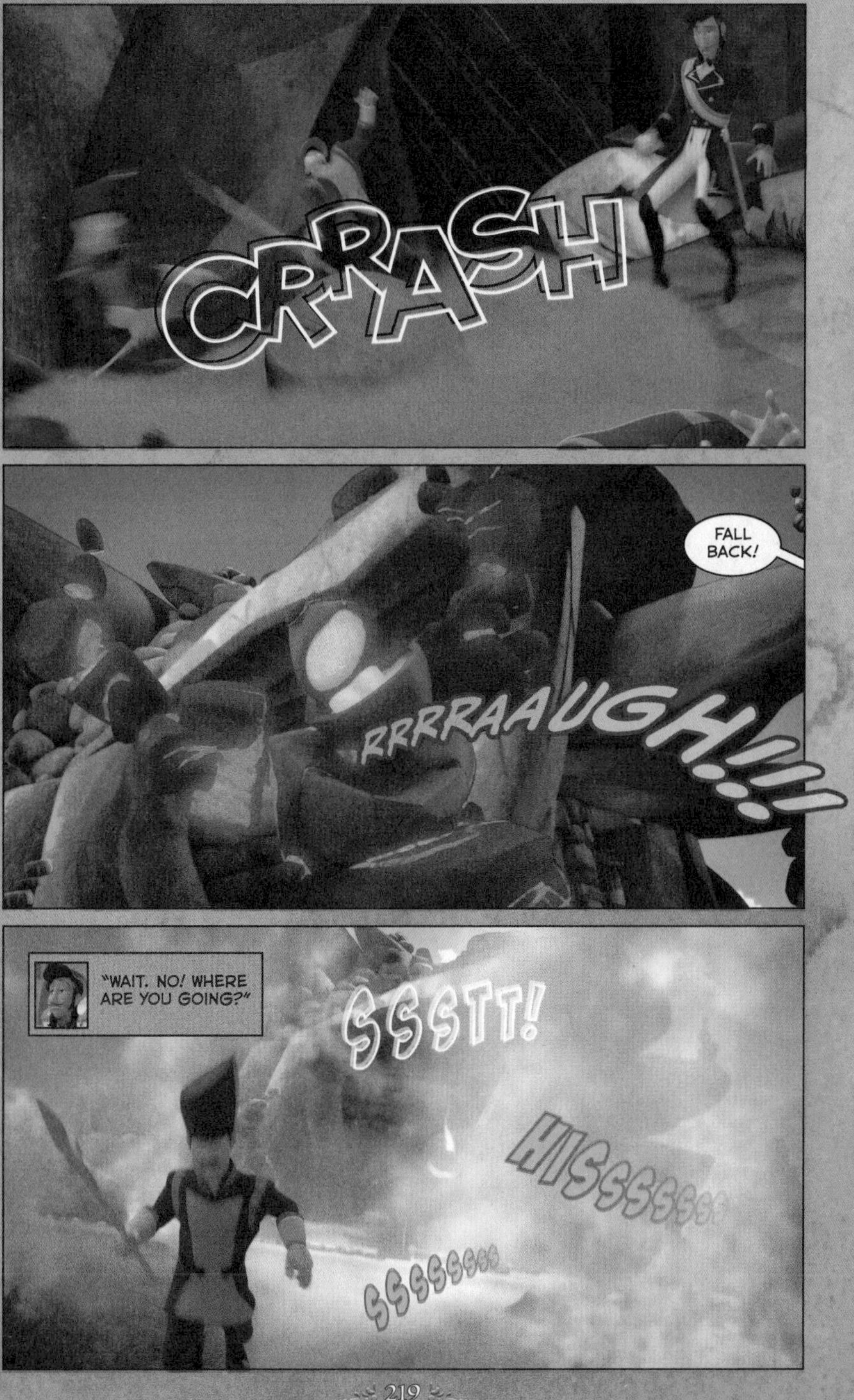
CRRASH
FALL BACK!
RRRRAAUGH!!!!
"WAIT. NO! WHERE ARE YOU GOING?"
SSSTT!
HISSSSSS
SSSSSSS

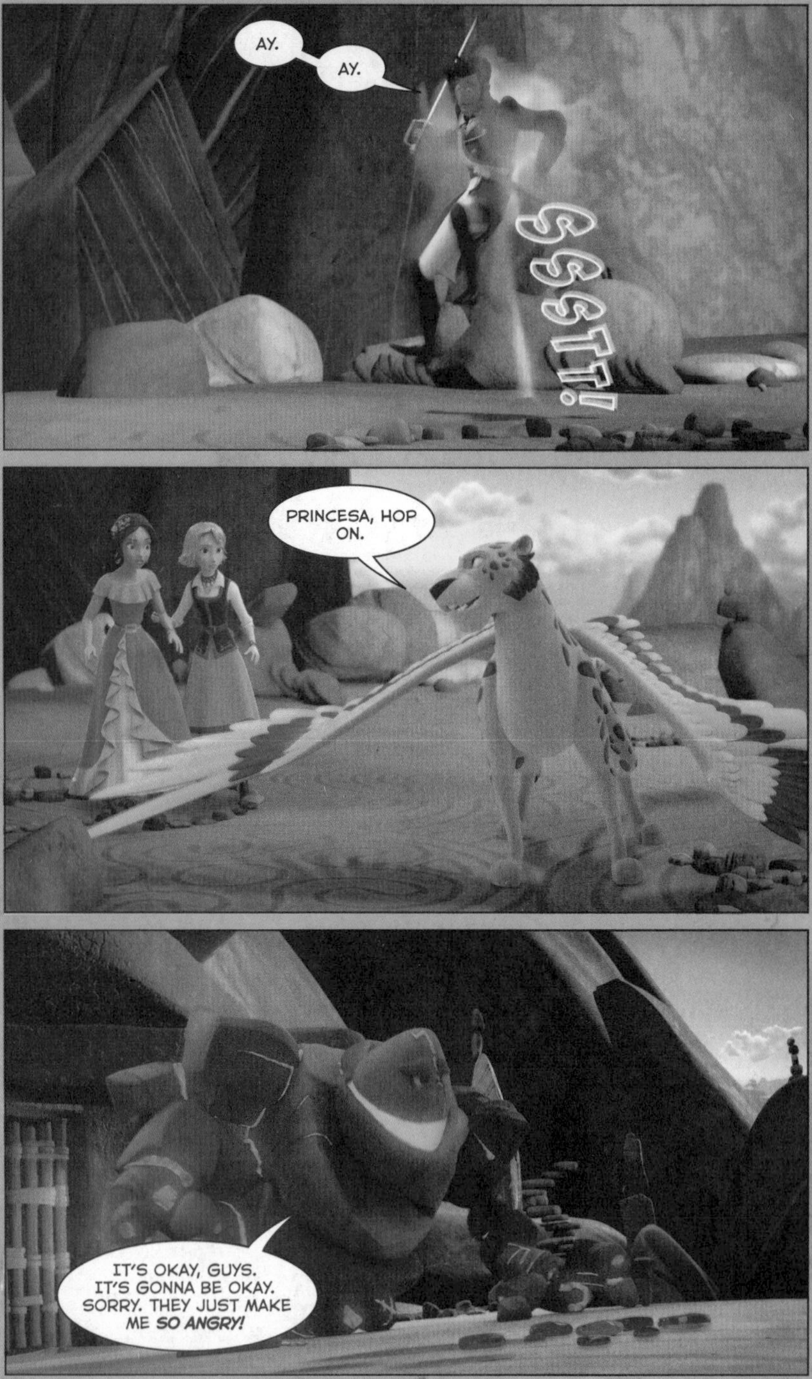
AY.
AY.
SSSTT!
PRINCESA, HOP ON.
IT'S OKAY, GUYS. IT'S GONNA BE OKAY. SORRY. THEY JUST MAKE ME *SO ANGRY!*

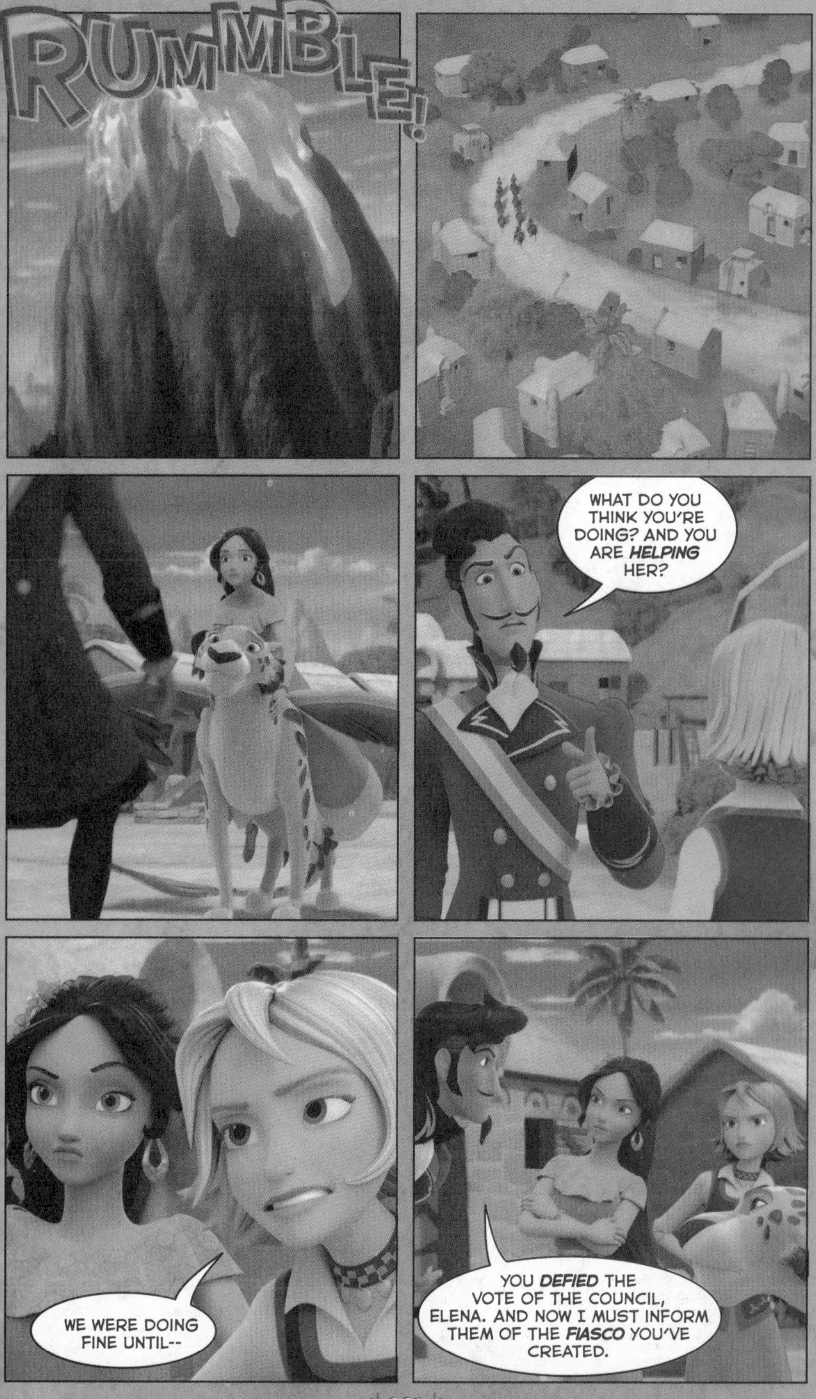
RUMMBLE!
WHAT DO YOU THINK YOU'RE DOING? AND YOU ARE *HELPING* HER?
WE WERE DOING FINE UNTIL--
YOU *DEFIED* THE VOTE OF THE COUNCIL, ELENA. AND NOW I MUST INFORM THEM OF THE *FIASCO* YOU'VE CREATED.

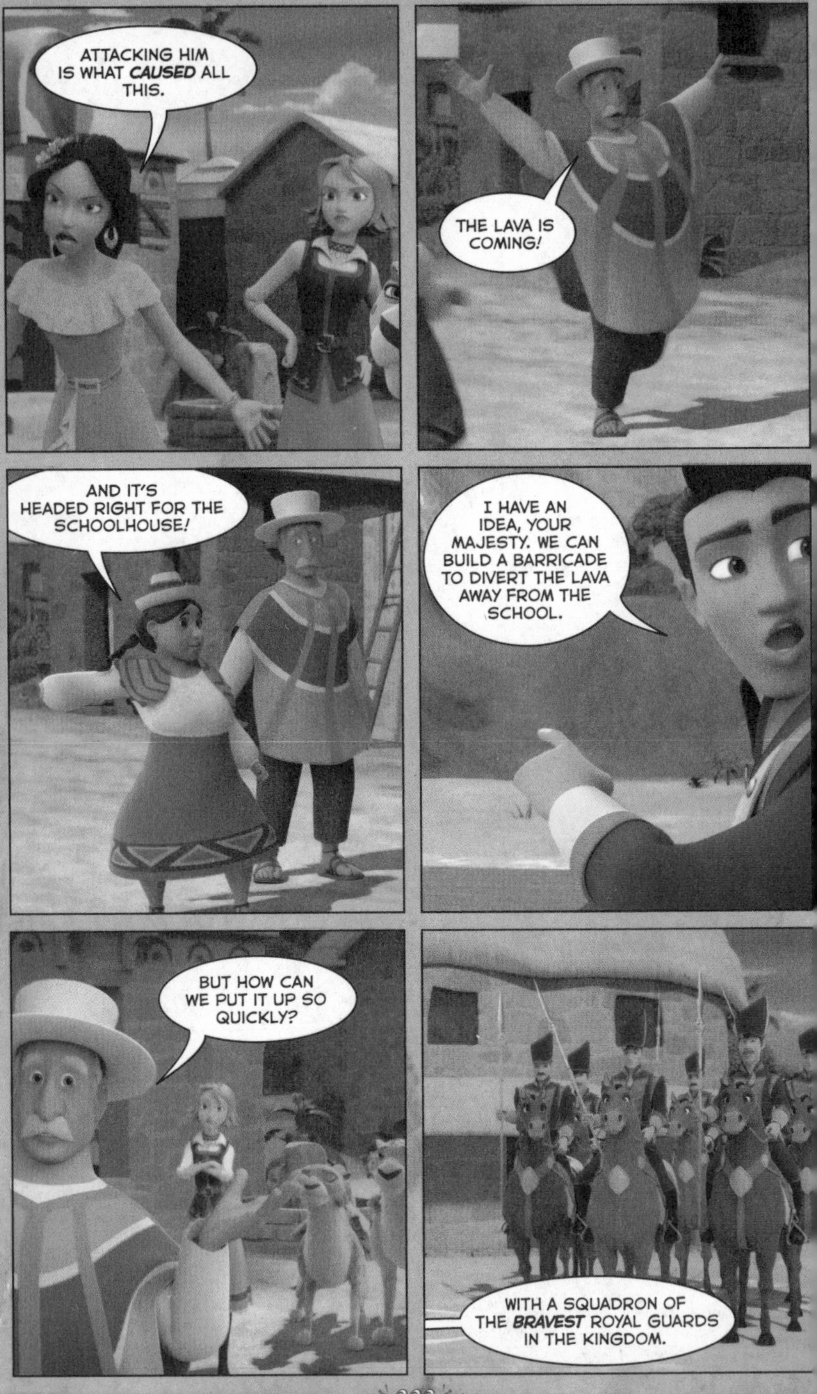
ATTACKING HIM IS WHAT *CAUSED* ALL THIS.
THE LAVA IS COMING!
AND IT'S HEADED RIGHT FOR THE SCHOOLHOUSE!
I HAVE AN IDEA, YOUR MAJESTY. WE CAN BUILD A BARRICADE TO DIVERT THE LAVA AWAY FROM THE SCHOOL.
BUT HOW CAN WE PUT IT UP SO QUICKLY?
WITH A SQUADRON OF THE *BRAVEST* ROYAL GUARDS IN THE KINGDOM.

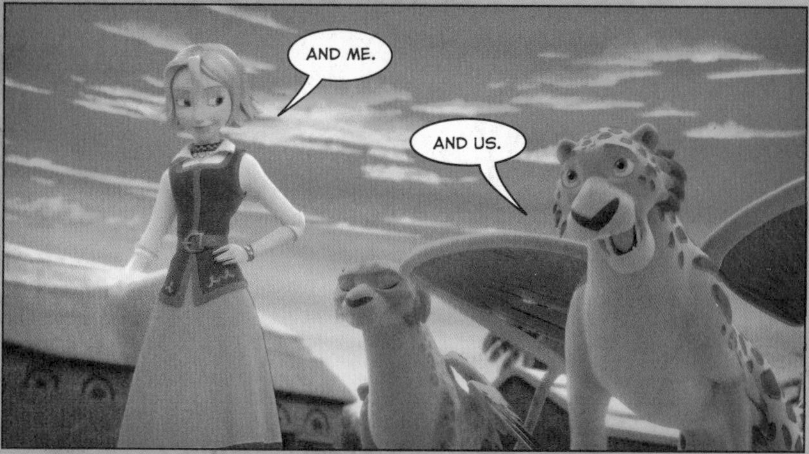
AND ME.
AND US.

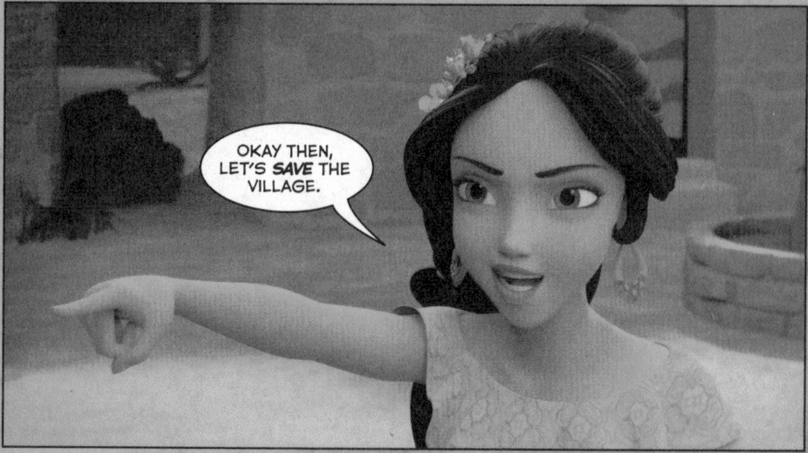
OKAY THEN, LET'S *SAVE* THE VILLAGE.

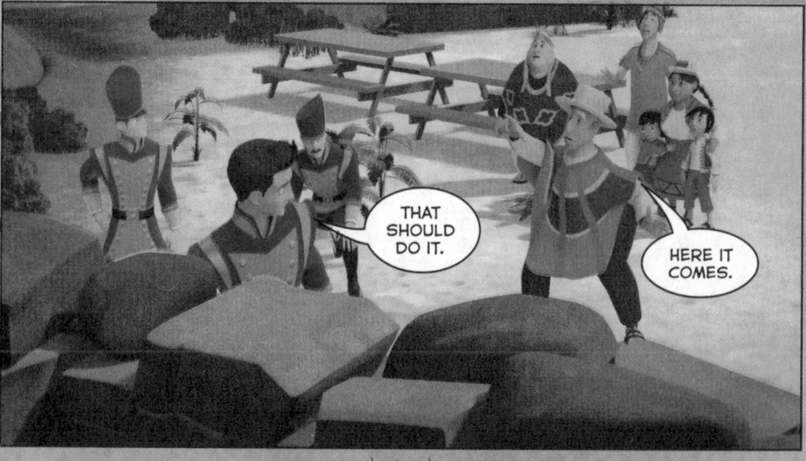
THAT SHOULD DO IT.
HERE IT COMES.

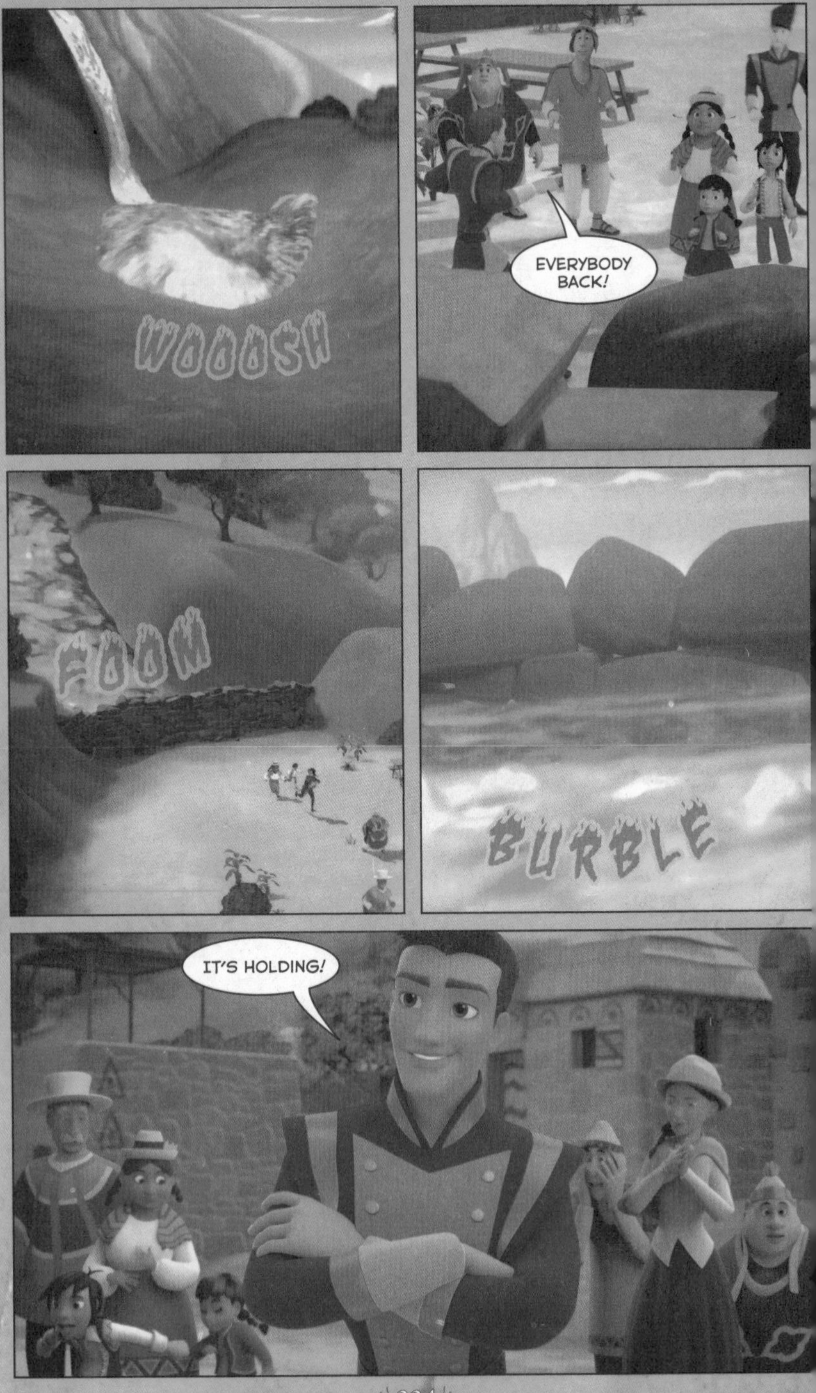
WOOOSH
EVERYBODY BACK!
FOOM
BURBLE
IT'S HOLDING!

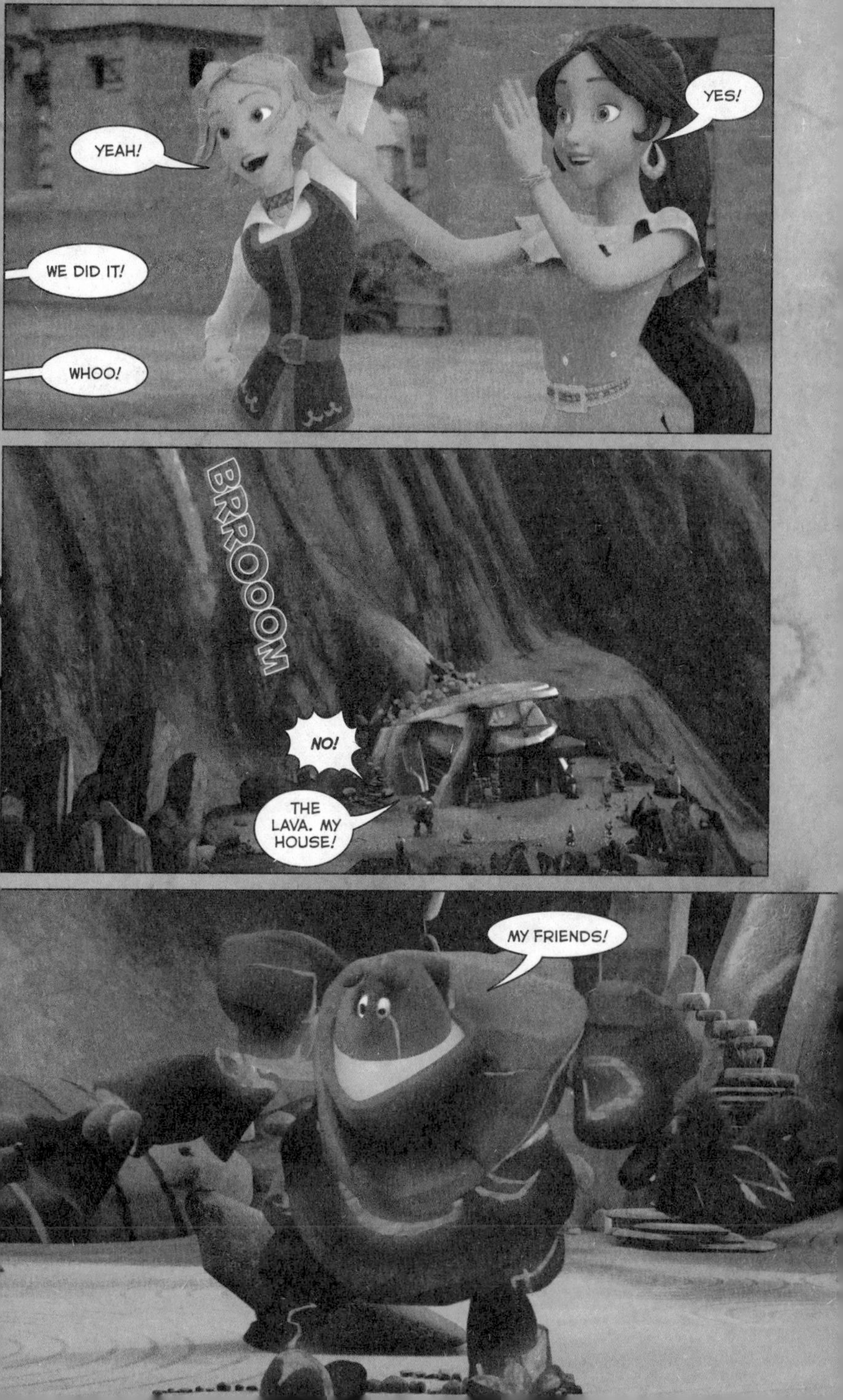
YEAH!
YES!
WE DID IT!
WHOO!
BRROOOOM
NO!
THE LAVA. MY HOUSE!
MY FRIENDS!

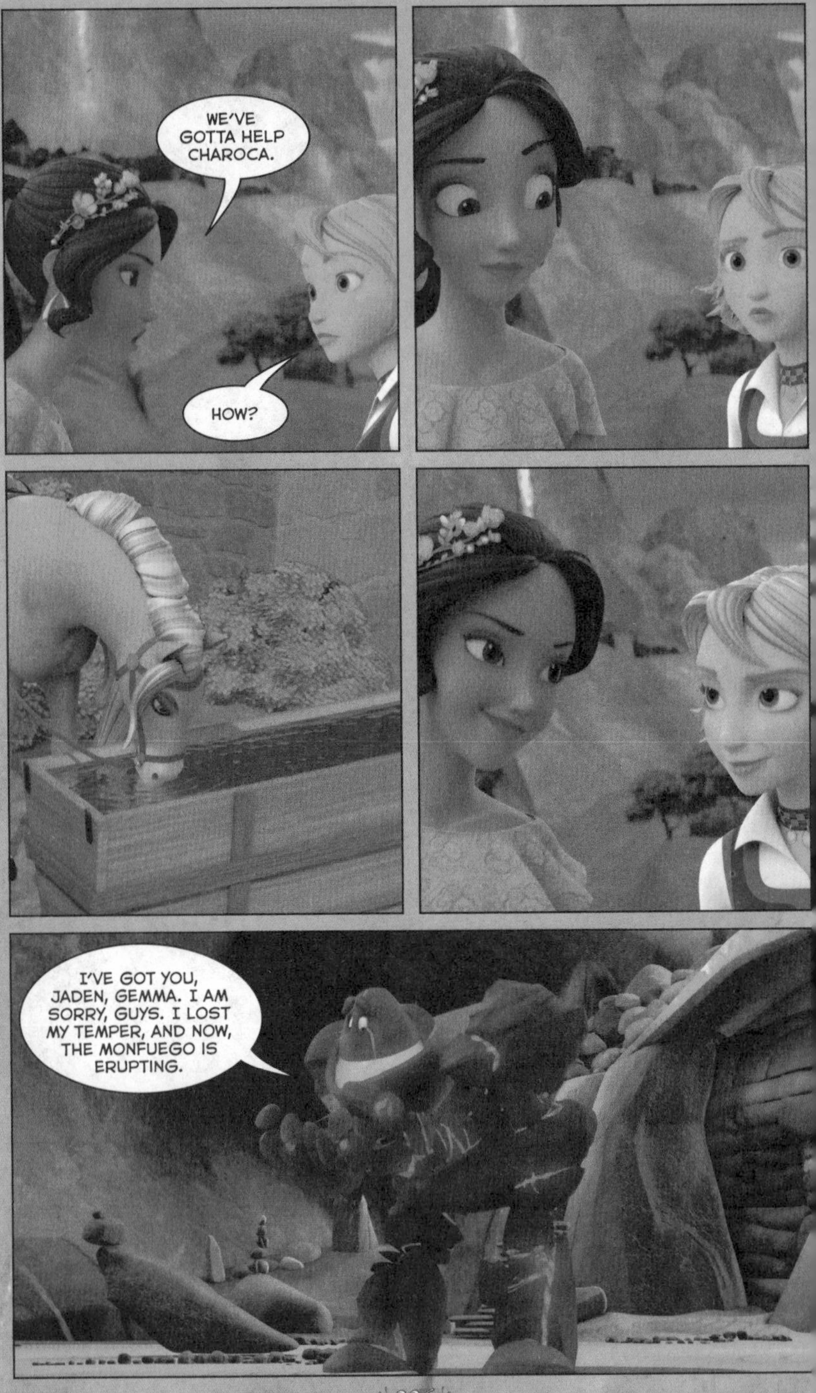
WE'VE GOTTA HELP CHAROCA.
HOW?
I'VE GOT YOU, JADEN, GEMMA. I AM SORRY, GUYS. I LOST MY TEMPER, AND NOW, THE MONFUEGO IS ERUPTING.

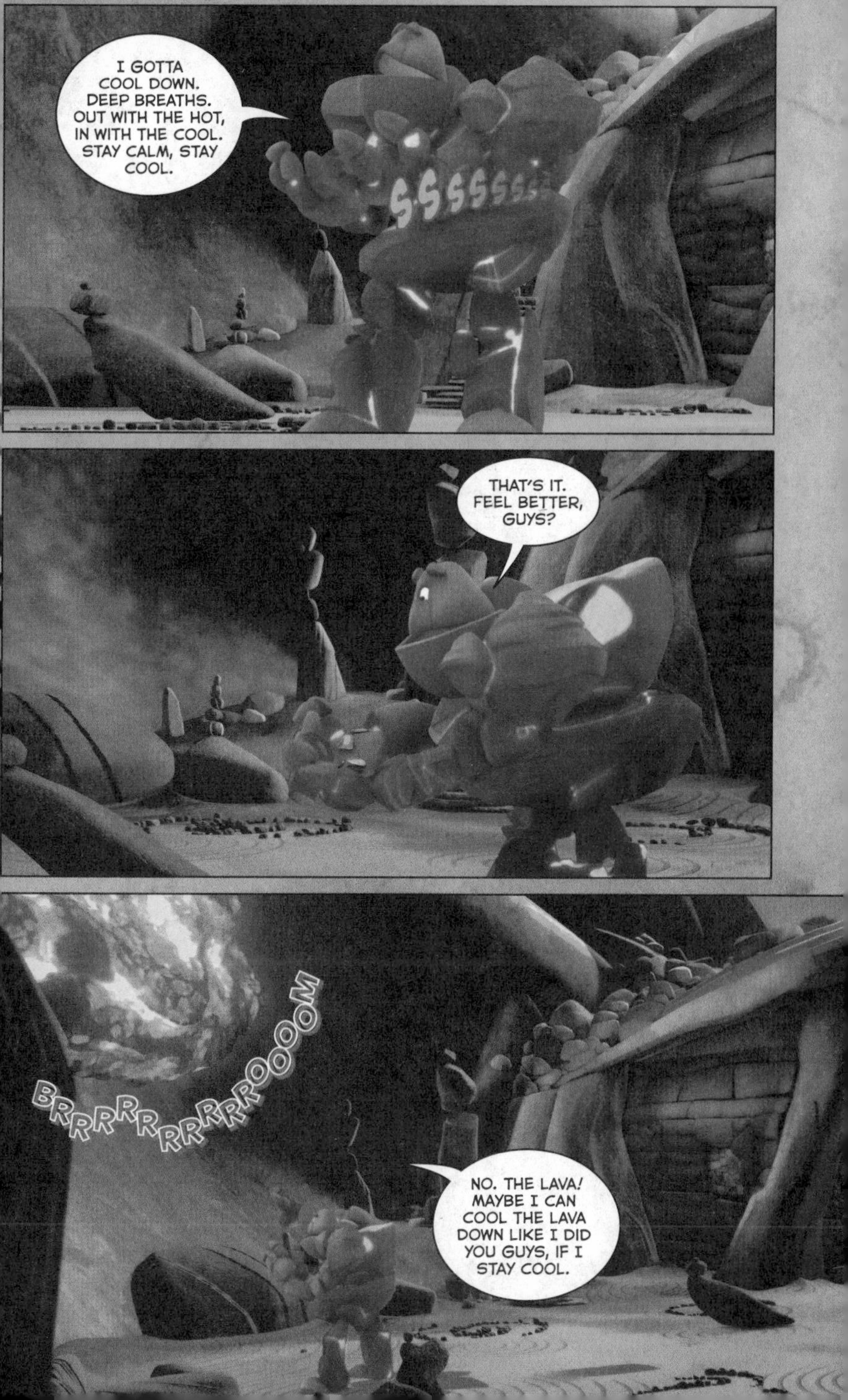
I GOTTA COOL DOWN. DEEP BREATHS. OUT WITH THE HOT, IN WITH THE COOL. STAY CALM, STAY COOL.
SSSSSSSS
THAT'S IT. FEEL BETTER, GUYS?
BRRRRRRRRRROOOOM
NO. THE LAVA! MAYBE I CAN COOL THE LAVA DOWN LIKE I DID YOU GUYS, IF I STAY COOL.

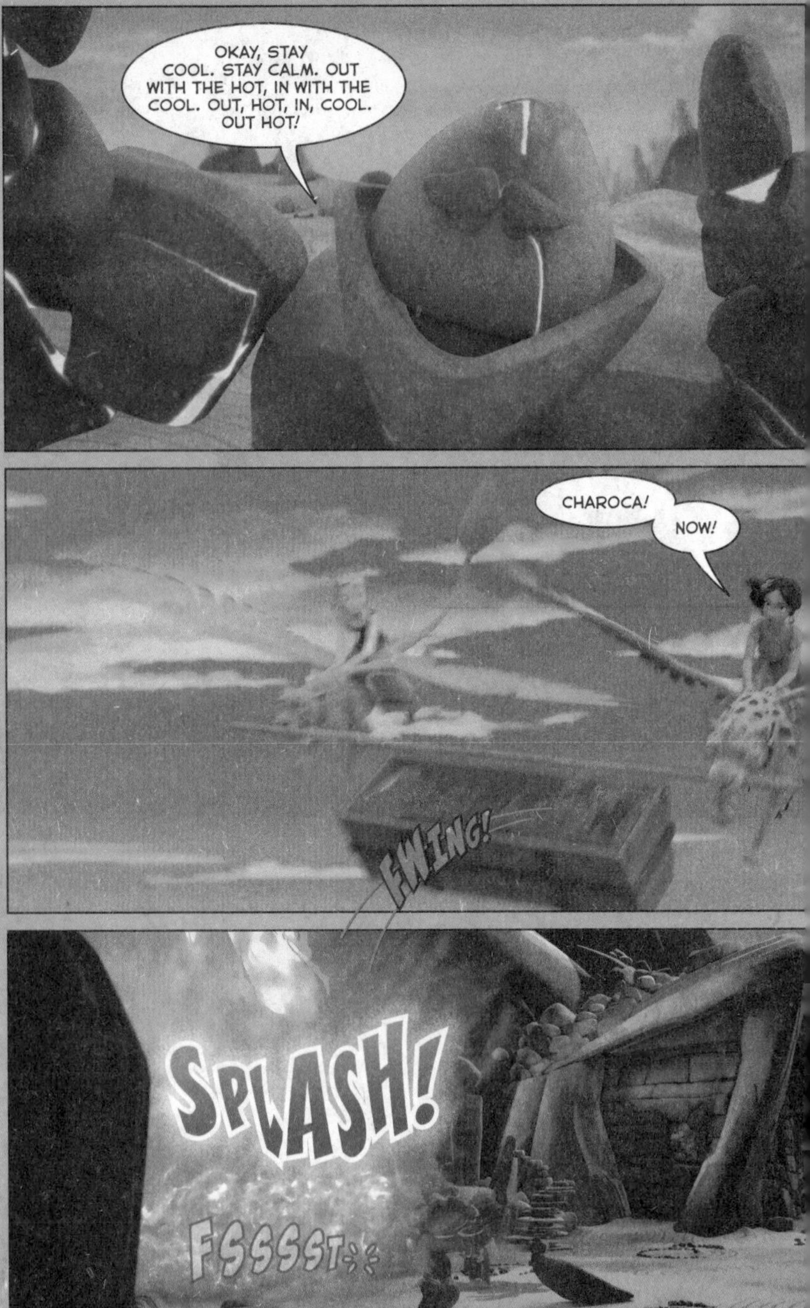
OKAY, STAY COOL. STAY CALM. OUT WITH THE HOT, IN WITH THE COOL. OUT, HOT, IN, COOL. OUT HOT!
CHAROCA!
NOW!
FWING!
SPLASH!
FSSSST...

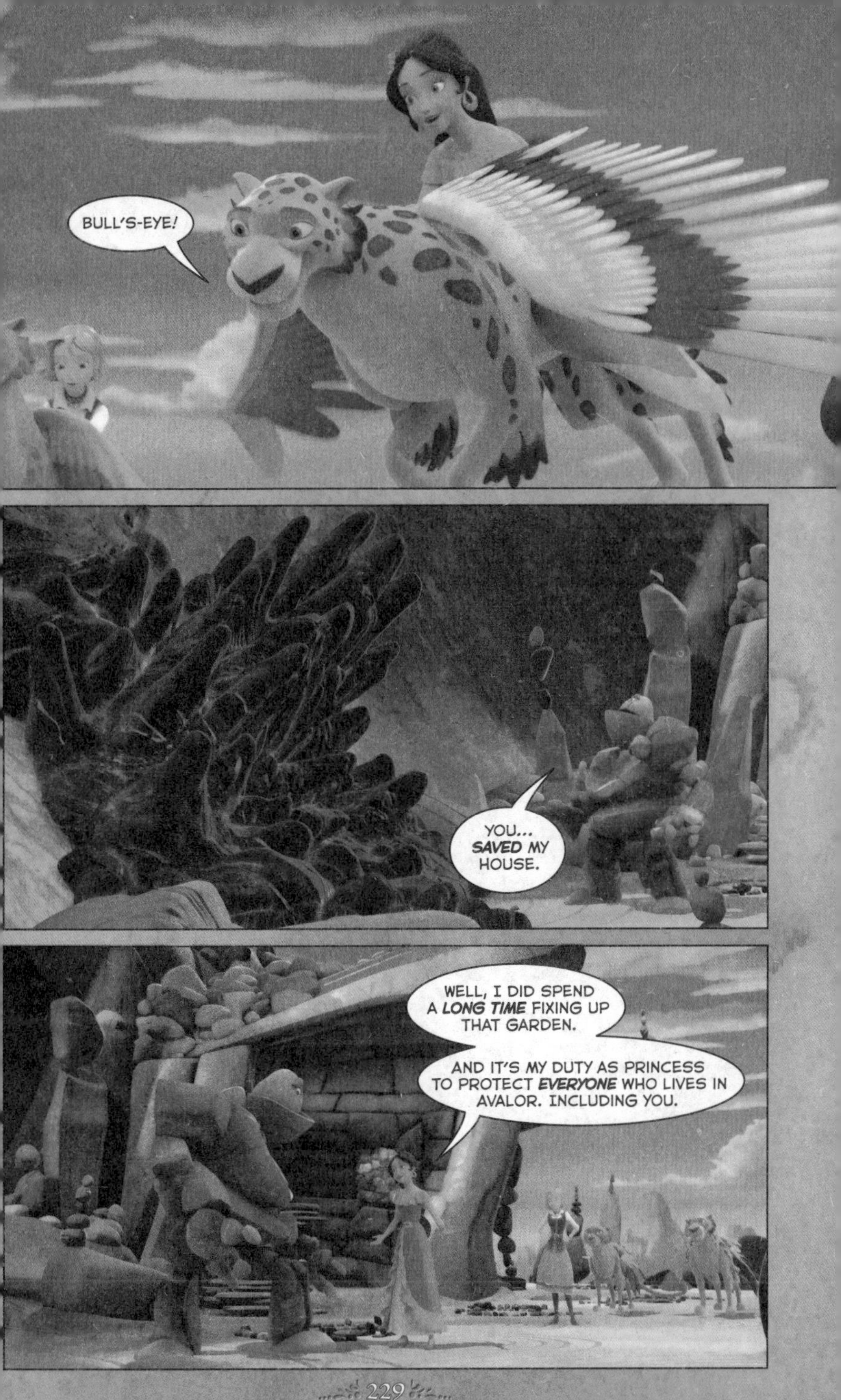
BULL'S-EYE!
YOU... SAVED MY HOUSE.
WELL, I DID SPEND A LONG TIME FIXING UP THAT GARDEN.
AND IT'S MY DUTY AS PRINCESS TO PROTECT EVERYONE WHO LIVES IN AVALOR. INCLUDING YOU.

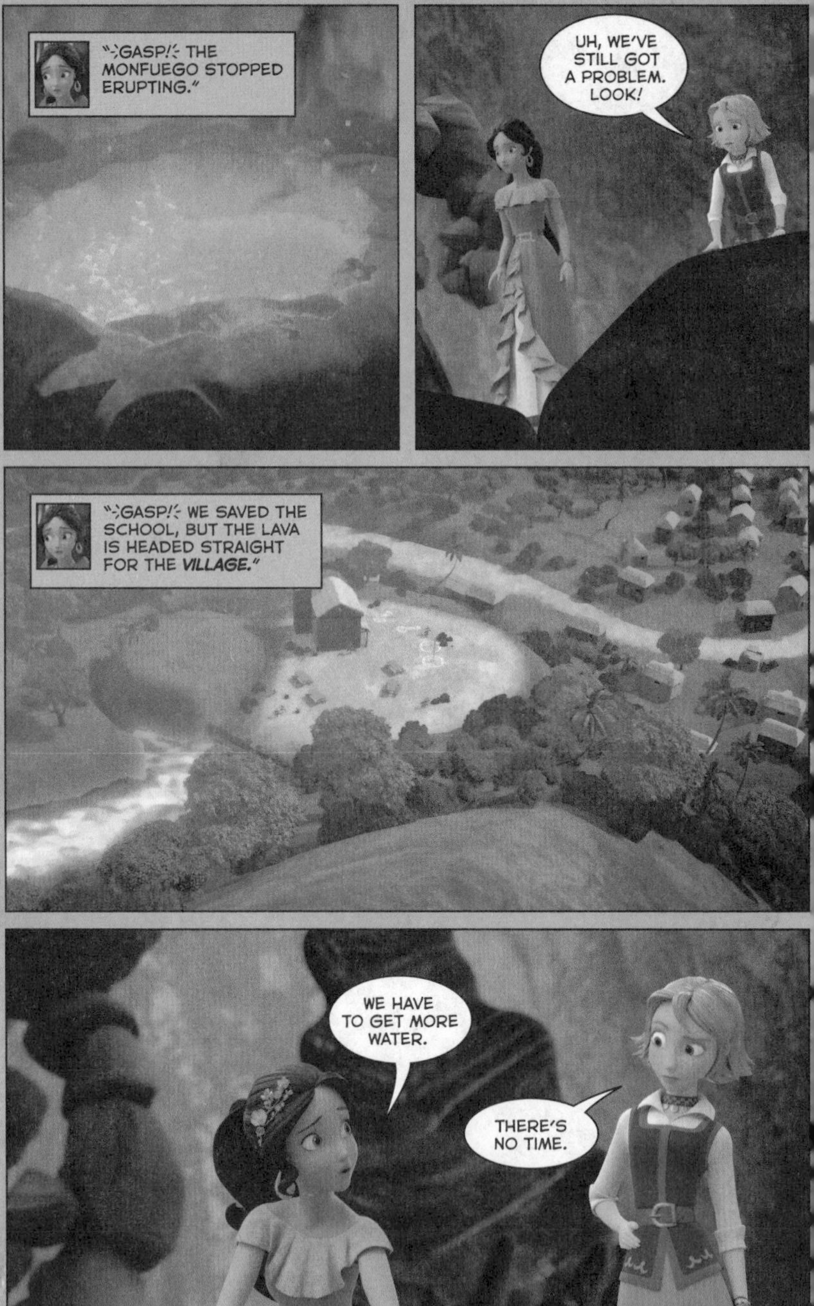
"*GASP!* THE MONFUEGO STOPPED ERUPTING."
UH, WE'VE STILL GOT A PROBLEM. LOOK!
"*GASP!* WE SAVED THE SCHOOL, BUT THE LAVA IS HEADED STRAIGHT FOR THE ***VILLAGE.***"
WE HAVE TO GET MORE WATER.
THERE'S NO TIME.

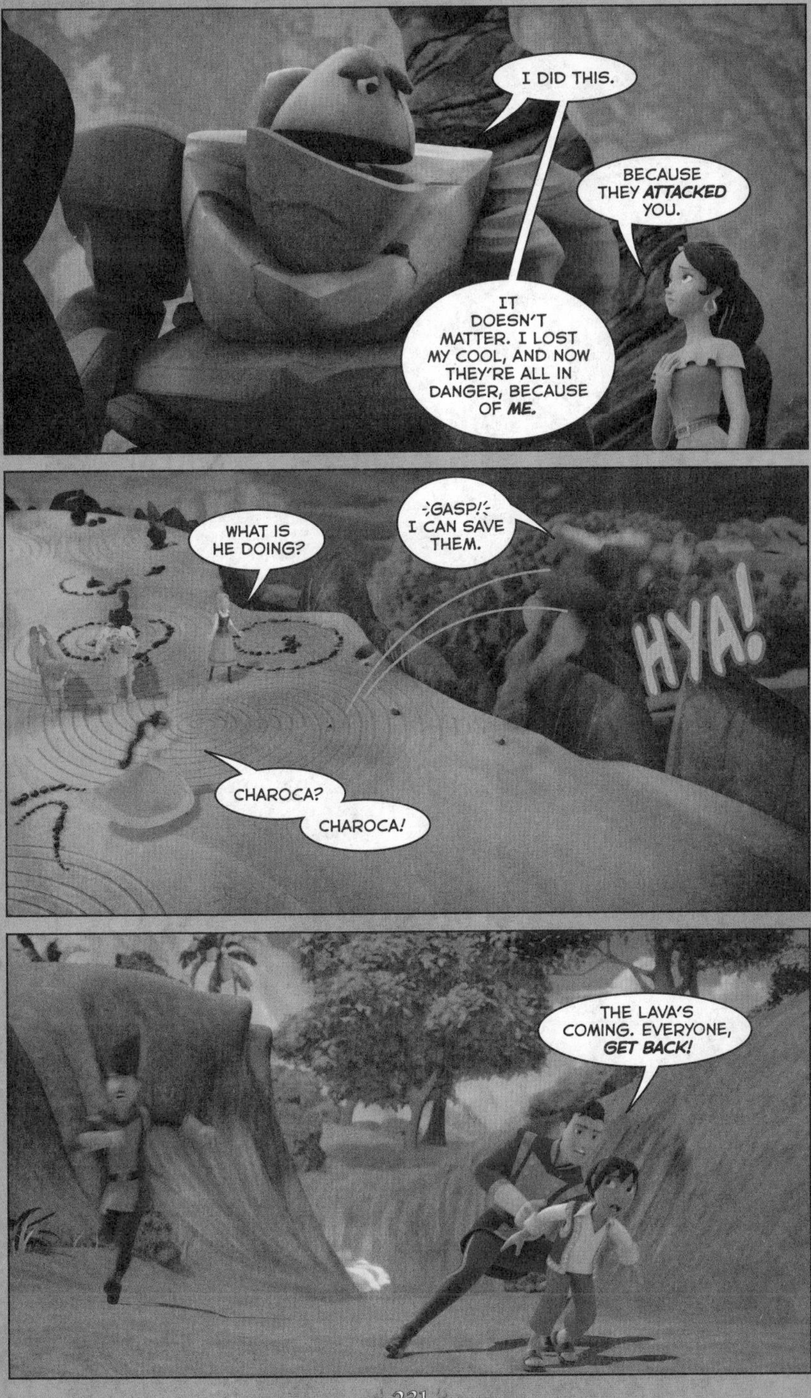

I DID THIS.
BECAUSE THEY ATTACKED YOU.
IT DOESN'T MATTER. I LOST MY COOL, AND NOW THEY'RE ALL IN DANGER, BECAUSE OF ME.
WHAT IS HE DOING?
-GASP!- I CAN SAVE THEM.
HYA!
CHAROCA?
CHAROCA!
THE LAVA'S COMING. EVERYONE, GET BACK!

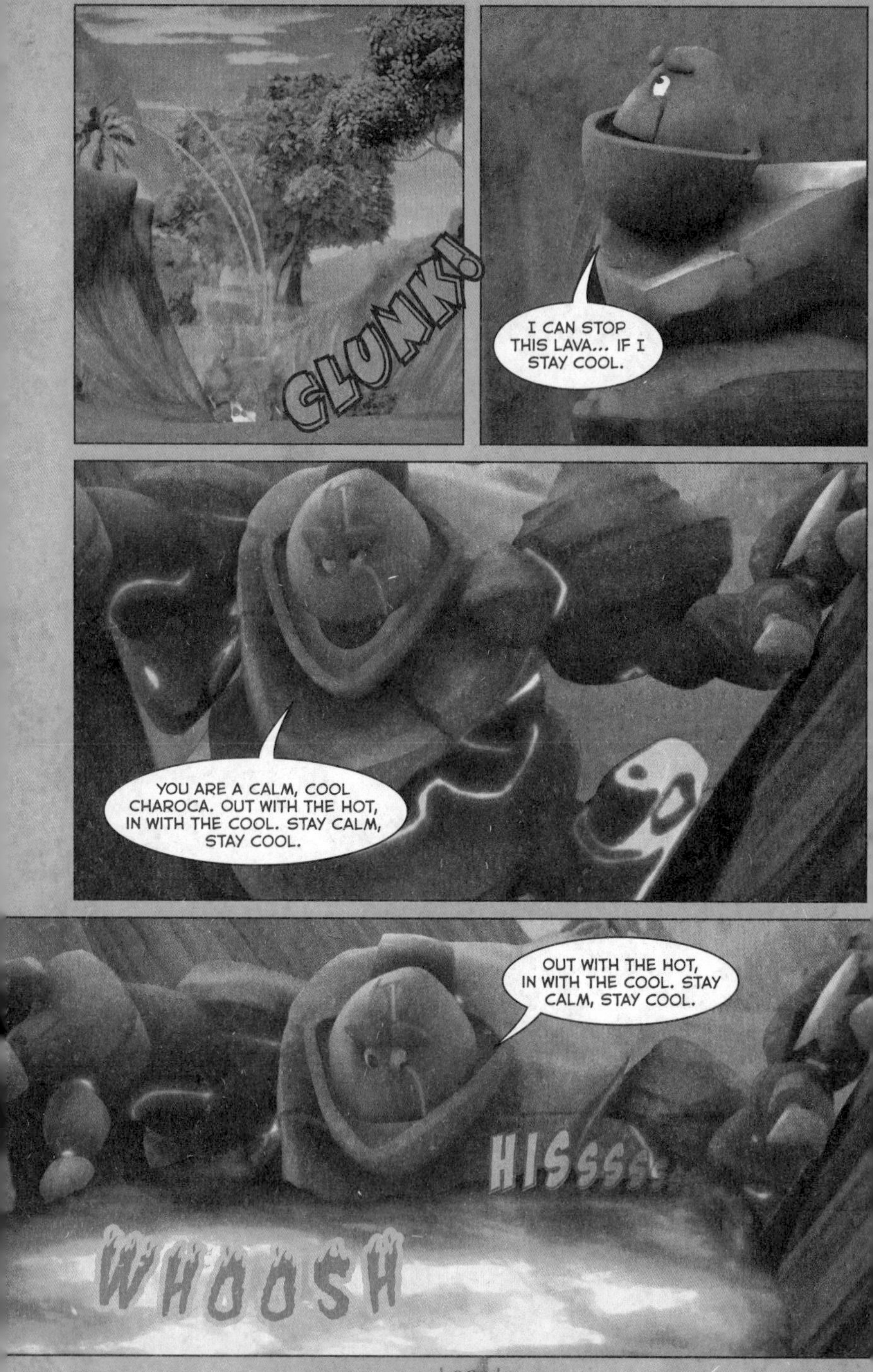
CLUNK!
I CAN STOP THIS LAVA... IF I STAY COOL.
YOU ARE A CALM, COOL CHAROCA. OUT WITH THE HOT, IN WITH THE COOL. STAY CALM, STAY COOL.
OUT WITH THE HOT, IN WITH THE COOL. STAY CALM, STAY COOL.
HISsss
WHOOSH

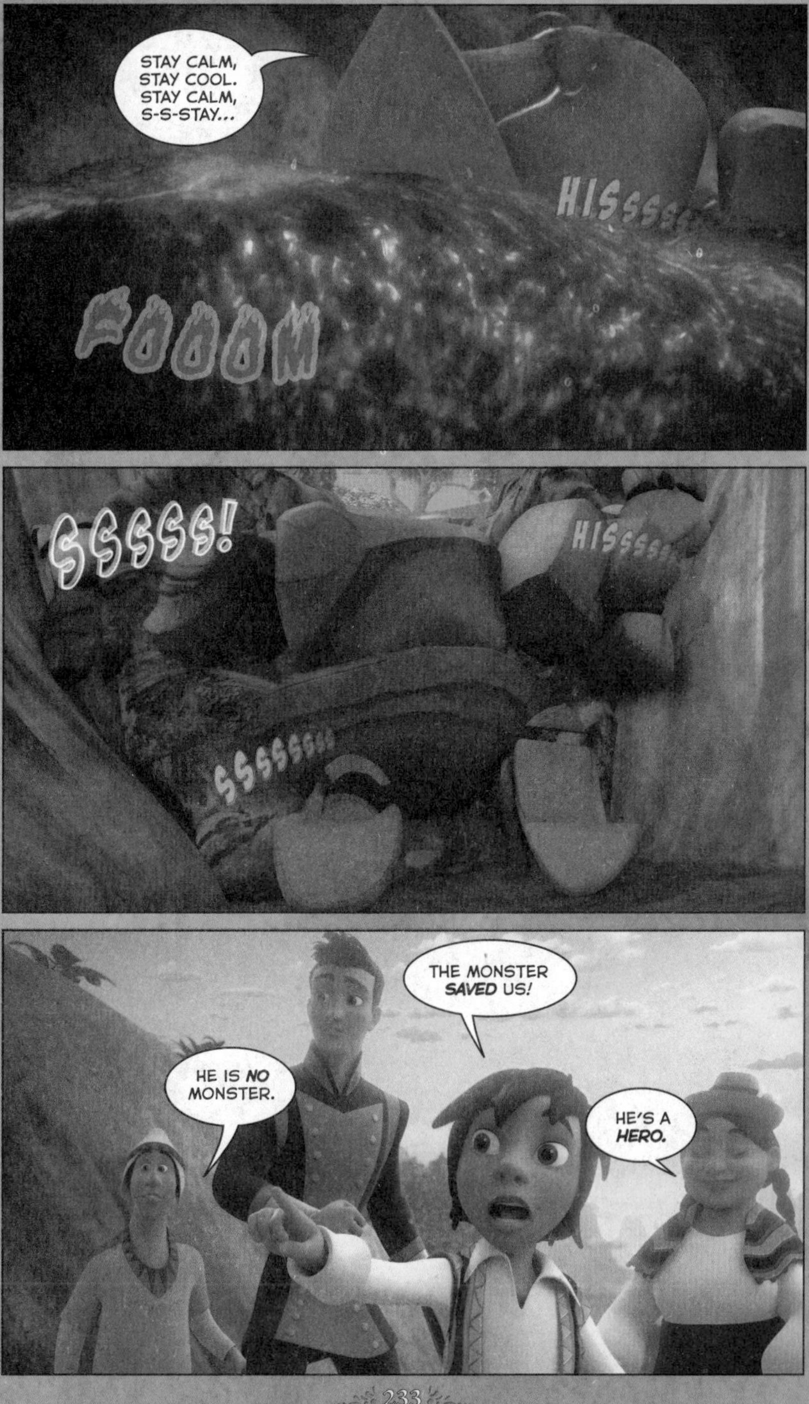
STAY CALM, STAY COOL. STAY CALM, S-S-STAY...
HISSSSS
FOOOM
SSSSS!
HISSSSS
SSSSSSSS
THE MONSTER SAVED US!
HE IS NO MONSTER.
HE'S A HERO.

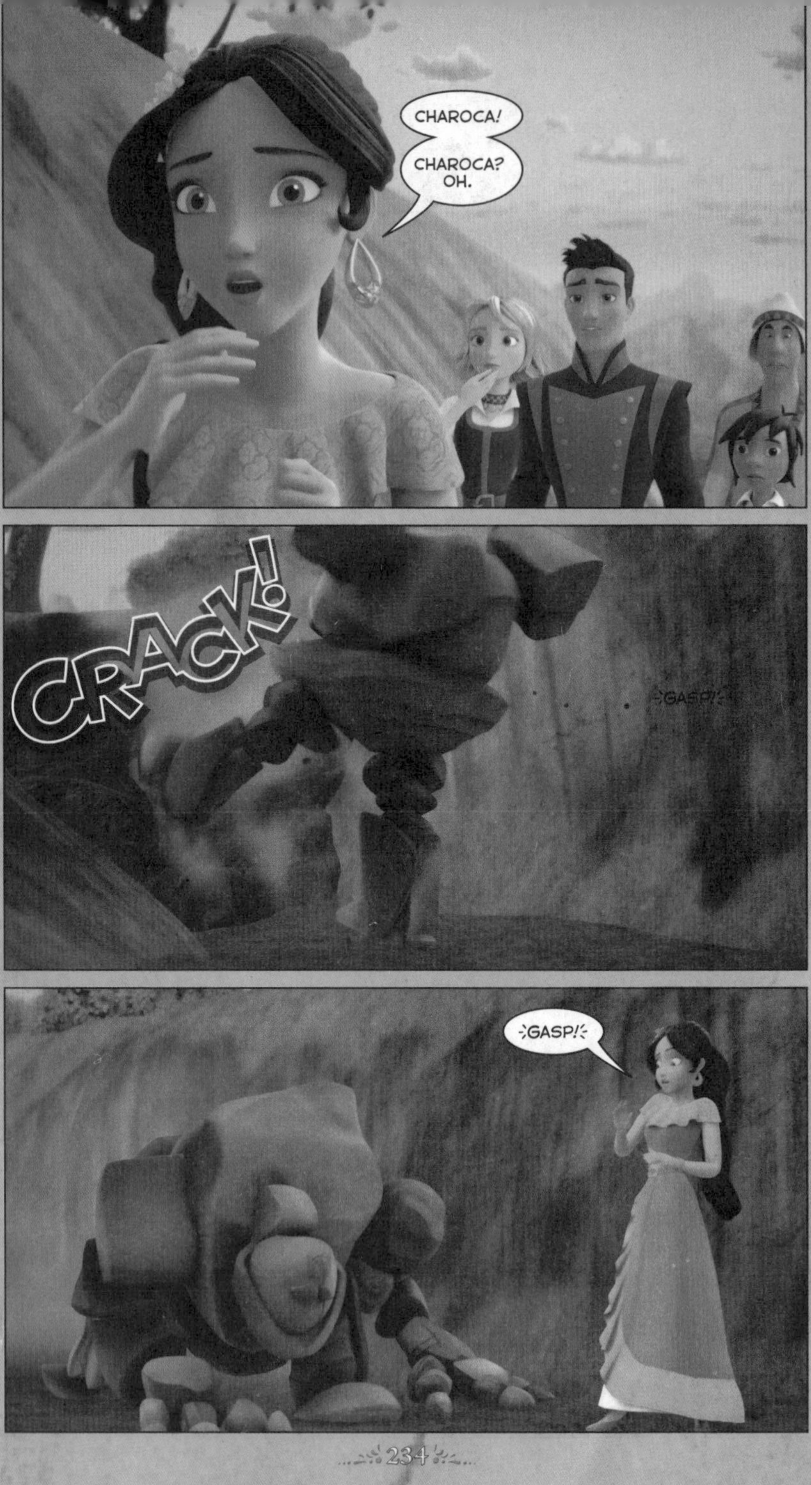
CHAROCA!
CHAROCA? OH.
CRACK!
GASP!
GASP!

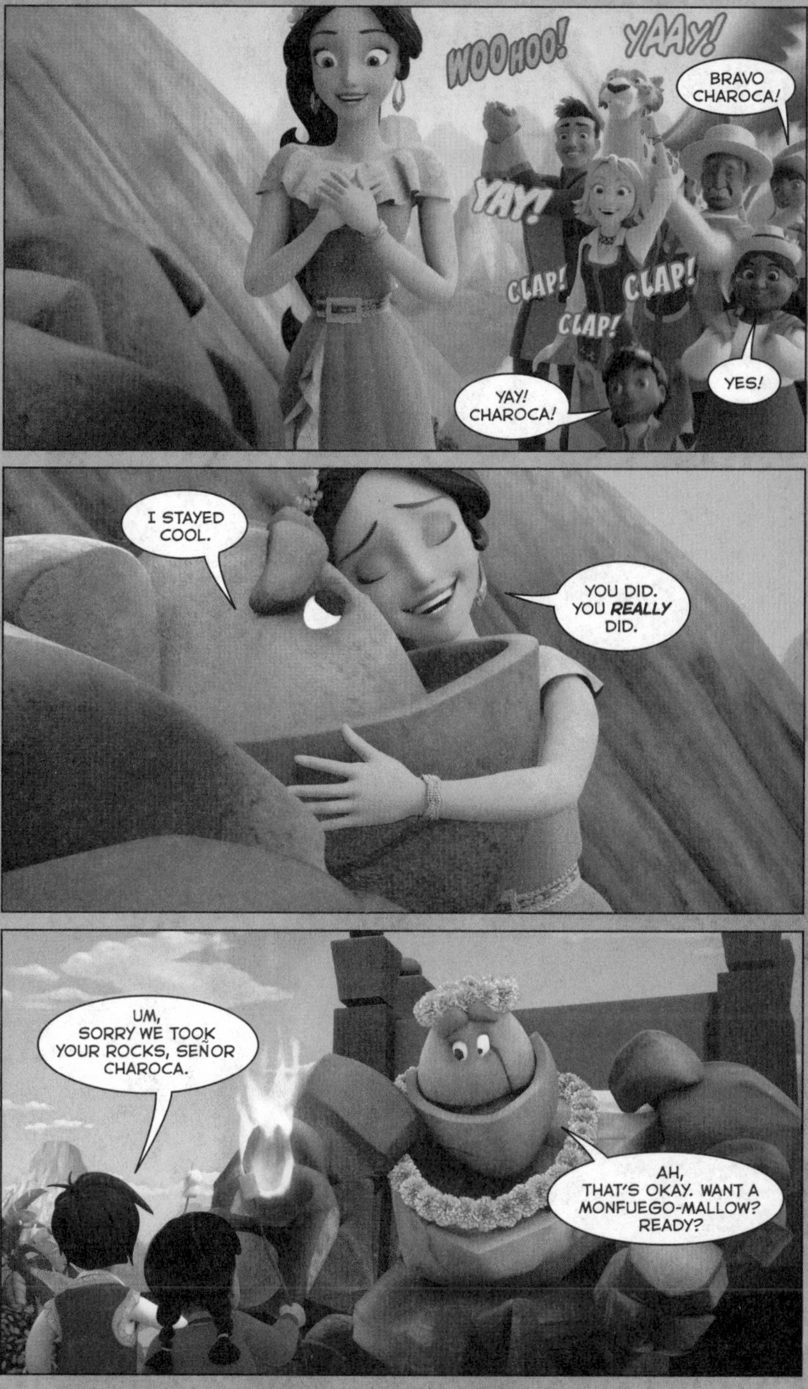
WOOHOO!
YAAY!
BRAVO CHAROCA!
YAY!
CLAP!
CLAP!
CLAP!
YES!
YAY! CHAROCA!
I STAYED COOL.
YOU DID. YOU *REALLY* DID.
UM, SORRY WE TOOK YOUR ROCKS, SEÑOR CHAROCA.
AH, THAT'S OKAY. WANT A MONFUEGO-MALLOW? READY?

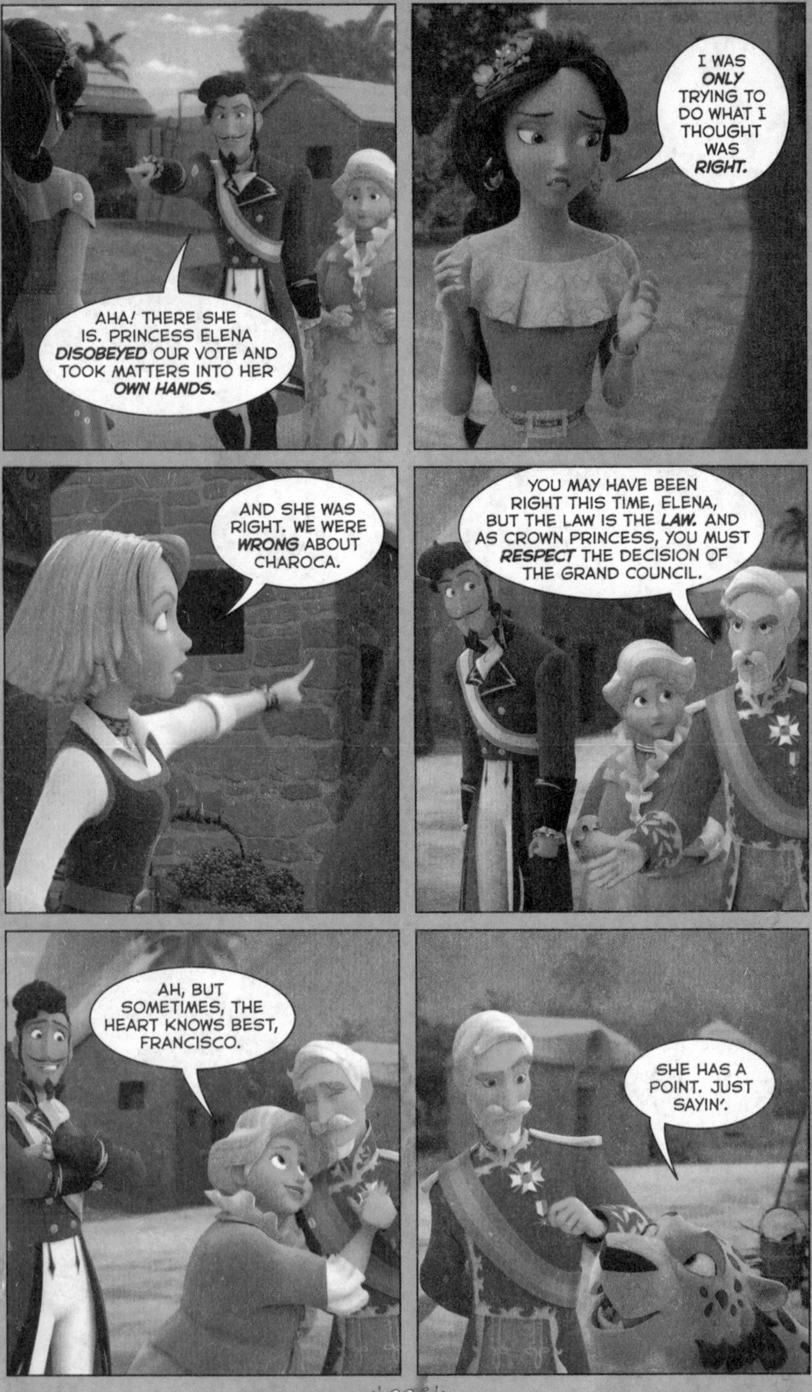
AHA! THERE SHE IS. PRINCESS ELENA DISOBEYED OUR VOTE AND TOOK MATTERS INTO HER OWN HANDS.
I WAS ONLY TRYING TO DO WHAT I THOUGHT WAS RIGHT.
AND SHE WAS RIGHT. WE WERE WRONG ABOUT CHAROCA.
YOU MAY HAVE BEEN RIGHT THIS TIME, ELENA, BUT THE LAW IS THE LAW. AND AS CROWN PRINCESS, YOU MUST RESPECT THE DECISION OF THE GRAND COUNCIL.
AH, BUT SOMETIMES, THE HEART KNOWS BEST, FRANCISCO.
SHE HAS A POINT. JUST SAYIN'.

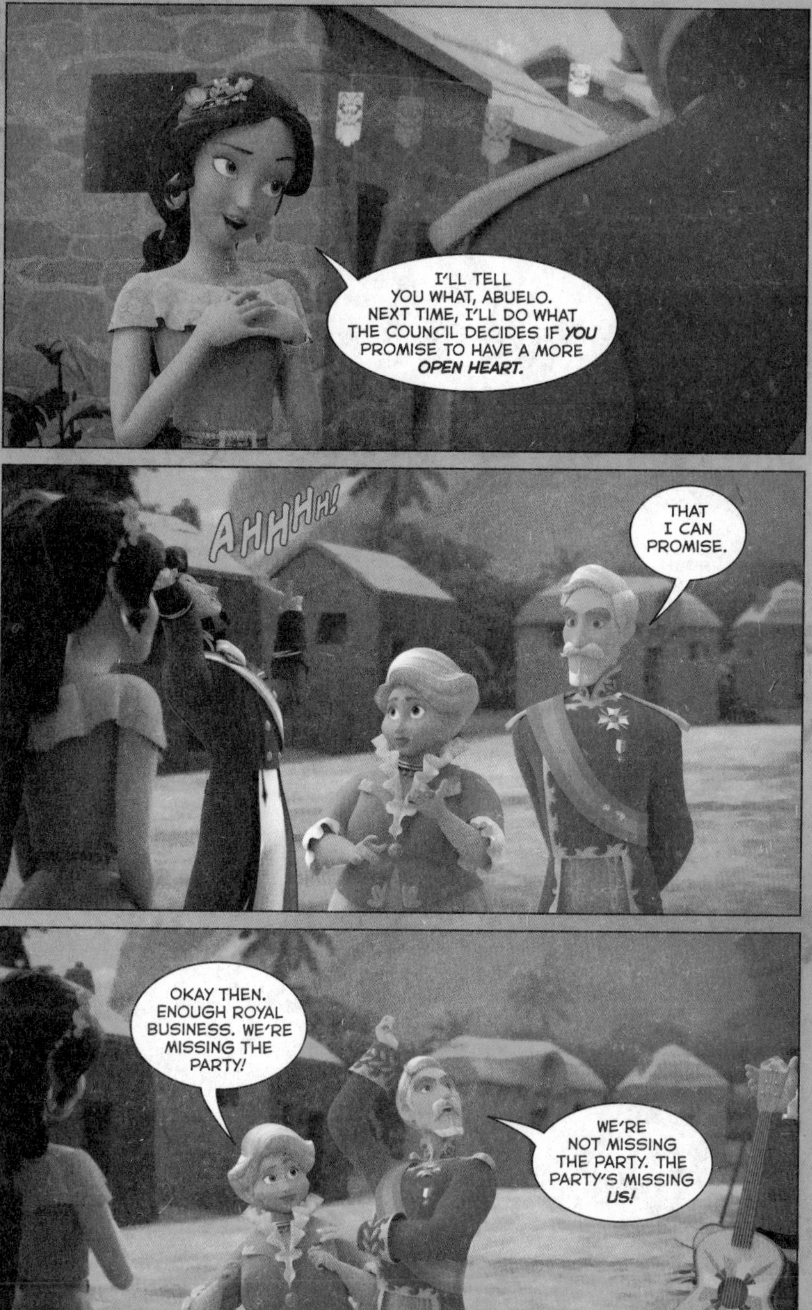
I'LL TELL YOU WHAT, ABUELO. NEXT TIME, I'LL DO WHAT THE COUNCIL DECIDES IF *YOU* PROMISE TO HAVE A MORE ***OPEN HEART.***
AHHHH!
THAT I CAN PROMISE.
OKAY THEN. ENOUGH ROYAL BUSINESS. WE'RE MISSING THE PARTY!
WE'RE NOT MISSING THE PARTY. THE PARTY'S MISSING ***US!***

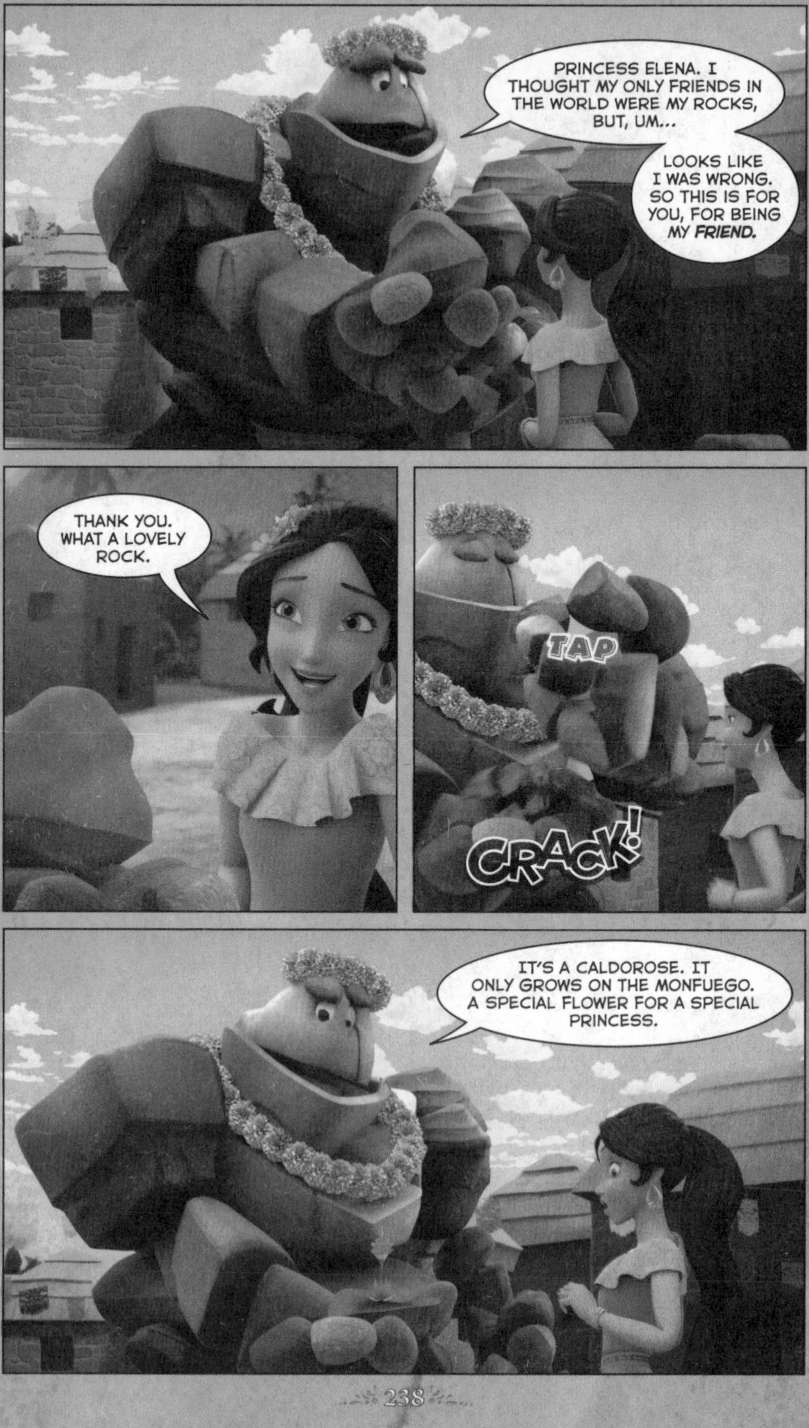
PRINCESS ELENA. I THOUGHT MY ONLY FRIENDS IN THE WORLD WERE MY ROCKS, BUT, UM...
LOOKS LIKE I WAS WRONG. SO THIS IS FOR YOU, FOR BEING MY *FRIEND.*
THANK YOU. WHAT A LOVELY ROCK.
TAP
CRACK!
IT'S A CALDOROSE. IT ONLY GROWS ON THE MONFUEGO. A SPECIAL FLOWER FOR A SPECIAL PRINCESS.

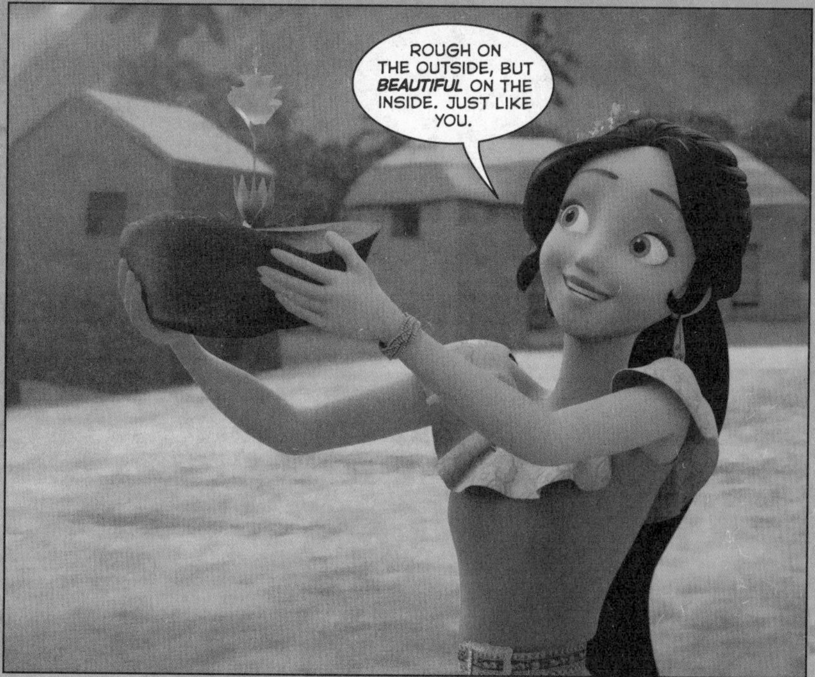
ROUGH ON THE OUTSIDE, BUT **BEAUTIFUL** ON THE INSIDE. JUST LIKE YOU.

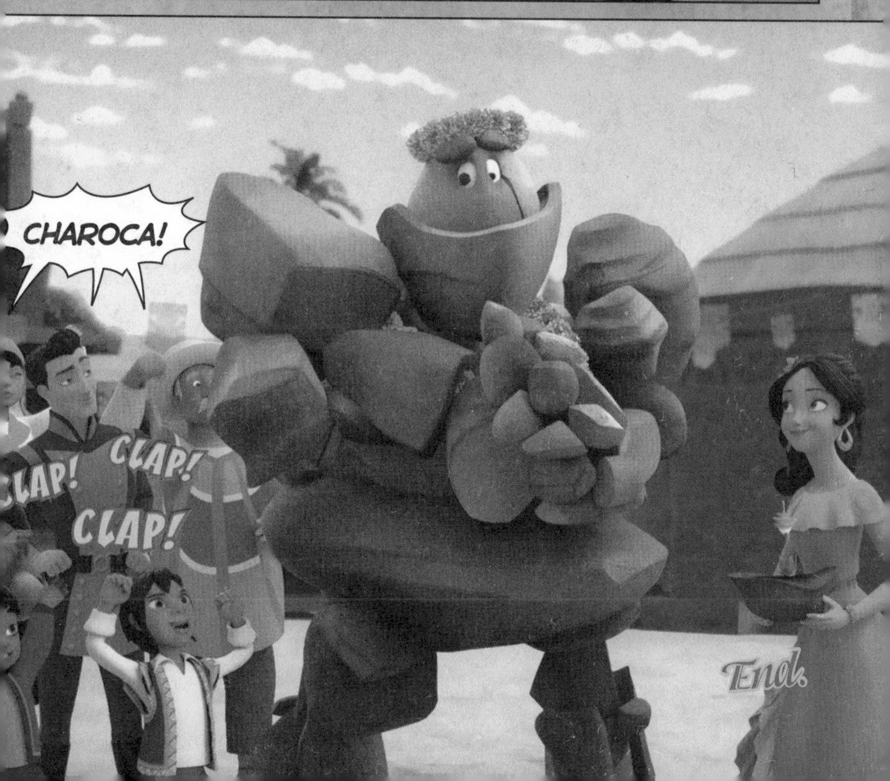
CHAROCA!
CLAP!
CLAP!
CLAP!
End.